the
mulligan

a novel by
NATHAN
JORGENSON

Flat Rock Publishing
Fairmont, MN

Flat Rock Publishing
P.O. Box 166
Fairmont, MN 56301
www.flatrockpublishing.com

Cover and interior design © TLC Graphics, *www.tlcgraphics.com*

2nd Printing 2008
Printed by Bang Printing, Brainerd, MN

ISBN: 978-0-9746370-2-0

For my Dad. Still my hero!

chapter
one

The first rays of sunlight splashed across the northern plains and threatened to bleed the deep greens of summer from an endless carpet of grass.

A little bit more of Joe Mix died every day now. Something that used to be vital and vibrant seemed to wither and then slide away from him every time he went to the office. He did insignificant things for people who really didn't care one way or the other. None of it had any meaning. He hated his job, and he was ashamed because the expectations of others would not allow that.

The countryside drifted by him slowly as he drove to the office. He cruised the rural highways every morning before his work day began, trying to avoid the inevitable turn that would take him back to the office. He wished he could just keep driving, keep going until he found a better place to stop.

Dr. Joseph Mix opened the car window and let the cool air of a fine spring morning rush inside. He put his left hand outside the window and felt the air flow between his fingers as he looked out at the small farms along the country roads.

Why had he done this? he asked himself yet again. He'd never enjoyed it. The life he led now had never been what he wanted. It had all just happened, as if he'd had no part in choosing it.

But he had chosen it. He'd let other people influence his decisions, but ultimately he'd chosen all this, and now he was stuck here, forever.

chapter two

A crimson droplet of blood swelled like a tiny red balloon when Joe Mix inserted the narrow blade into the gums, next to what was left of an upper molar. Some of the tooth had broken away long ago, and what remained was dark brown, with the brittle texture of rotting shoe leather.

Body odor, bad breath, and stale cigarette smoke had overtaken the little room. Even through their surgical masks, Dr. Joe Mix and his assistant were assaulted by the stagnant smell of neglect. The patient seemed to be defying them to continue, despite the fact that he lay on his back with his mouth open and eyes shut.

A dental X-ray, illuminated in a view box on the wall, showed a tooth surrounded by a large, dark semicircle; the bone support for the tooth had been destroyed by an infection that had gone untreated for many months. The adjacent tooth, like all the others in the patient's mouth, was covered with thick, brown tobacco stains, while a fuzzy layer of yellow dental plaque, mixed with food particles, surrounded all the teeth. When Dr. Mix pushed the surgical elevator a little farther into the sulcus around the tooth, he saw exactly what he knew he would see: the tooth moved easily—it was floating in a sea of infected tissue.

The latex glove on Joe Mix's right hand became taut as he applied pressure by twisting the handle of the surgical instrument ever so slightly. Pus began to ooze from the sulcus around the tooth, and the fetid odor of the room grew heavier. The patient opened his eyes and his glance began to dart about, first to the right, then to the left, with the anticipation that something bad was about to happen.

"Ahhh!!" The patient kicked both feet violently and jerked his head away from the steel instrument. His extreme response frightened both the dentist and the assistant.

Joe Mix slowly moved his hands away from his patient, as if he were holding some unseen force at bay, and leaned back in his chair. He took in a huge, deep breath, and when he let it out neither his patient nor his assistant could miss the anger that hissed along with it. Over the top of his eyeglasses and 2X magnifiers, Dr. Mix made eye contact with his assistant and passed along his anger.

"So, Dean, did that really hurt—what I just did?" Joe raised his eyebrows with the question.

"No, but I guess it felt like it was gonna hurt." Dean glanced at Joe first, then half smiled a nervous grin at the dental assistant and nodded yes.

Angela Fritz had worked side by side as a dental assistant with Joseph Mix for eighteen years and had never seen such anger in his eyes. In recent months she'd seen his moods darken, and he'd seemed frustrated by things that hadn't bothered him in the past, but she'd never seen anything like this. She leaned back in her chair, afraid of what she might see next.

At fifty, Dr. Joseph Mix still had the look of an outdoorsman. His angular face was tanned and his eyes always seemed to be searching for something. He kept his blonde hair cut very short. As a young boy he'd fallen and driven a sharp stick through the right side of his face. When the injury healed, it left a surprisingly small scar. But the incident had permanently impaired the muscles in his face, so when he smiled the little scar curled into a spectacular dimple that created an irresistible, asymmetrical smile. His blonde hair and light blue eyes, and that great smile, left him looking considerably younger than his years. However, middle age and twenty-four years of a sedentary lifestyle were beginning to change his body. His hairline was receding and he'd grown a bit of a potbelly over the past winter. During his twenty-four years of practice in Rochester, Minnesota, he'd earned a reputation as an outstanding clinician and a gentleman.

Joseph Mix always wore a white shirt with a red necktie, and Khaki pants with a sharp crease. The frames of his eyeglasses were round, always round, and they sat perfectly on his face. When he wasn't wearing his white gown in the clinic, his glasses gave him a scholarly, academic appearance, like that of a professor or trial lawyer. His shoes were always brown, always shined, and, like his glasses, they were something of a fashion accessory.

Dr. Mix took another deep breath, and as he let the second breath out he began speaking. His words came slowly, in a subdued tone, and all the anger of a moment earlier appeared to be gone. His voice was calm and reassuring. Angela was amazed at the sudden transformation in her boss. In the time it had taken him to draw a breath, he'd regained control of the anger that seemed about to boil over. When he made eye contact with the patient, his eyes were smiling over the top of his blue surgical mask. Angela knew him well enough to recognize that he was only hiding the anger.

"Scared me there, Dean!" he said, then chuckled softly. He rested the back of his gloved hand gently on the patient's shoulder in a subtle gesture intended to re-establish whatever goodwill might have been lost between doctor and patient in the last few seconds, when his anger had flashed.

"Me too!" Dean said with a smile. Dean Pope was a forty-five-year-old stranger who had walked into Dr. Joseph Mix's office about an hour earlier with a swollen face and a toothache. Joe had heard him announce loudly, for everyone in the office to hear, that he really hated dentists. He'd apparently gone without a shave and shower for several days, and on the front of his dirty T-shirt Joe could clearly see where parts of several different meals had been spilled. His greasy boots had left large, black stains on the carpet by the front desk.

Now, as Dr. Mix tried to reassure Dean Pope that things were actually just fine, he continued to rest his right hand on Dean's right shoulder while he spoke. "Yeah, that's pretty normal, to be a little scared, I mean." Joe raised his eyebrows and smiled again. "But you know, Dean, I do have to touch you in order to get that tooth out." He paused to give Dean a chance to think about what he'd said, then added, "I've got enough anesthetic in there that NOTHING should hurt you!" He was fairly certain that the tooth and the tissue around it were totally numb.

"Yeah, it feels pretty numb, Doc, that's for sure!" Dean agreed, then nodded. "I guess I just thought it was gonna hurt, that's all."

"That's what I thought," Joe said quietly. Angela could see Joe's face tighten slightly with disdain. She knew he was growing frustrated with

Dean Pope. She knew that, in Joe's mind, this stranger had come to represent the hundreds of other strangers who'd come before him—strangers who'd simply asked him to do the least that his training had prepared him for: to amputate the parts of their lives they'd neglected.

Joseph Mix had been a brilliant student, number one in his class in high school, college, and dental school. When he'd entered private practice, he'd expected to be a master in his profession and to change the world in some way. But over the years, he'd felt the creative energy in his heart being sucked away by the low expectations of so many patients and the money-driven bottom line of the health care professions.

"OK, Dean, I'm gonna just lift the tooth out and we're done." Joe brought a 301 Elevator to the side of Dean's tooth. The instrument had the look of a small screwdriver or a very small ice cream scoop. It had been designed so that a dentist could insert it next to a tooth and twist it, like a screwdriver, in order to elevate the tooth.

When Joe applied pressure, Dean began to groan. "Dean," Joe said softly, "is this hurting you?"

"No. But it seems like it should."

"Well, just tell me if it does actually hurt, OK?" Joe glanced at Angela and shook his head in contempt.

"OK," Dean said, then closed his eyes tightly as if he were in great pain, before Joe touched him.

But when Joe applied pressure, Dean began to groan again. Joe knew it was simply Dean's fear and apprehension; the tooth was numb. "Dean? No pain, right? You're just waiting for something bad to happen, right?" Joe said softly into Dean's ear.

"Uh huh," Dean replied. Then he relaxed—or at least tried to.

As he increased the pressure, Joe felt the tooth begin to move. Suddenly, it lifted out of its socket about two millimeters and made a small crunching sound, like a chicken wing being bent backwards.

When he heard the sound of his own tooth moving, Dean groaned loudly, kicked his feet, and jerked his head away from Joe. In the instant Dean turned his head, Joe deftly lifted the tooth out of the mouth and held it up for Dean to see.

The room filled instantly with an even deeper, more fetid, necrotic, foul smell that had been released when Joe had extracted the tooth, as if he'd pulled the cork from a bottle of bad wine.

For the third time, Angela could see her boss's eyes tighten with suppressed rage.

"Dean, did that hurt you?" Angela could hear the anger in Joe's voice. She knew there was no reason for Dean to have jerked away from Joe.

"No," Dean responded, then paused. "But it sounded like it was gonna!" Then Dean Pope smiled as though he'd said something hilarious. Angela smiled politely.

Joe turned away with a look of contempt. He flicked the bloody tooth into a wastebasket with a red liner that said "bio hazard," then threw his latex gloves into the same basket.

When he'd washed his hands and dried them, he turned back toward Dean. Angela was placing a fresh cotton dressing on the socket and giving Dean instructions on how to help the extraction site heal properly. Joe listened until she was finished

"So, Dean, in my world, if you wait until something hurts, you've waited too long. That's when things get difficult and expensive and you lose teeth. You should call right away when something breaks and come for regular check ups so we can take care of things before they hurt." Joe nodded "yes" and raised his eyebrows.

"When did that tooth break, Dean?" Joe tried to smile with the question.

"'Bout eight months ago," Dean mumbled through the cotton dressing, then smiled so that both Joe and Angela could see the bloody dressing between his teeth.

"Why did you walk around with all that infection in there for so long and not call me until today?"

Dean looked back at Joe and spoke in a condescending tone. "I told you, Doc, I didn't call you sooner because it didn't hurt." He shrugged his shoulders as if it were Joe who just didn't get it. Then he laughed and looked at Angela for approval, to see if she'd noticed his clever reply.

Joe looked at Angela, shook his head once, rolled his eyes for Dean to witness, then left the room without a goodbye. He knew it was rude to dismiss a patient in such a way, but he'd given the same lecture to hundreds of other patients and nothing had ever changed as a result. He felt tired and overwhelmed as he walked down the short hallway toward his private office.

"Doctor!" a small voice called from behind Joe, and he turned around to face Angela once again. "Marjorie Donovan is in treatment room two.

She's just here for a check up." Angela looked around her, then lowered her voice and whispered to Joe, "I think she still has a crush on you, Joe."

"She's seventy-seven years old," Joe whispered in reply. He knew Angela was right, but he tried not to think about it.

Angela shrugged, smiled, and swung open the door that led into a small dental operatory where Marjorie Donovan waited.

"Hi, Marjorie," Joe said when he entered.

"Hi, Doctor," Marjorie replied. Then, as she always did, she stood up from the dental chair and reached for the pitch black wig she always wore. The wig looked like something an aging and disoriented country singer might wear to her farewell performance at the Grand Ole Opry. She gripped the wig firmly and adjusted it as if it were the hood on her parka and she was about to step outside into a blizzard. After Marjorie's previous visit, Joe had told Angela that the wig looked like a hockey helmet, and now he struggled not to smile.

Marjorie had developed a strange ritual for her dental check ups. She waited until Joe was looking at her before she began a bizarre strip tease. She removed her eyeglasses and set them on a countertop. Then she removed her hearing aid and set it next to her eyeglasses. Next came her dentures; she placed them next to the glasses and hearing aid. Finally, she stood before Joe with her hands on her hips staring at him. "Would you like to see my new tattoo?" she asked.

"Sure," Joe blurted. But he began to regret his reply in a heartbeat.

Marjorie's hands reached across the front of her beige, polyester pant suit, and for one brief moment Joe was nearly strangled by the fear that she was about to remove her pants and show him a tattoo on a very private part of her body. His body temperature spiked, and he began to feel heat flushing up over his face as her hands came to rest on her hips. The image of seventy-seven-year-old Marjorie Donovan standing there with her pants pulled down, showing him a dragon tattoo on her ass, flashed through his mind. It would be just great, he thought, as a wave of panic spread through him, to have Angela walk into the room while he was looking at Marjorie's naked rear end.

But the fear vanished as soon as it had appeared, leaving only a rapid heartbeat and a few drops of sweat on Joe's forehead.

Marjorie lifted her pant leg and exposed a small, red rose on her ankle. Joe's mouth still hung open when Angela walked into the room.

"Oh, isn't that pretty!" Angela said cheerfully, then smiled a wicked smile at Joe.

"Yeah," Joe agreed. "That's really pretty." He sighed and then relaxed into his chair. Who would ever have thought that the most exciting thing he'd done at the office in months would be a check up for an old woman with no teeth?

———

Joe was seated at the walnut desk in his office, blowing on a cup of coffee and staring straight ahead, when Angela entered the room and closed the door behind her. Joe's private office was large and decorated with the feel of a man's library or trophy room. Oak bookshelves, antique bamboo fly rods, wicker creels, fly boxes filled with dozens of trout flies, and several graphite replicas of trophy trout covered the walls and tables. A leather loveseat sat in the corner behind Joe's large desk, and the wall behind it was covered with diplomas and various professional awards.

His desk was neat, so much so that it appeared unused. A phone and the day's mail sat in the center of the richly finished walnut desktop. On the left side of the desk was a photograph of Joe and his wife, Jess, with their two college-age boys, Ben and Chris. The photo had been taken the previous year during a ski vacation in Colorado. The entire family stood, wearing skis, on the side of a mountain. Both boys were taller than their father, and Ben was clearly older and more physically mature than the baby-faced Chris.

On the right side of the desk was an older photo that had been enlarged to fit an eight-by-eleven-inch frame. The enlargement had caused the small photo to lose some of its clarity, but Joe liked it that way. A cowboy wearing a white shirt, a jean jacket, and a white Stetson sat atop a fine brown horse. The cowboy had both hands on the saddle horn and was leaning toward the photographer. A cigarette rested in the corner of the cowboy's mouth, and he was smiling a tight-lipped smile that curved around the cigarette and caused everyone to smile back at the photo. The cowboy was weathered and handsome, a robust sixty-year-old man. He was Ray Mix, Joe's father. The photo had been taken the day before he died, twenty-five years earlier. Tucked into the frame was another photo, a tattered black-and-white picture of a smiling toddler wearing six guns and riding a rocking horse.

Now Angela stood with her back to the door, to guarantee privacy and to emphasize the fact that she felt she had something important to say.

"Are you all right, Joe?" She was asking as a friend, not as an employee, and she wanted an answer.

During recent months, Joe had grown weary of conversations with Angela. She always seemed to have questions that required direction or detailed answers. More and more now, he felt the questions were irrelevant or unimportant. Sometimes it seemed that she was simply pestering him. He remembered caring about her questions at one time, in the past. He used to enjoy discussing the small problems around the office and searching for solutions. But sometime during the past winter, he knew he'd stepped over some sort of bridge and he just couldn't go back across. He didn't care anymore. Now, Angela's questions about treatment plans and patients' needs were beginning to draw answers like "Who cares? What difference does it make?" and "I don't know." Sometimes, when Joe knew she was looking for him to answer a question, he actually hid from her or pretended to be on the phone so he wouldn't have to talk to her. In his heart, he knew that he wasn't really hiding from Angela or her questions. He could feel the apathy and emptiness in his own answers, and he didn't like the feeling. He knew he was hiding from his own fear of that emptiness.

"Joe! Are you all right?" she repeated herself.

He waited for a moment and blew on his coffee, but he never looked at her when he answered. "NO," he said flatly.

Her eyes tightened. She hadn't expected his answer. She certainly hadn't expected the bluntness of a simple "NO." She began to wonder if he was about to tell her that he'd been stricken with cancer or some terrible disease. Then she began to fear that he was about to describe some sort of marital trouble, perhaps some indiscretion on his part or his wife's. After all, she'd worked with him for all these years, and she had been noticing changes in him recently. A dark, distant, impatient mood had overtaken Joe during the long winter. She'd first noticed it many months earlier, but it seemed to descend on him more frequently now. Some days it never left him. It made sense that he'd tell her before the others if something dreadful had happened. She waited silently for almost a minute while he stared at his coffee and sipped.

"So what's wrong?" she asked when she knew he wasn't going to offer more.

"I wanted to shake that guy." He continued to stare at his cup. "It was all I could do not to holler, 'Hold still, DAMMIT!'" He blew on his coffee and sipped again, and his tone became apologetic. "I know he was just some scared guy with a toothache—and I feel bad that I got mad at him." He took a sip of coffee. "I wish I wasn't so short tempered; I never used to be." Then he looked up at Angela. "My God, Angela! Is this what I spent my life training to do—dig rotten teeth out of people's heads? I can do better than this! I was born for something more than this! There has to be some meaning, more than this." His voice trailed off and he took another sip of coffee. "I'm so sick of talking to people, of being the one who's supposed to care more about them than they do for themselves. I'm sick of people who don't care about themselves. I'm sick of the dishonest insurance companies, I'm sick of the government agencies sticking their damn noses in here." His voice was raising slowly. "But mostly, I'm sick of this place. Any moron can do what I'm doing with my life. When I started this practice I had such high goals. I was meant to do something better than this! I thought I'd go to work every day and be creative and insightful, and help people."

"You do!" Angela blurted.

"Hell I do," Joe said flatly. "I'm just some guy in the phone book that they call when some other guy in the phone book is busy. Some people like me enough to come and show me their tattoos. But I spend most of my time listening to people beg me to just do the least that I can do." He looked away and made a face like a dunce and began to repeat the things patients asked of him. "'Just patch 'er up, Doc,' 'I gotta be at work at three, Doc, just fix it up quick,' 'Just yank 'em out, Doc.'" Joe peered at Angela over his coffee cup, and his eyes challenged her to argue with him.

"OK," she said, "what about all those really difficult reconstruction cases that the other dentists send over here because they can't do them as well as you? And what about all those 'makeovers' that we do that look so great when they're done?"

"Angela," Joe said with a cynical smile, "you wanna know something? Those cases are pretty easy too. They're not so challenging; they just look difficult."

"Joe?" she asked softly, then paused. "What's happened? What about the passion you used to have for this place?" Angela's voice began to thicken with compassion as she finished the question.

"I just can't stand it anymore—the way people simply look for excuses so they can avoid doing the right thing. They show up here after they've grown a green sweater and some brown holes in their teeth. Then I GIVE them a fifty-cent toothbrush and show them a foolproof way to put me out of business.

"Six months, maybe a year later, they're back in here again with another sweater on their teeth, and a toothache, with a long list of silly-ass reasons why their problems really aren't their own fault: 'My mother had soft teeth' or 'I don't have time to brush my teeth.' I really like this one: 'I brush 'em three times a day, Doc!' Who do they think they're kidding? Just who are they lying to?" Joe paused for a moment. "I'm so sick of people not being willing to DO something in order to change their lives. Nothing I've ever done in this office has ever really meant anything to anyone.

"Hmph. Passion. Did I ever have any passion for this place? Or have I just been waiting my whole life, expecting the passion to arrive?" He stared at his cup for a moment, and Angela waited for him to continue. "So many of the things that I've been waiting for, expecting, just never came—not here, not at home either. Hell, I've lost interest in my own career—my own life," he mumbled. He averted his eyes from her and sipped at his coffee, unwilling, maybe unable, to continue.

Angela had heard the growing contempt in his voice during the past few months when he'd spoken privately about work. But just now, when he'd said the word "home," she'd been looking at his eyes and she'd seen something worse: apathy, complete apathy. His eyes had been empty.

"Maybe you need some time off?"

Joe continued to stare at his cup. "No," he said quietly, and blew on his coffee. "Six months ago we thought I needed some time off. That just made it worse."

His voice trailed off into silence, and Angela stood with her back to the door for another minute, waiting. When it was clear that her boss had nothing more to say, she opened the door. As she slipped out of his private office and into the hallway beyond it, she said, "I'll get ready for the next patient." Just as she was about to close the door, she remembered something. She pushed her face into the narrow opening between the door and the door jamb and tried to sound upbeat. "Hey, remember! You get to go play golf with Donny today, and then there's the party afterwards!" She hoped that the thought of playing golf with his brother and the formal party after that might cheer him up. But he still only looked at his coffee and nodded as she closed the door.

———

Just before noon, Joe Mix returned to his desk. The morning's schedule of patients was finished, but he still had some patient charts to write in, and his receptionist had prepared a list of things to do before he went to the country club for the rest of the day.

Joe poured himself another cup of coffee and stared at it just as he had earlier in the day. Then he opened the chart on top of the pile, grudgingly, and began making notes in it. Twenty minutes later, he finished writing in the last chart at the same moment he finished his coffee.

With his left hand, he picked up the list of things to do that had been prepared for him and read through it quickly. He rubbed his face with his right hand as if he'd been awake for forty-eight hours straight, and he called out, "Julie!" As he watched his receptionist walk around the corner and into his private office, he felt the same need to avoid her that he'd felt when Angela approached with questions. Every item on the list seemed so unimportant, and he wanted only to get away.

When Julie entered the room and stood next to his desk, he handed her the list. "Let's go through this," was all he said.

Julie took the list from his hand. "OK," she started, "the first item is to contact Lambda Dental Insurance Company with regard to their preferred provider program." She stopped and looked at Joe, her eyes questioning him.

"You handle it. Write 'em a nice note and tell 'em 'no thanks.'" He never looked at her. "They're a bunch of thieves, they're in bed with the crooked politicians in St. Paul, and I won't have 'em in this practice."

Julie looked confused. "You want ME to write that letter? I've never done that before."

"Well, today's the day. You'll do just fine. Next?"

"OK," she shrugged, then continued. "Next, we're supposed to call the clinic custodian and tell him about the problems with the air conditioning."

"You handle it. Next."

Julie turned to Joe with a look of disbelief and questioned him with her eyes.

"You handle it. Next!" He was more stern this time, and he looked at her and shrugged as though he didn't understand how she could question such a small task.

Every item on the list, from contacting the Minnesota Dental Association to responding to the State Environmental Protection Agency, was met with the same reply: "You handle it." And Joe's apathy grew with each question.

"OK, Dr. Mix, just a couple more things on the list," Julie said. "I know you don't like this stuff, but there are several personal issues among the staff." Julie's tone grew apologetic before she started to list the staff problems.

"Oh?" Joe sat back in his chair.

"Yes, well, Amy never takes the garbage out to the dumpster when it's her turn."

"Uh huh," Joe nodded. "Continue."

"And Erica doesn't like to clean her own instruments. She said she's a hygienist, and cleaning is a job for assistants."

"Uh huh," Joe nodded.

"And Sherry, she showed up today with a bunch of hickeys on her neck. I made her put her collar up to hide them. Oh yeah, and she and Amy have some sort of feud going between them over some incident at the bowling alley, so they're not talking. Just a few minutes ago, Sherry came and told me Amy passed gas in front of a patient this morning, twice."

Julie wore a confused look when Joe picked his car keys off the desk and walked to the door. He'd stood abruptly when she'd read the last item on the list, as if to emphasize that their meeting was over. As he slipped out the back door, he looked back at her one more time. She still looked confused and uncertain about what had happened. "You handle it, all of it!" He nodded and backed out of the office.

Joe knew that he should be the one to do the things on the list, but having to deal, once again, with issues like hickeys, and farting, and feuds among the staff felt overwhelming now. Instead of dealing with it all, as he had for so many years, he simply left the office. He felt like he'd just escaped from prison and was skipping through a meadow filled with flowers as he walked across the parking lot toward his car. He let a rush of joy spread through him as he started the car and drove away from the office. He actually felt a smile start to spread over his face—

one more day at the office was done. Then, as he gradually began to understand just what he was thinking, what he was doing, his heart began to feel heavy over the contradiction within him. He began to feel guilty, then sad. Grown men shouldn't be crossing off the days of their lives, like a jail term or like a child counts down the days until Christmas, but that's just what he was doing. Today was now just one more day of his life that he was done with. One more day at the office, done. Just beyond the reality of this moment, he became vaguely aware of one small, but absolute piece of truth: someday—perhaps on his deathbed, maybe before that—he would lament the fact that he had discarded so many days of his life, and he would know real sorrow because of it. But for this moment, the joy of being done at the office was actually greater than the guilt of counting down his life one day at a time. As he eased his car out of the parking lot, he pushed the truth and guilt out of his mind, again.

chapter three

The drive across Rochester and out along the river road on the way to The Oaks Country Club was smooth and easy. It was a fine spring day, and Joe enjoyed the way the sun warmed his arm as it rested on the open window of his car. He liked the way the country air smelled and the feel of a breeze on his face.

Just below the child-like joy of playing outside on a warm afternoon, the simmering uneasiness in his heart still churned. Joe knew there was something wrong about his feelings toward his job, maybe more than just his job.

He cupped his left hand and held it out the car window to catch the breeze, and he tried to let all thoughts of work fly away as he opened his hand and felt the wind rush between his fingers. He'd have a round of golf with his brother and best friend, Donny, and then their wives would join them for a formal dinner and dance, the first social event of the summer at The Oaks. Today would be a good day yet.

Joe really didn't care too much about the golf. He never had. But he did enjoy these afternoons with Donny. They'd become closer friends as adults than they'd ever been as children, and an afternoon of golf presented opportunities to talk with each other that didn't exist anywhere else.

Formal events like the one planned for this evening, however, had pretty much lost their luster for Joe. He acquiesced and attended them because he knew his wife, Jess, looked forward to them so much. Joe knew that Jess had been anticipating an elegant evening rubbing elbows with Rochester's finest for months. She'd be glowing with excitement by the time he met her in the dining room tonight. In his mind's eye, Joe could see Jess moving around the dining room tonight—laughing, flirting, gossiping, and loving every minute of it. As this vision played in his head, his face hardened and he reached into his pocket and switched off his cell phone. Then he let every thought of Jess fly out the window too.

When Joe arrived at The Oaks, he parked his car and went directly to the locker room. Even before he pushed the door open he could smell the stale dampness of the room and hear men's voices echoing. When he rounded the corner, he almost bumped into Donny.

Total strangers could identify Donny Mix as Joe's younger brother. He had the same blonde hair, blue eyes, and youthful smile.

Donny was five years younger than Joe. He'd taken some time off after high school, then some time off after college, and a little more time off after law school. During all the time off, he'd managed to see most of the world and acquire a laid back disposition that everyone seemed to enjoy. He'd followed Joe to Rochester because, well, because that's where Joe was. Clever and ambitious, Donny had been elected Olmsted County Attorney after only four years in practice. Unlike his brother and best friend, he found himself energized by his work.

"Hey, Joe, you still drivin' that old thing?" Donny pointed to the parking lot, where Joe had parked his Cadillac, then extended his hand while he flashed a huge smile, daring his brother to reply.

"Don't even start with that." Joe smiled weakly and shook his head. One month earlier, Jess had announced that Joe's three-year-old Cadillac and her two-year-old Mercedes 250SL were no longer adequate, and she'd ordered two matching BMW 760Li's. Joe was still angry that Jess had thought it so important to do such a foolish and pretentious thing. She'd been willing to spend a pile of money just so people around town could see her and Joe sitting behind the wheels of matching luxury automobiles. But he'd grown weary of arguing with her about such things, and when she'd announced that she'd made the deal for the cars, Joe had simply stopped talking to her for several days. Jess had developed an iron will when it came to 'things'—things she felt she needed or was entitled to. Joe felt that it had been impossible to reason with her about the cars; she simply would not be denied. He'd been angry and disappointed with himself for not squashing the deal for several weeks now, and Donny was the only person who could joke about the BMW deal and draw any sort of a smile from Joe. He felt weak every time he thought about the cars.

"So, Joe, when WILL the fleet be arriving?" Donny was still fishing for a better response about the new BMWs from Joe, and Joe heard the joy in Donny's voice when he used the word "fleet" to irritate him.

"I don't know. That's Jess's deal," Joe said without looking at Donny; he had no interest in the talk of cars.

"Hey, heard you got to see your girlfriend, Marjorie, this morning," Donny offered in order to change the subject.

This time Joe smiled and looked at Donny. "How'd you hear that?" he asked.

"I called to see if you were on time just before I left the office. Angela told me."

"She showed me her new tattoo," Joe offered, then shook his head in disbelief. He knew Donny wanted to talk about Marjorie Donovan.

"I can see it all now, Joe," Donny said as he leaned back and raised his hands. "There you are—you and Marjorie, that is—resting on silk sheets. As you lay her softly onto the bed, you gently remove her satin chemise, then her hearing aid, then her teeth, then her wig—that is a wig, isn't it? And then, just before you make love, you remove her absorbent undergarment and place it lovingly beside the bed." Donny stopped for a moment. "I think they make those in black lace now, for active seniors!"

Joe didn't answer right away; he was struggling to hide a smile. He finished tying his golf shoes, let the silence linger, and made sure Donny knew he was being ignored. Joe stood and looked at himself in the mirror, turned sideways, then sucked in his stomach while he looked himself over. He lowered his chin and tried to see just how far his hairline had receded. As he studied his belly, then the top of his head for a moment, he pursed his lips and furrowed his eyebrows with disappointment. Then he appeared to concede another hopeless argument, this one over the effect that middle age was having on his body. He let out his stomach and grabbed a hat from his locker. Not much he could do about the potbelly, but he could cover the thinning hair on his head and prevent sunburn.

"Women are attracted to me—I can't help it," Joe said as he walked past Donny, who was still sitting on a bench tying his shoes and waiting for an answer.

"It's your wild and reckless nature!" Donny said while he was still looking at his shoes. Then he laughed out loud at his own sarcasm.

Joe called back to Donny over his shoulder, as though he'd just remembered something important: "Oh yeah, that reminds me." He kept on walking, and his golf shoes clattered and clicked on the concrete.

"What?" Donny called as Joe was about to leave the locker room.

"Up yours."

Donny was still laughing when he caught up with Joe on the first tee. He could see that Joe wanted to cut loose and swear a blue streak, but the pressure to maintain his image around the country club kept him from it. The conservative veneer that Joe Mix wore all day at work weakened when he was alone with Donny, but seldom vanished. Joe never drank alcohol because he thought other people might think it was unprofessional. He seldom cussed for the same reason. But when he was with Donny, he was able to let his guard down and stop trying so hard to please others. He liked the little sense of abandon that came to him when he was with Donny; he could simply be himself. Joe liked himself better when he was around Donny, and he'd come to understand that it was because Donny expected nothing of him, only his friendship. He loved to be with Donny. They were standing shoulder to shoulder in front of the clubhouse by the first tee, watching the other golfers gather, when Donny leaned toward Joe.

"What's the matter, Joe? You OK? You look like something's really bothering you," Donny said as he gripped his driver and looked at his hands.

"Tough morning at the office," Joe sighed. "There has to be a little bit more to life than what I deal with every day."

"Whadya mean, Joe?" Donny bent at the waist and studied his grip on the driver.

"Just checked my voicemail," Joe started his explanation, then sighed.

"Yeah?"

Joe closed his eyes, then began to speak. "The mother of an eight-year-old patient called the office today and reminded Julie that we're not to use any fluoride in any of our work with her daughter." Joe stopped, then squeezed his eyes shut as if the words he was about to say were painful. "She said the Nazis put fluoride in the Jews' water supply to make them docile, so they wouldn't try to escape." Then he shook his head. "No fluoride for her!"

Donny pursed his lips and raised his eyebrows. "So the general public finally found out about that, huh?"

Joe simply nodded his head.

"Hell, Joe, she probably learned about the fluoride and the Nazis during her most recent alien abduction. Maybe she read it in one of the supermarket tabloids—they're usually the first to notify the public of things like that."

Donny waited for a moment, then changed direction. "Lighten up, Joe. Everybody has to deal with idiots."

"Issues with the staff, too," Joe offered.

"Such as?" Donny replied.

"Well, Amy doesn't like to take the garbage out," Joe said. "And she has a problem with farting around the office."

Donny stood straight and turned toward Joe. He nodded for a moment, implying that he was deep in thought. Then he shrugged, "Fire the bitch."

It was Joe's turn to nod, but neither of them would give in and smile. Joe continued. "Erica says she doesn't clean instruments—it's not her job."

His eyebrows knit together, and Donny brought his hand to his chin as if he were solving another riddle. He shrugged again, "Fire the bitch."

"And Sherry—she's the newest of the bunch, kind of pretty, too—she showed up this morning with a bunch of hickeys, and she won't talk to Amy, the farter, because of some conflict during bowling league," Joe continued.

"Fire all the bitches. Get new bitches on Monday," Donny offered as he pretended to address an imaginary golf ball and re-examine his grip.

"Thank you for that bit of insight in labor/management conflict resolution, Donny," Joe finally chuckled.

"No problem, Joe. But I just raised my fees; that professional advice is gonna cost you seventy-five dollars," Donny said, still looking at his hands.

"Send me a bill," Joe replied, still smiling.

Donny stood straight and looked his brother in the eye before he spoke: "I can't believe you let that shit bother you so much."

"Me neither! But I can't stop it! I have better things to do, more to think about than that stuff," Joe replied.

"Well, no, you don't—not really. Dealing with that stuff is what we do, all of us," Donny said. "Let it go."

"I can't live that way," Joe said as he shook his head. "There just has to be more to life than stuff like that."

Donny returned his attention to his grip on the driver but said nothing more for a moment.

"Hey." Donny touched Joe with his elbow. "Did you see who we're playing with?" Now there was added joy in his voice as he changed the subject.

"No." Joe turned toward Donny and raised his eyebrows. He knew by the tone of Donny's question that Donny did know who they were paired with, and that he wouldn't like what his brother had to say.

Donny tried to suppress a smile, or at least let Joe see him pretend to suppress a smile. He loved to give his big brother bad news and watch the reaction. "Lester Schultz and Omar Hagen," he muttered. Then, in a gesture done solely for Joe's benefit, Donny brought his hand to his face and covered his mouth, but laughed with his eyes. He knew he'd just thrown gas on a fire.

At first, it seemed as though Joe hadn't heard what Donny had said. Then, slowly, his head turned toward his brother and his face shrunk into a grimace. "You're shittin' me."

Donny shook his head. His hand still covered his mouth, and his eyes were glowing.

"A beautiful spring day..." Joe looked around. "And instead of going fishing, I have to play golf with two assholes." He squinted and looked at Donny.

"What about me?" Donny asked.

Joe shrugged his shoulders. "OK, three assholes." Then he looked away. "Jeez, Donny, what'd we do, lose a bet? Maybe somebody in the pro shop is pissed at us?" Joe turned his palms up and wrinkled his face with the question.

"C'mon, Joe, what happened to that boy who just does what he's told?" Donny raised his eyebrows and nodded 'yes' in a hopeless attempt to draw a smile from Joe.

Joe only grimaced and looked away.

—•—

Lester Schultz ran a very successful insurance agency in Rochester. He was totally unencumbered by professional ethics or personal integrity, and at forty-five he was a leader among the local set who liked to run hard. When he played golf, he drank too much, talked too loud, and bragged openly about marital indiscretions and shady business deals. Joe had once seen Lester Schultz pull an expensive-looking, gold ballpoint pen from his pocket and refer to it as his "golden harpoon" because he used it to stick the big fish. Then he pretended to "wipe the bullshit" from it and put it back in his pocket. Joe loathed him. Donny found him amusing, and he found Joe's hatred of Lester even more amusing.

Omar Hagen was a forty-five-year-old dentist and Lester Schultz's only friend. Omar was similar to Lester on most counts, but he lacked the bravado to let others see him for what he was. Worse than that, in Joe's eyes, Omar seemed to understand that there was a profit in his charade. He apparently understood that people expected him to look and act the part of a concerned, involved community member and professional. It was good for business to deliver that performance, and he intended to continue it. Several years earlier, Joe had told Donny that if Lester Schultz had been a little dumber, and a dentist, he'd be Omar Hagen. The only real difference between the two was that Omar wasn't as bright, and he at least tried to hide his lack of character. He was a womanizer and he was unscrupulous in business, but he was careful to avoid notice. He liked to walk into church a few minutes late and then sit in the front so everyone could see him, and he took every opportunity to be noticed at church and community functions. He was the type of man who volunteered to be on the board of directors for charitable and church organizations, then did nothing, but he made sure everyone knew of his involvement. Both Donny and Joe thought he was a pathetic phony.

"You know, Joe, what Omar really wants is for people to think he's just like you. He's just playing a part—you know, like Shakespeare said: 'All the world is but a stage, and all the men and women merely players.' Don't you think?"

Joe paused. Then, just before he stepped forward to greet Lester Schultz and Omar Hagen, he said softly, "Yeah, Donny, that's about it. But Shakespeare was right on the money there: 'ALL the men and women are merely players'—maybe he is just like me." Donny knew Joe was implying something more, but he didn't understand just what it was, and it was clear that Joe didn't plan to explain anything at the moment.

Joe turned, walked smoothly across the fresh-cut grass by the club-house, and greeted the others with a warm handshake and a smile while they waited in the midst of the dozen or so ancient white oak trees that still surrounded the clubhouse and the first tee. "Hi, Les. Hi, Omar. Beautiful day, huh?"

His countenance had changed entirely; he gave the others no hint of his true feelings toward them. To a stranger, it would have seemed that they were all close friends. Donny extended a similar warm greeting, but the smile he wore was not because he was glad to see Schultz and Hagen; he was simply amused by the way his older brother could hide what was in his heart.

Golf was a game that barely held Joe Mix's interest even on a good day. He was clearly the worst golfer in the foursome, and today his mind was far from his round of golf. It seemed that every time he struck the ball it landed in the rough or out of bounds. Although he really didn't care much about his score, he did enjoy striking the occasional excel-lent shot. On a good day, he could strike the ball for great distance but he never knew just how far off course it might fly. He took chances around trees, water hazards, and sand traps that players with his limit-ed skill should never take. He spent much of his time walking quickly from one errant shot to the next, trying to speed up his play so his part-ners wouldn't be upset with his slow pace. Each bad shot made the next one a little more difficult, but taking those chances hoping to make the perfect shot was the only thing about golf that he liked. Donny usually walked alongside Joe and tried not to offer advice. He only smiled as Joe took off his shoes and went after balls he'd hit into the water hazards or walked circles in the deep rough looking for his ball.

This day had been set aside for a sort of early-season kickoff for the summer golf season. Because of the formal event planned for the evening, a party atmosphere existed on the golf course. Several golf carts driven by pretty young women and loaded with tubs of beer and ice cruised the entire course, doing a brisk business selling beer.

The grass on the fairways was beginning to show the deep green of summer, but the leaves on the deciduous trees had not opened up to form the rich, dense hardwood forest that would shroud every hole at The Oaks later in the season. Some of the trees were about to unfurl the green of summer, but most of the woods around The Oaks still clung to the gray of winter or the soft yellow of early spring.

Joe's slow play turned out to be no problem, due to the crowd on the rest of the golf course. In fact, the foursome had to wait several minutes after each hole for the group in front of them to move along. Everyone was playing slowly.

Lester Schultz and Omar Hagen started out as cordial, pleasant golf partners. The men made small talk and kept the conversation to golf and community events. Play continued evenly for the first nine holes. But shortly after they made the turn at the ninth hole, Lester and Omar began to talk louder and laugh louder than they had previously. Schultz and Hagen rode together in an electric golf car and stocked their own cooler with plenty of beer for the back nine. The more they drank, the more their laughter and storytelling got to be a series of private tales that excluded Joe and Donny.

By the time they'd reached the thirteenth hole, Schultz and Hagen seemed busy with their own conversation. They laughed and talked mainly with each other, and they spoke to Donny and Joe only when it was time to record their scores after each hole. The lack of contact with their partners was just fine with Joe and Donny. The Mix brothers carried their clubs and walked the entire eighteen holes every time they played, so they always had plenty of time to talk.

The thirteenth, fourteenth, fifteenth, and sixteenth holes at The Oaks wound around several large, very irregularly shaped ponds. All four holes had a water hazard to deal with, and the thirteenth and fifteenth were long par threes. So even though play on the back nine was already slow due to the crowd, it was exceptionally slow on the thirteenth through the sixteenth holes because each foursome had to wait for the previous foursome to completely finish the hole before they could tee off.

After he'd finished play on the twelfth hole, Donny flagged down one of the golf cars driven by young women and bought a can of diet soda for himself and one for Joe. When he approached the thirteenth tee, there were three other foursomes already backed up and waiting their turn to play the thirteenth. Lester and Omar were sitting in their golf car, talking loudly and laughing with each other. The golfers from the other foursomes all stood in a large group, a few feet from Lester's car, talking quietly and waiting for the golfers on the thirteenth green to finish play and move on.

23

Donny walked across a wooden bridge that spanned a small creek separating the twelfth and thirteenth holes. As he stepped onto the soft grass near the thirteenth tee box, he saw that Joe wasn't talking with the other men. He was sitting on an old wooden bench, holding a four-iron and looking at the surface of the water on the little pond in front of the thirteenth green. Donny waved to the men and then turned toward Joe. He'd drink his soda and sit with Joe instead of chatting with the others.

"Want a diet pop?" Donny asked as he sat down on the bench next to Joe.

"Thanks." Joe took the can and opened it. He continued to look over the pond. Then he asked quietly, "You happy, Donny?"

Donny tapped the top of his can of pop, opened it, and took a drink. Then he turned and cast a suspicious look at Joe. "Now, why would you ask me something like that?"

Joe's eyes softened, but he still looked over the pond. "I'm just asking, do you like your job?"

"Yeah," Donny shrugged his shoulders. "I'd have to say that I like what I do. But then I fire a couple bitches every so often, then I just re-bitch on Monday. Keeps everyone on their toes!"

Joe re-entered the conversation when Donny's voice trailed off. Donny's words, as he'd intended, had drawn a smile from Joe, but the smile faded quickly. He seemed to stare over the horizon when he spoke. "Years ago, I used to leave for work a little early some mornings. Then I'd just drive out into the country with the car windows open and pretend I wasn't going to the office, you know? I'd just let the morning air rush by and think about not turning around. I'd just dream of driving right on down the road and not coming back. It was such a happy thought, not going to the office." He stopped and took a breath but continued to stare into space. "But then the kids were born, and I just set the plow in a little deeper, like Dad used to say, and I went to work. I just stopped thinking about stuff like not going to work." He turned and smiled at Donny after he mentioned his father, and Donny returned a wide smile in memory of their father. He understood and shared Joe's affection for Ray Mix.

"Yeah, the Old Cowboy was a believer in hard work," Donny chuckled.

Joe changed the subject back to work immediately when Donny looked at him. "I've been seeing a shrink for about five months, Donny. I found myself driving around again last fall and thinking about not going in to work. It's not about work. I like to work. I just hate what I'm doing; I always have." His statement about a psychiatrist, and about work, had a sobering effect on Donny. It was clear that Joe had been waiting for some time to tell him and was asking him to listen, truly listen. He was reaching out to Donny.

"Really?" Donny said slowly as he turned toward Joe.

"Yeah. I hate it—I mean, I really hate it. It isn't very often that somebody walks into my office and says, 'Hey, let's see the best you've got!' I have to beg people to want the good stuff, the nice work. And you know what happens after a few years of that? A dentist starts to dumb it down for patients, just encourage them to ask for less. That way they seem to like us more—for offering less. I don't get it." Joe sighed heavily, looked away, and waited a moment before he spoke again. "And what do you think it does to a man, inside, when he starts to be less, less than what he could be, less than what he is, because that's what people want?" Joe's question required no answer, but when Donny looked into Joe's eyes they were lifeless.

"Wanna know the thing I really like to hear from patients?" He was beyond frustration, beyond sarcasm. Joe was drifting somewhere between anger and despair when he answered his own question: "When somebody tells me they're allergic to Novocaine." He shook his head in disgust. "Then I ask 'em what happens when they have Novocaine, and they'll ALWAYS answer, 'My lip gets really numb.'" Joe grimaced and turned away while Donny laughed out loud. "I hear that once a week, every week! Glad I went to college for an extra decade so I could listen to that shit."

"Know the other side of that coin?" Joe continued with a blank stare. "So many of us think we know everything we need to know on the day we graduate from dental school. We never learn a new thing. Why should we? We already know everything. I'm tellin' you, Donny, what I do requires no creativity or insight. You could teach a damn monkey to do what I do. The profession is for small thinkers. Well, it's also a great profession for pompous people who never think at all." Joe's speech was animated, and he nodded his head yes as he spoke. "I'm not kiddin' you, Donny. If you're a thinker and you're practicing dentistry, you're so far out of the box that your colleagues, your patients, insurance companies, government agencies—everyone begins to resent you."

Donny returned a skeptical look and replied, "Yeah, right!"

"It's true, Donny! Just look!" And Joe pointed at Omar Hagen just as Omar burst into laughter at something Lester Schultz was telling him. "Hell, Omar's not even as bright as most chimps; he's the worst of all phonies; he's terrible. Hell, he's an ax murderer. His work is really bad. But he dresses and acts like the introspective, concerned professional. He doesn't know shit, his work is awful, and yet he's really successful. Go figure. Every morning when he gets up, he must think its Halloween; he dresses up like a dentist and people give him treats."

"Well, that's what I've been trying to tell you. He just wants everyone to think he's as good as you! But forget about him." Donny turned and straddled the little bench so he could look directly at his brother. "Joe, in a town full of doctors, world-famous doctors, your name comes to everyone's lips first. Everyone knows you're the best at what you do. If anyone asks about who's the best dentist in town, your name comes up first, you know that?" Donny ended his statement as a question and waited briefly for Joe's reply. But before Joe could answer, Donny spoke up again. "What about all those people who call you and ask you to do that Hollywood stuff—makeovers and shit—because guys like Omar just can't do it? You get a lot of that kind of stuff coming your way, don't you?"

"Yeah, I guess so," Joe sighed. "But it's just not enough anymore. It never really was what I thought it all should be. I've just been waiting all these years for it to be what I expected." Joe's voice trailed off. Then he added, "Hell, it's never gonna be, Donny. I wound up here because I allowed myself to follow the path of least resistance. I never wanted to do this; I've never liked it. Donny, do you remember Carl Yastrzemski, left fielder for the Red Sox—a GREAT player, a Hall of Famer? Well, I heard an interview with him once, and the interviewer asked him about his love of the game. Know what he said? He got a forlorn look on his face and replied that he'd never had any fun playing ball. At the time I heard him say that, I was shocked. I just couldn't understand how someone that good at such a cool thing could have no fun doing it. Well, I understand now. "

"Jeez, Joe. Don't you think everyone deals with frustration at work? Like you just said, people in every profession, every job, deal with burnout or whatever this is that you're feeling," Donny said.

Joe squeezed the grip on his four-iron and stared at his hands. "Thoreau said, 'Most men lead lives of quiet desperation.' I'm tellin' you, I understand what 'quiet desperation' means. I simply chose the wrong profession, the wrong life. I just chose the wrong thing, or maybe I just let others choose it for me. I don't belong where I am."

Joe turned and looked into Donny's eyes, but said nothing for a moment. "I hate it! I just hate it." He sighed heavily and looked at his feet. "Know why I chose dentistry? Really?"

"Why?"

"Cause Dad pushed and pushed and pushed me to be a doctor. He just thought that would solve all of my problems forever. You know—the doctor was the wealthiest, most respected man in town. You remember Dr. Sheedy, right?"

"Yeah. Nice man."

"Hell, he was a saint when we were kids."

"So why DID you choose dentistry, if Dad was pushing medicine?"

"Well, I actually was fascinated by the elegant design in human anatomy, and by the complex mysteries of human physiology. I always enjoyed the study of that stuff." Joe stopped, and his eyebrows bunched up while he chose his words again. "I guess I thought all that stuff was beautiful and I wanted to learn it…I just never wanted to spend my life trying to fix any of it." Joe looked at his hands for a moment and seemed to be listening to what he'd just said. "I just didn't want to deal with death. I couldn't stand the thought of telling someone that their closest loved one was dead, or having someone die in my arms." Joe looked away. "So I chose dentistry—didn't think I'd mind telling people they needed a root canal. Other than that, medicine and dentistry seemed to be six of one and half a dozen of the other, know what I mean?"

"Yeah, but what the hell does all that have to do with the Old Cowboy?" Donny asked.

"Let me back up a little bit." Joe paused and looked at his four-iron. "One day, when I was in college, I went into Dad's office at the stockyards. Told him I thought I wanted to come back to Kadoka and join him in the cattle business."

"Really? I never heard this before," Donny smiled. "What'd he say?"

"He had a shit hemorrhage!" Joe smiled now too, and when he looked into his brother's eyes, each of them could see that the other was holding onto the same image: Ray Mix, the Old Cowboy, stomping around his little office at the Kadoka Livestock Exchange and lecturing Joe about his career choice.

"Yeah, Dad looked like he'd swallowed a bug! Said he worked his whole goddamn life to try and give me something better than what he had. Said I was a fool to come back home and be a cowboy like him." Joe looked back through the years and smiled as he remembered his father's tirade. "He looked at me—he was damn near speechless—then he said, 'Jesus, boy, why the hell would you wanna come back here and shovel shit? You need to get an education, be a doctor! You're the smartest kid any of your teachers has ever seen. At least that's what they kept tellin' your mother and me!'" Joe grinned at Donny. "Can you see his face, telling me to be a doctor?"

"Yeah. So what did you say?"

"Said I just wanted to be like him." Joe hadn't stopped smiling. "Shit, Donny, I think that was all I ever wanted, to be like him. But you know, when I told him that—that I wanted to be like him—he just stepped back and stared at me for a second. He looked like he was disappointed in me—disappointed that I could set my sights so low." Joe looked away and shook his head. "I've never been able to understand why he would say that. He looked at his feet for just a moment, then he looked right into my eyes and said, 'Why the hell would you want to be like me? I'm just a dumb cowboy!'"

Donny waited for Joe to continue.

"I told him, 'Because you're my hero, Dad!' You should have seen him, Donny. He looked stricken. He slumped over and turned away from me. He just stopped talking about it.

"Everything sort of turned with that conversation. I just decided to do what he said I should. I chose this not because it was what I thought I wanted; I chose it because it was what I thought HE wanted for me. You believe that, Donny?"

Donny's face dropped. He looked at his five-iron, then tapped it on the ground. Each time the club hit the ground he said, "Joe, Joe, Joe." Then, in a tone that was meant to chastise his brother, he said, "I just don't get it. You have money, status, a great reputation, you're good at what you do—with the exception of golf—and people like you." Donny shrugged his shoulders and raised his eyebrows. "I don't get it! You've lived the American Dream."

"I know, Donny, and that's a scary thought, isn't it?" Joe raised his eyebrows and stared at his brother.

"Huh?"

"Nothing," Joe sighed. "Nothing."

For a moment, neither man spoke. Just beyond their silence they could hear the laughter of the other men on the tee box. And drifting across the golf course they could hear the occasional faint, agonized cry of "FUCK!" or "SHIT!" as some duffer shanked an approach shot or missed a short putt.

In an effort to steer his brother to a little rosier look at the world, Donny changed the subject. "Oh hell, Joe, everybody gets a little fed up with work from time to time. But remember: your wife will be here tonight. When she shows up with her blonde hair looking so fine, and wearing some sort of long evening dress, every guy here is gonna want to go home with your date."

"Well, be careful what you wish for; you just might get it," Joe sighed.

Donny leaned back and then cautiously turned to face Joe. He'd jumped from the frying pan into the fire. He grimaced, then shrugged his shoulders to exaggerate his need for an explanation. "Huh?" he asked, as though he couldn't believe his ears.

"All she does is work out and shop. She should look pretty good." Joe's voice carried disappointment, then anger, then an inclination to share another secret.

Donny was well aware of the reputation Jess had earned as a "rich bitch." Those in the community who knew Jess from a distance saw her as an attractive woman who also happened to be an energetic volunteer for dozens of local causes, and who was always available for fund-raisers and benefits and numerous community service activities. But through the years, always behind Joe's back, Donny had heard people who'd come to know her a little better talk in hushed voices about how Jess was just "somebody's wife" who really liked to be treated as if she were someone special—a princess—and who always had an opinion on things she really didn't know much about. Donny had been vaguely aware of a frosty distance that had gradually grown between Joe and Jess. He'd sensed an unkind silence from time to time when he'd been in the company of both Joe and Jess, but since Joe had never spoken of any disharmony in his marriage, and since he'd never seen them argue in public, Donny had been unable to come to any conscious recognition of trouble between them. Now, with one simple comment from Joe, Donny was aware that the scab had been picked off an old wound he'd never really noticed, and his brother wanted him to look at it. Only a few minutes earlier, he'd been surprised by his brother's need to share his frustrations about his career, and now it seemed urgent for Joe to share something far more personal. Joe appeared to have been waiting for an opportunity to talk about his marriage, too. Donny didn't try to hide the concern in his voice. "Jeez, Joe, troubles at home, too?"

"Not really. It's always been that way," Joe answered somewhat casually.

"What way?" Donny prodded.

"You know!" The way Joe said the words "you know" made it clear to Donny that he was aware of the way some people saw his wife. "Jess's possessions and Jess's appearance really do matter more than everything else, and it's getting old."

"Joe?" Donny grimaced.

"Yeah?"

"Has your shrink mentioned anything about midlife crisis?"

"Yeah, it's all she talks about. Well, she talks about sex a lot; I think she might be some sort of pervert." Joe smiled for the first time in a while. Then his smile vanished when he continued, "But that's not what's going on here."

"Oh?" Donny raised his eyebrows and made a point to question Joe's casual dismissal of the classic midlife crisis in men.

"Yeah! Of course, Donny, you're referring to the classic midlife crisis scenario, where a middle-aged man realizes that his life hasn't turned out as well as he'd hoped and dreamed, and he reaches out for a younger woman and a hot car to make up or compensate for something else that has passed him by. You mean that stuff, right? Well, here's the deal: I'm really good at what I do, and I'm making a lot of money doing it. But there's no joy in it! I hate going to work in the morning because I don't like my job and don't want it anymore. I never did want it. I wanna go and be good at something that matters, has meaning, and makes a difference—on some level. And wouldn't it be nice to find some joy at work? But I'm stuck here. I've got golden handcuffs holding me to a job I hate." Joe stopped. His eyes tightened and he continued. "And my wife? The lovely Jess? She's...hmph." Joe stopped himself. "Donny," Joe said softly as he redirected himself, "I do understand the midlife crisis thing. But this just isn't it. I'm not after a new woman or a car. And I'm not trying to recapture my lost youth. I've just begun to feel that I'm living someone else's life, and I want mine back. I lost something a long time ago, I don't even know what it was, but I want it back. And I want my life to mean something—to ME!"

Donny stared into Joe's eyes and understood for the first time that his brother was really struggling, and that he had been for some time.

"OK, you guys! We're up!" Lester Schultz called out to Joe and Donny. The other golfers hit first, and when Joe took his turn on the thirteenth tee he struck the ball perfectly. The sound of Joe's stroke was the precise, violent little "whack" that a well-struck golf ball makes. Joe's four-iron relayed the precision of the smooth stroke to his hands, and he knew even before his eye began to track the flight of the ball that he'd done something very well. The ball sailed high, and straight, over the water hazard and between the sand traps. It looked to be headed straight for the cup. When it landed, there seemed to be no bounce at all; it just appeared suddenly, about six feet to the left of the flag.

"Nice shot!" Omar and Lester called out in unison.

"I like my four-iron!" was all Joe said as he turned with a smile and picked up his bag.

"You should," Donny added. "It's the only club you can hit!"

"Up yours, Donny," Joe said cheerfully as he walked off the tee box.

Donny laughed out loud and hurried to catch up with his brother.

Joe proceeded to three-putt for a disappointing bogey. But all he talked about for the next few minutes was his fine tee shot. When they resumed play on the fourteenth hole, Joe hit a miserable drive into the water and followed that shot with a fairway wood that sliced all the way across the fairway and landed out of bounds on the right side of the hole.

Donny walked along with Joe as they moved from one errant shot to the next. "Do you ever want to take a mulligan, Donny? Just hit another ball and play that one instead?" Joe asked.

"That would be bad form. Keeping score would be a nightmare. No, you have to play that first ball no matter what," Donny replied as he sipped at a Diet Coke.

"Yeah. I guess so," Joe agreed.

After several more ugly attempts to approach the green, Joe found himself walking toward his ball for the ninth time. He tried to settle down, and he took several practice swings with his pitching wedge before he addressed the ball. His swing looked surprisingly smooth for a golfer who scored so poorly, and he struck the ball perfectly. It sailed over several trees and a large sand trap before it bounced once and rolled directly into the hole. He'd made an extraordinary shot; he'd pitched in from seventy-five yards away.

"A beauty!" Omar offered. He was chuckling over Joe's outrageous reversal of fortune when he held up the scorecard and questioned Joe with his eyes. Joe furrowed his brow and began to mentally replay the hole. He was concentrating as he tried to remember each time he'd struck the ball. He nodded with the memory of each stroke and counted on his fingers. Omar smiled as he waited for Joe to finish counting his strokes on the fourteenth hole. Finally, Joe answered.

"Nine!" Joe said with a smile. "Did you like that last one, Donny?"

"Yeah," Donny nodded and tried to hide a smile. "Did you use your four-iron?" He paused and let Omar and Lester chuckle for a moment. Then he added, "Jeez, Joe, you're the only guy I know who can score a quintuple bogey—a nine, for God's sake—and then stand there and smile like you just won the Masters. I don't get it."

"Well, I stroked a helluva shot! And besides that..." Joe paused.

"Yeah?" Donny prodded, hoping that Joe might let go and swear the blue streak he was stifling. "And..."

"And up yours," Joe smiled.

As they'd played the thirteenth and fourteenth holes, both Joe and Donny had been able to chitchat with their playing partners enough to observe the social amenities. But they were both eager for another opportunity to talk privately. Ever since Donny had seen the look in Joe's eyes when he mentioned Jess, he'd been unable to stop thinking about Jess. Donny had never been very close to her. Neither he nor Jess had ever had much interest in developing a friendship with the other. But every so often, Donny remembered something that one of the groomsmen in his own wedding had said to him at the reception afterwards. Several beers had given his friend the courage to confess, "Hey, your brother's wife is really sexy. But you know, I can't say if I think she's attractive or kind of ugly in a slutty, sexy way. That make any sense to you?" Donny had made a face and shaken his head "no," but he'd understood exactly what his friend was getting at.

"You know what I mean!" his friend had insisted. "All guys know what I mean. She's got that bleached blonde hair and athletic body. Maybe it's her big chin, maybe it's that I think she might be kind of dumb, I dunno. There's something about her that's hot and slutty and makes me want to have a run at her, but she's not really...pretty." Donny had simply smiled and waited for his friend to continue. "And the way she flirts, she reminds me of those sex monkeys that used to show up at frat parties looking for a good time, remember?" His friend had paused and added one final thought as he looked at Jess from across the room. "Yeah, can't tell if she's pretty or ugly, huh? Some women have beauty. Others just have sexuality. Know what I mean? Hell, all guys know what I'm talking about, right? She looks pretty good if she's had time to get ready, but I'll bet she looks really rough in the morning. One of those women that you love to take home but hate to wake up with. Just can't tell if she's ugly or sexy. Men understand that, but women don't." He was still trying to explain it all to himself, as though it were some cosmic mystery, when he'd wandered off to talk to someone else.

Donny smiled every time he thought of that conversation. And although he'd denied it, he knew his friend had found exactly the right words.

———

Play was backed up as it had been all day, and very slow, on the fifteenth hole, just as it had been on the thirteenth. The same small crowd of golfers was standing around and waiting by the fifteenth tee when Joe and Donny walked over from the fourteenth green.

Most of the golfers waiting around to play the fifteenth hole were friends or acquaintances of Joe and Donny, so the brothers took a brief moment to socialize with the group. As usual, men were laughing about bad golf strokes by their playing partners or telling jokes. When Lester Schultz began waving his arms and hollering to add a visual element to a dirty story that both Joe and Donny thought had descended from funny to pointless and stupid, they retreated from the group to a small bench by the edge of the pond that provided a water hazard for the fifteenth and sixteenth holes.

Joe held his four-iron and sat facing the water, tapping the club gently between his feet and staring blankly somewhere beyond it. When Donny sat down next to Joe, he was carrying a five-iron and took the same position as Joe, then waited for Joe to speak. After Joe had remained silent for a moment, Donny lifted his five-iron and tapped

Joe's shoe. Joe turned a sideways glance to Donny. He said nothing, but his eyes tightened slightly and asked the subtle question, "What?"

Donny chose not to speak either. When he looked at Joe's face, he turned his palms up and let his eyes answer, "I'm waiting." He wanted to pick up where the conversation had been interrupted earlier.

Joe smiled softly and looked away. He felt like he was holding a pitcher full of something, something heavy, and he wanted to pour it out and share it with Donny, but he was afraid that whatever came out might spill all over and he'd never be able to get it back.

"I almost called off our wedding, all those years ago," he started, looking out across the water. Donny could see that the laughter of the last few minutes had been good for Joe, and now he was willing to let go of a burden that he'd kept unspoken for years and was finally ready to share. The candor in his voice caught Donny off guard once again.

"No shit? How come?" Donny had never heard any of this before, and he'd never seen Joe act like this. The frustration in Joe's eyes told Donny that something unpleasant had been brewing in Joe's heart for quite a while.

"Hmph," Joe chuckled. "You know, I don't even remember anymore. I mean, I don't remember exactly what Jess did to make me so angry. But I do remember thinking I really didn't want to be married, for the rest of my LIFE, to her." Joe turned and looked at Donny. "Isn't that odd, Donny? I can't remember what it was anymore. But I knew, I knew I was making a mistake...marrying her." Joe shook his head and smiled an odd smile at Donny. Then his eyes hardened when he continued, "I'll tell you what I DO remember about that incident." He paused, then looked as if he might not continue. Whatever he'd begun to pour out of the pitcher was splashing now, and Joe felt anxious over what Donny might be thinking. But he needed to keep on talking, keep on pouring.

"Yeah?" Donny pushed.

Joe tapped his four-iron on the ground again several times before he spoke. "I do remember thinking that I couldn't call the wedding off, that it was impossible!"

"Why?"

"Cause we'd already sent the wedding invitations." Joe paused again. "And Mom would have been really embarrassed." He looked back at Donny. "You believe that, Donny? I mean, really. Can you believe I made a decision that important, and that wrong, for that reason? I married the wrong person because I knew that Mom—and other people, I guess—were expecting a wedding from me, and I didn't want to disappoint them."

"I never heard any of this before."

"Well, it's not the kind of thing you talk about, I guess." He'd reached the tipping point; he knew the story was splashing all over Donny, but now he had to empty everything out.

Donny felt a sinking feeling in his stomach. Joe's story struck him as so wrong and sad. "Jeez, Joe, did Jess know what was on your mind?"

"Yeah, I think so," Joe sighed. "When she realized how angry I was, what I was thinking, she began to understand that I just might call the whole thing off." Joe's eyes narrowed, and he smiled a wicked smile that seemed out of place. "That's when she sort of took control of things. She did that thing that women like her do in that situation: she applied so much sex that I got confused and gave up, like I always do. I guess I figured all that sex must translate into love somewhere along the line, or maybe I just figured that all that sex made everything else OK. You know how young men think at times like that." He smiled a faraway smile and shook his head at the truth in his own confession. But just beyond the smile, Donny could see his brother's anguish and regret, and he sensed the pain that Joe must have been feeling, just listening to himself say those words.

A burst of laughter and hollering erupted from the men on the fifteenth tee. One of the golfers in the foursome ahead of Joe and Donny had come within inches of scoring a hole-in-one. His ball had rolled to within a foot of the flag, and about half of the golfers were congratulating him on such a fine shot while the other half were joking about the custom that any golfer who scores a hole-in-one is supposed to buy a round of drinks for everyone in the clubhouse.

Joe and Donny both smiled, waved at the man who hit the shot, then turned back toward each other and sat down again on the little bench while they waited for the other foursome to continue.

After a brief silence, Donny leaned over toward Joe. "So how did you resolve everything—the issue that caused the anger?"

"Well, like I said, I don't remember that part of the incident. That's odd, I guess, isn't it? But whatever it was sort of went away, because of sex, I suppose. You know, Donny, that moment, that incident, sort of gives illumination now to everything that came before it, and after it, between Jess and me."

"What do you mean?"

"Well, here's the deal, Donny, the bottom line." Joe laid his four-iron on the bench and crossed his arms on his chest. "I just happened to be the one that Jess was dating when she decided to get married. She came from a poor family, really poor, and she just recognized me as a guy from a good home who was gonna make a good living, be good to her, and give her the life she wanted." Joe paused, then looked around. "This! You know! The country club, cars, house—stuff like that. I just represent a pretty fine bit of nest feathering, that's all. She just did whatever she needed to do in order to get the deal done. I think she traded love for security, or she at least grabbed hold of security and hoped that love would come along later. But it never really did." Joe paused and stared into the sky. "I'd have taken love. Well, I should have. I had my chance." Donny waited silently for the uncomfortable moment to pass.

"You really feel that way? Really?" Donny asked.

"Yeah," Joe said softly, and nodded. He felt bad, heavy, because of what he'd said, but he was glad to have said it.

Neither of them spoke for a moment. Just as Donny was about to ask a question, Joe blurted, "Do you kiss your wife goodnight?"

"Huh? Yeah, sure."

"Every night?" Joe asked.

"Yeah, pretty much," Donny nodded.

"Remember how Mom used to tuck us in bed like that? A kiss, and an 'I love you'?" Joe's question needed no answer. "I thought that's just the way people who love each other said goodnight."

"Jess doesn't do that?" Donny asked.

"Never!" Joe said with a slight grimace. "Not since we got married, anyway."

"Joe, c'mon. I deal with people and their marital problems every day, you know—divorce and shit like that. A kiss goodnight doesn't really amount to much one way or the other, you know? Besides that, you mean to tell me you've never been happy in twenty-four years of marriage, and you don't love Jess? Is that what you're saying?"

"Well, I've tried to believe we were in love. Sometimes it really seemed like it, mostly when we were on vacation. We seemed to be able to create the illusion of a loving couple, at least well enough so we could believe it ourselves for a while. But...no...well...I really don't know the answer to that one."

"Wow, Joe. Makes me feel bad to hear this stuff. You said you're seeing a shrink?"

"Yeah. Did I tell you it was a woman shrink?"

"Yeah. How's it going with her?"

"OK, I guess. She asks a lot of sex questions. You know, frequency, positions, fantasies, stuff like that."

"Have you told her all this stuff you told me?"

"Uh huh. More!"

"What'd she say?"

Joe turned his head slowly. His eyes began to smile first, then the dimple on the right side of his face appeared as his lips curved into an enormous grin. "Sent me a bill for $1,800!" Both men burst out laughing. Then Joe continued as his wicked grin reappeared. "Wouldn't that be a great job? Sit around and listen while people tell you dirty stories, then charge 'em $400 an hour? Another profession that beats the hell out of dentistry, eh?"

Donny saw Joe smile, then laugh openly for the first time in a while. And when he looked into Joe's eyes, he knew Joe had much more to talk about.

"OK, you guys, we're up!" Omar called from the tee box.

———•———

Sunset was only a few minutes away when Omar Hagen reached into the cup on the eighteenth green and retrieved his ball. Donny put the flagstick back in place and then extended his hand to Omar. "Thanks for a nice afternoon, Omar. Had a good time today! Lester, you too! Thanks for a nice time." He shook Lester's hand also. Suddenly, Donny's face blossomed into a huge smile as he remembered something. "Hey, Lester, you gonna sign this scorecard with the golden harpoon?" Everyone could hear the laughter in his voice. He found the imagery of the harpoon hilarious, but he'd deliberately asked about the golden harpoon just to aggravate Joe.

Lester Schultz returned Donny's smile, and he seemed to perk up with the mention of his harpoon. "Absolutely. In fact, I think we should all use it!" And much to Donny's surprise, Lester reached into his golf bag and produced a gold pen, then held it out as if it were a fine cigar.

Donny laughed out loud. The golden harpoon made him laugh every time he thought about it, and the fact that Lester took it with him to play golf struck him as even more outrageous. The icing on the cake for Donny was that Joe despised the whole golden harpoon thing. It seemed like Lester was flaunting his lack of integrity, and now Joe was going to have to sign his scorecard with it!

"You take that thing golfing?" Donny chuckled.

"You never know when you might stick a big one!" Lester smiled.

Joe faked a smile, signed the scorecard with the golden harpoon, then thanked Lester and Omar once more for the round of golf. When they walked off the eighteenth green, Donny put his arm around Joe's shoulder and called goodbye to Lester and Omar. He knew Joe had put up with all he could, and he was glad to be rid of them. "There, now. That wasn't so bad, was it?" Donny chided.

"Bout like having a catheter removed, I'd say," Joe answered with a scowl.

"Well, let's shower up and I'll buy you a drink before the girls get here!"

"I'll catch up with you, Donny. There's still a few minutes of daylight left, and I'd like to see if I can find a couple trout over in the creek behind the clubhouse." Joe's face bent into a faraway smile as he reached into his golf bag, produced a two-piece fly rod, and began assembling it. "If Lester can carry the harpoon, I guess I can carry this." Twenty-four summers earlier, Joe's first golf partner had given him the hand-made, bamboo fly rod after a very special round of golf.

"Jeez, Joe. You're the only guy I've ever seen carry a fly rod in his golf bag."

"It's my favorite club! I only use it when I find myself in a really difficult lie!" Now Donny could see some joy appear in his brother's eyes. "Carry my clubs back up to the locker room, will ya? I'll be right up. I just need to see what I can do down by the creek."

For just a moment, as the May sun softened and the yellow afternoon light flickered through the oak and cottonwood boughs that were still only threatening to open up into a curtain of green, Joe Mix found a glimmer of satisfaction. He stood at the edge of the tranquil creek and eased himself into the rhythms of the water and the wind. The trees swayed ever so gently in the early-evening breeze, and the surface of the water softened into an undulating, glossy sheet.

Joe found a clearing along the creek's bank that sloped gently to the water's edge. The place was fairly out of the way for any passing golfers, but it was visible from the clubhouse windows and from the ninth and eighteenth greens.

The custom-built rod in his hand was light and well balanced. Joe stood for a moment and held the rod while he admired it. The builder had been an artist. He'd created a light bamboo rod with a powerful spine and a fast action; most of the bend in the rod was out near the tip. It had been traveling in Joe's golf bag off and on for years so that he could always be ready for times like this.

Standing there beside the creek, Joe began to sense that people were watching him, and he stepped behind a tree in order to conceal himself from passing golfers or observers from the clubhouse. The current moved briskly along at his feet while he looked up and down the opposite bank, searching for trout rising to the surface to feed. He sneaked a look around both sides of the tree he was leaning against, but he couldn't see that anyone nearby was watching him. It shouldn't matter if anyone was watching, he thought. After all, there were no club rules about members fishing in the creek. But he knew that several of the older members, and even a couple younger members, had spoken up about his fishing in the creek from time to time. "Lack of etiquette," they'd claimed, or "distracting" or "it just doesn't look right."

Joe had grown self-conscious about it, and he tried to be as secretive as he could when he sneaked over to the creek to cast a fly.

Two lips suddenly appeared through the shimmering gray layer of film on top of the creek and sipped a gray-winged mayfly off the water's flat surface. Just as the ring of the rise widened in concentric circles across the top of the creek, a smile appeared and then spread over Joe's face.

The trout wasn't very big, but he was feeding in a difficult lie and seemed to be calling to Joe, daring him: "Here I am, Joe. Let's see who's better at this game, you or me." He rose again in the same place, just under a row of gooseberry bushes that hung over the far bank of the creek. It would be a difficult place for a fisherman to cast a fly, and the trout seemed to know it. He'd found a safe place to feed, with plenty of mayflies drifting by like pork chops on a conveyor belt, free for the taking.

Joe's first response was to reach for his fly rod and begin to strip line from the reel so he could start to false cast the line over his head. Then he looked at the brisk current in front of him and realized he'd have to do a little wading. The thought of walking through the cold water of early spring gave him reason to stop and think it all over for a minute. He didn't know what the bottom was like right here, during spring runoff, and he was afraid to step into the current and have it pull him downstream. More than that, though—much more than that—he was afraid that some of the members, here for tonight's party, might see him fishing in the little creek by the clubhouse and disapprove.

The trout rose again and called to Joe. "Maybe another time," Joe answered. He watched the trout rise several more times, then took off his golf shoes and socks and stepped into the creek up to his ankles. The cool water and the mud and the sand swirled between his toes and felt wonderful. He watched the trout rise for a while, and thought about all the conflicting expectations of others, before he turned away and walked to the clubhouse.

chapter four

Donny Mix straddled a wooden bench in the country club locker room. His tuxedo jacket was still hanging from his locker door, but he was almost dressed for the formal dance. He'd showered, pulled his pants on, and then sat down and talked with friends for the past half-hour. He leaned back and called out to one of the men standing at a sink, "So, Mike, why do we do this every year?"

"Do what?" answered the young man with a towel around his waist, as he wiped the fog off the mirror in front of him and combed his hair.

"You know. This 'prom night' thing at the country club," Donny responded.

"I don't know. My wife likes this dress-up stuff," replied the man. His voice echoed around the locker room.

Joe had been listening to the conversation between Donny and several other men while he dressed, but he hadn't been part of it. Donny and the others were not quite finished dressing yet—they'd been slowed by their conversation—but Joe was ready to be done with the noisy, steamy locker room.

Joe reached into the locker and removed his tuxedo jacket. He pulled it over his shoulders and walked to the large mirror by the door, then turned sideways and sucked his belly in again while he looked at himself. Ignoring the conversation around him, Joe moved toward the door and then called out, "Donny, I'll buy you a drink!"

"Be with you in a minute, bro," Donny answered. Joe could hear laughter from another, more distant locker room conversation as the door swung shut behind him.

Joe thought it felt good to step out of the noisy locker room and into the rich atmosphere of the stately clubhouse. Many of the people milling around the bar and restaurant area of the country club were unfamiliar to Joe. The restaurant area by the bar overlooked the first and the tenth tee boxes, and two large wooden doors separated the restaurant area from a large ballroom/banquet hall. The ballroom was paneled with dark oak and lit with about a dozen large chandeliers. Tonight the ballroom was set up with dozens of round tables, each set with linen tablecloths and elegant china place settings. One corner of the ballroom had been prepared as a dance floor and a bandstand. The members of the band were setting up their instruments and amplifiers, talking quietly amongst themselves.

As Joe approached the bar, he made eye contact with the bartender. "Hi, Slats," he said with a smile as he slid a barstool under himself.

"Hi, Doc," answered the ashen-colored little man. Slats Murphy had been the bartender at The Oaks as long as anyone could remember. For years Slats had been a postal worker during the day and worked the bar at The Oaks at night. After he'd retired from the Postal Service twenty-some years earlier, he'd continued to tend the bar at the country club. For many of the members, Slats seemed like the owner of The Oaks. He was always there, and he seemed to be the man in charge of everything. Although he was never really involved with the decisions regarding the operation of The Oaks, he knew everything that was happening from day to day, and he was the unofficial historian of The Oaks. He'd smoked cigarettes for about sixty years, and looked like it. He was thin and his face was always a pale gray. Surprisingly, his skin had retained a soft look, like a woman's, not the deep wrinkles and ruddy complexion that usually marks men who are longtime smokers. Slats always wore a bow tie, and a smile. "What'll ya have?" he asked.

"Diet pop for me and a scotch and water for Donny."

"How'd ya hit it today, Doc?" Slats asked as he poured the drinks.

"Moved a lot of dirt," Joe answered.

Slats laughed visibly but made no sound. It was just the way Slats laughed. His face twisted into a happy smile, and something seemed to move in his chest, but he made no sound of laughter. Joe looked at the old man and smiled. He'd always liked Slats. Now, as Slats fumbled with something under the bar, Joe looked beyond the frail old man and scanned the trophies and photos on the wall behind the bar.

His gaze stopped on one photo that had special meaning for him. On one fateful day during his first summer in Rochester, he'd been assigned to play in a men's day foursome with the best players at The Oaks. The golfer who usually completed their foursome had been absent due to illness, or business, or some other long forgotten reason, and at the last minute they'd allowed Joe to join them for the day since Joe was by himself and had no partners to play with. Joe had seen something special unfold that day.

A very young Joe Mix looked back at him from the photo. Joe saw himself with a shaggy haircut, a tight golf shirt with a huge collar, and hilarious plaid pants as he posed with the other golfers. Two of the golfers were older men, and they looked unhappy while Joe and the other man smiled openly. Joe was staring at the photo with a tiny grin of satisfaction when Slats reached up and put the drinks on the bar.

Slats caught Joe's eye, then looked over his own shoulder, behind the bar. He knew right away what Joe was looking at. "Helluva day, wasn't it?"

Twenty-four summers earlier, Joe Mix, Big Ben Monahan, Lyle Davies, and Win Westby had played a round of golf together. Win Westby had set the course record, a fifty-nine. Westby had shot a twenty-nine on the front nine and a thirty on the back nine. He'd chipped in four times and hit the two finest shots anyone could remember. He'd finished at twelve under par for the round.

Joe raised his pop to his lips, took a drink, and set the glass back on the bar. But he never stopped grinning at the photo. "I really liked Win. He was such a smart guy! He was different than the others!" Joe said.

"Yeah," Slats added, "he was a good guy. But the old-timers never really liked him, and the young guys never made him part of the group." Slats shook his head as if he didn't understand what went wrong.

"He was just different, Slats. He didn't need to be part of any of the cliques around here. He was just different." Then Joe started to tell Slats a story that he'd told many times before, and Slats listened as he always did.

"I'll never forget...we were on the second hole," Joe started, "and he hit his second shot over the green, about ten feet past the fringe on the back side of the green, probably the only bad shot he hit all day. It landed about six inches in front of a tiny tree. The only thing he could do was take a drop. But he walked up to the ball and then he turned to me. Know what he said? He said, 'I think I've got a pretty good game in me today!' And he turned around, pulled a four-iron out of his bag, and addressed his ball so that he was facing AWAY from the green, which was about twenty feet from his ball. None of us could believe what we were seeing. We thought for a minute that he'd lost his mind—didn't know where he was. He stood over the ball as though he was gonna hit it farther away from the green, but he was planning to BANK IT...OFF THAT LITTLE TREE! He took a nice, easy swing and hit his ball right at that little tree. Unbelievable! He hit that tiny little tree just perfect and the ball bounced back past him. Then it rolled onto the green and into the hole. He banked his ball off a tree the size of a horse's leg, deliberately, and knocked it in for a birdie!" Joe stopped, then started again.

"That's the way it went all day! And Win never stopped smiling. Everything he hit was true, and he got every bounce. But he saved the best for last. His drive on the eighteenth sliced into the rough. He knew that if he birdied the hole he'd have a sixty and tie the course record. When we walked up to his ball, he looked around and saw that he had a pretty good lie. But there were about six trees between him and the green. Hell, we all knew that the smart thing to do was hit safely out of the rough and then hope to go up and down in two. But when he got to that ball, he started to smile and he couldn't stop. He looked at me again, and he said, 'I got a pretty good round going here, Joe, I'm not gonna let up now. Besides that, trees are mostly air anyway, right?' And he took out a fairway wood, addressed the ball for about a half-second, and hit a rocket. It didn't carry the trees, though—went right through 'em! And never hit a thing! His ball landed about ten feet from the hole, and he made the putt for an eagle—a fifty-nine!" Joe smiled at Slats.

Slats had listened carefully as he always did when Joe told the story. He listened the way others did when HE told the same story, and he told it quite often too.

Both men were still smiling faraway smiles when Joe asked, "Do you still hear from Win?"

"Sure," Slats answered, "a couple times a year. And here we've been talking about him like he was dead or something. He asks about you from time to time. I think he liked you, too."

"Yeah," Joe grimaced. "I sort of lost track of him after that first summer." Joe looked away and shook his head. "I got real busy with work. And then he moved away. Boy, that really surprised everybody when he quit his job and moved to Georgia…to make furniture. He was some sort of electrical engineer, wasn't he?"

"He just wanted to make furniture, work with wood, stuff like that." Slats shook his head and shrugged. "I think he's sort of an artist; he just wanted to do things his own way." Slats paused for a drag on his cigarette, and a gray cloud of smoke slid silently through his lips when he continued. "He used to talk about how the grain of a piece of wood told him secrets, and that there was living history written in the wood." Slats stopped and laughed silently as more smoke puffed away from him. "People thought he was weird. Nobody thinks about stuff like that."

"I remember," Joe added. He also knew that, like Win Westby, he often thought about "stuff like that." Joe let that thought slip away when Slats spoke up again.

"My old man kept a willow switch above the kitchen door jamb when I was a kid," Slats laughed again as smoke billowed out of him. "He used it to tell me a few secrets about bad behavior when I was a kid." Smoke continued to drift from Slats for a while as he laughed.

"Know what else I remember about that day?" Joe's face bent into a grin.

"Huh!"

"I remember how much fun Big Ben Monahan and Lyle Davies weren't having! I think they were really pissed off that Win played so well that it seemed effortless, and he enjoyed it!"

Slats lit another cigarette and leaned against the counter behind him. "Big Ben—he was just a surly, fat old prick whose best days were way behind him when Win came along. But Lyle, he was good! Club champion seventeen out of twenty-one years! Lyle never seemed to like it out here, and I think he hated Win for having fun. Seemed like he was always angry, like he owed it to himself to come out here and suffer a couple times a week. Just imagine being that good at something and not liking it."

Joe stared at his soda.

"That reminds me, Joe." Slats looked suddenly embarrassed. He leaned forward and spoke more deliberately. "Some of the old-timers are upset about your fishin' on the creek. They think it's just not right, and one of the guys on the etiquette committee is gonna talk to you about it. He's gonna ask you to stop it. If Lyle was still alive, he'd be one of the guys bitchin' about it."

"Really?" Joe seemed surprised, but not angry. "I guess I could knock it off. There's plenty of good fishin' just down the road." He turned toward Slats and asked, "What do you think about it?"

Slats lit yet another cigarette, then paused before he answered. "I don't like it either—just don't look right. Shit, I sound like Lyle Davies, don't I?" As he laughed his silent laugh, smoke poured out of him. "Sorry, Joe, but it don't look right, it just don't!"

The idea of reproach from someone on the etiquette committee stung Joe at first. He felt embarrassed. Then he began to feel indignant and a little angry. But he said nothing more of it.

chapter five

Joe Mix sat alone at the bar while Slats held his cigarette in his left hand and leaned against the bar with his right as he laughed and joked with Joe. "Don't you get in trouble for smoking here, Slats?" Joe asked after a while.

"Not yet." Slats shook with laughter but still made no sound. "If I stand right here, by the door to the kitchen, the exhaust fan in there draws all the smoke and nobody really notices." He raised his eyebrows and smiled, and Joe couldn't miss the odd contrast in the little man. Slats Murphy had the thin, soft face of an old man, but bursting from that face was the open-mouthed smile of a young boy. Slats grinned like a high school kid who was getting away with smoking in the boys room.

"Yeah, but it just doesn't look right!" Joe teased.

Slats was smiling and nodding in agreement when Donny strode to the bar and sat next to Joe. Joe slid Donny's drink to him. "Scotch," was all he said.

"Thanks, Joe. Hey, by the way, how are your shoulders?" Donny asked Joe.

"Huh?" Joe stared blankly.

"Well, it's just that it looked like you might dislocate both of your shoulders trying to hack your way outta the tall grass on the eighteenth, and I never had a chance to ask about it." Donny took a sip and smiled with his eyes, and Slats laughed his ridiculous laugh as they waited for Joe to answer.

Joe made an introspective face as he tried to hide a smile. He raised his eyebrows and said, "Well, you know what everyone says about that?"

"What?" Donny asked.

Joe turned slowly and shrugged his shoulders. "Up yours...stupid!"

Slats's chest heaved, and he turned away and walked into the kitchen behind the bar. Donny smiled a broad smile and took another drink.

Joe stood up and motioned to Donny. "Hey, let's go check out the band; they're starting to play. The girls ought to be here soon."

As the men stepped between the small tables in the bar toward the large wooden doors that opened into the ballroom, Joe couldn't help but notice how much better he felt about things since he'd left the office. The time with Donny had been good medicine. He thought to himself that maybe just verbalizing his problems and frustrations to his brother had somehow made them less than they were before. Work didn't seem quite so bad now that he'd told Donny exactly how he felt. He felt a little better about Jess, also. Maybe that too was just because he'd spoken so openly to Donny. He felt as though he was ready to enjoy himself now. He tried to believe that maybe his morning was just about like everyone else's. He was ready to think that everyone had bad days at work, and that everyone had to struggle to hold a marriage together.

Joe reached his left arm around Donny's shoulder and squeezed him gently. "I love you, Donny," he said softly.

"Yeah. I love you too, Joe," Donny replied.

For a moment, as they stood looking around the ballroom at The Oaks, it seemed that maybe, just maybe, the world had turned for Joe Mix. He was waiting in the elegant ballroom of an exclusive country club, with his best friend, for his beautiful wife to appear. Soon they'd be partying with articulate, affluent friends. Maybe his life was pretty good and all the things he was so disappointed with were just part of growing older. Everyone probably felt that way.

Jess arrived with Donny's wife, Carol, shortly after the men strolled into the ballroom. Jess and Carol came in by way of the main entrance, next to the parking lot. They had already hung their coats in the coatroom when Joe and Donny noticed them walking through the growing crowd. As Donny watched Carol and Jess cross the room, he remembered the things his groomsman had said about Jess at his wedding and he smiled all over again. Jess did look attractive...but what was it about her? He remembered the phrase "sex monkeys" and laughed out loud.

Carol and Jess had always co-existed amicably, but neither of them had any great sense of friendship for the other. They were only friends because they were married to brothers, and Donny thought it was odd to watch them cross the room together. He was well aware of Carol's passive acceptance of Jess. Donny waved until Carol noticed, and the women turned and walked toward them.

Two other couples who'd been acquaintances for years were standing nearby, and all eight people began to greet each other at about the same time when Jess and Carol reached Joe and Donny.

Carol's lips were thin and her face was narrow and fine. Her dark hair was parted on the side, and the way it surrounded her face seemed to call attention to her dark eyes and perfect complexion. Carol had a rich, deep voice, and Joe had always thought it was a perfect match for her dark and delicate features. Sometimes, when he talked with her, he found himself staring at her fine features and soft, dark skin. He knew she possessed a quick wit, although she never had much to say while surrounded by large groups.

Carol stood in sharp contrast to Jess. Jess Mix was tall and fair, and she kept her hair as blonde as she could. Tonight she wore it on her shoulders, with a pearl necklace and a long, black evening dress. Her hair stood out even more next to the dark tan on her exposed back. Jess always liked to be noticed, and she liked to be the one to speak up or tell a story in front of a large group.

While the others exchanged greetings—"Hi's" and "Nice to see you agains"—Donny found his way to Carol and kissed her gently. "Hi, honey" was all they said to each other before they resumed greeting friends.

When Joe found his way to Jess, she was in the middle of a story. She was greeting the other two couples and telling them about the cars she'd ordered. For once Joe wasn't put off by talk of the cars. He was invigorated by the sight of his wife; he thought she was beautiful, and she was being charming for the crowd. Jess was laughing and explaining how Joe didn't want the cars but she'd just ordered them anyway. Just watching the beautiful Jess talk triggered the little twitch in his belly that made him think of sex.

He moved toward her slowly and put his hand on the small of her back. Then he gently pulled her in his direction. She turned to look at him but never stopped talking to the other couples. The others watched as he slowly moved his lips toward hers, expecting her to stop her story for a quick kiss and a "Hi, honey"—a public affirmation of her husband's affection.

But when Joe put his lips on Jess's, she broke his heart: she just kept on talking about the cars. His lips touched hers ever so gently for several seconds while she continued to describe the new BMWs and the deal she'd worked out. He felt Jess's breath blow into his mouth for several seconds. He could feel the words, "I just told them I wanted both cars in pewter" as they caromed around in his mouth. He felt her lips moving, but she never stopped talking, moved her head, or touched him. Joe realized that now he was less than invisible; he wasn't even worth stopping for. More than that, this was a message for him, and it hurt far more than he could have imagined.

He lowered his eyes and stepped away from her, then walked slowly back into the bar and sat by himself.

The six other people standing together nearby had all seen the kiss that never was. They'd all tried to laugh politely and hope that perhaps they'd misunderstood what they'd seen. Donny and Carol managed to hide their surprise and embarrassment, and they lingered in the ballroom for a while as other couples began to wander over and chat.

The format for the event was a typical formal dinner/dance. The members of The Oaks would mingle around in the ballroom for an hour. Then Eldon Monahan, the grandson of Big Ben Monahan and current president of The Oaks, would say a few words. After a dinner of prime rib, the band would play until the party broke up around 1:00 a.m.

Eventually, after all the couples had milled around the ballroom for a while, they all found seats at the dinner tables. A chair next to Jess was left empty for Joe. Donny and Carol elected to sit at the same table as Joe and Jess, and they waited nervously for Joe to return. The exchange between Joe and Jess had made Donny uncomfortable; it made him cringe every time he thought of it. Now he felt he needed to sit at the same table and remain close to Joe tonight, almost as if he needed to take care of his older brother, to be his friend if no one else would.

As Donny and Carol sat and waited for the evening to move along, they endured an uneasy vigil and watched for Joe's return. They were both anxious and uncertain if Joe would even rejoin them. Donny and Carol listened in surprise as Jess continued to tell stories, laugh, and flirt while Joe's chair beside her remained empty. Jess spoke of Joe from time to time, always fondly, and when someone asked her where he was now and then, she replied pleasantly, "He's around here somewhere" or "I think he's in the bar." But as they waited, Donny and Carol wondered if Joe's feelings were hurt so badly that he actually might not return.

Just before the lights were dimmed, the band stopped playing and Eldon Monahan stepped up to the microphone by the bandstand. Donny was about to go and find Joe when he appeared silently and took his place next to Jess. Donny was familiar enough with Joe to know what was in Joe's heart: he was expected to be there, and no matter how angry or hurt he'd been by Jess, he couldn't fail to fulfill the expectations of others.

Jess looked in his direction but never made eye contact with Joe. She smiled a thin smile and touched his thigh with her left hand just before she leaned back to listen to Eldon Monahan. Her greeting was designed for others to see but had nothing to do with Joe. Donny and Carol both stared at Joe until he raised his eyes toward them. Joe looked only at Donny and confessed with an empty stare that all he wanted anymore was for this evening to be over.

Eldon Monahan made his remarks about upcoming improvements to the clubhouse and the grounds, then previewed the social schedule before dinner was served. All through dinner Jess laughed and joked and told stories. Several times she got up and left the table in order to tell a story, or to flirt. It was clear to all that Jess Mix was enjoying herself, and that she liked to be seen and heard as she moved through the crowd. Joe Mix smiled pleasantly, although half heartedly, when he was supposed to, and nodded in agreement when he was supposed to. But he hardly spoke, and when dinner was done and people began to dance, he rose slowly from his seat and walked back into the bar, where he drank diet pop and talked with Slats until the party ended at 1:00 a.m.

Jess actually walked to the bar shortly after dinner and asked Joe if he was all right. Joe wanted to blurt, "What the hell do you care?" But he stifled the anger and frustration. It would do no good to confront Jess here, so he said he just didn't feel like socializing tonight. Jess simply turned and walked back to the ballroom. She made no attempt to lure him back to the ballroom, and she didn't ask for an explanation.

Donny and Carol hadn't really known what to do or say all through the evening. They'd tried to enjoy themselves, but Joe's misery was a burden they couldn't get around. Just before midnight, they gave up and decided to go home, and Donny went to the bar to find Joe. "Hey, Joe? Can I buy you breakfast tomorrow? I'll pick you up at eight. We'll talk, OK?" he asked.

"Yeah. That'd be good, Donny," Joe nodded, "that'd be good."

———•———

As Joe stood in his bedroom and undressed, he tried to find the words to tell Jess how she'd made him feel. He took off his tuxedo and hung it in the closet, then sat on his bed and looked at his feet.

Jess was standing in front of the large mirror in the master bathroom, taking off her makeup, when Joe entered the bathroom and stood behind her. The master bath had two sinks, both with gold faucets, set in a white granite countertop. A large bathtub with jets for a water massage rested on an elevated platform along one wall. When Jess took her bath, she could open a blind on the adjacent window and look down onto the woods and garden from her second-story bath. A large, glass shower stall was set in the opposite corner, separated from the tub by several white closet doors. Joe had never liked the way his voice echoed around the master bathroom. He stood there for a moment, staring at her back and waiting for her to say something. But she was busy with what she was doing and didn't speak. Joe wondered if she was ignoring him, or if she didn't know he was there, behind her.

"You hurt me tonight, Jess," he said finally.

"What do you mean?" she asked through the washcloth she was holding on her face.

"You know what I mean," Joe said passively. "I told you it hurts my feelings when you do that."

"Do what?" she said, still holding the washcloth over her face.

"You know what! That thing you do when I try to kiss you and you keep on talking! I told you the last time you did that I couldn't stand it again!" he said to her back.

"I was talking. Besides that, you interrupted me." Jess's tone suggested that she hadn't meant anything by it, or that she'd simply been in the middle of her sentence and she'd been unable to stop, like a train coming down the tracks. Maybe she was implying that it was all Joe's fault for trying to kiss her. In either case, Joe thought she had a weak defense for what she'd done.

"It hurt my feelings, Jess. I just wanted to kiss my wife, that's all. You hurt me, embarrassed me on purpose. Why?" Joe's anger was apparent, but he still seemed to be pleading for understanding.

Jess put the washcloth over her face once again and said coldly, "Let it GO!" as if she were giving an order or chastising a subordinate who'd spoken out of turn. She still refused to turn and face him. She'd talked down to him again, like he was not entitled to his feelings, and he felt the same anger and pain that he had earlier at The Oaks.

Joe turned and left the bathroom without a word to Jess. Something heavy and unwanted pushed at his chest again. When he reached his study, he flipped the light switch off and closed the door behind him. He stood with his hands at his sides for a moment and let the darkness of a quiet room restore some silence in his heart. One little thought crept back into his mind soon enough, and it triggered a cascade of similar thoughts that only added weight to his chest.

The darkness was hiding him from Jess, and soon one more argument, one more day, would be over. He recognized that he was counting down the days of his life with Jess too, and that made him even more aware of counting down so many other parts of his life.

He went to the window in his study and looked out at the night. The May full moon bathed his backyard with blue moonlight, and he could see the moon shadows of even the smallest oak branches. He saw his 1978 Ford pickup, with the snowplow still mounted, sitting by the dogwood hedge next to the garden shed. It looked almost new in the moonlight.

For just a moment there, the beauty of the moonlight in his own yard almost allowed him to set aside the anguish and hurt that swelled in his chest. He dropped heavily into a leather recliner and then raised the footrest as he leaned back. He was weary from a long day, and soon his thoughts wandered back to work, then to Jess. Then they began to swirl around like smoke drifting aimlessly, silently upwards into a dark void. As he sensed the moonlight flooding into his study, he realized that he felt worse now than when he'd left the office twelve hours earlier. His last conscious thought as he drifted off to sleep was how nice the old Ford looked in the moonlight.

chapter
SIX

Joe was sitting at the small desk in his basement den when he heard Donny open the kitchen door and let himself in at about 7:45 Saturday morning. Donny's footsteps struck the kitchen floor directly above Joe's basement hideaway, and he knew when he heard Donny stop to take a cup from the cupboard, pour himself some coffee, and then walk slowly down the steps into the basement that Donny was coming to find him.

Donny guessed that Joe would be in the basement tying flies while he waited to go to breakfast, and after he'd poured his coffee he found his way to Joe's den.

The room Joe had chosen for his happy place, as he liked to call it, was about twelve by twelve and had no windows. It was paneled in cedar and furnished with odds and ends. A small love seat with an end table and reading lamp sat along one wall, his fly-tying desk along another. Old photos and fishing tackle were pinned to all the walls, and a pile of fly rods and other miscellaneous fishing gear stood in one corner.

When Donny stepped around the corner and into the room, Joe was bent over a fly-tying vise attached to the desk. He was wrapping thread around a small fish hook, and he didn't look up when he heard Donny step into the room.

Donny leaned over Joe's back and briefly inspected the tiny insect that Joe was trying to imitate with feathers, fur, and thread. "Whatya tyin'?" was all he said as he backed up and then sat on a hard kitchen chair next to the desk.

"Baetis Emerger...size eighteen," Joe said softly as he stared at the fish hook.

Joe finished wrapping the thread, raised his head out of the dome of light created by the desk lamp above the vise, and leaned back in his desk chair. He reached for his own coffee, then nodded to Donny and said, "Morning, Donny."

Donny looked at the two dozen or so trout flies that were arranged like tiny soldiers on the desk in front of Joe and asked, "Been up for a while?"

"Couple hours," Joe sighed.

"So, Joe, is it as bad as what I saw last night?" Donny asked bluntly. Only a brother could ask such a question. He suspected Joe had been up most of the night, hurt by what Jess had done and possibly arguing with her. Donny had stayed up with Carol much of the night also; they had talked for hours about Joe and Jess. He knew the time had come for a long talk with Joe, and he knew his brother was waiting for him to try to help in some way.

Joe put his hands on his face and rubbed gently, then crossed his arms and looked around the room. The desk he was seated in front of was made of richly stained cedar, and every drawer was jammed full of feathers and patches of animal fur used for tying trout flies. Mounted on the wall in front of the desk was a shop organizer with dozens of small plastic drawers—the kind of thing most men put in their garage and fill with nails, and screws, and tools, and leftover hardware. But Joe had filled it with spools of colored thread, dozens of various sizes of tiny fish hooks, colored yarn, glass beads, and all the tools necessary for tying trout flies. The walls were covered with photographs of Joe and his sons, moments from three lifetimes spent fishing. Directly above the garage organizer, like a sentry overlooking the room, rested a large brown trout that Ray Mix had caught and stuffed many years earlier. The quality of the taxidermy had been poor to begin with, and now the trout seemed to be coming apart. Joe cherished the fish. It had lingered as a sort of connection to his father. Other than the bamboo fly rod in his golf bag, and his truck, the ratty-looking trout was his most valued possession.

The little room was truly Joe Mix's happy place; it had been for years. When they'd built their new home, Jess had allowed him one room in which to keep all his toys. Joe retreated to the little room most evenings, after supper, and read or tied flies until bedtime. Donny had always found him to be relaxed and comfortable when the two of them chatted in Joe's den. But now, as Donny waited for Joe to speak, he couldn't help but notice the anguish that twisted his brother's face, even here in the midst of his pleasant little room.

"Joe?" Donny asked again softly. "How bad is it?"

Joe sighed. "Pretty bad, Donny, pretty bad. That's what I was tryin' to tell you yesterday."

"Yeah, well, I think I understand now," Donny almost whispered, then sipped at his coffee.

"It's pretty much always been this way. But now, with both of the boys off at school—well, now it's worse."

Neither man spoke for several minutes. Then Joe broke the silence. "I've been thinking about this for a long time, Donny."

"Yeah?" Donny sipped at his coffee and waited for Joe to continue.

"I just don't know how much longer I can do this." Joe rubbed his face with his hands and breathed heavily once more. "Seems like I'm the least important thing in Jess's life. This house, travel, cars, things—hell, all of it is more important than I am. I'm just her roommate, the guy with the good job. Humph. And every time I say something, she takes the opposite point of view and then digs in for a fight. I don't get it."

"You need to see a marriage counselor, Joe," Donny said firmly.

"I don't know if I care enough anymore, Donny." Joe leaned back in his chair and folded his arms. "I think Jess is pretty unhappy too."

"You need to see a marriage counselor, Joe," Donny said again.

Joe ignored Donny and changed the subject. "I've been thinking about something else quite a bit too, Donny." Joe turned and raised his eyebrows. "There's something else going on here, something much bigger. I think it's all tied up together in this. Wanna know what I've been thinking?"

"Tell me," Donny said over the top of his coffee cup.

"Well, you know, Donny, Dad started out pretty poor. I mean, really poor. You heard all the stories about the orphanage, and not having any shoes, and all the hard times when he was young."

"Yeah?"

"How he was adopted by the Webster family and they gave him his first home. Then how hard he worked to get a leg up and get started." Joe raised his eyebrows and nodded yes, asking Donny if he understood. Donny answered with a nod.

"He and Ralph Webster made a fortune in the cattle business. They risked everything, and lost it all once, but recovered and wound up with a pile of money and land. You heard all the stories, right?"

"Many times. But so what?" Donny shrugged.

"Well, what made the Old Cowboy a great man?" Joe leaned back in his chair when he spoke to give the question more importance.

"I dunno," Donny said.

"He grew up real poor! He had to bust his ass in order to get ahead! He clawed and scraped and found a few opportunities. Then he hammered away at the world and made it fit his plan. He took chances! He made himself a success. He saw what he wanted and he went out and took it!"

"Yeah?" Then Donny grimaced with his own question. "So? What does that have to do with what I saw yesterday, and last night, and your marriage?"

"Nothing, and that's the point!" Joe paused, then drew in a deep breath. "Don't you see, Donny? Dad had one great goal when we were boys: he didn't want us to have to claw and climb our way up like he did. He wanted to give us a better start than he had, so life wouldn't be so hard for us. Are you with me?"

"Yeah."

"Well, I guess I should speak just for myself on this point, but in giving me all the things I wanted—cars, clothes, an expensive education— he deprived me of the thing that made him great, the thing that gave his life meaning. I never had a chance, or maybe I was never forced, to develop the kind of drive and character he had, because I had it too easy. I chose my career because it was what Dad wanted for me and it was easy, not because it was what I really wanted. I never had any struggles. I didn't know what I wanted, so I just let someone with a stronger will make that decision for me." Joe stopped and stared at Donny, then continued. "I feel like it's time for me to make my own decision, but I'm...afraid it's too late. I waited too long."

Donny looked at his coffee but said nothing.

"Same thing with the rest of my life—all the important decisions. I just let other people decide for me. Do you remember, Donny? I was dating Wendy Hample, from home, when I met Jess. My buddies at the time used to refer to Jess as Yoko because she took over my life so fast. Wendy was history in about ten days; I haven't seen her since. I just got rid of her because I knew Jess wanted me to." Joe smiled a faraway smile.

"Before I met Jess, I just assumed I'd marry Wendy and move back home." Then Joe's face darkened when he added, "That broke Wendy's heart, the way I broke up with her."

Donny still chose not to speak. He only waited for Joe to continue.

"You know, Donny, it isn't like some sort of fire went out with Jess. I don't think there ever was a fire. I just let a marriage happen that never should have happened. I let somebody else make that decision for me too. I've sorta been treading water and waiting to get happy in my marriage. It's never gonna happen, Donny. I think...I think maybe I've just been waiting for this period of my life to be over."

Joe sighed softly, then kept going. "Same thing with the boys, I guess. From the very earliest times, I remember thinking that things would be better when the boys got a little older. You know, when they were little babies and they were sick, or they just didn't sleep at night? They woke me up, and I had to get up and walk the floor with them. I kept thinking those miserable, sleepless nights would be over when the boys got a little older. Then, when they were a little older and some new problem arose—maybe a conflict at school, a bully on the playground, or a teacher I didn't like, whatever—I just got right back into that mentality where I wanted them to hurry and get done with this phase and get on with it, because life would be easier when that current stage was over. I thought like that all through elementary school, middle school, and high school. Well, now it's over!" Joe sighed. "They're gone. They're not comin' back. Those days are over!" Joe looked into Donny's eyes and couldn't hide the anger and regret.

"I've spent my whole adult life waiting for things to be over. Some of them were things I should have ended, and some of them were things I should have enjoyed. But I was so afraid, or weak, or lazy, that I just waited for things to change on their own."

Joe shook his head slowly. "I've let so much slip away. I've let it all slip away, haven't I?"

"Jeez, Joe, you're being kind of hard on yourself, aren't you?"

"Maybe," Joe replied weakly, just as he inhaled deeply. "But there's a sort of melancholy that's begun to cling to me. It's like something pulling at me that I can't get away from. I'm stuck. The thought of living this life out until I'm dead is nearly unbearable. I guess that's probably what I'll do. What are my choices now? I can go to work every day for the rest of my life, in a job I hate because it brings out the worst in me. I can stay in a marriage with someone who makes me dislike myself, and along the way I'll continue to be a poor father and make my children into less than what they should be. Or I can throw twenty-some years down the shitter and quit, move out. Everyone will think I'm a total loser, and I'll be alone, homeless in my middle age. Shit, Donny, I'm embarrassed to admit that I hate my job. People like me are supposed to stand around and puke up this happy horseshit about how much we love our profession and how much we love going to the office every day. I've been trying to do that for years. I can't do it anymore! I feel like such a failure if I tell the truth. Same for my marriage! So really—really—what are my choices?"

"I don't know, Joe. I don't know. But I do know you're gonna be OK. This will all be OK. I know it will. Let's go get some breakfast," Donny said as he stood up. "Let's get out of here!"

"OK," Joe agreed. "But let's take the truck. I just got the oil changed and I wanna drive it once more before I put it away for the summer."

Both men stood and stepped toward the door. When Donny reached the basement steps, he called over his shoulder. "Hey, let's try that new bakery out by the mall. It's supposed to be pretty good." As soon as he'd spoken the words, he became aware that Joe was not following him. He stopped and turned to look for his brother, and he was terrified by what he saw.

Joe Mix was ashen colored and clutching at his chest. He was leaning against the door jamb of his office as he slid toward the floor. Joe's eyes were filled with pain, and panic. He was calling to Donny but he made no sound. His eyes began to blink, but he couldn't clear away the panic in his face as his back slid along the wall and he shrank toward the floor.

"Jesus, Joe! What's wrong?" Donny called as he rushed back toward Joe.

Joe didn't seem capable of answering.

"Joe, are you choking?" Donny called.

Joe lowered his eyes and shook his head "no." When he hit the floor, he whispered, "Can't breathe" and clutched at his chest.

"I'm gonna call an ambulance, Joe!" Donny said, but he waited for his brother's response.

Joe nodded "yes," and Donny raced up the steps to the telephone in the kitchen.

chapter seven

Several different machines still beeped regularly while they monitored Joe's vital signs. His heart rhythms flashed across an oscilloscope, and his blood pressure was displayed on the same screen, next to his bed. All the other noises of a hectic hospital seemed to blend into something like road noise on a busy highway just beyond the white curtain surrounding Joe's bed in the emergency room. Joe could hear the doctor's familiar voice somewhere out there, across the emergency room. The doctor seemed to be moving closer by the minute. Joe kept his eyes closed and tried to listen for each step as the doctor moved his way. When the curtain was pulled back, the curtain rings that suspended it made their familiar small screeching noise as Dr. Harold Christensen stepped into Joe's little white tent in the ER. He slid the curtain closed behind him and smiled. "Sure didn't think I'd see you here today, Joe!" Dr. Christensen said with a big smile.

Joe smiled back at the doctor. He lay with his hands behind his head. His chest was exposed, and several wires were still attached to his torso. Jess stood on one side of his bed and Donny on the other. They waited nervously for an explanation of Joe's collapse.

"No, sir, I never expected to see you, Joe," the doctor said as he sat on Joe's bed. Joe had spoken briefly with Dr. Christensen the previous night at The Oaks, and Jess had made a point to visit his table for a while. He looked at Jess, then at Joe, before he spoke. "It wasn't a heart attack, Joe. That much I can tell you for certain. We've run all the tests! This was not a cardiac event of any kind."

"So what was it, Harold?" Jess asked.

Dr. Christensen smiled at Jess, then looked directly at Joe. "I don't know what it was. We're going to run some different tests, but I'm guessing I'll never be able to give you an accurate diagnosis." He touched Joe's leg with the chart he was carrying. "But I'll hazard a guess on this one." He stopped and looked deliberately at each of them over the top of his bifocals. "Joe, do you ever see things at your office that, well, you just can't diagnose? Things that leave you searching for an explanation?"

"Yeah," Joe replied.

"Me too. And like I said, we may never know just exactly what happened here today. But every now and then, I see a middle-aged man who thinks he's carrying the weight of the world on his shoulders. These guys will just sort of 'shut down' like you did. They sometimes collapse at work. Maybe they wake up in pain in the middle of the night—who knows. But quite often they have all the symptoms of a heart attack, only they really didn't have a heart attack. Then they need a few days, maybe a few weeks to rest, and they're back at it. Hopefully, they'll change their lifestyles some, in order to lighten the load, or reduce the stress if you will. It's like they've overloaded all their circuits. I believe it's a stress-related thing. Some rest and time off work seems to press the 'reset' button inside them, and they're fine." The doctor shrugged and smiled. "Sometimes we refer to this type of thing as 'Acute Fatigue.'"

"Acute Fatigue?" Jess's face bent with disbelief as she began to question Dr. Christensen. "How can that be? There's no stress in our lives, is there honey?" She looked at Joe and then reached over to gently stroke his cheek.

Joe never made eye contact with her and never reached out to touch her. He looked directly into Dr. Christensen's eyes. Joe made no movement of any sort, but while his lifeless eyes were locked with the doctor's he passed along all the information Harold Christensen needed. It couldn't have been more clear to the cardiologist that he was exactly right in describing Joe Mix as "a middle-aged man who thinks he's carrying the weight of the world on his shoulders."

Donny noticed the exchange between Joe and Dr. Christensen, and he understood that Joe had admitted to the doctor that his guess was probably correct.

"I need to call Carol," Donny said as he stood up and moved toward the hallway. He didn't have to call Carol, but he thought it might be a good time to leave the room and allow Joe, Jess, and the doctor to talk amongst themselves.

———•———

When Donny returned to Joe's bedside an hour later, he had a cup of Starbucks coffee in his hand. Joe still lay on his back, with his hands behind his head and several pillows under his back.

"Where's Jess?" Donny asked.

"Said she had to make a couple phone calls."

"Thought it might be easier for you all to talk a little more openly if I wasn't around." Donny waited for Joe to reply. When he didn't, Donny asked, "Did you tell Jess any of the things we talked about earlier?"

"No," Joe replied with no emotion, and looked away. "She's heard it all before."

Donny chose not to push that subject any more.

"How you feelin'?" Donny asked.

"OK," Joe shrugged. "Pretty tired."

"You look like shit," Donny said as he began to move back toward the little chair by Joe's bed. He stopped after one step and lifted the sheet that covered Joe's feet. Then he raised the sheet slightly and looked deliberately at Joe's crotch. He snickered as though he'd seen something hilarious and lowered the sheet.

Joe smiled a weak smile and looked toward the ceiling as Donny took the chair next to his bed.

"So what happened, Joe? I mean, exactly? How did it feel when you were looking so rough?" Donny asked as he leaned back in his chair.

"Well, I was having some trouble getting a good breath of air while we were talking, and I could feel, literally feel, a tightness slowly start to grip my chest. I just thought that if I stood up and got some fresh air, I'd be fine. But when I got up to leave, to follow you, it was like somebody, somebody really big and nasty, just reached inside my chest and started squeezin' my heart, I guess. It really hurt, and I couldn't draw a breath. Scared me!" Joe took a deep breath and smiled weakly when he exhaled. "There, that felt good."

"So how do you feel now? Any pain?"

"No, none now. I just feel really tired," Joe sighed. "I think Harold is gonna let me go home in a couple hours." Joe turned to face Donny. "Sorry I scared you, Donny," he confessed.

"No problem. The only thing I was worried about was that I might have to do CPR on you." Donny turned and pointed with his coffee cup and raised his eyebrows. "And there's no way I'm sticking my tongue in your mouth." His brow was furrowed and he shook his head.

"I don't think you do that with CPR, Donny," Joe said. He was straining not to smile.

"You do it your way, Joe, and I'll do it mine." Donny sipped at his coffee and maintained his serious expression.

"Jeez, Donny. Just the thought of your tongue in my mouth—who knows where that thing has been?" Joe reached to the table beside his bed and grabbed the vomit basin. He held it under his chin and raised his shoulders as if he were going to dry heave. "I can feel the bile rising just from talking to you, Donny. They should have you walk around and talk to people who've just swallowed poison."

Donny pointed his coffee cup at Joe. "Listen here, Joey, lots of ladies go to sleep every night just dreaming of that." Then he stuck his tongue out and pointed at it.

"Yeah, well, prison life is hard."

Both men smiled and looked away.

Donny took Joe's hand in his and squeezed it. "I love you, Joe," he said softly. Joe only nodded, and squeezed his little brother's hand.

Several minutes later, Donny was reading a magazine and Joe was about to drift off to sleep when both of them heard Jess's voice in the hallway outside the ER. She was obviously talking on her cell phone to one of her friends. "No, it's no big deal. We're going home in a few minutes." She paused and seemed to be listening to her friend. Then she added, "Yeah, this is really inconvenient for me. Now I'm going to have to change everything for book club this week."

Joe turned his eyes toward Donny. "Felt like a big deal to me."

The hurt in Joe's eyes was hard for Donny to look at, and he understood more completely now the anguish in Joe's words over the past twenty-four hours. He kept his silence; he could undo nothing and repair nothing. He let himself take hold of the fact that Jess saw Joe's collapse not as a serious harbinger of a larger problem, but rather as just another obstacle placed in front of her by her inconsiderate husband.

Donny watched Joe close his eyes and turn away.

chapter
eight

"How you feelin' today, Joe?" Donny held his office phone to his ear with his shoulder and shuffled papers into piles on his desk.

"Pretty good. I've been taking it pretty easy all week, like the doctor ordered," Joe replied. Dr. Christensen had insisted that Joe take a week off and rest. Joe had had no trouble following the instructions. He'd slept for three days straight, then felt some strength coming back. Now, on Thursday afternoon, he felt some of his old energy begin to return, and he was glad to hear Donny's voice.

"Jess been taking pretty good care of you?"

"Actually, yes," Joe replied.

"Well good! You wanna go fishin' tomorrow? Might do you some good to get a little fresh air, and I'm pretty sure I can get out of here for a day."

"Yeah," Joe said softly. "Yeah," he repeated with growing enthusiasm. "Yeah, that might be just the thing!" Donny could hear excitement rising in Joe's voice. He could sense that Joe was feeling better, and even though he'd been uncertain if he should call and suggest something like fishing so soon after Joe's collapse, he was glad he'd called now. "Yeah. The Hendrickson hatch oughta be going pretty good still. Pick me up at nine and we'll make a day of it."

"Where are we headed?" Donny asked. Joe could tell he was arranging papers on his desk while they spoke.

"Forrestville, where else? I love that place. There's also a chance that the Baetis hatch may be starting, and..."

"I'll be there at nine. I gotta go," Donny interrupted.

"See you tomorrow," Joe said. "And thanks for calling!" he added as the line went dead.

—•—

When 9:00 a.m. Friday morning rolled around, Joe Mix sat at his kitchen table sipping coffee and listening as Jess spoke to their boys on the telephone. Ben Mix was a junior at the University of Minnesota, and Chris was a freshman. They shared an apartment with two other boys from Rochester. Both of the Mix boys planned to go into medicine.

"No. Really. It's OK. There's no need to come home this weekend. Stay at school and study. Get ready for final exams. Your dad is just fine. Don't worry." She stopped to listen for a moment. "No, really, just get your studying done. We'll see you in a couple weeks when you're done for the summer. OK. Bye, boys."

Joe felt disappointed. He'd wanted to see his boys all week, ever since he'd collapsed, and he couldn't hide his disappointment from Jess. "Jeez, Jess, I told you I wanted to see the boys. Why'd you tell them to stay at school? Why do you do that? You know I wanted to see them!"

"They need to study!" Jess replied. Her words stung him as if she were rebuking him for being so selfish to expect them to come home and miss their studies.

"No, they don't! They're both A students. And they're an hour from home. It's no problem for them to come home, and you know it!" He felt she'd told the boys to stay at school simply because she knew he wanted to see them, or maybe because she knew they wanted to see their dad and she didn't want that.

"Good God, Joe! Let it go!" Her voice overflowed with contempt. "They need to study!"

"For Chrissakes, Jess, six days ago I thought I was dying on the basement floor! I just want to see my sons!" The volume and anger in his voice rose above hers.

"Oh, shit. You collapse on the floor because you can't handle a little stress, and now you act like it's a life-and-death thing! Harold even said it was nothing." She seemed to be mocking him.

"Well, it is a little stressful to put up with your selfish bullshit...your Beemers...your need to argue."

"Fuck you!" she said coldly, and then looked away.

Joe stopped talking. He stopped thinking, He stopped feeling anything. He stared at Jess from across the kitchen table. Their conversation had escalated and gotten out of control faster than usual, and Joe
felt more willing to confront her than he had in the past. But just before
his anger was about to erupt, he let it implode under its own weight.

He'd pulled it all back inside; he would not argue with her anymore.
He wouldn't talk to her anymore either. He took a deep breath and
looked away. Jess had raised the ante and overpowered him once again.
Something inside him wanted to stomp over to the kitchen sink and
smash his coffee cup. But he couldn't do things like that—he just could-
n't. He never had done things like that. He just regained control of himself and sipped at his coffee. His hands were shaking and his heart was
pounding, but he'd stifled his feelings again.

Jess waited for the silence to settle, then left the room. She slammed
her bedroom door behind her.

Joe raised his coffee cup again, and in the same instant he saw
Donny's car turning into his driveway. Before he could grab the duffel
bag with his waders and fishing gear, Donny was in the kitchen pouring
himself some coffee.

"You ready?" Donny called over his shoulder as he stood by the coffee maker, oblivious to what had happened just before he'd arrived.

Joe didn't answer. He fumbled with his gear and backed out the door.
Then he mumbled, "Let's go."

The smell of creosote hung in the air like a heavy cloud. The instant
they'd stepped onto the old bridge at Forrestville State Park, the thick,
unmistakable odor surrounded them. Joe breathed in deeply and filled
his lungs. "I love that smell—reminds me of the railroad bridge outside
of town when we were kids," Joe said with a smile, and memories of long-
gone summer days swirled briefly through his mind.

"Smells like shit. Remember the time we put a penny on the tracks
and waited for the train to squash it?" Donny really didn't want an
answer, and as soon as he'd said the words he let go of the memory of
the old bridge at home. He stopped walking, opened a box of trout flies,
and looked down at the river. He stood in the middle of the bridge and,
from a height of about twenty feet, he looked upstream at a large, flat
stretch of the Root River. The river was only about four feet deep here,

but it was gin clear, and the summer canopy of hardwood leaves would soon be closing it in like a green tunnel that could be opened only by a summer breeze.

Joe stood shoulder to shoulder with Donny and looked at the stream that was flowing underneath them. He could see trout moving and feeding. He saw birds in the brush and the trees. He saw insects drifting through the morning air. He looked to his right and saw the old brick house and store that had been abandoned a hundred years earlier when the railroad bypassed Forrestville. He saw the gravel road that emerged from the forest just beyond a green meadow and wound through the scattered buildings that represented the remains of Forrestville. There was seldom any traffic here; a man could stand on this little bridge and watch the river for several hours before a car might come along and clatter over the rough planks that had served for decades.

Joe saw beauty here—beauty in the slow pace of the way things used to be, and beauty in the trout stream that ran through the middle of Forrestville. Joe thought about the lives that had been spent here. People had been born here and died here, and now there was no trace of them. He wanted to believe that their lives had had meaning. It bothered him to think that they'd perhaps just existed, then died, and now all memory of them was gone. People's lives needed to mean something, he thought.

The stream, this place, gave him a chance to immerse himself, to literally and figuratively immerse himself in a riddle. Joe had never felt that the riddle needed to be solved; it only needed to be something he could participate in. The riddle seemed to involve the changing seasons, the passing of time, and the lives of the creatures and people that lived along the river. His own life had always seemed to be part of a river.

Donny saw only a quiet place to fish and a rundown old ghost town.

"Hey, let's just sit by the river for a minute and have a look at what's goin' on down there," Joe said as he nudged Donny with his elbow. Joe had fished all over the world—Russia, Alaska, Labrador, Argentina, Yellowstone—but this was his home water, and he liked to get reacquainted each time he returned.

They stepped off the bridge and moved through the tall grass and gooseberry bushes that lined the riverbank. When they reached an open area in the brush along the west side of the river, both men sat on the grassy slope and looked silently up and down the stream for a moment.

"Not much of a hatch going on yet, Donny. I think I'll try a pheasant tail nymph—a small one—and work the riffle above the flat stretch."

"Me too, but I'll head downstream."

Both men lifted small boxes that opened like books out of their fishing vests and began to poke through the dozens of trout flies. The flies were secure inside the boxes. Their hooks stuck gently into foam liners, and they were organized in rows according to their size and the specific stage in the life cycle of the aquatic insect they were designed to imitate.

A small mayfly called a Baetis, or Blue-Winged Olive, was due to begin hatching in the Root River any day now, and once the hatch began in earnest, thousands—maybe millions—of adult Blue-Winged Olives would hatch every day from about 10:00 a.m. to 2:00 p.m. for several months. During the early spring, there was also a heavy hatch of Hendricksons that would come later in the day. Joe had never learned the correct Latin name for the Hendrickson hatch that came off on the Root River. There were so many subspecies—Hendrickson had been good enough for Joe—but it was a larger gray mayfly, about the size of a small moth, and it only hatched in the early spring. When the adults of these or any other mayfly species hatched or emerged from their larval state in the Root River, they'd fly around by the river's edge for a couple of days, find a lover, lay some eggs, and die. The eggs would fall into the river, descend to the river bottom, and attach to the various weeds and pebbles. Then they'd spend the next year developing as the larval stage of the Blue-Winged Olive. Eventually, the larva, or nymph, would release its hold on the river bottom and be carried along in the river's current until it emerged to the surface film, where it would shed its nymphal skin and hatch into a mature adult mayfly with wings. The adult mayfly dries its wings on the breeze and flies away to look for a lover and repeat the life cycle. The emerger stage had always held the most interest for Joe. The mayfly had worked so hard to find its way to the surface, and was just about to sprout wings and fly away from the current. But it was more vulnerable then than at any other time, and trout made it a point to feed on them.

Joe pondered the life cycle of the mayfly as he looked through his fly box. He'd always seen beauty in it; it just continued on and on forever. He always thought it was curious that the mayfly spent a year developing in the river and then emerged from the river to live for twenty-four hours. One day to find meaning, he thought to himself. Just one day and a mayfly gets it done, while I've spent fifty years looking for meaning...the rest of my life cycle, and I can't seem to find it.

The thought of the mayfly's life cycle reminded Joe of something, and he turned toward his brother. "Hey, Donny, did you know that the Indians in these parts used to think that life was a circle? You know— each day just came around and ended where the next day started." Joe moved his finger in a circle. "And a month just came around and ended where the next month started. And each year did the same. Time was a circle they marked with the seasons and the phases of the moon, and they, the Indians, just got on and rode around for a while and then got off. They got on when they were born, and they got off when they died." He looked at Donny, and Donny continued to rummage through his fly box.

"So?" Donny asked without looking up.

"So the Europeans all think of time as a line that extends straight from creation to the end of time—just a straight line," Joe said.

"That's what it is. It's a line. That circle thing makes no sense." Donny still did not look away from his fly box.

"I used to think that too. But now I like the circle better—way better," Joe said as he lifted a tiny nymph from his fly box.

"Well, that's stupid," Donny said. Then he smiled. "Just trying to help, Joe." Donny shook his head. "I can't believe you think about shit like that—but it IS a line."

Joe smiled to himself and left the discussion of time and life cycles behind. He tied a section of monofilament fishing line to a size eighteen pheasant tail nymph. The fly was designed to imitate the nymph stage of the Blue-Winged Olive's life cycle. The fly Joe had chosen was so small that several of them could be placed on a dime and still not touch each other. His fishing line, or tippet, was delicate, so fine that it resembled a spider web. He bit off the excess tippet that extended past the knot holding his fly to the fly line, then leaned back to look at the river again.

Donny was still threading the tiny tippet through the eye of the tiny fishhook that his pheasant tail nymph had been fashioned around when Joe began to speak.

"You know, Donny, I thought I was gonna die the other day," he said, still looking out at the river.

It took Donny a second to withdraw from his preoccupation with the knot he was tying. He pulled the tiny knot tight with his teeth, and then he too spit out the tag of tippet material he'd trimmed with his teeth. He laid his rod against a gooseberry bush beside him and said to his brother, "You had me worried too!"

"Know what I was thinking about, Donny, when I was on the way to the hospital?" Joe raised his eyebrows and smiled.

"OK, tell me."

"I was afraid—afraid to die, afraid of being dead." Joe stopped and bent his knees up under his chin, then wrapped his arms around his knees and leaned forward. "You know I told you that I'd been waiting—waiting to get happy or waiting for some part of my life to end so I could get on to the good part." Joe paused. "Or waiting for my kids to grow up and grow out of some phase in their lives, because I figured the next phase would be easier?"

"Yeah," Donny said, inviting Joe to continue.

"Well, I started to feel really afraid that I was going to have lived my whole life just waiting for it to be over—that I'd come to the end of it with no joy and no meaning." Joe turned his face toward Donny. "There needs to be meaning to a man's life, and I think it needs to be the kind of thing that a man can actually feel and know he's gonna take along to the other side of the grave. That's what I need to find. Know what I mean?"

"Sort of." Donny squinted at Joe. "Well, actually...no."

Joe looked back toward the stream. "Odd little thoughts swirled around in my head too. You know that picture of me on the wall behind the bar at The Oaks? The one with Win Westby and Lyle Davies and Big Ben?"

"Yeah."

"Well, I was thinking I was gonna die, and then all that would be left of my life would be that picture. Before long, people would come along and say, 'Who's that guy?' and nobody would remember. All that would remain of my life would be that photo. I would exist for a while as a nameless face in an old photo, and then someone would throw the picture away and it would be as though I'd never lived. My life would have come and gone and meant nothing. It all kept coming back to that."

"You really think about shit like that?" Donny grimaced.

"Yeah. It's about all I think of anymore."

Donny and Joe sat silently along the quiet river for a few minutes, both of them thinking about Joe's answer: "Yeah. It's about all I think of anymore." The words drifted across the front of each man's conscious mind, and they both had a moment to themselves. Joe's thoughts blurred with the visions of a life that seemed to have missed the mark. Just how was a man supposed to find meaning, anyway? Something in Joe's comment had opened a portal in Donny's mind. For an instant, one brief moment, Donny began to question the meaning of his life— of everyone's life. The sun was beginning to warm the air and dry the heavy dew from the tall grass on the riverbank as both men drifted into private, silent dreams.

A red-tailed hawk screamed, flashed across the meadow on the other side of the river, and put an end to the moment. Both men watched as the hawk swooped from above the treetops of the hardwoods that sur- rounded the meadow and snatched a pocket gopher from the short grass. The hawk took flight on its powerful wings, clutching the gopher in its claws, and flew into the hardwoods. On its way, it passed by close enough so that they could see the gopher's futile struggle to escape from the hawk's grasp.

"Well, I guess that gopher's life sort of lacks meaning anymore, huh?" Donny said with a crooked smile.

"Do you believe that?" Joe asked.

"Sure do," Donny said. "The next phase of the gopher's life cycle is gonna be when he reappears as bird shit on someone's windshield. Does that have a lot of meaning for you?"

"Don't you see it, Donny—that moment we just witnessed? When the hawk killed the gopher just now, that was the merging of two life cycles. I take some comfort in that, in the poetry of that thought. Don't you see it?" Joe asked.

"No." Donny looked at his fly box again. "If I see anything meaning- ful there at all, it's a warning to go back to my office and work harder so I don't wind up as bird shit on someone else's windshield. Don't you see that?"

"I guess we just see the world a little differently, huh?"

"No shit," Donny said as he closed his fly box.

Joe only grinned, then reached for his fly rod "OK, let's get to it," Joe said as he stood up. He was ready to leave the talk of death behind them and get on with the day.

"Joe, if you get tired, just sit down and I'll find you. Are you sure you're even strong enough to wade in the current?" Donny asked when he stood up.

"I feel fine, Donny," Joe assured his brother with a smile.

"OK, I'll see you in a little while. I'm gonna check on my favorite hole down there beyond the bridge, where the river splits into some small channels."

"See you later, Donny," Joe said as he turned his back and walked upstream through the shady brush. The ground and short brush were still wet with dew as Donny watched Joe disappear on a narrow trail that led into the hardwood forest along the Root River.

When Donny returned to look for Joe two hours later, he followed the same path through the forest that Joe had taken earlier. The noise of gurgling water increased steadily as Donny neared the riffle where he expected to find Joe. When he reached the high bank on the side of the stream and the brush opened up to reveal the river, he couldn't find Joe. He looked right, then left, then backtracked to the main trail along the river and moved hurriedly upstream. He was beginning to feel panicky that he shouldn't have left his brother alone. His pace quickened and he felt his mind begin to race. What if Joe had collapsed again? Perhaps he'd fallen in the river and drowned. Perhaps he was lying on the river-bank and waiting for Donny to find him. Just as he was about to call out for Joe, he stepped through the thick underbrush and saw Joe in the middle of the Root River.

Donny stopped and smiled, and sighed a deep sigh of relief. Joe was kneeling on one knee in about two feet of water. The current was slow and the surface of the water was absolutely flat. Only the songs of small birds could be heard above the faint murmur of the water gurgling over rocks in a small riffle downstream from Joe. Donny knew that Joe was kneeling to keep a low profile and hide from a fish. He'd seen Joe do it a hundred times before. Joe would spot a nice fish rising regularly to take mayflies from the water's surface, then stalk that particular fish.

While he stared at Joe, Donny remembered a fine summer day, several years earlier, when he'd been fishing a calm stretch of water like this, unsuccessfully. The bright blue of the sky had been visible only intermittently, through the openings between deep green hardwood boughs that lined the stream. Even though the sun had been shining brightly, only a hint of yellow light found its way to the forest floor. The clear water reflected the green of the woods so perfectly that sometimes it was hard to tell where the river ended and the forest began. Joe had stepped into the river and moved cautiously to his side that afternoon. The water and the woods surrounding it were so quiet that Joe took extra caution not to splash and spook the fish away. He watched Donny fish for several minutes, and when he sensed Donny's growing frustration he finally spoke. "Donny, those rise forms that you're fishing—they're not rises; not really," he'd said in an effort to help. Donny had stopped casting and asked him to explain. "Well, when fishermen see those little circles in the water that trout make when they come up and break through the surface—rise forms...you know, circular ripples on the surface—they always assume the trout are taking adult mayflies—dry flies, off the surface, with their mouths. Sometimes they're not; they're actually feeding on emergers, the stage in the life cycle that's between the nymph and the adult mayfly. You know, it's the stage in the life cycle that isn't a nymph any longer but it's not an adult yet." Joe stopped and looked over where the fish were feeding. "It's funny: they only exist in the emerger form for a little while, just drifting along in the current, waiting to change into something else." Then he looked back at Donny. "Well, the emergers always seem to get eaten just below the surface, and when the trout take them they make something of a rise form—but it isn't...not really. Just look at what's going on over there." Donny had looked, then shrugged his shoulders. "Donny, look man. Those aren't trout lips coming out of the water. Those are dorsal fins breaking the surface as the trout feed a couple inches below." As soon as Joe said these words, Donny understood, for the first time, just what he was looking at. Joe's explanation had been perfect; as soon as Donny heard the words, it was as if a veil had been lifted and he saw exactly what was happening. "Here you go, Donny. Try one of these," Joe had said as he handed Donny two flies that he'd tied to look like adults, but with very small, immature wings. On the second cast, Donny hooked a trout, and Joe continued to give instructions as Donny reeled the fish in. "OK, Donny, now in a few minutes the adult mayflies are gonna start to hatch, to appear on the water's surface and in the air around us, and THEN the trout are gonna start taking them on the surface. You'll see mayflies in the air, and then you'll see fish lips, not fins, on the water when they rise and make a real rise form on the surface. All right, now this is how you pick out a big fish..."

Donny would always remember that conversation in the river. On that day, he'd seen something joyful in his brother, something deep and special. Joe Mix was a member of some fraternity that Donny didn't understand. Joe had insight, and passion, and skill far beyond his. Joe was in love with the beauty of this place. He saw something delicate and lovely in the cycles of the weather and the little lives in nature—the mayflies and the fish. He was drawn to it all. He found joy in the mastery of these difficult tasks.

A moment of clarity came to Donny once again as he watched Joe kneeling in the river. He understood that this was one part of Joe's life that existed without complication or anxiety. This was the one part of his life that he celebrated every time he came to it, with no waiting or desire for it to end. It really wasn't the fishing, although he obviously enjoyed that part. The fishing was just the thing that brought him here and allowed him to enter into all of this.

Donny knew that Joe was unaware he was watching, so he sat quietly on the riverbank and reached into his vest for his water bottle. He took a long drink, then put the top back on the bottle and watched his brother for a while. Joe looked about the river in front of him, scanning the surface for a rising trout. Donny could see the same sights as Joe; not very many mayflies in the air, and a few sporadic rise forms. But he couldn't tell if it was trout lips or dorsal fins that were disturbing the water's surface as the trout cruised the far bank. One trout appeared to be a little bigger than the others, and it was rising somewhat regularly along the far bank, under a large tree branch that hung about four feet above the water.

Joe opened a fly box and searched for the fly he wanted. Donny guessed that it would be an emerger. Joe would certainly notice the lack of adult mayflies in the air and use an emerger for that reason.

When he was ready, Joe made a series of false casts as he fed line into his casting motion. As Donny watched, Joe cast his fly line in long, tight loops just above the river. At just the right instant, he flicked his wrist and his fly line laid down on the surface of the water. Donny couldn't see where the fly had landed, but he watched for a response from Joe. Several seconds passed and Joe remained still as the slow current carried the fly over the fish's field of vision. Nothing happened. No trout struck at the fly. Joe waited until the line and the fly had passed downstream from the trout, and the fish would not be disturbed or spooked by the commotion caused on the water's surface when Joe flicked his fly line back into the air. Then, with an effortless movement of his right arm, Joe lifted the bamboo rod and thirty feet of fly line from the surface of the water. He began creating graceful loops over his head with it as he prepared to cast again.

A second cast went unnoticed, then a third, then a fourth. After Joe's fifth presentation passed over the trout with no result, he reeled his fly line in, held his bamboo rod under his left arm, and reached into his pocket for his fly box once more. He scanned the contents of the little box for a moment and then chose a new fly. He clipped the unwanted fly from the end of his line and placed it on the fleece patch on his vest so it would dry out in a moment and be ready if he needed to try it again. As Joe tied on a new fly, Donny could only guess what it might be.

Donny watched with renewed interest as Joe began to cast once more—tight loops, low and near the water. Donny noticed that Joe leaned forward. He knew Joe well enough that he could recognize both intensity and pleasure from his brother's posture. When he laid the line onto the water, it was perfectly straight and the fly fluttered to the water's surface about five feet upstream from where the trout had been rising. The current started carrying the fly toward the trout instantly.

When Joe saw the lips appear and suck the little fly under, he gently raised the bamboo rod in his right hand. A ten-inch brown trout felt the steel instantly and jumped out of the water twice in an effort to spit the hook. Joe's rod bent as he began to battle the fish. Then, in an instant, the resistance was gone and the rod straightened lifelessly; the trout had spit the hook.

Joe stood and turned toward Donny. He was walking toward the place where Donny sat when he noticed his brother waiting for him. Even as Joe had turned away from the battle with the trout and toward Donny, he'd been smiling. Now his smile only widened when he saw Donny and realized he'd been watching.

"Fooled him!" Joe called, clearly satisfied that he'd cast to a fish feeding in a fairly inaccessible place and then enticed the fish to strike at his offering. That was enough of a victory for him; he'd done a difficult thing, and he'd done it gracefully. Landing the fish was unnecessary. He moved out of the river with long, noisy steps as he walked steadily toward the shoreline. He was done fishing for a while.

"Baetis?" Donny asked.

"Yeah! Emerger! How about that! Go figure. I fished it dry...in the film. That's a trick I learned from an old guy on the Wisconsin Brule a few years ago! I love this little pattern. Started tying it last year. It always works," Joe said as he stepped out of the river and sat next to Donny.

Joe leaned back, took a deep breath, and let it out with a satisfied sigh.

"That was good. I love this place." He smiled at Donny and reached toward the large pocket in the back of Donny's vest. "Got any water left?"

"Yeah," Donny said as he lowered his shoulder and let Joe reach for the bottle in his vest.

"It's not about fishing, Donny. You know that, don't you?" Joe said as he fumbled around, reaching to pull a water bottle out of Donny's vest. "It was never about fishin'—about catching fish, I mean," Joe continued. "It's about this place!" he said, still reaching for the water bottle in Donny's vest. He pulled the bottle out and twisted the cap off before he took a long sip. "It's about coming here, to some beautiful place like this." Joe paused. "This is where life begins, Donny. This is where it all starts, maybe where it ends," Joe said, and then looked upstream.

"Nobody but you would say shit like that, Joe."

Joe smiled, then looked downstream.

"How you feelin', Joe?" Donny asked.

"Pretty good!" Joe replied. "It's been a fine morning!"

"You been catchin' fish?" Donny asked.

"Yeah. Caught about half a dozen in that riffle." Joe pointed downstream to the gurgling water. "I released a nice fourteen-inch brown just before I moved up to this flat stretch. Caught him right over there." Joe pointed to the far side of the river at the tail end of the riffle. "Nicest fish I've caught here in a while!" Joe paused. "How 'bout you?"

"Caught a nice rainbow. The hatchery must have dumped some rainbows in here. He was pretty stupid, like most hatchery trout—took a big old Royal Wolf."

Joe grinned when Donny said he'd used a Royal Wolf, a fluffy attractor trout fly that doesn't look like anything that occurs naturally in a trout's diet.

"Why were you using a Royal Wolf?"

"Cause the big, dumb hatchery trout like 'em," Donny smiled.

Joe ignored Donny's answer. He drank half the water in the bottle, then put it back in the large pocket in the back of Donny's vest. "Got any chocolate?" Joe asked as he felt around the bottom of the pocket.

"Yeah. Some jerky, too," Donny answered.

Joe withdrew two Snickers bars and started to unwrap one.

"Those are from last year," Donny said calmly.

Joe ignored that comment too. He ate one candy bar and put the wrapper in his own pocket, then began to unwrap the second. "Did you notice, Donny, that neither one of us asked the other for a score, like we do in golf?"

"So?"

"Well, think about it. Out here we measure success by the quality of the experience. The skill required to do some difficult thing correctly causes us to push ourselves to another level. And the satisfaction of completing something we had to struggle for—hell, that's priceless. Isn't that how we should measure success?"

"YOU think about it. In golf, you need to push yourself to develop your skills so you can have a good score, to measure your success— same thing as fishing," Donny replied.

"Good point, Donny. But we're talking about two different things. Some people play golf to accomplish a low score, others play because they enjoy the thrill of striking the ball perfectly. Some people fish so they can kill something, put it in the freezer, and brag about how many fish they caught. Others do this because they enjoy the game—the chase and the fine places the chase leads them to. They see something deeper. Know what I mean?" Joe paused. "The guy who plays the game for the wrong reason, just to keep score, misses the chance to really see the beauty in it all. He's just going through the motions, and he doesn't even understand that he's missing something. Worse than that, he thinks he's really getting something accomplished, but he isn't. He's just misleading himself. He probably goes to work every day and thinks his job is all about how much he gets paid, and not about how well he does his work."

"Well, Joe, the girl behind the cash register in the grocery store? She's keepin' score! And the guy who's fixin' your car? He's keepin' score. And Julie, at your office? I know she's keepin' score! Hell, we gotta keep score. That's how we measure our accomplishments." Donny shook his head and questioned Joe with his eyes. "And work IS about gettin' paid! You have to keep score!"

"Yeah," Joe sighed. "I guess that's true. But I'm sick of keepin' score. And I'm sick of hearing about other people's scores." He sighed again and changed the subject. He knew there would be no resolution to the issue of accomplishment today. "Let's go fish that long run, up there by the limestone bluffs!" Joe stood up and extended his hand to help Donny up.

Donny reached for Joe's hand and groaned as he stood up. His back had stiffened while they'd been sitting beside the river, and he was clumsy in getting to his feet. He stumbled slightly as he straightened his back, then stumbled again when his boot slipped on the soft ground. As he lurched to regain his balance, he dropped his fly rod onto a rocky shelf by the water's edge. "Shit!" he said softly. For just an instant, Joe thought his brother looked like a drunk, stumbling to get up off a street corner. When Donny finally stood up straight, he looked at Joe and scowled over his own clumsiness. "I look like you playing golf."

"C'mon, Donny, let's go. It's a long walk to the bluffs," Joe said through a smile as he turned toward the trail. Donny was smiling too, and he was about to reply as he bent over and reached toward the rocks to grab his fishing rod. Suddenly, a loud "HISS" jumped from the rocks near Donny's fly rod. In a heartbeat, his eye caught the movement of a large snake as it raised its head and opened its mouth. "SHIT!" Donny cried when he jerked his hand back and lost his balance. He stumbled backward down the riverbank for several steps and then fell into the river. He sat in about three inches of water with a stunned look on his face. "Look out! It's a fuckin' rattlesnake!" he called to Joe.

But when he looked at Joe, his brother stood motionless, with his hands on his knees. A strand of drool hung from the corner of Joe's mouth, and his chest was heaving with laughter. "It was a bull snake," Joe finally managed to say between fits of laughter. "They eat mice and gophers and stuff like that. A snake like that would almost never bite you. He's a nasty-faced SOB, but that's about it," Joe said as he wiped the tears out of his eyes. "Really, Donny, that snake looked mean, but he's harmless."

Donny stood up in the water and adjusted his hat, then his vest. Then he tried to smile as he confessed: "Scared the shit out of me." He laughed openly along with Joe, although a strange look of concern, or perhaps pain, would not leave his face. After several minutes of laughter and retelling of the snake story, Donny pointed to his fly rod. "Hey, Joe, hand me my rod, will you? It's right down there on the ground, right by where that great big fuckin' snake was a minute ago." Joe grinned, picked up the fly rod, and extended his hand toward Donny without a word. When Donny reached for it, Joe pulled it back, cocked his head sideways, and pointed to the grin on his own face. He was taunting Donny, demanding a smile. Donny smiled grudgingly and mumbled "thanks" as he took the rod from Joe.

As the brothers began to walk through the woods to the limestone bluffs a mile or so away, Joe offered over his shoulder, "You looked like that guy in *Psycho*—you know, when Norman Bates was stabbing him and it took forever for him to fall backwards down that flight of stairs?" Joe started laughing all over again.

"Yeah, that's really funny shit there, Joe," Donny said sarcastically. Which brought even heartier laughter from Joe.

———•———

"I'll just sit down here and watch for a minute," Donny said when they reached the gray cliffs. "You go ahead. I never catch anything in this stretch anyway."

Joe stepped into the pool directly in front of Donny and began to look around. The bank on his side of the river was low and easy to walk along. The far bank was sheer rock; the bluff rose from the river bottom and continued straight up for about seventy feet. He'd fished this spot for years and had never done very well either, but he liked the look of the place. He'd always suspected that the far side of the river held nice fish. But the good water was out of his casting range, and he just couldn't get close enough without stepping into deep water and fast current. So he'd always stayed on the safe side of the river.

He made several casts to fish rising sporadically just in front of him, then changed flies and tried again. He switched to a nymph and attached some lead weight to his tippet, about a foot above his fly. His plan was to bounce the nymph along the bottom and try to tempt any trout that might be holding tight to the bottom in the deep hole just in front of him. Two dozen casts resulted in no fish, no strikes, nothing.

Joe was growing frustrated when he decided to change flies one more time. As he searched his fly box, he realized he'd tried all the things that usually worked. He looked around to see what Donny was doing and saw that Donny was still watching him.

Then Joe looked over and noticed the small pool nestled along the bluff on the far side of the river. He'd noticed the pool for years. The pool seemed to be calling to him. He knew there would be fish waiting in that pool—fish that hadn't seen any fisherman. Joe looked upstream, then down. The far side of the river was beckoning; there had to be nice fish in that pool, and it looked so easy and pleasant over there. If he could only get there...

He looked upstream and downstream once more. Joe pursed his lips after he'd taken a deep breath. Then he stepped slowly, one small step, in the direction of the pool on the far side. He made sure his wading boot had a grip on the bottom, and he took another small step into the current. The water rose an inch or two and the current quickened. "Not so bad," Joe said out loud. He took two more small steps and felt the water rise above his waist. The current was pushing at his belly, and he raised his arms and leaned into it to help keep his balance.

This was the moment of truth. He'd arrived here by simply taking a few small steps out of his comfort zone. He knew that if he took one more step he'd be at the mercy of the river. He was tired of always coming to this impasse and then backing away. The bottom felt firm, and he didn't think it was too deep for him to cross, but he just didn't know for sure. He looked back behind him and saw that Donny was still there, watching.

Joe looked at the inviting, placid little pool on the far side. Then he looked at the river in front of him. "Do it!" cried a strange voice in his head. "Do it! For once! Now, do it! You'll be fine!" Joe paused and smiled at the way his own desire was pushing him. "Do it! What's the worst that could happen? You'll go underwater and get wet! No big deal!" the little voice in his head was coaxing. The current pushing at his legs and stomach seemed to be making his mind work faster. He looked across the water once more. "Do it!"

He leaned into the current, took another step, and the river claimed him. He was no longer in total control, and instantly he wished he'd stayed in the safer water. As the water rose to his chest, he had to take another step. There could be no return, not now; he was in too deep. He had to continue; the current was pushing so hard that he couldn't go back. He couldn't go straight ahead either; the current was going to alter his course and eliminate a retreat. There was no going back; he had to try to go forward. The current was pushing him downstream, but his feet still inched across the river bottom in short steps. Strangely enough, everything was much quieter now as he moved with the current instead of fighting it. In one sense, it was actually easier now that he was no longer fighting the current. Each step carried him closer to the other side, but each step carried him into deeper water, a deeper unknown, and placed him more firmly in the grasp of the river. He hoped he'd reached the deepest part of the hole, but the water seemed to rise a little closer to the top of his waders with each step. His pulse began to quicken and he felt fear tightening his chest.

If the water level reached over the top of his waders, he'd be in trouble. The Gore-tex waders would fill with water and pull him downstream. Joe's arms were above his head when he looked down and saw that the water was about an inch below the top of his waders. The next step would be his last if the hole was any deeper. He knew he was gasping as he took a tentative but irreversible final step on his tiptoes.

The bottom of the river came up to meet his right foot just as he was about to start swimming. He'd made it, and the river grew more shallow with the next step and the next. The current seemed to let up too, and when Joe stood in about two feet of calm water, next to the limestone bluffs, he stopped for a minute to compose himself. His pulse was racing and he was breathing quickly. The fear that had deepened with every step across the river had not receded as fast as the water around him.

As his pulse returned to normal and his breathing grew more regular, the fear that had accompanied him across the river began to morph into exhilaration. Hell, he'd done it! He'd crossed over, and it wasn't really that bad. He looked back across the river and knew he could do this anytime he wanted to now.

Joe took a deep breath and looked upstream for his brother. Donny was sitting on the riverbank looking at his fly box, and he seemed to sense that Joe was looking at him. He looked at Joe as if he'd heard Joe calling to him. He raised his head and looked directly at Joe. Donny smiled and waved. He had no idea what had just happened to Joe.

As the smile slowly melted from his face, Joe poked through the rows of trout flies in his fly box. When he glanced upstream again to check for insect or fish activity, he noticed a few adult mayflies—Hendricksons, he thought—flittering about over the water. Then he noticed dozens of them upright on the surface as the current carried them past him. A small pod of trout were rising just in front of them, and after he'd watched for a moment he could see that they were feeding on the Hendricksons.

The fish ignored the size fourteen dark Hendrickson that he'd chosen for several minutes. After a dozen casts, he tried a different fly that was designed to imitate the same mayfly, although with a slightly different look. The wings and body were a softer color, almost pink. On the third cast, he hooked a small trout, then another. But the fishing on this side of the river proved to be about the same as the fishing on the other side: not bad, but not what he'd hoped for.

After about half an hour, Joe began to feel the fatigue of a day on the river—his first day on his feet in a week. He reeled in his line and prepared to cross the Root River once more. This time, he walked a little farther upstream and struggled with the current much less than before as he crossed back to the other side. He was confident that, although the river would move him downstream, he could cross easily now, and he felt no fear as he came back to Donny's side of the river.

Donny was sitting on the bank, waiting for Joe when he approached along the path beside the river.

"I'm tired," Joe said as he sat next to Donny. "Just sort of hit me when I was over there." He pointed across the river.

"Yeah, you've probably had enough for one day. You OK?" Donny asked with obvious concern in his voice.

"Oh, yeah. Just tired." Joe paused, then asked seriously, "Any snakes around here?"

Donny leaned back against a tree and grinned at the memory of his misadventure, but he made no reply.

"Ever wonder what it would be like if you could do this every day—maybe be a fishing guide or a writer for some fishing magazine? S'pose those guys still enjoy it in the same way once it's their job? It's probably the same for pro golfers, huh? S'pose golf is work or fun for the pros...or both?" Joe mused.

"Well, I don't know, Joe," Donny said as he looked at the river. "But those guys sure as hell keep score!"

Donny could see that his remark about keeping score had carried Joe's thoughts away from the Root River. He could see that at the end of a fine day on the river, Joe felt the weight of his practice and his marriage return to him. In a couple days, he'd be back at work. Joe leaned back on his elbows and stared at the water. He listened to the water rush over the rocks in the riverbed and felt the growing weight of his other life nudge this day's good times out of his conscious mind. Neither of them spoke for a moment, and then Joe turned to Donny with the question, "Know what the worst thing about my life is, Donny?"

He knew that Joe was slipping back to the melancholy of the past few days, but Donny wasn't willing to let go of today's good times just yet. He tried to feign an introspective stare, then offered, "Hmmm...the worst thing in your life?" He rubbed his chin and looked at the sky as if he were trying to remember something. "Hmmm...having such a teensy little pecker?"

"No," Joe said slowly as a smile began to wrinkle the corners of his mouth. He knew Donny was only trying to hold onto the joy of the afternoon, but he'd already let go of it and he couldn't go back. He shook his head and confessed, "I was thinking that the worst thing about it all is that I chose it. I chose all of it."

Donny let go of the joke. "Joe," he said softly, "you have a good life."

Joe nodded silently and looked at his hands. "Yeah, I guess so." Then he sighed and said, "Let's go home."

"Keep an eye out for snakes!" Joe called, trying to sound serious as he followed behind Donny on the trail.

Donny raised his middle finger for Joe to see, but he said nothing and never turned around. He was hiding his smile from Joe as he walked the trail back, and Joe knew it. Joe smiled a satisfied smile too. He'd had a fine day on the river, one that would remain etched in his memory—not because of the great fishing but because of the joy of Donny's friendship. Joe was secure with Donny's love, and that seemed to balance the weight in the rest of his life, for now.

"Jeez, Joe. Why don't you get a new truck? Your backyard looks like a bunch of rednecks live here!" Donny said as he drove around to the back of Joe and Jess's sprawling brick home. Joe's old Ford pickup with the yellow snowplow sat next to a garden shed, poised and ready for work.

"I love my truck," Joe said indignantly.

"It looks like shit," Donny countered.

"Runs fine!"

"The windows don't open. There are holes in the floorboards. You've got the seats from my old Datsun bolted to the floor because your original interior fell apart. Shit, the snowplow on the front is worth way more than the truck." Donny scowled. "It looks like shit!" he reiterated.

"Aw, Jeez, those are such small holes. And the windows DO open. You just need a vise grip to turn the handle. I love that truck!" Joe said with a grin, as if he were defending the honor of an old friend. "And I just put that new...used...topper on the back to keep all my stuff dry. It's perfect!"

"Yeah, a green truck with a yellow blade and a red topper. It looks like Jim Brown's hat—like the dogs had it under the porch for a while!"

Donny laughed out loud over the comparison to Jim Brown's hat as his car rolled to a stop.

"Looks like the boys are home too!" Donny added. "Say 'hi' to everyone, will you?"

"Sure," Joe said. "Wanna come in for a minute?"

"Love to, Joe, but I still have things to do at home! I'll see you next week."

chapter
nine

The back door to Joe's house opened as he trudged up cedar steps that led to a large, wooden deck overlooking a flower garden and several acres of woods behind the house. "Hi, Dad!" Ben said as he stepped onto the deck in his stocking feet. Ben had a Coke in one hand, and he opened his arms wide to embrace his father.

"Hi, son." Joe held his son tightly and kissed him on the cheek.

"How you feelin', Dad?" Ben said softly into Joe's ear.

"Pretty good! Well, a little tired right now, but pretty good."

The sliding glass door that let into the kitchen opened once again and Chris stepped out, also in his stocking feet and carrying a Coke.

"Hi, Dad!" he said with a smile as he spread his arms.

"Hi, son," Joe said as he kissed Chris on the cheek too. He reached his right hand to the back of Chris's neck and stroked him softly as he held him. There was something warm and familiar and solid in the embrace for Joe, as if a pleasant memory had been restored. He still loved to hold the boys.

Ben and Chris were both lanky, physically mature young men. Every time Joe saw them nowadays, they seemed to change and grow up a little more. But they were still lost in that uncertain time between man and boy. Both had shaggy blonde hair and bony shoulders that held their clothes at odd angles sometimes.

"I didn't think you were coming home," Joe said as they all found cedar deck chairs and settled in to greet each other.

"Well, you scared us the other day, Dad. We had to come home and see you," Ben said. He was clearly concerned about Joe's episode in the hospital. "So what happened?"

Joe leaned back in his chair and began to describe the episode of "Acute Fatigue" to his sons. Soon the conversation turned to school, and summer, and summer jobs, and before long Joe was listening to the boys talk about sports, girls, and everything else in their lives. While Joe sat on the deck and chatted with his sons, the long afternoon shadows spread across the backyard, and a fine spring day stretched into evening.

Jess remained in the kitchen, sipping at a glass of wine and watching the TV on the kitchen counter.

"I think I need new tires on my car, Dad," Chris said in passing as Joe put several hamburgers on the barbecue grill and opened a can of diet soda for himself.

"OK," Joe said without looking up. "Next time you're home…"

"Jeez, Dad," Chris interrupted. "That guy at the car place? What a dose! Last time I had my car in there, it took 'em three days to get the right parts in! Really pissed me off."

"Yeah," Ben added, "he's really a dipshit."

"Are you talking about Sparky?" Joe asked. He turned to look at the boys.

"Yeah," Chris said. "He's the stupid fat guy at the front desk, right?" Then he laughed.

"Sparky's a good guy!" Joe said in defense of the service manager at the service center in the Ford garage. "He's always gone out of his way to take good care of us." Joe sounded as if his feelings had been hurt by his sons' comments.

"He's a dope, Dad. And he looks like a fool!" Ben replied. His words carried some added scorn for Sparky, and Chris laughed and nodded in agreement.

"Boys…" Joe was bothered by the disrespect and derision he was hearing from his sons. "That guy works hard, he's honest, and he's always been nice to me—and you. How can you be so hard on him?"

"Look at him, Dad. He's a stooge!" Ben argued, still smiling.

"Well, he's not exactly cosmopolitan, that's for sure," Joe conceded. "But he gets up and goes to work every day, he pays his bills, he helps coach his kid's hockey team. He's a man who deserves your respect!" Joe scowled and shrugged his shoulders. He was surprised by his sons' scorn for Sparky.

"You been hangin' around with him, Dad? You act like he's your buddy or something." Now Chris laughed at his own suggestions.

"He's just a man. Just like you and me. Maybe a better man!" Joe added.

"Yeah, right," Ben said sarcastically.

Joe realized he wasn't about to win the argument, so he turned back to the hamburgers and took a sip of his soda. It hurt him inside to see the way his boys seemed to look down on a good man. He'd seen that attitude off and on in both of the boys, and he felt it was getting worse over the past year, but he'd never had such a visceral response to his sons' behavior. Joe wished that he'd insisted on the boys getting summer jobs when they were younger. They'd probably have more respect for working people if they'd worked themselves, Joe thought. But Jess had always argued that there were other, more important things to do in the summer, and that they'd have the rest of their lives to work. Joe bristled slightly as he remembered Jess overturning his wishes that the boys work during the summer. He should have stood fast and made them work.

"So, Ben, how are your studies?" Joe changed the subject after a moment of silence.

"Pretty good. My GPA is still a 3.8-something, and I should be hearing about my score on the MCAT pretty soon. The Medical College Admissions Test is still an all-day exam, you know. That really makes for a long, stressful day. But I felt pretty good about the way the whole day went. I think I scored pretty well."

"Still sure you want to go to medical school?" Joe asked.

"Yeah, pretty much."

"Chris, how about you? Studies are going OK?"

"Yeah, no problem, Dad," Chris replied. Chris sneaked a sideways glance at his brother and raised his eyebrows when Ben returned his glance.

"That's good," Joe said without looking at Chris. "OK, Chris, tell your mom we're ready to bring the burgers in," Joe added as he took the hamburgers off the grill and put them on a plate.

Jess did manage to turn the kitchen TV off and join them for dinner. Virtually all of her interest and enthusiasm during the conversation over dinner was directed toward the boys' social lives, acquaintances from school, and plans for the summer. And as the boys answered their mother's questions, Joe began to notice that while Ben's comments were sometimes negative and spiced with the opinionated bluster of an overconfident young man, Chris's remarks about people and events at school were laced with outright contempt.

Chris seemed to think that his professors were all stupid, and that the classes he was taking were pointless. His classmates all lacked insight, and many of them were pseudo intellectuals or brownnosers. At one point, he seemed genuinely angry when he described how stupid and worthless the woman who'd waited on him at a McDonald's restaurant had been.

"Well, at least she's working. She's trying," Joe had responded.

Chris had only rolled his eyes and smiled at Ben.

By the time dinner was over, Joe's heart was aching over the unkind and critical comments of the boys, especially Chris. He'd also started to feel the fatigue of a long day. "I gotta shower and get some sleep," he said when he pushed his chair back from the table.

"Well, Ben and I are gonna go over to McNamaras' place. Ty's folks are gone and he's having some guys over for a card game," Chris said.

"OK. Behave yourselves," Joe said as he reached for his pocket. "Need any money?" He extended his open wallet, and both boys quickly reached in and lifted several bills out.

"Thanks, Dad," they both called out as they turned away from the table.

"Be quiet when you come home!" Joe said to their backs. They were already out the door.

The little boys who wanted to play ball in the yard after supper, or go fishing, were all grown up and gone now. It was clear that both of the boys thought their father had little to say that was relevant in their lives. Chris's arrogance and contempt had actually hurt Joe's feelings. Joe began to wonder if his wishing time away to just get on with things had resulted in lazy, poor parenting, and ultimately in two boys with pompous, self-centered personalities. Maybe this was just another phase he should wish would hurry up and be over. That thought brought a deeper sense of fatigue.

When he stood up from the table, Joe felt even more tired. "I gotta go to bed. See you in the morning, Jess." When he turned to touch her hand and say goodnight, or maybe steal a kiss, Jess lifted the boys' dishes from the table and turned away from him.

When she reached the sink, she turned the faucet on and stacked the dishes on the countertop. "You should have rested today. You don't need to overdo and wind up missing any more work," she said into the sink.

Joe sighed and walked slowly away to prepare for bed. He trudged up the stairs that led to the second story, and when he reached the upstairs bathroom he stripped off his shirt and turned the shower on. He looked at himself briefly in the bathroom mirror and sucked his belly in. As the mirror began to fog up, he turned and put his face close to it. He stared at himself and said, "Thanks for your concern, Jess. And yes, I had a nice day, and I feel good." When the mirror fogged over, he stepped into the shower.

The voices in the kitchen finally awakened Joe at about 10:00 a.m. on Saturday. It seemed as though he'd just settled onto the couch in his den a moment earlier, but fourteen hours had passed. He hadn't slept this soundly since college. Perhaps it would require some more rest to fully recover from the episode with fatigue. He stumbled into the bathroom and splashed cold water on his face in an effort to clear the cobwebs. His head seemed to clear as he was brushing his teeth, and the smell of coffee greeted him when he reached the top of the stairway that led back to the kitchen.

Jess and Ben were sitting at the kitchen table, waiting for a coffeecake to cool and speaking quietly, when Joe shuffled into the kitchen.

"Morning, Dad," Ben said. "You're looking good there!" he added with a smile.

Joe sucked in his belly and tried not to smile as he poured himself some coffee. He was wearing boxers with a blue plaid design, along with a gray T-shirt. His eyes still looked dull. He sat down heavily on the chair next to Ben when he reached the table.

"Morning," Joe said as he raised his cup in something of a greeting. Then he closed his eyes and took a sip.

"We've been talking about the boys' plans for the summer," Jess said. "Oh?"

"I still think they should travel, go to Europe, see the world!" Jess said. "Like we talked about a while ago."

Jess's words hit Joe like a fist. This morning's gathering over coffee now had the feel of a sneak attack. He and Jess had discussed Jess's idea that the boys travel through Europe. But Joe had been adamantly opposed to the idea, and they'd agreed not to discuss it in front of the boys until they'd talked it over some more and come to some sort of agreement. Initially, he had no reply to Jess's comment. He only stared at her.

"This really is the time to go," Jess added. "You'll never enjoy it more than now. We have so many connections there, with all the foreign students we've made friends with in the last few years when they've come to our high school to study for a year." She nodded her agreement to her own opinion.

"What about work? Summer jobs? Learning just what we want to do with our lives?" Joe asked. Then he scowled at Jess. "And what about our agreement?"

"They have their whole lives to work. And we don't need the money. They need to see the world." Jess's tone was intended to capture Ben's interest and enthusiasm, and it carried the unmistakable implication that Joe didn't understand the necessities of proper development and was actually the boys' opponent while she was on their side. The more Joe listened to Jess, the angrier he became. Several weeks earlier, when they'd discussed the idea of traveling in Europe, Joe had been emphatic that the boys needed to work—learn how to make, and save, their own money. Maybe they could discover some career they wanted to pursue, or avoid, when they were older. Jess had seen that Joe was serious in his disapproval of European travel this summer, and now she was trying to get around him by arguing her case in front of the boys. "They do need to see the world, Joe."

"They need to see the real world!" Joe said angrily. "And we agreed not to discuss this in front of the boys!" he added as he cast another stern look at Jess.

Just then, Chris walked into the kitchen. "Are we talking about traveling in Europe this summer, Dad? Mom told me all about it last night when we got home from McNamaras'. Sounds good to me."

Jess smiled a wicked smile and turned a defiant look toward Joe.

"Well, don't pack your bags just yet." Joe stifled the angry remarks he wanted to make, opened the sliding glass door, and stepped out onto the cedar deck in the backyard. He could feel that the morning would warm into a fine spring afternoon. But as he stood there in his boxers and bare feet, he noticed how soothing the cool morning air could be.

When he looked across the heavy dew on the short grass, he noticed his truck. And immediately it came to him that standing here on the deck like this, enjoying the cool air instead of arguing with Jess, was somehow the equivalent of driving around in the truck, avoiding his job in the morning.

He stood alone on the deck, watching small birds at the bird feeders in the backyard, sipping his coffee and allowing the cool air to soothe his anger. When he stepped back into the kitchen, the others were cutting pieces of coffeecake for themselves, and the conversation around the table involved only current events and some catching up on just what was happening in the lives of the boys' high school friends. Joe knew they had stopped talking about Europe because he was angry and wanted no more of it. His life experience told him they were still going to continue with their plans for a summer in Europe because...because they knew he'd cave in and then just wait for the whole thing to be over.

As Joe spread some soft butter on the cinnamon crust of the coffeecake, he listened to his boys tell stories about their classes, their friends, and their lives at school. It seemed to Joe that the boys didn't concern themselves with much outside of their own small worlds. All young men were probably as self-centered as Ben and Chris, Joe thought. But again today, when he heard the things coming from Chris, he felt bad. He noticed an unkind, condescending edge whenever Chris spoke of other people—especially when he spoke of people with blue-collar backgrounds who'd had far fewer opportunities than he. Ben spoke in much the same way, but Chris's comments seemed bitter and made Joe cringe from time to time. Chris just seemed to dislike and disrespect so many people. Although he had no life experience outside his home or college, he seemed to have all the answers. Finally, when Joe could stand no more of it, he spoke up.

"My God, Chris, how did you get so down on the rest of the human race?" Joe blurted.

"Me? Me?" Chris turned to face his father. "I've been sitting at this table listening to you rant about stuff like this for my whole life! You know, people from the office, the government, insurance companies!" Chris replied with a cynical grin. "I guess I learned from you!" he added.

Chris's words had the feel of a punch in the chest. The others all laughed as if Chris had paid his father a compliment—like father, like son. Joe lowered his eyes to the table in front of him but made no response.

Chris was right; Joe had created the problem. He'd been unwilling to do the right things, the difficult things. He'd given his boys too much because it was easy, and it was more fun to give them the things they wanted. But he'd never taught them to work. He'd told them all about the difficulties in his life and the ones they'd encounter too. But he'd never allowed them to resolve their own problems. Now it seemed like they'd never be able to find their way. He'd meant to be a good father, but by refusing to do the difficult things he'd repeated the mistakes of his own father.

As the coffeecake disappeared, Joe found himself staring into his cup and thinking about what Chris had said. The others picked at the crumbs in the cake pan and talked for a while longer, but Joe had dismissed himself from the conversation. He became a spectator at his own table, just watching his family but somehow existing apart from it.

Eventually the boys announced they had another party to attend this evening, back at the university in Minneapolis, and that they'd be leaving shortly.

Joe was still sitting silently at the kitchen table by himself, after he and Jess had cleared the dishes and prepared a package of food for the boys to take back with them. He looked out through the patio door and noticed Ben packing some things into his car before he and Chris returned to school. The realization that the boys would be leaving soon seemed to jar him back into the moment, and even though he was still dressed in boxers and a T-shirt, he stepped out into the driveway behind the house.

"Still lookin' good, Dad," Ben called out as Joe approached his car.

"Thanks," Joe whispered, and quickly dismissed Ben's reference to his clothes. He held a coffee cup in one hand and looked Ben up and down while his eyes asked a silent question.

"What? What is it?" Ben asked.

"What happened to my little boys?" Joe asked, as if it were a rhetorical question to be answered in a classroom.

"We grew up!"

Joe stared as though he hadn't heard Ben's answer. "It was easier when you were little! It was easier then. I kept waiting, but I was wrong." Joe didn't seem to be talking to anyone but himself.

"Huh?" Ben was bewildered by the look on Joe's face, and by his words. "You OK, Dad?" Ben gave his father a sideways glance with the question.

"Yeah," Joe nodded. "Yeah." There was nothing he could say now that would change things for Ben or Chris. They'd have to find their own way. "I was just thinking how much easier things really were when you were little boys."

"Well, it was easier for us, too, Dad. We were talking all the way home yesterday." Ben walked around the back of the car and approached his father. Joe thought Ben looked clumsy and uncomfortable for a moment. Gradually he sensed that Ben wanted to step closer to him. Ben stood near his father for a moment. He seemed uncertain of something, as if he needed permission to do what he was about to do. Then he suddenly wrapped his arms around Joe and pulled him close. Ben's display of affection surprised Joe, but he simply returned the embrace and waited for Ben to speak.

"We were worried about you, Dad. When Uncle Donny called the other day, we were really worried," Ben said softly into his father's ear. Joe could hear his son's voice tremble slightly, and he stroked Ben's back to steady him. "I was afraid you were gonna die," Ben whispered. "I don't want you to get old."

"I'm not old!" Joe said softly. "And I'm not gonna die just now. I've got some things to do yet." Joe stepped back and smiled at Ben. "Don't write me off just yet."

"I thought you were indestructible, Dad, and I still want to be like you," Ben said.

Joe Mix swallowed hard before he spoke. Suddenly, he was trying not to cry.

"Oh, Jeez, Ben, why would you want that? Don't be like me; don't try to be like anybody!" As soon as he'd spoken those words, it was impossible for him not to think of his conversation with the Old Cowboy when he was Ben's age.

"Ben? What I meant to say is that I want you to be something better than me. But you need to do the hard part. You need to go find out what it is that you love to do and who you really are. Don't choose something that you think I'd choose. Although I've probably been trying to do the hard part for you, I can't do that anymore. It'll only make things more difficult for you if I try to help you too much. Find your own way. Find what you want. Make your own mistakes. Do you know what I mean?"

"Yes," Ben said as he stepped away from Joe. "But it's a little scary sometimes."

"It's scary for all of us, son. I think it needs to be that way too."

Both father and son seemed to understand that some barrier had been breached, and that was all that needed to be said for now.

Voices from inside the house caused Joe and Ben to turn and look toward the deck outside the kitchen.

"Dad?" Ben said when he turned to face Joe again.

"Yeah?"

Ben looked back at the house to be sure they were alone. "Chris is gonna have problems."

"Whatya mean?"

"School is really easy for him."

"It's easy for you, too, isn't it?"

"It's not the same, Dad. It's really easy for him. He never studies anything. He just reads it once and knows it. They say he's like you."

"Huh?"

"He's like you! He's really smart." Ben smiled at the agonized look on his father's face. "It's true, Dad. Everyone sees it," Ben added. "And Chris? It's just too easy for him. He's starting to cut classes and party way too much." Ben looked at his own feet. "His grades are gonna suffer, though. He's just not trying."

Joe sighed and then asked, "You mean it's so easy for him that he doesn't value it, and he's gonna make some bad choices? Is that what you mean, Ben?"

"Yeah, I guess so. I guess he's not exactly like you."

"Maybe more than you know," Joe mumbled.

"Huh?"

"Never mind. You're a good boy, Ben. You need to understand something. It's nice that you're concerned about Chris, but all you can do is be his brother and love him. If he makes bad choices...well, that's on him and he'll have to learn from it. With me?"

"Kind of," Ben whispered.

"He's a good boy. He'll figure things out, like you," Joe shrugged. "He'll have to! Just help him when you can."

Jess stepped onto the porch with an armful of clean laundry. Chris followed close behind her with two grocery bags full of food. As they walked toward the car, Joe hugged Ben once more and whispered, "I love you, son."

When Chris had put the groceries in the car and was ready to say goodbye, Joe stepped close to him and held him.

"Bye, Dad," Chris said after a quick hug, and then he tried to release Joe.

But Joe refused to let Chris move away. He held his lips close to his son's ear and was about to whisper a bit of fatherly advice, like "study hard" or "be a good boy and do your homework." But instead, he simply held Chris close to him. He knew Chris didn't need or want a pep talk. He didn't need any charges about hard work, responsibility, and good behavior. Chris had heard it all before, and nothing Joe could say would make any difference now. Joe tightened his hold on Chris and said, "You're a good boy. I love you, son." Chris tried to step away from Joe once more, but Joe would not let go of him. He stroked the back of Chris's neck and kissed his cheek, and held him even closer for a moment before he released his son.

"Yeah, I love you too, Dad," Chris replied while a puzzled grin spread across his face, and he slid into the passenger seat and closed the car door. Ben made eye contact with his father over the top of the car, pursed his lips, and nodded.

"Bye, Mom. Love you," Ben said when he hugged his mother. Both boys waved out the windows as they rolled down the driveway and onto the road.

Jess turned and walked into the house when the boys were out of sight.

Joe tossed the cold coffee still left in his cup onto the concrete driveway, then slowly walked to the deck. He found a cedar deck chair and turned it so that the sun would warm his shoulders when he sat down.

This much he knew: he'd never count down another time in his life. He'd try to feel every moment from here on. And what his boys really needed now, he couldn't give them. He'd have to step out of their way and let them get it for themselves. Every man had to get it for himself.

The memory of his children's lives began to play in his mind's eye while he sat there in the cedar chair, and he stared a vacant stare while the boys laughed and played before him as if he were watching a video. Minutes rolled by and the memories kept coming. Joe saw toddlers playing in the backyard of their first home on the other side of town, Christmas trees, school events, and family vacations. He saw the boys fighting over toys and over all the other things that brothers find to fight about. Ben seemed to be the one who cried first when they fought—he could never break through Chris's tough exterior or win an argument with him.

The memories never sped up or slowed down, but they continued to come, and they continued to pile a heaviness in Joe's heart. He saw his children's high school friends parade through the house, ball games, conferences with teachers, graduations. His heart grew darker, and he felt more alone with each passing minute. Finally, he heard himself groan as he reached his left hand up to cover his eyes.

He'd done the same thing with his boys that he'd done with the rest of his life, and now he'd come to the sad end of that road. All along, at every turn, Joe had been counting down the moments of the boys' lives too. When they were babies in their cribs and began to cry, he'd been irritated that his sleep had been interrupted, angry that he'd had to walk the floor with one or the other of the boys. He'd wished that they would hurry and grow older, because surely, just a little further down the road, life would be easier. When the boys were toddlers and they'd made a mess around the house, or broken something, Joe had wished they would hurry and grow up a little, because the next stage would certainly be easier.

As the conscious realization of what he'd done settled over him, he heard himself groan and covered his face with both hands. He knew that the agonized cry he'd made was like a dam that had been holding back the knowledge of his failure as a parent.

Had he done everything wrong? Just how had he gone so far wrong in so many areas of his life?

Joe was still sitting on the deck an hour later—staring across the backyard, thinking about all the things that had been said during the past twenty-four hours, and letting the afternoon sun warm him—when he heard Jess open the sliding door and step onto the deck. When she walked over to the chair next to him and sat down, he looked at her, then looked away.

"What is it?" he asked.

"Are you all right?"

"Do you really care?"

"I want the boys to see Europe this summer."

He made no reply. He would not look at her.

"They're going to! They don't need some tedious summer job!"

"Did you hear those attitudes? Especially Chris? They need to learn to work, to respect people who work. They need to learn to respect all those people who work a lot harder than I do and come home with a lot less to show for it!"

"They need to widen their horizons," Jess spat back at him.

"Exactly! That's exactly right! And they need to do that by working, not playing, not living a life of privilege, not sampling fine wine and chasing pussy in Europe! Are you so shallow or selfish that you can't understand that?"

Her eyes narrowed and she leaned toward Joe. "Never...fucking ever...call me shallow or selfish again!" She pointed her index finger at him, and her eyes looked hateful, reptilian.

Joe sighed. "I'm sorry." He reached for her hand. Just before he touched her, she jerked her hand away and stood up to return to the house.

"Jess," he said firmly. She stopped and looked back. "I am sorry." He held out his hand, and his eyes begged her to sit with him again.

She stared at Joe for a second, then walked back into the house without another word.

chapter
ten

Joe was dragged from a fitful sleep when the alarm clock on his desk began to screech at 6:00 Monday morning. As usual when he didn't sleep well, he felt like he'd finally drifted off to a deep sleep just before the alarm went off, and now it took a moment for him to remember that he'd spent Saturday and Sunday night on the couch in his library. He'd had no interest in close contact with Jess.

He tapped at the alarm on his desk to stop the hateful noise. When he swung his feet onto the floor, he rubbed his face with both hands for a moment. He arched his back and stretched his arms toward the ceiling. "Ahhhh, shit," he groaned as he stretched.

The thought of returning to the office wasn't something that made him feel dark and heavy, but it wasn't exactly invigorating either. He leaned back, into the rich leather of his couch, and looked out the window. The eastern skyline was beginning to brighten, as it always did just before sun-up. Going back to work was just inevitable, he thought. It was unavoidable. He stood up and trudged into the bathroom for a shave and a shower.

———•———

A cloud of steam carried the heavy aroma of fresh coffee to him as he looked out the window. He stared ahead for a moment, then blew the steam away and sipped at the rich black brew. His white shirt, red tie, khaki pants, and brown shoes all said he was ready for work.

When he stood to pour himself one more cup of coffee, he glanced out the window and noticed his green truck with the yellow snowplow and red topper. He smiled at the thought of his old truck, and the dimple in his cheek deepened. He liked the way that old truck made him feel, and he decided to drive it to work.

The engine on the old Ford roared to life when he turned the key, and he couldn't help but smile again. He put his coffee cup into the cup holder he'd glued to the metal dashboard two decades earlier, then began to twist the vise grip that was necessary to crank the driver's side window open. The smell of grease and road dust lingered inside the truck. His smile widened as he pushed the hydraulic lever and raised the snowplow off the ground. When he hit the street, he was leaning back in his seat, his left arm resting on the open window, and grinning like the guy driving the homecoming queen's convertible in the big parade. He shifted into third gear and the truck lurched and bounced from the weight of the snowplow, and coffee spilled across the dash. Joe only smiled a bigger smile. He didn't need to be at work just yet. Maybe he'd just take a little ride in the country before work.

———

The small, steady noise of air rushing through the saliva ejector morphed into the gurgling rush of saliva and water and other debris racing though the gray vacuum hose, as Angela sprayed water and rinsed the floor of the old man's mouth. "How's it feel, Marvin?" Joe asked when he tipped the patient's chair to an upright position at the end of the appointment.

"It's numb!" the old man said with a twinkle in his eye, reminding Joe that he couldn't feel anything.

"Well, then, you just let me know if there's any problem when the anesthetic wears off in a couple hours, OK?" Joe said as he stood up and left the treatment room. "Bye, Marvin. See you in six months."

"Bye, Doc!" the man called as Joe stepped into the hallway that separated the small treatment rooms.

Joe felt a hand on his arm as he walked down the hall toward his private office. "Joe? How are you feeling? Are you OK?" Angela asked while she clasped her hand around his forearm.

"Sure." Joe thought the concern etched in her face was unwarranted and on the verge of melodramatic. "Angie, that was the seventh procedure I've done this morning, and they've all been pretty much the same." He smiled to assure her that he was grateful for her concern, but that the concern was unnecessary. "I'm OK. I'm not gonna drop dead or anything."

"Actually, those seven procedures were just about the same as the million other procedures I've done in the last twenty-four years. A monkey could have done them—just drill 'em and fill 'em!" he added as he turned toward his office. He looked Angela in the eyes and nodded to let her know that she should let go of his arm—he was all right; the day was going just fine.

As Joe nodded, he heard the front door of his office open, even though he was standing seventy feet away from it and was separated from it by a maze of hallways and countertops and small rooms. He was still looking into Angela's eyes when he heard the little voice cry, "I don't wanna be here!" The little girl's shrill scream was followed by loud crying, and Joe could hear a commotion, as if the child was struggling or wrestling with someone.

Joe's eyes fell shut and his chin dropped. "Oh, shit," Joe muttered without opening his eyes. "It's Meghan Loomis, isn't it?"

"Uh huh," Angela confirmed Joe's fears.

"And her mother?" His eyes were still closed.

"Uh huh. We wanted to surprise you; didn't want you to get all worked up just thinking about it. Remember, no fluoride! The Nazi mind control thing, remember?"

Joe sighed heavily and shook his head in disgust.

A few minutes later, Angela had eight-year-old Meghan Loomis seated in the dental chair when Joe entered the treatment room. Meghan was crying at about half volume, and her mother was hovering alongside the chair trying alternately to cajole, then threaten her daughter into appropriate behavior. Meghan's mother had been carrying a twenty-ounce bottle of Mountain Dew, which Joe assumed had been her breakfast. The Mountain Dew was resting on the windowsill, and Mrs. Loomis was trying to be heard above the noise Meghan was making. Joe thought her voice was way too loud, and very abrasive, as she struggled to be heard above the commotion she was causing. It sounded like there was a hostile crowd in the room instead of a little girl and her mother.

"Meghan, honey, if you behave, Mama will buy you a treat," her mother implored.

"Ahhh!" Meghan cried, and she started kicking her feet. She stuck out her lower lip, then lowered her chin until it rested on her chest, then scowled at her mother.

"Meghan? Sweetie? Now, you behave. 'Cause the dentist is gonna have to stick that big needle in your head, and it's only gonna hurt a little bit if you sit still, but it's really gonna hurt if you move around!"

"Ahhh!!" Meghan turned it up another notch.

Joe closed his eyes and shook his head in disgust again.

"Meghan, honey. Sit still and let the doctor fix your tooth." Joe thought her voice sounded like a barking poodle, but he kept silent. "I told the doctor that if he don't hurt you too bad, I'll let him fix my teeth too!" With that, Mrs. Loomis turned and smiled at Joe. All of her teeth were broken and had large, brown areas of decay. Her gums seemed to be throbbing with inflammation. Joe thought that if she ever touched them with a toothbrush she might bleed to death. Meghan's mother might actually be attractive, Joe thought, if it weren't for her brown, broken teeth and inflamed gums. But then every time she started speaking in that awful, grating, loud voice, she got uglier. Meghan was screaming even louder now, and her mother was still smiling at Joe when he finally spoke.

"It would be better if you went out to the waiting room," Joe said firmly.

"She wants me to be here. Don't you, honey? It'll be all right," she replied with fading conviction.

"No. You need to wait in the waiting room!" Joe said. Then he leaned back in his chair and waited for her to go.

"Mama will be just outside the door," she said as she took her Mountain Dew and backed out the door. Her body language told Meghan that she'd be waiting just outside the door, in the hallway, if Meghan should need her.

Meghan cried out angrily and reached for her mother. With that, Mrs. Loomis stepped toward Meghan.

"In the waiting room!" Joe said firmly. Meghan's mother appeared crestfallen, but she reluctantly obeyed Joe's order. When her face was just outside the door, she was still peering into the treatment room through the opening between the door and the door jamb. Joe kicked the door with his right foot and it slammed shut. "OK, Angela, it's time to send Meghan to a more distant orbit. Nitrous oxide, if you please."

Against all of Meghan's protestations at full volume, Angela placed a nose cone, which delivered laughing gas, over Meghan's nose. Joe and Angela sat quietly for a moment and adjusted the flow meter for the proper amount of nitrous oxide. Angela had been surprised by the way Joe had kicked the door closed, and she could see that he was so angry that his hands were trembling. She'd never seen Joe react to Mrs. Loomis with so much angst. But, as always, Joe stifled his anger and continued with his routine. Joe began speaking to Meghan in a calm, monotone voice. The nitrous oxide did most of the work, but Joe's slow, reassuring monologue also seemed to have a calming effect on Meghan. In a few minutes, Meghan Loomis had changed from a screaming banshee to a docile eight-year-old girl. She was talking and laughing with Joe by the time he finished the fillings she'd come for. The dentistry had been a non-event; only the assistance of Meghan's mother had been stressful.

Joe held his hand out and said "gimme five" as Meghan walked out of the treatment room. Meghan smiled and slapped his hand. Then Joe turned to Angela and said quietly, "Watch this!"

As Meghan walked into the waiting room, she was smiling and look-ing for her mother, hoping to show her the nice new fillings. Mrs. Loomis was sitting on the edge of her chair wearing a terror-stricken look, as if she'd just seen a ghost. When Meghan rounded the corner and made eye contact with her mother, the smile melted from her face in an instant. During her short lifetime, her mother had managed to condition Meghan to let her know when it was time to cry so that she could rush in and rescue her. The broad smile left Meghan's face in a heartbeat, and she ran to her mother. She buried her face in her moth-er's ample chest and began to sob. "That's OK, sweetie. You were so brave. We'll go buy you a toy now. Did it hurt?" Mrs. Loomis nodded her head "yes" so Meghan would be sure to know what to say. Meghan's mother needed, wanted, Meghan to cry and have a difficult time so she could rush to her daughter and appear to be a good mother. Joe felt that Mrs. Loomis had, in fact, used him to create an episode so she could further establish herself as Meghan's controller. Meghan's mother was obviously thrilled that she'd been able to bring her daughter to tears...so she could rescue her.

"That kid is an emotional cripple already," Joe whispered to Angela, "and she's gonna spend the rest of her life trying to live up, or down, to her mother's expectations."

Then he froze for a moment. His own words had made him think of the expectations he'd spent his life trying to conform to, and the expectations he'd placed on his boys. "I need a cup of coffee," Joe sighed as he turned toward his private office.

"Your next patient is here!" Angela pointed to the treatment room at the end of the hall.

Joe stopped and faced Angela. As he walked past her he said, "I never want to do that again! I didn't go to college for half my life so I could wrestle with a screaming kid and listen to her dumbass mother. Understand?" He turned his head to the side with his question. "Understand?" he repeated. "I'm never gonna do that again!" And with that he walked into the treatment room at the end of the hall to greet a new patient.

Angela stood by herself in the hallway. She'd never heard Joe talk like that. Was she supposed to tell Julie not to make any more appointments for Mrs. Loomis? Or was Joe simply blowing off steam? She didn't know what to do. But she'd never seen him like this before.

"Hello, I'm Dr. Mix" was all Angela heard before Joe shut the door behind him and disappeared into the treatment room with his next patient.

The young man seated in the chair was handsome and pleasant, and he began to tell a story of intermittent dental pain that stretched back for a few years. He began to relate a story of recent, all-night episodes, with throbbing pain in his lower jaw. Then he smiled and revealed a missing tooth. One of his front teeth, the upper central incisor on the right side of his midline, was gone.

Joe was confused and taken aback. This nice-looking young man was describing pain in his lower jaw, but his front tooth on top was missing. His smile was ridiculous, shattered. The man held his left index finger beside a lower molar when he described the pain.

Joe was still bewildered when he put his gloves on and tipped the dental chair back. He lifted the man's cheek away from his lower molar, and sure enough there was a tooth with a large decay staring back at him. When he set the man upright, he took a moment to examine the area where the missing front tooth had been.

"Yeah, there is a large decay, a cavity, in the tooth on the lower left. We can fix that," Joe said with a smile.

"Good," the man nodded.

"I can fix that other one too," Joe said as he pointed to the missing front tooth in the man's fractured smile.

The young man's face clouded over. Now it was his turn to be confused. At first he didn't seem to understand that Joe was suggesting that he replace the missing front tooth with a bridge or a dental implant. Then his eyes cleared, and he spoke as if Joe had suggested something ridiculous. "Why would I wanna fix that? I'm already married."

For the second time in this short conversation, Joe was caught so off guard that he didn't know quite what to say. "OK," he said after a short pause to collect his thoughts. He decided not to try to explain anything to this man. He reasoned that any man who was so content to have found a woman to wash his clothes and cook for him shouldn't have his world disturbed with talk of an ugly smile. In the past, on every other day of his life until this one, Joe would have lectured the man on the value of his smile, and how one missing tooth might cause the collapse of the others, and how a healthy, attractive smile might give him self-confidence and lead to more success at work. But today he didn't have the energy to care about this man more than he cared about himself.

"Oh, yeah, Doc. One other thing: I'm allergic to Novocaine," the young man offered.

"Really? What happens when you have Novocaine?" Joe asked. He knew what he was about to hear.

"My lip gets really numb," the man said, then raised his finger and touched his lip.

"I'll have my assistant take a couple X-rays, and we'll get after the tooth on the lower left. I'll be right back," Joe said as he went to get Angela. He stopped thinking about the man's broken smile the instant he left the room.

———————

Joe spent the lunch hour sitting at his desk, making phone calls, drinking coffee, and nibbling on an apple. The first day back at work after his collapse had picked up right where the previous twenty-four years had left off.

His first patient of the afternoon was a forty-five-year-old woman who was returning to have her dental makeover, as she called it, completed. Maureen Prokesh was a beautiful woman by any standard but one: she had ugly teeth. Her dark eyes, the perfect bones in her face, her long, dark hair, and her gorgeous figure all became invisible when she smiled and showed her teeth. She'd had some poor dentistry done as a child, but before that she'd been cursed with teeth that were rotated and misaligned. They'd been permanently stained when she'd taken the antibiotic tetracycline as a child. To top it all off, the teeth were all too small and there were spaces between most of them.

Almost a year earlier, Joe had mentioned to Maureen that perhaps she should take a look at the nice results he'd been having with some of the newer ceramic crowns and veneers. She began to show some interest—then the interest grew into enthusiasm, and Joe had started to treatment plan a makeover for Maureen. Dozens of hours of preparation in the laboratory and in the clinic had been spent in planning Maureen's case. She'd had orthodontics first and later some dental implants placed. Then, three weeks ago, she'd spent most of the day with Joe; he'd prepared her teeth, then made models for the laboratory to use in fabricating the crowns and veneers. He had made spectacular temporary crowns for her to wear while the lab finished her permanent, ceramic restorations.

There was an air of anticipation in the treatment room as Joe tipped Maureen's chair back and began to anesthetize her teeth. Joe knew that even if everything fit perfectly, he was in for several hours of intricate assembly of a puzzle inside Maureen's mouth. Maureen sensed that if things went well, she would be forever changed.

As the first hour passed, Joe seemed to emerge from the little world of crowns and implants and bridges. Things were all fitting together nicely, and Joe began to chat, then joke with Angela and Maureen. By the end of the second hour, Joe seemed animated. He was almost done and things were working perfectly. After two and a half hours, Joe touched the switch that set Maureen upright in her dental chair, then gave her a hand mirror and said simply, "Have a look."

Maureen raised the mirror and peeked at herself. Then she began to smile and turn her head from side to side. Joe stood off to her side, with his arms crossed, and watched her eyes. After she'd turned her head from side to side several times, her eyes slipped off her own image in the mirror and found Joe. When she made eye contact with him, he slowly raised his eyebrows and lifted his shoulders. "Well...?" he asked.

Maureen's lower lip began to quiver. She stepped out of the dental chair and put her arms around Joe. When she tried to speak, the words stumbled out between sobs. "Thanks, Joe. I love it!" she said. She held him with her cheek touching his and spoke in a low, intimate voice. "I always wanted this. Thank you so much!"

"Well, you're beautiful. This was easy!" Joe sounded as if the whole reconstruction of Maureen's mouth had been a simple procedure.

Maureen squeezed him tightly and replied, "Yeah, right." Then she let go of Joe and gave Angela a hug. In only a moment, she was at the front desk, showing Julie her new teeth, then hugging Julie and wiping away more tears.

The workday was nearly over, and Joe followed Maureen out to the front desk to say goodbye. After several minutes of small talk among Maureen, Julie, Angela, and Joe, Maureen began to move toward the door. She said goodbye and smiled at everyone, then paused for a moment and looked at Joe. He stood with his hands in his pockets and smiled at her. She looked him up and down one more time and then moved quickly back toward him. "One more hug!" she said. "Thanks, Joe." She was clearly moved by what had been done for her.

"Maybe you two should get a room?" Angela said in an effort to lift some of the emotion and provide Maureen with an opportunity to stop thanking Joe.

Everyone, even Angela, burst into laughter at the suggestion, and Maureen stepped away from Joe as she wiped her eyes once more. She was crying tears of laughter, and thankfulness.

"She can sure find somebody better than me!" Joe added.

Angela and Julie laughed out loud, but Maureen turned toward Joe, and as she spoke she smiled her new smile. "No. That's not true. I'll take you any day." Her voice had changed in only a few seconds, for the words drifted from her in a rich tone that carried a hint of something more. Although the words themselves could be interpreted any number of ways, they left everyone, even Joe, wondering if she'd issued a not-so-subtle, open-ended invitation. Maybe she was kidding, and maybe not. Joe really couldn't tell. The simple gratefulness for a job well done returned to her eyes in an instant, but the energy of a moment earlier never left as she said goodbye and opened the door to leave.

Joe was still smiling a sheepish smile over the exchange with Maureen and trying to avoid Angela's eyes when he heard the front door open again. He assumed it was Maureen returning because she'd forgotten something, and he looked toward the door.

To everyone's surprise, when the door opened, Dean Pope stepped through it. Dean's eyes widened when he saw Joe at the front desk. "Hi, Doc! I'm back!" The left side of Dean's lower jaw was swollen so that the skin was stretched tight. He looked like he had a golf ball in his mouth. "You done such a nice job on that other nasty one the other day. I thought I'd let you have a try with this one!" Dean smiled, then grimaced and grabbed at his cheek. "Ouch." The painful pressure that his smile placed on the swollen area caused him to flinch.

"Thanks, Dean," Joe said sarcastically as he turned to get ready for another extraction.

Dean's new abscess had a similar appearance to the previous one. On the dental X-ray, the lower molar had the look of a bow-legged cowboy, and there was a large abscess surrounding the entire tooth. Joe supposed that the swelling was due to a very localized pocket of pus and blood, just underneath the gums along the outside of the lower jaw. Dean was actually much easier to deal with on this the second time around. He was far less anxious now that he trusted his dentist not to hurt him.

"OK, Angela, get me the cowhorns," Joe said after he'd anesthetized the left side of Dean's lower jaw.

"The cowhorns?" Dean asked

"Yeah. Sounds odd, doesn't it? It's just what we call the forceps that we're gonna use to extract this tooth. The beaks on this little torture device look like cowhorns, don't they?" Joe held the forceps up for Dean to inspect, and Dean laughed at Joe's use of the phrase "torture device." His morbid joke seemed to relieve whatever anxiety remained for Dean.

"I'm gonna put one cowhorn in between the roots from the outside, and one cowhorn in between the roots from the inside, by your tongue, and then I'm gonna squeeze. The cowhorns should just lift that tooth right out of there. With me?"

"Yeah."

"Ready to have at it, Dean?" Joe asked.

"Yeah." Dean opened his mouth and closed his eyes as he had the other day. It looked to Joe as if the same food particles and plaque from ten days ago were still lodged between Dean's teeth, but the gums were even more inflamed.

The instant the beaks of the forceps slid between the roots of the tooth, Dean's gums began to bleed. As Joe added pressure, they began to bleed quite heavily. The soft tissue was very inflamed, and in addition to the blood, pus and plaque and food began to ooze from around the tooth and the forceps. Joe added just enough pressure so the tooth made a slight cracking noise, and Dean jumped.

"Hurt you, Dean?" Joe asked.

"No. Keep going. Just sounded bad." He sounded ridiculous trying to speak with a forceps in his mouth.

Joe began to increase the pressure on the forceps until he felt the tooth was about to lift out of the socket. But at the last instant he heard a loud crack. Dean's eyes popped open, questioning Joe.

"Your tooth broke, Dean. That's kind of a bad thing. Now I'll have to remove it in two pieces, maybe more." Joe was surprised at the way Dean remained calm and didn't overreact to the sights and sounds that had scared him only a week or so earlier.

After he'd used a scalpel to cut the attachment between the gums and the lower jaw, Joe peeled the gums back away from the jaw with an instrument that looked like a small spoon. The bone around the two fractured roots of the tooth appeared white and healthy as Joe began grinding it away with a dental drill. When he'd removed about three millimeters of bone around each root, he reached for a 301 elevator once more. He placed the tip of the elevator between the roots and twisted it like a screwdriver. As the front root began to move, a small flow of blood covered everything around the tooth, and Joe asked Angela to rinse and vacuum the area. When Angela sprayed water to wash the blood away, she used too much pressure and splashed blood and small bits of bone and plaque and pus onto Joe's clothing and mask and eyeglasses. Joe jerked backward reflexively and Dean Pope laughed out loud.

"Sorry, doctor," Angela said after Joe flinched. He leaned back in his chair, removed his gloves and surgical mask, washed his face, and then cleaned his glasses and put on new latex gloves and mask, but never said a word to Angela. Every time he got blood and spit splashed on his face, he thought about the young physician at Mayo Clinic several years earlier who had contracted hepatitis and then died from just such a splash. Wouldn't that be a poetic way for him to go, he thought—die from having the job you hate splash on you?

Joe reintroduced the elevator, twisting and digging at the two roots until they both loosened and then lifted out of their sockets. A flow of pus filled each of the sockets every few minutes, and Angela washed the area several times. When he'd checked to be sure that no root fragment remained, Joe placed two stitches in Dean's gums.

"Well, Dean, I think you've gotten familiar with me. You did fine today. Would you like the lecture on regular visits again today?"

"No thanks, Doc." Dean smiled through the gauze Angela had placed over his extraction site. Joe thought Dean's crooked smile, with the bloody gauze sticking out from between his lips, looked laughable.

"OK, then. I'll see you next time something hurts," Joe said with a shrug. Then he shook Dean's hand and said goodbye.

———•———

The day's work was done, and Joe sat at the desk in his private office and stared straight ahead.

Angela peeked into Joe's office as she walked past it on her way home for the day.

"Goodnight, Joe," Angela said as she pushed her face into his office.

"I hate this place," Joe replied, still staring.

"Huh?"

"The reason I chose to do this was to live up to someone else's expectations. Now I spend most of my time living down to other people's expectations. And I never liked doing any of this in the first place." Joe rubbed his face with both hands briefly, then continued. "Sometimes it sounds like I hate others for what they expect of me. But I hate myself for doing this—maybe for doing nothing about it. I need something more important than this. It needs to have some meaning."

"You helped all those people today," Angela said as if she were a teacher, correcting a wrong answer from an elementary student.

"I told you, a monkey could do what I did today," Joe replied.

"What about Maureen? You may have changed her life. The list of doctors who could do what you did…well, it's a pretty short list."

"Maureen was a dentist's dream—a beautiful woman with ugly teeth." Joe leaned back in his chair, and he appeared to be choosing his words carefully before he continued. "That was kind of fun, but it was an easy one. Don't get me wrong: that did turn out pretty nice, and that probably will make a difference in her life, and I guess there is some satisfaction in that." Joe actually smiled. "I think she likes me too!" Then his smile quickly faded. "All that stuff—that warm, fuzzy stuff—is nice. And it is satisfying to do nice work. But if the patient lives long enough, everything I do will wear out. It'll all fail someday. It's all just a nice service, but it has no meaning. Where is the meaning supposed to come from?" Joe sighed, then continued, "Besides that, I've already done all this stuff. Maybe I think I've made enough of a statement here. Do I have to spend the rest of my life doing all this over and over again?"

Angela stared at Joe while he slumped in his desk chair. She couldn't understand the despair in his voice, and she always felt lost and bewildered when he started to explain his need for meaning.

"But Joe..." she started.

"Angela," Joe interrupted, "it's not enough. How will it ever be?"

chapter
eleven

The coffeemaker was spitting the last of the hot water onto the finely ground coffee resting in the filter, and the scent of rich black coffee filled the kitchen when Joe rounded the corner and found Jess sitting at the kitchen table. Morning was beginning to break, but the backyard was still hidden by what remained of the night.

Jess never looked up from her newspaper. A bowl of strawberries rested on the table in front of her, and she picked at the strawberries while she scanned the morning paper. She'd risen early and worked out for an hour on the gym equipment in the basement. Her blonde hair was tied back, and the pink-and-white exercise outfit she wore looked as if it had been designed especially to show off her athletic body. Joe glanced under the table and noticed she'd taken off her white-and-pink tennis shoes and was wiggling her toes. Her white socks stood in sharp contrast to the dark tan on her legs.

"Coffee?" Joe asked as he poured a cup for himself.

"No," she said without looking up.

Joe looked out the window and tried to see into the sky beyond the trees in the backyard. "Looks like it's gonna be a nice day," he said, trying to draw some sort of response from her. It was the first time they'd spoken in three days.

Joe had risen early today too. He'd showered and shaved and stepped into his usual khakis, white shirt, and tie. He'd planned to have coffee and read the paper before work, and he was surprised to see Jess at the table. He assumed she'd stay in the basement and continue to work out until he left for work, like she did every other day.

She flipped a page in the newspaper but said nothing, and she did not look up when Joe sat on the chair across from her at the table. Joe sipped his coffee and looked at her for a moment. The fact that they'd argued on Saturday and not spoken for three days was not lost on him. When he stared at her there in the yellow light of the kitchen, he felt the weight of his confession to Donny—that after twenty-four years of marriage, he wasn't sure if he loved Jess, if he ever had. He heard his own words—"I really don't know the answer to that one"—and tried to stop staring at her, but he couldn't.

He looked at Jess and wondered, as he often had, just who that was sitting there with him, and how they'd been brought together, and what would happen in the years to come. He knew they had some baggage in their marriage—lots of it, actually. He also knew that they'd never found the closeness he'd always hoped for. They'd never really had it, but they'd flirted with it several times, mostly when they'd been on vacation, like he'd told Donny.

While Joe stared across the table at her and sipped at his coffee again, he realized that the part of his marriage that was missing was more important than all the parts that weren't. He had money, nice kids, security, and a pretty wife, but his marriage had always lacked intimacy—or maybe it was friendship.

"Jess?"

"Yeah?" She still had not looked away from the paper.

"I don't want to fight anymore. We fight all the time."

Finally she looked at him. "We don't fight all the time." Her reply sounded as if she thought they were pretty happy together and rarely quarreled.

"Jess." Joe smiled and shook his head. "We yell...hateful things. We go for several days at a time and don't speak. Much of the time we just sort of co-exist, like roommates. People who love each other don't live like this. They enjoy being around each other," Joe shrugged.

"We get along OK. Everybody has some problems in their marriage," she said.

"We fight too much," Joe said. He sensed that the conversation was about to take the same direction as a thousand others before it. Joe knew the predictable routine. Through the years of fighting and making up, their behavior had begun to follow a script: they'd fight, then not speak for a few days, then Joe would initiate some sort of truce, but nothing would ever be resolved. In earlier days, the truce would most often be ratified by sex. But in recent months, a verbal disarmament or cease-fire had usually been sufficient. Today Joe felt a need to not repeat the same old behavior that had brought them to this point.

"Jess, honey, why don't I sell my practice? We'll move someplace new. It's time for a change anyway. The boys are grown up. Let's sell and move on."

"What? Are you crazy? What we have here is perfect. Everybody wants what we have. Why would we change now? I don't want to move, or change anything." For the first time, Jess seemed interested in the conversation. She leaned back in her chair and moved her hands when she spoke.

"Jess, people want what they THINK we have. But the truth is, a lot of poor people—or at least people who don't make as much money as we do—have something we don't have. Truth is, we should envy what they have."

"And what's that?" Jess's eyes tightened with the question.

"Happiness, I guess. Maybe a loving marriage, instead of a never-ending argument." Joe paused. "Really, Jess, I could sell the practice and get a job teaching at the dental school. That company called last year to see if I wanted to get involved making teaching videos and writing text-books for continuing education courses. A change like that might even make my job enjoyable. I think I'd like to write, to do something creative." Joe's voice raised with enthusiasm as he suggested the changes. "Could be great!"

"You'd take a big cut in pay, right?"

"Yeah, but so what. If we were happy, wouldn't that be better?"

"No! I don't want to do that. I like things just like they are," she said, as if she were annoyed by the suggestion. "I'm happy."

Joe felt more weight—maybe it was just frustration with Jess's resistance to change. Anyway, something even more familiar and heavy settled in his chest, and he put both elbows on the table and stared into his coffee cup.

Jess rose and walked to the coffeemaker by the sink. She poured a cup of coffee for herself and said, "Joe, we're doing great here..."

"You are," Joe interrupted.

"What does that mean?"

"You have money, friends, status, and you like all this." Joe looked around the house. "But I'm just getting older, and more unhappy every day, in a life I don't really like," he sighed.

They were at an impasse, and they both recognized it. Lately, they found themselves at this same point every time they had discussions like this.

When Joe looked at Jess again, she was standing by the sink. He stared at her for almost a minute, but said nothing. Their conversation from a moment earlier was done. But Jess was still there, and she was the one he'd turned to for all these years. She was the one who was supposed to help him find his way. Even though it had seldom happened, she was the one he'd expected to comfort him and help make his troubles go away. Even now, after all the arguments and angry words over all the years, when he looked at her he felt the same need to ask her to help lift this weight from him. She was still his wife; she was still supposed to be the one he could turn to, wasn't she? He still wanted her to be the one. He wanted to try. He had to—Jess was all he had.

If he just held her close once, he'd feel better, wouldn't he? He needed a friend right now, and as he stood up he felt a little twitch of sexual energy somewhere inside him. He began to cross the kitchen, and his eyes locked with hers.

"The guy from the BMW dealership called yesterday," she said without moving.

Joe smiled to tell her that he wasn't interested right now, that he planned to put his arms around her, and if this little chat in the kitchen ended in sex, well, that was OK too; he was willing to let all that other stuff go away for a while.

She kept talking about the cars as Joe moved toward her. When he put his hands on her tiny waist, he felt a deepening stir of sexual tension. He pulled her close to him and brought his mouth to hers.

Instead of putting her arms around him, she kept her weight back and let her hands remain on the kitchen countertops. When his lips touched hers, she refused to kiss him; she just kept talking about the new BMWs. "He said the cars would be here Thursday and we could pick them up Saturday," she said as best she could while he pressed himself against her and softly kissed her lips. The words echoed around his mouth. Her warm breath and her words swirled around inside his mouth, and her lips continued to make more words as though he wasn't there kissing her.

Joe Mix's soul turned dark for a moment. There in the kitchen, in that moment, he felt as if he'd awakened from a long sleep and found everything around him foreign and malevolent. He felt himself releasing Jess from his life. For all these years they'd been connected somehow, fastened together, tethered, like two astronauts on a space walk. But now they'd come apart. Perhaps he was pushing her away. Perhaps she'd moved away from him and silently snapped the frail tether that had held them together for years. Perhaps the tie that bound them had simply given way. It didn't matter. Finally, and certainly, he was done with her. He could actually feel her soul separating, sailing away from his, and it was OK. Actually it was good; he didn't care anymore. His arms were still around her waist as he felt the anger begin to stir. He wanted her to be gone, forever. She could just drift off through the void, through life, without him. The sensation of release, and drifting, quickly gave way to real anger.

Joe closed his eyes and moved away from Jess ever so slightly. She had done this many times before. He'd never known if it was her way of saying "no, thank you" to sex or if it was a way of gaining control by castrating him emotionally. He'd never understood. Always, after she'd done it in the past, Joe would let her know that he was hurt. Then she'd assert that she was innocent of any unkind intentions. Joe had come to think that it was her way to establish dominance, and even to ignore his cry for a friend. He knew that, just now, she'd done it for the last time. He'd had enough—forever.

Jess was still talking about the BMWs. Her breath was still touching his face when he moved his head away from hers. As he did, he felt the scorching heat of a lifetime of frustration and indecision begin to build inside him. The heat grew quickly and then flashed, as if Jess had thrown a match into a gas can.

A riotous anger surged upward from his chest and blew away the weight that had been settling on him for years. In that instant, Joe Mix's old life came completely off the tracks. Joe turned away from Jess and walked back upstairs toward his bedroom.

Jess was seated at the kitchen table, just where she'd been earlier, when Joe entered the kitchen. He'd been upstairs for nearly twenty minutes when he returned to the kitchen. This time he was dressed in blue jeans, cowboy boots that he usually wore to cut the grass and work in the yard, a gray cotton sweatshirt that said "Gopher Hockey," and a maroon baseball cap with a large, gold "M" on it.

Jess looked up and her face curved slightly with confusion. "What are you doing?" she said, obviously surprised at Joe's change of clothes.

Joe didn't answer her. He dropped the two large, canvas duffel bags that he was carrying and sat at the table across from Jess again. He reached for the telephone and began to enter numbers on the cordless phone. There was no hint of anger in Joe's demeanor now; he calmly leaned back in his chair and waited for the phone to ring.

"What are you doing?" Jess repeated.

Joe didn't reply, and he wouldn't look at her. He glanced at his watch and waited. Jess noticed that his eyes cleared, as if someone had answered his call. After he'd listened for a moment, he spoke in a low, calm voice. "Julie, this is Dr. Mix...Joe. I won't be coming in to the office today, or any other fuckin' day, ever. You can cancel all the appoint..." He stopped in his tracks. "Hell, I guess I don't care what you do, but I won't be in the office, ever again." He hung up the phone and looked at Jess.

"What was that?" she said. She was totally surprised and taken aback.

"I just quit my job, Jess. It's OK, I didn't like it anyway. It made me unhappy. But I guess you wouldn't notice that type of thing. I've only been bitching about it for twenty-five years." He stared at her but said no more.

Jess stared back for a moment and stood up. She walked around to Joe's side of the table and reached out her hands to touch his face. "Joe, honey, we'll get you some help."

Joe brushed her hands away and stood up. "No, I'm gonna help myself today. I've been waiting all these years...all these years..."—he shook his head in disbelief—"...for you to be my friend. Now, it's too late." Joe picked up the two large duffel bags and brushed past Jess as he walked out the door.

The sun was beginning to rise, and the gray darkness of dawn was giving way to the greens and yellows of a May sunrise. Jess watched through the kitchen window as Joe opened the rear door of the topper on his old truck, then lowered the tailgate. He climbed in and pushed the two duffel bags to the front of the box. Then he stepped out of the truck and returned to the house.

Jess watched silently as he made six more trips out to his truck. Each time, his arms were loaded with canvas bags filled with clothing, large boxes filled with his fly tying materials from the basement, camping gear, and sleeping bags. Jess watched while he stopped by the hall closet and filled one medium-sized duffel bag with towels. He returned to the kitchen and poured himself another cup of coffee while Jess stood in silence and watched. From the look on his face, Jess thought he appeared to be planning something or going through a checklist. Joe sipped at his coffee and furrowed his brow. "Oh, yeah, I almost forgot!" He walked quickly to the basement and emerged with his father's ratty-looking trout that he'd kept on the wall in his fly-tying room. He put the fish in the back of his truck and returned to the house. Joe walked to the coffeepot and filled his cup. "Just gonna top 'er off...for the road," he said flippantly.

Joe knew that he'd crossed some invisible barrier. He enjoyed letting Jess see that something—something serious and permanent—had happened. He enjoyed the obvious fact that she was struggling to understand just what it was.

An eerie silence settled over the kitchen. Joe leaned against the kitchen counter for a moment and sipped at his coffee. He wanted Jess to know that she'd hurt him for the last time. He knew she understood that he was packing, and leaving; he just didn't want to spell it all out for her quite yet.

"What are you doing, Joe?" Jess said. Her voice was beginning to waiver with uncertainty.

"You know what I'm doing," Joe said with an edge to his voice. "I'm leaving. I just quit my job, and I'm leaving."

"Honey, I'm worried about you." Her eyes filled with tears. "What are you doing? I'm sorry. I need you. I love you." She moved toward him. "What about me?"

"You?" Joe said with contempt. "You? You never loved me. You're a mercenary, life-sucking bitch, and I'm taking my life back from you. You never really wanted me anyway, not all of me. Just my job, or the security, or the status you thought I'd provide. This is the final punch on your meal ticket. But don't worry, 'cause here's the wrinkle: you can have everything—the house, retirement money, the cars, especially the cars, your fucking Beemers! You can take it all and ram it up your ass. I'm not even gonna give you the satisfaction of a hateful divorce; you can have everything. But I get custody of me. I'm gonna do the worst thing I could do to you: I'm taking my life away from you, and you're gonna have to go through the rest of your life being you, without me!"

Jess began to sob.

"Save the crocodile tears. Right up until this morning that shit might have worked." Joe paused and watched the tears run down Jess's cheeks, but he remained unmoved. "I'm leaving now, Jess, and I'm not coming back, not ever! I'm gonna go find out what's left of my life. And you? I'm sure you'll soon find someone else and suck his life dry too!" He walked out the door and climbed into his truck. "I shoulda shot this dead horse a long time ago," he said loud enough to be certain she'd heard him. For the first time, he'd held nothing back. Only a half-hour earlier, as he'd walked up the stairs to his bedroom, the rage that had burned inside him threatened volcanic and murderous heights when it erupted. When it came, the eruption had simply given him a moment of clarity. Now he was actually enjoying the execution of several parts of his life that had spent far too long waiting on death row.

When the truck door slammed, he felt as though he was stepping out into another current, this was much stronger than the Root River. The exhilaration at what he'd said, and done, was powerful. But he knew that just behind that exhilaration, self-doubt, regret, and fear of the unknown were already lurking. Soon enough they'd be trying to rob him of this triumph in the same way that fatigue sometimes weakens the resolve of athletes and causes them to give up just as they stand on the verge of a great victory.

Joe looked over his shoulder and noticed that Jess had followed him out to the truck. Her behavior soon eased the self-doubt and regret further to the back of Joe's mind, and served to deepen the satisfaction in what he was about to do.

"You think the Old Cowboy would just walk out?" Jess hollered. She was standing about a foot from the truck and leaning toward Joe's window.

Joe turned the key in the ignition and the starter began to grind. He cupped his hand behind his ear as if he couldn't hear her, but he didn't open the window. He'd heard her clearly; he just wouldn't give her the satisfaction. He cupped his hand behind his ear again and shrugged.

"Ray Mix would never do this!" she shouted.

"Men like Ray Mix don't marry women like you," he said through the window as he shook his head and scowled. He let up on the clutch and started rolling away. He was angry that she'd referred to his father. It was odd, but he felt that she'd never earned the right to even talk about the Old Cowboy. Now she was trying to hurt Joe by mentioning his father. An odd parting shot, he thought, but he'd stolen most of her ammunition.

When he reached the end of his driveway, he looked in his rearview mirror just in time to see Jess take four steps and start screaming obscenities at him. He stopped for a minute and watched her tirade, then let up on the clutch and eased the old truck onto the road. When he shifted into second gear, the truck lurched and his coffee spilled. He looked away from Jess to clean up the spill.

"Donny, I think we need to have a talk," Joe said when Donny answered his cell phone. "Where are you?"

"Starbucks. Having coffee and reading the paper. My office doesn't open for twenty minutes." Donny paused, and Joe could tell he was looking at his watch. "Why aren't you at work?" Donny asked.

"We need to talk," Joe answered. "I'll be there in five minutes."

When Joe's truck rolled to a stop on the street in front of Starbucks, Donny was sitting at a table by the window, watching the street. Donny's face crinkled into a question, and he folded his arms when he saw that Joe was wearing jeans and boots as he walked through the door and up to the small table.

"So what's up?" Donny asked with a confused look.

"I just quit my job and left my wife." Joe nodded "yes" and raised his eyebrows. Then he sat down at Donny's table.

Donny stared for a moment, then realized that his brother might be telling the truth. "Are you serious?" he asked.

Joe nodded again.

"What the hell?" Donny asked. "Why? What happened?"

"I've had enough! I won't...I can't do it another day. Not with Jess, not with work. She's a bitch, and I never should have married her or stayed married to her. Same for my job! You know all about it, Donny. I've told you everything. It was time, I guess. I don't know how I put up with all that shit for so long! But I'm leaving." Joe was still nodding. "I'm leaving...I'm leaving all this shit."

"So where are you going? Is this a permanent thing? When are you coming back? Are you asking me about a divorce? Jesus, Joe! What are you doing?" Donny grew more animated as he spoke. Then he stopped and rubbed his forehead.

"Well, here's the deal, Donny, as I see it." Joe leaned forward and put his elbows on the table. "I want a divorce, and I want you to handle it or get somebody to do it. But I'm gonna make it easy. I don't want anything. Jess gets it all. I've got about $8,500 in my pocket. Jess needs to get the rest. Are you with me?"

Donny made a face like he had something in his mouth he wanted to spit out, and then he nodded yes as he looked away from Joe.

"And sell the practice. I don't care how much you get or what you do with it. Give all the money to Jess."

Donny closed his eyes and rubbed his face with the palms of his hands. "Did you fall on your head this morning?"

"No. But I had something of an epiphany, and I feel pretty good about this," Joe said. "I'm not asking for advice here, Donny, so don't start explaining shit to me. About an hour ago, part of my life—a big part—came to an end. I'm all right with that. I'm all done waiting for...whatever it is I've been waiting for. Now help me, OK?"

"You're fucking crazy! You want me to give everything you've worked for all these years to a woman you don't love?"

"Yeah, I do," Joe nodded. "The practice, the house...it all feels like it's got something on it, something sticky and unclean. I don't want to touch it again. It's better this way, for all of us," Joe said. He shrugged and questioned Donny with his eyes, asking for his brother's understanding.

"Joe. Now listen to me! Are you certain that all this isn't about a younger woman, a girlfriend, sex? You know, the middle-aged guy who's trying to reclaim his lost youth? The guy who just can't deal with growing old?" Donny leaned forward, rested his elbows on the table, and waited for an answer. "There's always a girlfriend hidden somewhere in these things."

"Donny, it's not about sex, and there is no girlfriend. But maybe you could use sex in order to see the heart and soul of all this," Joe said.

Donny tipped his head back and raised his eyebrows, as if he knew he'd turned over the rock where he'd find what he was looking for.

"When we were young, we couldn't wait to get home and get after each other," Joe smiled. "We were like two hockey players in a fight, each trying to pull each other's shirt over his head so we could really get after the other guy."

"Very romantic, but I do understand the analogy," Donny said.

"Hmph," Joe sighed. "After we settled into our married life, all that passion went away pretty fast." Joe looked up from his coffee. "I know now that Jess was using sex to get me to marry her, but during those early days she even seemed to look forward to it. Well, soon enough, sex was just something that came after about an hour of begging and whining...by me." Joe smiled openly and shook his head. "Then Jess got to be like Dr. Kevorkian," Joe said.

Donny grimaced and then turned his head sideways, silently asking for an explanation.

"You know, just a little mercy sex every now and then to put me out of my misery. It was the amorous equivalent of two shots in the back of the head." Joe looked into Donny's eyes. "She enjoyed using that power—using sex as a weapon, a means for punishment and control. Isn't it sad when the thing that we should look to in order to illustrate our passion becomes..."—Joe's voice trailed off, then added— "...becomes nothing?"

"You're a fifty-year-old loony! I'm thinking I should have you taken to a safe house and then have you deprogrammed! Jesus, Joe, it's like you turned into a hippie or some shit like that. Snap out of it! We're talking about a lot of money here, a lifetime of hard work!"

"No, Donny. It's OK." Joe's voice became calm. "This is the right way to do this. Jess is the mother of my children, and she was a good mother. A horseshit wife, but a good mother." Joe actually smiled softly. "Anyway, you need to look at this like some sort of business deal. That's what attorneys do, isn't it? Jess gets a pile of money, and I get rid of her, and my job, which I want to be rid of as much as her. It's a win-win deal."

"What are you gonna live on, Joe?" Donny pleaded.

"I told you—I have $8,500!"

"Joe, you spent more than that on a couple fishing trips last year! What are you gonna live on?"

Joe reached his hand across the table and touched Donny's hand. "Donny, my brother! Help me do this?" He nodded "yes" at Donny. "What the hell, Donny, it's only money. I can get up tomorrow and make some more! But once my life is over, it's over! You're keeping score again. This isn't about money; it's about everything else BUT money, I guess. Now, somewhere out there, I plan to find some meaning. Will you just help me dispose of my old life? Please? So I can get on with it all."

"You're fucking crazy," Donny sighed.

"Maybe. But…no…I'm fine. Really. This will be OK. Why is this any different than some corporate executive who quits a high-powered job to follow some goofy dream? People do shit like this all the time!"

"OK. So what's your dream?" Donny prodded.

"Haven't got that far yet."

"You are fucking NUTS! NUTS!" Donny rubbed his forehead again as he spoke.

"So I've made a little money and have a little status. Is that supposed to be enough to keep me here? I'm in a marriage that was never right, and I hate every minute of my job. I couldn't tell you the last time somebody asked me to think, to be creative, to do something special—you know, to do the best I can do. You've heard all this before, and yet you don't understand. You're the only friend I have right now, Donny. Isn't that enough to make you help me?"

Donny refused to answer for a moment. He stared at the table in front of him. Then he raised his face and looked into his brother's eyes. "So when are you leaving?" Donny asked. He shook his head sideways and closed his eyes. He'd given his approval, but only grudgingly.

"Right now," Joe shrugged.

"Where are you going?" Donny sighed.

"Well, I'm going that way"—he pointed south, down Highway 63—"'cause that's the way my truck is pointed," Joe said.

"You're crazy," Donny sighed. "Don't you think this is a little reckless?" he asked.

"Reckless?" Joe replied. "Reckless?" He paused again. "I should have been a little reckless a long time ago, before it came to this!"

"You're nuts," Donny repeated.

Joe answered with another nod "yes." Then he stood up and motioned for Donny to do the same. He put his arms around Donny and held him close for a moment. Then he kissed Donny on the cheek.

"No tongues," Donny whispered.

Joe's face curled into a smile.

"I love you, Joe," Donny added.

"I love you, too, Donny," Joe said softly. "My brother." Then he closed his eyes and pressed his cheek against Donny's one last time.

As Joe eased the truck out into traffic once more, Donny yelled from the street, "Hey, Joe?" When Joe looked back, Donny held his hand to his ear as if it were a phone. "Got your phone? Right?"

Joe held up his cell phone to show Donny and nodded "yes." Then he shifted into second gear and the Ford lurched away.

———————

The green pickup with the yellow snowplow and red topper rambled along in light traffic, and Dr. Joe Mix began to wonder just what he was feeling. All the morning drives in the country over all these years—all that time spent dreaming about just not going into the office—had finally led to this moment. Here he was, driving down the road on a clear morning, and he wasn't going to that damn office, ever again. He wasn't really going anywhere; he was just going away.

The sun was well into the morning sky, and just now the grass seemed a little greener than what he'd noticed before. The sky was bluer than it had been the day before, and yellow-green buds on the shrubs and trees seemed to hold the promise of summer in a way that he'd never noticed before.

He cranked the driver's-side window open by pushing at the vise grip he'd fastened to the broken window handle. Just opening the window on his truck required several awkward twisting movements with his left hand. For some reason, which he'd never been able to explain even to himself, he'd always enjoyed the process of opening the window with a vise grip so much that he'd never been inclined to replace the handle. As the warm air of the May morning rushed through the truck, Joe rested his arm in the open window and tried to understand just what he'd done, and what he should do now.

There was the unmistakable sense of euphoria that always comes with victory, but then he wasn't sure just what it was that he'd won. Sometimes he felt almost weightless, like a great burden had been lifted from him when he realized that he'd made the decision he'd hidden from for years. At last he'd done it—he'd broken away; he'd had the strength to make a painful decision. When he thought about the consequences of it all, he couldn't help but agonize and question his actions. Was he doing the right thing? He'd heard people say the words, "Be careful what you wish for, you just might get it" for years, and he thought he'd understood. But now, when he said those words out loud, he could actually feel them begin to tighten something in his gut. Now what?

He was still angry at Jess. He thought he probably always would be. He wanted her to be hurt. And yet, he felt sad when he thought that she might be sitting at home weeping, devastated by what he'd said to her. Some old, twisted part of his being was already nagging at him to go home and make it be all right with Jess. She hadn't meant to do all the things she'd done, had she? Yeah, she sure as hell had meant them, and only a fool would put up with the life he'd been living. He shook his head to try to dismiss all his conflicting thoughts.

People would think he was a failure; he couldn't even make it in dentistry. They'd say he was a real loser, like some of the professors back at dental school. All the guys had laughed about the middle-aged dentists who washed out in private practice and wound up teaching. Now, he was even worse than that: hell, he'd just run away from it. Nonetheless, he didn't want to turn around and go to the office. He knew—he knew in his heart—that this was the right thing to do.

But a small voice—like the voice from the river, way back in his mind—kept calling to him, telling him to turn around. The voice assured him that he could return home and things would be all right. Jess would understand. The women at the office would understand. He was just on edge after his heart problem. Everything would be back to normal, better than before, in a while. If he turned around and went home, he'd be safe and no one would be disappointed with him. If he kept going, he'd be leaving a lifetime of work behind, not to mention a pile of money and security. For a moment, Joe actually thought about crossing the centerline and turning around for home. Maybe he'd just had a moment of insanity, and now that it had passed he should go home. For a short time, there was no argument from inside Joe. He just listened to the voice and thought all the same thoughts that came to him all those other times when he'd almost stepped into the current.

He leaned back in the seat and took the wheel in his left hand. He couldn't remember ever talking to himself before this moment. But he assumed the demeanor of an attorney cross-examining a witness, and he pointed the index finger on his right hand at an imaginary hostile witness. The witness staring back at him was Dr. Joe Mix. "OK, Joe. Here's the question." He paused and pointed his finger to emphasize his own words. "Do you want to turn around and live your life on a leash? Do you want to get up every morning and have it be Halloween, so you can put on a costume and pretend to be something you're not? Do you want things to be back like they were, forever?"

If a passing motorist had seen Joe, waving his hand and speaking so emphatically, it may have been cause for concern, a few laughs at the least. For Joe, the question drifting around inside the truck had life-changing ramifications.

He relaxed in his seat and reached for his coffee mug as he prepared his own answer. He took a sip, swallowed, and then put the cup back into the cup holder on the dashboard. He put his right hand on top of the steering wheel as a confident, defiant look spread across his face. "No way!" he answered himself with a sneer. "And don't ask me shit like that anymore!"

When he reached Interstate 90, he turned and went west because—well, just because he thought it seemed like the thing to do. The sun was still climbing into a clear blue sky as he accelerated into traffic. He didn't know where he was going, but he was on the way there. As the entrance ramp merged with westbound traffic, an odd grin began to pull at the corners of his eyes, then spread to his lips. In a moment, the dimple on the right side of his face was at the center of his smile. "Oh, my God. What have I done?"

chapter twelve

Road noise quickly became an unexpected annoyance for Joe. The heavy tread on the snow tires was producing a painfully loud whine inside the truck. He tried rolling the window up, but the noise was only slightly less overpowering. Even though the truck was hardly airtight, having the window up made the inside of the truck stifling hot. Air rushed in through the two holes in the floorboard on the passenger's side and swirled a cloud of dust about the cab. The Ford had no air conditioning, and the vent, even assisted by the holes in the floor, just couldn't provide enough fresh air on a sunny day. Joe rolled the window down again and tried to ignore the whine from the tires.

The snowplow was providing another unexpected problem. Joe had never driven the truck at highway speed with the heavy yellow blade still mounted on the front. He hadn't realized that the extra weight up front would have such a negative impact on the comfort of the ride. The blade had been a great asset in the moving of snow, which was done at very low speeds, and the imbalance of weight had never been a problem. In fact, it had been a bonus when pushing snow. Now, as he cruised along at highway speeds, each seam between the concrete sections of the road surface caused a significant bump. This caused the overweight front end of the truck to bounce, buck, and rock the truck from front to back considerably more than it would without the weight of the blade. Joe felt that when his speed approached seventy miles per hour, the bumping and rocking of the truck was similar to crossing a rough, windswept lake in a small boat: you could do it, but you were in for a pounding. Also, the noise from the tires became almost unbearable as he approached sixty-five miles per hour.

Joe backed his speed to just under sixty-five and tried to adjust to the road noise and steady thump, thump, thump of the tires on the road as his thoughts quickly returned to the things he'd left behind. He began to lament the fact that he'd actually been the small-town doctor everyone admired and wanted their children to grow up to be like, but he'd never found any satisfaction in it. That bothered him. He should have been happy with what he was. He should have found some meaning in it all, but he never had. The road noise eventually made it difficult to think about anything, and he just bounced along into the afternoon.

Joe finally turned off Interstate 90 when he reached Albert Lea. The continuous thumping of tires on the concrete seams of the highway, the whack, whack, whack of the tires, and the nonstop bouncing of the front end of the truck had become too much to bear. He knew that before the interstate had been built, Minnesota Highway 16 had been part of the road that connected Chicago to Seattle. The road builders had used the route of Highway 16 as the path to cross Minnesota. They'd simply built a new four-lane road, roughly parallel to Highway 16. Upon completion of Interstate 90, there was no longer any use for a state highway. So the road was given to the various counties through which it passed. As it moved west into South Dakota, Minnesota 16 had become a South Dakota State Highway and then a Wyoming State Highway and so on as the old route wound its way to Seattle. Now, the smaller, local governments along the old road west maintained what was left of the roadbed.

Joe knew that if he stayed on what remained of the old road and wound his way west, he'd eventually find himself rolling through Kadoka, South Dakota, his hometown. He was beginning to admit to himself that maybe, probably, that had been why he'd turned to the west back in Rochester, when he'd had to choose a direction. He had to see his home again. He'd seldom returned since he'd left for college. He held the same curiosity about Kadoka, about his life there, that every man holds about an old lover. He wanted to know, especially in the light of the past twenty-four hours, just what, if any, promise remained for him—just what had changed and what would never change.

He knew immediately when he left the interstate that he'd made a wise decision in choosing the old two-lane road. He could cruise somewhat comfortably at fifty to fifty-five miles per hour. There was far less road noise and pounding at the lower speed, and there was almost no other traffic.

The most interesting and pleasant surprise was that the old road led him into little towns that he'd only known about because he'd seen their names on road signs along the interstate for years. Now, the road he'd chosen was taking him through places he'd assumed had been lost to urban development in the same way much of America had.

In the old days, every small community had built its commerce district on, or nearby, the highways that connected them to each other. Out here in the Midwest, in the little towns across the heartland, America was showing a little age. The beautiful old stone-and-brick buildings had once been banks, hotels, or creameries, maybe the occasional hardware store. Now, most of them sat empty, or they held video rental shops or small gift stores, the kinds of businesses that come and go without much notice.

He witnessed the parade of little towns and old buildings along the rural highway, but the countryside blurred as Joe struggled to get his mind around the fact that he'd just walked away from a marriage and the fruits of twenty-five years of hard work. He remained confident that he'd done the right thing, but as the afternoon deepened, the reality of what he'd done became a more serious companion.

He knew he needed to call the boys and explain what he'd done, even though he wasn't exactly sure how he could explain something like this to his sons.

When he reached Jackson, the road turned south and crossed a muddy little river. The little valley that sheltered the town had retained its rural charm, and Joe began to look around for a place to pull over and rest while he called his sons. The road took a sweeping turn to the right, and like every other little town it wound into the business district. Off to the left, across the river, he could see a pretty little city park about two blocks over. He took a left at a small stoplight and crossed the river once again. The sign said "Ashley Park," and when he pulled into the small parking lot under a grove of huge oak trees, he was the only person in the park. The little river didn't look so muddy from the park; it reflected only the deep blue of the May sky. The grass in the park had already taken back its deep green summer color. But the trees and shrubs still held onto buds that seemed ready to burst. The fullness of a new season was in the air, and a warm breeze carried the certain promise of summer.

The truck door creaked open and then made the usual metallic slamming noise that old trucks make when their doors are closed. Joe took the cell phone and walked to a red picnic table. He sat on top of the table with his feet on the bench and rested his elbows on his knees. He wanted to call his boys, but he was afraid to. He wanted them to understand what he'd done, but he didn't want to explain it. Joe was looking at his phone, gathering the will to call his sons, when it lit up and started to vibrate in his hands.

Caller ID told him it was Donny calling, and he answered immediately.

"Hi, Donny."

"Hey, Joe. Where you at?"

"Jackson. Sittin' in a little park."

"How you doin', Joe?"

"Pretty good, I think."

"Still planning to go through with everything?"

"Yeah."

"Not planning to turn around and be back here tonight?"

"No."

"Sure?"

"Yes."

Donny sighed. "All right. But you're OK, right?"

"Yeah, pretty much. Got a lot of shit going on in my head, as you might guess. But I'm OK with everything. How are you doing, Donny?"

"Interesting day here, Joe. I've spent most of my day working on this train wreck you left behind."

"Send me a bill," Joe smiled weakly.

"I spoke to Jess several times," Donny offered.

"And?" Joe replied

"She's a hard one to read. For the first half of our first conversation— which took place in your kitchen, by the way; I drove right over there after you left—she seemed concerned about your health." Donny paused for effect. "Then I could see that she was getting concerned about money, about fighting with you for money, dividing up your stuff, you know?"

"Didn't she tell you that I told her I didn't want anything—she could have it all?" Joe asked.

"No, and I didn't tell her that I knew that. I waited and watched her. At first, she seemed concerned about you. Then she started backing away from the topic of you and dancing around the money issues."

"Did she tell you that I told her I wanted her to have everything?" Joe asked again, impatiently.

"Yeah, took her about ten minutes to get to it. That was what she was really concerned about. I was kind of surprised that she never suggested that we go find you and bring you back because she loves you. She was pretty transparent with regard to her purpose. I'm sorry, Joe. I didn't know how bad it had become."

"No surprises here, Donny," Joe said calmly.

"Joe, I never told her that you'd told me not to contest anything. I didn't want her to know that yet, but I did tell her I'd be your attorney."

"Yeah?"

"That pretty much ended our conversation—almost seemed to end our friendship. When I got back to the office, some asshole divorce lawyer from Minneapolis was already calling." Donny's tone implied that Joe should be worried.

"So?" Joe asked.

"So, I think she's gonna try to cut your balls off!" Donny said.

"No." Joe smiled at Donny's words. "She wants money, not balls. So does the attorney. Just give it to them."

Donny sighed. "This isn't how it's done, Joe!"

"Donny, the only thing I have that I really earned, with the sweat of my brow, is this truck. I saved my money from summer jobs and bought it for myself. Everything else came pretty easy, and I did it all for someone else. Let it go, Donny!" Joe stopped, then started again. "It's OK!"

Donny breathed heavily into the phone. "Will you call me tomorrow?"

"Sure," Joe replied, and Donny hung up without a goodbye. Donny was clearly frustrated with Joe, and that knowledge bothered Joe. He expected something different, something more understanding and compassionate, from Donny.

Joe dialed Chris and Ben's apartment next. Several rings were followed by the click of the answering machine. "This is Chris Mix—leave a message" was all it said.

"Boys, this is your father. If you're sitting by the phone, please pick it up."

"Hi, Dad" came a voice from the other end of the line. It was Chris, and it was hard to tell from such a short greeting if he'd been told anything yet, but Joe suspected that Jess had let the boys in on everything hours earlier.

"Hi, Chris. Is Ben there too?"

"Yeah."

"Well, put him on the other phone. I need to talk to you and I don't want to repeat everything."

The line clicked as Ben picked up. "Hi, Dad."

"Hi, Ben," Joe sighed. "Have you talked to your mother today, boys?" His pulse was beginning to pick up.

"Yes," they said in unison.

"Did she tell you what has happened?"

"Yes."

Joe didn't know just what to tell the boys. He thought he'd had a pretty good explanation ready for them. But as he began to speak, he seemed to lose track of what he'd intended to say, and it felt like his heart was going to beat right out of his chest. His voice trembled slightly as he started out. "I left your mother today. I...we've been unhappy for some time."

He paused and tried to think of a way to say the words. How does a father tell his children that he doesn't love their mother anymore? How does he explain that all those images of a happy marriage and a happy home were just smoke? How does a father explain that his children should hold on to the happy times they had while living in his home when he's just thrown that happy home away? There was a conflict there, one that each of them would have to resolve.

"I never thought this would happen in our lives. I never thought I'd be saying these things to you. I'm sorry, boys. I failed...in so many ways." His heart was still beating in the back of his throat when he paused and took a deep breath. "You know, boys, everyone says this—I've heard it many times from other people when their marriages ended. But the one good thing your mother and I did—the one really good thing—was to have you." Joe waited, hoping that his heart would slow down. "There was so much wrong between your mother and me. It just...it just..." Joe had nowhere to go with his thought. It just...was over, and he couldn't really explain that to his sons. "I'm sorry, boys. I should have told you in person, not over the phone. I should have..."

"Dad?" Chris said cautiously. "We've seen this coming for a couple years. This is what we talked about the other night on the way back here from your place."

"Really? Was it that obvious...that something was wrong?" Joe noticed that Chris had referred to their home in Rochester as "your place," not "home."

"Yeah, it was getting to the point where it wasn't much fun to be around you and Mom at the same time," Ben added.

"I'm sorry, boys. I guess I thought I was hiding something from you," Joe sighed.

"Not very well, Dad," Chris said.

Joe let Chris's words settle for a moment before he replied, "Boys, there are some other things that I want to tell you." He stopped and took another deep breath, and noticed that his pulse was beginning to return to normal. "But before I say anything more, I want you to know that I think your mother did a fine job raising you and that she's a good mother, and she's always had your best interest at heart."

Neither of the boys replied. Joe couldn't escape the feeling that Jess probably hadn't been quite so generous in her remarks about him.

"This may be a hard time for her, so try to help her when you can. OK?"

"Yes."

"Yes."

"Now, having said that..." Joe stopped briefly, then spent the next thirty minutes explaining, or trying to explain, to his sons how he'd chosen so many things in life that were so wrong for him. That he'd made so many bad choices just to please others, not himself. He'd let others make important decisions for him because he'd been unwilling to displease them. He told the boys that now he had to make this choice, and it was the hardest thing he'd ever done. If he'd only made a few other difficult choices, he might not be here at this point in his life, doing this. He didn't know if any of it made any sense to his sons. When he finally ended the phone conversation, he knew that there was plenty of unfinished business with his boys, plenty of unresolved issues. He also knew that no matter where he was tonight, those issues with the boys would remain unresolved for some time. He knew that under the best of circumstances, the things the boys were pondering would probably take years to resolve. Perhaps it was all right that he wasn't with the boys tonight. In fact, it was maybe better for all of them this way. He wasn't sure what he thought about the future, so how could he tell them. The boys had each other to talk to, and he could be alone with his own thoughts.

Joe suspected that his boys would spend this night wondering about their parents' love for them. They'd wonder if that love could be withdrawn from them, too. But soon enough, they'd be secure with the knowledge that their parents' love was unconditional, wouldn't they? He'd assured them of that again today as he had throughout their entire lives. But they'd seen their parents assure each other of love all along, and now that was gone. They'd just have to wonder about all that and resolve it for themselves as best they could. Chris and Ben would probably wonder about a thousand other things too, things he couldn't begin to understand. There would come a time—someday, someday down the road—when the boys would be all right with this, wouldn't there? Joe clicked the phone shut and slid it into his pocket. He rubbed his face with both hands, then rested his elbows on his knees and watched some little birds fly along the river.

The sun was an orange ball on the horizon when Joe slid back into the truck. He found an older motel that had the unmistakable look of a mom-and-pop operation, and he booked a room. He'd been tired and ready to collapse into bed after the longest day of his life when he'd paid for the room and then moved his truck so it was just outside his door. But as soon as he swung open the door to the little room, he was struck by a sense of remorse, and he wanted to turn around and leave.

Every other time he'd stepped into a motel room, he'd either been with his family or in a hurry to call them and let them know where he was. Now, as he stood in the doorway and reached for a light switch, he was at once aware of the sudden absence of his family from his life. The boys were grown up and gone from home. In the light of his recent phone conversation, he felt they were further from him now than they'd ever been. He certainly wouldn't be calling Jess to see if she was all right or to report on his day away from home, ever again. A deep sense of melancholy began to settle over Joe as he tried to get ready for a few hours of sleep. He was totally alone, wading in the middle of another, far more powerful stream than he could have imagined a few hours earlier.

This long day had come suddenly, unexpectedly, and now it was winding down. It had been inevitable—Joe knew that much—but now, as the day slowed and became quiet and dark, he began to struggle with the slow, painful truth that in order to escape the things he needed to be done with, he'd had to throw away some happy memories.

He undressed, brushed his teeth, and then shut the lights off in his room. It wasn't right; it just wasn't right to be here like this. Shafts of light from the street's passing cars found their way round the edges of the heavy curtains and moved across the ceiling and the walls. Joe walked to the side of his bed and then lay on his back, with his hands behind his head. While he watched the lights from other people's lives move across the ceiling and around his room, he hoped they'd distract him from his thoughts. The small-town traffic died down around 10:00 p.m. and left only the steady glow of a streetlight that peeked around the edges of the curtains.

"God. What have I done?" Joe mumbled before he drifted off to his fitful sleep.

———·—

Joe's only restful sleep came in the last hour before dawn, so he stayed in bed and slept until well after sun-up. Initially, when he slid his feet off the bed and onto the floor, he felt guilty about sleeping so late. Then, when the cobwebs cleared, he remembered he had nowhere to go. It really didn't matter that he'd slept a few minutes later than usual. He realized that there was not much joy in this situation either. This was so far from his usual routine. Good God, was he simply a homeless person with a few dollars in his pocket? Was he about to drop out of the human race?

As he shaved, he tried not to think like that anymore. Maybe he could try to see himself in transition. That might work, he thought. He smiled to himself when he thought of the self-serving bullshit he'd allowed himself with that label. "In transition"—what the hell was that, he thought as he moved the razor across his face and looked in the mirror. People who said things like that were trying to candycoat the truth. He'd taken a hell of a step yesterday, a hell of a step into the unknown. Today he'd start to make something of it. He turned sideways and looked at his potbelly in the mirror. Then he sucked in his belly for a moment before he stepped into the shower.

———·—

As he dressed and packed his duffel bag, Joe decided he wouldn't stay in motels anymore. His room had been depressing. It had reminded him of things he'd lost. From now on, he'd simply camp out in his truck. After all, he'd spent many nights in the back of that truck. He'd taken it to the Brule River and the Kinny Kinnick in Wisconsin, the streams of Minnesota's North Shore of Lake Superior, to Yellowstone Park, the Pere Marquette and AuSable in Michigan. Hell, he'd taken it—or it had taken him—to many of the great trout waters of America. He could certainly sleep in it again, and all the small chores of camping would take his mind off some of the thoughts that came to him when he had excess time.

It wouldn't hurt to save a few bucks on motel rooms either. At this rate, his seed money would be gone in a hurry.

The sunshine and morning air were good medicine for Joe. When he stepped out of his room and into the parking lot, he was glad to be getting on with things. It seemed that fear, and pain, and anxiety went hunting for him during the night, but those things were weak hunters during the daylight.

Joe was hungry. He'd gone without supper the night before, and he cruised between the old brick storefronts on Jackson's Main Street until he came to the Mayflower Café. The Mayflower appeared to be something of a throwback. It had clearly been a restaurant for a couple of generations. It still had a soda fountain behind the counter, hardwood floors, and booths along one wall. It also had the look of a place that had found a new owner, and had been partially remodeled in the style of the newer coffeeshops that served the richer, Seattle-style coffee. He met two elderly women in the doorway who smiled at him as though he was an old friend. The woman behind the counter called out a warm "hello" and commented on the weather when she sold him a caramel roll with his coffee. He sat on a yellow leather couch and read the paper for a few minutes while he finished his coffee. This was a strange routine that he'd never had time for in his old life, and he liked it. It was nice to read, and think about the news for a moment, and not rush off to a hectic office. When he stood up to leave, he bought another coffee for the road. As he was paying for it, he noticed a small sign by the cash register that said "Puppies! 714 Sverdrup Avenue."

When the woman behind the counter handed him his change, he asked, "What do you know about these puppies?"

"Plenty. They're mine," she smiled as she wiped her hands on a towel. "Well, they're my husband's. Are you looking for a pup?"

"Not really. Well, I don't know. Yeah, maybe," Joe stammered, then smiled. "I hadn't thought about it until I saw the sign."

"Well, they're Labrador pups, and the only ones that are still available are yellow—two males and two females. They were born in March. My husband has this hunting dog that he thinks is so brilliant." She rolled her eyes. "Anyway, our neighbor's Lab had his way with her before we could stop them. The stud, he's a good dog, but he don't have papers so we really can't sell these dogs for very much. If you're looking for a dog with AKC papers, I can't help you," she shrugged. "But they should be good dogs. Wanna see 'em?"

"Sure," Joe smiled, carried off by her enthusiasm.

"OK." She leaned across the counter and pointed: "Take a right right there, then six blocks up that hill, then a left. It's a big old white house with green shutters and a garage around in the back. Look for an open garage set back away from the street, and a bunch of dogs!"

Joe was leaning forward in his truck seat, driving with one hand, sipping coffee with the other. He was peering to his left, looking for an open garage door as he crept along the quiet little street in the quiet little neighborhood. Eventually, he noticed an open garage door and a man sitting in a lawn chair, lighting a cigarette. When Joe stopped the truck in the street, the man stood up and waved to him as if they were old friends. He motioned to Joe to come on over. A red garden tiller lay half taken apart next to the man's chair, and tools covered the wall and a tool bench along the back of the garage.

The smell of a dog kennel, mixed with cigarette smoke and machine oil, greeted Joe before the man did. When he introduced himself to the man, the garage erupted with the noise of eleven puppies yipping and falling over each other, begging for attention.

"Joe Mix," Joe said as he shook the man's hand.

"Ron Matuska," the man said, then took a drag on the cigarette.

"Your wife sold me some coffee...down at the Mayflower." Joe held up the foam coffee cup in his left hand. "She said her husband had some puppies. Looks like I found the right place?"

"You sure did!" Matuska said. He was delighted that someone had come to look at the puppies, and he set out on an enthusiastic sales pitch. He emphasized the fact that both the parents were excellent hunters, well mannered, and such smart dogs too! As he rambled, Joe began to sense a subtle desperation in Mr. Matuska. It seemed to Joe that Ron Matuska had one fear and he was trying too hard to mask it: he didn't want to be stuck with a garage full of puppies. He continued with details of their accidental conception by the neighbor's lab, then the details of their birth, and then he began to repeat details of their superior intelligence. Joe nodded his head and tried to appear to be listening when he sat his coffee cup on a wooden crate and dropped to one knee beside the kennel.

Ron Matuska was still talking when Joe reached into the small, plywood box that held all the puppies. He picked up the closest one, the one that had been lying on its back sleeping with all four legs splayed in every direction. The yellow fur on its back had a reddish cast to it when the morning sun lit the kennel through the window. When Joe raised the sleepy pup to his chest, he thought its fur was the softest thing he'd ever felt. The puppy made a small whimper, snuggled against Joe's chest, and this deal was done, at least in Joe's mind.

Jess had steadfastly refused to let Joe have a dog, or to get one for the boys when they'd asked. She'd never liked dogs, and that had been a sore spot between them for years. She'd always said that dogs were dirty and stupid, so she would never have one in her house.

Joe sank his nose into the exquisitely soft, yellowish-red fur on the puppy's neck and breathed in heavily. He'd forgotten that smell. He hadn't smelled it since his father had taken him to a place just like this about forty years earlier. Joe was smiling when he looked over at Ron Matuska, but Matuska kept on talking until Joe interrupted, "How much do you want?"

"I've been getting $300," Matuska replied.

Joe's friends had told him they'd paid up to $2,000 for Labrador pups, so a price of $300 didn't seem too far out of line. Without another thought, he decided to pay for the puppy. Joe handed the pup to Matuska so he could use both hands to open his wallet. "That's a lot for a dog with no papers," Joe added with no real intent to dicker over the price; he was just making an observation.

Matuska appeared startled when Joe handed him the puppy. He thought Joe was telling him he wasn't interested in a puppy at that price. He immediately backed off the price of $300 and began to prepare a counteroffer. Then he noticed Joe was reaching for his wallet.

Ron Matuska found renewed hope for a sale, but it only lasted for a moment. When Joe opened his wallet, both men saw that he had only two twenties and two fives. Joe hesitated. He didn't think it was appropriate to withdraw the cash from his money belt in front of Matuska, so he rubbed his chin for a second.

Matuska, however, feared the deal was off once again because Joe obviously lacked the finances. He was literally holding a puppy that he was growing desperate to get rid of, and a look of resignation came to his face.

Before Joe could say or do anything, he noticed that Matuska stole a glance at his well-used truck, then looked back into Joe's nearly empty wallet. "Here, mister"—he handed the puppy back to Joe. "You just keep the pup!"

"Huh?" Joe straightened in surprise.

"Yeah, if you don't have the money, that's OK. I gotta get rid of some of these dogs. This is the first one anybody's wanted, and they're ready to go!"

"But your wife said..." Joe protested.

"Aw, she was just tryin' to get you over here to have a look. We thought if people would just hold one, they wouldn't be able to put them down," Matuska smiled.

"Worked for me," Joe said as he took the puppy back in his arms. "Well, here. Take this, anyway," Joe said as he gave Mr. Matuska the two twenties from his wallet. "And thanks."

"Thank you," Matuska nodded. "All sales are final," he added with a smile.

As Joe turned to leave, he called back, "Hey, is this a male or female?"

"It's a male. You picked the handsomest one!"

"Yeah, I just hope he's a good listener," Joe said as the truck door creaked open and he slid carefully inside.

Several minutes later, he was rolling down a two-lane highway and thinking about how much better today had started than yesterday. The timid puppy stood on the seat and shivered for a moment, then curled up next to Joe's leg. In only a few minutes, he lay twitching in his sleep. Joe's coffee was still hot, the country air was blowing through the truck, and he was having a hard time not staring at the sleeping puppy.

About an hour after Joe pulled out of Jackson, the puppy began to stir. He stood up on four shaky legs and started looking around. It took

Joe only a few seconds to pull over, grab the pup, and run to the ditch, but it was almost too late: he'd already started to pee on the truck seat by the time Joe had been able to catch him, and he finished his business in the ditch.

"OK. First of all, don't pee in the truck anymore!" Joe said as he placed the timid puppy on the seat next to him. "Also, you need a name," he said while he let the clutch out and started rolling again. He pulled back onto the highway. The puppy sniffed at his pants pocket for a moment, then plopped down on the blanket he'd spread out between the bucket seats. When Joe reached his right hand down to stroke the puppy's head, the pup licked Joe's fingers briefly, then began to chew on them with his very tiny, very sharp, deciduous teeth. He was so small that he was unable to put much pressure on Joe's fingers. So Joe let the puppy play for a while before watching him drift off to sleep again.

"Well, I think I'll need to see you in action for a while before you get a name, OK?" The yellow pup stretched and rolled on his back for another nap.

———•———

Joe's cell phone rang shortly before noon, just after his third stop with the pup. Before he answered the call, he slowed the truck to pull off the road so that the road noise wouldn't make a phone conversation impossible. "Hi, Donny," Joe said when he answered.

"Where you at, Joe?"

"Between Worthington and Sioux Falls."

"Did you find yourself yet and decide to turn around?" Donny asked.

Joe was hurt by his brother's attempt at humor. "Donny, if there's one person I need to be with me on this, it's you."

"I know. I'm sorry, Joe, but this is all sort of hard for me to put into perspective."

"How do you think I feel?" Joe sighed.

"Yeah, you're right. I'm sorry, Joe," Donny replied slowly. Then his tone changed abruptly. "OK then, Joe, we have two things to discuss. First of all, your soon-to-be ex-wife already seems to be a fast healer; she's already through the hurt feelings and lost love phase and into the HATE portion of all of this."

It was clear to Joe that Donny was acquiring some dislike for Jess already.

"Oh?" Joe asked.

"Yeah, she pretty much loosed the dogs on us today. I think her attorney wants all your money, all your possessions, even the truck and all the shit you took the other day. He wants you killed and he wants to sell your organs. Also, it's just a guess, but I'll bet Jess has already had your credit cards cancelled."

"You're right on the credit cards, Donny. I tried to gas up this morning and had to pay cash. That's OK. I knew that was gonna happen. But you know that her attorney won't have anything to fight over when he realizes I intend to give Jess everything."

"Are you SURE you want to do that?"

"I have to swallow hard, really hard, every time I think about what I'm leaving behind. But it needs to be done! So please do it, and don't ask me about it again." Joe sighed an audible, exasperated sigh.

"OK, just double checking. I'm gonna jerk this prick—Jess's attorney—around a little bit, just for the fun of it. I don't like him already."

"You handle it, Donny. Have fun. But give it all to her."

"OK, one more thing. Your practice. No matter what you want to do, Jess can't just sell your practice; only you can do that. In Minnesota, only a dentist can own a dental practice; it's a point of law. Only you can sell it, to another dentist. You can't give it to Jess as it is now. You have to sell it first, then give her the money. With me?"

"Yeah."

"So what do I do?" Donny asked.

"Call one of those guys who brokers deals like this. There's plenty of those guys around; they just offer the practice to the highest bidder. Takes a while to sell a dental practice that way, though, and the longer it takes, the more the value drops. A dental practice with no dentist isn't worth much. Each day that goes by it gets to be worth less."

"So you're saying that the more Jess's attorney jerks everyone around and delays things, the more he reduces the value of his own settlement?" Joe could hear the joy in Donny's voice.

"Yes," Joe said.

"OK then, Joe. I'm gonna make this prick wanna go to war—a long war—so he'll screw himself and Jess and drain the value of your practice as far down as possible. Is that all right with you?" Donny asked.

"Have fun, Donny," Joe replied. He smiled at the antagonistic world-view his brother lived with. "Is everyone your adversary?"

"Everyone but you!" Donny said slowly.

Joe knew that Donny would handle the disposal of his practice, and his marriage. He could hear Donny's affection, and his assurance that things would be all right.

"One other thing, Donny?" Joe asked.

"What's that?"

"The boys. Would you talk to them from time to time? They might be willing to tell you things they wouldn't tell me—you know, if something was...you know."

"Did that already, and I'll continue. Ben sounded pretty good. But I had a hard time reading Chris. They're good boys. They'll be fine. You know I'll stay in touch with them, too."

When the phone call ended, Joe drove on in silence, waiting for the pup to wake up and start looking for a place to pee. While the puppy slept, Joe was alone with his thoughts once again. The talk of Jess had stirred no feelings of loss; he didn't miss her or want to talk to her. But the fact she was actually more concerned about money than having him come back did make him angry. He wanted her to miss him; he didn't really know why. Perhaps he could feel like he'd won something if she felt worse than he did? Thoughts of Jess drifted from his mind soon enough while the rural countryside passed by him.

Joe was, however, surprised at his feelings of remorse over the end of his dental practice. He'd put a lot of time and effort into the building of it. Now, it was almost worthless without him. It was just a carcass to be cut up and consumed as soon as possible. He didn't want it back—he was still sure of that—but he felt bad over the end of it all. That conflict would probably take a while to resolve itself, he reasoned. As the road noise continued to drone in his ears, the thought of his practice being consumed by someone else seemed to underscore something he'd told Donny all along: even though he'd built a large practice, by this time next week, or next month, there would be someone else seeing his patients, and very few of them would miss him. Like he'd said to Donny, there was no meaning in it all.

———•———

The highway soon grew monotonous. All of his thoughts slowed until the only thing he was aware of was his own fatigue and road weariness. He wanted to stop the road noise and rest for a while.

Joe found his way to a small city park in Mitchell, South Dakota, as the shadows began to lengthen at the end of the day. He and the pup were making slow progress on the trip west. But then, since they had no place to go, maybe they were making good progress.

Now, as he prepared to spend a night in the back of his truck, that thought began to depress him too. As he stood by the tailgate and looked into the green truck's box, with the red camper top, he wondered if he was looking at his future.

"I can't think like that," Joe said as he leaned over inside the truck and rearranged his gear to prepare a bed for himself. The fear and pain and anxiety that repeatedly came hunting for him were always better hunters as the day moved along toward night.

He'd made a series of stops and filled a cooler with fresh fruit and some groceries for himself. He'd also bought a forty-pound bag of puppy food for the pup. Joe made a point to play with the clumsy puppy for as long as he would play, in order to tire him out completely; he wanted the puppy to sleep at the same time he did and not keep him awake like a crying baby.

Joe sat in the grass and threw toys for the pup to chase. Empty plastic bottles, a section of rope, a piece of paper...it didn't matter. The pup chased everything. Some things he pounced on and wrestled with. Others he returned with, his head held high as if he'd found a great prize and wanted to show it to Joe.

When he got particularly wound up, he ran around and barked a tiny bark and tripped over his own feet. Each time he stumbled, he seemed surprised, as if the earth had reached up to trip him.

He chewed everything, especially Joe's fingers. Joe found himself searching continually for something to hold between the pup's jaws, other than his own fingers. He smiled openly when he realized he'd been bitching for his entire adult life about coming home from work with spit all over himself, and now he was happy to have the puppy's spit on his hands and clothes. "Go figure that," Joe said to the yellow fur ball as he tried to tug a spit-soaked stocking away from him.

When he finally lay down among his belongings in the back of the truck, Joe began to think that just maybe he'd found a suitable companion. He was drawn to the dog in a way he couldn't have anticipated. The puppy needed Joe's love, and Joe needed to share it. The puppy had needed Joe to take care of him for most of the day. All the stops to pee and play had certainly slowed them down, but so what? His needs, and Joe's tending to them, had kept Joe's mind off the regrets and second thoughts that would surely have gnawed at him if he'd been alone.

The pup was curled into a ball, with his head resting against Joe's chest, when Joe noticed that he was making tiny noises in his sleep. He loved the way the puppy smelled and the way the pup wanted to be next to him. Joe lifted the tiny puppy and raised him to his face again. He just wanted to smell the pup—to feel that soft fur on his face once more. Then he laid his new friend back onto his bed.

A warm day that had been mostly golden sunshine, blue sky, and green grass cooled into a slate-gray spring evening. Heavy, dark clouds rolled over the distant prairie just before sundown and closed it in, like an endless dome. The cool air grew heavy with moisture, and all Joe could hear was the occasional car out on the highway.

A gentle rain began to tap at the aluminum roof of the truck topper as Joe's day drifted into darkness. So was this any improvement over a small motel room? Joe wondered. It wasn't very comfortable, and it made him think about what he'd left behind. That big warm bed, the leather couch in his library? They were pretty comfortable. And that great big nice home with the nice yard? What about all that? He'd never go there again, right? He closed his eyes and hoped for sleep to come.

The puppy lifted his feet, one at a time after each step, out of the short, wet grass. He looked at them as if he couldn't believe the odd sensation of wet feet. He had roused Joe from a not-very-restful sleep three times during the night while looking for a place to pee. He had peed on Joe's sleeping bag once—and done something far more serious by the tailgate—sometime not long before sun-up, without waking Joe.

The puppy was learning about wet grass for the first time while Joe sipped at a cup of coffee he'd made over a fire on the ancient camping stove he'd taken along when he'd packed the truck. Joe rubbed his eyes and tried to figure a course of action. His sleeping bag needed to be washed; the stink inside the truck was fairly pungent, and he had nothing to clean up with.

It was amazing just what a difference one night and a little rain could make. Everything was cold and damp this morning, and his truck smelled like dog shit. His back ached from sleeping in the truck too.

Sleeping in the truck never used to leave him so sore. Had he done something different to the truck? Had he aged that much? The truck had been a happy, comfortable home for him on countless fishing trips. Now, he felt like he'd slept on a pile of cinder blocks.

"OK, dog," Joe sighed. "After you finish your business, we're going back out to that big truckstop by the interstate and we're gonna clean up," he said as he watched the yellow puppy wander around by the truck and investigate every smell.

———•———

The hot water streaming over Joe felt wonderful. He stood under the shower nozzle at the truckstop for several minutes and let the hot shower restore his spirits. After he'd cleaned the truck and filled it with gas, he drove back into town and found a laundromat to wash and dry his sleeping bag. While he waited beside the large clothes dryers, he sipped at a Styrofoam coffee cup and watched the other people in the laundromat. It didn't feel right for him to have the time to do something like this; he kept thinking he should be going to work. He wished he had something to read so he wouldn't have to look at all the unhappy-looking women. Most of the women were there by themselves, and they showed no sign of joy or happiness. Two very young mothers with small children had obviously come in together. They sat smoking cigarettes and boasting about all the people they'd been telling off recently. Both of the women had tattoos covering the pasty white skin on their upper arms, and both wore too much eye makeup. One of them tipped her head back, blew some smoke into the air, and said, "...And then I told that bitch..." The other of the young mothers was teaching her little boy how to hold up his middle finger. Joe was glad to leave the place when his sleeping bag was dry. He felt glad, relieved, that he'd never again have to wrestle with a little kid like the one who was holding his finger up in the air, or listen to some woman, like these two, explain why it was impossible for anyone in her family to not have rotten teeth—after all, their mothers had soft teeth! He'd listened to that line of stupidity his whole life, and for just a moment he thought about saying something to the young woman. He imagined himself walking over to them and saying, "Pardon me, but I couldn't help but overhear your conversation, and I wanted to let you know there is no such thing as 'soft teeth'—only dumb bitches who have bad diets, don't brush their teeth, and want to blame their problems on someone else." But what good would that do? He just rolled up the sleeping bag and walked to the door. This stop had been a good one: he'd reaffirmed the rightness of his decision to leave it all behind.

As he eased out of the parking lot at the laundromat, a white sign with orange, handwritten letters and two small balloons fluttering in the damp breeze caught his eye. A piece of cardboard had been stapled to a stick, and the stick had been duct-taped to a "No Parking" sign in front of the laundromat. The sign said "Garage Sale - four blocks." Joe simply turned and followed the orange arrow, then several more signs with orange letters and balloons. Half a dozen cars parked in the street told him where he'd find the sale. He'd never stopped at a garage sale. In fact, he'd always thought they seemed like ridiculous affairs. But he was having a run of first times, so why not have a look? He still had nowhere to go and plenty of time to get there.

The previous night's rain had stopped, but the grass was still wet, so Joe carried his puppy in his arms. He didn't want to put a wet, muddy dog on the truck seat when they went back to the truck in a few minutes. Besides that, he didn't want the dog underfoot for the others at the sale. And to tell the whole truth, he didn't want everyone to pick him up and hold him either. He was Joe's friend, after all, and Joe wanted him close.

Joe kept to himself and wandered around the merchandise for a few minutes. On display in the driveway were men's clothing, some newer hand tools, power tools, some garden tools, and two tables covered with various glass trinkets and kitchenware. Joe was amazed at the odd things for sale: an ugly desk lamp, about a dozen already used paint cans, a NordicTrack exercise machine, a Kodak slide projector with twenty-some boxes of slides. Joe raised the puppy to his mouth and whispered, "What the hell would anyone want this family's slides for? And why would they want to sell them?"

He did find a nice plastic lawnchair with very short legs that looked like it would work well as a bed in his truck, and he bought it for two dollars.

Joe examined the men's clothes on the rack, then mumbled into the puppy's ear once again, "The guy who wore those clothes was about five-feet-nothing and weighed about 350. I'll bet the NordicTrack hasn't been used."

He turned to leave, and as he turned he stumbled on a cardboard box. The box was filled with paperback novels, and the cover of the one on top caught his eye. It was *Riders of the Purple Sage* by Zane Grey. Joe bent over, looked to see what else was in the box, and saw that it was all paperback novels by famous authors: Steinbeck, Hemmingway, Faulkner. He noticed *To Kill a Mockingbird* and several books of short stories.

"Sell you the whole box for $5, mister. There's a hardcover of *Lonesome Dove* on the bottom of the box!" A rotund woman was standing next to him. "But you gotta let me hold that pup for a minute," she added. The woman was huge. She wore a tent-like, flowered cotton dress, and she surprised Joe when she spoke to him. His own response, however, startled him more.

"Done," Joe said as he stood up. He passed the dog to the woman while he opened his wallet. She pressed the trembling puppy between her massive breasts and talked baby talk to him while Joe withdrew a five-dollar bill from his wallet.

Joe carried the books to his truck, placed them next to the two-dollar chair, and returned for his dog. He felt good about the bargains on the chair and the books. Maybe this whole garage sale thing could be fun after all, he thought.

"Yeah, my husband really liked to read. Said he always liked words." The woman wore a puzzled look when she turned toward Joe and extended her arms to pass the puppy back to him. "Said he always wanted to write a book." She paused. "Just never got around to it."

"He's...passed away?" The words were uncomfortable for Joe. They would have been even if he were alone with the woman, but about ten other people standing in the woman's driveway and garage could hear them speaking.

"He died about ten years ago."

"I'm sorry," Joe said. "What did he do for a living?"

"He was a dentist." She smiled a faint smile. "I guess that kept him too busy." She nodded. "And what do you do?" she asked sweetly, as a grandmother would.

"Construction," Joe blurted with no hesitation. It was the first thing that came into his mind after he decided not to tell the truth. The fact that the woman's husband had been a dentist had caught him off guard, and the lie just sprang to his lips. This was the first time he could ever remember telling such a lie, and he had to stifle a smile because he enjoyed the feeling.

"Are you from around here?" the woman asked.

"No, I'm just heading west. Just looking for work." Joe liked the story he was telling. He enjoyed the lie, but then again he wasn't sure if it was really a lie.

"Well, I hope you enjoy the books. My husband sure did. He always thought being a dentist was boring. He said he should have been a writer. He wanted to write books about his travels." She smiled and shook her head as she turned to take some money from an elderly man who was holding some hand tools and a shovel. Then she turned back toward Joe and smiled sweetly. She touched the puppy's head and looked into his eyes. "Enjoy the books. My husband sure did." Then she turned away again.

"Well, thank you for the books," Joe said as he turned to leave. But when he walked past the Kodak slide projector and the box full of slide carousels, he spun on his heels and called out to her. He had no idea why, but he was suddenly compelled to buy the slide carousels. Another lie sprang to his lips. "Hey! I need a couple slide carousels. Can I buy two of them?" he asked.

"Two dollars," the woman replied. When she took his money, she said, "I've got dozens more of them in the basement." And she turned back toward her chair in the garage and smiled again.

"You must be quite a photographer," Joe said. He wondered just why he was buying someone else's memories. It struck Joe as poignant and sad, but he'd simply needed to do it when he noticed the slides.

"My husband was. He photographed everything." She looked at Joe and shrugged her shoulders as she made a sad face, as though she'd resigned herself to the loss of her husband. "But who wants to look at all those old pictures, huh?" She took Joe's money once again, then sat down in her chair and looked away from him.

"That was odd, huh, buddy? Like she'd been waiting for us," Joe said to the puppy when he got back to the truck. The whole conversation between Joe and the woman had lasted for only a minute, but it did seem to him that it was all meant to happen. There was something unsettling, haunting in it for Joe. He'd felt as if he needed to buy the slides. But now he was bothered by the thought of carrying someone else's memories—the record of someone else's life away from its home. "Memories in a box," Joe said to himself as he started the truck.

The puppy slept off and on and forced Joe to stop and play several times. Eventually, the sky cleared into the bluest blue Joe could remember, and he got back on Interstate 90 in order to cross the Missouri River at Chamberlain. When he reached the west side of the river, he exited the interstate and found another small city park. The puppy didn't seem inclined to sleep, and Joe was getting tired of all the stops, so he opted for an afternoon off.

The tailgate creaked open as Joe lifted his new bed, or chair, or whatever it was, out the back of the truck. Then he grabbed one of the books from the garage sale box and proceeded to adjust the aluminum framework of the plastic lawn chair so he could rest in a sitting position while he read. As he adjusted the chair to the correct position, he kept a close eye on his puppy so he wouldn't wander too far away. The pup was careful to stay close to Joe, too. He stepped cautiously around some picnic tables, a flagpole, and several garbage cans, checking the scent of other dogs, before he found a suitable place to do his business. Then he found an empty plastic soda bottle and pranced back to Joe as if he'd claimed a great treasure and wanted to show it to him.

"OK, dog. They say that children develop a higher IQ if their parents read to them. So while you're getting a little exercise, I think I'll share *Lonesome Dove* with you." Joe raised his eyebrows, nodded, and held the book out for the puppy to see. He licked at the book, then clamped his teeth onto the back cover and tore part of the dustjacket off. When the dustjacket gave way, the puppy lost his balance and tumbled over backwards. He came to rest on his stomach and seemed to be enjoying the book cover as he chewed it.

"Everyone likes to curl up with a good book, eh?" Joe said as he turned to the first page. "OK, dog, now pay attention." Joe raised his knees to steady the book and started reading out loud. The puppy spat out the book cover and attacked the soda bottle. He was still pawing at it and chewing it as Joe read the first page out loud.

———•———

"Damn. He's good, huh?" Joe said when he finished the first six chapters and closed the book. He'd had to stop reading about a dozen times to retrieve the pup from over by the garbage cans near the parking lot.

But in general, Joe's voice had seemed to provide a homing beacon that the puppy was unwilling to stray from. Joe had found an old T-shirt and a piece of rope and tied them both to the chair. That had been enough to keep the puppy interested in staying close to Joe for an hour. He'd pulled and tugged at the T-shirt, then the rope, then the T-shirt again until he'd tired, and then he'd slept for a while underneath the plastic chair while Joe read.

"I don't think you were listening very well." Joe put his hand on the ground and leaned over to look under the chair. "You down there?" he said before he could see the dog. The yellow pup was lying on his back again, with all four legs splayed out in different directions. He never moved when Joe spoke.

"Well, dog, I have a name for you. You're lazy, and the only reason we got together for this long trip to who knows where is because a dentist died back home. I think your name should be Jake—like Jake Spoon, in the book. In case you weren't listening while I was reading *Lonesome Dove*, the only reason that whole story took place was because Jake killed a dentist; that's what started the whole adventure. Hmph." Joe smiled. "That whole great big adventure never would have happened unless the dentist had died. How 'bout that?" Joe leaned back in the chair and put his hands behind his head. "We'll talk about it more later...Jake!"

———•———

"Hi, Donny," Joe said when Donny answered his cell phone.

"Where are you, Joe?" Donny sounded busy and impatient.

"A city park in Chamberlain. I'm just reading and talking to a pretty little blonde I picked up the other day." Joe closed his eyes and tried not to laugh. He knew Donny would need a few seconds to digest what he'd been told.

"Just a minute, Joe, I'm gonna switch phones and take this in the other room." The line clicked.

Joe's face bent into a smile, and the dimple was at the center of it.

"Oh, jeez, Jake. The wheels are turning in Donny Mix's head right now!"

The line clicked again when Donny had found a more private place to talk. "A blonde?" It was a question and an accusation at the same time. He didn't wait for an answer. "I thought this wasn't about women and midlife bullshit." Donny was growing angrier as he spoke.

"That tickles—here, chew on this for a while." Joe turned his head away from the phone and talked to Jake, but said the words loud enough to be sure Donny could hear and understand them. He'd only said the words to aggravate and confuse Donny. His face could not have held a bigger smile. Then he waited to see if Donny was going to say anything. Joe knew his brother well enough to know he was fuming on the other end of the phone. He'd assured Donny that his leaving had nothing to do with young women. Now this phone conversation was sure to infuriate Donny. "There, that's better," Joe added, talking to Jake but for Donny's benefit. "Oh yeah! Chew on that. That's good."

Still Donny said nothing, and Joe waited—because he knew the silence was aggravating Donny.

"The nasty little animal shit in my truck last night too," Joe finally blurted.

"Pardon me?" Donny couldn't hide the confusion.

"Yeah, he's a handsome puppy, but he dropped a steamer in the truck last night." Joe waited for a second. "Oh, were you thinking I'd found a girlfriend? I just bought a puppy. Shame on you, you pervert."

"You're just a damn comedian, Joe. No wonder you wanted to be out of dentistry; you're ready for stand-up." Donny never laughed, but Joe could hear the relief in his voice when he continued. "You had me for a second there. I wanted to reach through the phone and choke you. Do you think all this shit is funny, Joe...jerking me around?"

"No, I sure don't. But I think maybe you're worried about me for all the wrong reasons. I just hit the wall the other day, Donny. But I'm not crazy!" Joe took a deep breath, then continued. "Lighten up, Donny. Everything is OK here, pretty much. There's a lot on my mind, but I'm OK. I think I'll spend the night here and then stop at Kadoka tomorrow."

Donny knew it was his turn to speak, and he waited a moment to emphasize the change of direction he was about to make. "Joe? I need to ask you again: have you had any sort of change of heart? Do you see yourself back here in a few days?" He stopped and said nothing more.

Joe waited a while to take his turn. Then he sighed deeply. "I'm not coming back. It's over. All of it," he said softly. Then he added, "And I AM all right with that." Joe said the words with confidence and finality.

"OK, Joe, just asking." Donny let that part of the conversation go. Then he sounded as if he'd just remembered something, and he changed the tone of the conversation again. "Hey! I spoke to a shrink today...about you. I've used this guy as an expert witness in several trials. Nice guy. He works over at the Mayo Clinic. Anyway, I was thinking about all this stuff yesterday, and I gave him a call and asked a few questions. He shed a little light on all this for me."

"Gonna share?" Joe asked.

"Well, at first he asked a few questions about you—about how you think, and what's been going on in your life, and your past. I told him about all that had been happening, and about our discussion of time the other day—about how you think that time is circular. It's a straight line, by the way." Donny interrupted himself, then continued. "I told him about all the obtuse bullshit you talk about and think about: life, death, time, mayflies—you know, all the weird things you said the other day when we were fishing."

"Thank you."

"You're welcome. Anyway, he started talking about people who use the left side of their brain for the majority of their thinking, and how they're more analytical. The people who mostly use the right half of their brain are more artistic. He said that if someone who was a right brainer, like you, got stuck in a profession that suited a left brainer, like dentistry, it might cause some significant frustration over time."

Joe did not respond when Donny stopped.

"You there, Joe?" Donny asked.

"I'm smiling."

"Well, he said some other things too, about how we think. He talked about people who think and reason through problems in a 'concrete sequential' way. He said they go straight from point A to point B to point C, and they need to put everything in its proper place. He also said a good example of this type of person might be an accountant, maybe a dentist. He went on to say that the opposite type of thought process was one called 'random abstract.' He said this is the kind of person who doesn't think in a straight line and tends to be all over the place with his logic—more artistic. Naturally, when he said that, I thought of your views about the life cycle of the mayfly and finding meaning in life, and all that same shit."

"How insightful of you," Joe said.

"Yes, it was, and thanks for noticing." Donny paused, then continued. "Then he said that the two thought patterns might be totally different, but could still lead to the same conclusion. However, the concrete sequential is probably better suited for a career in dentistry. I think you're the other—random abstract."

Joe did not reply.

"Still there, Joe?"

"Still smiling," Joe said.

"He said one more thing that really brought it all together—at least for me."

"Really?"

"Yeah, Joe. You'll like this. He talked for a while about how we deal with conflict, and the resolution of conflict. He listed several different styles of conflict resolution; maybe they were more like personality types. There were two extremes. On one end was something called 'power dominant.' I guess that's sort of self explanatory, but it sounded a lot like Jess. Anyway, that person always causes resentment when they deal with others. They either force their views onto others or just find a way to get things done their way. Are you with me?"

"Yes."

"OK, then. He named several other styles of conflict resolution— 'collaboration,' 'compromise,' 'suppression'—and he explained each of them. The guy actually talked a lot. Then he came to the last category: 'denial/withdrawal,' the opposite of power/dominant. He said that the person who deals with conflict by denying its existence and withdrawing from it only postpones the conflict and makes it more painful to deal with later. Sound like anyone you know?"

"Maybe."

"Well, we had a long, informative chat. I think I understand more clearly now some of the things you were trying to tell me. He put sort of an academic spin on all the things you had said, I guess."

"So you think maybe I'm not a loony now? Not a fifty-year-old hippie?" Joe asked.

"I didn't say that! He never said that either! In fact, his exact words were, 'I think your brother is crazier than a shithouse rat, and he just may be a whacked out, leftover hippie!' No, I still think you're nuts too. I just said I understand you a little better now."

"Did your guy ask you any sex questions, like the shrink I was talking to?"

"No! And I was pretty disappointed about that!" Donny said. He let Joe hear all the joy of their friendship return to his voice.

"It's probably better that way. You nearly shit in your waders when I tried to explain it to you," Joe said. He was sure Donny could see the smile on his face, even though he was hiding it at the other end of a telephone line. Like so many of their conversations, this one had changed in a heartbeat.

"I have to go now, Joe. Someone back here on Planet Earth wants to talk to me," Donny chuckled. "Call me tomorrow?"

"I'll call you," Joe said as he ended the phone call. He leaned back and grinned, thankful that Donny was at least trying to accept what he'd done.

Immediately after the phone call ended, Joe stood up to have a long stroll with Jake the dog. Jake toddled along like a young child and examined everything as he went. Cigarette butts, bottle caps, and birds that walked or flew nearby were all objects of wonder. He stopped to sniff every scent that had been left by another dog. He flinched when a butterfly passed above him. He stopped and barked his tiny bark at a clump of tall grass beside a pond. Then he laid his belly on the ground, as if he were about to pounce on an enemy, while he threatened to attack the same clump of grass.

Joe found himself smiling as he watched the puppy move from one small adventure to the next. He couldn't help but wonder what it would be like to see the world through Jake's eyes; everything seemed so new and exciting. Joe dropped to one knee and clapped his hands, and Jake scampered over to him. He held his face close to Jake's and breathed in deeply to draw the smell of puppy into his nose. "Maybe I'll try to see the world for the first time again. Can you help me with that?" Joe said with a faint grin. Jake struggled from Joe's grasp and ran until he found a small stick. He shook the stick twice, dropped it, and stumbled as he accelerated away toward a discarded paper cup.

An apple, peanut butter sandwich, and a bottle of water were enough for Joe at suppertime. He served Jake a handful of dog food on an old

Frisbee that someone had lost in the tall grass along a small creek in the little park. The Frisbee made a fine dog dish and doubled as a toy.

Before he was ready to bed down for the night, Joe took Jake for one more long walk around the park. Joe lay on the grass and wrestled with him. Then Joe threw things for him to retrieve. Jake was interested enough to chase most of the things Joe threw, and he seemed inclined to retrieve some of them. But Jake usually lost interest in the retrieve and just laid down to chew on whatever had been thrown.

The little stream with the tall grass along the banks, where Joe had found Jake's Frisbee, ran across the far side of the park. When Jake and Joe found a stretch of the creek with short enough grass that Jake could see into the water, he became wary and hunched over. He began to act as if he were stalking the creek, about to pounce into it. In short order, his manner became timid. He took several cautious steps toward the creek, then backed up a couple steps. His tail stopped wagging and sank between his legs. Eventually he moved to the water's edge, but he would not step into it or even touch it. For a minute or so, Jake looked like he wanted to touch his toes into the water. Then he just backed away. He only stood beside the creek and cowered.

"I think I know that feeling," Joe said after a moment of waiting for him to step into the water. "Let's go back to the truck and read some more," Joe said as he started back across the park. "You've got your whole life to jump in. You can wait a while."

Jake continued to stare at the water. But when he realized Joe was leaving, he jerked his head around to follow and reared up on his hind legs to make a leaping first step. He learned soon enough that he was unable to do such an athletic thing just yet. The force of his first step caused his front legs to buckle when they hit the ground. His chin bounced into the short grass when his front legs crumpled, but his hind legs kept on churning. He pushed his hind end over his own head and performed a not very graceful summersault. When he regained his balance, he looked around as if to ask just what had happened. Joe laughed out loud at Jake's clumsy enthusiasm and called to him. "C'mon, Jake, you look like someone threw you out of a car." He appeared to be caught up in a deadly serious race as he scrambled to catch up to Joe. He ran with a terrified expression on his face, as if a hound from hell was chasing him.

Inside the camper, Joe had arranged the plastic chair and the duffel bags so Jake could sleep beside him if he chose to. Joe lay on his back and clicked on the tiny light bulb in the dome of the camper. As he began to read chapter seven of *Lonesome Dove*, Jake slid himself off the duffel, where he'd been lying, and inched himself onto Joe's chair/bed. He rubbed his face against Joe's thigh, rolled over onto his back, and went to sleep.

Joe didn't know for sure, but he thought it was unusual for a puppy to sleep on its back with all four legs splayed out in different directions. He picked Jake up once more, ever so slowly, and smelled him, then put him back on the bed. It surprised him when he realized that his only thought at that moment, there in the back of the truck, was that he wished Donny could see how much his puppy liked him.

Joe read for a while, then switched the dome light off. Before he drifted off to sleep, he spent a few minutes weighing the recurring feelings of satisfaction at having left his old life and all the conflicting thoughts about failure in marriage and business. Those feelings of failure and loss were never far from his mind during the day, either. But now, in the darkness before sleep came, they always descended on him with the greatest strength. He was still comfortable with his decision to leave his old life, even though the strength of that conviction wavered quite a bit through the course of a day. He knew that most other people might think him a failure, though, and that would probably always bother him.

chapter thirteen

The road and the countryside began to look familiar as Joe's truck rumbled west along South Dakota's rural highways. As he drew near to Kadoka, he began to recognize familiar farms and ranches, the places where his friends and classmates had grown up. Some of the places looked abandoned now. Most of them looked like they were still in the process of dealing with hard times. The sad reality that this place wasn't his home anymore settled over him, just as it always did when he returned. He could never forget the eerie awareness that he felt the first time he'd come home from college. It had been Christmas break during his freshman year. He'd come home with every expectation that he'd just step right back into the comfortable home of his childhood, and that Kadoka would remain as it had been all during his young life. But as he drove into town all those years ago and looked around at his little town, he knew something had changed. Either Joe or Kadoka had changed, and the change was permanent. Kadoka was not his home anymore; it never would be again. He felt the same sadness now.

He didn't really understand his feelings or expectations as he and Jake closed the distance to Kadoka this morning. As he drew near to some of the happiness of his youth, he felt a balance of melancholy and joy. This place was the headwaters of his life, and he'd always feel some joy in the memories it served up for him, even if he couldn't hold onto them. There was an inescapable sadness in the way the years had changed the place, and him. Kadoka had not prospered. In some ways, at least, it seemed like his life—and the life of his old home hung in the balance now.

He wondered just what might have become of the boys who existed in the periphery of his life here—the kids who had been friends once, long ago, and then been lost and forgotten. He wondered about Wendy Hample and what had become of her—how she'd dealt with a broken heart. All he knew was that she'd returned to Kadoka and married one of the Benda boys from south of town.

When Joe reached the north side of town, he took a left onto Main Street. Several cars were parked along each side of the street, but he could see no traffic moving as he crept along a nearly deserted business district.

Backer's Western and Fleet Supply still occupied the largest store-front in town, and Joe noticed that the front door was wide open when he passed by. Three late-model pickup trucks were parked on the street in front of Backer's, but Joe couldn't see anyone moving around inside as he tried to catch a glimpse through the large window along the sidewalk.

An old woman with a bundle of mail in her hand walked toward her car and waved at Joe as she left the post office. Joe waved back at her. Everyone waved in Kadoka. They seemed to figure that if you were there, you were supposed to be there and they probably knew you. It had always been that way.

One car was parked in front of the Clover Farm Grocery Store. Macek's Clover Farm was a dinosaur, a throwback to the days before grocery stores evolved into supermarkets. In an earlier time, there had been small grocery stores on every little town's Main Street. Macek's was the only survivor Joe was aware of. A satisfied little grin began to pull at the corners of Joe's mouth when he realized that almost nothing had changed at Macek's Clover Farm in all these years. In a heartbeat he was taken back to his childhood. He saw himself standing with Donny in front of the small display that held the baseball cards. He remembered opening the packages and always having to give the first piece of rock-hard bubble gum to Donny, then listening to gum shatter when Donny started chewing. He remembered the anticipation that he might find the card of a superstar in those little packages, and the disappointment when he found the likenesses of players he'd never heard of. The store had only four aisles of groceries. Mr. Macek, the owner and butcher, displayed all the meat in an ancient, six-foot glass case that supported an ancient meat scale. As far as Joe could tell, Mr. Macek might still cut meat while customers watched, then wrap it and weigh it for them.

The truck rolled on past the Clover Farm store. When Joe turned his eyes back to the south end of town, he tried to look back through a lifetime to see things as they once were.

The business district was only two blocks long, but for Joe, the south end of it had always had a far different feel than the north end. When he was a child, the south end of town had been alive with ranchers, cowboys, and truckers. In those days, the stockyards and livestock exchange had done a brisk business, and traffic had been heavy, at least by Kadoka's standards.

On one side of the street stood the Stockman's Café, where all the ranchers used to gather for coffee and gossip every morning. They talked about the weather and local news while they rolled dice to see who would pay for the coffee. Joe could still hear the men's laughter, the sound of dice bouncing inside those leather cups, and the thumping sound those cups made when the men slammed them down on the tables as they poured the dice out of them. The Stockman's Café served eggs and bacon, or eggs and sausage, or eggs and ham, in every possible combination and style that ranchers and truckers might order. Joe supposed that maybe they served several different sandwiches at lunch, but the only noon meal he'd ever actually seen served there was a beef commercial—white bread covered with slices of beef, a big scoop of mashed potatoes, and brown gravy over the top of it all.

Directly across the street stood Bully's Bar. A large, malevolent, angry-looking neon bull hung over the door and could be seen all the way from Backer's Western Store. Bully's was dark inside, with a long bar, some booths along the opposite wall, and a pool table in the middle. Joe's earliest memory of Bully's was a fistfight that had spilled out the door and onto the street one afternoon when he was in town with his father. Joe had been holding hands with his father, so he reasoned that he'd been about five years old. Alex Grimsted and Nick Steinke had tumbled out of Bully's just as Ray and Joe were leaving the Stockman's Café.

Ray Mix had stopped on the sidewalk and stared for a moment as the two drunken men staggered and waved at each other with weak, sloppy punches. They appeared to be in more danger of falling down than being struck by the other man. Joe remembered the look of disgust on his father's face, and his words: "Now there's a couple of worthless sons-a-bitches! One o'clock on a Saturday afternoon and they already got a snoot full!" Joe smiled when he recalled the way his father always said the phrase "sons-a-bitches." Then he wondered if Alex Grimsted and Nick Steinke might still be alive and perhaps still sitting with their elbows on the bar at Bully's this very moment.

He supposed that the reason he remembered that day, and that fight, so well was because earlier in the day, he'd been begging his dad to buy him a cowboy hat. For some reason Ray had said no. Joe remembered that part of the day very clearly too. He'd been pleading to go down to Backer's and buy a cowboy hat like one of his cowboy heroes, and Ray had said no. He'd said no three times; the last time, he'd sounded angry. Maybe Joe already had a hat, or maybe he was being punished for something—he just couldn't remember why Ray had said no. That didn't matter. What he did remember was that he'd been angry enough about not getting a hat, not getting his way, that he never wore a cowboy hat, ever. It was his way of punishing his father, he thought. The details of the argument had been lost in antiquity, but Joe remembered how a decision that lacked any sort of logic or sense had become his mission.

Yeah, Joe nodded as he looked around, the town was all pretty much still here, but so much had changed too.

At the end of Main Street, a big one-story, wooden building with dull gray siding still stood. The building truly did represent the end of Main Street: it sat at the top of the "T" intersection. It was all that remained of the Kadoka Livestock Exchange. At one time, the Kadoka Livestock Exchange, the Stockman's Café, and Bully's had surrounded a busy intersection. Railroad tracks lay just beyond the building, and parts of two abandoned and rundown buildings still stood several hundred feet to the west. It hurt Joe to see how this place had fallen into such disrepair, but he knew it was a sign of the times. In the glory days, fences had run in all directions between the Kadoka Livestock Exchange building, the railroad tracks, and the loading chutes where semi trailers loaded and unloaded cattle. A generation or two earlier, this had been a bustling business, and both the Stockman's Café and Bully's Bar had done a brisk business because of it. But the cattle business had changed, and most of the cattle were now raised on huge feedlots to the south, in Nebraska, and to the west, in Montana. The rancher who raised a few head of fat cattle on a small working ranch had pretty much vanished from this part of the country.

Parked in front of the only door along the north wall of the gray building was an aging yellow Cadillac, conspicuous because it was all alone at the south end of town.

Joe had expected to see the sign that said "Kadoka Livestock Exchange." It had hung on the side of the gray building for as long as he could remember. But it was gone now, like so much of this place. The only reminder of its existence were a few screw holes in the side of the building and its faded outline on the wall.

The silence and the lack of activity inside the building only deepened Joe's sense of despair over the decline of the south end of town. When the door slammed shut behind him, Joe could hear only the echo of his own footsteps as he walked a narrow hallway. He'd halfway expected to smell the manure and diesel fuel that used to pervade everything around the Livestock Exchange, but now all he could smell was dust—the stagnant smell of a building that had become a bone yard. He looked into each room as he passed. All the small offices were empty except for the unused desks and office chairs that had been abandoned for a few years. As he walked along the hallway, he began to hear the faint noise of an AM radio station. At first all he could hear was the jabber of an announcer. Then he recognized that the announcer was reading current livestock and commodity prices on the Chicago Board of Trade.

Joe stepped tentatively into the doorway of the last office at the end of the hall, the office where the radio was playing. He put his hands in his pockets and waited to be noticed.

Seated at a well-used, metal office desk was an old man wearing a new Stetson and reading a newspaper, with both of his elbows resting on the desk. The window on the other side of the office was open, allowing a spring breeze to move through the room. Through the open window, Joe could see the rolling hills of the South Dakota countryside.

The old man wore a white-and-gray plaid shirt, cut in western style, with pearl snaps along the front, on the western-cut flaps that covered the pockets, and on the cuffs of the long sleeves. He wore a thin, rawhide vest, and even while the old man still looked down at the newspaper, Joe could see that his Stetson was tilted about five degrees to the right, the way old men wear their Stetsons when they want to add a little style to their look.

Joe stood for a moment, but the old man didn't notice him. So he cleared his throat and shuffled his feet.

The front brim of the Stetson lifted slowly to reveal the wrinkled and leathery face of Ralph Webster, Ray Mix's former partner and best friend. Ralph's eyes were still dark and sharp as he stared at Joe. He peered from under the brim of the Stetson and over the top of his bifocals. There was no recognition in his eyes at first. He couldn't seem to identify Joe. He stared at Joe for several seconds before his eyes cleared and his face relaxed into a smile.

"Well, well, well...The Kadoka Kid. What are you doing here, Joe?" Ralph said as he rolled his desk chair back and raised himself to stand.

"Just passing through, I guess," Joe said, while Ralph slowly stood and stretched to his full height. As Joe spoke, he watched Ralph struggle to rise from the chair. He didn't just stand up, like he always had in the past. He raised himself slowly, straining against the pain and stiffness in his old joints.

Ralph Webster looked every bit of his eighty-seven years this morning. He was feeble, and he was slow in getting around the side of his desk to greet Joe. Ralph's looks had changed significantly in the five years since Joe had last seen him, at his wife Millie's funeral. Even back then, at eighty-two, Ralph had carried himself as he always had, with the unmistakable swagger of the old-time cattlemen.

Today, however, Ralph Webster just moved like an old man. His eyes still sparkled when he smiled and spoke. The same intelligence and light that had always been there still shined. But his body had turned a corner; he seemed to be stuck in low gear as he shuffled his way around the desk to greet Joe. He'd always had spindly legs and arms, but he'd had a huge potbelly that looked like he'd lost a watermelon inside his shirt. He'd never been fat, but that amazing potbelly had always strained the pearl snaps on his western shirts to the point that Joe had worried that maybe one might give out and fly across the room so fast it would put someone's eye out.

The belly was gone now. His leather vest hung loosely in front of him as he slid his feet along the floor and inched his way toward Joe. Ralph's shirt and hat were neat and clean, as always, and his blue jeans had a crease. He still wore a belt buckle just a little bit smaller than the one that belonged to the heavyweight champion. Today's belt buckle was silver, with plenty of engraving and inlayed with a gold bull.

When Ralph rounded the desk and extended his hand, Joe was in for the biggest surprise of all: Ralph was wearing Nike running shoes instead of the alligator cowboy boots he'd worn for a lifetime.

Joe brushed Ralph's hand away and put his arms around the frail old man. "Nice to see you, Ralph," Joe said into Ralph's ear.

"Nice to see you, too." Ralph moved his head back and smiled.

Just being with Ralph had always provided Joe with a sort of vicarious kick. He wished he could be more like Ralph. The old cattlemen were a vanishing breed. Their style, their self-deprecating wit, the straightforward way in which they dealt with others, and the candid way they spoke to other old cattlemen all set them apart.

He remembered sitting in that very room, many years earlier, with his father and Ralph and several other cattlemen. The men were probably celebrating something—some big deal, Joe reasoned—because it was the middle of the day and a bottle of Cutty Sark Scotch Whisky sat on Ray Mix's desk while the men each poured drinks for themselves. Joe remembered laughter, and he remembered one thing Ralph said that drew a huge round of laughter from the men: "Yeah," Ralph had said as he sat back in his desk chair and raised his drink into the air. "Them guys raisin' hogs are makin' all the money, but we get to wear big hats and drink the good whisky!"

He'd always enjoyed Ralph's sense of humor and the confidence that seemed to radiate from him. They shared a unique friendship that could only be extended by a man so much older than himself. Joe saw quite a bit of his father's personality in Ralph Webster too. He felt that his time spent with Ralph gave him a glimpse of his own father. A subtle wave of joy rolled over Joe while he held the old man.

"So, Ralph? I gotta ask you," Joe said as he stepped back from Ralph. "What happened to your boots? I've never seen you without your boots on!" He shrugged and smiled and waited for an answer.

"Damn things hurt my feet! Started wearing tennis shoes a couple years ago. Just don't look right, does it?" Ralph was still holding Joe's hands. "Sure as hell feels good, though!" His back was bowed slightly in a permanent curve, he walked slowly, and his face was wrinkled. His belly was gone too, but he was still Ralph. He smiled a broad smile and squeezed Joe's hands. His eyes were as busy and sharp as ever.

Then Ralph's face changed, and he tipped his head to the side as if he were asking Joe to answer a question. "Donny called the other day...said you might be coming this way," he said.

"Yeah," Joe nodded. "Thought I might buy you lunch and tell you all about it."

Ralph only nodded and started walking out of his office. "Let's go. It's lunch time anyway." He didn't close the door to his office or lock the front door of the building when he stepped out.

"Aren't you gonna lock up?" Joe asked as he followed Ralph onto the street.

"What for?" Ralph answered without looking at him, as if locking the office was a stupid, unnecessary complication. Then he pointed to the yellow Cadillac and said, "Get in."

"Don't you want to walk over there?" Joe pointed to the Stockman's Café about two hundred feet away.

"Why the hell would I do that?" Ralph said as he opened the driver's door and eased himself inside the Cadillac.

Joe could only grin at Ralph's logic, then get in the car with him. The keys were already waiting in the ignition, and Ralph backed out into the street without looking behind him. Joe looked reflexively behind them, then relaxed. There wasn't a car moving on Main Street, and there seldom was anymore, he guessed. That was a good thing for Ralph, because he wasn't going to look back there anyway.

The Cadillac had almost rolled to a stop when Ralph jolted it into drive and the transmission clunked. In the instant before the car could lurch forward, Ralph looked out the window at Joe's truck and asked, "You drivin' that pile 'a shit?"

Joe nodded and smiled. Ralph stared at him for a second before he looked away.

In the time it took them to get into the car, cross the intersection, get out of the car, and walk inside the café, they could have simply walked from Ralph's office several times. But Joe knew it would have been pointless to argue with Ralph. Besides, he enjoyed the old man's eccentricities.

They sat in a window booth, and a young woman brought them coffee. The booths and tables hadn't ever changed as far as Joe could remember. The south and east walls were all windows, and the café was always flooded with sunlight. Each of the windows had white-linen curtains pulled to the sides. The tables were all plain with light gray, Formica tops. The booths and chairs had always been upholstered with pastel yellow leather. Even pale and cloudy afternoons had always seemed open and light in the café. In the summertime, the front door was usually left wide open. As the girl who brought them coffee walked away from the booth, Ralph leaned back and said, "I wish it was a class reunion or a fishing trip that brought you out this way." He reached for his coffee and stirred it with a spoon for a moment, although he'd added no cream or sugar. Then he looked up from his coffee. "Donny said...well, he said you just left?" Ralph said.

"What did he tell you, exactly?" Joe asked.

"Said you were unhappy, so you left. Just walked away."

"Did he tell you I was crazy?" Joe asked.

"I think that's what he was gettin' at," Ralph grinned.

"What do you think?" Joe said.

"Tell me what's going on first," Ralph replied.

"Well, Ralph"—Joe breathed in deeply and then leaned forward—"here's the story. I left Jess the other day. I want a divorce. I'll spare you the details, but there was none of the usual stuff with extramarital boyfriends and girlfriends; just a long, unhappy marriage." Joe moved his coffee cup in a slow circle on the table and stared at his hands. "Walked away from my practice, too. I hate dentistry. I've hated it for twenty-five years. I hated it after about two weeks of dental school. I just stayed with it because I didn't know what else to do, and I knew Dad would be so upset if I quit." He moved his cup slowly again while he thought for a moment. "All I've got is that green truck over there"— he pointed to the Ford—"and a few bucks in my pocket."

Joe moved the coffee cup around slowly for a moment, then looked over at Ralph, shrugged his shoulders, and said, "I'm not going back."

Ralph waited for Joe to continue.

"Know the first thing I thought of when I walked in here with you today?" Joe asked.

"What's that?" Ralph answered.

"I remembered one time when I came in here, to the café, with Dad. I must have been a junior in high school, something like that. I know it was over Christmas break. I was helping Dad with some things at the stockyards." Joe was staring out into the street, smiling softly at the memory of something from so long ago. "That was thirty-five years ago,

Ralph. Doesn't seem possible. Anyway, when we walked in, you were sitting at that table right by the coffee pot. You were sitting with Richard and Raymond Eggiman, and one of the Fransen boys."

"It was Russell—Russell Fransen," Ralph interrupted.

"You remember?"

"Sure do," Ralph nodded.

"I remember that Dad got up and left me. He walked over and sat at your table for a few minutes and talked to you guys. Then he came back and sat with me, and we had breakfast. You know what he said to me?" Joe asked.

"I got a pretty good idea," Ralph replied as he sipped his coffee.

"Dad had an odd, excited look on his face, then he started to grin a little. He looked at me and he said, 'A million dollars just changed hands at that table. Did you notice anything odd over there, Joe?' I said no, and Dad got this really satisfied look on his face. He said, 'A million dollars! There was no signing of contracts, or even handshakes. In fact, those men would have taken it as a sign of distrust if anyone needed a hand-shake, or a contract, to cement the deal. They'd have been insulted! Those guys gave their word; and that deal is goin' down just like we all agreed. There's no other business like the cattle business. Those boys don't need anything but their word, and their word is always good!'"

Joe was fighting back tears when he continued. "Goddammit, Ralph. That was what I wanted to be. That was it...just Ray Mix." Joe wiped his nose with the back of his hand. "I'll never make it now. I'll never be as good a man as my father. He made a fortune out here, and I flopped at dentistry, where nobody fails! He had integrity, and I walked out on my wife and my business." Joe wiped his nose again and took a deep breath to steady himself. "So can you see why it's a little hard to sit here and tell you about myself—to tell you the truth? If the memory of my father's unwillingness to break his word over a livestock deal puts a lump in my throat, how do you think I feel about telling you I walked away from my career and broke my wedding vows?"

Before Ralph could say anything, Joe started again. "Maybe what I wanted was the joy that he seemed to get from the ranch, the cattle business, his friends, or his life with my mother...I don't know. He just seemed to enjoy his life so much. But I never went after what I wanted. I just went out and did what he wanted me to, and I hated it. I probably should resent him for steering me away from this place, this life, but I don't. I resent my own behavior, I guess—the fact that I never pursued what I wanted. I wish I'd have come back here. I guess I started letting other people choose things for me. I want something with some meaning...for me!"

"OK, Joe. Now back up a little bit. Fill in the details between that day in the café and today. Tell me how you got here," Ralph said calmly.

The Stockman's Café still did a pretty brisk business during the lunch hour. Dishes clanked, and people came and went all around them for the next ninety minutes while Joe tried to explain to Ralph all that had happened at work and between him and Jess. He told Ralph all the things he'd told Donny, and more.

Joe and Ralph were the only patrons still seated in the café when Joe finished his story and turned to Ralph. "There, that's how I got here. That's how I took the long way around the barn, as Dad used to say. Made quite a mess of it all, haven't I?" He folded his arms on the table in front of him and leaned forward. "You wanna know the kicker here, Ralph? I still don't want all that stuff back. I don't want a chance to go back and make it all right. I don't want my wife, or my job, or my old life back. I just want to go find what I should have found all those years ago. I want something with some joy and passion and meaning!"

Joe shook his head and looked away, as if he were laughing at his own words, when he continued softly. "I'm afraid of what I'll find next."

"So you think you need to be poor in order to find what you're after? That why you left everything?" Ralph asked.

"No, not really. But I think traveling light—maybe being poor—seems to clarify a man's needs. That make sense?" Joe answered.

Ralph stared at the table in front of him for a moment when Joe finished. "Joe, maybe you made a few mistakes, but your problems don't sound any different than a lot of men I know."

"You know a lot of men who've failed at a job that's a lead pipe cinch for success, and then made a mess of their marriage?" Joe asked.

"Well, yes, I do. A lot of GOOD men did those things, as a matter of fact. I've learned that nothing is a lead pipe cinch, either. You're being a little unfair to say those things about yourself. But more than that, before you go comparing yourself to your Dad, maybe you should know all the facts."

"Oh?" Joe said.

"Let's go on out to my place." Ralph started to slide out of the booth and seemed to want to change the subject for a while. "We'll talk some more later. You're gonna stay with me tonight, right?"

"Got a room for me?" Joe asked.

"Sure do."

"I have a traveling companion, Ralph—a puppy," Joe smiled.

"Long as he don't shit in the house, we're OK," Ralph smiled.

"Hey, Ralph?" Joe chuckled as they stood up beside the booth and prepared to leave. "Whatever happened to Wendy Hample?"

"I thought you knew," Ralph said over his shoulder while he walked toward the cash register to pay for lunch. "She married one of the Benda boys—I think it was Del, the oldest one. They run some cattle out on the home place, out south of town. They run a pretty nice cow/calf operation. Those Bendas always ran a nice place. They bought the grocery store from Gene Macek too!" Ray added as if it was big news. "Gene was about to close up. He was gettin' too old. Anyway, Wendy and Del wanted to keep the grocery store open, so they bought it. I'm glad they did too! We'd have to drive fifty miles for groceries if the store had closed." Ralph added, "I don't think they're making a lot of money, but they're committed to keeping our town together. I thought you knew all this," Ralph said when they reached the street.

"No, I didn't know," Joe said.

"Hell, there she is, right there." Ralph pointed to the street in front of the grocery store, about a half-block away. "That's Wendy."

Just down the street, a short woman with frizzy salt-and-pepper hair stepped out of the Clover Farm Grocery Store. It was Wendy Hample. Joe raised his hand to cover his face when he recognized her. He stopped in his tracks and stared.

She was about twenty pounds heavier than the last time he'd seen her. He couldn't look away from her uncomfortably tight-fitting blue jeans. She wore a white cotton turtleneck sweater under a red fleece vest, and she wasn't really fat but thick in the middle. Her eyeglasses had a heavy tint, and when she spoke, Joe noticed that her teeth were too big. He'd never noticed that before. He'd been treating teeth like hers for twenty-five years, but he had no memory that Wendy's teeth were so unsightly. How odd, he thought. He couldn't take his hand away from his face while he stared at her.

Wendy was carrying a grocery bag in each arm, helping a woman with two small children load things into their car. She put the bags on the floor in the back seat of the car, then did something Joe couldn't have expected: she kissed the woman. Then she kissed each of the children.

My God, Joe thought, that's her daughter and her grandchildren. He was speechless. His old girlfriend—the girl he'd always assumed to be in his alternate life—was a frumpy, not very attractive grandmother who worked here in Kadoka at the Clover Farm Store. Wendy's life, just like his own, had raced along while he'd been counting down the days.

The young woman drove away, and Wendy Benda—not Wendy Hample—walked back inside after she waved goodbye to her family.

This was unsettling, way too unsettling, Joe thought. It just wasn't right—none of it. He'd just recently disposed of his other life, back in Rochester, and he hadn't dealt with all the conflicting thoughts and feelings of that experience yet. Now this?

He was forced to admit to himself, while he stood there next to Ralph's yellow Cadillac, staring at the Clover Farm Grocery Store, that he'd been hoping he'd find Wendy to be a classy-looking, fifty-year-old beauty who'd been pining away after him for her whole life. Today, she should have told him that she'd thought of him every day since he cast her aside. Not that he wanted that to happen; he'd just been thinking that would be what he'd find here. It was a pleasant myth, that Wendy still needed and wanted him; it was another part of his old life that hadn't been left behind yet. It was gone now! Damn—she'd just gone on and had the life she was determined to have, with or without him.

As Joe had watched and listened to Wendy, he'd understood something for the first time: if he'd married Wendy, he'd simply have come here to live and fulfilled Wendy's expectations. He'd be a fifty-year-old guy married to her, wishing he'd gone on to dental school and married someone like Jess. All he'd have done by staying with Wendy all those years ago would have been to allow someone else—someone other than Jess—to guide his life along a different path, still not the one he really wanted.

"You wanna ride with me?" Ralph asked, jolting him back to reality. The whole thing with Wendy had lasted maybe fifteen seconds, but it had reached far into Joe's heart.

"I guess I'll just follow you home, Ralph. I'll drive my truck to your place," Joe replied. "My puppy's waiting in the truck."

"See you there in a few minutes," Ralph said when he opened the driver's door of the Cadillac.

"Aren't you gonna lock up the office?" Joe asked.

"What for?" Ralph said just before he slammed his car door and started the engine.

Joe was still smiling at Ralph's lack of concern for the security of the livestock exchange when he opened his truck door and woke Jake from a long nap.

"What was I thinking?" Joe said to Jake when he scratched Jake's ears, let the clutch out slowly, and started to follow Ralph's Cadillac. He knew that in his selfish heart, he'd expected to find Wendy beautiful and unhappy because he'd chosen someone else all those years ago. He'd actually wanted her to be waiting for him to take her away from all this and live out another destiny. How could he have been so wrong and stupid? he thought. All he knew for sure was that he wouldn't be seeing Wendy Hample ever again, and that his ideas about an alternate destiny were all wrong.

Websters' Ranch looked about the same as it always had, as far as Joe could remember. After Ralph Webster and Ray Mix had made a fortune trading commodities, they'd each hired significant improvements to be made on their ranches. Ralph had remodeled the old ranch house and added several outbuildings and a new horse barn, but nothing else seemed to have changed since then.

"I gotta take a little nap, like I do every afternoon nowadays. I'm bushed, Joe," Ralph said when he reached the top of his front steps and stood on the porch. He pointed to the large grove, the outbuildings, and the woods along the creek that ran behind the house for about a mile. "You can take that pup for a long walk if you want to. Should be plenty for him to see out there." Then he shrugged, "Do what you want, but I need to have my nap. We'll eat around six."

The sun had slipped below the rolling hills to the west several hours earlier, and a large, nearly full moon was climbing into the night sky when Ralph, Joe, and Jake stepped onto the porch. The moon was casting gray shadows across a blue prairie, and a light breeze whispered through the evening.

"That was a fine steak, Ralph. Thank you!" Joe said.

"Remember that girl you brought home for dinner one time?" Ralph asked as he settled into the cedar swing on the porch.

"Which one?" Joe asked.

"The one who asked for catsup to put on her steak. Just some girlfriend from college, I suppose," Ralph laughed.

"Sure do." Joe laughed with him.

"I remember when she asked for catsup, I just knew what your dad was gonna say." Ralph still chuckled. "'Hell, no, you can't have catsup! You don't put catsup on a fine cut of meat like that!'" Ralph said with the proper gusto as he quoted Ray Mix. "He was just kiddin' that poor little girl, but she damn near started to cry."

"Yeah, I thought that was pretty funny too," Joe added. "But I remember my mother telling Dad how it wasn't funny and how he'd scared the poor girl. My girlfriend laughed about that too, Ralph, after she got to know Dad a little better. Actually, she thought the way Mom scolded Dad was funnier than what Dad did," Joe laughed.

"Whatever happened to that girl?" Ralph asked.

"Don't know. I sort of lost track of her. It was just after that when Mom got sick," Joe answered. Neither man spoke for a moment as they settled into the evening.

"You said before that I needed to know all the facts about my dad. What did you mean by that?" Joe asked.

Ralph sipped at his scotch before he answered. "I think there are some things you need to know, given the place you find yourself just now. Maybe if all this hadn't happened, you'd never have needed to know." Ralph sipped at the scotch again.

"So tell me," Joe said.

Ralph rested the tall glass of scotch on the arm of the cedar porch swing that had hung from two heavy chains on the Webster porch for seventy-five years. He leaned back into the chair and listened to the wood creak and groan as it had on thousands of other summer nights. "I don't drink much scotch anymore," he said to no one in particular. He was gathering his thoughts before he continued.

Joe sat on the porch floor and leaned against the house so Jake could curl up in his lap. He scratched Jake's ears and waited.

"Yeah, you maybe need to know a little more about just who your dad was before you wear yourself out chasing him." Ralph stopped for a moment and seemed to be choosing his words. Then he started slowly, "You know, Joe, the one thing your dad really wanted for himself was for you to come back here and take over the ranch. But he knew, he just knew this life wasn't for you."

"Wait a minute," Joe interrupted. "I told Dad that I wanted to come back here, and he made a face like he'd just stepped in something. He told me not to even think about it."

"Yeah, he told me about that many times." Ralph nodded as he spoke. "He told me how hard it was for him to push you away. But he felt so strongly that you had bigger things to accomplish than this. He wanted you here, close to him, but he knew that you needed to go on and do something bigger." Ralph paused again. "That was hard for him, Joe, really hard. He talked about that quite a bit, right here on this porch."

"He never told me that," Joe said.

"He never wanted you to feel obligated to stay. It broke his heart to see you leave. He knew it was the right thing for you, but it was breaking his heart. He wanted you here, but at the same time he was so damn proud of how well you were doing in school."

"He wanted me here? Never wanted me to feel obligated?" Joe smiled at the irony.

"Yeah, he did. But he thought that was selfish, and that it would be wrong for him to ask you to deny yourself the great things you were meant to accomplish away from here."

"Hmph. Isn't that strange? He didn't mind making me feel obligated to do something else that I didn't want to do." Joe stroked Jake's fur softly, then added, "Good thing he isn't here to see what I've done, huh?"

"Your life isn't over yet! This whole thing isn't finished!" Ralph answered.

After several quiet minutes, Ralph sipped at his scotch and leaned back on the porch swing. "Know my best memory of your dad?" Before Joe could answer, Ralph continued. "He told me over and over and over about how you used to ride on a little red rocking horse. The horse was made of plywood and rested on four springs." Ralph looked at Joe. "Do you remember it?"

"Yes," Joe said softly.

"He'd get this sappy look on his face, this great smile, and tell me how whenever the Gene Autry TV show would come on that old black-and-white TV, you'd run like somebody was chasing you to jump on that red rocking horse. You'd start rocking to beat hell, trying to catch up with Gene Autry, and you'd holler, 'Wait for me, Gene!'" Ralph stopped and smiled to himself. "Ray told me that same story a thousand times, and every time he got that same look on his face. He called you 'The Kadoka Kid.' Do you remember that?"

It was all Joe could do to answer with a soft "yes." He hadn't thought of that old red horse in years; a lifetime had passed since he'd last thought of it. But now, as Ralph told the story, he had a visceral, palpable memory of the red horse. He could feel himself rocking. He could hear the springs creaking and the wooden horse groaning softly. He could see Gene Autry and his horse Champion kicking up a cloud of dust as they rode across the old TV screen. He remembered the great thrill—the joy that little Joey Mix, The Kadoka Kid—had felt all those years ago.

"Wow, Ralph. You took me back a ways there," Joe sighed. "And I guess I never thought about what he was thinking. I was always proud of HIM."

"Yeah. I guess it's good that you're proud of your dad; we all need to be proud of our fathers. Your dad was a good man, the best friend I ever knew, but he wasn't perfect, and he sure wasn't very proud of HIS father." Ralph's tone made it clear that he had plenty more to say.

"What do you mean, Ralph?"

Even the dark blue veil of moon shadows couldn't hide the anxiety on Ralph Webster's face. He wanted to tell Joe something, but he was struggling with himself.

"What is it, Ralph? This is no time to hide something," Joe said.

"Well, yes, it may be a good time to hide something, but I'm gonna tell you anyway." Ralph tipped his scotch back, and the last ounce slid over his tongue. He closed his eyes and savored the taste for a second, then swallowed. "Like I said, there's so much more you need to know before you chase your dad any farther—so much more. Did your dad ever tell you about your grandfather?"

"Grandpa Mix? Only that he died and left Dad an orphan."

"That's what I thought, Joe." Ralph's face tightened. "That's not true. Well, it's only partly true." He shook his head slowly. "Ray's dad was a bad man—a bad man, a worthless man. The story I got from my dad was that Ray's dad used to beat him. Ray's mother, your grandmother, died real young, and nobody seemed to know much about her. Ray and your grandfather showed up in Rapid City and lived above a bar for a while. Ray grew up in a bar and on the street. His dad beat him a lot, then abandoned him. We heard later that the old man died in the silver mines in Arizona, but nobody knows for sure. Ray was about seven years old and runnin' the streets alone. My dad was a friend with the sheriff in Rapid City. He wrote to Dad and asked if we might take Ray in to live with us—give him a decent home. That's how he wound up here. Did you know that?"

"No." Joe shook his head and admitted his surprise.

"Well, I'm sorry to tell you that, Joe. I know your dad wanted that information to die with him. God forgive me, but I think you should know some of this in light of what's going on in your life."

Joe nodded "yes" in agreement. "Well, Ralph, you know, I think that down deep I've always suspected something like that. Dad was so secretive about his side of the family. He used to act like he just didn't remember things when we asked him, and Mom did the same. Maybe I just wanted to believe what he told me."

"Yeah, people do that. We all do that. We believe what others tell us because it's easy to just go ahead and believe it." Ralph sighed, then sat quietly before he continued. "If you ever want to go find out more details, you'll need to know something else, too: your dad's name wasn't always Mix. I don't remember now just what your dad's last name was. It was some long, Polish name—Kopewski or something like that. He changed it, you know, a long time ago. You can probably look it up at the courthouse in Rapid City."

"So how did it get to be Mix?" Joe asked. He was scratching his head and squinting.

Ralph smiled, then laughed openly. "I guess you'll like this," Ralph said. "After your dad came to live with us, he and I got to be pretty close, like brothers. We were still little boys. We used to go into town on Saturday night, like everyone else in those days. When it got dark enough, Mr. Miller, who owned the drugstore, used to show silent movies on the north wall of the creamery. It was a white stucco wall, so it was perfect to show movies on. People would pull up park benches and watch those old movies. 'Cept they weren't old movies then." Now it was Ralph's turn to look out across the prairie and into the past.

"My dad used to give both Ray and me a nickel, and we'd go into Millers' Drugstore and buy a Three Musketeers candy bar. We'd nibble on those things slowly and save 'em like they was gold—made 'em last all night. Anyway, one night the movie was a western. The star was Tom Mix, an old-time cowboy hero. He must have killed fifty bad guys, ridin' and shootin' and just bein' the good guy. Your dad didn't say much after the movie that night. But the next day, after church, we were having Sunday dinner, and he asked my dad if he could talk to him in private." Ralph sighed and shook his head as though he couldn't believe what he was about to say.

"Well, my dad took him into the parlor, but we could all hear him from the dinner table. I remember this because your dad made my mother cry that day." Ralph smiled at the memory of his mother. "From around the corner we heard him say, 'I don't want my dad's name no more. I was gonna ask if I could have your name, Webster, but I think I'd like to be like that man last night. He was a good man, wasn't he? I want to be a good man, like him—like Tom Mix! Can I change my name so I can be Ray Mix? I'll be a good man.' Sounded like he was promising my dad.

"My mother got all choked up and laughed and cried at the same time. I didn't understand why she was crying at the time. Maybe that's why I remember it so well." Ralph smiled. "He was a good man." Joe couldn't see Ralph's eyes, but his voice seemed far away for a moment. "He was a good man, my friend Ray, and damn he cut a wide swath through this ol' life." Then Ralph seemed to remember himself. "Did you know any of that, Joe?"

"No, never heard it before."

"Thought not. I hope it's all right that I tell you. Ray was so ashamed of his father, of what he'd done. He never spoke of it with me but once. He asked me never to tell you and Donny what I just told you."

"I'm glad you told me, Ralph."

"I don't know why, but I thought you should know that story."

"It only makes me admire him that much more."

"Joe, no one would argue that your dad was anything but a good man. I only told you that because I thought it might do you some good to know your dad a little better. But he wasn't perfect." Ralph's tone was more reluctant than before and carried the promise that he had more to share.

"You didn't know your dad as well as you think. Oh, he was a good man, that's for sure. He was a good father; he loved you boys. But he was just a man, just like you." Ralph sounded as if he were trying to convince himself.

"What are you getting at, Ralph?" Joe could hear the reluctance in Ralph's words. Ralph seemed as if he were standing in the shadow of a dark room, wanting to step into the light.

"Did your dad ever tell you how he made his money? How he got his break?" Ralph asked.

"Said he scored big in the futures market a couple times."

"That's true. And he made a fortune for ME, too. But, oh, he walked a fine line between disaster and fortune, between aggressive business tactics and thievery. He could have lost everything...everything!"

"Really?"

"Yeah. It was pretty simple, Joe. We'd been dabbling in the livestock and grain futures markets for a while after we opened the livestock business in town here. It's a pretty natural extension of the business, but it can be like playing with fire. We made a few bucks, but we were always afraid to get tangled up in the speculative sport of the futures trade. You can lose SO much money so fast! Well, anyway, we started to play the futures some, and we did make a little money. Then your dad got a little more aggressive and actually started to make some real money. You might say he was gambling, just like in a casino. Well, one thing led to another. You were in about the third grade, and your dad had a few pork-belly trades go bad on him. So he doubled his position and got back in the market—you know, he bet even more money. He thought he couldn't lose. But he lost, again. So he doubled up on that position and figured for sure the market would turn. It didn't turn, and he was about to lose everything—everything—and take the livestock exchange and me down with him. Hell, he'd lost everything. They just hadn't come and actually taken it all away yet.

"Well, about that same time, cattle prices were really low—I mean, really low—so we talked some banker from Rapid City into lending us money to fill up our feedlots. We just had to find a way to make back some of the money that he'd lost in the futures market. We figured once the market turned, we'd have cheap cattle ready to sell at higher prices.

So at that time, your dad was hiding from the futures broker in Chamberlain—not answering his phone calls, things like that. He owed way more than he could ever repay, and he borrowed about the same amount for these cattle. It was crazy! I was in debt way over my head, but your dad? It was crazy, just how strung out he was. Then, one night, we were sitting right here on this porch. We were actually waiting for the sheriff to pull in here and get us so he could start selling our things to pay our debts. We just didn't know what was gonna happen next.

"We were drinking scotch and worrying about whether we'd ever get out of the hole we were in, and Ray says, 'We're gonna go long on some cattle futures. I know the market's going up.' I thought he'd lost his mind. I said, 'Ray, we already own the damn cattle, why would we want to leverage ourselves out even further and buy more cattle futures on the board of trade? We'll make things a hundred times worse.'"

Ralph smiled again. "You should have seen his face. He looked at me and said, 'We'll make a damn fortune!' He was grinning like it was already a done deal, like the money was in our pockets. He KNEW he was right. He knew it was gonna happen. But he had to go all the way to Sioux Falls before he could find a futures broker who didn't know how strung out for cash he was. You could do that in the old days. Anyway, he bought some cattle contracts on the board of trade, and sure as hell the cattle market began to turn. He used his profit, which existed only on paper anyway, to buy more cattle futures, and so on and so on as the market went up. There was a long run-up of prices, and we rode it all the way up. Finally, we sold our live cattle and made one fortune. We sold the futures contracts and made a far bigger fortune. By that time, your dad had paid off the money he'd lost on the pork-bellies disaster, and he had a pile of money still left over. That's when he did the thing that set him up for life: he took all his profits from the cattle trades and put them back into the cattle market. Except he took a short position— you know, he sold a huge number of cattle contracts at a very high price, on the gamble that he could buy them back when the price dropped. He just knew the price of cattle was about to take a tumble! Well, the price absolutely fell out of bed, and he made another fortune ridin' the market down! He looked like a genius. That's what paid for his ranch and your college and everything he left you."

"I pretty much knew all that stuff, Ralph. Well, I didn't know he was that strung out for cash, but I knew it was a close call. Maybe that narrow line between hero and villain is the kind of thing people write books about, huh?"

"Yeah, I guess so," Ralph conceded. He was tired now, and he realized that by sharing the truth about Ray's fortune, he'd created an even bigger pedestal upon which Joe could place his father. He'd added the mystique of a schemer; he'd made Ray into a lovable rogue. Ralph's intention had been just the opposite—to allow Joe Mix to understand that his father was a man, an ordinary man, who had once been a desperate man who had just been lucky to steady himself. He just wanted to let Joe get on with whatever it was he was doing and not let his long-dead father guide his decisions any longer. Ralph would have to tell all the truth now.

"I'm tired," Ralph sighed.

"There's more to all this, isn't there?" Joe asked.

"Let's talk in the morning, Joe."

———•———

Ralph Webster's simple guest bedroom seemed more luxurious than any expensive hotel Joe had ever stayed in. Clean sheets and a warm bed felt so fine that Joe actually moaned with pleasure when he pulled the covers over himself.

He lifted Jake onto the bedspread and then put his hands behind his head as he stared up at the ceiling. The full moon was setting now; it was low in the sky, and moonbeams reached into the room through a small window.

For the first time in several days, he was really comfortable and secure. But laying himself down in this warm bed made him think briefly about his old life. And, as usual, the same regrets of the past and fears of the future began to press on him. This little bed in this little room was comfortable, but it wasn't his. Here he was, a middle-aged man sleeping in the guest room of an old friend he hadn't seen for years—and it was the only real home he could think of where he'd be welcome. He should be sleeping in his own bed, he thought, not hiding here in Ralph Webster's home. The past few days had made him feel like he'd been standing outside in bad weather looking for shelter. Well, now he'd found shelter of a sort, and that didn't seem to provide any real peace either. He had to move on, farther out into the current, and he was afraid of it. He was glad to be at Ralph's house, but he'd found only temporary relief here.

"A couple yesterdays seem like a long time ago, huh Jake?"

chapter fourteen

Jake and Joe wandered onto the porch shortly after sun-up and found Ralph sitting in the swing again, looking out over the rolling prairie. Ralph was wearing his bathrobe and slippers. What was left of his wispy gray hair was mussed, and it swayed in the soft morning breeze. Ralph looked old, and a little bit lost without his Stetson.

"Morning, Ralph."

"Morning, Ray," Ralph answered.

Joe's head turned back slightly when Ralph called him Ray. He looked at Ralph and wondered if maybe he was lost in a daydream and thought he was really talking to Ray Mix. Joe sat on the top step so he could hold Jake. There was no point in correcting Ralph, so he kept silent.

"Called you Ray, didn't I?" Ralph said after a while, as if he'd only just noticed it himself.

"Yeah," Joe said.

"Gonna be leaving today, moving on?" Ralph asked slowly.

"Yeah," Joe nodded.

"I may not see you again after today," Ralph said. He looked away from Joe and Jake.

"Shouldn't talk like that, Ralph!" Joe said.

"It's all right. I know I'm old. I don't feel good every day anymore. I have a lot of bad days. Yesterday was a good day." Ralph sighed. "I used to have a day's work done by this time when I was young. Now, it's all I can do to get out of bed and watch the sun come up."

Joe tried to look into the old man's eyes, but Ralph was staring across the plains.

"I'm worried about you, Joe! This thing you've done? It could turn out to be a good thing, but it could be all wrong, too. I don't know if I understand just what you're after, but I'm afraid you're still chasing your father, tryin' to satisfy him. Think I could be right, Joe?"

"No. Maybe. Yes. Hmph, I don't know."

"He was just a man, Joe, but no better than you. I loved him, and I miss him every day still. But he was no better than you, maybe not as good."

"What do you mean?"

"I mean when he risked everything it was easy for him; he didn't have much. What the hell difference would it make if he lost it? All that crap about integrity? It was important, it was good, it was a nice thought, but it would have all been so much bullshit if he'd gone down financially. His creditors would have been screwed. He'd have ruined some other lives besides his. I don't think he could have climbed out of that hole. Maybe he was brilliant, maybe he was lucky, but his integrity was riding on a bet—a big bet.

"But you...look at you. You went out and did something that not every man could do, and then you left the money behind to go look for something better. Hell, your dad would wish he was you. I wish I was you!" Ralph tightened his brow and looked at Joe. "You're a better man than you know just yet."

"I left my wife, Ralph. I failed at marriage. I failed at marriage."

Ralph shook his head slowly. His eyes were dark, hard, and set, his face tightened. "OK, Joe. You think you need to start out poor in order to justify your fortune if you ever make one. That's all right, I guess. Maybe it even makes some sense. But do I have to take another treasure away from you—make you bankrupt on another, deeper level—to get you to see the world clearly for the first time?" Ralph seemed upset, and he brought both hands to his face as though he was sorry for what he'd said, or was about to say. Joe had never seen such a gesture, and such reluctance, from Ralph.

"What is it, Ralph?"

"Your dad died in my arms. He was the one great friend of my life, and I swore I'd never tell." Ralph stopped and rubbed his eyes again. "I thought about this all night."

Then his eyes turned calm and still, as though a storm had passed, and he looked at Joe. He folded his arms across his chest. Behind Ralph's eyes, Joe could see that he'd found the words he was searching for: "Your father loved another woman, and the stress of hiding it all is what killed him."

Joe's face lost all expression.

"It's true, Joe. When your mother was so sick for those last couple years and he took care of her…that was terrible for him. He loved your mother, and it broke his heart and spirit the way she withered and died." The thin gray hairs on top of Ralph's head stood straight up in the tiny breeze. He raised the collar on his bathrobe and waited for Joe to respond.

"I don't believe it," Joe snapped.

"Well, it's true. I wish it wasn't, but it is," Ralph said softly.

"Bullshit! Not the Old Cowboy. Not Ray Mix. Not my dad!" The anger in Joe's voice rose.

"Maybe I shouldn't have told you." Ralph looked away. "But it's true."

"How do you know?"

"Ray Mix was my friend. In many ways, I was closer to him than you were. He sat right here and told me everything. It's true, Joe. It's true."

Joe put his left hand on his forehead, rubbed his scalp for a moment, and let the truth settle in. He knew Ralph Webster wouldn't lie to him. Then he slumped visibly.

"Jesus, Ralph, why would you tell me that? Why would you tell me that now?" Joe asked softly.

"I told you, Joe. You're about to go off chasing a dead man, trying to live up to something that never existed. You had to know this. I guess if you'd stayed in your old life, you'd have had no need to know. Oh, hell, I don't know…maybe I shouldn't have told you, but Ray Mix was just a man. Maybe all this was easier for Ray—ever think of that? He didn't have any false dreams to live up to. He was just trying to be a good man, lead the best life he could. He deserves all your love and respect just because he was your father, and he was a good father; he loved you. But he was just a man, like any other man."

"So why did he do it? What happened?" Joe asked.

"Like I said, his heart was breaking," Ralph said.

"So he found a girlfriend?"

"It's not that easy, and you of all people should be starting to get a feel for just how easy life ISN'T. I suppose there are plenty of people wondering how you could do what you did!" Ralph waited for Joe's response, and when none came he continued. "He met a woman who'd lost her husband. Her husband was a rancher from out west of here a ways. Your dad met her at a bank of all places. She was a fine woman, and she was lonely too. They started out as friends. Then one thing led to another. She had integrity too, Joe. She was a good person. They were just two lonely people, and they needed each other."

"How do you know all this?" Joe asked with a scowl. He looked as if he wanted to cover his ears and hear no more.

"Because your dad and I sat right here, where you and I are now, and talked about it many times. Many times," Ralph explained.

"I thought he loved my mother," Joe blurted again. He was spitting out fragments of thoughts as they came to him.

"He did, Joe. You know that. And don't you dare start judging your father now either. Can you imagine the feelings he was having? No, I doubt you can. He nursed your mom at home, and he ran a business. You and Donny were both in school. He was so lonesome." Ralph stopped and looked at Joe, questioning him, asking for understanding. "After your mom died, I thought your dad would marry Rose—that was her name, Rose. But your dad died so soon after your mother." Ralph sighed. "I wish you could have heard some of the things he said right here on this porch. I thought the guilt and shame of hiding his feelings for Rose might kill him. I suppose it did. But he did love Rose, and that was a good thing for him." Ralph paused to consider his own words. "Yeah," Ralph added, "after some healing, I thought for sure he'd marry Rose.

"Rose couldn't even come to your dad's funeral. She said she was afraid someone would have seen her grief and figured it all out. She told me she sat in her car and watched. Can you imagine how she felt?"

Both men sat silently for several minutes.

"That was the hardest time in my life, Joe," Ralph said.

"Mine too, up till now," Joe said. Neither one of them was really talking to the other.

"There was so much death. Your dad was just sitting next to me at the office, and he slumped over and died. I guess that was when I started looking for meaning in all this, sort of like you are now."

"So did you find any…meaning?" Joe asked after a while.

"Yes. I guess so. But I'm glad I had a lot of time—a long life, I mean."

"What did you find?" Joe asked. "Where's the meaning in all this?"

"Hmmm," Ralph sighed. "That's the hard part, isn't it? For one man to explain the meaning of it all to another man. It's probably a little different for each of us, too! For me, the meaning exists in little pictures of the moments of my life. I feel love, and hate, and I can smell and feel things, but there are no words to go with my pictures. I don't think words would give them meaning. I think words might even make the picture vanish, so I'll keep them to myself." Ralph grinned and tilted his head. "Maybe that's what you're bound to do, son. Maybe you'll find the right words so you can pass them along to others."

Ralph stood up and shuffled inside the house. When he returned a few minutes later, he was fully dressed and wearing his Stetson and alligator boots. The Stetson was tilted about five degrees to the right.

"It's a good day for boots!" Ralph announced to Joe. He stepped close to Joe and hugged him. "You need to be on your way, Joe. You're a good man. And your father was a good man. He always did the best he could. That's all you can ask of a man." Ralph stepped back from Joe. "I may not see you again, son. I'm sorry if I told you something I shouldn't have. I truly am."

"You're a good man, Ralph." The words brought a lump to Joe's throat, and he embraced Ralph once more. Joe felt like he had his arms around his dad. He knew he'd never feel this feeling again, and he held Ralph tightly. "My dad would thank you for telling me. He would, Ralph. He would!"

"I hope so, boy. I hope you find what you're looking for, too!"

"I love you, Ralph," Joe whispered before his chest heaved once. "I always have, always will."

"I love you too, Joe." Ralph stroked Joe's back with one hand and squeezed him with the other. "Ray would be proud of you. But he's gone, and you can't spend the rest of your life trying to make a dead man more proud of you."

Joe nodded and stepped back from Ralph. He walked to the truck, with Jake bouncing along at his heels. When he'd started the truck, he turned toward Ralph and raised his left hand. "Bye, Ralph," he said as the truck started to roll forward.

Ralph raised his hand with the same gesture. "The Kadoka Kid!"

During the drive from Ralph's house into town, all the ghosts of Joe Mix's childhood had been shouting for him to take one last drive through Kadoka before he returned to the road.

When he turned north onto Main Street, he felt the ruins of the Kadoka Livestock Exchange brush by as if they were reaching for him. Then he turned for a glance at the Stockman's Café. Then Bully's. And then they were all behind him.

He began to feel that this Kadoka, the one he was traveling through right now, was part of his present life—and that oddly enough, the old Kadoka, the little town of his childhood, was somehow separate, gone forever, and it existed only in his past.

Joe crept north on Main Street one more time. He made a point to look away from the Clover Farm Grocery when he rolled by it.

Just as he was about to accelerate and leave Kadoka behind, one last lingering memory flashed through his mind. He cramped the wheel and turned sharply into a parking stall in front of Backer's Western and Fleet Store. He walked quickly inside and found a young clerk. The kid looked like a Backer, Joe thought. Old Man Backer had died a few years earlier, and his son was a few years older than Joe...so this must be a grandson of Old Man Backer. "Can I help you?" the kid said.

"Are you a Backer?" Joe asked.

"Yes. I'm Dean Backer." The kid extended his hand.

"Joe Mix," Joe said as he shook hands.

The young man's face went blank. "From around here?" he asked.

"I used to live here, a long time ago," Joe sighed.

The kid just smiled and waited for Joe to continue; he wasn't interested enough to ask Joe any more.

"I'm looking for a hat. A cowboy hat. You know the kind of hat that Robert Duvall wore in *Lonesome Dove*?"

"Oh, a 'Gus' hat! Sure, we can do that!"

The floor inside Backer's was hardwood, like an old gymnasium, and it creaked when the men walked over to the hats and found a light gray Stetson made of 4x beaver that fit Joe perfectly. Dean Backer remained uninterested in conversation with Joe, but he steamed the hat, and worked it, and steamed it some more until it had the shape and look of a "Gus" hat.

Joe watched silently for twenty minutes while the Backer kid, who didn't care who Joe was and didn't particularly want to talk to him, steamed his hat. It was all right to have lived here once. And now, it was all right to let it all go, too.

The wooden floor creaked under Joe's feet as he walked from the back of the store to the front. He stepped through the open front door of Backer's Western Store into the bright May morning, wearing his new hat. Forty-five years had passed since he'd told his father he wasn't interested in any more hats. Today, finally, after all these years, maybe he'd start to pick a few things up where he'd left them so long ago.

chapter **fifteen**

"So how do I look, Jake?" Joe asked the yellow puppy sitting on the seat next to him as he let the clutch out and started rolling down the entrance ramp onto I-90.

Jake tilted his head one way, then the other, then passed along the bewildered look that dogs do.

"Hard to find the right words, isn't it?" Joe said to Jake the dog. Then Joe leaned to the right and looked at himself in the truck's rearview mirror. "Handsomer than shit! That's what I'd say," Joe nodded.

Kadoka was disappearing beyond the horizon behind him when Joe reached his right hand over and began to rub Jake's belly. Jake simply rolled onto his back and tried to chew on Joe's thumb. "That little stop didn't exactly settle anything, did it, Jake?"

In short order, Jake was asleep with his muzzle resting beside Joe's thigh as the truck bounced westward along the interstate highway. Joe had taken I-90 west in order to put some miles behind him. He needed to be far from Kadoka, and he was so deep in his thoughts that he didn't even notice the road noise that had bothered him before. All the events of the previous week kept darting through his mind in a continuous, tumbling mass of unrelated memories.

He tried to imagine his father in the arms of another woman. Then he tried not to think about it. He was angry at his father for being unfaithful to his mother. Then he wondered if he was more angry at his father for being unfaithful to him and his memories.

Joe thought of his mother withering for several years while Ray took care of her. He couldn't help but wonder if his mother knew about the other woman, Rose. And what about Rose? If his father had loved her, she must have been a good woman. But how could she allow herself to come between two married people? What kind of person would do that? Joe remembered the way they'd all stood around at his mother's funeral, and then his father's funeral. He tried to imagine where Rose had been—if he'd noticed her, looked right at her maybe, and just not seen her. Joe considered calling Ralph and asking for Rose's last name so he could go and learn something more about her. He wondered what she looked like, and he wanted to see a photo of her. But after a moment of reflection, he knew he had to let it be. He'd never know her anyway, and he didn't need to. It all just needed to be over. Shit, why did I have to find out about all this? Joe wondered. A son wasn't supposed to have to rewrite his father's life story twenty-five years after his death.

The way Ray had risked his integrity for money began to bother Joe after a while too. He'd known a little of Ray's close call between rags and riches. But now that he understood the way Ray had risked everything, even his integrity, for money, Joe saw his father in a little different light.

Did Ray have to be a hero, or was it enough to simply be Joe's father? Was it all right for Joe to love his father simply because he was his father? Oddly enough, it was getting to be easy to love Ray with a deeper, more compassionate love now that he'd stepped down off that pedestal.

Joe hoped his boys could come to the same understanding someday.

And Wendy, what about her? He'd wanted to use his father's legacy, the warmth of his hometown, even the lost love of an old girlfriend as parts of a cornerstone upon which to build a new life, and it hadn't worked. It was no good to rewrite the past. It had all become so muddled and confusing—he'd just have to let it all be the past; that was enough.

The inside of the truck grew warmer, but the road noise remained apart from all the thoughts rolling around in his head. Joe felt he might run out of road before he found the answers to his questions. The current he'd always been so afraid of seemed to be rolling him down this road, too, lost and maybe out of control.

Faster traffic streamed past Joe and Jake as they bounced and plodded along on Interstate 90. While he'd been driving, Joe had gradually sequestered all of his thoughts, memories, and expectations and taken them to that place somewhere behind his eyes. He was driving through traffic, and the country around him was changing from the flat, rolling hills of the eastern Dakotas to the more rugged landscape of the western plains. He could assign part of his brain to drive the truck, to navigate the highway, and maybe to notice the world changing, but the rest of his brain was busy trying to make sense of all this new information. It was as if the man organizing the incompatible ideas and experiences chasing around in Joe's head was a separate person from the man driving the truck.

Jake's needs for water, food, and exercise gradually became a welcome distraction for Joe. Whenever Jake needed to stop, Joe was forced to shut down that place in his mind where he was wrestling with himself. He had to emerge and play with a puppy, who had become his only friend. Jake needed Joe right now, not later when Joe got around to it. At every stop, Joe would open the cooler and withdraw a diet soda. At the rest stops, he'd walk Jake into the tall grass or shrubs provided for pets, and he'd play with Jake, and he'd talk to Jake while he drank his soda. Joe didn't take the time to read to Jake today. He was impatient to get farther down the road, and he didn't feel like reading or relaxing. Even though he felt a need to get back in the truck and think—just think, and drive—Joe was thankful for the change of scenery that came with each stop. For just a few minutes, he was able to play like a little boy, and he found himself laughing out loud at Jake's enthusiasm.

About an hour before sunset, Joe began to search for a place to spend the night. He'd found no great insight or understanding after a day of thought. He was tired, really tired, and once again he felt like he'd been standing outside in a storm.

South Dakota had become Wyoming a couple hours earlier, and the country had become even more rugged. A small road crossed under the interstate and ran along a pretty little river up ahead. When Joe slowed down to exit I-90, Jake's head lifted off Joe's lap, and the yellow puppy began to look out the window and wag his tail. He could sense a change coming. About a mile down the narrow blacktop road, Joe found a gravel parking area overlooking the little river. Several dozen large cottonwood trees surrounded the place, and Joe decided to spend the night there. He didn't know if it was legal to sleep there, and he didn't care.

A cold supper of potato chips and a sandwich from the cooler didn't do much to help Joe's sense of well-being. He sat on the ground by the riverbank and opened his last bottle of diet soda while Jake attacked a dead tree branch laying beside him.

"Shit, Jake. Do you know what's going on here?"

Jake gnawed at the tree branch.

"You don't even know your name yet, do you?"

Jake looked at Joe, bounced back from the tree, then pounced on the branch again.

"You're a poor listener, Jake. But I need to ask you something, so listen up." Joe took a drink from the soda and leaned forward so his elbows rested on his knees. "You think I'm nuts? You think I pissed away everything? You think I shoulda stayed at home and tried to find a way to make it work? Just be a better dentist and a better husband?" He took another sip of soda. "Well, I'm beginning to wonder."

Jake made a hideous wretching sound and vomited up three cigarette butts. "I'll take that for a no," Joe smiled.

The sun had disappeared beyond the hills, and like every other sunset recently, this one was followed by fear, loneliness, self-doubt, and all the demons that tempted Joe to go back home. He had no place to go and no friends. He had no useful skills except for dentistry. The only job he could get with a degree in dentistry was doing dentistry, and that was out of the question, wasn't it? So what was he to do, really? How could he pull this off? This leaving home and finding something better might have been just a tragically dumb idea after all. The more he thought about it all, the closer he moved to despair.

Joe took his cell phone from his pocket and turned it on. As the phone came to life, it beeped and played several musical notes. Jake stopped playing with his stick and looked at Joe's cell phone and the hand holding it. He'd noticed the noise from the phone, and his head spun to look at it. He hunched over, dropped to his belly, and started to slink like a predator about to attack the phone. "Whadya think, Jake? Think I should call Donny and talk about surrender? Think I should talk to him about calling this off and coming home?" Jake took the stealthy posture of a killer about to spring and watched Joe's hand working the cell phone. As Joe punched in the numbers, the phone made small beeping noises, and with each beep Jake's ears twitched. "OK, Jake. Do we call Donny? I mean, really! Do you know where all this is headed? Am I just an old wannabe hippie who's flipped out?" Joe's own words made him sad.

Joe turned his hand and pointed the phone at Jake's face as though Jake might actually have something to say. "So what is it? Yes or no?"

Jake leaped at the phone. His mouth was open and his ears were back. One of his teeth actually hit a key on the keypad and made a beep. Joe flinched and pulled the phone back, laughing as he lost his balance, and rolled onto his side. Jake immediately forgot about the phone and rushed to Joe's face. He licked, and barked his tiny bark, and bounced back away from Joe so he could set himself to leap again.

"So was that a yes or a no?" Joe laughed.

Jake leaped again, this time content to chew on Joe's fingers while Joe held the phone up with the other hand.

"Looks like you have some time to think about it. We don't have a signal here anyway," Joe said, and then put the phone back in his pocket.

———·———

When the dark of night was deepest, an intermittent breeze blew through the cottonwood boughs above him, and Joe settled onto the plastic chair in the back of the truck. If only the leaves had already opened up for spring, they could have whispered to him as he laid there and tried to sleep. Ray Mix, the Old Cowboy, moved in and out of Joe's thoughts as he closed his eyes and tried to sleep. Ray was followed by Jess, Ralph Webster, Chris and Ben, Wendy, the dental office, and Kadoka. It was no use to try to sleep. Joe opened his eyes and put both hands behind his head. He drew in a deep breath, searching for the smell of the yellow puppy lying against his chest. "What have I done, Jake?" he whispered.

chapter
sixteen

The sign read "Ranchester," and an arrow pointed to the south. "I need a hot meal. How 'bout you?" Joe said to a sleeping Jake when he pulled off the interstate.

Several eighteen-wheelers and a handful of pickup trucks surrounded a small diner along the road just outside of Ranchester, Wyoming. Joe had always assumed that truckers all knew where to find good food, and that they shared that information freely with each other—and so if he saw trucks by a small restaurant, he knew it was probably a good place to stop.

The Ford raised a thin dust cloud that swirled into the cab, and the gravel in the parking lot crunched under his wheels when he rolled to a stop outside Ike's Café. Wyoming seemed even drier than South Dakota. He thought it was too early in the spring to be so dry.

Joe fed and watered Jake, then took him for a long walk in the tall grass on a hillside overlooking the road. As Joe and Jake walked back to the truck, Joe bent over and picked up an old shoe that lay along the shoulder of the road, next to the restaurant parking lot. "Ever wonder why you just see one shoe laying on the road, Jake?" he asked as he dangled the shoe in front of Jake. "S'pose there's somebody rolling down the road right now wondering what the hell happened to their other shoe?" Jake snatched the scuffed, brown-leather shoe away from Joe and pranced away with it held high, like a treasure.

"You think about that while I go eat," Joe said, then lifted Jake and the shoe onto the truck seat and rolled down the window. Jake shook the shoe so hard he fell off the truck seat and onto the floorboards, then curled up around the shoe and began to chew on the toe.

Before he reached the café, Joe could see through the screen door, and he noticed a row of wide-bodied, overweight truckers sitting on round stools that were fixed to the floor in front of a long counter. When the wooden screen door slammed behind Joe, one of the truckers turned around to see who was there, and when he saw Joe he simply turned back to his meal.

Joe seated himself at a small booth and looked around the place quickly. There were several other empty booths and several tables occupied by ranchers wearing cowboy hats and talking just low enough so that Joe couldn't pick up any of what they were saying. He put his elbows on the table and cupped his hands over his face. As he rubbed his face, his cowboy hat lifted up off his brow, and he was reminded that he was wearing it. He liked wearing it. He thought he looked good with it on, but he knew he was an imposter sitting in a room full of real cowboys. He wondered if the cowboys around him knew it too. He rubbed his face again to massage the fatigue out of his head.

While his hands were covering his eyes, he could hear a truck engine shifting gears and accelerating, moving out into traffic, and then another truck crunching gravel and slowing to a stop in the parking lot. It was odd, he thought, to have only a screen door on the front of a restaurant; it let in so much of the outside world.

Joe leaned back in the booth, still rubbing his face, and stretched his back. When he finally took his hands from his face, there was a young woman standing next to his booth with a notepad, waiting to take his order.

"Tired?" she asked as if she'd caught him sleeping in school.

Joe smiled a sheepish smile. "A little," he answered.

"Want some coffee?" the woman asked with no enthusiasm. She wasn't really that interested in Joe or what he wanted.

"Yeah, that'd be good," Joe said, and the woman turned to get the coffee.

While Joe waited for her to return, he scanned the other booths. The men all looked like truckers and ranchers. The ranchers appeared to be doing business among themselves, but Joe had no way to know for sure. The truckers were all quiet, alone with their meals.

"What would you like?" the woman said when she placed Joe's coffee on the table.

"A big hamburger and some fries, Diet Coke," Joe said.

The woman turned away without a smile, and Joe reached for the newspaper that rested on the booth behind him. He was flipping through the paper, trying to get a glimpse of just what life was like here in Ranchester, when he heard another truck roll to a stop in the parking lot. He was searching for some respite from the worry of finding something—a job, a place, a person, some meaning to his life—before he ran out of road, or money. The worry over what he'd done was never far from his mind. He was glad he hadn't called Donny last night. He had felt better about things this morning when he woke up. But now, sitting here, separated from the lives of all the people around him in the diner and far away from everything he was familiar with, his mood flip-flopped and he began to feel lonesome again. He wondered if maybe he should call Donny after all and talk about coming back. What else could he do? He knew—he just knew in his heart—that he shouldn't go back and didn't want to go back. But where was he to go?

The voice startled Joe. "Hey, Virginia!" the man called loudly from the screen door. "I'm a little ripe today!" Joe looked up to see a large man wearing filthy clothing standing just outside the screen door. The man used his thumb and index finger to pinch his own shirt and pull it away from his chest while he made a face. He smiled and continued. "Can you make me a sandwich? I'll eat it out here so I don't drive everyone away."

"Sure, Mike!" the waitress called from behind the counter. "I'll bring it out."

"Thanks, Virginia! I'll be sittin' in the shade."

With that, the man disappeared around the side of the café and sat at a picnic table in a small shady area beside the restaurant.

Joe's eyes moved out across the gravel parking lot, and then he understood why the man had said what he'd said to the waitress, and why she'd smiled: the man in the dirty clothes had driven up in a rendering truck. Apparently, he was a driver assigned to go out to area ranches and pick up dead animals. He'd been gracious enough to park his truck as far from the restaurant as possible. Joe could see into the back of the rendering truck from where he sat, and it appeared to be about half full. A tangled, grisly mass of hooves and bloated carcasses lay strewn about inside the cargo box of the truck, and it was all visible from the café window.

Joe had to smile. This was such a strange vignette of the rural west—a guy parks a truckload of dead, stinking cattle outside a restaurant full of cowboys, then orders a sandwich from outside the restaurant because he stinks so bad himself that he knows he can't come in, and the waitress smiles at him like he's an old boyfriend. Maybe he was an old boyfriend. Then he'll just ignore his own stench and have a pleasant meal in the shade. The dimple on Joe's cheek deepened as he smiled and sipped the coffee.

Joe couldn't help but remember the guy who'd driven the rendering truck around Kadoka. His name was Nooky Steinke, and just the thought of him sent Joe's memory racing back to his childhood days on his father's ranch. Joe and Donny had watched in amazement many times as Nooky had interrupted their play, or work, parked his truck by the barn, then stepped out of the cab and walked around to the back of the truck. A heavy winch was mounted inside the box of the big dump truck. Nooky would get into the box of the truck and then make his way from the back of the truck to the front, crawling over whatever sort of dead critters were in the box until he'd reached the winch cable at the front. Then he'd unlock the winch and pull the cable back across the rotting cargo in the truck until he reached the back. He'd then jump down onto the ground and fasten the cable onto the unlucky animal he'd come to pick up. Once the winch cable was secured to the dead cow or horse, Nooky would climb back up inside the truck and crawl over the dead critters until he got up to the front of the truck once again, where the winch controls were mounted. He'd turn on the electric winch and haul his fare into the box. At last, he could loosen the cable from the dead animal and jump out of the box—unless there were more customers waiting, in which case he repeated the whole process for each critter that needed a ride to the rendering plant. Nooky always smelled bad—real bad. Joe laughed out loud at the memory of Nooky Steinke climbing over dead cattle. Then he laughed even louder when he remembered Nick Steinke, the drunk he'd seen stumble out of Bully's Bar all those years ago—Nooky's brother. Maybe somewhere there was a Mrs. Steinke who had two little boys, Nick and Nooky.

Joe's cell phone rang while he was still laughing. When he saw that it was Donny calling, a tiny wave of uncertainty flickered through him. Last night he'd nearly called Donny and undone everything. This morning, when he'd woken and looked around at the little stand of cottonwoods by the river, he'd been relieved that he hadn't been able to talk to Donny in a moment of weakness. During a fine sunrise this morning, as he'd walked with Jake and then driven back along that little road along that river, he'd thought about how it would feel to be driving back to the office. The memory of driving around, wishing he wasn't going to the office, made him sick. He knew he'd done the right thing in leaving, and he was thankful for his failure to contact Donny last night. Seeing that the call was from Donny only reminded him of his worry and apprehension over his future, but he was still glad he wasn't back in his old life.

"Hi, Donny!" Joe answered.

"I was getting worried, Joe. It's been two days."

Joe could tell immediately, by the edge in his tone, that Donny had something important to say. This was the tone of voice that delivered bad news.

"Yeah, I had a nice day with Ralph Webster, and I just didn't get around to calling. I couldn't get a signal yesterday. Sorry." He waited for Donny to tell him whatever it was he had to say.

"Where you at, Joe?" Donny asked. He had no time or inclination for chitchat.

"Ranchester, Wyoming. A little café on the…"

"You need to get back here right now!" Donny snapped.

"What's the matter? Are the boys all right?"

"Yes. They're fine. But the Minnesota Board of Dental Examiners is going to take your license away if you don't get back here. Soon!"

"Oh?"

"They're going to charge you with abandonment. Do you understand?"

"Yes."

"They're going to take your license away because you abandoned your patients. That's serious shit, Joe! Unless you're here to meet with a couple of those guys next week, explain this, and offer to get some couch time, they're gonna take your license away. So put an end to this bullshit and get back here! Enough of this happy horseshit! This is for real. Do you understand?"

"Listen, Donny!" Joe's voice rose in volume and carried a ring of anger and stress. "I know this is for real!" Joe stood up beside his booth and raised his voice even louder. "I'm the guy that's living it! Every fuckin' night when I try to fall asleep, I look around me and know how real it is!" Several of the cowboys seated at the other side of the café turned and looked at him. "Now, you listen to me! And you understand this! I'm not comin' back!" Joe was pacing alongside his booth now and stabbing his index finger in front of himself as if he were trying to poke Donny in the chest. "Listen, Donny. Listen to ME! I can't believe you said that! There will be no going back!" Then he paused for a moment and felt himself swallow. "In 1519, when Hernan Cortez reached the new world, he assembled his men on the shore and made them watch while he had their ships burned! He made it clear that there would be no retreat! Now we're gonna burn the goddamn ships! Understand? No retreat! You tell 'em I don't give a shit what THEY'RE gonna do! This is what I'M gonna do. I don't care if I'm broke and homeless—I'm not comin' back! YOU UNDERSTAND?"

"Goddammit, Joe! Dad would roll over in his grave if he knew what you were doing!"

"WHAT!! WHAT DID YOU SAY TO ME?" Joe shouted, challenging Donny to repeat himself. Everyone in the diner turned to look at Joe. Donny's words had triggered anger that Joe had never felt toward his brother. Joe stomped out the screen door and into the dusty parking lot.

"You heard me!" Donny said, returning Joe's challenge. "The Cowboy would shit if he could see you now. He'd roll over in his grave! You're letting everyone down—your boys, yourself, and your dad!"

The anger inside Joe boiled over, and he felt the heat flash up into his face. As he began to speak, his strides grew longer and faster and heavier. He was walking toward the rendering truck, and his anger had stolen the awareness of everything but this phone conversation. All the cowboys and truckers, even the waitresses and the cook inside Ike's Café, were watching Joe now. Each of his steps kicked up a small cloud of dust, and they thought he looked like he was trying to hurt the ground, he was walking so hard.

"Goddammit, Donny! Don't you EVER, FUCKING EVER, tell ME about the Cowboy again! YOU GOT THAT? FUCKING NEVER!"

Joe Mix seethed with white-hot anger. He skipped once as he wound up his throwing arm, like a baseball pitcher, and his boots kicked up another cloud of dust as he hopped into his throwing motion. He threw the cell phone as hard as he'd ever thrown anything. He stumbled forward when he let go of the phone, and it rocketed toward the rendering truck. It glanced off a hoof protruding from the tangled mass of bodies that pointed to the sky, then exploded against the inside of the truck. Joe stopped in his tracks and bent over with his hands on his knees. He was more angry now than when he had left Jess. "Fuckin' Donny," he hissed. Then he picked up a rock and threw it after the phone. He was shaking and breathing heavily. The silence in the dusty parking lot was all Joe could hear for a moment, and then the anger began to drain from him.

He had nothing now—no ideas, no place, no friends, no Donny, no phone. Just Jake and the truck. He stood up straight and stared into the midday sun. Now what? Everything was suddenly so quiet. The anger had flashed, and now it had receded, below the boiling point, anyway. It was just sliding out of him, away from him. Joe walked slowly back toward the café. Just before he reached the screen door, his waitress appeared. She was carrying a paper sack, and she walked right past him without comment while she delivered the sandwich to the stinky guy driving the rendering truck. She put her eyes down slowly, as if she was afraid of Joe.

When Joe sat down at his booth, he covered his face with his hands once more and breathed a huge sigh. He stared at the table in front of him. What was happening? How could Donny say something like that? How could his father go and change on him? How could his marriage have turned out so wrong? How could he have found a career he hated as much as he hated dentistry? Jesus, how could he plug away at all that stuff for most of his life before he hit the wall? How could he find himself sitting here like this?

"Your burger is ready, mister. Are you all right?" His waitress was standing next to him holding his meal and a bottle of catsup. She tried to smile a timid smile. She still seemed afraid of him.

"Yeah. I'm OK. I'm sorry for the commotion!" Joe apologized. Then he smiled weakly and gave her permission to relax.

"It's OK." The woman smiled finally. "I never seen anyone do that with a phone!" She was still smiling when she walked away.

Joe took a sip from the water at his table and stared at his hamburger. He wasn't very hungry anymore. He pushed the plate away, put both elbows on the table, and then brought his right hand up to support his chin. Now what? he wondered.

———

Room-temperature french fries seemed like they'd just come from the freezer. They tasted flat, with a mushy texture, and he wanted to spit them out. The catsup and salt added just enough taste to overcome the unpleasantness of cold fries. Joe wasn't sure how long he'd stared at his food, but only one table full of cowboys remained in the diner. All the others had left the café and gone back to work. When the phone call with Donny had ended, he'd come down from some sort of anger-inspired high and remained all alone in his tiny world there in the booth. He'd sat there and considered his life, as it lay around him in smoking ruins, for a while—he wasn't sure how long. Then he'd sort of slipped into neutral. He just sat there and stared until he snapped out of it.

The hamburger wasn't too bad cold, but damn, the fries were hard to eat. Joe decided that the next one would be his last. As he raised it to his mouth, he noticed that the last table full of cowboys was leaving the diner—except for one guy.

A large man, a shade over six feet tall, was walking toward Joe's booth. The man looked to be about sixty-five, but he moved like a much younger man. He was bowlegged and had the swagger of the old cattlemen. His shirt was white, with pearl snaps. His Stetson was tilted just a bit to the right. It was clear he'd been working earlier in the day because his jeans and his shirt were marked with several dirt smears, and his boots were scuffed. He walked up beside Joe's booth and stood there for only a second before he spoke.

"That your truck?" he asked. Then he pointed to the Ford.

Now what? Joe thought. He leaned back in his booth and looked at the man before he nodded. "Yes," he answered softly.

"Lookin' for some heavy weather?" The man smiled, but only with his eyes. He was referring to the snowplow.

"Well," Joe sighed, "you never know when things are gonna turn to shit."

"Can I join you?" the man asked as his weathered face bent into a grin.

Joe gestured for him to sit on the other side of the booth.

"Jim Crossman," the man said as he sat down and extended his hand.

"Joe Mix," Joe answered, then shook his hand.

"I couldn't help but overhear some of your conversation," Crossman offered.

"Sorry."

"It's OK. I seen worse." Crossman smiled. "Hell, I've done worse. But from what I heard—and I truly wasn't listening on purpose—you was talkin' pretty loud..."

"Sorry." Joe smiled and shrugged.

"Like I said, it's OK. But I couldn't help but notice that you were a man of conviction...and no job, nor place of your own?"

"Maybe." Joe furrowed his brow and tilted his head. His eyes asked Crossman just why he'd want to know about that—just why he thought that was any of his business.

Crossman leaned back and showed Joe the palms of his hands. His gesture implied that he really didn't care much about Joe's past, and that he was getting to something else.

"I run some cattle up in Montana, and I'm short of hands—real short. I came down here this morning to get two of my boys outta jail. But it looks like they're gonna be spending the summer indoors, if you know what I mean."

"Yeah. But so what?" Joe asked bluntly.

"So if you can sit a horse, I can put you to work. You can do other work than slammin' doors and throwin' phones, can't you?"

"Yeah." Joe squinted at Crossman for a long minute. "You're offering me a job...as a ranch hand, a cowboy?"

"Yeah, temporary."

"But you don't even know me." Joe stared.

"I ain't lookin' for a brain surgeon," Crossman said quickly. "I got work to do and I'm short of help."

The dimple appeared, and Joe answered Crossman with a grin.

"You can sit a horse?" Crossman asked.

Joe nodded. "It's been a while." He thought thirty years since his last time in the saddle qualified as "a while."

"You can do work?"

Joe nodded again.

"Police ain't lookin' for you?"

Joe shook his head and smiled.

"When can you start?"

"Let's go!" Joe answered.

Crossman took a napkin from the table and drew a map so Joe could find the Crossman ranch. He wrote his name and phone number on the napkin too, then looked at Joe and chuckled. "Lotta good that's gonna do you; your dern phone is gonna be soap on a rope before long." As the two men stood to leave, Crossman snatched Joe's lunch ticket out of his hand and walked to the cash register. "I gotta tell you, Joe Mix, I enjoyed your phone call more than anything I seen in a long time." He was still laughing after he paid for Joe's lunch. "I hope you wasn't talkin' to a friend," Mr. Crossman offered as they walked together across the gravel parking lot.

"Nah," Joe mumbled, "fuckin' lawyer!"

"Oh," Mr. Crossman chuckled, "that explains it."

"Hey, Mr. Crossman?" Joe called out as he opened the door to his truck. "I have a dog here, a puppy! Is that all right?"

"I'll be keepin' you pretty busy during the day! But I'm sure my daughter-in-law will be happy to take care of that yellow pup!" Crossman said as his truck rolled out into the road.

This was all pretty odd, Joe thought while he fed Jake a handful of his leftover french fries. The exchange with Donny still bothered him. On the heels of everything else that had happened during the previous weeks, it had touched off an explosion. Joe didn't regret the explosion either; he was still angry with Donny for the things he'd said. It was bad enough that he'd said them at all, but he'd spoken in ignorance, and he was smug in the certainty of his position. Joe had heard his little brother talking down to him, explaining the situation. It was a situation that Donny didn't even understand. Anger rose slightly in Joe's chest every time he heard the tone of Donny's voice playing in his mind. "Fuckin' Donny," Joe growled. "I guess we'll just see about hurrying back. Huh, Jake?"

The abandonment thing? Well, that would be OK too, probably. Even though he was uncertain—no, actually he was afraid of the future—he knew now, after the words he'd heard himself holler at Donny, that he would never return to dentistry. The divorce thing? That would just have to be whatever it would be too, he thought. The demons that usually assaulted him at night, before bed, were circling him right now because of Donny's words. But he was determined, more determined than ever, to go ahead and find his way. "Damn, this road is long and empty," he said after a few minutes of silence.

Crossman's map fluttered in Joe's hand. His ranch seemed like it should be a fairly easy place to find. But why had Crossman come to him? And now what? If he'd thought about it at all over the past week, he'd sort of assumed that he'd find a job selling something he knew about, like medical supplies. Maybe he'd get a real estate or securities license and deal with money somehow. But now the thought of spending his days making deals or selling tax-free municipal bonds and mutual funds to little old ladies, then listening to them bitch about how his commission was too high and their rate of return was too low, swirled around in his head for a moment. His dimple reappeared. Hell, that stuff wasn't as bad as dentistry, but it was pretty bad. He'd always hated that kind of thing too; it was just more keeping score! So why in the hell had he assumed that something like that would be his next career? Would he ever get anything right?

He smiled a faint smile, shook his head over his own lack of insight, and drove north to Montana.

chapter
seventeen

For Joe, the winding road to the Crossman Ranch began to feel like a TV documentary in which several anthropologists spend days wandering deeper and deeper into the Amazon rainforest in a small boat, getting more and more lost and isolated every minute. He felt certain he was reading the map correctly, but he'd left I-90 an hour earlier, and he couldn't avoid the self-doubt that began to creep up on him. The two-lane, blacktop road had carried him twenty miles from the interstate. He'd been sending up a trail of dust from a narrow dirt road for thirty more minutes as he wound deeper into the rolling hills of eastern Montana.

The dusty road just kept getting narrower and he was about to turn around to retrace his steps when he cleared the crest of a hill and saw a large cluster of buildings and equipment in the little valley below.

A large wooden sign beside a gate made of logs announced the entrance to the Crossman Cattle Company. Joe crept along the lane into the compound of buildings and looked around for Jim Crossman's pick-up truck. It was parked in front of an odd-shaped building with two huge overhead truck doors. The doors appeared tall enough to admit the biggest of the ranch trucks and tractors, so Joe surmised it was a repair shop. Two five-hundred-gallon gas barrels sat off to the side of the shop, and several smaller pieces of equipment that seemed to be in various states of disrepair lay scattered around the shop. A gravel parking lot, large enough for an eighteen-wheel truck to turn around in, lay at the center of all the buildings.

A split-rail fence marked the boundary of the lawn, which surrounded a large, attractive, ranch-style home with cedar siding and cedar shakes.

To the south of the ranch house were two much older and smaller houses with almost no landscaping around them. Both of the small, older homes appeared to have been moved onto the ranch site within the past few years. Just to the south of the second small house sat a doublewide mobile home that was showing its considerable age and use.

Two new barns, connected by a series of fences and corrals, had been built into a hillside with a gentle slope to the south, away from the other buildings.

As Joe stepped out of his truck and walked toward the shop in search of Mr. Crossman, he looked to his left and noticed that a series of fences and feedlots extended for about a quarter of a mile to the west, away from the barns and along the hillside.

While Joe had been driving in search of this place, he'd reasoned that Jim Crossman was probably cut from the same cloth as Ralph Webster, an insightful person who sized up other men in short order. If it appeared that the other man had any value, he proposed his business in a straightforward manner so they could just get on with things, one way or the other. By the look of Jim Crossman, Joe had guessed him to be a hardworking man who ran a big operation and a pretty tight ship. He could tell by the amount of machinery and buildings that he'd been right about one thing: somebody was running a pretty big operation.

He'd been tempted to ask Mr. Crossman how many cattle or how many acres he ran. But Joe knew that was bad form. Men like Jim Crossman didn't care if you knew approximately how big their place was, but they sure as hell weren't going to tell you, and they took it as an insult if you asked. Maybe that was why Crossman hadn't asked any more about him, either: he knew it wouldn't do him any good to know any more, and Joe Mix's past was none of his business anyway.

Joe was looking around the place tentatively with Jake sniffing along at his heels. He was just about to walk through the main door on the side of the shop when Mr. Crossman and another man stepped out of it.

"Hello, Joe Mix," Crossman said warmly, and he extended his hand. "Welcome to the Crossman Cattle Company!"

"Hello, Mr. Crossman," Joe said.

"Joe, this is my son, Robert! He lives in the big house over there, and he's in charge of the stock on this place!"

"Hello, Robert," Joe said as he extended his hand.

Robert Crossman hardly looked at Joe. His handshake was lifeless. He only managed to grunt a hurried "hello" before he walked off toward the ranch house. Robert appeared to be about forty and either unhappy or stupid—Joe couldn't tell which.

"Joe's the fellow I was tellin' you about, Robert!" Crossman called to his son's back.

Robert turned a blank face to Joe and said, "Uh huh. Have him put his stuff up in the bunkhouse." Then he turned and walked away again.

"C'mon, Joe. I'll show you where to put your things."

Joe wondered if Mr. Crossman had noticed that his son was rude and aloof. He collected his personal things and followed Crossman into the shop, then up a bleak plywood staircase. At the top of the stairs was a door that opened into a grim-looking room with a plywood floor and plywood walls and four single beds. There were hooks on the wall for clothing and towels, but there were no closets. The only mirror was on a small vanity in the small bathroom.

"Home, sweet home! You can have any of these three beds. James is the only other wrangler living in here for now. Like I told you, two of my hands are gonna be staying somewhere else for about a year."

"Yeah," Joe said as he dropped his duffel onto the bed farthest from the one that appeared to belong to James. He really didn't want to know what the two cowboys had done to earn a year in jail. As he looked around at the spartan accommodations, he wasn't so sure if he wanted to stay here either.

"C'mon. I'll show you around some before supper. Mary—that's Robert's wife— she'll be bringing you some sheets for the bed. See those two little houses over there?" Mr. Crossman asked as he pointed across the turnaround. "The Duncan brothers each live in one of those. They're for hands that have been with me for a while or hands that have a family."

Joe nodded his understanding.

"The houses were each deserted for a couple years. They sat on a couple small ranches not far from here. I bought 'em for a song and had 'em moved in here. They're nothin' special, but the Duncan boys each get a little privacy this way."

Joe nodded and kept on walking.

The corral nearest to the barns held about sixty horses. All the other fences, which cordoned off a total of about five acres, seemed to serve no purpose since there was no other livestock on the place.

Just off to the south of the other buildings, two semi trailers had been disconnected from their tractors. Each stood next to an older shed that had no doors.

"I think your job for the next couple days is gonna be unloading them two trucks," Mr. Crossman said.

"See that older mobile home over there? That's the kitchen. That's where you go for meals. Breakfast is at 6:00 a.m. for now, but once the weather gets hot we'll start the workday real early and try to be finished up by early afternoon so we can avoid the hottest part of the day. It's tough on the cattle to move 'em in the heat. It's no fun for us, either. We don't have any breakfast on those days." Crossman stopped himself. "Supper is usually around 6:00 p.m."

Joe and Mr. Crossman walked back toward the house, and Jake followed at their heels, stopping now and then to check whatever scent or prize he might find along the way.

Paint was peeling from the windowsill and the door jambs of the big house, and Joe could see that it was a twenty-some-year-old house that was in need of some minor maintenance. He guessed that when it was new, it had been immaculate and well kept, but during the past several years someone had failed to notice the little things that were calling out for repair.

Crossman knocked on the door and then turned to Joe. "My wife and I live about five miles over that way. Robert and Mary moved into this house a few years back, after we moved to the new house. Mary must be down at the kitchen. Let's just walk over there," Mr. Crossman said when no one answered the door.

A sign that read "Cowboy kitchen" had been hung above the door of the mobile home. When they swung the door open, the first thing Joe saw was the back of a woman who was standing on her toes reaching above her head, trying to put something onto the top shelf of a kitchen cupboard.

This mobile home had received a utilitarian, but not very aesthetic makeover into a kitchen/dining hall for the ranch hands. The front door now opened into a large room that had originally been the living room. A large, cheap kitchen table made of aluminum with a blue

Formica top and eight aluminum chairs occupied the room. The carpet had been removed during the makeover, so the floor was now covered with only plywood. Two rocking chairs sat along one wall, separated by an end table and a lamp. A narrow countertop separated what was now the dining area from the kitchen. The kitchen looked worn and appeared to sag with fatigue. Large pots and pans covered the kitchen table and hung from the ceiling. Whoever did the cooking here was used to cooking for a crowd.

"Hi, Dad," the woman said when she turned and greeted them.

"Hi, Mary. This is Joe Mix. I just hired Joe today." Crossman paused while Mary shook Joe's hand. "Joe, this is my daughter-in-law, Mary. You met Robert before."

Mary exuded warmth and welcome. She smiled pleasantly as she brushed her brown hair behind her ears. Then she reached into a grocery bag as she asked, "Where you from, Joe?"

"Minnesota," Joe said quickly.

"So what were you doing...before this?" Mary's face was inside the refrigerator when she started the question, and by the time she'd finished it she was looking at him and smiling.

"Oh, a little of this and a little of that." He hoped his answer would be good enough; he really didn't want to explain his recent history.

"Well, welcome to Montana," she said as she continued to stock the shelves with groceries.

Crossman put his hand on Joe's shoulder. "Joe, I'm gonna leave you here with Mary. I think she's about to start making supper, and I need to get home to my place before my wife gets upset. Mary can help you with anything you need. The other hands will be in here soon for supper, and your boss, the man you'll be taking orders from, will be here tomorrow for breakfast. You'll meet him then. His name is Preston Murdock; everybody calls him 'Murdo.'"

Mary chuckled at the mention of Murdock's name, but she never turned around.

Crossman shook Joe's hand again. "If you need anything, just ask Mary or Murdo. I'm glad I ran into you today, Joe! I'll be around the place all week. We'll see you later."

Joe sat in one of the aluminum chairs and watched through a window as Crossman pulled out of the driveway.

"Can I help you with anything, Mary," Joe offered.

"No. I pretty much have things under control now. By the way, I'm frying hamburgers for supper. That OK with you?"

"Sure."

"So how did you meet Dad, exactly?" she asked.

"Well, we sort of had lunch together in Ranchester," Joe said slowly.

"Were you in jail?" she asked politely without looking at him.

"No," Joe grinned. "No. I've never been in jail."

"Well, that's where Dad went this morning, you know? To see if he could get two of our hands out of jail." Mary couldn't hide her disappointment when she spoke. "Two of our hands, good hands, got drunk and then robbed a little store. They just broke in after the place had closed and stole some things. They took the cash register, too—left their fingerprints all over it and then threw it in a ditch. Smart guys! They both had records with the police. Took the cops about two days to find 'em. Even when they were sober they weren't exactly pillars of the community, but when they were drinkin' they got mean." Mary shook her head, then added, "Do you drink?"

"No," Joe answered. "I don't drink. I guess I was always afraid of what others would think if they saw me drinking, or that I wouldn't be at my best if someone had a..." He was just about to say "toothache," but he caught himself and said, "Well, I just don't drink."

"That's good," Mary said. She evidently hadn't thought his sentence sounded too odd because she'd just let it go. They chatted about the ranch and the cattle business for the next half-hour while Mary made supper for the ranch hands.

———•———

Heavy footsteps thumped along the small wooden deck outside the mobile home, just before the door swung open and a big-boned young man stepped into the dining hall. He stared into Joe's eyes first, with a confused look.

"James, this is Joe. He's our new hand," Mary said from the kitchen. The fog seemed to lift slightly, but James looked as though he didn't like new information, and he held onto the confusion for a moment. Joe guessed him to be twenty years old or less. His head was huge and square, his brown hair cut short. He apparently didn't wear a hat because his face and head were very tan. When he finally did smile at Joe, he showed square teeth with extra spaces in between them. His gums were inflamed—bright red—and Joe guessed that even gentle pressure with a toothbrush would draw blood.

James was wearing tennis shoes—hightop tennis shoes with holes where the tongue was pulling loose. Neither shoe was tied very securely, so every step James took landed heavily as he clomped the big, ill-fitting shoes around. A cowboy with no hat and no boots? Joe thought. That just didn't look right. James was the only man within miles who wasn't wearing boots and a hat.

After he'd greeted Joe, he walked awkwardly to a chair on the other side of the table and sat down. James had such an unusual walk, Joe thought. James's head bobbed when he walked, but it bobbed in a rhythm separate from his footsteps, as if his head was so far from his feet that they couldn't communicate. When he sat, he looked at Joe and asked, "How old are you?" as if he couldn't understand some riddle.

The dimple in Joe's face was showing when Mary looked over at him. "I'm over thirty," Joe answered. Then he quickly asked James, "How old are you?"

"Eighteen," James answered.

"My truck's older than you," Joe smiled.

"That your truck out there with the snow blade? That's way older than me!" James looked at Joe for a moment, then added, "But your hat ain't old. It's new, ain't it?"

Joe raised his eyebrows and nodded.

"It's a nice one!" James added.

Initially, Joe had figured James as a dumb kid because of the way he looked and moved. But after only seconds of conversation, he knew James might be young and probably uneducated—certainly a bit of a hayseed—but not dumb. There was curious intelligence in his eyes, and kindness. He came off as an unassuming, easy kid to like.

Two men, both recently showered and cleaned up for supper, stepped into the dining hall. Joe hadn't heard them approaching, so he guessed they hadn't been speaking with each other while they'd walked across the yard. Powerful-looking men, both in their early thirties, they wore cowboy hats and blue jeans. Each of them had engine grease ground into his hands. Both men stopped and stared at Joe, just as James had, but neither of them spoke.

Mary introduced the two men, Junior and Norm—the Duncan brothers. She explained that they were mechanics and maintenance experts.

They kept a fleet of pickup trucks, several semis, several farm tractors, and all the other equipment working, as well as helping with the repairs on the barns and other buildings. Neither of the Duncan brothers was particularly interested in talking to Joe. They just ate supper quietly and left. The Duncans didn't seem unfriendly; they just kept to themselves. They did ask a few questions about Joe and his past, but they didn't really seem to listen to his answers. Joe figured they'd probably seen many other hands come and go, and they weren't about to invest the time to get to know him until he'd proven he'd be around a while.

James, however, made some conversation and shared some information about the ranch, and before long he began to treat Joe as if they had something in common.

Mary left the men to finish supper by themselves shortly after she put it on the table. So when James and Joe were through eating, there was little else for Joe to do except stow his gear, talk to James, and play with his puppy. The friendly overtures from James actually made Joe begin to feel welcome after a while. The new friends sat on a couple of cinderblocks outside the shop, got to know each other as best they could, and played with Jake the puppy until dark.

———·———

Joe found himself staring at James while he brushed his teeth and prepared for bed. When they'd walked into their room above the shop, James had kicked his hideous tennis shoes off and stripped down to his briefs in the time it had taken Joe to find his toothbrush. James sat on the side of his bed, wearing just his tighty-whitey cotton briefs, and then set his alarm clock. Eighteen-year-old James had shoulders like an ox. His arms and hands were huge. When he stood, the skin on his legs appeared to be stretched over the muscles underneath, and his feet sounded like hams that had been dropped off a kitchen table when they struck the floor. Joe stood by his bed, brushed his teeth, and stared at James for a while longer. When he walked toward the bathroom, he kept looking at James. James's hands and face were suntanned to a dark brown, but the rest of him was white, pale as death, the whitest white skin Joe had ever seen. He thought James looked like The Incredible Hulk without the green skin.

"Hey, I think your puppy likes me!" James said. Jake had been trying to play with the clothes James had laid over the chair next to his bed, and now he was chewing on James's toe. "Quit that. It tickles!" James laughed as he reached toward Jake. The yellow puppy lowered his head, snatched a sock off the floor, and ran away with his head held high. "He likes me!" James said joyfully. He turned away from Jake. "There's clean towels in the bathroom. Mary likes us to shower before supper!" James called from his bed as Joe stepped into the bathroom to finish brushing his teeth.

Something about James's comment struck Joe as odd, like a child repeating an order given to him by an adult, but he let it slide for now. He walked back over to his bed and unrolled a sleeping bag. He knew he'd feel more at home and sleep better if he was inside his familiar old sleeping bag, not between some stranger's sheets. Nonetheless, he still felt out of place, a little lost and maybe even a little afraid as he let himself settle into his bed.

This little plywood room above a machine shop that smelled of engine oil and gasoline was turning out to be a fine place for all the demons to attack him. It wasn't really comfortable, and it wasn't home. Only one week earlier, he'd been a fairly affluent guy, living in a fine home. He'd had friends and comfort. Tonight, he was holed up on a ranch in Montana, sharing a spartan little room with James. No doubt about it: he missed the comfort and security of the life he'd left. Just being in another new place like this for another dark night only renewed his fear that he'd done the wrong thing and maybe he was on the road to his own undoing. He wanted to run back home. He wanted to be home. He wanted these feelings of loneliness and fear to go away. All those new people and this strange new place—he was downright lost and afraid. He felt like he had as a little boy when his parents had sent him off to camp—only much worse.

He snapped his fingers and Jake jumped onto his bed. Jake turned slowly in a small circle several times, as dogs do before they lie down. When he settled into a ball, he was resting against Joe's chest, and he sighed as he tucked his paws beside his head. Suddenly, Joe was thankful for the warmth and reassurance that came with Jake's touch. It was soothing and pleasant, and Joe reached a hand to stroke the yellow dog cuddling next to him. No one had touched Joe for...how long was it? Joe wondered. Maybe it had been weeks since anyone had touched him and passed along any affection. Tonight, Jake the puppy was suddenly Joe's oldest friend, and he was so grateful for that friendship. He'd never really understood the value of another's gentle touch until this moment.

When James emerged from the bathroom, he turned off the room light and dropped heavily into his bed. Only a few seconds went by before he called out across the darkness between them. "Hey, Joe?"

"Yeah?"

"What's your last name?"

"Mix. Joe Mix," Joe answered. "How 'bout you?"

"Bond."

Joe thought for a moment, as if he were waiting for the punchline. "James Bond? You're kidding."

"Everybody calls me James, but my name is Darnel." He stopped as if to ponder the mystery of it. "People just like to call me James; it's my nickname, I guess!"

"Yeah, how 'bout that?" Joe chuckled. But once again he'd heard something odd in James's words. Before he could say anything more, the sound of James's soft and steady snoring told him the conversation was over.

Here I am, Joe thought, lying here above a machine shop, with James Bond and Jake the dog. What have I done?

chapter
eighteen

The large, gravel turnaround area in the center of the building compound at Crossman Cattle Company was dark and silent when Joe and Jake walked across it toward the ranch house at 5:30 a.m. Joe fed Jake and walked him around the buildings, then sat on the cinderblocks where he had the night before and played with Jake for a while. A yellow glow was just beginning to spread along the eastern horizon and hint that sunrise was coming when he walked to the dining hall.

Parked in front of the dining hall was a late-model, white Chevy pickup pulling a horse trailer. The truck said "Crossman Cattle Company" on the doors, and the box was full of hand tools and bundles of wire. Joe suspected he was about to meet another Crossman employee when he stepped into the dining hall.

When he swung the door open, he knew immediately that he'd found his new boss. Preston Murdock—Joe knew it could be no one else stood just inside the door, sipping at his coffee and chatting with Mary, who was leaning over the stove working on breakfast.

Joe stopped in the doorway for a moment while Preston Murdock looked him up and down. "Preston Murdock," the man said, and then thrust his hand toward Joe.

"Joe Mix."

"You must be the phone thrower from Minnesota?"

"Yeah," Joe nodded as he shook Murdock's hand. Apparently Murdock had spoken with Mr. Crossman.

"Everybody calls me Murdo," he said while he pumped Joe's arm with an iron grip, and Jake jumped up at his ankles. "Nice lookin' pup," he added as he reached down to pet Jake. Standing there in front of Joe was the residue of one hundred years of American cowboy history and folklore. Murdo was smiling at Joe. His black cowboy hat was pulled so far down on his head that the tops of his ears were bent over, and his eyes were barely visible from under the brim of his hat. Joe could only catch a fleeting glimpse of Murdo's teeth when he spoke because his mustache, which drooped over the corners of his mouth onto his chin, had grown over his upper lip and covered his teeth, too. He'd let the whiskers on his lower lip grow into a soul patch, and the rest of his face had gone unshaven for a day or two. Murdo was wearing a red-and-gray, cotton plaid shirt and a jean jacket. His boots were scuffed and worn, and his blue jeans bunched at the ankles.

Joe guessed Murdo to be about forty years old, but he'd clearly put some hard miles on himself. His face and hands spoke of a lifetime of hard work in the outdoors.

"Nice hat!" Murdo offered, then pointed his coffee cup at Joe's hat.

"Thanks," Joe nodded.

Heavy footsteps preceded James's appearance in the doorway of the dining hall. Joe heard, and felt, James's last dozen or so steps before he reached the door. He opened the door, let it slam behind him, walked past Joe, and mumbled, "Mornin', Mary...Mornin', Murdo," then sat heavily on one of the aluminum chairs.

"Goddammer, James, you snuck up on us again!" Murdo said.

James did not reply. He poured himself some coffee and stared at it for a moment. "We makin' fence today, Murdo?"

"I b'lieve you and Cletto will. We need to get that stretch finished up there on the Dawson Ranch before we start branding. You load your truck full of posts and wire, and Cletto'll do the same. Two days up there, maybe three, oughta be enough to get 'er in good shape."

James nodded in agreement as the Duncan brothers stepped into the mobile home and sat at the table.

"Mornin', boys," Murdo said with false enthusiasm.

"You're kinda hard on the equipment," Norm offered in place of a greeting.

"Well, there's alotta gals that have said that same thing to me"—Murdo's eyes sparkled before he finished—"but they was all grateful for the fine work I done with the equipment." He nodded in agreement with himself.

Norm Duncan covered his mouth to avoid revealing his smile, but his brother Junior took up the conversation. "We're on our third transmission in your truck, Murdo; you do push things pretty hard!"

"Well, as I like to say to them gals, thanks for noticing. But Mr. Crossman asked me to keep you boys busy over there in the shop, and I aim to do just that!" Murdo nodded again.

Mary walked past Murdo with a huge bowl full of scrambled eggs. Then she returned to the stove and brought a plate mounded high with bacon and another plate covered with toast. She seemed to be in a hurry, and she turned to leave as soon as she had breakfast on the table. "Save some for Cletto. He'll be here in a minute. Just leave the dishes; I'll be back and clean up later," she said as she stepped out the door and walked to the ranch house to get breakfast ready at her own house.

"Thanks, Mary!" all the men called when she was outside the dining hall.

"Later, boys," came her faint reply from just outside the trailer.

"So where's Cletto?" Junior Duncan said with a mouthful of eggs.

"He had to pick up a couple things before he can get after that section of fence up there on the Twins," Murdo replied. "Should be here by now."

"So what are you gonna break today?" Norm Duncan asked Murdo.

"I ain't decided yet. But I'm sure I'll find something." Murdo grinned at Joe, then turned back to Norm. "Do you boys have them tent poles welded yet? We're gonna hafta start settin' things up for the horse sale purty soon."

"They're done. They're out back of the shop," Norm replied.

A cool morning breeze carried the noise of an approaching truck engine into the trailer. As the truck slowed, it grew louder and closer. It was accompanied by the noise of gravel crunching under its tires.

"That'll be Cletto," Murdo said.

A dark-featured, Hispanic-looking man of about fifty appeared in the doorway. His cowboy hat was tipped up, exposing most of his forehead. He stopped himself in the doorway, stuck out his chest, and greeted the group with a huge, joyful smile. Joe couldn't help but notice his beautiful white teeth. When he smiled they became the center of his face. They were spectacular. He smiled as though he'd returned to his family after a year on the road. Joe felt good, glad to see this man even though they'd never met. This guy has the most sincere, friendly face I've ever seen, Joe thought.

"I hope you saved me some eggs!" Cletto said as he seated himself at the table. Cletto seemed to be smiling all the time. He was pouring coffee for himself when he turned his face toward Joe. "Cletto HomenDeMello," he said, and then extended his hand to Joe.

"Joe Mix."

"Welcome." Cletto's smile grew even more. "Where you from, Joe?"

"Minnesota."

"Glad to have you here!" Cletto said. Then his head spun toward Murdo. "What happened to Jason and Bradley? Mr. Crossman couldn't get them out of jail?" Cletto was still smiling.

"No, them dumb asses are gonna be busy for a while," Murdo said through a slice of bacon.

"Do you know about those two?" Cletto said to Joe.

"Yes. Some," Joe offered.

Cletto only smiled bigger and then turned toward Murdo. He was deferring—giving the next comment to Murdo. And Murdo picked up on it immediately.

"Yeah, Goddammer. Them two was a couple regular hombres! Stole a case 'o beer and a two-hundred-pound cash register with no money in it." Murdo swallowed his last mouthful of eggs and washed it down with coffee. "I didn't want them two back here anyway; never felt I could trust 'em. Hell, they oughta go to jail just for bein' stupid—steal a damn empty cash register," Murdo mumbled as he leaned back in his chair. "Cops found it right in a road ditch up here about ten miles, right where them desperados threw it." He shook his head in disgust.

Cletto looked at Joe and raised his eyebrows, as though he enjoyed listening to Murdo and he wanted Joe to know it.

"OK, boys!" Murdo said as he stood up. "Cletto and James, each of you load a truck with fence posts and wire and head for the fence line up there on the Dawson Ranch when you're done eatin'." He looked at Cletto and nodded.

Cletto smiled to confirm he understood.

"Junior and Norm, I'm gonna run out and break some shit right away so's you don't have to sit around so much."

The Duncan boys ignored him and finished their coffee.

"And Joe, you come with me. I got something very important for you to do." With that, Murdo was out the door. It seemed to Joe that he'd better follow closely. He jumped up from the table and hurried after Murdo.

"Hope you're ready for a little exercise," Murdo said when Joe caught up to him. Murdo walked fast; he seemed to be in a hurry all the time. He talked a lot too, and the ranch hands clearly enjoyed listening to him. His wit and sincerity drew people closer to him. Joe had noticed that when he spoke, his mouth didn't seem to move. Well, Joe couldn't really say that for sure because Murdo's mustache drooped over his lips and obscured whatever lay behind it. Joe had stared at Murdo's face over breakfast, looking for signs, trying to get a read on this man that was now his boss. The only thing he came away with from his first meeting was that he liked Murdo, and it seemed that the other hands did too.

"Well, that there's your job." Murdo pointed to the two semi trailers and the large, three-sided shed they were parked next to. "You just take what's in them trucks and stack it in that shed."

Murdo stepped to the back of the trailer and swung open the large doors. "Forty thousand pounds of mineral!" He reached under the trailer and pulled out two heavy planks. Then he rested one end of the planks on the inside of the trailer and created a ramp so a man could walk up into the truck.

All Joe could see inside the truck were large bags, stacked neatly in piles. "What is it?" Joe asked.

"It's mineral. It's a diet supplement for the cattle. We take it out to various feed troughs around the ranch and feed it to the cattle. The grass they're eatin' is good, but they need this to gain weight and stay healthy. It's just some mix of minerals and other shit. It's like takin' a vitamin, I s'pose. Anyway, your job is to unload these two semis. Stack them bags in piles over there inside the shed, on top of them wooden pallets. Understand?"

"Sure," Joe answered.

"Well, have a nice day, then." Murdo chuckled and walked hurriedly toward the barn. He stopped about ten paces from Joe and turned on his heels. "I'll check back with you in a while. There might be some rough-looking fellers come drivin' in here in Crossman trucks wantin' to take some of that mineral. Just let 'em have what they want. They work over on the west side of the Crossman Ranch. They'll be checkin' the feeding stations today." Then he turned away, nearly running as he approached the barn.

Joe and Jake were alone before the sun was even above the horizon, with a job to do. Joe shrugged his shoulders and walked up the planks into the truck. Each of the bags of mineral weighed forty pounds. That meant a thousand bags of mineral in each truck. Two thousand trips up and down the ramps. Oh well, Joe thought, here we go, and he started back down the ramp.

He carried the bags on his shoulders, alternating sides with each return trip. It wasn't hard work; he could do it. But he knew he had to pace himself. Five bags, then ten, then he'd finished his first rectangular, neatly stacked pile of fifty bags inside the shed. He was sweating, but he felt pretty good. He could do this. When his second pile was finished, he stopped and rested his hand against the side of the shed. The inside of his hatband was sweaty, and he was breathing heavily.

Joe finished the third pile of fifty bags and sat down for a minute. The sun was rising in the sky, and he could hear the Duncan brothers clanging things around over in the shop and talking to each other. He wondered what Cletto and James were doing. Making fence, he thought he'd heard Murdo say. He noticed that Murdo's truck and horse trailer were gone. He must have been concentrating on his own job so intently that he hadn't noticed Murdo leaving.

He made a fourth pile of bags and sat down again for a moment's rest. His hands were sore from grabbing the bags and holding them while he lifted them onto his shoulders. The muscles in his forearms were beginning to burn, just like the muscles in his back. Luckily, the sun hadn't risen high enough yet that he had to work entirely under direct sunlight. Each trip into the shed afforded a little walk in the shade along the back wall, and he found himself looking forward to that cool respite from the growing midday heat.

Fatigue began to press at his hands, forearms, and legs as the first few hours wore on. He stood outside the truck and looked inside when he noticed the first of his muscles begin to burn. "Only eighteen hundred more bags," he said out loud.

He turned and walked to the dining trailer. A drink of cool water might help, he thought. Joe could hear dishes clicking against each other when he rounded the corner on the outside of the trailer. When he swung the door open, he was surprised to see Jake lying on the floor of the kitchen. Mary was humming softly while she did the breakfast dishes, and Jake was sprawled out on his back, sleeping.

"Hi, Mary," Joe said softly. With that, Jake sprang to his feet and attacked Joe. Jake was wagging his tail so hard that it seemed to be throwing him off balance, and Joe dropped to one knee to play with him.

"Hi, Joe. I bet you're thirsty," she said when she handed him a glass of water.

"Thanks," Joe said.

"I hope it's OK with you that I'm playing with Jake," Mary said.

"That's fine. I thought he was up here sleeping. He got tired of following me up and down those ramps after a hundred trips. Are you sure it's OK with you—taking care of Jake, that is? Don't you have enough to do already taking care of your own family?"

"It's just Robert and me, so that's not much work. I'm just filling in here. Our old cook left us a while ago. But I just hired a woman who lives nearby to come over and make two meals a day. She'll be starting in a couple weeks," Mary explained. "Besides, I like working like this."

Joe handed the empty glass back to Mary. "Thanks," he said again. "For the water and for watching Jake." Then he turned to leave.

"My pleasure," Mary said. "It'll be lunchtime pretty soon. I'll make some sandwiches. Just come on back when you're ready for lunch."

———•———

Joe walked to the truck and started another pile of bags immediately. The cool water had been good for him, but his hands, arms, and back continued to tire with each trip back to the shed. Jake followed him back to the truck trailers and even made a few trips up and down the ramps with him until he decided to lay down in the shade and take a nap.

Joe's thoughts during the morning had been mostly about the job at hand. He'd been timing himself and doing the math. If he didn't wear out and fall way behind his current pace, it would take him three days to unload the trucks. He knew already that he'd be sore when he was finished. His body just wasn't used to this kind of work.

As he started to stack the sixth pile of bags, his thoughts turned to Donny and their ugly phone conversation twenty-four hours earlier. He was still upset with Donny for the things he'd said. Damn, Donny had ordered him to come home, as if Donny had some authority to do that or some insight that gave him the right to push. What would Donny say if he knew what I know? Joe thought. Joe wondered for a while if perhaps Donny already knew the things Ralph had told him. Probably not. Ralph seemed to be letting go of that knowledge for the first time.

All the images of Ralph, Kadoka, Jess, Wendy, the dental office, and Ben and Chris began to flutter through Joe's mind again. As usual, there was no resolution to any of it. Joe's conversations with the people in his life just played and replayed in his mind, and his memories of incidents from the past did the same as he lifted bag after bag of mineral onto his shoulder and carried them into the shed. Now and then, his feelings of guilt and failure over leaving his job seemed to barge through his mind and take a malicious swing at him. Occasionally his thoughts came to rest on Jess for a while. He remembered the white-hot anger he'd known as she continued to talk when he tried to kiss her, and that, in turn, triggered the recollection of a thousand other unhappy memories of her. But mostly when he thought of Jess, he remembered the feeling of drifting away from her, like the astronaut who'd lost that tether holding him to his spacecraft. He saw her drifting slowly but surely away from him again, and he didn't care. She existed separate from him now, and it felt as if they'd been separated for a lot longer than a few days. He thought of the unkind things he'd said to her before he left. He felt no sadness or regret for having said them. In fact, if he could go back and do it again, he'd say worse things. He still wanted to hurt her. "Mercenary, life-sucking bitch," he said out loud. Then he smiled, "That was good!"

Murdo's truck pulled into the gravel turnaround area about 12:30, just as Joe was walking down the ramp, carrying another bag. Joe lifted his free hand in greeting but kept on walking as Murdo approached. He found Murdo standing with his hands on his hips looking into the semi trailer when he returned from the shed.

"You're makin' a helluva dent in that mineral, Joe. Goddammer, you're doing all right. You tired?" Murdo asked.

"A little," Joe replied.

"Well, let's go have some lunch," Murdo said as he turned to walk to the dining trailer.

Joe had to hurry to catch up to Murdo. When he did, Murdo looked over his shoulder at Joe. "I'll tell you one thing. Them second thousand bags is gonna be a shitload heavier than the first thousand!" Then he chuckled over the job that lay ahead of Joe.

Junior and Norm Duncan were just getting up from the table when Murdo and Joe stepped into the dining trailer.

"What's for lunch?" Murdo asked in a loud voice. He obviously liked the Duncan brothers; Joe could hear it in his voice.

"Mary made some sandwiches and cookies," Norm said as he walked past Murdo.

"Cookies! Goddammer, that's good! She musta knew I'd be here," Murdo laughed.

Junior stopped in the doorway as he was about to walk back to the shop and changed the subject away from cookies. "I fixed that fencepost driver—how in the hell do you knock the top off one of those things?"

"Well, Junior, I swing that hammer purty hard. Course, any of the gals around'll tell you that!" Murdo said as he reached for a sandwich.

Junior smiled and walked back to work in the shop. Norm walked along at his side, still finishing one of Mary's cookies.

"Them two boys is workin' fools. They can fix anything, too. Mr. Crossman is lucky to have them two. You want a can of soda?"

"Yeah, sure!" Joe said, slightly confused by the speed at which Murdo had changed thoughts, and then walked to the refrigerator.

"So you're doin' all right?" Murdo asked again as he handed Joe a Coke.

"Sure. But explain something to me here, Murdo: what's goin' on here? I can see this is a pretty big spread, but where are the cattle? Can you tell me a little bit about the big picture here?" Joe took a bite from his sandwich and questioned Murdo with his eyes.

"Well, this is a big spread. Mr. Crossman runs alotta cattle and owns allota land."

"How many cattle?"

"Thousands."

"How many acres?"

Murdo sighed, "Well, under a million. But I'm just guessin.'"

Joe raised his eyebrows in surprise.

"No shit! Told you it was a big spread." Murdo shoved the last of his sandwich into his mouth and washed it down with a swig of Coke. "It ain't all one big chunk of land. There's two ranches up north of here a few miles—the Dawson Ranch and the Mills Ranch. They sit side by side, and Mr. Crossman owns 'em both. One is about two hundred thousand acres and the other is about one hundred thousand. We call them two 'The Twins.' I live in the old house on the Mills Ranch, and Cletto lives on the Dawson Ranch. I'm in charge of the operation up there at the Twins, and I work here alot too."

"This ranch down here? We call this the Crossman Ranch, but that's just so's we don't get this operation confused with the Twins. It's really all the Crossman Ranch. Understand?"

"Yeah."

"Mr. Crossman's father, the old man, he bought up three ranches right around here and then ran 'em all together, back about seventy-five years ago."

"So where's all the cattle, Murdo?"

"You'll find that out soon enough! They're spread out all over the grassland up on the Twins and down here on the rest of the Crossman ranch too. We'll be gathering cattle, getting ready for brandin' in just a few days. 'Cept first we got this great big damn livestock sale here next week, and we got too damn much work to do to get ready for it!"

"Livestock sale?"

Murdo stood up and moved toward the door. "We got work to do, Goddammer. You ask alotta questions! Every other hand I ever been around just wanted to know when was payday and what did I want him to do next."

"Sorry," Joe said as he stood up and followed.

"It's OK. Just stay close to me and you can learn alotta shit. Now, give 'er hell on them mineral bags!" The slam of Murdo's truck door punctuated his parting sentence, and his truck roared down the driveway out of sight.

A trail of dust from Murdo's truck was disappearing over the horizon when Joe returned for another trip inside the semi trailer. The bags didn't seem to be getting any heavier, but the day was getting hotter. He'd try to keep a steady pace and not allow fatigue to settle in with each rest stop. Thankfully, his thoughts began to drift from this mindless labor to the place where he'd landed.

Murdo certainly was an interesting character, Joe thought. He was profane, but kind. He was hard working, but he seemed to know how to have a good time. He was always teasing the hands, but they all enjoyed his banter. In one moment, he was one of them, joking and telling stories. In the next instant he was their boss. He gave sharp orders and the others obeyed.

Soon enough, Murdo slipped from Joe's mind, and his thoughts slid back and forth between this ranch and his old life. He wondered just what things from his old life he was done with and what things he'd have to deal with yet.

The day wore on, and on, and Joe resolved not to stop except for a drink of water from time to time. Even then he wouldn't sit down. His hat began to feel heavy during the peak of the midday heat. When he checked it, he noticed that he'd sweat through the hat all the way around, about an inch up from the hat band. It wasn't a new hat anymore. It seemed like such a good idea to sit down and rest a minute. But each time he'd tried resting, it only got that much harder to get going again. He'd just keep moving. Moving at a slower pace was still far better than stopping.

Two men pulled into the yard about 3:00 p.m. driving a flatbed truck with "Crossman Cattle Company" printed on the side. They introduced themselves quickly and then began to stack bags of mineral onto the flatbed truck. "We need summa this over on the west range!" one of the men said when they left. They'd loaded two hundred bags on that flatbed in what seemed like a minute or two. They worked as fast as Murdo, almost, and Joe was glad to see those two hundred bags roll out of sight. It only meant that much less for him to unload.

As the day wore on, Joe continued to measure the time it took him to unload fifty bags of mineral and stack them. He'd thought at first that it would be difficult to get both trucks emptied in three days. Now, he was sure he could do it in less. This simple job required only enough concentration to stay on task but nothing more. He could let his mind wander from Rochester to Kadoka to the Crossman Cattle Company. He only had to stay focused on the mineral bags enough so he didn't fall off a truck. From time to time, it was easy to dwell on the regret and fear that had nagged at him since he'd left Rochester, and be overwhelmed by the demons that had been assaulting him since he'd left home. He was also beginning to feel badly about his conversation with Donny. Donny had indeed said some things that infuriated Joe—they still did, every time he thought of them. But he needed to call Donny and repair the damage, and let Donny know where he was.

"OK, Joe, it's five o'clock. Time to wash up for supper." Mary and Jake stood at the foot of the ramp. "We're having roast beef tonight," Mary added with a smile. "Cletto and James will be here any minute." She was shading her eyes with one hand when she looked up at him. She looked pretty just standing there. Her cotton shorts exposed shapely legs, and he couldn't help but notice that the pink knit top she wore seemed as if it had been designed to feature her perfect breasts. Her short haircut made her appear younger than Joe thought she could be. When he reached the bottom of the ramp, he noticed her perfume.

"I guess I'm ready for the end of this day," Joe said while he bent forward and stretched his back.

"Looks like you got a lot of work done," Mary offered. "It's always nice to get that first day done with, isn't it?" she added.

"Oh, yeah," Joe smiled, and he thought of the day he'd left Rochester.

Jake was jumping up on Joe's leg, begging for some affection, and he knelt to play with his puppy before he spoke to Mary. "It was a good day," Joe confessed with a small grin. "Thanks for helping take care of Jake."

"That was my pleasure!" Mary replied. "It's so much fun to watch him learn about the world for the first time."

"Yeah, I can relate to that too," Joe sighed as he stood up.

Mary was still holding her hand above her eyes to shade them, and she stared at Joe for a moment, considering his words: "Yeah, I can relate to that too."

"S'pose I could shower before supper? Do I have time?" Joe asked before Mary could find the words to go with her thoughts.

"That's the idea. I have to remind James and the Duncans every so often, but it's kind of a rule around here. Last I heard, Murdo's going to stay for supper too, so there'll be entertainment tonight."

———•———

Joe eased himself slowly into his chair in the dining trailer. The hot shower had been wonderful, but now muscles in his arms and back were beginning to ache. He was surprised by the stiffness in his calves and hamstrings.

"Tired?" James asked when he noticed Joe's face tighten.

"A little," Joe replied. Then he raised his voice. "Mary, can I help you with anything?"

The Duncan brothers looked at Mary immediately. They'd both been buttering slices of bread when Joe had asked Mary if she needed help. Judging from their reaction, Joe guessed that the only time one of the Duncan boys would help a woman in the kitchen would be if she caught fire or was in danger of ruining their supper. Both men returned to their bread once they realized Mary was in no danger and that they weren't going to have to help her.

"No, thanks," Mary answered without turning around. She was busy putting the roast beef on a large platter.

"Well, that's probably good," Joe smiled. "I don't know if I could get up," he added weakly.

Cletto, as always, spoke with a happy smile when he said, "You got quite a bit of mineral unloaded today! You should be tired."

Mary was making her second trip to the table with an armful of potatoes when Murdo stepped into the trailer. "Hello, girls! I hope you ain't finished eatin' yet."

"Just starting, Murdo," Mary said.

"Good. Good timing!" Murdo swung his leg over a chair and sat down. Then he did something Joe had seen done only once or twice before: he put a wad of tobacco in his mouth BEFORE he started eating. Joe blinked in surprise, but none of the others seemed to even notice. He turned to Cletto and asked, "How'd you boys do today?" Joe simply stared in disbelief, unable to back away.

Cletto explained that he and James had had a productive day; they'd made several long stretches of new fence up at the north end of the Mills Ranch. He also said that much of the fence up there was in need of repair before they dared to run any cattle on the north end. All the while Cletto spoke, he retained that happy countenance of a young boy describing a day on the playground. James listened to him but added nothing.

"How 'bout you, Norm? Gimme some o' them potatoes, would ya? You two get the tent ready and set up everything in the barn? Is that slow cooker fixed?" Murdo even asked questions fast.

"The tent's ready," Junior said. "And so is the cooker; that's been ready for a long time. But we didn't get to the barn at all today. We had a little problem with the hydraulics on that old skid loader. We'll start out in the barn tomorrow."

"That'll work," Murdo said, then turned to Joe. "Looks like you done all right today." He pushed a huge bite of roast beef into his mouth and waited for Joe's reply.

Joe had only been able to think of one thing since Murdo had sat down. He hadn't taken his eyes off Murdo. He knew it was his turn to respond to Murdo, but all he said was, "Jesus, Murdo, did you put tobacco in your mouth BEFORE you started eating?"

Cletto laughed out loud. The Duncan brothers looked up, smiling. Even James raised his head from his meal. "Well, Goddammer, Joe, that's where all the flavor comes from," Murdo replied. He was smiling now too. "Would you like some?"

"Just seems like putting dog shit on your shoes before you pick up your date. Just doesn't look right," Joe blurted, then wished he hadn't.

When the Duncan boys and Cletto burst out laughing, along with Murdo, Joe was relieved that his spontaneous outburst had been well received, and he laughed too.

Murdo leaned back in his chair and smiled. "What are you, some kinda half-assed doctor or something? Or are you worried about me offending the sensibilities of my colleagues?" Everyone at the table, even James, chuckled at Murdo's response.

"I'll be back later to clean things up," Mary said as she walked out the door. She'd been straightening up in the kitchen, and she'd heard the conversation at the table. She flicked the back of Murdo's hat when she walked behind him. "My sentiments exactly, Joe!" she said from outside the trailer.

"Thanks, Mary," Murdo called over his shoulder. Then he turned his attention back to Joe. "I'll give you a little sample of chew before work tomorrow—you'll have that second trailer done by noon. Just a little pinch'll give you energy for the whole mornin."

"No thanks, Murdo. I think all the puking might slow me down."

"Suit yourself."

"Hey, Murdo!" Junior Duncan interrupted excitedly, "You s'pose your girlfriend will be comin' to the livestock sale again this year?"

Murdo's face went blank, and his head drooped in what looked like a confession of guilt. He seemed embarrassed, Joe thought, but he looked like he was about to smile too, and the others all laughed even louder than before.

"Tell Joe about your girlfriend! He'll probably get to meet her before long!" Junior chided.

Murdo started talking while he looked at his plate and stirred his food with his fork. "'Bout two years ago, I was up in Billings. It was my night off, and I was playin' pool and having a good time…drinking a few beers, too. Anyway, this gal just walked up to me and give me something. It was a little package, and when I held it up to the light I seen it was a rubber." Murdo looked at the anticipation on the faces of the cowboys around him before he continued.

"What did you do?" Joe asked.

"Well, what the hell could I do? I went home with her. I had to," Murdo shrugged. "Anyway, turns out she was a talker and…"

"A talker?" Joe interrupted. Even the Duncans were smiling now.

"OK, Joe, in case you didn't know, there's four kinds of gals. There's moaners, you know—they moan when you're workin' 'em." Murdo raised his eyebrows to ask Joe if he understood. Joe pursed his lips and nodded.

"An'nen there's talkers. They like to talk dirty and tell you what to do when you're workin' 'em." Murdo raised his eyebrows again, then continued. "'Nen there's screamers; everybody understands that one, right?"

Everyone at the table chuckled softly.

"What's the fourth kind, Murdo?" Joe asked.

"Triple threat! They do all three—moan, talk, and scream, in that order. My favurt kind!"

Joe laughed out loud, maybe because of the serious expression on Murdo's face, maybe because the words Murdo had spoken struck him as bizarre. But he laughed a deep laugh from down in his belly. Joe hadn't felt the cleansing effect of a belly laugh in a long time—since he'd been fishing with Donny.

"Anyways, I thought she was about to shift from a talker to a screamer when I give her the Velvet Half-Nelson…"

"The Velvet Half-Nelson?" Joe interrupted again.

"It's a secret amorous embrace. I can't tell you any more than that, but it drives women wild!" Murdo had both forearms resting on the edge of the table, and he leaned forward a little bit farther with each of his own sentences. "Only a very few of us know how or are able to use it!" Murdo appeared to be deadly serious. He raised his eyebrows and nodded to Joe. Cletto, however, was smiling uncontrollably, and he winked at Joe.

"Anyways, like I said, I give her the Velvet Half-Nelson and finished the job, then took a little nap. When I woke up, I looked over at her and I seen that the beer had affected my judgment—she looked like ten miles of bad road." Murdo shook his head. "She wanted another try at the Velvet Half-Nelson too." His eyes were twinkling when he looked up. "I had a hard time gettin' outta there."

All the ranch hands were laughing as they ate.

"The best part was when she showed up at the livestock sale out here about a month later," Cletto interrupted. "She brought Murdo flowers!"

The table erupted in laughter again. Even Murdo struggled to hide his laughter.

"Murdo made me tell her he was married!" Cletto said. "But she said she didn't care; she wouldn't tell."

"So what ever happened to her?" Joe asked.

"I just convinced her that my heart belonged to another."

"It wasn't your heart she was after!" Norm said, and triggered another explosion of laughter.

———·———

When Murdo finished his supper and finished entertaining the others with stories of his amorous past, he quickly reviewed the next day's routine and let everyone know what was expected of them. Then he bolted for his truck. James and the Duncans left the dining hall soon after Murdo, leaving Joe and Cletto alone, sitting at the table covered with dirty dishes.

"Hey, Cletto. Should we do the dishes and clean up for Mary?"

"Sure," Cletto replied. The two of them went to work busing dishes and drawing water.

"So why are you here tonight? I thought you lived at the Mills Ranch," Joe asked when he had the sink full of hot water and soapsuds. "I'll wash, you dry?" he added.

"James and I are making one more day of it on the fences up there tomorrow, and we're going to take one truck. I didn't want to drive up there, then back down here, then back up there tomorrow. So I stayed here. And Mary made roast beef! I always stick around for that." Cletto smiled his great smile and dried dishes while he talked.

When the dishes were done, Cletto poured two fingers of scotch into a coffee cup and then dropped two ice cubes in after it. He sat on one of the aluminum kitchen chairs and leaned back so that the front legs of his chair came off the floor as he took a sip of the scotch.

The ache in Joe's muscles had intensified during supper, and he groaned when he let himself settle into the rocking chair in the corner of the dining trailer. Cletto lifted his cup of scotch in a silent salute to Joe. Joe returned the salute with a Diet Pepsi.

"So, Cletto, what's your story? You must be from somewhere south of Montana, but your accent, it doesn't fit. It's close, but it doesn't fit. Your first language isn't Spanish, is it?"

"Portuguese."

Joe raised his eyebrows. "Really? How did you wind up here?"

"I was born in Brazil...raised on a cattle ranch," Cletto smiled. "Your government used to send agricultural advisors to Brazil to help us learn better methods of farming. One of these men became good friends with my father. One day, he arrived at our ranch with his beautiful young daughter. She was the most beautiful girl I'd ever seen. Several years later, we married and moved to Montana, her home."

"Where is she now?"

"In Heaven. She died six years ago."

"I'm so sorry," Joe said.

"We had a good life together. Very good!"

"Any children?"

"No."

For the first time since he'd met Cletto, Joe noticed he wasn't smiling. There was no light in his eyes. He looked into his small glass of scotch as if there was no bottom to it.

"So how did you wind up here, working for Mr. Crossman?" Joe asked.

Light flickered back into Cletto's eyes, and his lips curled into a smile. "I don't really work for Mr. Crossman. I own some horses, and Mr. Crossman lets me keep them at the Mills Ranch, and I live there too. In return, I help him out during branding time and whenever he needs some help." Cletto sipped at the scotch. "I'm partners with him on this big livestock sale, too. Many of the horses that we sell next week will be mine. We'll draw a big crowd—you'll see! It's almost like a party, but it's a lot of work!" Cletto's smile returned to its usual splendor.

"How big of a crowd?" Joe asked.

"Maybe three hundred people a day, maybe more, for three days. We sell some bulls on the first day, then horses on the next two days. People come from all over, but mostly the western states."

Cletto tipped his head back and poured some scotch over his lips. "What about you, Joe? You're not like the cowboys Mr. Crossman usually hires. You made friends faster than any of the others. Even the Duncans like you."

"How can you tell that?" Joe asked.

"I can read men's faces pretty well."

"Well, then, what do you see in my face?"

"You're an educated man. You're a good man, and you're hiding something," Cletto replied.

"That's pretty good," Joe said softly. "I can live with that."

"You're not going to tell me anything more, are you, Joe?" Cletto asked.

"No."

"I can live with that too." Cletto tossed back the last of his scotch and walked to the door. "I'm sleeping up there with you and James tonight. I've slept up there before, so I can tell you that you'd better get up there and get to sleep before James starts to snore," Cletto said.

"I'll have no trouble sleeping tonight. But I'm gonna sit here and read for a while. My pup likes me to read to him before bed. It's still early."

"See you in the morning," Cletto said before he stepped out the door.

An hour later, Mary approached the trailer after she'd fed her own family. She usually needed about forty minutes of cleanup in the trailer before she could return to her home for bed.

The light was still on in the dining trailer. Through the window she could see someone sitting in the rocking chair. As she drew near to the window, she recognized it was Joe. When she heard a man's voice, she began to step quietly so she could hear what was being said before she disturbed whatever was going on. She stopped, leaned her shoulder against the side of the trailer, and listened for a moment.

Joe Mix was reading aloud from *Lonesome Dove* while Jake chewed on a plastic milk bottle with a rag tied to the handle. He was a good reader, and he put emphasis where it belonged, as if Jake might understand the story better if it was read properly. What kind of man reads to a dog? she wondered. Now that Mary had crept so close to the trailer, she couldn't just barge in; she'd startle Joe. He'd know that she'd been eavesdropping, which might embarrass him. She peeked around the corner and stole a glance into the kitchen. When she recognized that her work for the night had been done by someone else, she felt a wave of gratitude. It was as if someone had extended her a rare and extraordinary compliment. It must have been Joe, she thought: none of the others had thought to do something like that before. Only a man who reads to his dog could be so thoughtful, she reasoned, and she had to thank him now.

Mary stomped her feet several times in an effort to announce her approach, then pulled the metal screen door open. Joe was sitting in the rocker with an uncomfortable expression on his face, and Jake instantly bounced over to greet her.

"I thought you'd all be in bed by now," Mary said. "Look at that—you did the dishes and cleaned up! Thank you, Joe!"

"It was nothing. We were just trying to help. Supper was great!" Then Joe stood up and began to walk toward the door. He couldn't hide the pain and stiffness in his back and legs. Mary thought he moved as if he was walking barefoot over a gravel road.

"Stiff? Sore?" she asked.

"A little." Joe was obviously trying to hide his pain, and he tried to smile. He walked past Mary and out the door.

"See you in the morning, Joe, and Jake," she called. No one had ever thought to do the dishes before. That one simple act of kindness made her feel as though Joe had dropped to one knee, kissed her hand, and told her she was beautiful. She wore a faint smile as she got a few things ready for breakfast and wondered just who Joe Mix really was.

chapter
nineteen

The grating, hateful buzzing noise from James's alarm clock shattered Joe's sleep. He wasn't sure just where he was at first, but the faint smell of gasoline, coupled with all the metallic odors of the machine shop beneath him, permeated the barracks he was lying in, and he remembered this place before James turned the lights on.

A gripping pain stabbed at his arms, back, and legs, and barked at him with every movement. The last time he'd felt like this was the day after basketball practice had started in high school. The byproduct of a day's hard labor, lactic acid, had built up in his muscles, causing this pain and stiffness. He remembered that much—the reason for the pain—but he'd forgotten the way the pain grabbed at him when he tried to move. It was a good pain—not like he'd just taken a beating or broken a bone; just the result of a very hard day's work. A little bit of exercise would work things loose again. It always used to, anyway, he thought.

It was no use trying to play with Jake this morning; he could hardly pull his own boots on, let alone roll on the ground with a puppy. Joe simply fed Jake and walked over to the dining hall. Jake ran along in front of him on the way. Joe was glad no one was watching him walk. It hurt so bad just to shuffle along that he couldn't keep up with Jake.

When Joe finally reached the dining hall, it took several feeble steps to cross the dining room and find an empty chair. The other hands were all seated and eating while Joe put some biscuits and gravy on his plate, then yawned.

"Sore?" Cletto asked.

"No," Joe lied. "Where's Murdo?" he asked, partly out of curiosity and partly to remove his physical condition from the conversation.

"He had to run up to Cowboy Camp! Had to drop a few things off and do a little maintenance before you start gathering cattle!" Mary said. Then she set a cup of coffee by Joe's plate and touched his shoulder as she passed by. Her touch was deliberate, and firm, and it triggered a rush of pleasure across his back. It was warm and friendly and seemed full of promise. He wanted to lean backwards and follow her touch. He wanted her to touch him like that again, but with both hands. He tried to steal a glance at her to see if there was a message in her eyes, but she was walking away from him, back toward the kitchen. If it feels that good for a dog to snuggle up against me at night, I suppose the touch of a pretty woman ought to feel pretty good too, he thought.

"Thanks, Mary," Joe said as he lifted his coffee cup. Then he turned toward Cletto. "What's Cowboy Camp?"

"You'll find out soon enough," Cletto said. "We run a lot of cattle up on the Twins, and we have a place up there on the north end where we gather them and brand them in the spring—Cowboy Camp! It's a pretty remote spot, so we have a shack up there, and we just stay there 'till the branding is done instead of trucking cattle all over the place."

"It's Murdo's favorite place," Junior said, staring at his biscuit.

"Surprised he don't bring his girlfriend up there!" Norm added, and everyone chuckled softly at the memory of Murdo's girlfriend.

Preston Murdock seemed to be the ideal foreman for these men. They all respected his knowledge of ranch operations. They took his orders seriously and were willing to comply with whatever he wanted. But they liked him too and enjoyed his company. Murdo was one of those rare men who could be boss in one instant and a buddy the next. These men let him decide when he would be one or the other.

Joe thought Murdo might be among the most profane and foul men he'd ever known, but when he turned profane and foul he became even more likeable. Murdo had a gift: other men liked him and were willing to follow him in all situations. He could give stern orders in such a way that men clearly understood his expectations and knew there would be unpleasant consequences if they weren't met. But the men never harbored any resentment for the manner in which Murdo spoke to them.

Cletto had been thinking the same thing about Murdo. He interrupted the short silence around the table to add, "You know, Murdo's a rare breed. A couple years ago, I saw him tear into one of the hired hands! He just ripped that poor guy a new asshole. Then, in the next breath, he borrowed some chew and asked the guy about his family."

"I saw that too," Junior said. "I'd 'a thought that guy was gonna start cryin' or take a swing at Murdo. But the two of them wound up talkin' nice."

"So whatever happened to the guy Murdo was talkin' to?" Joe asked.

"He fucked up again and Murdo killed him!" Norm blurted. As the other men laughed at Norm's comment, Joe knew he'd heard Norm describe exactly what it was that drew the men to him. Murdo respected the men who worked so hard on the Crossman ranch and carried out his orders; he expected results, but he respected all the hands. Joe smiled to himself when he thought of Murdo's girlfriend showing up here, at the big livestock sale, with flowers for him.

When the Duncans were finished with breakfast, they stood up and left together, as usual. Cletto stood soon after and so did James. But when James stood up, he quickly carried his dishes to the sink. "Thanks, Mary," he said when he clomped out the door, dragging his tennis shoes with each step.

Joe had barely started eating when the others got up and left. He made an effort to hurry up and get to work at the same time as everyone else. He shoved a biscuit in his mouth and slid his chair back.

"Whoa! Slow down! Finish breakfast," Mary said as she sat down across the table from him and poured herself some coffee. "Another minute or two won't make any difference."

Joe slid his chair under the table and nodded.

"How did you sleep?" she asked.

"Like a rock. Never thought once about..."—then he stopped himself—"...anything."

Mary noticed that Joe had nearly said more than he intended for her to hear, but she decided not to ask any more about it. "Thanks for cleaning up last night," she said. "Did you notice the way James carried his dishes over to the sink this morning? All I did was mention how much I appreciated it that the kitchen was cleaned up last night."

"What's the deal with James?" Joe asked. "He seems to think of you like a mother. He craves your approval, doesn't he?"

"James? He came from the worst of homes." Mary shook her head in despair. "He grew up in Billings. A girl I went to college with was teaching school there, and James was a student in her fifth-grade class. One winter day, he came to school in his pajamas and bare feet. His father had beaten his mother during the night, and he'd run away. He didn't know where else to go except to school, so he stood on the front steps until the custodian opened the building. It was so sad. After a few years in and out of foster homes, he wound up here. I've tried to give him some order, rules, and a little friendship; maybe I've become a mother figure to him. He's a good kid, but I don't know what kind of a future he has."

"He's not stupid. You can see that much right away," Joe said. "But he's not exactly worldly. He doesn't even understand why everyone calls him James—at least I don't think so. You know...'Bond, James Bond,'" Joe said in his best Sean Connery imitation.

Mary's face crinkled in surprise. "Really?"

Mary seemed to still be contemplating James's naïveté' when Joe stood and moved toward the door.

"Thanks again for cleaning up last night, Joe."

"You're welcome. Hey, if you listen I'll bet you can hear my joints creaking," Joe said as he tried unsuccessfully to hide his stiff back from Mary.

Jake loped along at Joe's heels as he approached the semi trailers filled with mineral. He walked directly up the planks and into the truck without any hesitation, right behind Joe.

The shed and the semis loaded with bags of mineral had become Joe's private challenge. So far, it was the only place and the only task he'd been assigned, so he went right to work. He intended to get this job done correctly. After all, what sort of statement would it be if he couldn't even unload a couple trucks properly? It was the most menial, entry-level job on the ranch, and it was probably all Murdo and Mr. Crossman trusted him to do just yet. After a dozen or so trips up and down the ramp that led into the first truck, Joe's muscles began to ache less. After another several dozen return trips, he'd worked up a light sweat and he felt pretty good. The key still seemed to be keeping a steady pace.

His footsteps echoed inside the empty semi trailer as he carried out the last bag of mineral well before noon. He'd planned to have a small celebration when he'd finished the first truck, but now he simply moved the planks over to the other truck and continued carrying bags into the shed. By mid afternoon, he'd made good progress on the second truck. He was thrilled when the two guys from the previous day reappeared and took two hundred more bags off the truck for him.

His hands were beginning to tire again, and along with the fatigue came some pain. He felt steadily weaker as the day wore on, but he knew he could finish early tomorrow. He'd tried to carry a few bags on his right shoulder, then a few on his left. He'd carried some in the crook of his right arm, then his left, then both. As various muscles in his arms and back grew weary, he began to worry that he might overdo and wind up with some sort of ache or slight injury that would leave him unable to work. The thought of having no value to Murdo or Mr. Crossman was disconcerting, and he began to wonder just what they might do if he was unable to work. He'd made an effort to exercise every muscle that he could and not overdo or abuse anything. His hands and fore-arms got a workout with each and every bag, and he could feel the growing weakness in his grip. Even his fingertips and fingernails were getting sore from gripping the bags.

He'd thought several times that he should call Donny and tell him about this place. But then he wondered just what to say, so he decided not to call.

Just before five o'clock, Murdo's truck rolled into the yard, pulling a large horse trailer. Murdo waved as he drove past Joe, then backed the trailer up next to a fence by the barn. He got out of his truck and motioned for Joe to come over to the barn.

By the time Joe reached the fence alongside the barn, Murdo had released six horses into the corral—three mares, each with a colt. Each of the horses had a six-digit identification number shaved into the hide of its left hip.

"Looky there, Joe," Murdo said happily. "Those are some fine cuttin' horses! Those animals were bred to cut cattle." Joe couldn't miss the admiration in Murdo's voice. "Goddammer, Joe, those are some fine ponies! You're gonna see some fine horses start rollin' in here tomorrow."

Joe put his hands on the fence and nodded. "Yeah, well, all horses smell about the same, don't they?"

His left arm was still resting on one of the planks in the fence when Murdo turned to face Joe. He lifted his hat off with his right hand, then used his sleeve to wipe the sweat from his own forehead. "I seen a lot of hands over the years, Joe. Some of 'em was just about like you. They showed up here with new hats and acted like they was in love with the cowboy life, but they didn't last very long around here. This ain't easy...this life out here," Murdo said. "Just so's you understand, Joe. I need to know that I can count on you to get things done when I tell you. If you can't, well then, Goddammer, you'll be outta here faster than them two hardened criminals sitting down 'ner in jail in Ranchester. This ain't a vacation for you or some shit like that, is it?"

"Well, just so you understand, Murdo," Joe started. "I pretty much jumped off a runaway train about a week ago, and this is where I stopped rollin'. I need to be here, 'cause this is all I have. I need to work." Joe paused for a moment. "And whether or not I can do the job around here, I guess that's what we'll find out in the next few weeks." Joe's voice softened noticeably. "I'll do the best I can; I'll be all right. Like I said, I can already tell the difference between horses and cattle..."—Joe closed his eyes and sniffed—"...with my eyes closed."

Murdo turned his head slowly and smiled at Joe's honesty, and ignorance. "Me and Mr. Crossman figured that was about all you knew. Yer gonna get an education in the next few weeks!"

"Well, I already know a lot about stackin' mineral bags. I'm probably ready to move on to new challenges!"

Murdo turned and looked back through the fence and watched the horses for a minute. "I'll help you," he said softly while he was still watching the horses.

"Can I use your cell phone and call my brother, just to let him know where I am? I lost my cell phone the other day," Joe said after they'd stood alone together by the fence for a while.

"Yeah, I heard about that," Murdo chuckled. "You can use my phone if you promise not to throw it, but you won't get a signal out here. There's a landline in the barn. Follow me. You can call from the office in the barn."

When the door to the barn swung open, Joe saw something he'd never seen: one end of the large barn was set up like a theater, with bleachers and a balcony above the bleachers. In front of the bleachers was an elevated pulpit, as if this was a giant cowboy church with a dirt floor.

"This here's the auction pit, and the auctioneers stand up there in that pulpit." Then Murdo pointed even higher, to a huge window behind the pulpit. "That up there...that's the office. The stairway to the office is up there 'round the back of the pulpit. You gotta go out through that door behind the wall. That's where the stairway is."

"Jeez, Murdo, this is kind of a big operation!"

"No shit. I told you that the other day! Make your call and get ready for supper." With that, Murdo turned and left.

Joe sat at the spartan little desk in a plywood office overlooking a livestock sales arena and looked at a stack of blank recipe cards beside a black desk phone. A small TV with a built-in VCR sat on the desk with a handful of videotapes. He tried to imagine what to say to Donny for a moment. He still didn't want to talk to Donny yet. He only wanted Donny to know that he was safe and where he could be reached in an emergency. He still bristled when he thought of Donny's reprimand, so he decided to call Donny's office and leave a message on the answering machine. He simply told the machine that he could be reached at the Crossman Cattle Company, in Montana, and gave the phone number.

———·———

The sound of dishes clinking and men talking greeted Joe as he stepped into the dining trailer, and Jake tumbled in after him.

"You're late," Murdo said.

"Sorry," Joe apologized as he found his chair. "The shower felt pretty good and..."

"Mary don't like it when we're late for supper!" James said. It was the first time Joe had noticed James say anything at the table. He was almost scolding Joe. He definitely wanted Joe to know that Mary expected him to be at supper on time. He seemed to think it was important for Mary to know that he was trying to help enforce her rules.

"I'm sorry," Joe said again.

Cletto caught Joe's eye and winked. In an effort to remove himself from any more scrutiny, Joe changed the subject as he lifted a large helping of meatloaf onto his plate. "Hey, Murdo. When I was leaving the barn after I called my brother, I walked around a different way and saw a small corral with one horse in it."

Murdo pushed a forkful of mashed potatoes under his mustache and withdrew a clean fork. "Uh huh."

"The horse was kind of a funny color, and he looked like there was something wrong with him. And he just stared at me the whole time."

Cletto's face brightened, but Murdo answered. "That was Billy—Blue Billy. He's a blue roan."

"Yeah, he looked like he was sort of dark blue with white splashed all over. Had big ears too!" Joe added. "Looked like a mule, sort of."

"That's Billy," Murdo said flatly. "He's a bucker! He ain't ever been rode!" Then he shook his head and smiled. "Goddammer, that ol' Billy, he's a bad one to buck!"

"So what does he do? Why is he here?" Joe asked.

"'Cause ever now an' 'nen some cowboy thinks he'd like to have a try at that ol' jughead."

"Maybe someone will buy him this week at the sale and break him," Joe suggested as he plopped a spoonful of potatoes onto his plate.

"No. He's not for sale. He's just gonna be Billy for the rest of his life. He's just gonna stay here and be Blue Billy, the horse that never got rode."

Murdo leaned back from the table and chose his words carefully. The talk of Billy just being Billy forever seemed to have sent Murdo off somewhere in his private world for a moment.

"You know, Cletto," Murdo started slowly, "I don't know if Mr. Crossman is ever gonna figure out how slow and expensive it is for us to brand cattle the way we do. I like it up there at camp. I always have. I love this life, and I love workin' with the stock. But Goddammer, we work too hard up there and don't get as much done as we should. You know, Cletto, you and I and James—or even Joe, who can only tell horses from cows by the way they smell—could brand three hunnerd head a day if we modernized and bought a chute," Murdo sighed. "But we're gonna go up there with a crew of seven or eight, and then brand one hunnerd'n fifty head a day. We're gonna rope and throw and brand 'em by a fire, like we've been doing it for a hunnerd years!"

"Cows run slower and sound different when they talk," Joe interrupted. He didn't mind making himself the butt of a joke by exaggerating his own ignorance. Scattered laughter spread around the table as the men continued eating.

Murdo ignored Joe's comment. He wanted to smile, but he wasn't finished making his point just yet. "We need to modernize SOME of the things around here, but Mr. Crossman just don't think like that. I guess maybe he likes the tradition of the old ways."

"Well, it's hard for most of us to give up on something we've grown used to, even if we know it's not working anymore." Joe couldn't help but smile when he realized he'd just described his own life. Joe looked at Murdo and nodded. "I know it's true in dent..."—he caught himself just in time. "Well, I know it's true in most businesses that it requires a pretty significant paradigm shift in order to abandon an old management philosophy or system and then adopt new methods and technology." He lifted a forkful of potatoes to his mouth when he was done, but when he looked around the table all the cowboys sat staring at him with open mouths.

"What the hell are you talking about—a pair of dimes? Sorry, Mary," Murdo apologized for swearing in front of Mary. "I'm talkin' about branding cattle." The irritation in his voice grew. "What the hell are you talking about? Sorry, Mary!" Murdo's face looked like he'd just spent an hour trying to read a book he didn't understand.

"Nothing—just some bullshit I read about once," Joe said. He tried to hide his own smile, and he hoped the conversation would just move on by him. He wouldn't bother with any more lectures on business management. His job was to stack mineral bags, not run the ranch.

Joe raised his water glass to his mouth. As he tipped his head back, he caught Mary's eye. She was staring at him, grinning, and when he looked into her eyes she smiled openly. She'd understood what he'd said.

Jake was chomping a plastic Coke bottle and chasing it around the dining hall while Joe read to him from *Lonesome Dove* when Mary returned to the trailer two hours after dinner and the chat with Murdo.

"Thanks for doing the dishes again!" Mary said. She raised her hands from her sides and smiled. "I guess my work here is finished! Thanks, Joe!"

"James did it all himself tonight. I think he picked up on how much you appreciated the dishes being done. He aims to please you!" Joe answered. "He was about to give me hell for being late!"

Mary put her hands in her pockets. "Do you read to your dog every day?"

"I like to," Joe answered. "Don't know if Jake knows what's going on, but I like to think that it helps us bond a little if he hears my voice like this. Also, I've sort of rediscovered the written word in the past week or two."

"What have you been doing special in the past week or two that you would rediscover the written word?" Mary asked. She was curious, and her curiosity was directed at more than Joe's appreciation for the written word. She was trying to find some insight into Joe's past—just who he was and what had brought him here.

"Oh, just since I got Jake and started reading to him. That's all I meant." That was a pretty quick recovery there, Joe thought; much better than throwing up an obvious roadblock or telling a complicated lie. Mary didn't need to know anything more about his past couple of weeks.

Mary looked back at him as if she might ask another question. She stood with her hands in her pockets and stared briefly. She was petite. With her short hair and her youthful figure, she looked like the proverbial girl next door. But the way she looked, standing there with her feet spread slightly and her hands in her pockets, seemed to suggest something more to Joe. He thought of her touch the other day at breakfast, and he felt a tiny stirring of sexual tension.

"Well, I gotta get Jake out for a walk, then get to bed," Joe said as he stood up from his chair and started toward the door.

"You're not quite as sore as last night?" Mary asked.

"Yeah, I think I feel worse, but I'm just more tired. Goodnight, Mary," Joe said as he walked past her and out into the night.

chapter
twenty

James and Joe had the last of the mineral bags stacked by 10:00 a.m. Joe had thought that some sort of celebration might be in order, but one job simply rolled into the next, and the two of them loaded some wire and tools into the back of a Crossman Cattle Company pickup truck and started out for the Twins. James made a point to drive.

The fresh air swept through the truck and cooled both men. Each of them had a sandwich and a soda while they were en route to their next job so that they could start to work immediately when they arrived.

James didn't usually have a lot to say, but today in the truck he was fairly talkative. He told Joe which of the horses he liked the best and which jobs he enjoyed the most. "Gathering cattle, that's my favorite!" he'd said several times.

"So what jobs don't you like?" Joe had asked just for the sake of conversation.

"I like 'em all," James answered.

Joe leaned back in the truck seat and put his left arm across the top of the seat. When the conversation waned from time to time, he'd steal a glance at James. James drove with both hands on the wheel and a serious look on his face. He never exceeded fifty-five miles per hour, and he was concerned about obeying all the rules of the road. Joe couldn't look away from James sometimes. His hands and forearms were so big, and his feet, with those huge, clumsy-looking tennis shoes, looked almost like part of a clown costume. "What size shoes do you wear, James? Just out of curiosity. I mean, you've really got a pair of gun boats there!" Joe finally blurted. It irritated Joe the way James dragged those ugly damn tennis shoes when he walked. But he couldn't say anything about the shuffling. James was such a good kid, and it might hurt his feelings.

"Size 15EEE," James said with a smile. "They're hard to find!"

Joe nodded in agreement and watched the road roll by at fifty-five miles per hour until James Bond signaled he was about to leave the highway.

"I'll get the gate," Joe offered when they pulled off the road and stopped in front of a sign that said "Dawson." When James drove the truck through, Joe swung the gate shut and locked it again.

"Are we anywhere near Cowboy Camp?" Joe asked.

"We're closer than we were this morning, but we're still a ways away. It's up that way." James pointed to the north. He'd only driven the truck a short way along a barbed-wire fenceline, and up and down several hills, when he stopped again.

"This is the place, Joe. Camp is up ahead a few miles. We got fence posts to pound right here," he said with some enthusiasm. James left his truck door open when he stepped out of the truck. He pointed down a long draw to a series of metal fence posts that had been hammered into the ground. The fence posts had been placed several hundred feet apart from each other, and then a string had been tied to them to provide a visual aid for the alignment of the other fence posts. Once a straight line had been established along a series of widely spaced posts, all that was required to keep other posts in the same straight line was to follow along the string and pound all other posts on that line.

"OK, Joe, grab a couple posts and one of those post drivers, and start pounding. We'll move the truck every now and then to catch up with ourselves," James said. With that, he started driving a fence post into the ground.

Joe picked up the other post driver, a heavy, steel sleeve about four inches in diameter, open on one end with a heavy steel weight welded on the other end. The fence maker's job was simply to slide the driver down onto a fence post several times, hard enough to drive the post into the ground. Then pick up another post, place it along the string about fifteen feet from the last post, and drive it into the ground also.

The pounding of a fence post wasn't very difficult, but the cumulative result of carrying posts and the heavy driver, then pounding fence posts with the driver, walking on down the line, and repeating the chore for hours was physical exhaustion. A man's back, hands, forearms, shoulders, and legs all received a workout that could never be duplicated in any gym.

After two hours of making fence, Joe began to wish he were back at the ranch stacking bags of mineral. The ache in his hands was getting painful, and he was barely able to raise the post driver above his head. The muscles in his shoulders were exhausted.

Joe and James drove fence posts for several hours until all the posts in the back of the truck had been used. "There, that worked out pretty good!" James exclaimed when they'd driven the last post into the ground. "The fence line is ready. Let's start the wire!"

"How the shit are we gonna do that, James? I don't have any feeling in my hands anymore."

"That's easy. We're gonna wind it around these double-creosote posts with diagonal braces that Cletto and I put in the ground over the last couple days. Then we're gonna use a come-along and tighten the wire. But that'll be easy. It's puttin' the electric wire and all the insulators on the fence that's gonna be hard on your hands and forearms."

Joe did what he could to help James. He found that stringing the electric wire was actually fairly easy. But grasping the hard wire that held the insulators to the fence posts and then bending it into place with a pliers was out of the question. He could only watch while James took a pliers in his right hand and wrapped the heavy wires around the posts. Several times he tried to do what James was doing, but the pliers just fell from his hand. The strength to grip and twist the wire connectors was gone from him.

James talked to Joe while Joe watched him build several gates through the fence. He explained that Joe's hands and forearms would be all right before long—it took time to build strength to do this. Joe simply handed James whatever tools he needed and watched with awe as the young man twisted and snipped the ends off heavy wires, then stretched the loose ends of the wire gates until he could fashion another interlocking section of wire from the other side of the gate.

When the last of the electric fence insulators had been fixed to the fence and the electric wire had been fastened to the insulators, Joe dropped his pliers on the ground.

"James, if I had to piss right now, you'd have to unzip me and whip it out for me. I got no strength left in my fingers. My forearms feel like Popeye's—feels like the skin is gonna split open," Joe said. A cloud of dust billowed away from him as he sat heavily onto the dry ground.

"I told ya," James said. "Good news is we only got one more stretch of fence to finish tomorrow, then we're done for a while. Bad news is, it's kind of a long run of fence, a little longer than this one. It's just over that hill."

"I don't want to think about that. Any Coke left in that cooler?" Joe asked.

"Here." James extended his hand toward Joe after he'd retrieved a Coke for each of them.

"You'll have to open it."

James looked accusingly at Joe and furrowed his eyebrows.

"I'm not shittin' you, kid. I'm outta gas."

"You're outta shape, Joe. What did you do before this?"

"Stacked bags," Joe said. Then he belched out loud. "How 'bout you, James? What's your story?"

"I came out here to Crossmans after high school—actually, it was during my senior year. I've never done anything else."

Each of the tired men were more concerned about not telling anything more than they were about learning about the other, and they fell silent for a moment.

"This is a good place to work," James offered.

"What do you think you'll do when you grow up—or, should I say, when you're thirty?" Joe asked.

"This," James answered.

"Why this?" Joe asked.

"I like the horses and the cattle, I guess." James stopped and looked across the hills to the south. "I feel like I'm home when I'm here. Know what I mean, Joe?"

"Yeah, maybe," Joe said.

"Where do you feel at home?" James asked as he opened another Coke.

"Hmph," Joe sighed. "I don't know yet."

"You never had a home yet?" James asked.

"Yeah, I had a home for a long time, but now I'm looking for a new one."

"Maybe this will be your home," James said.

"Yeah, maybe." Joe sat for a moment and then grinned when he stood up straight.

"What's that smell, James?" Joe finally asked.

"What smell?"

"Smells like industrial waste—a real pungent, heavy odor. It feels like it's all around us. I've been smelling it all day. Can't you smell it?" Joe asked.

James's stare was blank for a minute while he sniffed at the air. Then his face cleared with recognition. "You mean the sage. That's just sage. It's gonna get a lot stronger in June and July when the pollen is in the wind. It gets like it's on your skin and in your hair almost; it'll be all over us. You can almost feel it—like the air is sticky sometimes. Yeah, that's just sage."

The instant James said the word "sage," Joe recognized it. "Oh, yeah, sure it is. I just never smelled it like this. Sage." He drew in a deep breath. "Sure can see why the cowboys wrote songs about it."

"You probably never walked through it all day long before today either. That's why you didn't recognize it, I bet."

"Lots of firsts recently," Joe said to himself.

———

The supper dishes were clinking together in the sink when Joe settled into the rocker and started reading to Jake. James did all the supper dishes by himself once more, and when he was finished he walked to the dinner table and sat down. The others were long gone, and Jake was lying on his back on the floor sleeping while Joe read aloud.

"That's a good story you're readin," James offered. He'd been listening while he did the dishes. "You're a good reader, too. I'll bet Jake likes it!" he smiled.

"*Lonesome Dove!*" Joe nodded. "Seen the movie?"

"Huh uh. What's it called?"

"*Lonesome Dove!* Aren't you familiar with it?"

"Heard of it, I guess," James said.

"Well, I'm getting near the end now. Instead of me reading the end and spoiling it for you, why don't you just take it and read it while I start something else. I'll bet it really doesn't make much difference to Jake there. And I've read this a couple times."

"You mean you read the same book...over again? Why would you do that?"

"Sure. I really like it," Joe answered.

"But you already know what's gonna happen."

"Yeah." Joe paused and nodded. "But I really enjoy the way the author uses words to draw me into the story. It's good every time I read it. That's the way good books work." Joe closed the book and smiled at James, then threw the book to him. "Here. It's yours. When you're finished with it we'll have a book discussion. OK?"

James's eyes tightened with confusion and surprise.

"What's the matter?" Joe asked.

"I don't have any books. You're giving this to me?"

"Sure! You read the English language, right?"

"Yeah," James smiled. "But I never read a book with chapters and no pictures—a book like this—before."

"Well, that's a helluva good one to start with," Joe said.

"You're giving it to me?" James asked again.

"Sure. I may need you to open my Coke cans for me or help me piss tomorrow. Then we'll be even."

"Thanks, Joe." James still seemed a little confused. "I think I'll start it right now. But what are you gonna read?" James sounded as if he needed someone to sit and read with him—like he just couldn't do it if he were left alone. Just beneath that, Joe thought he felt James reaching out to him, like it was a confirmation of their friendship to read together.

Joe stood up to go to his truck and find another book. "I'm going out to my mobile library right now. I have a box of books in there." Joe's legs and back still hurt so badly that he walked as if he were crossing hot coals with his bare feet. He leaned against James when he walked past him. "Can you actually hear my muscles tightening like banjo strings when I walk, or does it just feel that way?"

"It'll get better," James said.

"Hope so," Joe replied from just outside the door.

When Joe returned to the dining hall, Mary was sitting at the table with James. "That's a good one, James; you'll like it," Joe heard her say before he stepped through the screen door.

"Thanks again for doing the dishes!" Mary said to Joe.

"He did them," Joe said as he pointed to James. "My hands hurt too bad." In his left hand Joe was carrying *Riders of the Purple Sage* by Zane

Grey. Under his right arm he was carrying the two slide carousels he'd bought at the garage sale in Mitchell.

"Are we going to have a slide show tonight?" Mary asked.

"No. Well, maybe. I bought these two boxes of slides at a garage sale a while back. It was the strangest thing. I just felt like I should buy them. I don't want the carousels, and I don't know what's on the slides. I just felt like I should buy them."

Joe set the carousels down on the table and lifted the top off one of the boxes. "Wanna see what's in here?" he asked Mary and James as he lifted a slide out of the box.

Joe held the slide up to the light above the kitchen table. He looked at it for a long moment, but he said nothing as he handed it to Mary and reached for another. When she looked at the slide, she saw a fat, bald man standing at an airport. She handed the slide to James when Joe passed another one to her. The second slide showed the same fat, bald man standing in front of the Sphinx in Egypt, and when she'd looked at it for a moment she passed it to James. Joe kept taking slides out of the box and holding them up to the light, then passing them to Mary.

Occasionally, Joe would say something like "hmmm" or "how about that?" But for the most part, he just looked at each slide for a moment and then passed it along to Mary.

The images that passed in front of their eyes were astounding. The same fat, bald dentist appeared in almost every slide. He smiled as he held the head of a trophy deer that he'd just shot. He stood on the edge of the Grand Canyon. His family—or at least Joe thought it was his family—surrounded him at weddings, graduations, and birthday parties. He'd obviously taken a trip to Europe because he'd been photographed in front of the Eiffel Tower, Big Ben, castles in Scotland, and the fjords of Norway. Several slides showed the various stages of construction of what must have been his home. The man's biggest smile came as he stood on the pontoon of a floatplane; he appeared to be on a fishing trip.

When he'd looked at the last of the two hundred slides, Joe leaned back on his chair and stared into Mary's eyes. All expression had drained from his face, and he said nothing.

"Isn't it wrong that someone would be selling their memories—all their nice memories?" Mary asked.

"Yeah, it kind of bothers me, too. This guy's life is over. I bought these images from his widow." Joe paused as if there might be some insight to be found in that thought if he waited for a while—but none came. "They're just someone's useless memories now; they don't mean anything to anyone else. That is odd…isn't it sad? This guy is dead now, and here's his life in front of us. I wonder if he found any meaning while he was having all these pictures taken?"

Joe shook his head and left the table. He thought of Ralph Webster's wordless pictures that only had meaning for Ralph. "We shouldn't be looking at this. It's not right to be looking at this." He crossed the room, put his hands in his pockets, and turned to Mary once more. "Think about what we just did. We just held another man's life up and examined it. We were looking for something, but what? It's just not right to re-examine a dead man's life. I hope he found some meaning in his life. Maybe it's there in those photos—who knows? But, sad as it is, that guy's life is over, and we shouldn't be looking at it. It was what it was. Now it's all over."

James was still holding slides up to the light when Joe and Jake disappeared out the door.

Mary wanted to follow Joe, but she sensed this wasn't the time to talk more. He seemed distant and depressed when he walked out the door. She would have liked to talk to him and ask just exactly what he was thinking. She didn't know anyone like him, and he'd just taken the words from her mouth when he'd asked about the old man finding meaning.

———

Several cups of coffee and a slow walk around the yard after breakfast had been enough to take the edge off the pain in Joe's back, arms, and legs. He swallowed four aspirin to help with the stiffness in his hands and forearms, then brought the aspirin bottle along when he and James left for one more day of fence building at the Twins.

"How do your hands and forearms feel, James? Aren't you a little sore from twisting and clipping all those strands of electric wire and barbed wire yesterday?" Joe asked.

"No," James replied.

Joe looked across the seat of the pickup truck while they bounced along toward another day of making fence. James shrugged and smiled when he realized Joe was staring at him. "Not really. I feel good," he added.

It hurt for Joe to make a fist. His fingers felt like they were all too big—like they were swollen. Even his fingernails hurt when he clenched his fists. He hadn't used his hands like this in a long time. He didn't really like the feeling of fatigue in his hands, but he was happy to be getting this type of physical work, and he knew it was good for him to find out how other men felt after a day's work. But he liked the idea that his hands were able to do delicate, precise things that other men couldn't. The idea of leaving dentistry behind was just fine, but he began to worry somewhat about his hands—if they would ever be the same again.

Cool morning air rushed in through the open truck window and made Joe think of all the times he'd driven along the river road at home and dreamed of just not going to work. He should have been ready to go to work back then. He was young and strong. It all should have been easy. But it just hadn't been easy. Now he was old, stiff, broke, and homeless, and he was looking forward to a day of manual labor. Life made no sense sometimes.

A cloud of dust swirled softly around the truck as it rolled to a stop along an unfinished fence line at the top of a grassy hill. "See, Joe, we just gotta run this fence over that hill and partway up the hill on the other side. Then we're done," James announced. "If you get too sore, just stop drivin' posts in. You can just carry 'em out there along the fence line and I'll drive 'em," he said as he stepped out of the truck.

"Oh, bullshit!" Joe called from the other side of the truck. When James looked over the top of the truck box, he couldn't see Joe but he could hear Joe talking.

"I'm a little stiff, but I can keep up with you!"

James stood on his tiptoes to look over the top of the truck and saw that Joe was bent over, stretching.

"Ow! Shit, that hurts!" Joe said when he straightened up. "I'll do my share!" he said in a businesslike tone as he reached into the truck and lifted some fence posts and a post driver out. Then he lifted his head and smiled. "But like I told you yesterday—you just might have to help me piss later." He turned and carried the posts away while he laughed at himself. "So we both have that to look forward to, huh?" he called out. He knew James was still staring at his back, wondering about him.

The pain in Joe's shoulders and back ebbed as the sun climbed in the sky. His continuous work with the post driver burned the stiffness away. Except for his forearms and hands, he was feeling fine by midmorning.

However, his hands had been pushed far beyond what they were able to cope with. He had enough strength left that he could squeeze the post driver and raise it over the fence posts, but that was about all. He knew that by afternoon, he'd be reduced to being James's assistant. He'd never be able to twist the heavy wires with a pliers and secure them to the fence posts. His hands and forearms were already aching, more than he could ever remember them aching before.

Shortly after noon, they'd driven all the fence posts into the ground, and it was time to start stringing barbed wire and electric wire from post to post. "Let's take a lunch break first, Joe," James suggested.

"OK," Joe said as he straightened his back. "But let's take the truck over by that tree, down by that little creek," Joe said.

As the truck bounced slowly over the open ground, the men jostled from side to side with each bump. Joe tapped James's arm and asked, "Know what kind of tree that big one is?"

"No," James answered.

"It's a Piss Elm! They call 'em Piss Elms because the cowboys like to stop and piss under 'em!" Joe laughed at himself. "My dad said that every time we came near one of those big old trees like that. A Piss Elm! Hmph."

"What did your dad do—what was his job?" James asked.

"He was a cowboy," Joe said, and his own words carried him swiftly back to his childhood.

"Really? Is he still alive?" James asked.

"No. He died pretty young. Had a heart attack and died one day."

"Was he a good man?" James asked.

Joe turned and smiled at James. "Now, why would you ask that?"

"Just wondered. You turned out to be a good man. I just wondered about your dad."

"Hmph. Well, I'm not so sure what I've turned out to be. But my father? Yeah, I guess he was a pretty good man. He did the best he could, and he was good to me. Turns out I didn't know him as well as I thought I did. But yeah, he was a good man, a very good man." Joe looked at James. "How 'bout your dad?"

"He wasn't such a good man," James said when he reached the shade of the Piss Elm. He turned off the truck engine and sat quietly. Joe could see the boy agonizing over his father and what he might say next.

Joe reached into the cooler and took out a sandwich for himself, then passed one to James. "Well, James, my grandfather—my father's father—was a terrible man. He was a wife beater and a child beater! No one really knows what happened to him. He may have died in prison for all we know. But his son, my father, turned out pretty good. There doesn't seem to be any rules about who's gonna turn out good or smart or handsome."

"Your grampa was a bad man?" James asked again.

"Yeah, that's what they say." Joe took a bite from his sandwich. "I never met him. He abandoned his family."

"My grampa was a nice man." James seemed to be talking to himself.

"Well, there you have it, kid. Maybe we can choose what we want to be, huh?" Joe sighed.

"I'm gonna go have a Coke and a cookie or two and sit over by that tree," Joe said as he stepped out of the truck. In a moment, James was sitting beside Joe on the ground near the tree.

"We got all of the really hard work done this morning, Joe. We can have the wire strung in a few hours and be all finished," James said optimistically. "You did good this morning."

"Well," Joe said slowly, "I did do pretty good, didn't I?" Then he smiled a wicked smile at James. "But I was right." With his left hand he pointed at the zipper on his blue jeans, then said, "I need some help now; my hands are too tired."

James's eyes narrowed as he smiled. "You're on your own, Joe. Maybe you should just piss yourself and let the wind dry you off while we work."

"No," Joe groaned as he stood up. He stepped over by the little creek, turned his back on James, and peed. When he was finished, he called out, "Oh oh! Can you help me put it back, James?"

"Too tired to put yourself back together?" James said as he climbed back into the truck.

"No. I just don't think it's healthy to touch that thing!" Joe called over his shoulder. As he zipped up his zipper, he laughed out loud. It really didn't make any sense. This labor was so hard that he'd lost all the strength in his hands. His back and shoulders were sure to be sore again tomorrow. But he couldn't remember the last time he'd had so much fun at work.

—•—

When the men gathered for supper that night, the talk revolved almost entirely around the livestock sale that was to begin in two days. Most of the corrals were now filled with horses, some with bulls that had been arriving continuously during the past two days. The Crossman place was beginning to buzz with anticipation.

Murdo had nearly finished giving the men their instructions for the next day, and he was about to get up from the supper table when Joe asked, "Hey, Murdo, next time you're in Billings will you buy a new cell phone for me?"

"You can buy one for yourself. You're goin' there tomorrow. You're gonna make a run for some last-minute groceries and other supplies. Mary'll give you a complete list later." With that, Murdo was out the door and gone in search of other chores to do, and the Duncans followed close behind him. Joe was thankful to have a little less physical job for a day.

"You gonna read for a while tonight?" James asked as Joe was busing dishes from the table to the sink. The enthusiasm in James's voice was clear. He wanted to sit with Joe and read books tonight.

"Sure. For a while," Joe answered. "But I'm a little tired tonight."

James seemed to need a pattern to follow. The act of reading for the sake of reading was obviously new to him. Joe could see that James was trying to watch his every move to see just how this reading thing was supposed to be done. When Joe pulled a rocker into the yellow light under a table lamp in the corner of the dining hall, James did the same thing.

After an hour of reading, sleep pushed Joe's eyes closed several times, and his head bobbed forward into *Riders of the Purple Sage*. Joe knew he had to turn in for the night. But before he stood up and prepared to leave, he stole a glance at James.

James Bond was staring a hole through the pages of *Lonesome Dove*. He looked at each page as if the secret of life had been laid out for him.

"How's the book?" Joe asked.

"It's like I'm right there with these guys!" James said.

"That's the idea. McMurtry tells a great story, doesn't he?" Joe said as he stood up. "I gotta get some sleep. C'mon, Jake."

"Hey, Joe. There's a guy in the book named Jake—Jake Spoon!" James said.

"Yep. That's where Jake's name came from. Someday we'll talk." Joe moved slowly toward the door. "You coming to bed?"

"I'm gonna read for a while longer."

"Hey, I need you to snore me to sleep," Joe said from the door. When he looked back at James, he was already reading again. He hadn't heard what Joe had said; he'd returned to the world inside the book.

———

The long drive into Billings seemed different than the long drive across Minnesota, South Dakota, and Wyoming: Joe had someplace to go and someplace to return to. The day off from hard labor was a good thing. It was even more difficult to make a fist today, although the stiffness in the rest of his body was beginning to subside.

None of the stops on Joe's list took much time. He picked up six hundred hamburger buns from a baker and twenty-five cases of Coke and Diet Coke from a grocery store. He bought himself a new cell phone. An auto parts store had several large boxes waiting for him, and he made a stop at a western store for some tack Murdo had requested.

He was carrying the tack to the cash register when he noticed a display of cowboy boots by the front door. They were just plain boots, like the ones all the cowboys wore for work. But he stared at them for a moment and thought of James. James really needs some boots; he can't keep wearing those stinky, grubby tennis shoes with holes that let the dust and cow shit in, he thought. In the back of his mind, he heard the sound of James clomping and dragging those ugly tennis shoes around. He thought it over for just a moment and then asked a salesman if they had the boot in a size 15EEE. The man said he'd have to look in the back, and then about five minutes later he emerged from the storage room with a smile and a box under his arm. "None. But I got one pair of size 16EEEs! Will that work?"

"That'll work. Little Sasquatch may still be growing!" Joe stroked his chin for a moment, then asked, "What size hat goes with a 16EEE boot?"

"That's a good question, mister," the man said, then he shrugged.

"OK. Do you have a size eight that looks like mine sort of?" Joe asked.

"I gotta go look in the back again," the man said as he turned around. The second trip to the back room took as long as the first, but when the salesman returned he was smiling once again. "You got a big cowboy at home, ain't ya?"

"Yeah. If you look out there in that truck, you can see the groceries I picked up for him just now."

The clerk peeked out through the glass doors and saw hundreds of hamburger buns and several dozen cases of Coke and Diet Coke. Then he looked at Joe again.

Joe nodded at him and added, "Little Pee Wee...sixth grade's been hard for him!"

The clerk turned and walked away. Joe smiled at himself. He was having fun. He hadn't had this much fun in years. The only times he'd been able to relax and joke like this had been when he was with Donny. Now, he was finding little bits of pleasure everywhere he looked.

As Joe stood at the cashier's counter and waited to pay for the tack, boots, and hat, he happened to look over at the things that had been placed next to the register to entice impulse buyers. There were candy bars, nail clippers, batteries, and some cheap toys. Then Joe noticed a rack of old movies on VHS tape. Joe reached over and flipped through the movies, not really intending to buy anything, until he came to *Goldfinger*. He smiled and put the tape on the counter next to James's new boots. While he stood there and waited his turn to check out, he began to wonder if he was doing the right thing, buying boots and a hat for James. Maybe he was sticking his nose into James's personal business. If James wanted boots and a hat, wouldn't he already have them by now? Joe figured he'd find out soon enough. This was a thing that needed to be done.

chapter
twenty-one

While Joe had been in Billings earlier in the day, a large tent, open on all four sides, had been set up just outside the auction arena in the south barn. A large, black, heavy-steel meat cooker, which traveled on four car tires and needed to be pulled around behind a truck, had been rolled under the tent.

"There! Everything looks like it's ready," Mary said. "We'll be up early to put some beef on the rotisserie, and we'll be serving beef sandwiches by midmorning! There's plenty more beef in the cooler, and everything else is set." Mary smiled at Joe. She'd stacked napkins, paper plates, and plastic cutlery on a table next to the cooker. Now, she glanced around with a satisfied look. "Murdo told you you're to help me tomorrow, right?" she asked. "You'll be helping me serve food out here, right?"

Before Joe could answer, Murdo stepped around the corner of the barn.

"I've already told him, Mary. But I'll need him from time to time, like right now." Murdo looked at his watch. "This happens every year, Goddammer! Here it is 10 o'clock and we still got stock to move around. C'mon, Joe, I got some work for you." With that, Murdo returned in the direction he'd come from.

"Goodnight, Mary," Joe said as he turned to follow Murdo.

"Beef! It's what's for breakfast!" she called to him. "See you in the morning!"

Joe jogged a few steps to catch up to Murdo. Before he could speak, Murdo answered the question he was about to ask. "Gets to be a damn train wreck every year the night before." He seemed to be talking to himself, not Joe. "There is a plan—a system we use for runnin' them bulls and then the horses into that arena, Goddammer. But every year, them dumb cowboys roll in here with stock and then put it in any ol' damn corral. 'Nen we wind up moving it around all night, puttin' it in the right place for mornin'. If them dumb-ass cowboys could read the signs we put up for them, we wouldn't have to stay up all night fixin' their dumb-ass mistakes!" Murdo stopped, then pointed. "Move them horses into that other pen over there. Can you do that?"

"Sure," Joe replied.

"Come 'n get me when you're done. I got more o' that shit for you to do!" Murdo snapped.

James, Norm, Junior, Jim Crossman, and two hands Joe didn't recognize were doing the same thing: moving several horses at a time, walking behind them and whistling while they chased them through a maze of fences into the proper corral. All the gates had small signs with ID numbers for the horses inside. A program had been printed for buyers sitting in the arena, and it was important for the correct horses to be in the proper corrals so that the Crossman hands could move them into the auction pit in precise order by the number assigned to them in the program. Also, many of the buyers liked to wander around the corrals and have a leisurely, close-up inspection of horses they were interested in before the horses reached the auction pit.

About 1:30 a.m., Joe heard Murdo from across the other corrals. "Goddammer, I b'lieve that's it, Mr. Crossman! Fuckin' dumb cowboys!" It made no sense, but every time he heard Murdo cuss, he felt good. Most of the time, Murdo's cussing actually drew a smile from him. There was something comforting in the way Murdo complained and cursed.

Joe looked over and saw Murdo standing on the second plank of one of the fences so that he could see across the corrals. The big yard lights mounted on a tall pole beside the barn cast Murdo's shadow in several directions. As Joe looked on, Murdo counted livestock and compared what he saw in front of him with the information on the piece of paper in his hand. He mumbled profanities and counted with his index finger. Finally, he said, "That'll do 'er" and jumped down.

A smile creased the corner of Joe's lips as he walked toward Murdo. If any other man spoke to him in the harsh way that Murdo did, he'd hate the man. Yet he was drawn to Murdo. He thought once more of the power of words. Murdo was able to spit out words in simple combinations that everyone understood, while the next man might say the same thing in an abrasive or hurtful way. Joe's smile widened as he considered that thought.

"What the fuck are you smilin' about?" Murdo said, trying to hide his own smile. Even that small question could have come across as mean-spirited, but Joe could hear and see the joy Murdo sent with it.

"You. You're not so tough!" Joe smiled openly and put his arm around Murdo's shoulder as they walked along a plank fence toward the barn.

"Well, don't tell them others. They think I'm twisted fuckin' steel!" Murdo chuckled. "You better get some sleep. It's gonna be a long day tomorrow—I mean today!" Murdo said. Then he walked quickly to his truck and drove away. He waved with his index finger as he drove past Joe.

Mr. Crossman's truck followed closely behind Murdo's, and the Crossman ranch fell silent as Junior and Norm walked over to the little frame houses they lived in. From behind him, Joe could hear the heavy thumping of James's enormous tennis shoes as he dragged them across the gravel parking lot and clomped toward his bedroom above the shop.

"Hey, James! Come here, I've got something for you," he called out. When he'd retrieved the packages from his truck, he led James up to the little room above the auction arena where the TV with the VCR still set on the little wooden desk.

"What's up?" was all James had said as he'd followed behind Joe.

When they reached the little room, Joe turned to James. "All right, kid. I took the liberty of buying you some things. If you don't want them, that's OK. I'll return them. But I thought you needed this stuff. All right?"

"Yeah?" James nodded.

Joe reached into the large plastic bag and withdrew the box that held the boots. "Try 'em on!"

James took the box and returned a confused look.

"Cowboys don't wear tennis shoes!" was all Joe said.

"For me?" James asked.

"Damn right."

"Where'd you get the money?" James asked.

"Never mind; I've got money," Joe answered. "Try 'em on."

"They're perfect!" James said as he walked a few circles in the little plywood room. "Where'd you get 'em?"

"Western store in Billings. Now try this," Joe said as he pulled the hatbox from the same plastic bag.

James's eyes narrowed. He turned his head slightly sideways. With his left thumb he lifted the lid of the box ever so slightly and tried to look under it before he actually removed it. Joe knew what James was thinking. He could see that it was a hat box, and he wanted desperately for there to be a hat inside it instead of some other thing delivered in a hat box. But James's eyes told Joe that he felt he had no right to hope for such a great thing. When he'd lifted the lid far enough, he leaned forward and looked. He closed his eyes in thankfulness when he realized what he'd been given. Then he flipped the box top on the floor and held the brown Stetson while he looked at it.

"Hope it fits!" Joe said.

"It's perfect!" James said. He stood up and walked around in his new boots and hat, but said nothing.

"You look like you're seven feet tall, cowboy," Joe said with a smile.

"Why did you do this, Joe?" James asked solemnly.

Joe didn't answer immediately. He sighed once, then said softly, "Because you needed it."

"Thanks, Joe." James nodded as a grin curled his lips. For just a moment, Joe thought he looked like his own sons used to look on Christmas morning, giddy with excitement. James Bond looked like he wanted a hug or was about to run over to show the Duncans his new look. He offered Joe an awkward handshake and a crooked smile instead. "Thanks, Joe."

"My pleasure! I have one more thing, then we'd better get some sleep, cowboy," Joe said as he fumbled with the videotape. "Do you really NOT know why they call you James?" Joe asked.

James only shrugged. He seemed to be unwilling to admit that he didn't know the answer to Joe's question. "It's my nickname."

"That's what I thought." Joe unwrapped the movie and slid it into the VCR on the desk. The VCR clicked several times, and in a moment *Goldfinger* was playing on the TV. "They call you James because of this guy, in this movie. The hero is a spy named James Bond, same as you, and he's the coolest guy on Earth. He's handsome, smart, and he has a license to kill bad guys, and all the babes want him. Kind of like Murdo, only dressed up nice! Here, watch this." Joe stopped the tape at the exact spot where Sean Connery first says his name is "Bond, James Bond." "That's why everyone calls you James—because your name reminds them of this guy. His name is James Bond. Get it? It's just like Sherlock Holmes," Joe shrugged. "I never knew anybody with the last name of Holmes whose buddies didn't call him Sherlock. You know Sherlock Holmes, right?" Joe nodded yes.

James shook his head no.

"Well, there's some more reading for you, then," Joe said, and he tried to hide his surprise at James's lack of knowledge. Joe guessed that James Bond had had his feelings hurt enough already in his short life, so he didn't say anything. Joe hit the eject button and gave the videotape to James. "Let's get some sleep. You can watch that whole thing when you have more time."

Darkness and the faint scent of machine oil permeated everything as Joe settled into his sleeping bag on his bed in the room above the shop. Jake stretched once, then curled up against Joe's chest and sighed. Sleep was coming for Joe, and there were no demons to drive away tonight. Joe was free tonight, and as he was settling into a deep sleep, he heard a voice from the darkness.

"I'm likin' that book you gave me, too," James said softly.

"Good. Reading will make you a better man," Joe mumbled.

"Thanks, Joe," James added.

"Uh huh," Joe mumbled again as sleep settled over him.

The last thing Joe Mix heard that night before he drifted off to sleep was his roommate repeating the words, "Bond, James Bond."

"Never had a beef sandwich for breakfast before!" Joe said to Mary as he pushed the last of his sandwich into his mouth.

"Where's Jake the dog this morning?" Mary asked.

"Left him behind closed doors in the shop. He doesn't need to be underfoot all day. I was worried he might get run over, what with all the truck traffic in the yard," Joe answered. He picked a scrap of beef off the knife Mary was using to cut sandwich meat and tossed it into his mouth. "What would you like me to do first, Mary?"

"Start putting Coke in those big buckets, then cover them with ice. Next, bring out the napkins and paper plates. This place is gonna get busy in a little while."

By 9:00 a.m., the driveway of the Crossman ranch was lined with two hundred cars and trucks. Mary had already given away several dozen sandwiches. Some cowboys stood under the tent and ate as they renewed old friendships. Others wandered into the auction arena and bid on livestock.

Robert and Jim Crossman, along with another man that Joe had never seen, sat in the little office where he'd given James his hat and boots only a few hours earlier. They looked out at the crowd in the bleachers and the balcony and made notes while they watched the auction.

Two auctioneers stood in front of them. They took turns calling out for bids while a very pretty young woman, dressed in cowboy attire, moved the bulls slowly in front of the gallery of bidders sitting in the bleachers.

Joe thought the young girl was stunning. She had red hair and thin features, and she was an expert at parading the bulls through the auction pit. Her eyes were sharp, and she kept her distance from the massive critters. She moved the bulls with a whip that she handled like a willow branch as she tapped them on the backside and coaxed them to strut in front of the cowboys. She wore buckskin-colored chaps with fringe all down the legs, and a white shirt with light blue fringe on the arms, across the back, and on the breast. Joe had crept into the auction several times, presumably to look at the bulls and watch the auction in progress, but he'd really wanted to watch the red-headed cowgirl.

"That's Sherry Lanning. She lives over by Ennis. Her grandfather is a friend of Dad's," Mary said. Joe hadn't seen Mary approaching, and she startled him.

"Who?" Joe said sheepishly.

"I saw you looking," Mary smiled.

"I wasn't really looking. I'd say I was noticing..."

"Forget it. Everybody looks at her," Mary interrupted. "I just came to get you because Murdo was looking for you. He says he needs a little help moving some horses. He's over there." She pointed in the direction of the corrals.

"OK. I'll be back when he's done with me. You need anything before I go?" Joe asked.

"No. But when you get back, we'll have to put more beef on the spit."

"OK. See you in a while," Joe said as he turned to leave.

"Hey, I just saw James!" Mary called after Joe had turned and taken several steps. "I didn't recognize him!"

Joe turned to face Mary. "Oh?"

"He's so proud of the way he looks in his hat and boots! I was talking with Murdo when James walked right past us. Murdo wasn't sure who he was at first either!"

Joe pursed his lips and nodded. "Yeah, he needed that stuff." Then he turned away.

"That was a nice thing to do, Joe!" Mary walked over to Joe and took hold of his arm. "A fine thing!" she added, then stroked the back of his arm to acknowledge the kindness he'd shown to James.

"Yeah, well, it needed to be done, I guess," Joe said sheepishly before he walked away. Mary's touch had been warm and soothing. He'd wanted to put his arms around her for just a moment. He let out a huge sigh when she returned to the sandwich table.

He walked around the side of the barn and started looking for Murdo. Old men, young men, even some women stood around in small groups holding Coke cans and beef sandwiches, talking to one another, while others walked in and out of the arena. It seemed to Joe that there might be two distinct groups of livestock buyers here today. Some of these people were ranchers looking for bulls or horses they could use to work on their ranches. Others appeared to be more affluent and were probably there looking for riding horses. They wore nicer clothes, didn't show quite as many hard miles on their faces, and, judging from the license plates in the lot, some had come quite a distance.

When he rounded the corner on the north side of the barn, he was surprised by the scale of activity in front of him. Several dozen men wearing cowboy hats and boots wandered back and forth along the pathways between all the corrals containing livestock. Some of the men were employees of the Crossman Ranch, moving horses to and from the auction pit. But others were trying to get a close look at animals they planned to bid on later in the day, or perhaps the next day, in the auction pit. Joe figured there were about five hundred bulls—big, fine-looking bulls—in one area of the feedlot, and perhaps four thousand horses. The horses had been arranged according to their color. All the blacks were in one series of adjoining corrals, the buckskins in another, and so on.

Joe noticed several cowboys standing in a circle and talking near a pen full of red roans. When he walked a little closer, he saw that Murdo was part of the group and appeared to be telling a story. Joe walked directly toward the men, and as he drew closer he could see that, as usual, Murdo was entertaining the group. Joe edged close enough to hear the conversation. He guessed that he'd arrived just in time for the best part. Murdo was gesturing with both hands, palms down, and moving them in small circles. "I was a-working this gal, and she was a big ol' gal, too. Anyways, before long I got everything going in the same direction." He stopped to raise his eyebrows, and all the others laughed.

He recognized Joe and then interrupted himself to say something. "Don't go nowheres. I got some shit for you to do!"

The cowboys glanced at Joe. He nodded that he understood, and the cowboys turned expectantly back to Murdo.

"So anyways," Murdo continued, "I'm a-workin' this big ol' gal, an' ever'thing is movin' together—all the parts. So I was gonna rearrange things a little bit an' try to give her the Velvet Half-Nelson. Well, one o' them big titties was a swingin' like this here"—he waved his hand back and forth in front of his face—"and sure enough, I leaned into it! Hit me right square on the side o' the head! Sounded like somebody dropped a watermelon off'n a bar stool! Purt near knocked me silly! All I could hear outta my left ear for a couple days was the ocean!"

The cowboys had been laughing all along, but the laughter exploded when Murdo finished the story. One of the cowboys looked around as if he was searching for someone and then asked, "Maybe she'll bring you some flowers today?" And the cowboys laughed even louder.

"I told her I was you, and I give her your phone number!" Murdo said.

"Well, she must not have been that impressed. She ain't called."

"She's probably waitin' for your hearing to improve!" Murdo replied.

The group's laugher grew with each man's reply. Finally, Murdo stepped away from the others. "I gotta go to work. See you boys later!"

In an instant, Murdo and Joe were walking quickly toward the stock pens adjacent to the auction pit. "You gotta give Norm and Junior a break so they can go get something to eat. Follow me. They're over here mindin' the gates by the arena."

The Duncan brothers were working "backstage." Each one of them was minding a gate. Junior was in charge of the door that opened into the auction arena. Norm was operating the gate that led out of the arena, and Junior's job was to make sure that only one bull or horse got from the pen he was watching and onto the stage. Norm's job was to make sure that once a bull or a horse had left the arena, it never got back in there. "Why don't you give Norm the first break?" Murdo said, loud enough for Norm to hear. "He looks like he's getting faint with hunger."

"Where'd you find him, Joe? Tellin' lies?" Norm asked when he walked past.

"Hurry back, Norm," Murdo grinned. "I ain't sure Joe can grasp the complexities of this job!"

Norm only smiled and walked around the outside of the barn in search of a sandwich and a Coke.

Joe waited, then slammed the gate shut after a black bull lumbered through. Then he leaned on the fence and tried to see through a crack in the plank wall into the auction arena. Murdo leaned on the fence beside him and said softly, "James looks handsomer than shit in his hat and boots. That was a nice thing you done!"

Joe never looked at Murdo; he just peered through the small crack in the wall. "Yeah, he's a good kid. He needed a hat and boots. Besides that, he took pretty good care of me the last couple days while we were making fence." He turned his head to get a better look through the gate and asked, "Do you know that girl with the red hair? She's beautiful!"

"Sherry? I know her! She's a wild one!" Murdo stopped, then started again.

"That was a thoughtful thing, Joe, buying him those things. I wish I woulda done it!"

"Well, that makes us even, I suppose—'cause I wish I'd done a lot of things you've done!" Joe turned and raised his eyebrows.

Murdo smiled a surprised and innocent smile and stepped away from the fence. "Yeah...well...you know what they say?"

"What's that?" Joe asked.

"I don't know either. You caught me off guard there," Murdo muttered when he walked away. "Give Junior his break when Norm gets back! Then check with Mary," Murdo said as he disappeared through the door of the barn.

Joe moved from one job to the next for the rest of the day. He helped Mary put more beef on the spit. He helped the other men move live-stock. He spent some of the afternoon driving a feed truck out to the horse corrals.

The crowd at the auction began to thin out about 6:00 p.m., and by 8:00 p.m. the only job that remained before the next day was to clean up the mess under the tent, bag the garbage, and burn it. The day had been easy for Joe—a well-needed rest for his aching hands, forearms, legs, and shoulders. He'd been assigned to clean up the tent area and the arena. He went about the end-of-the-day chores by himself. When he'd carried a dozen large, bulging plastic bags full of garbage to a rust-ed, fifty-five-gallon barrel behind the shop, he put two bags in the bar-rel and started them on fire.

He stood upwind and watched the flames from the garbage fire flick-er. He couldn't help but think how far behind he'd left his home and life in only a couple weeks. It was quite a distance from his home and his life in Rochester to this place in Montana. But it was even farther from the ballroom at The Oaks to burning garbage behind the shop. He'd had a good day—a pleasant day with no regret or longing for something else. He watched yellow flames and then gray smoke and tiny ashes drift into the Montana evening. He felt just fine. He knew this wasn't his final destination, but it wasn't bad for now. He was beginning to come alive, and he knew it.

chapter
twenty-two

Mary cut thin slices of sizzling beef and let them fall from the huge rotisserie onto the plate she held under them. "Getting sick of beef sandwiches for three meals a day?" she asked James and Joe when she handed them each a paper plate with two large sandwiches. The second day of the sale had dawned clear and fresh, and all the hands were having breakfast under the tent once again.

"Not yet," James answered quickly. He'd been sitting with Norm and Junior while they prepared for another day.

"Never!" Joe added. He was looking forward to another day. He knew his place was to help a woman give away beef sandwiches, and to open and close gates so livestock could pass through. It wasn't very cowboy-like, but he was just fine with that. He understood he was harboring what seemed to be a serious inconsistency. He'd been weary and unhappy over a job like dentistry, which carried status and provided an excellent living. It made no sense, but he was enjoying the simple chores of a ranch, where his main intellectual challenges seemed to be not stepping in shit and not spilling beef onto the dirt floor under the tent.

The other men finished their breakfast, threw their paper plates into one of the large garbage cans, and wandered off to their assigned jobs to prepare for the day.

The first pickup trucks of the day began to arrive while Joe was placing paper napkins and plastic forks on the long table under the tent. Only horses would be sold today at the sale; buyers who wanted to wander around and look at the horses before the sale started began to arrive several hours early. The men who began to sift through the corrals at Crossman Cattle Company today were a little different from the men of the previous day. There were ranchers and cowboys in the mix, just as there were yesterday. But today, there was a much larger contingent of a different type: many of the men wandering around this morning looked as if they'd just stopped at western stores and purchased fine, expensive western clothing. Many of the men wore new jeans with sharp creases, new, stylish boots with leather accessories, and new hats. About half of today's well-dressed men were accompanied by women.

Several times, Joe actually did a double-take when he noticed a woman. Most of them were younger than the men they were with, and they all seemed to be dressed as if they were about to appear in a country music video. Their clothing was cut to accentuate their cleavage and their butts, and Joe made a point to enjoy the view. Almost all of them wore expensive cowboy hats and plenty of makeup.

As the cowboys and couples began to filter past the tent where Joe and Mary were preparing sandwiches, some of them stopped to visit. Many of them knew Mary, or at least knew she was a Crossman. They paused to exchange greetings and chat about other friends they had in common. Many of them seemed to have been regular visitors at past Crossman Cattle Company livestock sales. Several of them smiled or laughed openly when they asked just where they might find Murdo.

Mary was a charming hostess, and she greeted everyone as if they were old friends. When strangers approached her, she was friendly and always welcomed them to the Crossman Cattle Company Livestock Auction before she gave them permission to wander around and look at the stock.

"You're pretty good!" Joe said to her during a lull at the sandwich table. "You should be in there selling horses. People like you. They'd pay extra for a horse just for the pleasure of buying it from you."

Mary never smiled. She just turned to the big, black rotisserie with a knife and a plate and sliced some more beef from the spit. "That's Robert's job," she said when she turned back toward Joe.

Joe didn't like Robert, and he didn't see how anyone could—especially Mary. He was totally self-absorbed. The only time Joe had seen him speak to anyone or show any enthusiasm was when he'd greeted the auctioneers and some of the more affluent-looking livestock buyers and their women. He could be engaging and pleasant when he chose to, but he only chose to be gracious to the beautiful people. He'd passed by Joe several times during the first day, nearly touching shoulders with him, and he'd looked away and said nothing. He'd stopped by the tent to pick up a sandwich twice and hadn't spoken to Joe or Mary either time.

"So, does Robert like the cattle business?" Joe asked while he dumped some ice into a cooler filled with Coke. Mary didn't answer for a moment. Joe thought she hadn't heard him, and he was about to ask the question again when Mary answered.

"I don't know," she said with a faraway look in her eyes. "He was studying to be an architect when we met in college. But Jim persuaded him to come back and take over the ranch." She looked at Joe and raised her eyebrows. "And that was that!" she said. Her face couldn't hide a simmering unhappiness, or the fact that she had more to say.

A jolly sixty-year-old rancher with a big belly and a big hat strolled up to the table and asked for a sandwich. Joe was thankful the man had interrupted Mary's story because he didn't want to ask her any personal questions, and it was clear she'd given him the green light to do just that.

"Say, can you tell me where I could find Murdo? I always like to talk to him—or I guess I should say listen to him." The man's round face bent into a big smile.

"I just heard him laughing over there." Mary pointed around the corner of the barn. "Just follow the trail of bullshit; it'll lead you to Murdo."

The old man said "thank you" and walked in the direction Mary had pointed. He raised his paper plate up just under his chin and held it there with his left hand. He held his sandwich in his right hand and chuckled at Mary's directions as he ate the sandwich and disappeared around the corner of the barn.

Joe watched the man walk away and hoped Mary had lost her inclination to talk about Robert.

"I could tell you more. But it would be like looking at slides from my life, like those slides the other night." Mary was staring at Joe when he turned to her. Her sad eyes were stealing away some of the girl-next-door beauty. Her short, brown hair and pleasant face and perfect, small figure were easy to look at. If Joe had met her under any other circumstances, he thought he'd have been attracted to her. But she had an unhappy, vulnerable look about her that made Joe uneasy.

"Mary...I...those slides...there's a lot going on...," Joe stammered.

"Somebody left a message for you last night," Mary said flatly, "on the phone at the house." She seemed like a trial attorney who'd abandoned one line of questioning and taken up another. "The caller was looking for Dr. Joe Mix?" Mary stopped and tilted her head with the question, then added, "Said he was your brother and wanted you to call him." Mary had asked a question as she'd delivered Donny's message, and Joe knew he must answer it now. It was time to tell her the story.

Joe drew in a deep breath, then looked to his right and left to be sure no one could hear what he had to say.

"About three weeks ago, I sort of hit the wall with my life. I guess I had what they used to call a nervous breakdown. It felt like a heart attack, but it wasn't, I guess." He shrugged but still looked at the ground when he spoke. "The doctor said it was 'Acute Fatigue,' whatever that is. Anyway, I'd been really unhappy with my job, my marriage, my life. It seemed I was gonna die if I didn't make a change." He stopped and looked at her before he went on. "One day, I just flipped out. Took the things I wanted and left. I quit my job and left my wife—told her I did-n't love her anymore. I've been on the road ever since then. The only thing I know for sure is that I don't want any of my old life back. I'm happy I'm here, for now. Well, at least I'm happy I moved on—that I'm not there anymore."

"And you're a doctor?"

"Dentist."

Mary made a face.

"Sorry," Joe said.

Then Mary smiled. "No, it's not that. I just don't understand. Were you having money trouble or problems with your health or your mar-riage? If I can ask...sorry."

"It's OK. I was just so unhappy I thought I was gonna die from it. Just a failed marriage and a job I hated. Like a lot of other men, I suppose. I don't know if I could put it into any other words."

"Your wife—how's she?"

"I don't know. I guess she'll be fine. We sort of lost track of each other."

"Kids?"

"Two grown sons. Pretty much grown, anyway. That really bothers me—that I probably haven't been a good father." Joe paused. "That and the idea that I failed at so many things." He stopped himself and looked away. He shook his head in frustration.

"Joe…" she started.

"Look, Mary. I left all that because I was miserable, and I guess I was looking for some meaning. I'm just some guy who ran away. I don't have anything profound to say. No answers to life's questions. No keys to happiness." He paused again. "Meaning? Shit. I don't know anything about that." He looked at her and shrugged as though he'd given up. "I don't know anything. I don't need a pep talk or a lecture. I just need to find my own way. I really don't need to talk about it—not now, anyway."

Mary nodded but said no more.

"I hope you'll keep this between you and me?" Joe asked.

"Sure," Mary answered.

Nothing more was said, by either Joe or Mary, about anything but sandwiches and livestock, or just who some of the buyers were that were milling around the ranch. Mary explained that about half of the people at the sale were locals and the other half came from all over the West and Midwest. Several of the people she knew because she saw them every year at the livestock sale, and they'd become friends. Some of the people she recognized because she knew they'd spent a lot of money at the Crossman sale every year, but she'd never spoken to them.

Even though there was no talk of anything other than the job at hand, both Joe and Mary began to sense that their friendship had moved to another level since Joe had confided in her. Joe thought that maybe if the subject of his past came up again he'd share a little more with Mary.

"Would you like to take a break, Joe? You can wander around for a while if you'd like—just have a look at the sale and relax for a while," Mary said during a quiet stretch.

"Sure. Then I'll come back and you can have a break," Joe answered.

He walked slowly through the corrals and watched as the prospective buyers looked at the horses and talked to other buyers. The cowhands all said hello to Joe. Several asked him questions about a particular horse or pen full of horses. Apparently, the cowhands had noticed that he worked at Crossman Cattle Company and assumed he knew something of the business. Joe always smiled when he confessed his ignorance, and had a chuckle with the cowboys.

The affluent types, on the other hand, seemed to think Joe was invisible. Some of the well-dressed buyers who were alone or with another cattleman would exchange a greeting with Joe. But none of the men who were accompanied by women seemed able to see Joe. He began to stand close to them when he could and listen to their conversations.

Some of the men seemed arrogant and a little rude to the women with them. They strolled and strutted among the horses, then leaned close to their woman's ear and explained all that was wrong with a particular horse. They seemed so serious, almost angry, as they looked at horses. It seemed to Joe that it was very important for them to convince the women of their special knowledge and insight regarding horseflesh. Many of the women seemed to understand that it was their duty to hang onto every insightful word and profound utterance of their cowboy.

Some of the women were a little smug too, Joe thought. As Joe walked along between the corrals, his eyes moved from one woman to the next. Oftentimes the women would make eye contact with him, but as he smiled and said hello, they usually looked away as if they hadn't seen him.

Joe walked through the corrals and then found his way into the arena. The redhead from the previous day was working again, looking even more beautiful than the day before. Her buckskin vest and chaps were almost white, and she wore a blue shirt under the white vest. Her red lips, red hair, and green eyes created an image Joe couldn't look away from. She liked what she was doing, and she smiled openly at the cowboys in the bleachers as she moved horses through the auction pit. Joe didn't realize it, but he was grinning all the while he watched her work.

"You're gonna drool on yourself there, cowboy!" Murdo's words surprised Joe. Joe wiped his chin with a napkin and smiled at Murdo to confess he'd been caught staring. "She's beautiful, Murdo!" Joe said.

"Yeah, she's a wild one too. I seen her up in Billings once..."

"No, you don't get it," Joe interrupted. "She's just beautiful! I don't want to run down there and hump her. I just think she's a beauty, that's all."

Murdo's brow crinkled into a pile of eyebrows under the brim of his black hat.

"Look like you stepped in shit," Joe said.

"Junior needs a break." Murdo shook his head and walked out the back of the arena with Joe at his heels.

"You're an odd one, Joe," Murdo said when they were outside walking together.

Joe stood several inches taller than Murdo as they walked shoulder to shoulder around the outside of the barn. "There's a lot of attractive women around here, Murdo. You can't want to hump every one of them," Joe said.

"Oh?" Murdo asked.

"Really, Murdo. What do you guys look for in a woman? Hell, where do you find women when you're not having livestock sales?" Joe asked.

Junior Duncan had heard Joe's question, and his face took on a grin as he waited for Murdo to answer.

"Well, Joe, we usually go into Billings, to bars and such," Murdo answered. Then he stood on the bottom plank of a fence and leaned over the top plank.

"I like natural beauty in a woman, just like you or any other man does, like that'n and that'n." He pointed to several women. "And I like 'em to know something about horses, but I don't like 'em too ranchy."

"Too ranchy? What the hell does that mean?" Joe asked.

Murdo was preparing his answer when Junior blurted, "He don't like 'em to chew or to look like James."

Murdo laughed out loud, then spit. "Goddammer, that was a good 'un, Junior."

"How about you, Junior?" Joe asked.

"There's girls around. Murdo hasn't ruined 'em all! I'll be back in a little while. Thanks, Joe."

Joe watched Junior walk back around the corner of the barn, and he was about to say something to Murdo when he turned around. But Murdo was staring intently at something across the corral.

"Whatya lookin' at, Murdo? You in love again?" Joe asked.

"Looky there." He pointed to a corral some distance away. "Look at that. That 'ol Billy just stares at everybody who walks by him. Seems like he's tryin' to pick a fight with everyone. Goddammer, that 'ol Blue Billy, he's a bucker! I'll see you later, Joe." He jumped off the fence and walked away.

The remainder of Joe's day passed pretty much as the previous day had. When the sale day ended, he cleaned up the area around the tent and prepared things for the final day of the sale. He burned several large bags of garbage as the sun was setting, then took Jake to the dining hall for some playtime and reading.

Joe was reading *Riders of the Purple Sage* to Jake while Jake chewed at a bone next to Joe's feet. He was surprised at how much he was enjoying a novel that had been written nearly one hundred years earlier. The night was dark, and Joe supposed he'd remain alone in the dining hall until he chose to go to bed. But off in the distance, he heard the growing noise of heavy footsteps, and he knew James was coming to join him.

"Hi, Joe," James said with a smile. Then he held up *Lonesome Dove* for Joe to see. "Thought I'd read for a while before bed."

"Where have you been for the past couple hours? I thought you were in bed," Joe said.

"I was over watching *Goldfinger* on the TV in the auction arena," James said with a huge grin. "Did you know James Bond—the other James Bond—his girlfriend's name is Pussy Galore?" James had the look of a junior high school boy who had just learned about the facts of life.

"Yes, I knew that. Great name, huh?" Joe added.

"Yeah!" James giggled, and looked even more childlike.

Both men read silently for another ninety minutes. Jake was spread-eagled on his back and sleeping soundly when Joe finally yawned and closed his book.

"How far along are you, James?" Joe asked as he stretched his arms above his head. "How far into *Lonesome Dove* are you?"

"I think the boys are gonna head for Montana pretty soon. They just stole some horses. How's your book?"

"Well, it's pretty good. It's really good! I used to think that Natty Bumpo, in *The Leatherstocking Tales*, was the greatest hero in American fiction. He's the guy who sort of morphed into the Lone Ranger, Roy Rogers, and then John Wayne, maybe even Clint Eastwood." Joe stopped himself. He could see by the look on James's face that he'd left James far behind. "Are you familiar with *The Last of the Mohicans*? It's part of James Fenimore Cooper's *Leatherstocking Tales*. The hero is Hawkeye, or Natty Bumpo, and his Indian friend is Chingachgook. It's a great story." Joe knew what James's answer would be.

"No," James admitted.

"Well, that's OK, 'cause you got some great books waitin' for you," Joe said. "Anyway, Zane Grey, the author of *Riders of the Purple Sage*, may have created an even better character—a real man's man. This first chapter might just be my favorite in any book." Joe looked at James and saw only a blank stare.

"You can have this book when I'm done with it too!" Joe said. "But let's talk about great books some other time. I'm going to bed." Joe stood up and Jake scrambled to his feet also.

"Me too," James added when Joe stood up. He followed Joe out the door and over to their little room above the shop.

As they crossed the gravel turnaround area and passed under the yard light, James asked Joe, "Have you read all those books? Really?"

"Sure! Lots of people have read them!" Joe replied.

"Do you know where I could get 'em?" James asked softly.

"Sure, James. You know, you can go to a library. I'm sure they have a big library in Billings. You just get yourself a library card. Then you can check out any book you want and take it home for a couple weeks."

James looked as if that was an impossible task.

"They've probably got about a million books just waiting for you, James. And a bunch of librarians who'd be glad to help you find whatever kind of books you're looking for. And it's all free. They can't say no to you," Joe explained.

"Really? That would be OK, I guess," James said. His eyes flickered with a sense that just maybe it could be possible for him to claim something more than this little life he found himself in. Joe stared for a moment and wondered if he was helping James open the door to a bigger place.

"Yeah, go get yourself a library card next time you're in Billings. You can do that," Joe urged. "It's free, you know?"

"Sure, I could probably do that," James said.

When darkness settled over Joe Mix and he heard James Bond start to snore softly, he thought back through the years. He remembered the time when he'd made a point to read one chapter of *The Leatherstocking Tales* every night, then repeat that chapter as a bedtime story for his boys the next night. Ben and Chris had laid awake and listened to each word of their father's stories. Chris had listened with a furrowed brow, as if he were waiting for something to disagree with, while Ben had been spellbound, sitting with his mouth open much of the time. Chris had interrupted him over and over again with questions about the Indians, or whether Hawkeye was really the best shot with a rifle, or why Chingachgook never got lost in the woods. Those were good days, Joe thought—great days. Maybe he hadn't been such a failure as a dad after all. But he wished he could have those days back again; he'd do better. He wondered why he'd been in such a hurry for those days to end. But then maybe there was still time to do better. He drifted off to sleep thinking about good times for a change.

———•———

"You know, I haven't seen Cletto for two days!" Joe said to Mary as they put one last cut of beef on the spit and started to prepare for the final day of the sale.

"He's been around, but he's pretty busy. He's going to make a lot of money this week," Mary said. "He's bred a lot of fine cutting horses, and people know about him. They come here from all over."

Joe reached down to pick up a box of buns, and Mary put her hand on the middle of his back. "Did you call your brother?" she asked quietly.

Her touch sent another wave of something warm and comfortable rushing off to every pleasure center in his body. He wanted to turn and put his arms around her waist and see what that felt like. Instead, he straightened his back and stepped away from her.

"I forgot! Is it OK if I go call him right now? I won't take very long."

"Sure. Go. I can set this up," Mary answered.

Joe walked quickly behind the shop where his truck was parked and tried to use his cell phone, but as Murdo had told him, there was no signal. He hurried back to the auction arena and hoped Robert Crossman would not be sitting in the little plywood room with the phone and the TV, overlooking the auction pit. When he reached the little room, it was empty. So he dialed Donny's home number as fast as he could.

"Hello," Donny answered.

"Hi, Donny," Joe said softly.

""Oh, jeez, I'm glad you called. Are we OK, Joe? I know you hung up on me the other day, and I'm sorry I barked at you. Are we OK...you and I?"

"We're OK, Donny. But I don't want another lecture. What's done is done. There are things we're just not going to talk about, ever. Well, someday we'll sit down together and talk, but for now...no more lectures. All right?"

"All right. I shouldn't have gotten after you like I did. I'm sorry," Donny said.

"It's done. It's over, Donny. What's up?" Joe asked.

"Well, there's a lot to tell you. But first of all, where are you?" Donny said.

"I'm living on a ranch in Montana still, for a while. Nice people. I'm OK. I'm OK, Donny. Don't worry about me."

"How's your heart? Any trouble with that heart thing or Acute Fatigue since you left?"

"I feel great. I still have a lot going on in my head, though. I've been getting a lot of exercise and fresh air. I feel great." Joe paused, then asked, "What's going on back there?"

"Plenty. Are you ready?" Donny asked.

"I guess so."

"The Minnesota Dental Examiners revoked your license..." Donny waited for a reply.

"OK. What else?"

"Jess filed for divorce..." Donny waited again.

"Who?" Joe said as though he'd never heard of Jess.

"Ooo—good one, Joe," Donny chuckled. "But the bitch is gonna get everything?"

"No. Like I said, I got custody of me, and that's all I wanted. What else?"

"I got her to sign off on any rights to your future earnings if you sell the practice right now and give her everything."

"That sounds good. You have a buyer?"

"Yes. But remember: I said EVERYTHING," Donny continued.

"And I said no more damn lectures."

"OK, I understand."

"Who's the buyer?"

"You'll like this:"—Donny stopped for emphasis—"Omar Hagen! He's gonna pay a fortune, too!"

"Really? He's in way over his head with my practice," Joe said. "He can't do the work."

"Does that mean anything—what you just said?" Donny asked. "As long as he's got the money?"

"No. It was just an observation." Joe smiled a weak smile.

"OK. Jess gets all the money from the practice, and you'll be divorced in about ninety days. You all right with that, Joe?"

"Seems a bit final, doesn't it Donny? But yeah, I can live with it. It's OK."

Robert Crossman and another man stepped into the little room.

"I'm sorry, Mr. Crossman. I had a family emergency," Joe said.

Robert simply stared at him and waited.

"Are the boys OK, Donny?" Joe asked hurriedly. Then he looked up at Robert Crossman.

"The boys are great. I had dinner with them last night. They're..."

"I gotta go, Donny. I'll call you later," Joe said as he hung up.

"Sorry, Mr. Crossman," Joe said as he left the room and walked down the plywood steps.

Robert Crossman said nothing as Joe walked past him.

When Joe reached the dirt floor of the arena, he noticed Junior Duncan leaning on a gate and drinking coffee from a foam cup. "You OK, Joe?" Junior asked. "You look like you just got some bad news."

Joe shook his head and tried to smile. "No, nothing like that." But he offered no more.

"Well, at least you look better than Murdo. He's got a toothache!" Junior said.

"No shit?" Joe said. "Where is he?"

"He's around somewheres," Junior replied.

Joe found Murdo standing by the table at the sandwich tent, rubbing his face. "It don't hurt now—don't hurt at all—but it kept me up some last night," he said to Mary.

"Toothache time?" Joe said as he greeted Murdo.

"Yeah. I broke this tooth about a year ago. It acts up on me ever' now an' 'nen. Goddammer, it really hurt last night for a while, but it's OK now," Murdo smiled.

"Why don't you call a dentist?" Joe asked. How ironic, he thought, to have to listen to this, only minutes after he'd been informed that his career in dentistry was in fact over. He knew exactly what Murdo was about to say.

"It don't hurt all the time!" Murdo replied.

"So you're just gonna wait until your face is all swollen and you have pus running out of a draining fistula on your face?"

"Goddammer, Joe. You some kinda half-assed dentist, too?"

"Nope," Joe smiled. "Not even half-assed." He turned and briefly made eye contact with Mary before he walked away. He walked into the auction arena where he could be alone for a moment. The conversation with Donny had a certain finality that left him feeling heavy. It was all gone now. His old life was pretty much gone without a trace. It had happened with more speed than he'd anticipated. It should have drawn out longer; it should have had a more dramatic end, he thought. Instead, he just felt like something had drained all the strength from him and left him empty. But it was done now, and it didn't seem right to be reflecting on it all here in a livestock arena. Joe took a deep breath and let it out in a big sigh. Then he turned to go back to the sandwich tent and help Mary.

When he turned, he was face to face with the beautiful redhead in the white buckskins; they were inches apart. Joe put his eyes down and stepped out of her way. "Excuse me," he said without looking at her again.

"Hi," she said as if they were old friends. "And excuse me!"

Joe lifted his eyes to meet hers and saw that she was even more beautiful at close range. Her lips curled around perfect teeth, but the center of her beauty was her green eyes. She just smiled at Joe for a moment as she turned sideways and began to brush past him.

He felt his own lips bend into a smile, and he saw her eyes brighten even more when she noticed the dimple on the right side of his face. He stepped back again to make way for her, but he still said nothing.

As she began to step past him, he did something totally out of character. He'd never done anything like it before, but he had to do it now or the moment would be lost forever.

"Wait. Wait a minute, please," Joe said while she was almost touching him.

"Yes?" The redhead stopped and faced Joe again.

"I have to tell you. I just have to tell you. You're the most beautiful woman I've ever seen." He stopped and swallowed heavily. "I just had something unexpected happen to me a little while ago, and I was feeling bad for a minute there. But when you smiled at me like you did just now, you made all that go away. Thank you. I don't know if you have any idea how good that felt for me. So thank you. Thanks for shining some of that beauty on me for just a moment." He stopped, then shrugged. "That's all."

Sherry Lanning, the lovely, redheaded cowgirl from Ennis, had no idea what to say. She stared at Joe for a moment, then stood on her tiptoes and kissed him on the cheek. Joe had never been kissed while wearing a cowboy hat, and he didn't know enough to turn his head a little. As her lips rested briefly on his cheek, she knocked his hat off, and it was sitting almost sideways on his head when she disappeared back into the crowd in the arena.

It seemed that no one had seen their brief exchange. But it had been real enough for Joe. Whatever had made him do that? Damn, this was a strange world, he thought. One little smile from that woman had lifted his spirits away from the melancholy of the loss of his old life. Then he remembered what he'd said to her. Unbelievable, Joe thought. Two weeks ago, that little exchange would have been absolutely impossible for him. It was innocent enough, and he'd needed to say it, but it was unlike anything he'd ever done before. Maybe he was changing; maybe some current was carrying him to new, better places. "I don't believe I just said that," Joe said aloud as he walked back to the sandwich tent, shaking his head and grinning.

For the rest of the day, Joe moved quietly around the auction, helping whoever needed help. He seemed to divide himself as he'd done on the drive after he'd left Kadoka. Part of him was doing the work that was required, helping Norm and Junior when they needed help, running errands for Mary, moving horses for Murdo. But the other part of him was trying to make sense of all that had happened and all that might happen.

That afternoon, for the first time that he could remember, the weight, or pressure, or whatever it was that had always pushed him to go out and do something or be something he didn't like, began to lift. He felt a little flicker of happiness that he hadn't known before, and he could only guess that it was what he'd been hoping to find during those long drives before work all those years ago.

Joe's whole afternoon drifted along like a cloudy dream. He did his job but thought about other things. The dream snapped back into reality when the day's work came to an end and he burned garbage behind the shop. He'd been alone in his own world most of the day. Now, he watched ashes, sparks, and smoke drift into the sunset again, and he was startled by the loud rattle of a diesel engine. A huge, silver-colored Dodge pickup with an abrasive, ear-splitting diesel engine rolled to a stop just behind him. He turned to see just who was driving it. The redhead in the white buckskins stepped out of the driver's side and walked over to Joe. He wore a puzzled look and was about to say something to her when she tilted her head and lifted one index finger in a gesture telling him to remain silent. She was much shorter than Joe, and she only stopped walking when she was almost touching him.

Joe questioned her green eyes for a moment, and those eyes answered with a heavy, sensuous tranquility he'd seldom felt. He couldn't stop his gaze from wandering over the soft skin covering the firm lines of her face. He could smell the auction pit on this beauty, and he was sure he could smell alcohol; she'd almost certainly had a drink or two with the real cowboys when the sale had ended. It made no sense that he longed to touch this woman who smelled of horses and bourbon, but he did.

Then she put her arms around his waist and pulled him close. She kissed him full on the mouth and searched for his tongue. She pressed herself against him, and he felt her breasts against his chest as she held him. He reached his hands and arms around her. The feel of her tiny waist and the firmness of her back were wonderful. She was causing him to feel something he didn't think he could feel with his clothes on. She held the kiss for a long moment, then stepped back. "What you said—that was nice," she said.

Joe drew in a breath as if he were about to reply, and she quickly reached her index finger up to his lips. She shook her head to tell him not to speak while she looked into his eyes and rubbed her finger around in the wetness on his lips. She got into her truck, and while she backed away, she looked at him, smiling softly and nodding. Then she was gone.

The loud diesel engine rattled and barked while Joe watched the truck ease out of the parking area, down the lane, and out of sight into the Montana evening. He leaned on the garden rake he'd been using to stir the garbage fire, smiled, and licked his lips in search of another taste of Sherry Lanning, the redheaded cowgirl.

———·—·———

Riders of the Purple Sage was open in Joe's hands, but he wasn't reading. He'd taken his boots off an hour earlier, and he was rubbing Jake with his stocking feet while he rocked and thought about all the things that had happened in the past three weeks. James was sitting beside him reading.

There had been no supper for the hands tonight. They'd eaten the last of the beef sandwiches and made preparations to leave for Cowboy Camp in the morning.

When Mary walked into the dining hall, she looked at Joe and James briefly before she said anything. "James, would you leave Joe and me alone for a minute?"

"Sure, Mary," James said when he left. "See you in the morning."

"Goodnight, James," Mary said.

"Are you all right, Joe?" she asked when James was gone. "You weren't yourself all day after your phone call. Robert said he heard you say you'd had a family emergency?"

"I didn't think Robert knew who I was."

"Well, he does. Are you all right?" Mary asked again. Joe saw genuine concern in Mary Crossman's eyes. He sensed it was time to open up and respond to her offers of friendship.

Joe breathed in deeply. "Yes, I'm fine. But I had a big day. Would you really like to know about it?"

"Yes."

"Well, Donny—that's my brother; he's my attorney also; he's handling all the details of the train wreck I left behind—he told me that my wife had filed for divorce and it would be final in ninety days or so. He said my practice was now in the hands of an idiot. Everything I worked for these last twenty-five years now belongs to my soon-to-be ex-wife. None of that really bothers me except for the finality of it all. There is no going back—just like I've been telling myself all along. It just felt odd for someone to actually say it to me."

"What happened with Sherry Lanning?"

"Nothing, really. I just told her she was pretty," Joe smiled. "We'll never see each other again, but she sure gave me a lift. That was nice."

"I don't understand," Mary said.

"I don't either. I don't want to," Joe shrugged. "That can just be what it was."

Mary turned to leave.

"Don't go, Mary. I want to thank you, too. You've been so nice to me."

She came and sat in the rocker next to Joe but still wore a puzzled look.

"What's going on here, Joe? Really," Mary asked.

"I wish I knew," Joe sighed. "I think a man needs to slay a few dragons and rescue a few maidens. He's not supposed to back into a safe and easy life. I know that doesn't make any sense, but I had to get out of a dead marriage and a dead life. When I walked out the door and left my home, I think I walked through a door of opportunity that I never knew existed." He paused and then finished. "There's a lot going on out here that I just don't understand yet, but I'm liking my life for the first time in a long while."

chapter
twenty-three

A thick layer of brown dust already covered the dashboard of the pickup truck, so it didn't matter to anyone that a fresh cloud of road dust swirled into the open windows of the pickup truck as it bounced across the hard ruts on the way into Cowboy Camp. Cletto drove the truck slowly along a dirt road that wound over and through rolling hills. The road was nothing more than tire tracks created by crushed grass—two dirty ruts weaving across the grassland of eastern Montana like an endless ribbon.

The three days of the livestock sale had been a fine time for Joe to rest physically and take a while to reflect on all the changes of the past few weeks. Now that the sale was over, he was rested and ready to get on to Cowboy Camp, whatever that was.

Joe sat between Cletto and James, and each time one of the truck tires struck a rock or a rut, he was jostled to one side or the other and he bumped shoulders with one of them. Jake had curled into a ball at their feet and slept since they'd left the ranch. Occasionally, they passed some cattle grazing on the lush, spring grass. Even though the weather had been dry for several weeks, it was still spring and the grass was thick and green. Most often, the cattle stood along the small creeks near the shade provided by scraggly cottonwoods that grew by the side of the creeks. Several times Cletto had to stop and cross a fence line. Then James would jump out of the truck and open a gate to allow the truck to pass through. While Cletto and Joe waited in the truck on the other side of the gate, he'd shut the gate behind them and get back in the truck.

They'd all lost interest in conversation a while earlier, so they just bounced and jostled along in silence, each of them left to his own thoughts. Sometimes when they turned into the wind, all the dust was carried away from them by a soft breeze. But when the road wound back again, the truck and the horse trailer it was pulling stirred up so much dust that it was difficult to breathe or even to see the road, because the breeze carried their own dust over them.

"Doesn't all this dust bother the horses?" Joe asked Cletto as he squinted and tried to cover his face. Jake was curled up on his lap, trying to sleep, but he'd sneezed several times.

"Don't think so," Cletto answered. "But I never asked."

"How come we're crossing so many fence lines?" Joe asked.

"We've crossed the same fence line six times," Cletto smiled.

"Really? Why?"

"Just sort of worked out this way over the years. The road was here before the fence." Cletto pointed to the north with his right hand. "Up here, on the north end of the Twins, there are five large pastures. They're all pie shaped, sort of," Cletto shrugged.

"At the center of the pie is Cowboy Camp. Years ago, Mrs. Crossman's father dammed up a section of Mills Creek and created a large reservoir of water for the livestock. He kept so many cattle up here in this area that he just started branding them here every year instead of moving them south with the others. Pretty soon he built some fences, then the shack. Turns out that Cowboy Camp is a pretty good spot to gather cattle, then brand 'em. After we brand 'em, we just have the cattle trucks drive right into camp and load out the ones we're gonna sell or move to another pasture."

Cletto turned to Joe and smiled. "Then we run some bulls in here, and when they've done their job, we turn the cows back into the pastures." He shrugged. "When the grass in one pasture starts to look a little thin, we move the cattle."

"How do you move 'em?"

"On horseback. You know, like cowboys." Cletto smiled his enormous smile. "That's what we do—we're cowboys."

Cletto slowed the truck almost to a crawl, then crept across a creek bed that was nearly dry. When he'd crossed the creek bed, he accelerated quickly to establish momentum to power the truck and trailer up the slope of the far side of the creek bed. The truck bounced heavily, and the trailer made a loud clanging noise as it bounced along, then rolled over a large rock in the left tire track.

The bump pushed Joe into Cletto first, then back into James. "Four-wheel drive is nice," Cletto said.

Joe glanced to his right and noticed that James appeared to be sleeping in spite of the rough ride.

"So how come we brought so many horses?" Joe asked.

"We're gonna be spending a lot of time on horseback. Horses get tired too. We may just need them all."

Joe nodded his understanding but said nothing more. The conversation ended when Cletto reached for a Coke from the small cooler on the truck floor. Cletto and Joe watched the country roll past them in silence for the next twenty minutes while James seemed to be sleeping, even though his head banged against the door of the truck with each bump in the road.

"It's just over this hill," Cletto said as the truck crested a small ridge. James sat up straight and rubbed his eyes.

The two ruts that were the road disappeared over the top of the ridge, and when the truck reached the ridgeline, Cletto stopped to let Joe have a long look at Crossman Cowboy Camp. A small valley, maybe four miles long and less than a mile across, stretched out in front of them. The hills on the far side of the valley were covered with scattered pine trees, while the hills on their side were smooth and grassy, with an occasional outcropping of rock. The valley in between stretched north to south with a small stream meandering through it. A manmade dam blocked the flow of one branch of the stream and created a small lake about twenty acres in size.

Several hundred yards from the lake sat an odd arrangement of plank fences, misshapen piles of lumber, and used equipment, next to a weathered cabin. Not far from the cabin were two white pickup trucks connected to large horse trailers. It appeared to Joe that about ten horses were standing beside a horse shelter, which had only three walls and a roof. Wire fences ran in all directions and demarcated several corrals. At three separate places, heavy plank loading ramps had been built into the fences to facilitate the loading of cattle onto large trucks. The only solid-looking plank fences were the ones surrounding the horses.

"Wow. Looks just like I thought it would, I guess. Where are the cattle? I still don't see any cattle."

"That's what we're here for!" Cletto's teeth flashed with his smile again. "You'll see cattle tomorrow!" He eased the truck down the hillside, along the dusty ruts and toward Crossman's Cowboy Camp. "Looks like everybody's here and getting ready to go to work."

Murdo, Mr. Crossman, and the Duncan brothers had arrived about an hour earlier and were busy preparing to gather and brand cattle. The Duncans were in the three-sided stable arranging saddles and tack, while Murdo and Mr. Crossman carried groceries into the cabin.

"Hello, girls!" Murdo called from the front steps of the cabin. The siding on the cabin appeared to be cedar. It was mostly weathered gray, with some areas of deep brown where the sun didn't strike it directly. The roof was made from cedar shakes, and a small, covered porch extended along the entire front of the cabin.

"I'll start unloading our gear. You two get the horses out of the trailer and into the corral. OK?" Cletto said.

Joe watched what James did and tried to do the same. They led the horses, one at a time, off the trailer and into the corral. When the trailer was empty, James found a shovel and cleaned the horse manure from each of the trailers.

Joe simply wandered around by the trailers and the stable for a few minutes. He'd been waiting for instructions but had received none, so he took the opportunity to look around camp. An outhouse stood about thirty yards from the cabin, and several other mysterious-looking structures that appeared to be on the verge of collapse completed an irregular semicircle of Cowboy Camp buildings. "Looks like Ranch Henge," Joe mumbled to himself as he approached a small, rickety-looking wooden windmill. Next to the windmill was a large, oblong, galvanized water tank. The sides of the tank were about three feet tall, and the tank was approximately twenty feet long and six feet wide. Log posts had been driven into the ground around the tank. The logs supported a plank roof over the tank, which had apparently been built to provide shade. The tank rested in the middle of the yard where no cattle could reach it to drink from it. It made no sense.

Off to the south, about forty feet from the covered stock tank, four more large cedar logs had been driven into the ground. Resting atop the logs was what appeared to be the wing of a military airplane. The wing rested about eight feet off the ground and looked completely out of place. The paint on the wing was a faded army green, and Joe thought he could make out some numbers that had been stenciled onto the wing with white paint, but they had been nearly erased by weather and time. A boardwalk made of cedar planks had been built beneath the wing, and several ropes hung down from the wing.

Joe stood with his hands in his pockets and stared at the stock tank, the wing, and the windmill.

"Hey, Joe! C'mon in and stow your gear," Cletto called.

The cabin smelled musty, and the footsteps of the men echoed slightly against the exposed two-by-four-and-plank walls. The floor plan was pretty simple. Joe understood the simplicity of the design even as he stood on the threshold of the door. The cabin had two rooms, a kitchen and a bedroom. The kitchen was large, with a roughhewn table and eight chairs. The running water in the kitchen sink came from a large pump with a red handle. The wastewater drained through the sink onto the ground outside the cabin. A small, permanent icebox had been built into the kitchen wall. Outside the cabin, a portable generator supplied electricity that powered an icemaker, which made ice to cool the insulated walls of the icebox. All the cooking was done over a propane stove, and the garbage was burned in an old fifty-five-gallon barrel just outside the front door.

The other room was a narrow bedroom with eight single beds along one wall. One window on the east wall allowed some afternoon light into the room. The bedroom walls, like the kitchen, were exposed two-by-fours that supported plank siding on the outside of the cabin. Nails had been driven into many of the two-by-fours, presumably to provide places to hang hats and clothing.

Half a dozen hurricane lanterns hung from hooks on the walls. One other lantern sat on the kitchen table. Several boxes of groceries were stacked along the kitchen wall, next to the wooden doors that opened into the ingenious icebox.

"We got no power for a freezer," Murdo said when he noticed Joe staring at the plywood doors to the icebox. "So we built that icebox from Styrofoam and plywood. The double walls are six inches thick, with space for a six-inch layer of ice on the inside. We use that gas generator to power the icemaker that we salvaged from the high school cafeteria over in Hardin. The ice in them walls will keep food cool for a couple weeks in the middle of summer! When it melts, we just fire up the old generator and make some more ice." Murdo turned back to the stack of grocery boxes and two cases of whisky that he was arranging.

Everyone seemed to have a job, and to be hard at it, except Joe. He looked around at the strange, unfamiliar camp, trying to find some place to fit in.

"We're gonna have an early supper. Then we're gonna find you a horse to ride tomorrow. We'll see just how you sit a horse," Mr. Crossman said as he unpacked groceries.

"Yeah, great," Joe said softly. He was growing apprehensive about the horseback riding. It had been thirty years since his last ride. He hadn't been much of a horseman even when he'd lived on a ranch with his parents. He just never cared much about it one way or the other. It certainly was odd that he'd felt at one time that his destiny was to return to Kadoka and take over the ranch, because he'd lost interest in horses quite some time before he'd gone off to college. "Yeah, that'll be great, Mr. Crossman," he said as he turned to the window and grimaced.

———

Murdo threw a blanket over the horse's back. "This here is Tom," he said. He lifted the saddle on top of the blanket and began to cinch it into place. "Tom's a fine cuttin' horse," he said as he tugged on the leather strap that crossed under Tom's belly.

"Yeah, he smells like a good one," Joe said. His apprehension over this ride was growing.

Murdo had both hands on Tom's saddle when he turned to smile at Joe. He looked up and down for a moment and asked, "How tall are you?"

"About six-one," Joe answered.

Murdo simply loosened the strap that held the stirrup, then lengthened it.

"Thought so," he said when he walked to the other side of Tom and lengthened the other stirrup. "The last feller to use this saddle was one of them runty little desperados sittin' in the Ranchester jail right now. A man your size would look like a monkey humpin' a football if I hadn't let them stirrups down."

With that, Murdo handed Joe the reins to the big, brown horse. "Let's go."

The others were all mounted, waiting for Joe and Murdo when they walked out of the corral, leading their horses. The plan was simply to take an evening ride and be sure that their gear was in order for a day of gathering cattle tomorrow.

"Ready, Joe?" Mr. Crossman asked. His hands rested on his saddle horn, and he leaned forward.

"Yeah, I guess so," Joe said. "It's been a while for me. I was hoping you had a horse about like my truck," Joe said apprehensively. He watched Murdo mount his horse as he gently stroked Tom's neck.

"We don't have no horses like that around here," Murdo said as the leather saddle groaned under him. "When our horses get to lookin' like your truck, we let 'em ride around with your phone!"

Murdo and Mr. Crossman looked at each other and laughed. Everyone was laughing. Obviously they'd all heard of his phone-throwing display in Ranchester.

Joe nodded, smiled, and then felt himself swallow heavily. Here goes, he thought. He put his left foot into the stirrup and swung himself into the saddle while the others watched. The rich, warm sound and feel of the saddle settling under him briefly sparked a comfortable memory. But at the same instant, he felt the power and then the energy of a strong horse begin to pulse underneath him. At first he wondered if Tom could sense his fear, but when he felt Tom's skittish response, he knew. Tom lifted his front feet quickly, one at a time, and Joe understood very well that Tom was in charge. Tom knew it too. Joe noticed Cletto take a quick sideways glance at Murdo.

Murdo turned his shoulders to his right and pulled his horse's reins to the right also. His horse turned with him, and they seemed to move as one. "Let's go," he said calmly as he raised his heels into his horse's sides. Murdo leaned forward slightly in the saddle as he started out across the valley to the north. The others followed one at a time until only Joe was left.

Tom had been straining to go along with each of the other horses, but Joe had held him back. He'd felt Tom's power and eagerness surging, growing beneath him, and now he had to let it go. There was no reason to hold Tom back any longer. Joe simply lowered the reins. Before he could raise his heels to nudge his horse, Tom had taken several stutter steps and begun running to catch up with the others.

Joe's sense of panic was visceral and immediate. Tom understood very well that he was in control of Joe, not the other way around. Tom lurched and was out of control the instant Joe lowered the reins. His first several steps caused Joe to bounce out of the saddle and lose both stirrups. Joe knew he looked like a ragdoll being thrown around by an angry dog. The only feeling he could remember and compare it to was the time many years earlier when Donny had grabbed him by the ankles and pulled him down a flight of stairs so that his ass slammed into every step all the way down. He managed to stay in the saddle for several seconds, but he was at the mercy of a headstrong horse. He struggled against what he knew was an overwhelming power. Tom was able to ignore what little force Joe could exert on the reins. Just as he was about to slide off the right side of his saddle, Joe leaned back heavily on the reins in one last effort to slow the horse. Tom jumped slightly in response to the reins, and Joe was airborne in a heartbeat. Just when Tom's hooves struck the ground, he arched his back slightly upward. At the same instant, Joe's backside bounced back into the saddle, and Tom's arching back catapulted Joe upwards.

The violent impact with the saddle hammered at his ass, and his chest felt like it might collapse from the force of it. Then, for a brief moment when he left his horse and rose into the Montana sky, he felt weightless and calm. The horizon began to turn. He saw the world moving, but in slow motion, and Joe knew he was about to strike the ground. Before he had a chance to brace for impact, the world sped up and he crashed to the earth. He heard himself grunt and felt all the air explode from his chest. His own breath and the concussion of his hard landing blew up a cloud of brown dust in front of his face. He felt the prairie dirt fly into his nose, mouth, and hair. He was aware that his hat was rolling away and that he was lying on his right arm.

The urge to breathe was powerful, and he felt panic descend over him when he was unable to draw a breath. In the same instant, he felt a sharp pain in his ribs. For just a second, he thought he might die. Then, slowly, he understood that he'd only had the wind knocked out of him. Just like every other time he'd had the wind knocked from him, there was a brief moment when he knew intellectually that he was going to live and breathe again. But there was also a very real fear that was driven by the fact that he actually wasn't breathing and couldn't draw a breath just yet.

Joe lay still for a minute, assessing which of his body parts might be broken and which ones still worked, while he allowed his lungs to fill.

When he heard a rider coming, he struggled to one knee and tried to hide the pain and the embarrassment.

"You OK, Joe?" Cletto was far above him, looking down from atop his horse. He looked concerned, then embarrassed for Joe, which only deepened Joe's shame.

"Yeah. It's just my wind."

"I told Murdo not to give you such a fresh horse."

"It's OK," Joe said as he stood up and put his hat back on.

"Hey! You never let go of the reins!" Cletto exclaimed. "That was good."

"I was too scared!" Joe said. He stepped back into the stirrup and swung his leg back over the saddle. He winced noticeably when he sat in the saddle. His ribs and his arm still hurt, and the sense of panic over not being able to breathe had not completely passed yet.

"Are you sure you're OK, Joe?" Cletto asked.

Joe looked over at Cletto and noticed he wasn't smiling. The other riders were about a hundred yards away and were making no effort to approach Joe. But they were all watching.

"Yeah, I'm OK," he replied. He knew that neither he nor Cletto was at all sure about that. He took a deep breath and looked at Cletto. Then he turned back to Tom. "OK, let's go." When he turned Tom's head with the reins, Tom bolted again.

The same out-of-control, bouncing sensation started again, and Joe lost his right stirrup immediately. He knew he'd be back on the ground again in only a second if he didn't act quickly. For one brief moment, he even considered jumping off Tom's back, abandoning ship. But he felt a rash of anger swell inside him in the next second, and he was disappointed with himself that he could even consider such a cowardly thing as letting go. In that instant, he remembered something from his days on his father's ranch.

He slid his left hand along the rein on the left side of Tom's head and neck. When he'd almost reached the bit in Tom's mouth, he pulled back with his left hand as hard as he could. Tom's head jerked violently to the left until he was almost nose to nose with Joe and facing backwards. The big horse stopped in his tracks. Long ago, Joe had been told that horses would stop in this situation because they don't like to run if they can't see where they're going. In any case, Joe was relieved when Tom came to a complete stop. He'd won a small battle with his horse and established control for the moment, at least. But he knew he could never win the war this was shaping up to be. Joe held Tom's nose close to his own with an iron grip and spoke softly to the spirited horse. "Easy, Tom. Take it easy on me. Easy, now."

"OK. You SURE you're OK?" Cletto was at Joe's side again, and the others were still watching.

"Yeah," Joe answered without looking up. He was afraid of Tom and afraid of what might happen in the next few minutes. He knew he had to act decisively, and soon, or give up the cowboy façade. He was tempted to admit his fear and embarrassment and give up on horses. This stuff with Tom simply couldn't be allowed to continue, Joe thought. He couldn't go on like this, but he couldn't just quit, either. He knew all the men were watching, waiting. He remembered his fear while standing in the Root River and not knowing what to do next—the water was rushing by him again, and the prize was just on the other side of it. He swallowed heavily once again and felt the pressure of time slowing down because of his fear and indecision. He had to DO something, soon. He stroked Tom's neck. "Easy, Tom. Easy."

"Joe, you want to go back?" Cletto offered.

"Tom likes to run, huh?" Joe ignored Cletto's question, and his eyes narrowed. He knew the thing he had to do.

"Yes," Cletto replied.

"What's the ground like between here and that ridge up there, to the northwest?"

"Smooth. Nice, short grass." Cletto looked perplexed. "Why?"

"No gullies to jump?" Joe asked.

"No," Cletto said.

Joe reached his right hand to his hat and pushed it down onto his head until his ears bent over. Then he turned Tom in the direction of the ridge he'd pointed to, took a breath, and held his eyes shut for a second. He knew his only chance—and it probably wasn't a very good chance—was to run some of Tom's energy off. He just had no idea whether he could stay in the saddle for such a ride. "All right, Tom, let's do this," he whispered. Then he lowered the reins and barked "HYAH!" as he raised his heels into Tom's flanks.

A sleek, brown bomb exploded beneath Joe Mix. Tom's first several steps were rough, and Joe knew he was barely in control of himself, let alone the big horse. In a heartbeat, Tom seemed to rise above the earth and race on a cushion of air. Joe kept his weight in the stirrups, and Tom's rhythmic steps began to feel like feathers stroking the earth as it screamed by beneath them.

The dry Montana air rushed past Joe's face and pushed at his hat. Tom the horse could run like the wind, and Joe Mix was merely along for the ride. But it was the ride of his lifetime, and Joe knew he was on the edge. He wasn't much of a horseman. It would require every bit of skill and luck he could muster just to stay in the saddle for the next few minutes. For the first few seconds, he thought he'd never be able to ride this one out. But then he began to rediscover the subtle skills of balancing himself in the saddle. Tom had the sort of stride that made it easier for Joe to stay with him at full speed. Joe remembered other horses like Tom: at lower speeds, the rider's ass took a pounding; but at a full gallop, Tom was silk.

His reasoning when he'd given his heels to Tom had been that it was better to risk failure or humiliation or injury or even a violent death than to hold back and struggle with Tom anymore. This horse would only wrestle all the joy from the experience slowly. Better to find out just what there was to be found out right now than to let it slip away one small crash at a time.

The ground streaked past him in a blur as Tom continued to stretch his stride. Joe's sense that he might be near death began to subside, and he slowly found his own balance. "HYAH!" he hissed several times, and each time Tom accelerated.

The crest of the ridge that had seemed so far off was close at hand now. The fear of a moment earlier had given way to euphoria, which was quickly turning into ecstasy. There was a joy that seemed to be filling Joe's chest and the back of his throat. When he crested the green ridge, Joe stood in the stirrups and leaned back on the reins. "Whoa, Tom," he said softly. Tom eased to a stop, and Joe was thrilled at the feel of the saddle and the fine horse under him. He turned Tom back in the direction of the others. They were far across the valley—a mile away, perhaps two, where they'd been all along—still looking at him. He reached up, grabbed his hat, and waved it at the other men, and tried to drink in the beauty of that little valley in front of him. Then he pushed his hat down tight once more. Joe patted Tom's neck softly for a moment, then looked back again at Crossman's Cowboy Camp and the valley surrounding it.

"All right, Tom, still got any piss and vinegar left? Let's take 'er home. HYAH!" Once again, Tom exploded underneath Joe, and the grass seemed to separate beneath Tom like a river of green. It even made a gentle hissing noise, like water made when it brushed by him in a trout stream.

A sense of exhilaration began to swell inside Joe as he raced back toward the others. The joy in his chest grew too large, and he started to smile uncontrollably. He laughed out loud. Then there was someone riding with him suddenly. He could feel the other rider—behind him, maybe just beside him, but somewhere very close, racing along with him. The joy continued to grow and grow. He laughed out loud because he knew the rider was right there with him, and he knew who the rider was: it was the Kadoka Kid!

He knew that rider. Mounted on a red, plywood rocking horse and wearing his matching six-guns was four-year-old Joey Mix. Somewhere, somehow, all those years ago, that little boy had ridden off on that red pony, and Joe had lost him. He hadn't even known the little boy was gone until now. Life hadn't been the same without him. It had been all right but not like it should have been. Just now, when he saw that little boy, he knew he'd recovered a lost treasure. Joe couldn't say when that little boy had gone away; it must have happened one day when Joe was busy with something someone else expected him to do.

By God, he was back—after all this time! Joe was thrilled to see him, and he knew he'd never let that little boy ride off again. Little Joey Mix had returned to help him slay the dragons and rescue the maidens. Tom ran, and the red, plywood rocking pony ran, and Joe Mix laughed all the way across the valley. Joe was laughing out loud when he stood in the stirrups and reined Tom to a stop in front of the other riders. Joe put both hands on his saddle horn and continued to laugh. The laughter was rolling from him uncontrollably as the other riders continued to stare. Joe couldn't remember feeling such joy, ever—just pure, childlike joy.

"Goddammer, Joe. I never seen nothin' like that before. Looked like a big dog shakin' a cat when you and Tom took off!" Murdo said. Then he looked at Cletto and shrugged. Cletto could only return the shrug and a look that confessed he didn't understand what was going on either. Mr. Crossman looked at Cletto, then Murdo, then Joe, then he shook his head.

Joe continued to laugh, and to look around at the way the setting sun turned the hills in the rim of the valley yellow—and at the way his new friends stared at him.

The boundless joy in Joe's heart began a mysterious transformation while he sat a horse and laughed. The joy he'd found had flowed uncontrollably through him, and now it had weakened an old dam that had held back many other long-forgotten emotions. It was wonderful to find that little boy at last; there was real, visceral joy in finding him. He'd missed out on all those years, so much of Joe's life. The little boy hadn't been there to see his parents die. He'd never met Jess, he'd never met the boys. He'd missed the heart and soul of Joe Mix's life. How different would Joe's life have been if he'd never lost track of the Kadoka Kid?

The joy and sweet laughter suddenly morphed into an overwhelming torrent of grief, sadness, and regret. So many things he didn't understand pulled and tightened the back of his throat. All those years had passed, and little Joey Mix had been lost. Oh, Jesus, Joe thought. Why did that little boy just ride away all those years ago? I let him go! I grew up, Joe thought.

Joe's face twisted as a lifetime of remorse and regret pushed its way out from inside him. His face tightened and his eyes filled with tears. It happened slowly at first, but then some force began to push huge sobs out of his chest. The laughter changed into anguish. He cried heavily, as he'd done only at his parents' funerals. He couldn't hold back what was flowing from inside him anymore. He put his face in his hands and sobbed heavily. He didn't care that the others were looking at him; he couldn't stop this anyway. He hadn't shed a tear since he'd left his home and his old life behind. But these tears were for his father, his mother, his sons, for himself, and for all that had been wasted while he was waiting to get on with life.

While the others watched, Joe continued to weep. Then he wiped his face with the back of his hand. He turned Tom back toward the little shed at camp without a word of explanation. Tom walked slowly while the other riders stared at Joe's back and listened to his muffled sobs. They stared at each other, each of them asking the others for an explanation of what they'd seen.

Half an hour later, Joe was still leaning against Tom when he heard the other horses returning to the corral. He'd taken Tom's saddle off and brushed Tom for a few minutes. Then he'd put the palms of his hands against Tom's back and rested his face on Tom's side while he breathed in the smell of a fine horse and tried to understand all that had happened.

He stood with his face against Tom's side while all the other riders silently took the saddles off their horses, brushed them, and went into the cabin.

Murdo reached over and touched Joe's back as he walked by in a gesture of support, but he did not speak. Joe could hear the faint voices of men talking in the cabin, but he stood with his face resting against Tom's side for a while longer. The smell of horses had improved in the past hour. Tom smelled good, Joe thought. He stood there with Tom as the shadows from across the valley spread over the corral and darkness descended.

Jim Crossman hesitantly returned to the corral after about twenty minutes of waiting in the cabin. When he saw Joe still standing beside Tom, he asked. "Are you all right, Joe?"

"Yeah. I'm OK. I'm sorry about all that, Mr. Crossman." Joe raised his head and smiled sheepishly. "I had a lot of shit happen in my life recently, and I just haven't dealt with it all yet, I guess." Joe nodded. "But I'm OK, really. I had sort of an epiphany out there today too. It's hard to explain, but it's good. I'll be OK."

"Do you want to talk about it, Joe?"

"No."

Mr. Crossman nodded his agreement that it was all right not to talk if he didn't want to, then turned toward the cabin. "Would you like a drink?" he said over his shoulder.

"No thanks, Jim," Joe said softly.

Jim Crossman never turned around. He just nodded, waited for Joe, and listened while Joe did an odd thing: Joe turned his cheek and held it against Tom's back for a second. Then he stroked Tom's neck and said, "Thanks, Tom! You're the first one who's demanded the very best from me in a long, long time."

He turned away from the horse, stepped out of the corral, and started walking toward the cabin with Mr. Crossman.

"Hey, Mr. Crossman? Just what is this, anyway?" Joe asked when they passed by the steel water tank.

"It's a hot tub!" Mr. Crossman said as he turned to face Joe. "They were drilling for oil around here about seventy years ago, and they struck hot water, way down there. It's kind of like a natural hot spring. We use it to help with aches and pains when we're here at camp."

Joe was digesting the idea of the hot tub, and he'd taken only a few steps more when he stopped and asked, "OK, what's that?" He pointed to the airplane wing suspended above the logs.

"That? It's a shower! During World War II, the Air Force was training bomber pilots out here. Turns out one of the bombers had a rough landing about ten miles east of here. That wing was about all that survived. It has a big gas tank inside it. My dad and I found that wing and salvaged it. We cleaned it up, put it up on those timbers, and now we pump water into that gas tank in the wing. The sun heats up the water, and then we have hot showers. But down there in that little compartment at the base of it, that's where we keep the pump to pump water into the hot tub." Mr. Crossman smiled and turned his palms up. "Understand?"

"Sure! And what's that?" Joe asked again

"What?" Mr. Crossman didn't know just what it was that Joe was asking about.

"That! That piece-of-shit old windmill!" Joe said.

"Oh, that. That's a piece-of-shit old windmill." And Jim Crossman turned toward the cabin. "We just keep it for good looks."

———•———

Several hurricane lanterns burned inside the cabin, and a thin, yellow glow illuminated the kitchen. Junior, Norm, and Murdo sat at the kitchen table and watched Cletto shuffle a deck of playing cards. Each of them had a cup filled with ice and whisky.

James leaned back in a kitchen chair and held a book close to his face, just beneath a lantern that had been hung in a corner away from the table.

When Joe and Mr. Crossman stepped into the cabin, all eyes turned to Joe.

"I'm all right," Joe said "You don't need to worry about me." He took his hat off and hung it on a nail protruding from a two-by-four near the door. "I've just had a lot happen to me lately, and what you saw—well, that was a lot of...well, it was things I need to work out for myself. I'll be all right."

The men at the table nodded to Joe but said nothing.

"Would you like a drink, Joe?" Mr. Crossman asked.

"Diet soda," Joe replied.

It was James who first began to let things return to normal. "Hey, Joe, I got your book for you, and Jake is waiting for you too." Jake was curled up on an old blanket at James's feet.

By the time Joe settled into the chair next to James, the men had resumed their card game. James had *Lonesome Dove* tipped toward the lantern, trying to get better light onto the pages. Jake raised his head, then lowered it and rolled onto his side when Joe leaned back in his chair and made eye contact with Mr. Crossman.

Jim Crossman raised the cup in his right hand, and Joe heard ice cubes sloshing around in the whisky, clinking against the cup. A slow nod from Jim Crossman told Joe not to worry; things were all right.

Joe raised his diet soda and returned the nod. Then he opened *Riders of the Purple Sage* and tipped it toward the same lantern James was using. He stared at the page and collected his thoughts for a moment before he started reading. The current he'd stepped into back there in Rochester was carrying him someplace good—someplace he needed to be. He felt certain of that. But just where was that place?

chapter
twenty-four

During the night, Joe heard the others turning in bed and moving about. But there had been so much snoring, farting, and rolling around in bed there in the bunkhouse bedroom, all through the night, that he didn't give it much thought when he heard someone stirring again. But when he heard shoes walking across the floor, he lifted his wrist in front of his face to check his watch. Before his eyes could focus on the glowing numerals in front of his eyes, a hurricane lantern hissed and spattered to life, and the bedroom was awash with yellow light. Murdo and Mr. Crossman were both fully dressed, and Cletto was putting his boots on. "Three o'clock, girls. Time to get to work," Murdo said as he walked out of the bedroom and lit a lantern in the kitchen.

The cool, morning air finally brought them all to life when they began saddling their horses and loading them onto trailers. "So why do we do this in the middle of the night?" Joe asked Cletto while they stood beside their truck and waited for the others to load up.

"It's gonna get hot today—really hot. It's just nice to be done with a day's work early instead of working through the hottest part of the day. It's tough on the cattle and horses to move 'em when it's real hot too. That's why we left your pup in that little shed. It's cool in there and there's plenty of water. Don't worry about him. This heat would kill a young dog if we made him run along behind us all day."

"How can we do anything? It won't be light for two hours yet," Joe asked.

"Jump in. You'll see," Cletto said. James and Joe stepped into Cletto's truck while Mr. Crossman, Murdo, Norm, and Junior packed themselves into the other truck and drove off, away from them.

Headlights fluttered, bounced, and sprayed light along a fence line as Cletto's truck crept slowly on the grass next to the fence. Now and then, he'd hit a small rock or a rut and jostle everyone about inside the truck. The truck seemed to wander forever, and Joe saw only barbed wire fence, grass, rocks, and cow pies.

"Coffee?" Cletto asked after about ten minutes.

"No thanks," Joe said

"Well, get me some anyway!" Cletto chuckled.

Joe poured coffee from a thermos and tried not to spill on his lap. "So what's the plan here?" he finally asked when he handed Cletto the cup.

"We're gonna let James and his horse out here, just a ways farther," Cletto said.

"It's the middle of the night," Joe answered.

"Not really. He's gonna stand there and wait until the sun comes up, though. As soon as it's light enough to see, he'll start riding back toward camp and gather whatever cattle he sees along the way."

"Really?" Joe asked, not sure if he believed Cletto.

"That's right. Then I'm gonna let you and Tom off a ways down this fence line and you're gonna do the same thing. Then I'm gonna be right about where I need to be when the sun comes up, and I'm gonna do the same: get on my horse and drive cattle back to camp."

"What are you gonna do with your truck?"

"When we get back, Mr. Crossman will bring one of us back out here in his truck and pick up this truck. It's pretty simple." Cletto nodded and smiled. "OK, James, let's get your pony out!" Cletto said as he eased the truck to a stop.

When James had been left in the darkness behind them, Joe turned to Cletto and asked, "What if his horse gets away before sunup?"

"What you mean is, what if YOUR horse gets away before sunup, right?" Cletto said.

"Yeah, pretty much," Joe agreed.

"Don't let that happen," Cletto said flatly.

This was the darkest night Joe could remember—no moon and some cloud cover. When Cletto unloaded Tom from the trailer, Joe was anxious about just what was going to happen. "OK, Joe. When it gets light enough so you can see, just ride straight away from this fence. Gather any cattle you can find. The cattle will know what to do—so will Tom— even if you don't. You should reach camp before two o'clock. You all right with that?"

"Yeah," Joe answered, trying to hide his apprehension. It was so overwhelming, Joe thought. He was about to be abandoned in the middle of the great plains, in the darkness, with a horse he was still afraid of.

"And don't lose your horse," he heard Cletto chuckle as he slammed the truck door. In only a few minutes, the tail lights from Cletto's truck and horse trailer disappeared over several hills and into the darkness.

Joe held his hand in front of his face and couldn't see it. "Shit," he muttered to himself as he shook his head. "What the hell have I done?"

He felt as isolated as he'd felt since he'd left home in Rochester, and he allowed himself a few moments to think about all that had happened. He certainly didn't wish he was about to go back to the office; he was totally comfortable with the idea that that was never going to happen again. But he couldn't have removed himself much further from that life.

Darkness still covered everything around him. He could smell Tom, but he couldn't see him just yet. He decided to draw in a deep breath and make an effort to appreciate this odd little moment in his life. The remorse and regret over leaving his other life really was drifting away from him, just as he'd felt Jess drift away. His discovery about his father actually seemed to be making things easier, like Ralph had said. When he did think about Ray Mix, he was beginning to forgive him for just being a man, like himself. Life is hard, and nothing ever really seems to be exactly what we expect, Joe thought to himself. Thoughts of his sons came to him again. He'd spoken to them several times on the phone. They seemed to be doing just fine despite all the changes in his own life. He found some comfort in that realization. Even though he wished he could go back and have the chance to be a better father, his boys had turned out all right. Maybe they'd turned out just fine in spite of his poor parenting.

What about the Kadoka Kid, the little boy who rode a rocking horse back into Joe's life? Joe understood that he'd had a look at the "child within" that writers had written about for years. He didn't really understand it all yet, but he was willing to accept the Kadoka Kid as a harbinger of good fortune—as an indicator that he'd actually taken the right road on this odyssey.

He thought about the power of words, too. He remembered the way it had hurt when Jess had said, "Fuck you!" And then he remembered how it made him laugh when Donny said the same thing. Words were funny; they did have great power. Joe remembered Ralph Webster lamenting the fact that the images of his life had no words with them, so he couldn't share them. He thought of the vivid word pictures that Larry McMurtry had painted in *Lonesome Dove*. Then he smiled at how all this really hadn't been able to start until the dentist was dead. Maybe he had died on the basement floor? No, that was too much to think about right now.

He hoped Jake was all right. He should be resting in a plywood kennel, in the shade of the horse shelter, with a bucket of water and a handful of food.

Ever so slightly, the eastern skyline began to lighten. The black sky eased into a deep blue. Then a rim of light appeared on the eastern hills. By the time the eastern horizon glowed with a hint of yellow, Joe could see pretty clearly out over the valley below him.

There were dark, gray green hills out there in front of him when he turned to Tom. He hoped last night's adventure had taken away some of Tom's need to run. "OK, Tom. I don't feel like running right now. Can we do without that this morning?" Joe asked. At that exact instant, Tom spread his legs and pissed a yellow river down the hillside.

"I'll take that for a yes," Joe said with a smile, and he swung himself into the saddle. Joe looked all around to get his bearings, then eased Tom away from the fence and toward a ridge between two hilltops, far to the south. Tom started in a slow walk and showed no need to stretch his legs this morning.

———·———

About two hours after he started riding, Joe's ass began to ache. Shortly after that, the inner sides of his thighs and calves got sore from rubbing on the saddle. He turned often to shift his weight in the saddle, but nothing helped. He knew he was in for a long day.

At the start of his third hour of gathering cattle, he still hadn't seen a single cow or calf. He'd made it a point to ride far to the east, then far to the west over every little hill and ridge, searching to be sure he wasn't leaving any cattle behind as he moved south toward camp.

Tom's hooves rested on the edge of a large ravine that was so steep it appeared to drop straight off in front of horse and rider. As Joe looked out over the edge, he was uncertain if he could ride Tom down the slope, or if Tom could even keep his footing on the way down. But there was no other place to cross in either direction, and there were tracks of other horses that seemed to have made the descent.

Joe lowered the reins and allowed Tom to make the decision. Tom stepped cautiously over the edge, and Joe felt a lump tighten in his throat immediately. Every movement Tom made seemed designed to flip Joe forward over Tom's head and down the ravine. He leaned as far back as he could and began to clutch for something to hang on to. He felt he was going over the top at any second. He was leaning so far back that his shoulders were almost touching Tom's rump when they drew near to the bottom of the ravine. He was breathless when he reached the bottom. He'd been terrified that Tom would stumble on the steep hill, roll forward, and crush him. But there was no time for a moment of gratitude when he reached the bottom of the ravine, for he discovered that Tom was sinking in soft mud. He felt another rush of anxiety as Tom struggled before he escaped the mud and found good footing on the far side. Joe was still unsteady in the saddle. Every time Tom struggled or stumbled, Joe realized how easily he could be thrown from his horse. He was literally just along for the ride, and he'd stay mounted only if Tom wanted him to.

Tom was easing his way up the far side of the ravine, walking slowly toward a thicket surrounded by some scraggly cottonwoods, before Joe's heart slowed down. He just didn't know what Tom was capable of, and that awareness of his own ignorance bothered him. As Tom meandered along a little trail in the direction of the thicket, Joe looked right and left, hoping to spot some cattle. Then he wondered just what he'd do if he actually came upon some cattle in this thicket. He'd probably be able to turn Tom, but he wasn't so sure about herding the cattle. Hell, he knew he couldn't drive them out of this place if they didn't want to leave; who was he kidding?

He was wondering if maybe he'd just ignore the cattle and tell Murdo he hadn't seen any if he did find some now when he realized that Tom was about to walk under a scraggly tree, with some very low-hanging branches, and scrape him from the saddle. If he didn't act quickly, he'd be brushed off like a fly. Joe had only an instant to duck. He lay his stomach on Tom's neck. The low-hanging branch knocked Joe's hat loose, then dragged over the top of him. He was able to catch his hat before it fell to the ground, but the branch scraped all the way down his back and made him grimace in pain.

His face was almost touching Tom's mane when Tom passed under the tree and came to the steep upward slope of the ravine. Tom jumped suddenly in order to clear a little ledge on the slope, and Joe thought his saddle horn might be driven through his chest. "Ugh," Joe groaned, then sat up with his eyes closed when Tom reached the top of the ravine. "Jesus, Tom," Joe said in agony. "Gene Autry's horse never did shit like that. Take it easy." He rubbed the spot where the saddle horn had hammered at his chest. His face was still twisted with pain when he straightened his back. "This cowboy shit looked way easier in the movies."

Joe rode in all directions for the rest of the morning and worked his way south, but he never saw any cattle. He grew more than a little worried that he was doing something wrong as the morning wore on. Then he got nervous and started to worry that he was lost and riding in the wrong direction. Shit, he thought, everyone would laugh for sure.

Sweat had soaked through his shirt and his feet were hot inside his boots when he finished his second, and last, bottle of water. As he put the bottle into his saddlebag, he noticed a fence line off to his right. He hadn't seen a fence all morning. He rode over to the fence, and when he reached it he couldn't help but examine it to see if it was as straight and sturdily built as the fence he'd helped James build.

He decided to keep the fence within view for a while, since he reasoned the fence had to lead somewhere. If he followed close by it for a ways, he knew he couldn't be too badly lost.

A small bunch of rocks protruded through the prairie grass at the top of a little hill, as if they'd grown through it, and he rode slowly over the rocky hilltop to have a look. Then he felt as if he'd discovered gold: three cows and three calves, just beyond the crest of the hill, raised their heads and looked at him with big, dumb cow eyes.

He was trying to decide what to do next when one of the cows turned and started walking away from him. In only a second, all the others followed the first cow.

"That was easy," Joe said out loud. "Nice work, Tom."

The cattle walked slowly toward the south as Tom followed slowly behind them for several hundred yards. If they began to veer to the east, Joe would lead Tom a little farther to the east; then the cows would veer back to their original course. If they would start to move to the west, Joe would move Tom farther to the west and turn them back. Several times, the cattle decided to slow down and stop. But when Tom closed within a few feet of them, they started moving again. "Shit, I'm a cowboy," Joe said out loud.

The six cows were about to crest a ridge that extended between two tall hills when Joe began to wonder again just where he was. His ass was beginning to burn in several places, no matter how he shifted his weight, and he was growing more uncertain about being lost. He got his answer when he reached the crest of the ridge.

Far below him, across the valley, lay the Crossman camp. It looked to Joe as if there were several hundred cattle in the large pen that surrounded the small lake. A tide of joy and satisfaction swelled in Joe's chest. "Regular Pathfinder, just like Hawkeye in *Last of the Mohicans*! That's what I am, Tom! I found camp!" He raised a hand, in case anyone could see him, as he let the feeling of satisfaction settle over him. The others had found all the cattle, but by God, Joe Mix had found camp! He laughed out loud when he patted Tom on the neck and said, "OK, Tom. Let's take these dogies and skedaddle on down to camp! The Kadoka Kid is bringing this herd in!"

The six cattle Joe had found seemed to understand exactly where to go when they cleared the ridge and saw the large herd of cattle in front of them. Joe and Tom simply followed them into camp.

Tom walked slowly, and Joe rocked gently in the saddle with each step as the camp grew closer. Joe's ass and the inner surfaces of his legs were so sore from the saddle, and the way he'd bounced around on it all morning, that he thought he might cry. But still, he couldn't stop smiling over what he'd done. There was no position he could shift into that resulted in anything but a raw, burning pain somewhere below his waist. He'd sweat through his blue jeans hours ago, and his salty sweat only made the blazing sores on his ass that much more uncomfortable.

Joe looked at his watch and saw that it was 2:30 p.m. Then he glanced up and saw what looked like Mr. Crossman walking from the corrals over to a gate on a barbed wire fence. Mr. Crossman waved to Joe, signaling him to bring the cattle toward the gate he was standing beside.

"We were getting worried about you, Joe!" Mr. Crossman called out when Joe was within earshot.

"My ass hurts!" Joe replied.

"We figured your ass would hurt! We were worried you were lost!"

"Well, technically I was. I just tried to ride south. I never saw any cattle until about fifteen minutes ago."

"Yeah, it just works out like that sometimes," Mr. Crossman said.

Mr. Crossman opened the gate and the cattle walked through. When he'd shut the gate, Mr. Crossman looked up at Joe. "You OK, Joe?"

"My ass hurts."

"But everything is OK?"

"Yeah...no...my ass hurts."

"Well, climb down off that horse!" Mr. Crossman smiled.

Joe crawled off Tom and stood still for a moment. He took a step with a stiff leg, then stopped. "Feels like I've been pounding fence posts with my ass!"

Before Mr. Crossman could respond, both men heard the front door of the cabin slam. When they looked up, they saw Norm and Junior Duncan run from the porch to the stock tank. Both men were completely naked except for their cowboy hats and boots. Each of them carried a bottle of Jack Daniel's in one hand as they ran. They kicked off their boots and hollered just before they jumped into the stock tank.

"Did I just see that? Really?" Joe asked.

"What?" Mr. Crossman said, trying not to smile.

"The ghosts of Norm and Junior running to get drunk in the stock tank?"

"Close. Those pale, white asses still belong to Norm and Junior, not their ghosts. We just decided that since it was so hot and everybody has a bit of a sore ass, we'd fill the stock tank with hot water and relax for the rest of the day. It's damn hot, ain't it?"

The cabin door slammed once more and Cletto, Murdo, and James ran naked, except for hats and boots, toward the stock tank.

"Hey, Joe! 'Bout time you got here," James hollered.

Joe turned an incredulous look to Mr. Crossman.

"It's been a long day—a good day for all of us, Joe—and we're gonna be branding tomorrow. That's damn hard work. Put your horse away and get him some oats and water. Then come on over for a soak. You'll like it."

Ten minutes later, after he'd put Tom in the shade of a lean-to by the corral, Joe emerged from the front door of the cabin. He wore his hat and boots only, and he had a can of Coke in each hand. When he drew close to the stock tank, all six naked cowboys sitting in the tank turned to look at him.

He smiled and put both cans of Coke in front of his crotch. When he reached the tank, he saw Jake curled into a ball sleeping in the shade. The men all looked at Joe while he stood beside the tank, but no one said anything at first.

"Jake likes to swim, but he's pretty tired now," James said.

"We was getting worried about you," Murdo said. "But I guess it took you some extra time to bring in that large herd." All the men chuckled.

"No, it wasn't that," Joe said as he stepped one foot over the side of the tank, then the other, and slid into the tub next to Murdo. "I was captured by fifty wild Indians. They took me prisoner, and then they all beat my ass bloody with cedar switches. That's what kept me." The men laughed even louder, and when the laughter subsided, Joe said, "It's true! Here. Look!" He stood up and bent over and put his bare, blistered ass about six inches from Murdo's face. "See?"

The roar of laughter that resulted could be heard across the valley. With that one gesture, Joe Mix had let himself into the small fraternity at Cowboy Camp. He laughed at his own behavior. He knew he'd never have been willing to do such things in his other life, before he'd started riding with the Kadoka Kid again.

When the laughter finally subsided, Junior Duncan had one last thing to add. "You know, Joe, when you bent over like that? And you sort of turned everything my way? Well, I thought you looked like that gal that brang Murdo flowers!"

For the next hour, the cowboys laughed out loud and told about their day's experiences on the trail.

———•———

Cigarette smoke swirled lazily into the silent twilight. The cigarette resting between Jim Crossman's fingers sent up one line of thin smoke while he sat on the steps of the cabin and stared across the blue hills of eastern Montana. A cool evening was about to settle over the little valley, and Jim Crossman always liked to watch the darkness descend like this.

He could hear the murmur of voices and subdued laughter coming from the kitchen table, where the men were playing cards. When he raised up a bit and craned his neck to the left, he could see Joe through the window in the front wall of the cabin. Joe was leaning on the right armrest of his chair, holding his back close to the hurricane lantern that hung between him and James.

"Hmph," Mr. Crossman sighed as he smiled and blew out a small cloud of smoke. Joe Mix was different than the other men he'd hired, that was for sure, but he was getting along quite well.

The cabin door opened and Jake tumbled out, with Joe right behind him. Jake was wagging his tail so hard he almost knocked himself over when he licked at Mr. Crossman's right hand. Mr. Crossman still held the cigarette in his left hand, and he raised it above his head so Jake wouldn't burn himself.

"Does your dog smoke?" he asked Joe when Jake jumped for the cigarette in his hand.

"Not unless he's on fire. But he does enjoy eating cigarette butts and sheep turds…stuff like that," Joe replied.

Mr. Crossman took one last drag on the cigarette and smashed the butt into the porch. Then he flicked the butt away onto the dirt in front of the cabin. Joe sat on the porch too and let his legs dangle off it.

"Thanks for offering me this job, Mr. Crossman. This has been good for me."

"It's gonna be a hard day tomorrow."

"Don't have to use my ass for anything, do I? No saddles involved?"

Mr. Crossman smiled softly. "We're gonna be branding cattle. We're gonna put in a longer day than today. You ever help with branding before?"

Joe shook his head.

"You don't know shit about the cattle business, do you?"

"No."

"Don't really care about the cattle business either, do you?"

"Not really," Joe smiled. "At least I don't see it as my calling, if that's what you mean. I do like this place and these people and the work."

"So how in the hell did you wind up in that restaurant in Wyoming?"

"Hmph…boy," Joe sighed. "I took a long road to get there." Joe reached over and pulled Jake away when he seemed to be pestering Mr. Crossman. "What are we gonna do tomorrow? How do we brand all those cattle?" Joe still wasn't ready to give the answer to the question about how he got there.

"We don't brand 'em all; the cows are already branded. But the calves were only born a few weeks ago, so we brand 'em while they're young and easy to handle. They'll be about a hunnerd to a hunnerd and thirty pounds." Mr. Crossman stopped and looked at Joe. "You're gonna start out as a 'wrassler'—that's what you call an 'entry-level position' around here. You know what that is...a wrassler?" he asked before he lit another cigarette.

"No." Joe shook his head.

"You better get some sleep," Mr. Crossman chuckled, and then he coughed on his own smoke when he laughed.

chapter
twenty-five

Sun-up was still twenty minutes away when the cowboys spilled out of the cabin and walked across the camp toward the horse corral.

"Murdo, Cletto, and I will saddle up and start separating cattle at sun-up," Mr. Crossman said. "We'll put the young ones in that trap over there." He pointed to a fairly small area that had been fenced in by barbed wire. Then Mr. Crossman turned to Norm and Junior. "You two set up the branding pot and get everything else ready. Try to explain to Joe how this works." With that, Mr. Crossman, Murdo, and Cletto walked around the corner of the lean-to in the corral and began to saddle their horses.

Joe leaned toward Norm Duncan and asked, "What's a trap?"

"Just a smaller fenced-in area, so they don't have to chase cattle all over hell."

"What's a branding pot?" Joe asked.

"You'll see. Take a step back there, Joe," Norm answered. Then he opened the topper on his truck and started lifting equipment out. He handed a small table to Junior. Then he lifted a large, cardboard box and gave it to Joe. "Put it over there, in that trap. Just follow Junior."

Joe took the cardboard box through a gate Junior had opened. He set the box beside the table Junior had carried in. Norm had a propane tank in one hand and a heavy steel rack with a cover in the other. James followed closely behind with another large cardboard box.

"OK, Joe," Norm said, "you pay attention. This here is a branding pot. It's just a stand that we use to hold several branding irons. That propane tank is what we use to heat the branding irons. In the movies, you'll see the old-time cowboys using an open fire to heat the irons. We're actually kinda surprised that Mr. Crossman has gone high-tech and quit usin' the open fire." Norm chuckled and looked at Junior.

"Now, look over there, Joe." Norm pointed to the table where Junior was displaying stainless steel syringes and bottles of medications. "We'll also immunize the calves today. There is a cocktail of drugs in each of those syringes, and we inject the calves at the same time we brand.

"One more thing, Joe. See that box that James is opening? There's a tool in there that stretches a big rubber band. When we get the bull calves on the ground to brand them, we place one of those rubber bands around their nut sack. It's called an elasterator. We used to cut 'em, but this is easier and less stressful for the bull calves."

"Sounds kind of stressful," Joe said.

"Well, it slows 'em up a little bit at first," Norm smiled

"What do you do when you need a bull with nuts?" Joe asked.

"The guys down on the west side of the Crossman ranch handle the breeding stock. We make all these bull calves into steers," Norm answered.

Joe heard the whoosh of the propane burner when James lit it. Then he saw Mr. Crossman riding out of the corral, followed by Murdo and Cletto. Murdo rode his horse over to the little table and asked, "Got everything you need, Norm?"

"Think so," Norm replied. "Give us a few minutes to get the irons hot."

Murdo reached his left hand up to his face and grimaced.

"You OK, Murdo?"

"Tooth hurts," Murdo said as he turned and rode away.

The sun had barely broken free from the eastern horizon when Mr. Crossman rode up to the crew at the table. "OK, boys, Murdo and Cletto are gonna finish separatin' the calves into the trap. I'm gonna go rope one and we're gonna show Joe how it's done."

Mr. Crossman lifted the rope from his saddle horn and moved his horse slowly toward a bunch of calves huddled along a fence. James and Norm stood side by side about ten feet apart from each other and waited while Junior walked to the table.

As Mr. Crossman approached the calves, one of them broke and ran. When the calf turned, Mr. Crossman spun the rope over his head several times and then threw it toward the calf. It looked to Joe as if Mr. Crossman's aim was bad; the loop missed the calf's head. But in only a heartbeat, Mr. Crossman lifted the rope firmly, and the calf fell to the ground. His aim had been perfect; he'd been trying to catch the calf by the hind legs.

Mr. Crossman deftly wrapped the rope around his saddle horn and began to drag the calf by its hind legs. As he approached James and Norm, he passed in between them. When the calf's hind feet were about even with them, James grabbed the rope holding its feet and pulled it firmly toward himself while Norm grabbed the calf's tail and pulled in the opposite direction.

The calf raised and turned and dropped heavily onto its right side. James instantly dropped to the ground with it. James held the calf's left hind leg firmly in his hands and pushed it forward. He wrapped his right leg around the calf's leg and put his boot firmly on the calf's right thigh and pushed backwards.

Joe had been watching only James. He could scarcely believe how fast he'd immobilized the calf. He hadn't even noticed that James had removed the rope from the calf's feet and thrown it loose so Mr. Crossman was free to go rope another. Joe had also failed to notice how quickly Norm had stepped over the neck of the calf, sat down, and bent its right front leg at the knee to prevent standing and struggling by the calf.

Junior appeared with a hot branding iron and did the deed. The calf bellowed, then fell silent. Junior walked back to the table, put the branding iron back in the branding pot to keep it hot, and picked up two stainless steel syringes that looked like pistols. He walked quickly over to the calf and injected the medicine just under the skin on its neck. The calf made no noise and didn't seem to feel the injections.

Then Junior returned with a tool that resembled a pliers, but it had a blue rubber band stretched around its beak. Junior walked to the rear end of the bull calf and looked for a second. The calf's balls lay by its left thigh, and Junior quickly encircled the scrotum and let the rubber ring slip off the pliers.

The instant Junior was finished, James let go of the calf's legs and rolled away. Norm released his grip on the calf's front end. The calf jumped up and walked back toward the other calves.

"There. That's how it's done, Joe," Junior said with a smile. "That one took forever, though. When Cletto is done separatin', he'll join us on the ground, and you're gonna get your hands dirty too. Why don't you start out doing the immunizations? You have any problem with giving the shots?"

"No," Joe smiled.

"Well, just don't immunize Norm," Junior said. "Or yourself! I'll handle the branding and the elasterator 'til Cletto joins us."

Mr. Crossman appeared with another calf in only a moment, and Joe hurried over to the table to get the syringes ready while Junior showed him what to do. James and Norm had the calf on the ground in what looked like two effortless wrestling moves. The calf bellered when Junior lowered the hot iron, and the stink of burning hair filled Joe's nose as he knelt beside the calf and finished the injections. Joe couldn't help but stare once again when Junior placed another rubber ring around the calf's scrotum.

"That calf is walking kind of funny," Joe said to Junior when they let the calf up. "S'pose that hurts?"

"Fuckin' right!" Junior laughed. "But it hurts less than cutting 'em like we used to do."

"Cuttin' them?" Joe asked.

"Yeah, we used to castrate with a knife. That just takes a lot more skill, an' it's still hard on the calves—bleedin' and all," Junior said with a shrug.

"Look at the way that one walks now," Joe said as he pointed to the most recent calf to be branded.

"Yeah, they kind of hunch up like that until it goes numb."

"Then what?"

"Then, after a while—maybe in a few days—his balls just fall off."

Joe looked at Junior with a strange, pained expression and stared for a moment. "Kinda like being married, huh?"

Junior stared a blank stare, smiled, then started chuckling slowly and didn't stop laughing for ten minutes as Mr. Crossman returned several times and the cowboys repeated their chores. Every time he was about to stop laughing, he looked at Joe and then started all over again.

Joe looked around several times as the cowboys settled into their jobs. He was a little overwhelmed by the action and the sights and the smells around him. Hundreds of cow pies and horse turds had dried and then been stomped into the dust inside the corral. The dust swirling around him carried the smell of sage and shit and burnt hide. James's shirt was smeared with dirt and dried shit and the blood from a small cut on his own hand. His face was covered with dust already, and a calf cried as it ran away from the branding pot. There's a lot going on here, Joe thought to himself.

When the separating was done and all the calves had been removed from their mothers, Cletto returned his horse to the corral. He joined the men working on the ground to help with branding, immunization, and castration. Mr. Crossman and Murdo roped calves and dragged them over to the 'wrasslers' every few minutes as the morning began to wear on. Cletto handled the branding, Junior the elasterator, Joe did the injections, and James and Norm 'wrassled' for the next hour. All the jobs seemed to be running smoothly when Norm finally said, "My ass is draggin'. Somebody spell me."

"Me too," James said.

"OK, Joe, this is your turn. Front end or the back?" Junior asked. "We're gonna switch with those two. You ready?"

"I guess so," Joe replied. "I'll try the hind end?"

"Hold on!" Junior warned him as Mr. Crossman approached, dragging a heifer calf. When the calf seemed to be in the right place, Joe grabbed the rope and pulled firmly. The heifer's feet lifted nicely, and the calf landed on its side when Junior used its tail to turn it. But as soon as the heifer hit the ground, it started to struggle before Joe had a good grip on its leg. The calf was just about to wriggle free and run away when Cletto lunged across Joe and pinned its hind leg back while he lifted the other leg. "Never let go of this leg, and be quick about pinning that one back. Can you feel now how much force it takes?" Cletto asked. He even smiled when he gave instructions regarding wrasslin'.

"Yeah, I think so," Joe said, as the first calf's branding and immunizations were finished quickly. When Murdo arrived with the next calf, the same struggle took place and Cletto had to help Joe a second time.

"You gotta hang on better right here," Cletto said as he pointed to the calf's left leg. "Hold on, Joe. You'll be all right. It just takes practice." Cletto smiled and nodded again.

"Thanks, Cletto," Joe said. He was embarrassed over his difficulty in doing a job that James had made look so easy.

Mr. Crossman approached with another calf in tow, and Joe grabbed the rope and lifted just as before. This time, he lost his grip almost immediately, and the calf jumped to its feet and ran away.

"Just hang on better with that left leg and lock that right one backward right away," Cletto said. Then Cletto nodded his encouragement. The other hands said nothing; they only waited for Murdo to approach dragging another calf.

"You're OK, Joe," James finally called as the calf was pulled directly in front of them.

Joe looked into Murdo's face and was about to smile and say something when Murdo's eyes turned cold. "I don't wanna hear no fuckin' excuses! Just wrassle these sonsabitches down and hold 'em. Goddammer, Joe, ever'body else is working too damn hard for you to fuck it all up! Now, get 'er done right, with no fuckin' excuses!" He'd spoken very loud and pointed his finger at Joe when he finished.

Joe's anger flashed in an instant. He was embarrassed, and he felt as if he'd been betrayed by a friend. I'll show you, you prick, he thought as he swung the bull calf to the ground. He wrapped his leg around the calf's leg and had it immobilized instantly. He lifted Murdo's rope off the calf's hoofs and threw the rope at Murdo. When the branding was done and the elasterator was in place, he let the bull calf scramble to his feet and run away.

"Nice one, Joe," Cletto said. "You've got it now."

Joe could only nod a slight thank you. He turned to face Mr. Crossman as he dragged another calf over to be branded. Joe grabbed the rope and flipped the calf over in one firm motion, then threw Mr. Crossman's rope clear and watched the others finish their jobs.

Anger still burned at the back of Joe's collar, and he was so upset at the way Murdo had spoken to him that his throat tightened. When Murdo approached with another calf at the end of his rope, Joe stared into his face, and Murdo returned the stare. Joe grabbed the rope, flipped the calf over, and held it with no problem while the others finished their tasks.

The morning wore along, and Joe refused to let go of his anger at Murdo. He made it a point to take extra turns at wrasslin' just because it was the hardest job. He tried to stare into Murdo's eyes each time he approached with another calf. He wanted to reach up and pull Murdo off his horse and punch him. He knew Murdo was right in what he'd said, but the words hurt. He had been justified in yelling, but Joe still didn't like to be spoken to like that, and Murdo's rebuke still stung. He'd show Murdo, by God. He'd put these cattle on the ground so well that Murdo would feel bad for yelling at him.

By mid afternoon, the crew had branded about 150 calves. No one had taken a break for lunch, but they'd all had several bottles of water or soda. "We'll finish the last little bunch right here; that'll be about 175 for the day," Mr. Crossman announced as he removed his hat and wiped the sweat from his forehead. "Turned out to be a hot one today. Let's have a soak when we're done, boys!"

During the day, Joe had become competent at all the jobs on the ground. He could wrassle on either side of the calf, the immunizations and the elasterator were easy, but he'd found himself holding his own nuts—as if to protect himself—after the first few times he'd placed a rubber ring around a calf's scrotum. The other cowboys had noticed him immediately and laughed out loud.

The job that surprised him the most was the branding. He'd grown used to the smell right away, and it looked like it should be pretty easy when he'd watched others do it. But there were several things the man with the branding iron could do wrong. He'd held the iron on one calf's rump a little too long and burned the poor calf through his hide. Several times, he'd accidentally slid a hot iron and smeared a brand, as if he were writing on the critter's hide with a burning pen. Overall, however, he felt he'd learned something and been a real contributor, almost as valuable as any of the real cowboys.

The only thing he knew he couldn't do was rope the cattle. He could see that Murdo and Mr. Crossman were very skilled; they just made roping look easy because they were seasoned by a lifetime of experience. Neither of them had missed many times during the day.

When Junior stood up and threw Murdo's rope free after the last calf of the day had been branded, Joe made a point to stretch his back and raise his arms above his head. He was still finding new muscles to abuse, but he knew he was beginning to get stronger, in many ways. He helped to carry the branding pot, the table, and the other supplies back to Norm's truck, and then he followed as the cowboys straggled over to the cabin.

Seven naked cowboys sat in the stock tank under the shade of the plank roof and soaked their sore muscles for an hour or so. The stock tank was an unexpected luxury, Joe thought. "I figure it'll take about three more days at this rate and we'll have this bunch done. That sound about right to you, Murdo?" Mr. Crossman asked.

When Murdo didn't answer right away, everyone turned to him. All that could be seen of Murdo above the water was his hat and his eyes. He'd sunken the lower half of his face below the water and was rubbing the left side of his upper jaw. He hadn't heard Mr. Crossman's question because he'd been so preoccupied with the pain in his tooth. When he realized everyone was looking at him, he raised his head above the water and said, "Huh?"

"Tooth botherin' you again?" Norm asked.

"No shit. Hurt off and on all day. Then it was fine for about an hour. Now she's a throbbin' again," Murdo said.

"Why didn't you see a dentist?" Joe asked.

"I guess I'll have to now if it don't stop hurtin!" Murdo answered.

That's not my worry anymore, Joe thought.

"I seen a dentist one time," Junior said. "He stuck a damn needle in my head, musta been this long." He held his hands about six inches apart. "Sonuvabitch that hurt! Then he just took out my tooth before it was numb. I wanted to kick his ass."

"Ever had a root canal?" Norm threw the question out for anyone to answer, then finished his own thought before anyone could respond. "I had one a couple years ago. Goddamn, that was the worst thing I ever had! Shit, I'd rather have a baby."

The men all fell silent for a moment and looked toward Norm Duncan. After the pause, Murdo twisted his face and said, "Now that's the dumbest fuckin' thing you ever said, Norm! Even for you, that was stupid! You mean you'd rather watch your wife, if you had one, have a baby instead of you havin' another root canal? Right?"

"Yeah, I guess so!" Norm smiled. "Sounds good to me."

When the laughter over Norm's comment subsided, Murdo asked, "What should we make for supper tonight, Mr. Crossman?"

"I thought we'd fry up some hamburgers, maybe some fried potatoes, and Mary made a bunch of that three-bean casserole, too."

"Can you imagine how that bedroom is gonna smell in the morning?" Cletto offered for everyone to think about.

When the dishes were done, James and Joe sat on opposite sides of the same hurricane lantern reading their books while Jake played on the floor with a bone. The other five men all sat at the table, playing cards and sipping at small glasses of whisky before bed.

"Say, Joe?" Murdo asked after a moment of silence around the table.

"Yeah?" Joe replied. Then he closed his book and looked over at the table.

Murdo turned his chair slightly and looked at Joe. "You done good today after that shaky start. You done real good," Murdo nodded.

"I didn't like it when you yelled at me. You pissed me off," Joe said flatly.

The other men all stopped and listened to the exchange between Joe and Murdo, wondering if the words might escalate into a confrontation.

Joe had forgiven Murdo hours earlier. He knew Murdo had been correct to scold him. But he was growing to enjoy these little verbal sparring matches with Murdo. He'd never done things like this before, and he felt himself beginning to look for opportunities to step into these conversations.

"If I hadn't barked at you, we'd still be out there chasin' cattle around." Murdo raised his eyebrows and grinned at Joe.

The silence grew heavier as the men waited for Joe's response.

"Yeah, that's probably true. But you know tonight when you and I were showering out there by the tank?" Joe asked.

"Yeah?" Murdo replied.

"While you were standin' there washin' your hair and talking to me under that old airplane wing? You know?" Joe asked again.

"Yeah?"

"I was pissing on your leg!" Joe said.

The whole group burst into laughter. Before Joe's face dissolved into a smile, he held his stare just long enough that Murdo couldn't tell if he was joking or if he'd really been pissing on his leg. Joe savored the suppression of the truth just long enough so he could see the doubt in Murdo's eyes, then confessed his lie with a smile.

—·—

"Damn, it's hot today," Junior groaned while the wrasslers waited for Mr. Crossman to rope and drag another calf over to them. After three days of this routine, Joe had mastered each of the jobs, and the crew had become quite efficient.

The men all waited with their hands on their hips while Mr. Crossman swung a rope above his head and then let it fly. He missed the calf he was chasing for the third time. "That don't happen very often," Junior said.

"He makes hard work outta this," Norm added. Then he took his hat off and wiped the sweat from his forehead.

"So there's an easier way to do this?" Joe asked. "Is that what Murdo was talking about over supper a while ago?"

Norm and Junior had been wrasslin' the calves, and they were standing a few feet in front of Joe with their backs to the rest of the crew. Norm turned around to face Joe and said, "If we modernized just a few things..."—he paused and looked around the trap—"...three of us could do all this work in a couple days." There was no sense of anger or frustration on his face, as there had been on Murdo's when he'd spoken about the way Mr. Crossman chose to brand cattle.

"So why do we do it this way?" Joe asked.

All the hands fell silent and turned their attention to the task in front of them when Mr. Crossman dragged another bull calf over to them. The Duncans wrassled the calf onto its side as the others went to work quickly. Joe stepped away from the calf after he'd placed the elasterator around its scrotum, and the calf scrambled to its feet.

"Hotter than hell for this early in the year, ain't it Norm?" Mr. Crossman said as he gathered his rope into a large coil and rode away.

"Yeah. I b'lieve a soak will feel pretty good later," Norm answered. Mr. Crossman acknowledged his agreement by pointing his finger at Norm, then rode away in search of another calf.

When Mr. Crossman was out of earshot, Junior turned to Joe and answered his question from a few minutes earlier. "We do it this way because Mr. Crossman says so, and he's the boss. He likes this—all this roping and cowboy stuff. Hell, we all do. But it's work, and there's ways to work more productive."

"How?" Joe asked.

"Run all the calves through a steel chute. You just clamp 'em in a lit-tle fence that looks like a gate, which holds 'em still. You hold 'em still without wrasslin', then you do all this work while the calf is standing up. You don't have to rope 'em or wrassle 'em, and two men can do all the work on the ground while one man on horseback drives 'em into the chute," Junior said. "We could do twice the work in half the time."

"Seems like a no-brainer," Joe replied. "Why won't Mr. Crossman change?"

"Well, Murdo thinks he just don't get it," Junior answered. "But me? I know Mr. Crossman ain't a fool. He does it this way because he come out here long ago and done it this way with his grandfather and his ol' man, and he just don't want to let go of it. He loves this. He just does it like this...because he still can." Junior shrugged.

"You can bet your ass that when Robert takes over, this shit is history!" Norm added. "He'll never do this. He'll just sit up there and smoke them big cigars until he's run this place into the ground."

Murdo dragged another calf up to the crew, and the men suspended their conversation of the moment while they went to work. "Goddammer, she's a hot one today, huh Junior?" I b'lieve I'm so dirty I could leave a ring around the stock tank after a soak today."

"How's the tooth?" Joe called out as Murdo rode away and gathered his rope from the ground.

"Pretty good! How's your ass?" he answered. Then he smiled and spat tobacco juice onto the ground.

"Much better, and thanks for asking!" Joe replied. He was chuckling to himself as he placed another rubber band on the elasterator tool when he noticed Cletto standing next to him. Cletto was holding a syringe in each hand and waiting for one of the ropers to bring another calf to the crew, but he wasn't smiling.

"You OK, Cletto?" Joe asked.

"Sure."

"You're pretty quiet today."

Cletto pointed both of the pistol-style syringes into the air so that their needles looked like smoking gun barrels. "I was just listening to you guys talking about Mr. Crossman." Cletto stopped and stared across the trap while Mr. Crossman and Murdo searched for calves to rope. "I've known him for a long time..." Cletto seemed as if he needed more time to finish his thought.

"Yeah?" Joe prodded Cletto.

"There's men who do things the hard way because that's how they live their lives. Can you see how happy Mr. Crossman is? This is the most fun he has all year. His is the old way; it's what makes him happy. This is when he connects with what he is and what came before him. He needs this. How could we ever do this any other way?"

Joe glanced at Mr. Crossman and watched for a moment while he lit a cigarette, then hollered something to Murdo. He smiled and hollered again when Murdo missed a calf with his rope.

"See, Joe?" Cletto said when Joe turned back to him. "He needs this, just because it's the hard way! I don't know for sure yet, but I don't think you're any different," Cletto said, then stepped out of the way as Murdo dragged a heifer calf between the wrasslers. Cletto was immunizing the calf when he looked up and caught Joe's eyes once more. This time, he stared for a moment, then walked away without a comment or even a smile.

When the midday heat began to intensify, Joe took another turn as a wrassler. The job had become routine, and he'd learned the proper amount of force required to turn the calves and hold them. He grabbed rope after rope, flipped the calves, and then held them securely while the other men did their jobs. He'd grown confident and comfortable in this job. Now, after several days of this, he'd reached the point that he could do this job easily while his mind wandered.

A bull calf struggled while Joe pinned his legs, and Cletto's words played over again in Joe's head while a hot breeze carried the smell of burning hide and cow shit past him. The hard way? Was that what he was searching for to prove himself? He had felt that until now, he'd always taken the easy road. Maybe Cletto was right. He let go of the calf and scrambled to his feet, then wrestled another to the ground.

Jess crossed his mind just now. The fact that he was lying on the dusty Montana ground, using his boot to hold a bull calf's leg back and both his hands to hold the bull calf's other leg so it didn't kick his teeth in, never occurred to him anymore. He was just able to go about his job and daydream about other things. He didn't miss Jess; that would probably never change, he thought. He did still enjoy the thought of maybe hurting her feelings. He was still angry. But his reason for being angry was so big that he could hardly get his mind around it. He was angry at her because...she'd married him? Or was it because he'd been foolish or weak enough to...what? To willingly suspend his knowledge that she was the wrong one? She'd made him do it, hadn't she? Or had he just been young and been part of the mistake too? No, he wanted it to be her fault. She was the one who actively pursued someone she didn't love, after all. It still needed to be her fault.

The boys? He thought of the boys often but less and less all the time. They seemed to have reached that point in life when they didn't want to rely on their father for too much—certainly not for advice. He talked to the boys regularly, and they seemed to be all right. The phone calls were always pleasant, and the boys seemed busy with their own lives.

What of the old life he'd left behind. He'd grown comfortable with the routine of a white shirt and tie every day. He didn't really like it, he didn't want it back, but he had grown comfortable, and he sometimes missed the comfort of a familiar routine.

The office? Dentistry? Shit! he thought. What had he been thinking? He'd never really enjoyed that. Yet he'd hammered away at it until it had almost killed him. Why? Why do men do that? he thought. Then he remembered his need to please others—the way he'd talked himself into believing that the office, the practice, and dressing up like a dentist every day was what he needed to do to please others. He'd allowed himself to believe that that life was the one he was supposed to live. But why? The smell of burning cowhide filled his nose as he let another calf get up and scramble away.

He thought of Wendy Hample and how he'd tried to make her into his alternate destiny. That was a good one! He'd almost thrown his life away in order to please Jess, and even after a gut-wrenching breakup with her, he'd assumed that having spent that same amount of time trying to please someone else would have made him happier. Maybe he was just a fool. Norm and Junior were laughing about something, and James was just behind him, coughing and complaining about the dust and the heat.

What about the Old Cowboy? What about Ray Mix not being perfect or not being what Joe had wanted him to be? That still bothered Joe some. But now that he'd had the time to let it settle in, maybe it was like Ralph Webster had said: maybe Ray Mix was just a man, no better than his son.

Another calf bellered and ran away while Joe's mind wandered over the horizon. He wondered if there were fish in any of these creeks. After all, it was getting to be summer out here, and Montana was home to a lot of fine trout streams. Maybe there were Indian artifacts along some of the streams. And the Indians' view of time as a circle? It was easy for Joe to understand how the Indians could be pretty thoughtful—how living in this place would lead them to search for a deeper understanding of life.

He worked right along with the others, still lost in his daydreaming, and the picture of himself standing next to Win Westby, Ben Monahan, and Lyle Davies materialized in his mind. Win had been the first man he'd ever known who had talked about the simple joy of a thing well done. He'd always said...

"Goddammer, girls! That's it for today!" Murdo hollered, and Joe quickly returned from his daydreams. He was still lying on the dusty ground about to release a heifer calf when Murdo announced the end of the workday and startled him back to reality.

Murdo leaned on his saddle horn and looked down at Joe. "How's our ass today, cowboy?"

"Just a minute and I'll show you," Joe answered.

Murdo chuckled and turned his horse toward the corral. "Soon as I put my horse away, I'll have a look. That's the thing about you, Joe: put a couple diet sodas in you and you want to show all the cowboys your ass!"

Joe watched and smiled as Murdo's horse took several steps back and began to turn to the side. Behind Murdo, across the compound, Joe's gaze shifted when he saw Junior open the door to the small shed where Jake was kept while the men worked with livestock. He knew instantly what was about to happen, and he knew he was powerless to stop it. All he could do was watch as the entire horrific incident played itself out in slow motion.

Jake exploded through a small opening the instant Junior opened the door and sprinted directly toward Joe. His ears were back, and he was racing at full speed when he approached Murdo's horse from behind. The horse spooked from the sudden commotion at his feet and kicked Jake flush on the side.

A tiny, painful yip hung in the air for a second, and the limp puppy sent up a trail of dust as he tumbled across the ground. He came to rest in a twisted, grotesque form about twenty feet from Murdo and his horse.

Joe had seen the whole thing happen. He'd seen the smile melt from Murdo's face and be replaced by a hollow, blank stare filled with guilt, pain, and shock. He'd seen the playful puppy's life take a dreadful turn in only a heartbeat.

Joe ran to Jake. He appeared to be dead. He should be dead, Joe thought. Junior arrived next and dropped to his knee next to Joe. "Oh, Jesus, I'm sorry, Joe. I just opened the door. Jake just...oh, Jesus, I'm sorry."

Cletto was next on the scene. He arrived while Junior was still talking, and he turned Jake onto his side without saying a word. Then he bent down and put his ear against Jake's chest. "He's alive," Cletto said when he straightened up. "Let's get some shade for him."

Junior ran to get the small table, returned quickly, and set it up to cast a shadow onto Jake.

By the time Murdo had put his horse in the corral and returned, Jake had opened his eyes and begun moving his head. Several minutes later, he lifted his head from the ground and appeared to want to stand.

Cletto watched Jake's every movement and moved even closer to Jake when he began to whimper. His hands seemed so confident, Joe thought, as Cletto reached toward the puppy and began to examine the trembling pup. Jake flinched and let out a painful yelp when Cletto touched his left front leg.

"Broken leg, I think," Cletto said. "But it might not be so bad if that's all that's wrong." He touched the leg once more and Jake yelped again. "It don't look like a compound fracture. There's no bone sticking out anywhere. This might be something that will heal. Hey, Junior, would you get the medicine kit in the cabin?"

When Junior returned with a shoebox full of tape and BAND-AIDs and a few bottles, Cletto removed the tape and fashioned a splint from two wooden tongue depressors. When he was finished, he carefully lifted Jake to his feet. Jake's tale dropped between his legs and he held his head low, but he stood up. He seemed to have only enough strength to hold the splinted leg up off the ground.

"He might be OK," Cletto said. "Let's get him a drink, pat him down with some cool water, and let him rest in the cabin."

Joe picked the puppy up gently, carried him into the cabin, and let him lie on a blanket by the door.

"He might be OK!" Cletto tried to reassure Joe and the other cowboys. "I'm sure he's hurtin', but he's been rightside up and he just took a drink! That's good. All we can do is wait."

"I'm sorry, Joe," Junior whispered.

"Me too," Murdo added.

"It's not your fault," Joe said. "It's not anybody's fault. Stuff like this just happens." He reached down and touched Jake ever so gently. "He's gonna be OK."

Joe sat on the floor beside Jake for several hours and watched him sleep. He hadn't realized it until now, but he loved his puppy and he needed him. He watched Jake's little breaths lift his chest rhythmically, and he was thankful for each breath. He just hadn't understood how much he loved his puppy until he'd watched the terrible accident and stood over Jake's limp body. Several times Jake drew in a long breath, then sighed heavily. Joe had to choke back tears several times as he watched the yellow dog sleep.

The cowboys were cleaned up, sitting around the cabin and waiting for supper, when Murdo walked to the frying pan and stuck a fork in a piece of hamburger. He walked slowly to the blanket where Jake lay sleeping and sat down on the floor beside the pup. Murdo smiled at Joe, then held the piece of meat in front of Jake's nose for a moment.

Jake opened his eyes, licked his lips several times, then raised his head off the floor. He stared at the hamburger briefly, then ate it in one bite.

Murdo grinned and raised his eyebrows at Joe. He reached for the femur of a long-dead cow that Jake had been playing with for days. Usually at this time of night, Jake would be tugging the bone around the cabin. He liked to pick it up in his mouth and shake it until he lost his grip. Then, when it flew across the room, he'd chase it as if it were trying to escape.

The femur hung from a section of twine as Murdo bounced it on the floor about a foot from Jake. He was tempting Jake to go get it.

Jake stared for a moment, then climbed gingerly to his feet. He stood on three legs for a while, then walked tenderly over to the cow's bone, without putting any weight on his left front leg. He picked up the bone with his mouth, walked back over to his blanket, and laid down again. He chewed on the bone for almost a minute while all the cowboys stared at him. Then Jake looked at Joe, tilted his head, and seemed to ask, "What are you lookin' at?"

"I think he's gonna make it," Murdo said.

Several hours after supper, the cowboys were playing cards and Joe was sitting under a light reading when Jake climbed unsteadily to his feet once more. He stood still for a moment while everyone watched. He walked slowly to the front door, peed on the floor, then walked back to his blanket and laid down again. He chewed on the bone for a moment, then went back to sleep. "First time I was ever happy to see a dog piss in my cabin," Mr. Crossman said.

"That's a tough dog, Joe," Murdo said with a smile.

Murdo had watched earlier when Joe had sat beside Jake's blanket and waited. He'd seen the hurt and fear in Joe's eyes. Now, he was only too happy to joke about a different hurt in Joe's eyes. When he looked at Joe, he noticed that his weight was shifted to one side; he was sitting on his pillow while he read, leaning far to his right. Murdo knew that Joe's discomfort was the lingering result of that long first day in the saddle. "You all right, Joe? You look a bit uncomfortable." He was teasing Joe, trying to get him to admit his lack of experience once more.

"Yeah," Joe sighed without looking up from his book. "This is the first time reading ever made my ass hurt," he said as he turned a page.

Junior was rearranging the cards in his hand. Without looking up, he blurted, "Jesus, must be some hard words in that book, Joe."

The room fell silent once more, and Murdo's face twisted with disdain as he glanced at Junior, then looked back at Joe.

"Goddammer, Junior, you better just stick to havin' root canals," Murdo said.

"Huh?" Junior said, still looking at his cards.

"Nuthin," Murdo sighed.

"Well, that root canal...that fucker hurt!" Junior still stared at his cards.

At that point, Joe closed his book and raised his glance. He made eye contact with Murdo, who simply smiled, then shrugged as if it would do no good to say anything to Junior because Junior really didn't understand what he'd said. Joe exchanged a smile with Murdo—the kind of smile that comes without plan or purpose and serves to deepen the mutual understanding of the people who share it.

Three more days of branding cattle came and went without incident, and Joe began to master all the jobs around camp. The ache in his arms and back slowly turned into strength. He enjoyed these men and this labor, and he could feel a deeper strength building in him.

twenty-six

They looked like lawn ornaments, fixed and motionless. Several dozen black cows and calves seemed to be frozen in place when Joe crested the small ridge. Tom was only walking, moving at a very slow pace. Joe had been enjoying the quiet, peaceful ride across the prairie, but he reined Tom to a stop and looked out over the little green valley in front of him.

Joe put both hands on the saddle horn, leaned forward, and drew in a deep breath. Several cows turned to look at him, then turned away, unimpressed by the appearance of a rider. Then two of the calves began to walk toward the cows, looking for the safety of their mothers.

Two hours earlier, Joe had stood along a lonely fence line in the darkness and held tightly to Tom's reins before starting another day of rounding up cattle. He'd been crossing hills and gullies since daybreak, wondering just what he'd do if he ever came upon a large group of cattle.

The morning was clear and soft and carried the powerful summer scent of sage. Joe felt good to be sitting alone in this place. But he couldn't help but wonder if he was up to the job in front of him. "All right, Tom," Joe sighed, "let's go do some of that cowboy stuff." He lowered the reins and Tom began walking slowly once more, directly toward the group of cattle. The cattle looked at Joe, then looked away. Several of them turned and began to walk slowly in the same direction Tom was walking. They moved like glaciers at first, then picked up the pace and ambled south. Tom simply followed. He seemed to be leading them from behind. They know the way home, Joe thought.

Soon, all the cattle had turned away from Tom and were walking together in a small, slow-moving parade. "Nice work, Tom," Joe said as he followed behind the caravan. "That was easy, huh? Looks like those little dogies know how this is done. I'll just leave you in charge."

From the top of the next ridge, Joe saw more cows directly in front of him and another cow, with her calf alongside her, about two hundred yards off to the west. Short, scraggly-looking evergreen trees were trying to grow along the hillside in front of him. Rocky limestone outcroppings, which lay across the hillside like scattered railroad cars after a train wreck, poked through the grassy slope.

The black cow and her calf off to the west didn't seem interested in joining the other cattle, but the half dozen or so cows and calves directly in front of him turned away from Joe and began to walk in the correct direction at the head of Joe's parade, as though they already knew the drill too.

Joe turned Tom's head to the west, and they moved off in a long, circular swing to approach the lone cow and calf from the west, then push them back toward the main bunch of cattle. When Joe and Tom were still about thirty yards from the stragglers, the cow lifted her head and began to trot toward the other cattle. Her calf followed her, just as Joe had hoped.

The whole thing certainly seemed easy, Joe thought. There was no galloping and waving of hats, no whistling and hollering, no shooting of pistols in order to drive cattle, like in the movies. All Joe had to do was approach the cattle from the opposite direction he wanted them to go. He was at once relieved and disillusioned; he knew he wasn't a good enough horseman to do the job, but nonetheless he'd hoped to do some hat waving and galloping.

The cattle were moving along, basically in single file. The closer Joe approached to them, the more they sped up. The crest of the next ridge revealed yet another valley just about the same as the one they'd just left. Several dozen more black-and-white cows, accompanied by their calves, were grazing along the small creek bed in the middle of the valley.

"OK. C'mon, girls, let's move along," Joe said as he approached the cattle. This time, however, some of the cows looked at Joe and began to act skittish, while the others began to edge slowly away from him toward the small, meandering herd Joe had assembled.

Suddenly, the skittish cattle, about eight of them, bolted and ran off, away from the others. Joe thought they'd stop running after a little burst, but they continued to move across the floor of the valley.

The other cattle had joined the small herd that Joe had already assembled, and they continued to move slowly to the south. Although Joe was glad that the majority of the cattle were so obedient, he HAD been looking for a chance to lope over and do some of that cowboy stuff while he herded the strays back. This was his opportunity.

Joe watched for a while longer as the small group of cows and calves continued to run away from the others. Then he smiled when he understood what he had to do. "OK, Tom, let's go get 'em," he said as he turned Tom's head to the right and raised his heels gently into Tom's flanks. Tom's response was not an explosion as it had been before, but Joe could still feel power and a sense of purpose beneath him. Tom knew what to do, and Joe wasn't quite sure if he was giving Tom directions any longer or if he was just along for the ride.

Tom's pace was quick and smooth. He made up ground quickly as he circled around to the west of the runaway cattle. The cattle reacted to Tom's pressure just as Joe knew they would: they began to turn back toward the other cattle that had fallen in with the herd, and soon they were walking slowly toward the next ridge.

Suddenly, one black cow and her calf bolted away from the others once again, and Tom turned quickly when Joe leaned on the reins to direct him to the right again. Joe was thrilled with the swiftness of the pursuit and with his own horsemanship. This cowboy stuff wasn't so hard, Joe thought.

For a second time, Tom cut sharply. He circled to the right of the running cattle and began to turn them back to the left as he approached. The cow planted her front legs and kicked up a small cloud of dust as she turned to the left. The calf did the same. Much to Joe's surprise, so did Tom.

Tom's stop, and his turn, were sudden and violent, and as the force of his own motion began to lift him, Joe knew he was about to leave the saddle quickly. This time, there was no sense of weightlessness or floating on air. Joe left the saddle as if he'd been ejected from a moving car. He clutched at the saddle horn as it whizzed by but it was no use. He felt like a giant tornado was blowing him sideways across Montana. Luckily, he lost both stirrups as his momentum carried him off Tom's back at what he thought was a shocking speed. Joe hit the ground on his right side and rolled over several times. He'd lost his grip on the reins, and his hat flew off as he impacted the dusty ground.

Joe's first thought when he stopped moving was to assess the damage to his body. This fall had been much more sudden and dangerous than the first one, but surprisingly, nothing hurt. He rose quickly and drew in a deep breath, then picked up his hat and examined the grass and dirt stains on the shoulder and sleeve of his white shirt.

The cattle he'd been chasing were now walking slowly toward the other cattle, and Tom stood about twenty feet from Joe, looking at him.

"OK, Tom, we're not gonna tell anyone about this, are we?" Joe said as a smile creased his lips. He walked slowly toward Tom and picked up the reins that hung to the ground. Joe wasn't quite sure what he was feeling as he swung his leg over Tom's back and settled into his saddle, but the smile wouldn't leave his face. He wasn't really embarrassed at having been thrown from his horse. In fact, he imagined it had probably been a pretty funny thing to see. He was satisfied in some way that he just couldn't identify. This was fun—even getting thrown off his horse was fun. He wished Donny was here to see this. He'd never felt it as an adult. He was just happy to be there, in that place and time. A strong man sittin' on a fine horse, most of the time, anyway. The sun felt warm on his shoulders, and he was breathing in a clear Montana morning. That was enough. Hell, maybe that was everything—all he'd ever wanted, really. Damn, he felt good, and he decided to stop wondering why. He just lowered the reins and let Tom follow the stray cattle over toward the others.

"You tell me if you're gonna do any more of that shit, OK?" Joe's smile curled across his whole face. "Bad horse, Tom."

———

Joe guessed he could see fifteen or twenty miles from the top of the hill. It was only about fifty feet higher than the other rolling hills on this part of the ranch, but when he reached the top, Joe felt as if he'd climbed to the summit of a mountain. All he could see were more hills and valleys, with rock outcroppings and scraggly pine trees covering some of the hilltops. From the top of the hill, it looked like this country continued in all directions and covered the whole world.

During the first several hours of today's roundup, Joe had gathered about two hundred cattle. Other than the one little bunch that had run off and resulted in him being thrown from his saddle, the cattle had been so easy to drive that he wondered if they'd been trained. Even now, after he'd left them and ridden to the top of this hill, they continued to wander slowly to the south as if they knew the routine.

Joe reached into his saddlebag and found his new cell phone. This hill had roused his curiosity. Besides the fact that he wanted to see the view from the top, he wondered if he might be able to get a signal and call Donny from here. Sure enough, when he turned the phone on, the signal was strong enough for a try. So Joe dialed Donny's cell number and waited.

"Hello."

"Donny?"

"Joe?"

Joe felt a familiar pleasure at the sound of Donny's voice.

"Hi, Donny!"

"Where are you, Joe? Can I call you back?" Donny asked.

"Probably not, Donny. I'm sitting on a hill in the middle of nowhere, and I don't know when I'll have a signal again. Might not be able to call again for a while," Joe answered. Then he heard Donny excuse himself from whatever it was he was doing and carry his phone into a more private place.

"So how are you, Joe? Everything OK? Jeez, I can hear you clear as a bell," Donny said.

"Yeah, things are good, Donny. I just wanted to call and say hi."

"What are you doing?"

"Well, I'm sittin' on a big brown horse named Tom. I'm lookin' out over some fine country. I'm rounding up cattle. We're gonna brand 'em tomorrow. You believe that?" Joe paused, but only briefly, and Donny had no time to answer before Joe asked another question. "You remember how we laughed that last day we were together? You know, when we were fishing? It was like we were little boys. Remember, Donny?"

"Sure," Donny answered.

"Well, I just fell off my horse, and when I climbed back on I felt good about all this. I felt like I did that day with you—like I used to when we were kids—and I decided to call, that's all."

330

"You felt good when you fell off your horse? Did you whack your head on the ground?"

"No," Joe smiled, but he said no more as he looked out over the prairie.

"Still there, Joe?" Donny asked. He wondered if the call had been dropped or if Joe had put the phone down.

"Remember the Kadoka Kid?" Joe asked. He raised up in the stirrups and looked all around.

"Yeah, sure," Donny replied, but he was clearly surprised by his brother's question. "Why do you ask?"

"No reason," Joe replied. He'd decided he didn't want to share any more about the Kadoka Kid.

"You all right, Joe?" Donny asked.

"Never been better," Joe replied.

"So do you think you want to be a cowboy now? Is that where all this is headed?" Donny asked.

"No, I didn't say that," Joe smiled. "This isn't my final destination. My future still lies somewhere down the road. But I'll stay here for a while. I'll know when it's time to leave. I like these people, and I want to see just what it is that allows these guys to work this hard, for slave wages, and love every minute of this life. It's funny: these cowboys have given me something. Might even be the thing Dad was trying to protect me from. Maybe if Dad would have given it to me, I would have made a lot of choices differently.

"You're getting a little philosophical again, Joe. Pretty soon you'll be talking about mayflies again," Donny said.

"Maybe. But it's true, Donny. These guys have allowed—no, demanded—that I be a little wild and live somewhat dangerously. Dad always seemed to push me away from danger. It was as if he thought that being safe, mild mannered, and boring was the same as being insightful and wise. Hell, so did I! I thought that for most of my life."

Donny had no reply. He only waited for Joe to continue.

"I had to leave, Donny. I had to." Joe held the phone to his ear and looked across the Montana prairie. "I knew something was really wrong when I started to lament the fact that life was so long. I'd sit there at my desk at the office and think, 'Why does life have to be so long? I wish it was over.' You believe that? That's when I knew I had to make a change—a big change."

"Yeah, I could see it coming, Joe."

"But you know, Donny, it's funny. I thought there were gonna be dragons to slay, noble causes to fight for, and maidens to rescue, shit like that. Maybe that's yet to come. For now, I'm likin' things here."

"Jesus, Joe! Dragons to slay? You don't think you slew a few dragons?" Donny sounded incredulous. "Every men's day at The Oaks, about a dozen guys wander over to me and ask about you. They don't want anyone to know it, but they think you're a hero!"

"Really?" Joe said, unable to hide his surprise. "Everyone doesn't think I'm a loser...a failure?"

"Yeah, lots of people think that, too!" Joe could hear Donny chuckle. "But some of the guys want an update every time I see them. Slats Murphy says hello, by the way. He laughs that crazy laugh, and smoke pours out of him every time I mention your name."

"Say hi to Slats, will you?" Joe said.

"Sure," Donny said. "I'll say hi to Jess, too, although she hasn't asked about you in a while," Donny said sarcastically. Then he waited for Joe's response.

"Well, you know, Donny, I can't really blame her for everything. The failure of our marriage wasn't totally her fault. I want it to be her fault, but I had something to do with it all failing too."

"Pardon me?" Donny said.

"Well, think about it. When we first met, Jess was just a young girl who was afraid of the future, like we all were, and she was just trying to make her way. She hadn't changed into the malicious, mean-spirited Jess we all know now. She was just trying to build a good life for herself, and she took hold of me because I probably looked like the easiest, safest way to a decent life. She must have thought that love and happiness would naturally follow along someday. It just didn't work out that way. She never should have chosen me either, and she probably harbors a fair amount of resentment toward me. I can't blame her for that, I guess. I didn't like me either."

"So you want to put an end to this divorce thing and take her back?" Donny asked sarcastically.

"No. I didn't say that. No matter what I'd have done, Jess, in the final analysis, would only have been interested in what I could do for her. But by being the safe, boring imposter that I was, I just made her realize how much she hated being married to me. She was done with me, too!"

"Imposter? I don't get it, Joe."

"You know, Donny. Like all those guys who sit in the front of church and try to spend their lives convincing others of their religious fervor. All the while, they know they've got serious issues that they're terrified to deal with. So they just ignore them and go on pretending to be fine, boring Christians. Know what I mean?"

"Yeah. But aren't you still an imposter, even now? Haven't you just changed your costume?" Donny asked. "Aren't you just dressed up like a cowboy now instead of a dentist?"

"Good question, Donny. But the answer is no. This isn't what I'll be; it's not what I am. In fact, I try not to think of myself as anything except a man anymore. No more labels if I can help it."

"You're getting philosophical again!" Donny said.

"Yeah, and my cattle have stopped moving too. I'd better go."

"Joe, hold on! Before you go...you're OK, right?"

"Yes."

"No regrets?" Donny asked.

"None." He paused for a second. "None, Donny. In fact, that's why I called—just to tell you how good I felt."

"You'll be fine. Take care, Joe. I love you!"

"Love you too, Donny," Joe said.

When Joe rode around the curve at the bottom of another small hill just before 2:00 p.m., he saw that all the cattle he'd gathered had fallen into a single-file line and were walking along a dusty trail at the bottom of a ravine. Each cow seemed to be urging the one in front of itself, and the one at the front of the line simply followed the trail. The line of cattle curved up over the bank of the ravine, then crossed over the crest of the far side so that Joe lost sight of them. He knew he had to be close to camp, and while he waited to cross the ravine, his thoughts turned to Jake. He'd only worn the splint Cletto had made for two days. Then he'd been able to walk, albeit gingerly, without the splint on the following day. Cletto's guess was that the leg was never broken, just very bruised and sore. Jake's injury had brought the cowboys a little closer too. Joe laughed out loud when he remembered how quickly Junior had forgiven Jake for chewing a hole in his boot. All of the cowboys, even Mr. Crossman, had spent time crawling on the floor of the cabin and playing with Jake since the day of his accident.

Joe daydreamed about playing with Jake and waited his turn at the end of the line of cattle he was driving. When he followed the last calf over the top of the ravine, he saw that he was only about a quarter-mile from camp.

In the distance, James Bond was standing in his stirrups, waving and flashing a smile as Joe and Tom stepped into view. The two hundred or so cattle Joe had gathered swelled the size of the herd in front of him to about eight hundred, he thought. Joe waved back at James and drove his cattle into the trap where the other cattle waited.

"Seen Murdo?" James called out when Joe was close enough.

"No."

"He's usually the first one back here," James said.

"He'll be along soon enough," Joe answered with a grin. Just the mention of Murdo brought a smile to Joe's face now. In his mind's eye, he could see Murdo's face as he told a story about his day in the saddle or described an indecent act.

But Murdo didn't come, and Joe began to worry about Murdo after two more hours had passed and there was still no sign of him. The other cowboys, however, had no such concern for Murdo's safety. They were naked except for their hats and soaking in the hot tub when the first of a large group of black cattle appeared in the distance. Murdo rode slowly over the horizon about ten minutes after the first of the cattle came into view.

"Looks like four hundred head," Junior said.

"He'll have some stories to tell," Norm added.

But when Murdo finally walked up to the stock tank after he'd pushed his cattle into the trap, taken the saddle off his horse, and stripped down to his boots and hat, he was unusually quiet. After a short, silent walk from the cabin to the hot tub, Murdo stood over Jake for a second and watched as Jake wagged his tail and limped over to him and begged for some affection. He bent down and held Jake's face close to his own for almost a minute while Jake licked his neck and cheek. Then he rubbed his swollen cheek over the soft fur on Jake's back and stood up.

He held a bottle of Jack Daniel's in one hand and softly passed the other hand over the stubble on his face. "Tooth hurts" was all he said when he kicked his boots off and stepped into the tank.

chapter
twenty-seven

Hot, dry, cloudless days were the only constant for the next several weeks while the Crossman cowboys continued to gather and brand the cattle from the north range of the Twin ranches.

Days of wrasslin' cattle in the dust and nights filled with card games, reading, and ridiculous banter in the stock tank brought the men together in a way Joe could not have predicted. They'd had enough work to do so that they'd discovered they needed each other. They'd had only enough free time to learn to accept each other's likes and dislikes and sense of humor. Joe felt that if they'd had too much free time to spend, they'd all have learned to dislike each other. The only constant complaint from any of the men was that Norm and Junior were bored with the seven-year-old pornographic magazines in the outhouse.

Other than the dry weather and the stale pornography, the other consistent topics of discussion had been Murdo's toothache and Jake's recovery. Junior seemed to enjoy lavishing attention onto Jake more than the others, but all of them took turns playing on the floor with Jake at night. Every one of them enjoyed sneaking scraps of food to Jake, even though Joe asked them not to.

They all enjoyed asking Murdo about his tooth also. Sometimes he'd groan, "Fuckin' tooth hurts!" and sometimes he'd just turn away, but all the cowboys enjoyed speculating about when Murdo would be ready to go and get it taken care of. Every other day or so, Murdo would complain of tooth pain—or at the very least he'd seem distracted— and Joe could read the pain in his eyes.

On the day the last bunch of cattle had been gathered, Joe was removing the saddle from Tom and placing it on top of a fence inside the barn, next to all the other tack, when Murdo walked around the corner.

Murdo was walking his horse at an unusually slow pace and dragging his boots along the ground when Joe turned to look at him. He moved as if he was exhausted or sick. Murdo raised his face and made eye contact with Joe, and Joe noticed the swelling immediately. The left side of Murdo's face was swollen, and the skin was pulled so tight it was shiny.

"Fuckin' tooth hurts," Murdo groaned. His mouth was fixed in a grimace.

"Jeez, Murdo, it's time to get that looked at." Joe could hide his concern no longer. "I do know something about that kind of thing. You need to see a dentist. Now! Well, tomorrow. Just go, Murdo. In the old days, people died of infections like that. Go into Billings and see a dentist. Tomorrow."

"Yeah, maybe," Murdo mumbled.

"I'll put your saddle and tack away, Murdo. Go on and have a soak. You look like shit."

"Thanks, Joe," Murdo said as he handed Joe the reins to his horse and shuffled off toward the cabin.

All through the ritual of a hot soak in the stock tank, and all through supper, Murdo only stared straight ahead and grimaced.

"All right, Murdo, this is it," Mr. Crossman finally ordered. "Tomorrow you get up bright and early and head into Billings. You get that tooth fixed, then pick up some supplies for the last few days out here. Understand?"

Murdo nodded, got up from the table, and poured himself a tall drink. For the first time Joe could remember, Murdo remained quiet all evening. He sat by himself and tried to deal with the pain in his face.

All through the next day during Murdo's absence, the branding crew spent most of the time speculating as to Murdo's well-being and waiting for his return. The day's work came and went. When supper was over and the dishes were done, there was still no Murdo. Mr. Crossman sat on the front steps and smoked cigarettes and looked for Murdo's truck lights to appear on the horizon until after midnight. But Murdo did not return.

Only Joe was still awake when Mr. Crossman stepped into the cabin. "He'll be here in the morning," Mr. Crossman said when he closed the door behind him.

Joe closed his book and asked, "Are you worried?"

"No. Hell, no. It's just not like Murdo to waste time," Mr. Crossman said. "He must have had some problem with a vehicle or the supplies. He's probably sleeping in his own bed tonight and planning to roll in here for breakfast."

Breakfast was long done and half the morning's work was finished when a trail of dust appeared on the horizon. Joe noticed Cletto and Junior exchange smiles when they noticed the growing dust cloud.

"That'll be Murdo," Mr. Crossman said as the dust cloud drew closer.

After five minutes of peeking over their shoulders and tracking Murdo's progress, the men saw a white pickup pulling a horse trailer roll over the crest of the ridge and begin the gradual descent into camp.

Mr. Crossman dismounted, tied his horse to the fence, and walked toward the truck when it rolled to a stop. Joe put the branding iron back in the branding pot. Cletto put the syringes back on the table. Junior rested the elaserator on the cardboard box with all the rubber bands in it, and James and Norm dusted themselves off. Then they all followed Mr. Crossman over to Murdo's truck.

Murdo was standing beside his truck, leaning over the front seat, when the men reached it. He was still leaning into the truck when he called to them over his shoulder, "I got some ice cream in this cooler! And I got some new fuck books for the shithouse!"

The others didn't seem to notice, but Joe smiled and shook his head at the bizarre sentence Murdo had just uttered: "...new fuck books for the shithouse!" Joe laughed out loud. What a strange combination of words. He grinned and waited for Murdo to turn around.

But when Murdo stood to show the men the stack of dirty magazines in his arms, all they could see was that his face was just as swollen as when he'd left.

"Shit, Murdo! That dentist was pretty rough on you, huh?" Junior said.

"Lemme see them fuck books," Norm said as he took the magazines from Murdo. "You still look like shit, Murdo," he added.

Murdo's swollen face didn't have the look of post-surgical trauma to Joe. It still looked like a growing infection. "Did you even see a dentist?" Joe asked.

"Well," Murdo tilted his head, "that turned out to be a big problem."

"Goddammit, Murdo! You took a day and a half off work and then you never seen the goddamn dentist? What the hell is wrong with you?" Mr. Crossman blurted. Joe had never seen him angry, like he was at the moment. Maybe he was angry with Murdo for wasting time, or perhaps he was frustrated and concerned about Murdo's infection. Joe couldn't tell.

"Well, it's more complicated than that, Goddammer. I went right to see the dentist yesterday morning. Everyone said he's supposed to be the best one in Billings. Anyway, he got me right in there and took a look, then said to come back at 4:00 and he'd take the tooth out. So I ran some errands and picked up some supplies. My tooth was feelin' pretty good, too, and the swellin' was down some." Then Murdo's tone became apologetic, and he hung his head when he continued.

"My work was done and I had some time, so I went into a little bar for lunch and a game of pool. You know the place, Cletto. It's called Beeches. Old man Beech sits in there and bullshits with the cowboys. We been in there a couple times." Murdo seemed to be looking for a place to hide as he continued. "Well, goddammer, wouldn't you know—there sat Dorothy Buck."

"The woman that brought you flowers?" Cletto asked. Joe had never seen him smile such a huge smile.

Murdo nodded shamefully.

"The one who didn't care if you was married or not?" Junior added above a smattering of laughter.

"Yeah, it was her," Murdo continued. "Well, what could I do? I still had some time, so we went to her place. She lives in a trailer park down by the highway. One thing led to another, and that's when I run into some trouble."

"What happened, Murdo?" Anger and frustration oozed from Mr. Crossman with the simple question.

"Well, I think I told you fellers she's a screamer, right? Anyways, right there at the end, I give her the Velvet Half-Nelson and she started screamin'. I mean, loud! One of her dumb-ass neighbors called the cops." Murdo shrugged. "Apparently she thought Dorothy was bein' murdered. Well, anyways, the cops showed up about the time she stopped screamin', and then everything turned to shit."

"Keep going, Murdo," Mr. Crossman said.

"Well, it seems Dorothy had been sort of livin' with one of the cops who answered that call. I guess you can imagine how surprised he was to find my boots beside his bed."

Even Mr. Crossman started to laugh at the tortured look on Murdo's face. "So what happened?" Joe asked above the laughter of the cowboys.

"I spent the night in jail with a bunch 'o drunks who smelled like vomit. Dern cop was pissed! Obviously, I missed my dental appointment, and I decided to just come back to camp." Murdo looked from side to side, nodding and searching his friends' faces for understanding.

"So what about your tooth?" Mr. Crossman asked over the laughter.

"I'll get 'er fixed in a couple weeks."

Joe moved close to Murdo and surveyed the swelling at close range. The infection looked as if it was going to turn ugly. He was about to ask Murdo if he had taken any antibiotics when Mr. Crossman hollered, "Back to work! Saddle up, Murdo! We've got work to do!" He was angry and disappointed with Murdo.

As Murdo moved to the back of the horse trailer, he smiled a crooked smile. His swollen face would only allow his mustache to curl up on one side.

"Looky here, Cletto, I brang 'ol Blue Billy just in case we get some time for a little bronc ridin' before we finish up here." Cletto shook his head and smiled his great smile while Murdo hurriedly led Billy to the little horse barn and saddled up his roping horse.

During supper that night, Joe continued to observe the severe swelling on the side of Murdo's face. By breakfast the next morning, Murdo's eye was beginning to swell shut. The men branded cattle all day, and Joe watched as the skin on Murdo's face grew tighter and tighter, then became pink.

The air temperature began to drop near the end of the afternoon. The western sky darkened for the first time in weeks, and the dark blue clouds turned gray, then nearly black, as the hours passed.

When the work day was finished, Joe went to Mr. Crossman privately and told him that Murdo needed immediate attention for the infection on his jaw. "He's got to go now, Mr. Crossman," Joe said. "Maybe I should drive him?"

"Yeah, I just told him the same thing." A rumble of thunder rolled above them, and large raindrops began to splatter on their hats. "But now we've got another problem. It's gonna be rainin' like a cow pissin' on a flat rock in about one minute. Hell, it's already rainin' hard south and west of here. You're never gonna get no truck out to the highway tonight. We're stuck here. After it's been so dry for so long, these roads are gonna be nothin' but grease, and all the little cricks are gonna be full." A bolt of lightning ripped across the sky, and thunder crashed at almost the same instant. Water began to fall from the sky in sheets just as Mr. Crossman had said "like a cow pissin' on a flat rock." Now, there was even a chill in the air, as the temperature had dropped even more on the front edge of the approaching bad weather.

The noise of a hard rain striking the cedar shingles on the cabin was loud enough that Joe had to raise his voice to be heard when he asked Murdo how he felt.

"Fine. Purty good," Murdo said as he nodded his head and tried to smile. He was obviously lying. He was seated at the kitchen table, and his mustache was twisted at a grotesque angle by the swelling in his face. James sat next to him with Jake on his lap. He was feeding the puppy small nuggets of dog food and staring at Murdo.

Joe pulled up a kitchen chair, sat next to Murdo, and looked closely at the swelling. Then he turned and looked behind him. The only light in the cabin was coming from six hurricane lanterns that burned oil and produced a soft, yellow light. "Any flashlights around here, Mr. Crossman?" Joe asked. He sensed that the time to reveal himself might have come.

Mr. Crossman went quickly to a kitchen cupboard and removed two large flashlights powered by six-volt batteries. When Mr. Crossman returned to the kitchen table, he stood next to Joe and faced Murdo. The other men gathered behind Joe and Mr. Crossman. Joe took one of the flashlights and then sighed heavily. He reached a finger to Murdo's chin and gently tilted Murdo's head back.

"Open a little, Murdo, would you?" Joe said as he shined a flashlight into Murdo's mouth.

"What are you, a fuckin' dentist?" Murdo lowered his chin and tried to laugh.

Rain clattered heavily on the shingles, and thunder boomed intermittently in the distance, then nearby, while Joe waited to reply. He turned off his flashlight and stood up. Then he walked to the pump on the kitchen countertop. Darkness had settled completely over the cabin. Scattered lightning flashes revealed only glimpses of the world outside.

Without the lightning, the men would be unable to see anything, and all the world seemed to have shrunk inside this dim little outpost.

Joe stared back at his audience. He smiled softly at the way fate had brought him to this place. Jake the dog was playing with the femur of a dead cow over in the corner. Through the yellow light of several oil lanterns, six men stared at him, waiting for him to speak. Rough, unshaven cowboys stood and stared at him across the kitchen, waiting. It was time for life to take another twist; there was no choice. As he started to explain, a bolt of lightning turned the black of night into a bright blue world. Then thunder crashed and Joe jumped with fright. He smiled to admit the way the thunder had scared him. Then he started again.

"Yes, Murdo, I am a dentist. Up until a few weeks ago, I was practicing in Minnesota and I was pretty successful. I'm actually pretty good."

"So what the hell are you doing here?" Murdo mumbled through his swollen lips.

"I was really unhappy. Hated my job, hated my wife." Joe thought about it all for a moment. "I had a nice house, a beautiful wife...had some money, too. But I was SO unhappy. I just knew there had to be something more than all the material things men chase. I had to find some meaning in this life. So I quit and left all that behind. I set out to find something of lasting value—maybe to find myself. Sort of like Don Quixote, tilting at windmills."

Joe raised his eyes to the group, expecting to find some acceptance on their faces after his honest, heartfelt confession. But there was no acceptance. All he saw in their faces was confusion. Only Mr. Crossman showed any understanding. He covered his mouth with one hand and furrowed his eyebrows. Then he stared at Joe, probing with his eyes. Cletto crossed his arms and tilted his head. He seemed to be trying to digest the words Joe had spoken.

Murdo, James, Junior, and Norm stared dumbly at Joe. They looked like Joe had just asked them to answer a complicated mathematical problem. They had no idea what to say and no frame of reference from which to analyze Joe's words. They stared, open-mouthed, as if Joe had addressed them in a foreign language. The cowboys, except for Mr. Crossman, were totally at a loss, with no hope of understanding. Joe was looking for meaning? What the hell was he talking about? The reference to Don Quixote went WAY over their heads.

"Don't you get it? Don't you understand?" Joe tried once more. "All those things that the world values, and that other people value, really have no meaning, and they certainly don't bring happiness. So many of us just get up every day and set out to fulfill the expectations of others..." Joe paused. "There was no meaning in my life."

There was no hope. Mr. Crossman still held one hand over his mouth but was nodding in agreement. The others looked stricken while they waited for Joe to explain himself more clearly. Junior Duncan's face began to contort visibly in confusion. He looked as if a bad smell was rising into his nose.

As Joe surveyed the mass confusion there in the kitchen, he realized these men would probably never understand what he'd said. They just didn't think like that. In that moment, he decided to tell a story they were sure to understand. A smile tugged at the corners of his mouth, but Joe stifled it as he set out to tell them all a lie they wanted to hear, and that they'd understand for certain.

"I can't fool you guys, can I?" Joe started. He slumped his shoulders and allowed them to see they'd caught him in a lie. "You saw right through that stuff about the meaning of life, didn't you? Of course you guys knew the truth already." He nodded and tried to look guilty of what he was about to confess. "I started using all those drugs around my office, then alcohol, then sex. That's right—I was having my way with all the women around the office and I got caught. You could tell, couldn't you? I should have known better than to try to fool you guys."

Murdo's eyes cleared and he nodded, then nudged Junior with his elbow. Junior nodded his understanding and exchanged a knowing glance with his brother. James nodded too; even he understood those vices. A smile tightened across Mr. Crossman's mouth, but he said nothing, and Joe thought that maybe Cletto's eyes revealed the knowledge of the truth. But he wasn't sure.

"Well, there it is. It's out in the open now. I'm here because I ruined my life with drugs, alcohol, and sex," Joe said. He was enjoying this moment more than any he could remember. He kept a straight face and continued. But this time he told the truth. "But Murdo, you've got a problem. You have a serious infection in your head, about that far from your brain." He held his thumb and index finger about an inch apart. "If it spreads much farther, you're fucked, cowboy. You're dead! And I'm not shittin' you. You need that tooth outta there!"

"Can you get it out, Doc?"

"First of all, never call me 'Doc!' Understand? It's Joe."

Murdo nodded. His smile was long gone.

"And yes, I can get it out, I think," Joe answered. "Want me to have a go at it? Or do you want to wait till your head explodes from all that pus?"

Murdo looked around for a moment.

"You can wait until the rain stops and the roads clear—might be a couple days; you might live. What the hell were you thinking? There are a hundred dentists in Billings. They each spend about 240 days a year sittin' around waitin' for the phone to ring. And you, numb nuts, you wait 'til you're almost dead. This tooth broke, what, a year ago?"

"Yeah, about that," Murdo admitted.

"Well, what the hell were you waiting for?"

"It didn't hurt," Murdo replied.

"Jesus, Murdo, if you got a flat tire on your truck, would you drive it around on the rim until the sparks made the whole undercarriage of your truck hot and it burned your ass? Or would you fix it right away?"

Rain pelted heavily against the roof of the cabin as the cowboys waited for Murdo's response and Jake wrestled with the cow's femur over in the corner.

"I'd fix it right away," Murdo replied

"Exactly! But you'll neglect your own health until you're nearly dead? Then you'll piss and moan because some guy who was the smartest guy in his class all through ten years of college, and who borrowed a half-million dollars to set up a practice so he could have a place to sit around and wait for you to call him, who goes home every day with blood and spit splashed all over his face, charges you a couple hundred dollars to save you from yourself? You dumb shit! You deserve a toothache!" Joe was loving the show he was putting on, although he wasn't sure if it was a show. He'd always longed for the freedom to say these words to a patient.

"Will you take the tooth out?" Murdo asked again.

"Love to," Joe replied. Then he turned to Mr. Crossman. "Will you start boiling some water? And Cletto, while the water's boiling, will you put an edge—a really sharp edge—on the small blade of your Swiss Army Knife? Junior, you find me a small screwdriver—an old one with good steel; regular, not Phillips! Maybe you've got one with a wooden handle? Those old ones like that have good steel. Murdo, if I was you I'd have several drinks! Oh, Junior! I want you to take a rasp or a sharpen-

343

ing stone to that screwdriver, and I'd like you to put an edge on it. I'll show you."

It took about forty-five minutes to sterilize and prepare a wooden-handled screwdriver so it resembled a 301 elevator. It had also taken about that long for Murdo to get sufficiently drunk. "All right, Mr. Crossman, please hold the flashlight so it shines right there if you would." Murdo now lay on the kitchen table with a pillow under his head. Each of the cowboys held a hurricane lantern and leaned over the table to catch a glimpse of the imminent surgery.

"Odd, isn't it, Murdo?" Joe said as he wiped his hands on a towel. "I washed my hands for twenty minutes just so I could put my fingers in your mouth. Does that really make any sense?" He shook his head and laughed softly.

"OK, everyone stay out of Mr. Crossman's way and my way," Joe said. Then he leaned over and placed the dull blade of a butter knife inside Murdo's cheek. He used the knife simply to lift the cheek away from Murdo's teeth in order to look inside his mouth.

Then he leaned back suddenly, away from Murdo, and slumped his shoulders. He sounded like a teacher, disgusted with a hopeless student: "Jesus, Murdo, you have tobacco in there! Where the hell would you put that tobacco if you ever went to see a real dentist?" Then he stood back. He couldn't believe Murdo had left his chew in place.

Murdo smiled, turned his head, and spit the brown glob of tobacco into an empty paint can that Mr. Crossman held beside his head as a spittoon.

It had been sort of a rhetorical question, just what Murdo would do with his tobacco if he went to a dentist. Joe wasn't really expecting an answer about the tobacco, and silence fell over the room while everyone considered the question. Then, from the midst of the gallery standing directly behind him, he heard Norm Duncan say softly, "Well, he ain't circumcised. I seen that when we was in the tank. And judging from the pecker on him, he could keep quite a chunk of chew down there."

Joe was just beginning to move the screwdriver toward Murdo's tooth again when Norm spoke, and he started chuckling at the same time everyone else did. In a moment, the screwdriver was shaking because he couldn't hold it steady, and Mr. Crossman turned off the flashlight because he too was laughing. Murdo's eyes tightened with a smile, and before long the entire cabin resounded with laughter. Even

Murdo sat up and laughed. Several times the laughter died down and then started up again.

"OK," Joe said after a few minutes. "Let's try that again. That was a good one, Norm." He repositioned Murdo on the table and then adjusted all the lights again. "All right, you ready, Murdo?"

"Uh huh," Murdo grunted.

"Cletto? Gimme that Swiss Army Knife, will you?" Joe said. When he'd lifted Murdo's lip away from his teeth once more, he slowly brought the fine tip of the small blade inside Murdo's mouth. At the top of the tooth, where the gums curl over and become the cheek, Joe poked the blade—just the tip of the blade—into the skin. His movement was followed by a soft but audible "pop," and a yellow/gray mass spewed from the incision. The material gushing from the incision had the texture of cottage cheese, and the first bit of it flew all the way to Murdo's boot. Murdo said nothing, but none of the dental assistants could stay silent.

"Aw, Jesus! That green shit is everywhere," Junior groaned. The others only mumbled in disgust. Initially their heads had all jerked backwards. Then they quickly moved forward for a better view. All the cowboy hats closed in together above Murdo as if they were all petals on the same flower, about to close up for the night.

A torrent of pus was running out of Murdo's mouth and into the old paint can Joe had prepared for just that purpose. After about a cup of pus had drained into the paint can, the small incision began to bleed and a fetid odor spread across the room.

"Stinks in here...smells like that infection was in your ass," Junior mumbled from somewhere in the back of the crowd.

"Go ahead and spit that blood and pus and shit into the can, Murdo—that's good," Joe said. He helped Murdo sit up for a moment and spit more pus into the can. "There was a lot of pressure behind that, Murdo. Pretty soon you're going to start spitting a fair amount of blood. Your body pumps a lot of blood into an area like that in order to fight the infection. It's gonna bleed now for a few minutes."

"This ain't so nice as the little toilet my dentist used to have right beside his chair," Murdo said as he spat another mouthful of blood into the can.

"Should let up bleedin' soon," Joe replied.

"Didn't hurt a bit, Doc—er, Joe. In fact, it feels better already," Murdo said after he'd spit several more large mouthfuls of blood into the paint can.

"That's good, Murdo. But I'm not even close to finished yet," Joe said. "I just did that to let some of the pressure off."

"Give 'er hell!" Murdo said when he laid down on the table once more.

"OK, Mr. Crossman. Now I need the light," Joe said as he moved the tip of the screwdriver toward a brown, broken nub of a tooth. "Keep it on the tip of my instrument now," Joe coached.

He touched the tip of the screwdriver on Murdo's gums, next to the tooth, and Murdo jumped. "Ouch! That hurt!" Murdo said as he flinched and pulled his head away from Joe's hands. Joe's back straightened as he stepped away from Murdo. He knew he was about to say the words he'd longed to say for twenty-five years.

"All right, goddammit! That's enough, Murdo! This is all your doing, not mine. Now, behave yourself and sit there like a man! You keep jumpin' around like a pussy and someone's gonna get hurt. Whadya think…this is my dream job, twisting this nubbin out of your head? Think I need you to jump around like a little girl just to make it more difficult? Now, sit still, shut up, and take your medicine. The reason we're sittin' here like this is because of you, not me! So man up a little!"

Joe worried that his challenge had been a little harsh, but he knew he needed to make Murdo angry enough to overcome the pain he was about to endure, just as Murdo had needed to scold him while they were branding. He truly enjoyed saying the words for a change too instead of just thinking them. There was one great difference between Murdo and all the others who'd complained through the years: the whiners and complainers back in his office had been completely numb; they were bitching about pain they only imagined. Joe was about to do dentistry in a life-and-death way, as it must have been done for thousands of years until modern times: with no anesthetic.

Murdo's eyes closed tightly in pain as Joe pushed the tip of the screwdriver between the tooth and the gum tissue surrounding it. This time Murdo held still and made no sound. Blood swelled around the tip of the screwdriver, and pus oozed from the crevice around the tooth when Joe twisted. Murdo's eyes squeezed more tightly, and Joe twisted the handle harder. The tooth moved, and everyone in the cabin heard the crunch as the attachment of the tooth gave way. Still the tooth would not come. Joe twisted hard, one more time, and pumped the handle of the screwdriver as if he were trying to pry a nail from an old board. For a moment, Joe thought he'd have to let go and get a new grip, and hurt Murdo even more. But at the last instant, the tooth made the dreadful, familiar sound like a chicken wing breaking and rolled out of Murdo's mouth, into the paint can James was holding.

"You're done, Murdo," Joe said softly into Murdo's ear. Another stream of pus, nearly half a cup, flowed from the empty socket. Before long, the pus changed to blood again. Joe reached up and pinched Murdo's nose shut with his thumb and forefinger and looked into his mouth. "OK, Murdo. Try to blow your nose—gently, OK?" Murdo tried to blow and Joe said, "Good, now close on this." He placed a small cotton rag over the socket, between Murdo's teeth. "This will slow the bleeding. If it's still bleeding in twenty minutes, we'll have you close on a tea bag. That always stops the bleeding."

Murdo closed his eyes and rested.

"So why did you plug his nose like that, Joe?" Cletto asked.

"Just checking to see if I pulled the floor of his maxillary sinus out too. If I had, he'd have been blowing bloody little bubbles through that socket, and when he ate lunch tomorrow he'd be blowing hamburgers out his nose. We're fine. He's gonna heal up nicely," Joe said.

Joe's explanation caused all the cowboys' faces to go blank. They just stared at Joe and waited for him to continue.

"Hey, Murdo? Can you hear me?"

Murdo opened one eye and looked at Joe.

"Just so you know, cowboy, what you just did was the gnarliest thing I ever saw anybody do, ever! I was just trying to make you angry enough to sit still when I called you a pussy. But I never really thought anybody could do it! I'm impressed. And I'm sorry if I embarrassed you."

The kitchen fell silent for a moment while everyone tried to digest what they'd just seen and heard. Joe Mix still held the screwdriver in one hand while he looked into the faces of the men around him, and a smile began to spread over his face so the dimple in his cheek appeared. He raised his hand and stabbed the screwdriver into the table as he said, "There! That's the first time I ever enjoyed dentistry." Then he leaned back into a kitchen chair and grinned at everyone.

Murdo sat up on the table and reached for the drink he'd been working on at the moment his surgery began. His feet were dangling from the table when he looked at Joe, then pointed his finger at Joe. "I gotta ask you something, Doc," Murdo mumbled through a blood-stained rag he held between his teeth.

Everyone still huddled around the table, and they all listened to hear whatever it was that Murdo wanted to know. The rain still pounded on the shingles as Joe prepared to answer Murdo's question. He assumed Murdo was going to ask about post-operative care of his surgical wound.

"So, Doc? Did you ever do two of them nurses at once?" Murdo asked. His drunken eyes were pleading for an answer.

"Huh?" Joe asked. His eyebrows tightened in confusion. All the cowboys sat there open-mouthed and waited for Joe's answer also. They turned toward Joe in unison and looked like puppies at feeding time. They'd all suddenly found that they shared Murdo's interest as he'd asked the question about sex with two nurses at once.

This was so odd! Murdo had just endured a very painful extraction, and the cowboys had watched the whole thing. Now, they were all more interested in a ménage à trois in a dental office.

Only a few minutes earlier, Joe had released a deluge of bullshit onto his friends, not unlike the rain that was finally falling, and he'd enjoyed it. The cowboys had sat there and believed the outrageous lie he'd told about drugs, alcohol, and sex and the end of his professional life. And Joe had enjoyed the moment when he'd held their attention too. They'd needed him to tell a lie, because they'd never understand the truth, and he'd felt a thrill in leading his listeners along. Now, they were begging for more. It was true that the audience for his story was a semi-literate bunch of half-drunken cowboys. But nonetheless, he was intrigued by the invitation to continue.

They sat still now and waited expectantly for him to answer Murdo's question. Clearly, they all shared Murdo's curiosity; they wanted more. Murdo, somewhat impaired by alcohol and staring at Joe with a bloody rag protruding from between his lips, seemed to be insistent that Joe answer the question about having sex with two dental assistants at once. He removed the bloody rag from his mouth, spat a bloody wad into the paint bucket he held in his lap, and took another drink.

Joe scanned the faces in the small audience as he considered his answer. Norm and Junior Duncan both wore similar expressions. They stared blankly at Joe as one shared thought began to crystallize for them: "Yeah! Why didn't I think of that?"

James Bond was in over his head, experiencing some type of sensory overload. His jaw hung open, and he looked back and forth between Joe and Murdo. He clearly didn't know what to think; he'd never seen or heard anything like tooth extractions with a screwdriver by a runaway dentist. Now, all the talk of sex, and all this after a couple drinks. He wasn't stupid—just innocent and very inexperienced.

Cletto appeared deep in thought. He wasn't smiling for a change. He seemed to be quite interested in Joe's answer too.

Mr. Crossman, on the other hand, sensed what was about to happen. He walked to the kitchen cupboard and produced a bottle of Cutty Sark Scotch Whisky. He opened a cooler, filled a glass with some ice, and poured some scotch over the ice. Then he smiled a sly smile and raised his eyebrows at Joe. Moments such as this were what brought him back to Cowboy Camp every year. This was as important as the cowboy rituals of rounding up cattle and branding. Joe could see it in his eyes when he raised his glass to salute what Joe was about to do.

Joe Mix looked around once more, then broke the anxious silence and stepped into unknown waters again. "How did you know about that?" Joe asked earnestly. "About the two nurses at once, I mean."

"I knew it!" Murdo exalted. "Goddammer, I knew it!" he mumbled through the bloody rag in his mouth. Then he elbowed Junior.

"Pretty hard to hide something like that from you, I guess," Joe conceded. Then he stopped and nodded and looked away as if that was the end of it, deliberately trying to draw a response from Murdo.

"Well, goddammer, Joe! I wanna hear about that shit!" Murdo demanded.

"Oh, OK," Joe said slowly. He pointed to the kitchen cupboard and said, "Would you make me a drink like yours, Mr. Crossman?"

"That's right—I guess you're quite a drinkin' man, huh, Joe?" Mr. Crossman replied with a sly smile.

"Haven't had a drink in quite some time!" Joe said when he took the glass from Mr. Crossman. "Been on the wagon, you know."

"OK, boys, what did you want to know again?" Joe asked. When he turned to look at the group, they were all sitting on the edges of their seats, staring intently.

"Start at the beginning," Norm blurted.

Joe Mix had never so much as touched one of his employees. He'd never even been tempted. So he started by repeating a story that one of his colleagues had shared about an affair with his dental assistant. Then he began to improvise. He combined another true story that his friend had shared and a story he'd seen on TV, except that he made himself the star of each story. He took small sips from his drink between stories to stall for time while he remembered, or created, another story.

Joe remembered that over the years, when he and Donny had made long drives together on fishing trips, Donny had discovered that a good way for the two of them to stay awake was to buy dirty magazines like the ones Murdo had just purchased. Donny read the outrageous letters to the editor out loud while Joe drove. Sometimes, they'd laughed all night at the bizarre sex stories in the magazines.

Now, as the cowboys leaned forward to listen even more intently, Joe began to recall dirty letters to the editor from those road trips with Donny, and he simply inserted himself into the action. He told stories of dental hygienists and wicker baskets, dental assistants with electric toy-train transformers wired to specific body parts. He told of sex in the office with laughing gas as a stimulant, sex in the car, sex in the hospital emergency room, and dental study club meetings gone wild. He had a hard time not laughing out loud at the ludicrous thought of those incredibly dull dental lectures turning into orgies. He told story after story as if he were sitting around a campfire, telling ghost stories to terrified Boy Scouts. With each story, he enjoyed the experience more.

His lips were beginning to feel numb—he presumed it was from the Cutty Sark—when he leaned back and took a deep breath. "Course...all that stuff got really crazy when I hired the twins!" With that, Murdo actually slid closer, and Joe went on for twenty minutes with sex stories about the dark-haired, long-legged Knutson twins. In reality, the Knutson twins had been beady-eyed trolls from the playground in Kadoka, but Joe enjoyed changing them into vivacious, sex-starved dental assistants and using them to torture these cowboys.

"Is that what finally got you in trouble? Them twins?" Junior asked at the end of one particularly outlandish story.

"No. No, it wasn't them," Joe said sadly as he tried to manufacture one more spectacular sex story for a finale. "Mr. Crossman, would you fix me another drink?" Joe asked in an effort to stall while he created one more story. His nose was getting numb.

"Thanks, Mr. Crossman," Joe said when he reached for his drink. "No. My downfall..."—he paused while he sipped at his drink—"...was

Wanda, Wanda Wolf." He had no idea where that name had come from, but he liked it. "Wanda was older—about forty-five. So she had no need to hide what she was after, and she was warm for my form." Joe looked up and saw Mr. Crossman standing behind the cowboys. He was smiling openly while the others leaned forward and hung on Joe's every word.

"Wanda was an aerobics instructor when she wasn't working in my office. She was—well, she was...shall we say...taut? She was in good shape, and she was real tall—all legs! She could reach up like this and scratch her ass." Joe held his hand behind his head and waited for them to laugh, but the men were already lost in their own fantasies.

"Anyway," Joe continued, "Wanda was always ready. We even used to get after each other between patients. We'd just close the door after we finished with a root canal and have a little party." Joe turned his head and tried to manufacture a faraway look. He nearly smiled at his own overacting, and he had to take a drink to compose himself once more. "Wanda did one thing that drove me wild!" Joe said as he tightened his eyebrows and shook his head. "She liked to wear that little paper nurse hat, and ONLY that, when we were...you know!" He raised his eyebrows and smiled. "Drove me wild!" Joe sighed.

Murdo rubbed his face with both hands and leaned forward in his seat. "No shit, Joe! Me too!" He seemed to be cheering for Joe.

"Ahhh, Wanda," Joe sighed. "She's the one who brought me down." He took another drink, and the cowboy hats moved closer, as they had during Murdo's extraction. "One day, just before lunch, she asked me if I'd fill a cavity for her." Joe turned and looked, but none of the cowboys got the joke. They were staring—they looked like they were waiting for Joe to deliver Christmas presents. "Anyway," Joe continued, "I told her I'd like to pull the uppers and fill the lower." Still nothing from the cowboys.

"Well, a few minutes later, she was wearing just that paper nurse's hat and I was workin' up a sweat." Joe paused. "That was when my wife walked in. You know the rest! Divorce, bankruptcy—my wife got everything but my pickup truck."

The cowboys stared in silence, unwilling to accept the fact that Joe's long story was over.

"So what's Wanda doing now?" Norm asked.

"I don't know, Norm. I sort of lost track of her after my second time through rehab," Joe answered.

"Too bad," Norm said under his breath. The idea that Joe had just described the total destruction of his marriage and business was lost on Norm. He simply returned to his own fantasy of Wanda Wolf.

"Can I take another drink here, Doc—er, Joe?" Murdo asked. "A drink won't hurt this bleedin' tooth place here, will it?"

"Go ahead," Joe said as he sipped at his own drink. "It's a good antiseptic rinse, but then be sure to swallow," Joe added. No one got the joke but Mr. Crossman. Most of Joe's face was tingly now, and he liked the sensation the alcohol was providing. He sat down heavily in a kitchen chair.

"So, Doc," Murdo called to Joe from over by the kitchen countertop, still holding a bloody rag between his teeth. He was making drinks for everyone now. "Have you done stuff like this before? I mean, have you taken teeth out with screwdrivers before?"

"No," Joe answered "But I guess I saw something almost as strange once before!" Joe noticed that his words were slurring. Nonetheless, he still liked the numb feeling on his lips and face. "One time, when I was fishing in British Columbia, I saw one of the other fishermen sit down on an old bed spring in a cabin about like this one. One of the springs poked through that shitty old mattress and sliced my buddy's scrotum. Really opened him up; left about a two-inch gash in his nut sack. Turns out the guy was a doctor! He was just a little bit more drunk than I am now, and he took out a needle and thread and sewed up his own nut bag. He just lifted his jewels up with one hand and stitched himself with the other! Up until tonight, that was the greatest thing I ever saw. I think it took more grit for you to let me pry a tooth out of your head than it did for him to sew himself up!" Joe sipped at his drink and continued. "I guess it's hard to compare teeth to nuts. Hmph—there's a sentence I never thought I'd build," Joe added, speaking to himself while his world continued to blur.

"Well, here's to you, Doc. You done good, goddammer!" Murdo said as he raised his glass in salute. The other cowboys did the same, and Joe swallowed the last of the scotch in his glass too. Murdo seemed faraway and blurry all of a sudden.

"Hey, Cletto! You remember that big Polack that used to work down on the south range for a couple summers?" Murdo said loudly as he took another drink.

"Yeah, but I don't remember his name," Cletto answered. "He used to ride a big buckskin, though. I remember that!"

"I don't remember his name either, but who cares. What I do remember is the time he came ridin' that big buckskin into the barn. He was really haul assin' down the road to get in out of the rain." Murdo stopped and laughed at his own story. "Anyways, he come ridin' up as fast as he could, and then he reined up on that buckskin. He decided to show off, so he jumped off that horse before that big ol' cloud of dust in the barn cleared. Dumb fucker landed on a pile of scrap lumber and drove a couple nails clean through both of his feet from the bottom of his boots right through the top. Shit, he looked like he nailed his skis on, walking around there with them planks nailed to his feet. I drove him to the hospital. Laughed the whole damn way."

Murdo's story sounded so irrelevant all of a sudden. Joe heard the other men laugh, and he thought he heard Junior start to tell a story about a cowboy who pissed on an electric fence. He knew they were laughing louder, but their voices grew faint. His world slowly became quiet and dark.

When Joe finally slumped over in his chair, the cowboys carried him in to his bed and then returned to the kitchen. They told stories at full volume and drank for several more hours while the rain pelted the shingles above them.

———•———

Before Joe opened his eyes—even before he felt the pain in his head—he heard the sound of a gentle rain tapping on the window and the shingles. Still raining, he thought as the weight of a drunken slumber began to lift. When he opened his eyes, the pain of his first hangover began to press against his skull. The narrow slits that were his eyes seemed to let something awful and painful rush into his head. Every part of his head throbbed like a sore thumb.

Then he realized it was light inside the little bedroom at Cowboy Camp. It had never been light before when he woke up. Every other day, they'd all had breakfast and been working for a while before the sun cleared the horizon. Now, although it was overcast and raining outside, it was clearly well after sunrise.

Joe sat upright on the bed and swung his feet onto the floor. Jake was gone, and that was unusual. But Norm and Junior and James were still sleeping. He tried to rub his head, but the pain only got worse. The little alarm clock said it was 8:30 a.m. Where were Murdo, Cletto, and Mr. Crossman? Something was wrong.

His bare feet brushed across the wooden floor as he shuffled out to the kitchen. Several empty Jack Daniel's bottles sat on the kitchen table, and the empty bottle of Cutty Sark lay on top of the garbage can near the front door. Norm's boots rested on the kitchen countertop, surrounded by a group of empty glasses.

"Mmmm," Joe moaned as he rubbed his head and reached for a coffee cup. The coffee pot was still hot, so Joe poured himself a tall cup before he wandered out the front door onto the porch.

The smell of cigarette smoke greeted Joe as he stepped out into the cool, wet air. He was wearing only his boxer shorts and a T-shirt when he dropped into the plastic lawn chair next to one Mr. Crossman was sitting in. Jake had been sitting at Mr. Crossman's feet, chewing on the femur he'd come to prize very much. He wagged his tail and scampered over to greet Joe. His leg looked almost normal today.

"You OK, Joe?" Mr. Crossman asked.

"I think I have the flu."

Mr. Crossman smiled and lit a new cigarette. "You caught it from that bottle of scotch!"

"This is what a hangover feels like?" Joe asked.

Mr. Crossman answered with a nod.

Joe raised his coffee to his lips with one hand and scratched his nuts with the other. His head hurt too much to respond to Mr. Crossman.

"That was quite a load of bullshit you forked down everybody's well last night, Joe."

"I enjoyed it too, right up to the part where my head blew up about ten minutes ago," Joe said.

"That was your first taste of liquor? Really?" Mr. Crossman asked.

Joe closed his eyes. It hurt too badly to nod. Then he sipped at his coffee again.

"So that bullshit about losing your license because of drugs and alcohol? That was all bullshit too?"

"All bullshit," Joe nodded, then sipped his coffee again. "Those guys didn't want to hear about my quest for the meaning of life or anything like that."

"Well, you gave 'em a helluva show. You are a dentist, though, right?"

"I was."

"Well, I never seen anything like that show you put on last night, and I seen a lot of shit here at camp!"

"Where're Murdo and Cletto? And how come we slept in?" Joe asked softly in an effort not to hurt his own head.

"You was all still drunk when it was time to go to work. Hell, James just stopped pukin' about an hour before sun-up! None of you was fit to work. We'll take the day off today. That was a helluva party last night. Besides that, we been runnin' pretty hard. We needed a day off. We're almost done with the branding. We'll just say we had our celebration a little early."

"Sounds good to me, but where're Murdo and Cletto?" Joe asked again.

"Oh, hell, it don't matter what time those two go to bed, they get up and go early every day. They saddled up about an hour ago and rode out to see how high the water was getting in the little creeks." Then Mr. Crossman turned and looked to the western sky. "I think it's gonna clear up and get warm later."

The small pitter-pat of rain on the roof of the porch was a soothing sound for Joe. He raised the hot coffee to his face and let the steam warm his nose and eyebrows. He sipped at the coffee, leaned back in his chair, and looked over the world in front of him. Here he was, sittin' on the front porch of the bunkhouse at Cowboy Camp. Hell, he was a cowboy, and he'd been rounding up cattle with real cowboys. Right over there was the little horse barn filled with horses, saddles, and tack. And over there was a…shower, where grown men pissed on each other, made from the wing tank of a crashed bomber. Next to that was an aluminum stock tank the cowboys had converted to a hot tub by using the hot water from a failed oil well. Good God, he thought, there was so much more to this life than what he ever could have found if the dentist hadn't died. He sipped at the coffee and scratched himself some more.

"All right, Joe, will you tell me the true story about how you wound up in that diner in Wyoming?" asked Mr. Crossman.

The cold air and hot coffee had begun to clear Joe's head. He stared off into the gray clouds for a moment before he answered. "Pretty simple. I had a normal life. I was a dentist in Rochester, Minnesota, like I said. I tried to tell the truth last night, you know. I had a pretty wife— she was a bitch—and a nice house. Everything I ever did in my whole life I did because I thought it was what other people expected of me. I hated my job and my marriage. The thought of being there until I died made me wish for this life to just hurry and be over. I knew that was wrong. One day, my wife just pissed me off enough that I threw in the towel and hit the road—left everything behind. Wound up in my home town, a little wide spot in the road back in South Dakota. I found out that most of the dreams and memories I'd been holding onto were about as feeble and phony as the life I'd built." Joe shrugged. "So I guess I'm out here looking for...something else."

"So what are you gonna do? I mean, what are you gonna do with your life when ya find it?"

"I dunno," Joe shrugged. "What are you gonna do with yours?"

"Sit here and smoke cigarettes and rope cattle. That's all I EVER wanted to do." Mr. Crossman looked at his hands for a moment, then started to speak again. "It's funny, Joe: I know that after I'm dead and gone, my son Robert will drive this ranch into the ground and lose it. But that's OK because I'll have had my turn, and Robert will have his. I hope someday he gets happy, but who knows. I hope the next man who owns this land loves it as much as I do."

"Do you see any meaning in all that, Jim? Do you see any meaning in this life?" Joe asked.

"No. I don't think so, Joe. I see joy, and sorrow, love, and tears...maybe that's all we get?"

"Yeah. Maybe." Joe stopped, then shook his head. "No, there's more than just that."

"You're gonna be leaving soon, ain't you, Joe?" Mr. Crossman asked.

"Why do you say that?" Joe turned to look at Mr. Crossman. He sipped his coffee with one hand and rubbed his forehead with the other. The idea that he should be leaving had been circling around in his clouded brain since he'd sat down on the porch a few minutes earlier. But he was taken off guard that Mr. Crossman had raised the question just now.

"I've seen other men do what you're doin'." Mr. Crossman took another drag on his cigarette. He blew the smoke out slowly, then resumed his thought. "I've seen men take some huge turns in their lives, then stop before they found what they was looking for. I think they was just so happy they made a turn that they forgot to keep going until they found out for sure why they turned." He pointed his cigarette at Joe and paused a moment, then added, "If you stay around here just a while longer, you're gonna wind up stayin' here way too long—maybe forever."

He flicked his cigarette butt onto the dirt in front of the porch and lit another one. Joe was going to say something, but it looked like Mr. Crossman had only interrupted himself and still intended to finish his thought. "Now, I like you, Joe Mix," he said as he drew on the cigarette. "We've become friends. You've changed just in the time you've been here. I'm not sure just what I seen—that first wild ride with Tom and the way it affected you? I know there was a lot goin' on in your head. I've seen you smile a little more all the time. That show you put on last night? Hell, I'll never forget that." He drew on his cigarette again. "But that phone thrower I met in Wyoming? He ain't done with his journey yet. This ain't the end of your road...not yet. I'm right, ain't I?"

After a long moment, Joe began to nod. "Yeah. Yeah, Jim. You're right. I do need to keep going, and after last night things won't be the same anymore, will they? I think maybe that rain last night washed away something else: a veneer that covered a lifetime of trying to be something I never was. That storyteller last night? That was me, Jim." Joe stopped, sipped his coffee, and leaned back. Then his face curled into a huge smile and exposed the dimple in his right cheek. He smiled openly and waited until Mr. Crossman turned to him.

When Jim Crossman made eye contact with Joe, he began to chuckle. "You're a helluva storyteller, Joe Mix!" Then he broke into laughter.

"Damn near killed Murdo, didn't I?" Joe said through his own laughter.

"He believed every word you said," Mr. Crossman laughed.

"I liked making him believe it too," Joe said.

chapter twenty-eight

Preston Murdock sat a horse like no man Joe had ever seen. As he loped toward camp, Joe thought Murdo could pass for Lassiter in *Riders of the Purple Sage*. Murdo was what every cowboy wanted to look like. He seemed beyond comfortable in the saddle; he looked like an extension of his horse.

"Well, looky there!" Murdo said with a smile as he reined his horse to a stop beside the front porch. "How's your head, Joe? I'm thinkin' it oughta feel about like your ass did a couple weeks ago." Murdo smiled and looked into Joe's eyes.

"How's YOUR head?...speaking of hurtin' things." Joe returned Murdo's smile.

"Purty good, Doc. Right after you fainted last night, I put some tobacco in there and got the healin' started. Feels fine today!"

When Murdo smiled, Joe could see that the swelling was mostly gone already, and Murdo had only a small bruise on his cheek. His smile was nearly back to normal.

"I told you never to call me 'Doc'! I'm not a dentist anymore."

"Well, goddammer, you done good last night!"

"If you call me 'Doc' again, I'm gonna send you a bill!"

Murdo turned, as if he'd been caught off guard by Joe's comment. He stared blankly for a moment, then smiled broadly. "I got something I can give you!"

"I was kidding, Murdo."

"Well, I ain't! I'll pay you later!" Murdo looked excited about the prospect of paying Joe.

"You and Cletto put your horses away. We'll have breakfast in a little while," Mr. Crossman said. Cletto had arrived with Murdo but had said nothing yet. As usual, he'd been smiling and listening to the conversation.

When Murdo turned his horse toward the barn, Cletto leaned over his saddle horn and said, "The creek isn't too swollen, Mr. Crossman. That storm last night sounded worse than it was. We didn't get that much rain." Then he followed Murdo to the barn.

———————

Silverware clinked against the dishes while the men ate and passed a large bowl of scrambled eggs around the table.

"I think a soak will feel purdy good after lunch," Mr. Crossman said. "Some of you boys still look a little rough."

"Sounds good to me!" Murdo said with a mouthful of eggs. "The ground oughta be dry by tomorrow, and we can finish brandin' in a couple days and close up camp. Ain't that right, Mr. Crossman?"

"Yeah, I guess so," Mr. Crossman replied.

"My head still hurts," James said softly. "S'pose some aspirin would help?"

"Try a little 'hair of the dog that bit you,'" Murdo smiled.

"Huh? What's that?" James asked.

"Another swallow of Jack Daniel's or whatever made you sick," Murdo answered.

James's face twisted into a grimace. "Jeez. Makes me sick just to think of that," he groaned.

"Sick?" Norm groaned. He was staring ahead with his elbows on the table, only playing with his food and rearranging it. He still looked ashen-colored. "I still feel sick." Then he raised his head and said to Junior, "No wonder I was sick last night, Junior. There was puke in my stomach!"

"Goddammer, Norm! You say a lot of stupid shit! You better just stick to havin' root canals and watchin' your imaginary wife have babies! We all got puke in our stomachs, you dumb ass. We just ate."

Norm turned to Murdo and all the color drained from his face. His chest began to heave. Everyone at the table sensed what was about to happen. Norm jumped to his feet and ran out the front door of the cabin, then proceeded to vomit for several minutes.

"I guess I'm done eatin," Mr. Crossman said, and dropped his fork onto his plate.

"Sounds like he's gonna turn inside out, don't he?" Junior said with a smile as the men listened to Norm dry heave.

"Shoulda got some tobacco in there right away this morning! That woulda helped!" Murdo called to Norm out on the porch.

"S'pose I could have the rest of his eggs?" James asked.

Joe had been waiting for the right moment to announce he was leaving. But just now, he felt the right moment might never come with this bunch. This was as good a time as any.

"Well, I know I may regret this—I'll certainly miss our intellectual discussions at mealtimes—but I'm moving on today," Joe announced to the cowboys' surprise. "I need to get going. Will that be all right, Mr. Crossman?"

"I'll send a note with you. You can draw your wages. Mary will write you a check." Mr. Crossman nodded yes. "We're nearly done here."

"Thank you."

"How come? Why do you have to leave? What's the big hurry?" Murdo asked.

"Yeah," James added.

"No hurry, really. It's just time to go. I didn't really have a plan when I set out, but...well, it's just time to move on. That's the best I can explain it," Joe answered.

"Cops ARE lookin' for you, huh?" Junior added. "Hell, this is the safest place you can be. They'll never come lookin' here."

"Sorry to disappoint you, Junior, but I'm not a fugitive. I truly have enjoyed some wild behavior since I got here, but I'm just not a criminal yet. Sorry," Joe shrugged.

"It was that drinkin' and tellin' us about them women, wasn't it, Joe? Sort of opened up an old wound, huh? Now everything's changed, ain't it?" Murdo said and then nodded in agreement with himself.

On every other level, Murdo was insightful and perceptive. But when the subject turned to women and sex, he became so absorbed in it that he was totally willing to suspend his grip on reality—to believe stories like the ones Joe had told last night.

The other cowboys had believed Joe because they were basically gullible and drunk, and because Joe had discovered a hidden talent as a storyteller. But Murdo, he'd believed all Joe's stories because he wanted to. He wanted for Joe to have done all the things he'd claimed to have done. He seemed to think that Joe's exploits only deepened their friendship.

"Yeah, I guess you could say I sort of fell off the wagon last night." Joe sighed and suppressed a smile. "I just need a change now, I guess."

"I understand," Murdo said softly.

Mr. Crossman and James were doing dishes when Joe began to pack his duffel bag. He was looking around for his book when he stood straight and said, "I think I need to say goodbye to someone else before I forget." Then he walked out the front door and went directly to the barn.

Tom was standing by the fence, just inside the little barn, when Joe stepped through the gate. He walked slowly toward Tom and spoke softly with his hands up. He touched Tom's neck first, then began to stroke the soft, brown hair on Tom's side and back. In just a moment, he moved toward Tom's head, still softly stroking the big horse. He drew in a deep breath and tried to take in the smell of Tom so deeply inside him that he'd never forget.

Then he rested the side of his face against Tom's neck. It seemed important to pass some sort of message to Tom—or maybe to receive a message, he wasn't really sure. But he pressed his face against Tom for several minutes and said nothing. He only stroked the soft, brown hair on Tom's neck.

"Thanks, Tom," he finally said. "You made me a better man, and I'll never forget you." Then he lifted his head away from Tom's neck and patted him softly. "And you're a fine ride, every bit as good as my old red rockin' horse!" He patted Tom once more and turned away from him so that he could finish packing, say goodbye to the others, and leave.

When he turned, Blue Billy stood only a few feet from him. Blue Billy, the nasty-tempered jughead blue roan, was looking at him from between the top two planks of the fence that was separating them. Blue Billy—"The Horse That Ain't Never Been Rode" was what Murdo had called him. Now, Billy stared at Joe. There seemed to be an ornery challenge in Billy's eyes.

"You want to have a go at it, Billy? You and me?" Joe reached his hand toward Billy and Billy tried to bite it. Joe jerked his hand away and jumped back a step. Then he smiled and tried to stare deeply into Blue Billy's eyes. There was a whole mysterious life in there behind those eyes, and Joe could make no sense of it.

"So what if you threw me and broke a few bones? What would that prove?" Joe's brow furrowed and he spoke quietly to the horse. "I'd just be another dumb cowboy with a story to tell, maybe a scar to brag about. Maybe that's the point, huh?" Joe paused and stepped closer but kept his hands to himself. "No, Billy, I guess there's a few challenges that don't need to be met. I already know how good a cowboy I am. I don't need you to beat my brains in to prove it to me."

Joe stepped closer, but this time Billy stepped back. "And think about this, Billy. What if I got on and rode you? Then we wouldn't have Blue Billy, 'The Horse That Ain't Never Been Rode,' anymore. Either way it played out, somebody would be keeping score, too, and that wouldn't do for either of us. We both need to think about that, Billy." With that, Joe turned on his heels and left the corral.

The Montana air smelled fresh. Rain had washed away a summer's worth of dust and left a clear sky filled with sunshine and the scent of sage.

"There you are!" Murdo called out from beside the windmill. He was bent over fumbling with the pump, trying to get more hot water to run into the hot tub.

"C'mere," Murdo said, "I got something for you. I was gonna give it to you as payment for takin' my tooth out. But now I'll make it sort of a goodbye present too." Murdo raised himself straight—he'd been resting his elbows on his knees while he bent over and started the pump. He extended his hand, and when Joe took it he said, "Goddammer, Joe, I wish you wasn't leavin'. I really got to like you."

"Yeah, me too. But I'll know where you are. I'll stop back again. I'm not taking any money from you, either. It was a pleasure to stab you in the head with a screwdriver!" He smiled and pumped Murdo's hand.

"I'm not offerin' money! I got something more valuable. And a man like you? You'll understand the value of it!" Murdo looked around to be sure no one else was within earshot. Then he hunched his shoulders and stepped close to Joe. "I'm gonna give you the secret of the Velvet Half-Nelson!" Then he nodded, as if to assure Joe that this gift of all gifts was actually going to be given to him. "I learned it from a drunk Frenchman a long time ago. I was just a kid, an' I was in this bar in San Francisco." Murdo looked over his shoulder again. "I seen this big fella start pushin' this little Frenchy around. Turns out the Frenchman had made advances to this big guy's date while he was away in the bathroom or something. Anyways, he was pushin' the Frenchman around, so I walked over and tried to get in between 'em. The big guy took a swing at me! Pissed me right off! So I throwed a punch—turned out to be a good one too! I dropped that big fella like shit from a tall cow. Anyways, that Frenchman was so thankful, he bought me some drinks. And then, before he left, he told me about the Velvet Half-Nelson...how it drives women crazy. He was sure as hell right about that! He called it somethin' else, though, something French, but I couldn't say it. So I give it my own name. You'll know why I call it that after I tell you. OK, you ready?"

"How could I refuse? Shoot," Joe smiled.

"OK. First of all, you need a lot of room to do it right. You can't do it in a truck or nuthin' like that. Well, you can, but you gotta be good, and it just ain't the same." Murdo paused and looked expectantly at Joe.

"Keep going. I'm listening," Joe smiled again.

"OK. Well, when the time is right, you know, you put your one hand..." Murdo talked for fifteen minutes. He described every possible nuance and variation of the Velvet Half-Nelson. He warned Joe about how some women "start in yellin' an' thrashin,'" and then he explained how to overcome any possible complications due to overstimulation—and, last but not least, how to drive women wild during the grand finale.

"That's it! You don't want to go tellin' just anyone about this. But then, I don't think just anyone can even do it," he said when he was finished.

In only a few minutes, Murdo had described something Joe had never heard of—never even dreamed of. Just Murdo's explanation actually left him with sort of an amorous twitch in his belly.

"Jeez, Murdo, I thought you were kidding! Who would have come up with that?"

"Hell, I don't know! But I ain't kiddin'!"

"Well, thanks, Murdo." Joe couldn't hide the dimple in his smile. "That information may have made twenty-five years of unhappiness worthwhile. Maybe a career in dentistry wasn't wasted if it led me to the Velvet Half-Nelson. I guess we'll see, huh?"

"You're smilin', but I ain't shittin' you, Joe. You'll see, goddammer, you'll see!" Murdo said as he turned and walked to the hot tub.

When Joe entered the cabin to finish packing his things, he assumed he'd be able to find a minute for private goodbyes with each of the men. But that idea was soon abandoned. He met Cletto and Junior just inside the door, wearing only their hats and boots. They were on their way to the stock tank. Junior brushed past Joe and just kept going. But Cletto stopped and smiled his great smile. "Are you leaving soon, Joe?" he asked.

"Pretty quick. Soon as I finish packing," Joe replied.

Cletto thrust his hand forward. "Good luck, Joe. Keep us posted wherever you wind up, OK? You can come back anytime!" Then Cletto stood there and smiled for a moment, as if he wasn't sure what to say next. "Well, I'll be out in the tank when you leave, Joe," Cletto said as he stepped out the door and walked directly to the tank.

Joe turned and watched Cletto. This was so strange. He watched Cletto walk happily across the camp, wearing only boots and a hat. Cletto's ghostly white back, legs, and ass looked so strange, so out of place.

"Just have some water to drink!" Mr. Crossman called loudly to Norm Duncan again. "The reason your head hurts is because you're dehydrated. That's what a hangover is, Norm!"

"I'm goin' back to bed. I think I've been poisoned," Norm said as he turned around and shuffled back to the bedroom. Joe heard him tumble into bed a moment later.

"Norm don't take advice very well, does he?" Mr. Crossman said to Joe. "I've been trying to help him for twenty minutes, but he just don't listen."

Joe shrugged. "What can you do?"

Mr. Crossman nodded and smiled a faint smile. Then he reached into his shirt pocket and pulled out an envelope. "Here, give this to Mary when you get back to the ranch. She'll write you a check."

"Thank you...Jim. You've been good to me. Thank you. I hope we'll meet again."

"You're welcome. It's been an adventure getting to know you. Every step of the way, from throwin' your phone to slingin' bullshit to watchin' you fly off horses, it's been a dern adventure. You can come back to camp and tell dirty stories every year, Joe. I know Murdo would love it!"

"Might just do that, Jim."

Mr. Crossman extended his hand, and while they shook he said, "I'll be out there with the others when you leave. Just go ahead and take any one of the trucks. I'll see you in a few minutes." And he walked out to the tank.

As Joe was stuffing clothing into his duffel bag, James appeared at his side. "I'm gonna miss you, Joe. You're my best friend."

Joe stopped and looked at James's eyes. He sighed heavily; this was the goodbye he'd been dreading. He knew he'd become something of a friend and father figure for James. "I'm gonna miss you too, cowboy." There were words Joe wanted to say. He wanted to be funny. He wanted to be serious. He wanted to tell James how much he'd enjoyed him, and he wanted to give him some advice. But words would only trivialize all the things he had to say. He stared at James's sad face for a moment, then put his arms around the boy. "You're a good man, Darnell Bond! A good man. Thank you for being my friend. We'll stay in touch, OK?" Joe patted the thick muscles on James's back as he spoke. He kissed James on the cheek, like he had his own sons.

"Thank you for all you done, Joe—the hat, and boots, and for readin' books with me and everything." James stopped for a moment, then added, "I wish my dad would have been like you."

Joe felt his throat tighten the instant James said the words. A few minutes earlier, Joe had thought he'd have to console James because he was sure to cry during their goodbye. Now, he was wiping away his own tears. "Thanks, James. That's the finest thing anyone has said to me in a long, long time." He swallowed once, but his voice wasn't there when he tried to say more. "You're a good man," he whispered finally.

"I'll be outside with the others when you get done packing," James said. Then he walked away, clomping his feet heavily against the floor, just as he had since the day Joe had met him.

Joe's duffel still wasn't full when he'd gathered all his things; he'd learned to travel light. He took one more look around the bedroom, checking for any personal items. When he was satisfied he was ready to leave, he kicked the bed he was standing next to and said, "Norm! I'm leaving now!"

Norm Duncan was still in serious pain. He brought a pillow over his face with one hand and raised the other to shake Joe's hand. He never lifted the pillow from his face. He just laid on his back with his pillow covering his face and raised his right hand straight off the bed.

Joe took his hand, pumped it, and said, "See you, Norm!"

A very muffled "good luck, Joe" escaped the pillow covering Norm's face, and when Joe let go of Norm's hand, it fell back to his side.

So much for dramatic goodbyes, Joe thought as he turned and whistled for Jake. He walked out of the bedroom, out of the cabin, and across the middle of Crossman's Cowboy Camp.

Jim Crossman sat on an old aluminum kitchen chair, smoking a cigarette and talking to his hired hands. Apparently he didn't plan on a soak today. He just intended to sit and smoke and talk with the boys.

Cletto, Murdo, and James all sat naked once again, except for their hats, in the stock tank. The sight of Junior lent a particularly odd note to the moment. He was naked also, but he was beside the tank on his hands and knees playing with Jake. Apparently he'd planned on a soak, but one final chance to play with Jake had distracted him.

Joe raised a hand to cover his eyes and protect himself from what he'd see if he glanced over at Junior again. He tossed his duffel bag in the back of one of the trucks, then walked over to the tank. He simply stood and looked at the men for a moment.

"Norm and I changed the oil in your truck a while back. That old piece 'a shit still runs good, Joe," Junior offered, still on his knees playing with Jake.

"Thanks, Junior. And if Norm lives, would you thank him, too?"

Joe whistled for Jake to join him. He opened the door of the truck so Jake could get in, then sat down himself and closed the door.

Joe looked at all five of the men for a moment, then started to nod. "Goodbye, boys" he said as he raised his right hand. "Don't get up! I don't need to see that ever again!" Joe said with a smile.

When he'd started the truck, Joe turned for one last glance. Jake stood with his paws on Joe's lap and looked out the truck window at the men too. Mr. Crossman was drawing heavily on a cigarette and pointing at Joe with his other hand. The four naked cowboys all smiled and waved like children. What a parting shot, Joe thought.

Maybe he should have stayed for a while longer. That thought descended on him as soon as he felt the truck rolling out of camp. He was all alone again and not so sure if he liked it. He held the steering wheel in one hand and lifted Jake up to his face with the other. In some ways, he was back at the beginning, right where he'd been when he'd left Rochester and then Kadoka. He tried to reason with himself. He had to leave the Crossman Ranch; his future wasn't here. He thought of Tom the horse and then the extraordinarily white asses on the naked cowboys as they walked to the stock tank for a soak. He remembered the bizarre conversations over meals, and he knew he'd never forget the adventure with Murdo's tooth. He smiled as he thought of extracting a tooth with no anesthetic or light, during a thunderstorm, with a screwdriver!

Had he gained anything from his time on the ranch? he wondered. How does a man calculate things like that? He had found some joy in work—that was a new thing for him. He'd smiled, and he'd actually enjoyed work for the first time he could remember. He'd regained some physical strength from the hard labor, and he'd grown confident in his renewed strength. The potbelly was gone, his jeans hung on his hips, and his shoulders had begun to reappear. He felt that on two occasions, he'd broken through some barrier and claimed a prize. The first time he'd let Tom stretch his legs at full speed—that was a special thing. It was the night he'd seen the Kadoka Kid for the first time in...hell, in a lifetime. He'd found something of himself, something that had been lost for a long time, that had to be a good thing. He was done with dentistry and glad of it. That much was behind him now, no doubt about it.

He'd let go of all his inhibitions just last night and been a storyteller for the first time. He'd truly enjoyed that. Maybe it was just the alcohol? That was all right too. He certainly intended to try that again before long. For whatever reason, he'd liked the telling of a story. He'd made people listen intently and laugh and believe things that weren't true. What a kick, he thought. His only regret was that he hadn't been able to have a try at Blue Billy. Oh well, he thought, it's all right if some things just stay dreams.

———·———

The old Ford was parked right where it had been left several weeks earlier. It looked older than what he remembered. The Crossman Cattle Company truck that he was driving was much nicer in every way. When he flipped his duffel into the back of the Ford, he also opened the driver's-side window to let some of the hot air out of the cab. As he looked around, he was reminded of the rough shape of the interior of the Ford—no window handles, about half the knobs gone from the dashboard controls, and the holes in the floor and the seats.

"Oh well, Jake, it's all ours," he said as he took the keys from the Crossman truck and the letter from Mr. Crossman and walked toward the ranch house in search of Mary.

The door to the ranch house swung open before Joe could knock. "I saw you pull into the yard. Is everything all right?" Mary said before either of them could utter a greeting.

"Sure. Everything's fine," Joe shrugged.

"So why are you here—by yourself?"

"Oh, well, I'm gonna be leaving today. Gonna be on my way. It's a long story. I guess you know most of it. Anyway, it seemed like today was the day. Feels odd. But it's time." Joe reached into his shirt pocket and got the envelope Mr. Crossman had given him. "This is from Mr. Crossman. He said you'd write me a check for my wages. These are the keys to that white truck. He wants you to drive it up there in three days and help them close up camp."

Mary took the envelope and the truck keys. "You're leaving?"

Joe nodded. "As soon as I can get all my personal stuff out of my room above the shop."

"Just like that?" Mary said.

"Yeah, it happened pretty suddenly, I guess," Joe offered.

"I'll write the check and come find you," Mary said as she closed the door.

She was waiting for Joe when he stepped out of the shop door with a paper bag full of clothing under his arm. "Nice luggage, huh?" he laughed as he held the grocery bag in the air.

"I didn't think you'd leave like this," Mary said, oblivious to his laundry. Her eyes were curious, uncertain, and Joe thought she might even be angry. She handed him a check. "He gave you a little extra. He likes you," she said with no feeling.

"What's the matter?" Joe asked.

"I think you know. I think you've known for some time," she answered. Mary obviously had more to say, but she stood there stone-faced and stared at the check she'd just handed to Joe.

Joe knew she wanted an explanation, and he saw she was hurt that he could just leave like this. He had no idea what to say, so he just stood there for a long moment and waited.

Eventually, Mary reached a reluctant hand toward Joe and took his hand in hers. She wiped away a tear with her other hand, then sniffled once and looked up at Joe.

"You want to come with me, don't you?" Joe asked.

Mary lowered her eyes. "I thought I would, but I don't know," she sighed. Then she brought both hands up to cover her face and blurted, "I don't know!" as she bagan to cry.

Joe threw the paper bag full of laundry into the back of his truck, then put his arms around Mary while she cried for a moment. Her face was twisted with anguish, and her eyes were red when she looked up at him again and shook her head. "I don't know," she said again.

"OK. What's wrong?" Joe asked. He lowered the tailgate of the old Ford, sat down, and motioned for her to do the same. When she sat next to him, he took her hand in his again and asked, "What's wrong?"

Mary spent the next half-hour describing a marriage with little chance of redemption. She told Joe there was no longer any affection between her and Robert, and that she suspected he had girlfriends. He was in Denver for the week and hadn't called her for three days. Joe listened while Mary described Robert's bouts with depression and her alternate feelings of inadequacy and then anger as Robert refused to get help. She sobbed heavily for a while and then seemed quite angry twice. When she finished her story, or was too disappointed to continue it, she took Joe's hand in hers and kissed it. "You understand all of this, don't you?" she asked.

"I think so," Joe replied. "But I don't have any answers or advice for you. I don't think I'm the one to be giving advice."

"Joe, the first day you showed up here, I knew you were different. The way you talked to the others, the night we looked at that old man's slide collection. When you bought those things for James. You're different. You asked if you could help me. No one else ever did that."

She squeezed his hand and wiped another tear from her eye.

Joe raised the back of Mary's hand to his mouth and kissed it. "Mary, you want a man to ride in here on a white horse and rescue you, don't you?"

She looked away and rubbed her eyes again, then nodded slowly.

"I wish it could be me. I'd like to be that man. But I'm not. I'm just some guy trying to find my own way. I'm lost too." He kissed her hand again. "This is what I think: I think maybe you want the same thing I do, but you don't want me—not really. You want to take a risk. You want a man to slay a few dragons and take you away. You're almost willing to take a chance that I might be that man. But down deep, you know better, in spite of how much you'd want that to be true. Think I might be right?"

Mary nodded slowly.

Joe kissed her hand again. "Yeah, I'd like to be that man. You were my friend when I had no others. And just so you know...I hope I won't embarrass you, but I've spent so many hours dreaming of my hands and mouth moving all over you. You're a beautiful woman, and I could take you right now and have a hard time believing there was something wrong in doing it. I could take you with me when I leave, but it wouldn't be the right thing. We weren't meant to be lovers. We're just two people who are gonna brush past each other while we're both looking for our lives. We're gonna take a long look at each other and then wonder how it all might have been. That's all. Sounds sad, but it's true, isn't it?"

Mary put both hands on her face for a moment, then slipped off the tailgate and stood in front of Joe. "You have to go now, Joe," she said.

Joe stood by her briefly, then shut the tailgate. He put his arms around her and held her for a moment. Then he kissed her on the lips—just a gentle kiss, not like a lover would kiss her—and both of them wondered how a kiss could taste so sweet and leave them both so empty.

"Goodbye, Mary," Joe said as the truck rolled down the gravel road and out toward the highway.

"Goodbye, Joe," she whispered.

chapter
twenty-nine

If only Murdo knew how different Joe's real life was from the one he'd described at Cowboy Camp. He'd be so disappointed, Joe thought. The pickup bounced along as it had all the way from Minnesota. Just now, as his truck tires howled along a narrow blacktop road once more, Joe Mix wasn't thinking about dentistry or Jess or failure or the meaning of life. He was trying to understand just what he'd felt as he'd said goodbye to Mary Crossman. In the movies, she'd have jumped into his truck and they'd have driven away and lived happily ever after. But this life of his just wasn't turning out like the movies. That strange goodbye, which he hadn't really expected, only served to exaggerate the loneliness and uncertainty of being on the road again. He felt bad for Mary and hoped she found her way through things too.

He supposed he really had done the right thing. Holding Mary and talking to her and kissing her had tempted him to take the next step with her. But when he imagined how it would be if she were sitting here with him in the truck right now, he knew he'd done the right thing in saying an awkward goodbye. "Makes me lonely just to think about it all," he said to Jake.

He hadn't wanted to leave this time—not really. But it was the thing to do. Mr. Crossman had been right on the money when he'd recognized that Joe had something yet to do. If he stayed any longer, he just might never get on with it. Joe had known it too, but when Mr. Crossman said the words "this ain't the end of your road," that was when Joe understood it was time to move on. But the fear of the future was threatening to return for the first time in a while, and he didn't like the feeling very much.

Now where? Joe thought as the green pickup with the yellow snow-plow rolled along the highway. Where would this road lead him? he wondered. Jake was snoozing on the front seat again. The rhythmic motion of the truck plodding down the interstate always seemed to rock him to sleep. He'd turn off the interstate and onto some back roads after the next gas stop, he thought.

Jake took up quite a bit more room than he had several weeks ago. Joe enjoyed watching him grow and learn about the world. Although he was growing up, he still saw the world through innocent eyes, and there was plenty of puppy left in him. He was long and lanky now, clumsy and curious at all times. The fur on Jake's belly was still puppy soft as he stroked the sleeping dog.

Joe continued to wonder about his own decision to push on down the road. He'd been angry and certain of his need to go when he'd pulled out of Rochester. He'd been satisfied that there was nothing left for him in Kadoka when he'd left; there had been no doubt that he had to go.

Now, he thought that leaving the Crossman Ranch seemed like the right thing to do, but he wasn't sure about anything. He was back to sleeping in his truck, and he had no place to go. He just couldn't deny that he felt a little fear about stepping into the current again. At least at the Crossman Ranch, he'd had a roof over his head, something to eat, some friends, and a job.

Joe smiled broadly when he remembered the eager, drunken eyes Murdo had turned to him as he clamped his lips over a bloody rag and waited for his stories to continue. That last night had been pretty mem-orable. The whole time at the Crossman Ranch had been good, Joe thought. He couldn't get the image of those cowboys' eyes out of his mind. They were all good men, and they'd been anxious to hear about all the wrong things Joe had done, not the good things. It made no sense, but still Joe smiled every time he thought of them.

The cattle country of southeastern Montana seemed endless as Joe wound his way west into the green hills. The mid-afternoon sun was high, and there was almost no breeze when Joe crested a hill and saw Hardin, Montana spread out before him along the highway. "Let's gas up, Jake. We'll fill the cooler with some 'health food' from one of these truck stops," Joe said. When Jake heard his own name and felt the truck begin to slow down, he scrambled to a sitting position on the seat next to Joe. Jake had grown enough during the summer that he could easily see over the dashboard. He stared so intently that Joe thought he was trying to decide which truck stop he wanted to try.

When Joe stopped the truck in the shade provided by an aluminum canopy above the gas pumps, he inserted the gas nozzle into the Ford's gas tank and leaned against the door.

"That's a handsome pup you have there!" the man at the nearest gas pump said to Joe. When Joe made eye contact with the man, he smiled and pointed at Jake, who was standing on the driver's seat, looking out of Joe's window.

The man looked to be about Joe's age, but he was heavier set. He was putting gas into a Suburban from the next pump. Three other men sat in the Suburban and talked amongst themselves. The man was dressed like an affluent outdoorsman on vacation. He wore expensive loafers, Khaki cargo pants, a pastel, salmon-colored wind shirt with his glasses hanging from a lanyard around his neck, and a navy blue baseball cap that said "Big Horn Adventures" across the front.

"Thanks," Joe said and returned the man's smile. "Been fishing?" he asked.

"Sure have!" The man smiled a bigger smile and nodded.

"Must have had good luck?" Joe asked. He could already see in the man's eyes just what his answer was going to be.

"Hell, I've fished all over the place—been to Alaska several times, been to all the western rivers, out here. I've never seen anything like what we saw here!"

"Really?" Joe prodded.

"Yeah. Took us about a day to figure it out." Laughter erupted from inside the Suburban, and one of the men hollered something about how it hadn't taken all of them so long to figure it out. A huge smile covered the man's face immediately, and he turned toward his buddies who were all laughing and said, "Fuck you, guys!"—which brought another round of laughter. He closed the door of his Suburban and looked at Joe again.

"Like I said," the man continued, "took us about a day to figure things out, but after that we all had the best several days of fishin' we ever had."

"What do you mean, exactly? Ten fish? Twenty fish?" Joe asked.

"Hell, I had a fish on the line more than I didn't have one on!" the man said. Joe expected the man's buddies to harass him for making such a bold statement. Instead, all three men nodded and smiled. "Best trout stream I ever saw. You headed that way?" he added.

"How far is it?" Joe asked, surprised at his own question.

"'Bout forty-five miles down that road." The man pointed behind him. "It's not a real pretty drive, but it's a helluva river once you get there!" he said as he climbed into the Suburban's driver's seat.

"Maybe," Joe shrugged. The men pulled out of the gas station, and he waved goodbye when the men drove past him. "Yeah, maybe," he said to himself.

After Joe paid for his gas and bought a supply of food for his cooler, he sat in his truck for a moment and looked at his road map. "Well, what the hell, Jake," Joe said as he folded the road map. "Let's go see a new river." Jake stared at the half-eaten piece of beef jerky in Joe's hand as a long string of drool ran from the corner of his mouth.

Joe grinned, tossed the jerky to Jake, turned the Ford onto Montana Highway 383, and eased the old truck down the road.

It seemed logical to Joe that the highway would run alongside the river until it reached Fort Smith, the end of the line for fishermen. But to his surprise, the road remained quite a distance from the Big Horn River. The road just meandered along through some very flat, arid-looking farmland and never came within several hundred yards of the river. Usually it was miles away.

After nearly an hour of winding through the Crow Indian Reservation, Joe saw a small water tower off in the distance. When he was close enough to read the writing on the water tower, he slowed down for a close look. The tower said "Fort Smith Trailer Park." About two hundred mobile homes lay scattered around both sides of the narrow, two-lane highway.

Not one other car was moving, and Joe could see no sign of human activity. "So this is the jumping-off point for the greatest trout stream in the world—the fabulous Big Horn," Joe said out loud. The place reminded him of one of those scary movies in which some unknown force had killed off all the other humans in the area and only one unsuspecting stranger is left to solve the mystery.

Joe noticed a small grocery store with two gas pumps and several small fishing outfitters' storefronts on the left side of the road as he pulled off the highway. The sound of gravel crunching under his wheels made the place seem even more desolate as the Ford rolled slowly to a stop in front of a sign that read "Big Horn Adventures." Joe stepped out of the truck. Still there was no sign of life anywhere else in the little town. A small, handwritten note taped to the inside of the glass window said "Guide wanted, apply inside."

The door to Big Horn Adventures was wide open, and Joe stepped cautiously into the place. He was still wearing his boots, jeans, white shirt, and his 'Gus' hat when he walked through the door. He felt a little out of place immediately. He'd entered a surprisingly upscale fly shop and outfitter store. A large display of expensive graphite fly rods occupied the wall on his left. Several dozen rods by Sage, Loomis, Scott, and Winston stood on two mahogany racks. Next to the fly rods was a display case holding expensive, top-grade fly reels by manufacturers like Bauer, Ross, and Abel. In the middle of the shop sat a large table with hundreds of small compartments. Each of the compartments held dozens of tiny trout flies. The store was loaded with displays of various sizes and shapes of fly lines, waders, rain gear, clothing, and gifts. One entire wall was dedicated to a display for fly tying supplies—tiny spools of colored thread, hooks, colored feathers, tinsel, and beads. Small patches of colored animal fur lined the wall.

Along the back wall of the store, a woman sat on an antique chair in front of an old-fashioned writing desk and flipped through what appeared to be a catalog. Joe couldn't see her very well since the only light in the corner of the room where she was sitting was a reading lamp directed at the catalog on the desk. The woman turned and looked at him, nodded and said "hi," then turned back to the catalog.

As Joe's eyes scanned the merchandise in the shop, a man appeared through a small open doorway behind the cash register.

"Hi," the man said as he walked around the counter and shook Joe's hand. "Heard you roll up. It's always a little quiet around here in the afternoon when everyone is fishin'. My name is Marsh Clements. Can I help you?"

Marsh Clements looked to be about sixty-five years old, Joe thought. He was dressed in faded blue jeans, cheap, moccasin-like slippers with rubber soles, a gray T-shirt that said "Big Horn Adventures" across the front, and a gray baseball cap that said the same thing. He sort of shuffled when he walked, like a man who was getting older and losing some of his physical strength. But when he spoke, his eyes and voice were sharp. He was clearly the man in charge of Big Horn Adventures.

"No, not really. I just wanted to have a look around. I've heard so much about the Big Horn and never seen it," Joe shrugged. "I just wanted to see the Big Horn." Then he remembered to introduce himself. "I'm Joe Mix. I'm just passing through," he said as he shook Marsh's hand.

"Aren't you gonna fish?" Marsh asked.

"I really hadn't even thought of it," Joe admitted. "Just wanted to see the river."

"Well, you sure as hell drove all the way to the end of the road. You better fish it now! Didn't come all this way to stand there and look at it, did you?" Marsh smiled as if he thought his question was funny.

"Well, no," Joe replied slowly. "But I didn't come all this way just to go fishin', either," he said to himself as he turned away.

"Huh? What did you say?" Marsh asked.

"I said you have a nice store here, Mr. Clements," Joe answered. Then he turned and walked out of the fly shop. "Very nice!"

"Thank you," Marsh Clements said to Joe's back. Then he turned and passed a confused look to the woman at the antique desk.

Joe walked slowly to his truck while Marsh Clements and the woman watched him. He opened the cooler, took out a plastic bottle of Diet Coke and two pieces of jerky, then returned to the shade of the covered boardwalk in front of Big Horn Adventures. He sat down on a wooden bench, opened the soda, and started chewing on one piece of jerky while he let Jake gnaw on the other. For the next fifteen minutes, he sipped at the soda, nibbled at the jerky, and played with Jake.

The woman at the desk went back to her work on the catalog, and Marsh straightened some things at the cash register. But each of them continued to peek at Joe every so often.

When Joe finally stood up and walked back into the store, he walked directly to the cash register and stared at Marsh for a moment. He swallowed once and said, "I'd like to apply for that job as a guide—the one you have posted in the window." Jake had followed him into the store and now sat on his rear end and scratched behind his ear with his hind leg.

Marsh looked at Joe for a moment, then bent his face into a question before he said the words, "Didn't you just say you've never seen this river before?"

"Yeah," Joe nodded, then smiled until the dimple in his cheek was visible even to the woman in the corner. Joe hadn't had to ask for a job since...forever. Just the simple act of asking for work had given him a sense of vulnerability he'd never experienced before. He'd just always been the boss. Three months earlier, he wouldn't have been able to do something like ask for a job. He wouldn't have been able to bear the disappointment if he'd been told no. But after his time on the road and at the Crossman Ranch, that fear of failure was beginning to fade. Now that Marsh had instantly identified a fairly important shortcoming, like never having seen the river, Joe could only smile. "Well, you got me there. But I am a pretty experienced fisherman, and I can keep a boat right side up in pretty rough water. I'm not stupid. This has got to be about like any other trout stream. I'll find the fish. I guess you're not lookin' for a brain surgeon, are you?" Joe smiled just as Jim Crossman had when he'd said the same thing months before in the diner in Wyoming.

Marsh's face wrinkled with concern as he turned a questioning look toward the woman in the corner. The woman pursed her lips almost imperceptibly and nodded her head yes. Her eyes said, "Talk to him...see what he's like."

"OK," Marsh said. "Be here tomorrow at 9:00 a.m. You and I are gonna take a boat down the river, like a job interview. If you can handle things all right, you can start working the next day."

"Do I need to bring anything?" Joe asked.

"Waders and a fly rod," Marsh answered.

Joe extended his hand to Marsh Clements and said, "See you at nine. Thanks, Mr. Clements."

The look of concern hadn't left Marsh's face, and his eyes betrayed a puzzled curiosity as he shook Joe's hand. "I'll be right here waiting," he said.

The door to Joe's truck creaked loudly, then slammed. He started the engine, raised the snowplow up off the gravel parking lot, and waved at Marsh as he pulled out of the parking lot in front of Big Horn Adventures. Then he turned to Jake. "I think we should go find someplace to play instead of sitting back there by the shop like two homeless bums, eh Jake? Seemed like the wheels were really turning in Marsh's head there. He probably doesn't need to know just yet that we really are just two homeless bums."

When darkness fell, Joe eased the Ford back into the parking lot in front of the Big Horn Adventures fly shop. He'd driven past the place several times to make sure the lights were off and no one was still inside. Since his conversation with Marsh Clements, he'd spent the time at a boat landing three miles downstream, playing with Jake and reading. Now that it was time to sleep, he returned and parked his truck in the parking lot between several other trucks—probably trucks belonging to guests of the Big Horn Adventures Motel. Joe wanted his truck to be as inconspicuous as possible, so he parked it among others hoping no one would notice he was sleeping in it. He prepared his bed on the plastic lawn chair inside the small topper on his pickup.

After a long swim in the Big Horn and plenty of play time along the river bank, Jake was ready to curl up next to Joe and sleep for the night. In just the past few weeks, Joe had begun to find comfort in the smell of a wet dog. Jake was his only friend. Jake needed him, and it was already clear that the only thing Jake the dog wanted to do in life was to play with and please Joe Mix. It was odd, Joe thought, that the aroma of a still-damp puppy carried with it the security of home and an old friend. Joe had grown to need Jake next to him at night too. Jake's touch was reassuring, and Joe loved the little noises and twitches Jake made in his sleep.

It had been a long day—a long day indeed, Joe thought. It seemed like a long time ago since he'd left the Crossman Ranch, but he'd only left this very morning. He was only a few miles away, but the ranch seemed far behind him now. He clicked off the little dome light above his head and lay in the darkness. Jake sighed a huge sigh, then curled up for the night, resting his back against Joe's side as he began to twitch and chase things in his dreams.

Joe's last thought before drifting off to sleep was that he hoped he'd found work on his first try. He wanted to stay here and see the place for a while. He was proud of the way he'd asked for work. It would be quite a drop in pay from what he'd done for twenty-five years, but it was work.

chapter thirty

Marsh Clements stepped slowly into the front seat of a fiberglass drift boat and began speaking to Joe. Joe had already backed the boat and trailer into the river, unloaded the boat, and moved the truck and trailer. Then he prepared the boat for a day on the river by checking for lifejackets, securing the anchor, and placing both oars in the brass oarlocks.

"Nice work, Joe," Marsh said when the boat was ready to shove off. "Looks like you've done this before?"

"A few times," Joe smiled. Then he asked, "Are you sure Jake is all right staying up at the shop?" He knew Jake's injury had healed, and he'd be full of energy and want to play all day.

""Sure! Molly will love him. Besides that, I never let guides bring their dogs along when they're working. Some clients just don't appreciate a dog in the boat. Don't worry. Molly and Jake will get along fine. Now, before we shove off, there are a few things I'll share with you just because you need to know."

"OK," Joe nodded. Several other drift boats were stacked up at the landing while anxious fishermen jostled their gear into the boats and pushed off into the current. Joe pushed Marsh's boat onto a gravel area beside the boat landing, sat down in the seat facing Marsh, and said "what?"

"The Big Horn is a tailwater fishery. That means the water that flows here is being released from a dam."

"I knew that. You mean that enormous concrete thing right there, correct?" Joe pointed to the dam about two hundred feet from their boat and smiled.

Marsh ignored Joe's reply. "The Yellowtail Dam was built in 1969, about five miles up that canyon. This little dam behind you..."—Marsh pointed over his shoulder at the dam about two hundred feet away from them—"...that's the Afterbay Dam. That's the secret. That's how they accidentally created the greatest trout stream on earth. The way the big dam and the Afterbay Dam work...they're able to release a fairly steady flow of cold water, year round, from the bottom of the reservoir. That cold water runs through all this limestone, which provides the perfect pH at the perfect water temperature with very little fluctuation in water level, to produce incredible numbers of aquatic insects, which God created strictly to feed the trout! Are you with me?"

"Yes," Joe smiled.

"There are no motors allowed on this river for the first thirteen miles beyond the Afterbay Dam. All river traffic is drift only. There is a river access at about three miles from this Afterbay Dam and another river access at about thirteen miles. There are other accesses every so often all the way to Hardin, but we pretty much only use the three-mile and thirteen-mile river access."

"Jake and I visited the access at three miles yesterday," Joe offered.

"Once you put our boat in here, you can't take it out until you reach one of the access points. Before you leave for a day of fishing, you always tell us where to shuttle your truck and trailer. We'll have it waiting for you at the end of the day, wherever you want."

"Sounds good," Joe said. "How far are we going today?"

"Thirteen miles," Marsh answered. "Shove off!"

Joe stepped out and gently dragged the boat over the small rocks and gravel by the river bank until the fiberglass boat was free from the river bottom. He climbed over the gunwale, took his seat in the middle of the boat, leaned heavily on the oars, and at once felt the mighty river pull at the boat. The Big Horn River had its first grip on Joe Mix. He loved the way the gin-clear water wrestled with him for control.

He'd learned long ago, while piloting other boats like this one on streams all over the world, that the way to navigate downstream in a drift boat was to point the bow of the boat where you didn't want to go and then row backwards. He pulled hard on the oars until the boat was in the middle of the river, about 150 feet from either bank.

Marsh leaned back in his boat seat, scanned the river bank on both sides of him, then turned back toward Joe. He looked Joe up and down while Joe worked the boat into the current. "You like to use bamboo, huh?" Marsh asked, then pointed at Joe's fly rod.

"Yeah, I do." He pulled on the oars and looked back at Marsh. "I know that these big western rivers are better suited for bigger graphite rods with faster spines, but a special friend made this for me and it's a work of art," Joe shrugged. "So I use it all the time."

Joe turned the boat slightly and looked over his shoulder, then offered, "You know the character Natty Bumpo in James Fenimore Cooper's *The Deerslayer*? He had a special rifle—called it Killdeer. Never missed with it!" Joe grinned and looked over his other shoulder. "I always liked that story—like it more now than ever. So this old bamboo rod is my Killdeer."

"Never had a river guide discuss nineteenth-century authors before," Marsh replied. "You a professor or something like that?"

"No." Joe shook his head and sighed. "You?"

"Not hardly. Got a degree in English Literature, though." Marsh paused for a moment before he continued. "But I spent most of my college days partyin' and protesting one thing or another."

Joe grinned, turned the boat a little, and waited for Marsh to continue. But Marsh folded his arms across his chest and stared at the river for a minute. Then he began to prepare his fly rod but said nothing more.

"OK, what now?" Joe asked.

"Just gimme a good drift," Marsh said as he flipped about thirty feet of floating fly line into a pile beside the boat. "The Big Horn produces so many aquatic insects. It's primarily a river for nymphing; most of the fish we catch here will be on nymphs. This is your standard Big Horn rig, right here," Marsh said as he lifted his line off the water for Joe to see. A small strike indicator—just a piece of red cork, like a bobber—was fixed near the end of the fly line. About ten feet of tapered, monofilament leader extended beyond the strike indicator, and several small pieces of lead were attached near the end of the leader. Three feet or so beyond the lead, a small fly was attached to a very fine piece of monofilament line. Joe had seen lines rigged like this hundreds of times before. The idea was simply to have the cork remain visible and free floating on the surface while the lead carried the little fly to the bottom of the river, where the trout were waiting for lunch to tumble by. When the trout struck at the fly, they'd disturb the red-cork strike indicator the fisherman was watching and he'd set the hook. The trick in it all was for the guy rowing the boat to keep the boat moving along at the same speed as the fisherman's line. Moving the boat and the fly line at two different speeds created "drag" on the fly, which warned the fish that something wasn't natural.

Joe turned the boat slightly and held it in a perfect drift for several minutes. Joe looked to his right, then his left. Like most other western rivers, this was big water. There would be no green canopy of hardwoods shrouding this river. The wind might play hell with a fly caster here, but heavy overhead tree cover certainly wouldn't. Joe breathed in deeply, then smiled to himself.

"You've done this before, haven't you?" Marsh called over his shoulder. He was standing in the front of the boat, balancing himself in the little perch created for fishermen.

"'Bout a million times," Joe answered.

"Take me over there." Marsh ignored Joe's answer and pointed across the river.

"Now take me through that run again," Marsh ordered, and Joe paddled upstream for several minutes until he'd returned the boat to the head of a nice section of the river.

"Again," Marsh ordered. "Again..." And Joe returned. "Now over there." And Joe moved the boat downstream and across the river. "OK, now run me right through that slot over there between those two islands." Joe moved deftly through the current again.

"OK, get me a good run right over there along those trees on that bank," Marsh ordered. Joe turned the boat once again. As he did, he felt the current carry him close to the river bank. He corrected his mistake but quickly felt the boat moving too far from the bank. "Jeez, Marsh, I'm sorry. I..."

"I know you're sorry, goddammit, but I don't care. I wanna fish right there. So save your excuses and get me there!"

The orders Marsh had given up to this point had been cautious, and they were designed to see if Joe had the skills and the strength to pilot a boat like this on a big, western river. But this outburst at drifting too far from shore...this was strictly to test Joe, to see how he'd respond to a demanding client. Marsh was just pushing him to see what he'd do, and it reminded Joe of the way Murdo had scolded him. He dropped the end of one oar into the water and pulled back hard. The boat spun violently to the left, and Marsh nearly lost his balance.

"OK," Joe said. "You wanna do this right-handed?" He stopped for only a second, then dug the other oar into the water. The boat spun even more violently to the right, and Marsh was thrown back the other way. "Or left-handed?" Joe said as he raised his eyebrows, feigning innocence. He held eye contact with Marsh, grinned slightly, then dug both oars into the water, pulling on one and pushing on the other. The boat spun 180 degrees and was facing upstream. "Wanna run this next riffle backwards..."—he spun the boat violently one more time—"...or sideways?"

Marsh sat heavily into the boat seat in front of Joe, then turned to face him as he reeled in his fishing line. Joe was staring into Marsh's eyes as Marsh laid his fishing rod in the front of the boat. "OK," Marsh said calmly. "Pull 'er over on that grassy bank over there." Then he crossed his arms and stared back at Joe until the drift boat slid to a halt on the riverbank.

"OK, who are you?" Marsh asked in the same calm tone of voice as a moment earlier.

Joe didn't answer.

"Only a couple other guides on the river can handle a boat like you can." Marsh paused. "So who are you? Some cowboy comes ridin' into town drivin' a snowplow in July and wants a job guidin' on a river he's never seen before. Can you see why I might have a little trouble with this?"

"Maybe," Joe smiled. He saw something open and honest in Marsh—something he'd seen in little bits and pieces up until this moment—but Marsh was putting all his cards on the table now, asking Joe to do the same.

"Cops after you?" Marsh asked flatly.

"No," Joe smiled again. "Everyone in Montana has asked me that."

Marsh continued to question Joe. "Some personal shit happened then, right?"

"Personal shit. Yeah. Personal shit. I like that," Joe nodded. "That's about right," he admitted.

"So you're runnin' from something?"

"I guess so. Running from or running to something. I don't know."

"Well, you'll fit right in here. Everyone in Fort Smith is running from something," Marsh said.

"You and your wife—you running too?" Joe asked.

"My wife?"

"Molly, the woman at your fly shop."

"Oh, Molly! She's not my wife. But yeah, I suppose she's running too."

Marsh stopped himself, folded his arms again, and leaned back in his boat seat. He studied Joe for a moment, then began to speak. "So, Joe Mix, I guess I really don't need to know about your personal problems; we all have 'em, huh? What I do need to know..."—Marsh leaned forward and rested his hands on his knees before he continued—"...is whether or not you really want to do this. I don't want to spend the time training you and then have you run off. Know what I mean?"

"Yes," Joe nodded.

"So you think you're going to stay around for a while?" Marsh had laid himself open in the last few minutes. He wasn't angry, and he wasn't trying to deliver any sermons about what he expected of Joe. He was just asking for the truth. When Joe looked into Marsh's eyes and listened to him speak, he thought he saw and heard the same type of integrity he'd heard from the cowboys and ranchers like Ralph Webster—men who had sat around and done business in the little booths at the Stockman's Café. "What's it to be, Joe? I'm only trying to find out what your intentions are. It's obvious you can handle the boat. Do you want me to finish this? I'll be glad to float the river with you and show you where to find fish, but is it what you want—really? Don't waste my time, and yours, if you're just gonna leave in the middle of the night."

Joe looked upstream and then down. The only sound he could hear was the gentle gurgling of the river as it surged through the little riffle behind him.

"I have nowhere else to go," he said, just loud enough to be heard over the noise of the river. He'd lowered his guard too, and he was comfortable with that feeling, much as he had been at the end of his time at Cowboy Camp when he'd told Jim Crossman the truth. He turned his eyes directly toward Marsh and blurted something that surprised even him: "I think maybe I've always had nowhere else to go but here." Then he leaned forward and continued. "So yeah, I'd like to stick around if you'll have me." He raised his eyebrows and grinned crookedly at Marsh.

"OK, then, let's go fishin," Marsh said with an emphasis that separated everything that had been said in the previous few minutes from all that he was about to say. A deal had been struck between the two men, and that was the end of it. Marsh's word and Joe's: that was it; all that would be needed. Each of the men had his first look into the other man's character.

"Here's a fairly detailed map of the river. As we move along for the rest of the day, I'll point out good spots and we'll make notes on the map. We'll stop and fish a few of the holes. I'll try to show you a couple places that always hold fish when the usual spots aren't working." Marsh reached for his fly rod and then held it as if he were waiting for something. "OK, Joe, you're the guide. Take me fishing."

The tone in Marsh's voice had changed entirely since before they'd stopped on the bank to talk. Before that, Marsh had been a little short with Joe, as if Joe needed to be kept on the outside of some club or fraternity. After Joe's eyes had flashed and he'd spun the boat in the current, then confessed he had nowhere else to go, Marsh seemed to open a door slightly and let Joe stand on the threshold.

"Just run 'er right down the middle of this flat water. Then pull up on the left bank up there. That's a helluva riffle up ahead about a quarter-mile." Marsh talked as he fed fly line effortlessly into his casting motion, then laid his line onto the water about thirty feet to the right side of the boat. "This is pretty slack water in this stretch, but it holds some fish. Just gimme a good drift through here."

The boat responded smoothly to Joe's maneuvering with the oars, and the two men eased away from the small riffle where they'd stopped. They began to glide silently along on the current of the cool stream, as if they were sailing through clouds. The Big Horn River was about two hundred feet across here, and its surface was flat as glass for the next several hundred yards until it narrowed into a small rapids about fifty feet across.

At the rate they were moving, it would take about ten minutes for the boat to reach the bank where Marsh had told Joe to stop next. Both men sat in silence and watched the strike indicator at the end of Marsh's fly line. A rooster pheasant called from just beyond a thicket on the right bank and interrupted the silence, but neither man seemed to notice.

"So where you from, Joe?" Marsh asked without looking away from his strike indicator.

"Minnesota, South Dakota," Joe said as if they were both the same and it didn't matter anyway.

"You didn't learn to handle a boat like this in South Dakota."

"No," Joe smiled. "But I've been around some—Alaska, Labrador, Russia, Argentina, everywhere else in the states, all the famous western rivers. I spent a lot of time in drift boats. Just never been here before. Just never got around to it," Joe shrugged.

"So what's the rest of your story? How did you earn a living before you became a fishing guide?"

"You wouldn't believe me," Joe said. Then he deliberately turned the conversation. "What's your story, Marsh? How did you come to own a fly shop and hotel out here?"

"I doubt you'd believe..."—Marsh sputtered, then raised his right hand quickly as his fishing rod bent in half. An instant later, a rainbow trout leaped from the surface and then splashed loudly when it returned to the current. Marsh reeled the fish in after a short battle, then removed his fly from the fish's mouth with a hemostat. He held the fish up for Joe to see. It was a pretty, silver-sided rainbow about sixteen inches long. "There. That guy's a little small, but he's almost a typical Big Horn trout.

"He's a trophy where I come from," Joe smiled.

"Catch 'em like that all day long here," Marsh said while he fed line into his casting stroke and returned his fly to the river.

"You were saying...?" Joe said when Marsh had finished casting.

"Huh?"

"About your past. You doubt that I'd believe..."

"Oh, I doubt you'd believe my story either," Marsh smiled. "I grew up in Vermont. Learned to fish with a bamboo rod, and never really wanted to do much else but fish." Marsh turned a devilish grin toward Joe and went on. "Then I went off to college and found that I also wanted to drink beer, maybe smoke some pot, and chase girls. Sort of left trout streams and trout fishin' behind me for a while there. After I graduated from college, I took a job in L.A. and wound up selling widgets for a large widget manufacturer. Didn't have much use for my degree in English Literature." Marsh smiled, then continued. "Lots of travel and corporate politics. Started makin' a lot of money too! But I was real unhappy—I mean, real unhappy. I got sick of the travel and bullshit and bored with my job. Well, actually, I hated my damn job and everybody

I worked with. They all hated their jobs too. I started to feel bad about feeling bad—guilty, maybe? Felt like I was in prison."

"Yeah, I can understand that," Joe smiled.

"Anyway, I was thinkin' I'd just stick with the old job and make the best of it. Then I came here for a couple days of trout fishing shortly after the river opened." Marsh looked at Joe, then turned his attention back to his strike indicator. "After the second day," Marsh shook his head and chuckled, "I walked over to the pay phone outside of the Yellowtail Grocery Store. Still had my waders on." He paused and seemed to be enjoying something. "Picked up the phone and quit my job. Told 'em I was gonna stay here and open a fly shop."

Joe turned the boat gently and replied, "That took some stones!"

"Not really," Marsh answered while he untied a knot. "I'd been thinkin' for a long time that I'd made a lot of wrong choices and that I had to correct things before it was too late. OK, pull over here, Joe," Marsh said before Joe had a chance to ask him any more. "This is a great run through here. All the area up here at the head of this run?" He held out his hand and waved it over the flats at the top of the first run. "This all holds fish—nice fish. All that over there on the other side? That's good too. But I like this side better. OK, now, this is how you fish this spot up here."

Marsh spent thirty minutes with Joe at the top of the run...then another few minutes showing him how to find fish in the middle of the run...and another half-hour on the tail end of the run. Each spot required the men to make subtle adjustments with tackle and technique in order to place their flies in front of the fish. "If you're not bumping the bottom, you won't catch fish!" Marsh had said several times.

When they'd finished fishing the calm, flat water where the river widened after the narrow channel, Marsh gave the order to get back in the boat and move on. He was sitting in the seat at the front of the drift boat when Joe pulled on the oars and moved the boat out into the current.

Every time Joe eased the boat into the river, he looked forward to the feeling as the current took hold of the boat and pulled it along. The flat water at the tail of this run was calm and silent, but the current was steady. Joe turned to look as a Great Blue Heron lifted itself noiselessly out of the water along the shore and flew off somewhere downstream. Earlier, when they'd been fishing in the whitewater at the middle of the run, Marsh had almost needed to shout in order to be heard over the noise of the rushing water. But now, as Joe teased the boat into the current, the water was silent. Joe liked the river both ways, but the shallow runs, where the water only gurgled softly over quiet riffles—that was the water he liked best.

"Here," Marsh interrupted Joe's thoughts. "Here's a map of the river channel, and I've made some notes for you." Marsh held out a printed map with handwritten notes for Joe to see. "Right there, that's where we just were."

Joe leaned forward and smiled. "Says 'Marsh's Run' on the map?" It was an observation and a question at the same time.

"Yeah. It's my favorite hole. I was right there, right where we pulled over at the tip of the run, when I decided I was never leaving. The other guides just started calling it Marsh's Run after that. During those first couple years, I fished it hard. OK, now, after this next flat stretch, we're gonna come to some islands. Pull over at the top of the first island and I'll show you around," Marsh continued before Joe could ask any more questions about Marsh's Run.

Marsh spent the rest of the day giving orders to Joe about where to stop, making notes on the map about how to fish the various holes, and telling stories about triumphs and disasters on the river.

The trees along the bank were beginning to cast cool shadows across the river channel in late afternoon. Joe was relieved by the soft comfort of a shady cottonwood tree every time they passed behind one. The skin on the back of his hands and neck felt uncomfortably hot every time the sun struck them directly. "Gotta watch out for sunburn out here!" Joe offered.

"Yeah, the sun will really take it out of you by the end of a day on the river. But it's a great way to feel: tired after a day on a trout stream."

"Yeah, but you know..." Joe stopped, then interrupted himself as they drifted around the tip of a narrow island and reached the confluence of three river channels joining back into one channel. Several dozen Mallards flushed straight off the surface of the river as if they'd been lifted by invisible strings. All the banks were lined with Russian Olive trees, and behind them stood tall cottonwood trees. The water was so clear and calm, it held the reflection of the trees perfectly. The bank was so green that it was hard for Joe to tell just where river ended and forest began. Then, back off in the woods on the right bank, a small cabin appeared. It would have been easy to miss because it had been built in a stand of cottonwoods.

"Jeez, what a great little cabin—a perfect spot!" Joe sighed.

"It's my place," Marsh said, but he offered nothing more for a moment as they drifted silently past it. The cabin was sided with dark cedar boards, and a screened-in porch and several large windows faced the river. A boat exactly like the one they were in had been pulled up on the bank and was tied to a tree.

From the river it was difficult to see, but Joe thought he could make out a small clearing on the riverbank about ten feet above the water line, just in front of the cabin. The clearing appeared to have a red wooden bench and several signs or markers around it.

Marsh's place was nearly past them when Joe turned his head to look at the far side of the river. Dozens of large cottonwood trees grew from a carpet of short green grass, and several black cattle grazed while a few others stared dumbly at the boat drifting past them. "A cow pasture?" Joe asked.

"Yeah," Marsh said. "They keep the grass over there nice and short—just the way I like it." Marsh looked at the pasture, then his cabin, then looked away.

The boat and the men drifted on in silence for about ten minutes until the next run of gurgling water, then Marsh began to give instructions again. By the time Marsh and Joe had completed a thirteen-mile float, the sun was getting low in the sky and Marsh had filled all the margins of the river map with notes and symbols.

"OK, Joe. When you reach this boat landing with your clients, we'll have your truck and a trailer shuttled down here waiting for you. You just put this boat back on the trailer and bring it back to the fly shop. Can you handle that?"

"Sure," Joe nodded.

———

Jake's tail was wagging so hard that he had a difficult time with his balance when he saw Joe walk through the door of the Big Horn Adventures fly shop. "Molly, would you do the paperwork so Joe can be a legal employee tomorrow? You know, the social security stuff?" Marsh said as he followed Joe into the shop.

"Sure," she answered. "C'mere, Joe, we've got a little paperwork to do," she said while she pulled some papers from a cabinet behind the cash register.

This was his first real conversation with Molly. They hadn't really introduced themselves the previous day. Now it was too late for that; they already knew each other... sort of.

While Molly's back was turned, Joe couldn't help but notice her narrow hips. Her blue jeans looked slightly worn but still had a sharp crease, and she wore woven leather shoes with no socks. Her white, cotton blouse served to deepen the sun tan on her arms and face.

But the thing Joe noticed more than anything else—the thing that jumped at him—happened when she smiled. On the previous day and every time today when he'd looked at her, she'd seemed stern and distant. Her eyes were hard and dark. Joe had assumed that she'd taken an immediate dislike to him.

Just now when she smiled, her eyes softened and explained that he was welcome in this little world. He felt a palpable sense of relief—she wasn't so bad. Her smile, the way her lips curled around her teeth, was so inviting and so unique. Her teeth were white and nicely shaped, but one of her central incisors—her upper front teeth—overlapped the other one ever so slightly. It created just the right amount of character or individuality in her smile. The thing that really caught Joe's eye, however, was that a small area of her upper lip, just off to the left of the midline, seemed to remain stationary when she smiled—as if she'd just come from a dentist's office. Her lip curled a little higher on the right side of her face when she smiled and provided a slight facial asymmetry that Joe found very attractive. It was this kind of defect or imperfection that other dentists tried to eliminate. Joe, however, had always tried to build these types of aesthetic nuances into his makeover cases.

He relaxed for a moment and let his eyes drift down to the papers Molly was writing on. He noticed immediately that her fingers were long and thin. She looked graceful just filling out tax forms.

She wasn't Marsh's wife. But she must be his significant other. What else would keep a woman like her in this place? She did seem to have a close relationship with Marsh—Joe could see that much. They must be together, he thought.

Joe leaned against a countertop and answered her questions as Molly read them from the printed forms. It took only a minute to fill in all the blanks, but Joe hesitated when Molly asked him for his address. He had no address, and he didn't know what to say for an uncomfortable moment.

"Want me to use the license number for your truck?" she asked with a skeptical smile. She was teasing when she raised her eyebrows.

Joe tried to answer with a grin to hide the fact that Molly's eyes and her question had surprised him. He was embarrassed, and he felt like he'd been caught in a lie.

"I saw you get out of bed this morning—or should I say out of truck? I was out for a morning walk and I happened to see you. Were you going to just live in there?" she asked, clearly referring to the back of his truck.

"Well, I guess I hadn't really figured that out yet," Joe confessed.

"Marsh! Come over here," Molly called. "Joe has no place to stay," she announced bluntly when Marsh found his way to the counter where Joe and Molly were standing. Marsh looked first at Molly, then turned a questioning look to Joe.

"I just got here," Joe shrugged.

"It's all right, Joe," Molly said. Just the tone of her voice told Joe and Marsh that she already had things taken care of. "I thought this might happen, so while you two were on the river I opened your old trailer, Marsh. Got some fresh air in there, put clean sheets on the bed..." She paused, then added, "It's been a long time since anyone has stayed there!"

"Good idea, Molly. That's why you get the big bucks! You wanna take him over there and show him around? I've got some phone calls to return. Be here tomorrow at seven, Joe." With that, Marsh disappeared into the tiny office behind the cash register.

"OK," Molly shrugged when the rest of her paperwork was finished. She looked around the empty shop and added, "Let's go! I think Marsh can handle the crowd in here for a few minutes."

Molly walked past Joe, through the door of the shop, and out into the gravel parking lot. While her back was still turned to Joe, she pointed to the south and said, "Your place is way over there, on the south side of town!" Then she turned and said, "Follow me" as she got into an older green Subaru and started the engine.

Joe started his truck and followed her out of the parking lot, onto the unpaved street in front of the shop. Joe noticed that none of the streets in Fort Smith were paved. In fact, there were only three streets on the south side of the highway in Fort Smith. Each of the streets was lined with an irregular arrangement of older mobile homes. As they crept slowly along onto the southernmost street, Molly turned left and inched along a narrow alley. Some of the places had junk in the front yard—maybe an old car or two, a propane tank, a pile of scrap lumber, or a drift boat on a trailer. One place had an aluminum garden shed with a broken front door. The shed seemed crammed full of garden hose, lawn ornaments, and other junk Joe couldn't recognize.

Molly stopped her Subaru in front of the last place on the street. It sat in the very southernmost corner of town. The lot on which the trailer rested was covered with a small, scraggly lawn. It was bordered with a handful of large, scruffy old cottonwood trees and surrounded by a chicken-wire fence. Beyond the lawn was nothing but miles and miles of the Big Horn Valley, and out there beyond the valley lay the Big Horn Mountains.

"Not much, is it?" Molly said when Joe and Jake stepped from the truck and walked toward the trailer. Joe could only stop and stare and try to process what exactly rested on this lot. It looked to be a single-wide mobile home, about 1955 vintage. It was beige, with faded aqua trim and rust-colored streaks extending down from all the windows. The lines appeared to be straight, so Joe assumed it was structurally still all right. The most striking feature of the trailer—the one that set it apart from all the others Joe had ever seen—was its roof. Some years earlier, the roof must have been leaking, because a carpenter—a carpenter with pretty limited skills, Joe thought—had taken some two-by-fours, some plywood, and a hodgepodge of different-colored shingles and built a pitched roof over the entire trailer. Exposed two-by-fours still showed on both ends of the thirty-five-foot trailer, and the shingles were beginning to curl. At first Joe wondered if it was a practical joke, but he could see that the windows had been opened earlier. Molly seemed totally serious. When she read the trepidation in Joe's eyes, she smiled. "It's actually pretty comfortable, and that roof WILL keep the rain out." The sudden transformation that came to Molly's eyes when she smiled told Joe this place really was for him.

Jake walked cautiously and sniffed at everything when Molly opened the door and let Joe inside. The trailer was about nine feet wide, and it creaked when they walked around on the worn red carpet. The front door opened into a room that functioned as a kitchen and living room.

A tiny kitchen table with two chairs, a tiny desk, a sagging love seat, and a well-worn, overstuffed chair were the only furniture.

"It's small, but it's clean," Molly said. "Doesn't look like much, does it?" she added.

"It'll do," Joe smiled.

"Bedroom and bath are down there." Molly pointed down the narrow hallway beyond the small kitchen.

"Thanks, Molly," Joe said. "It's nice. Thank you."

"See you at seven, Joe," she said as she turned and left.

Joe sat on one of the aluminum chairs at the kitchen table and watched through the screen door as Molly's Subaru wound its way back to the fly shop. He couldn't help but chuckle when he saw her stop and walk back into the shop. His trailer was all the way across Fort Smith from the shop, but he was pretty sure he could hit a golf ball from here to there.

He moved some of his things into the trailer, then ate a can of peaches from his cooler and fed Jake. It had been a pretty fair day. He'd actually had fun with Marsh. He felt that he and Marsh had found some sort of mutual understanding. He was looking forward to getting to know Marsh better. And he was thankful, very thankful, to have this little trailer for his home just now. For tonight, at least, he and Jake weren't homeless bums.

The silence and the sense of isolation there in the little trailer, however—in the tiny town in the middle of the prairie—reopened an empty place in his heart. He was still all alone. He'd felt the same way when he left Rochester and then Kadoka.

But just the fact that he had this place—this odd little place—to call his own for the time being gave him a glimmer of hope that he hadn't felt since he'd left everything behind.

The sun's rays were bright and harsh as they streamed in sideways from just over the horizon and through the kitchen window of the trailer, moments before sunset. Joe looked around at the amber hue inside the kitchen and living area. He actually liked the mood created by the last yellow sunlight of the day when it struck the faded brown cupboards and paneling in his new home. It did seem like a place where he might be comfortable. But it was so quiet, and he was so alone.

"C'mon, Jake, let's go have a look around outside," Joe said when he stood up from the kitchen table and stepped out into the gentle greens and blues of early evening. The sun rested just above the horizon, and the western sky seemed hazy, full of the afternoon's dust. The hills on the far side of the valley were golden, the grass already turning in the summer heat; it looked like harvest time did back in Minnesota. A large cottonwood marked the corner of the property line, and the leaves rustled in the warm breeze while Joe walked around to the stark little backyard. He noticed a small pit surrounded by a ring of stones, then a stack of firewood and two rickety-looking lawn chairs folded against the wood pile.

By the time the sun disappeared beyond the horizon, Joe had built a small fire inside the circle of stones and seated himself on the sturdier of the lawn chairs. The sun was gone for the day, and the sky had faded to a softer blue. It wasn't dark yet, but the day was over and the air began to cool as it whispered through the cottonwood leaves around him. This evening's summer wind carried a sense of well-being. He was alone, but the feeling that he might be home began to settle over him. Joe was poking at the fire with an old broom handle when Jake walked over, nudged him, and began to beg for Joe to scratch his ears.

"OK," Joe sighed as he scratched the young dog's ears. "Look what we've done, Jake. Tomorrow I'm gonna get paid to go fishing. How 'bout that? And we have this place here—this might not be so bad." Jake plopped to the ground and rolled over onto his back, begging to be scratched on his belly now, as a moment of clarity dawned for Joe Mix. He leaned back in the lawn chair and kept his right hand on Jake's stomach. "After all I left behind, life is funny, huh, Jake? I mean, here I sit, living in a trailer that makes my truck look pretty good. Two days ago, I thought we'd probably be sleeping in a city park or a truck stop tonight. I ate supper out of a can, and all I have to do for fun is sit by this fire and scratch your nuts." Joe smiled at his own sentence. "But you know what, Jake? I feel good."

chapter
thirty-one

Several small groups of eager-looking men were milling around inside the Big Horn Adventures fly shop when Joe and Jake arrived at 6:45 a.m. Joe stopped in the doorway and quickly assessed the fishermen.

Most of the men were already wearing Gore-Tex waders. Some hadn't made their final preparations yet and were still wearing blue jeans or Khakis. There seemed to be a fair amount of gray hair in the room, Joe thought. Several of the men were talking and laughing, while others were staring intently at the display case filled with flies.

When Joe looked at the cash register, he noticed Molly was staring at him. Molly smiled softly and pointed her index finger at him. Then she began to motion to him with her finger—the universal signal for "come here." When Joe walked over to her, she leaned over the counter and put her lips close to his ear. "Those two young guys over there...you'll be guiding them today," she whispered.

Joe was thankful for the information. He turned his eyes toward them quickly. Even before he'd had a chance to look at the two dark-haired young men, he'd had a brief, unexpected rush of pleasure. Molly's eyes had softened again when she'd smiled at him. When Molly leaned over to speak to him, he'd felt her breath on his ear, turned sideways, and allowed her to lean close to him when she spoke. His eyes had been turned down as he bent slightly to listen. He couldn't help but notice her long fingers and delicate hands on the countertop. Neither could he avoid noticing the way her full breasts filled her cotton blouse, and she smelled so nice too. Her perfume wasn't the really expensive stuff that Jess had always bought. A softer scent drifted into his nose while he stood beside her. The whole exchange with Molly had taken only about five seconds, but it felt to Joe as if it were happening in slow motion.

He was already having a good day, but it was time to forget about Molly and concentrate on the day ahead of him. "Thanks, Molly," he said as he stood straight. "Jake's OK with you again, right?"

He looked at the two men for a moment, and he was about to walk over to them to introduce himself when Marsh called out, "All right, Mike and Jay, your guide is here! You ready to go?" Then he introduced Joe to his first clients and sent them all on their way. As Joe was about to climb into his truck, Marsh touched his arm. Joe turned a puzzled look back at Marsh. Marsh wished him well by raising his eyebrows and smiling. "We'll have a chat tonight. Good luck," Marsh said when he shut the door on Joe's truck and watched Joe and his clients drive off.

———·———

"So where are you guys from?" Joe asked as he strained at the oars and eased the drift boat away from the boat landing. Another long pull and Joe felt the current take hold of the boat and begin to move it downstream.

"Iowa," Jay answered.

"New Jersey," Mike added.

"How'd you meet?" Joe asked.

"College," Jay replied. "University of Michigan. Turns out Mike is kind of stupid, so I did his homework for him. Even bought some shitty clothes and dressed up like him so I could disguise myself and take exams for him a couple times. I got him through school."

"He just followed me around to meet women," Mike said to Joe.

"Well, that part is true!" Jay added, and both men laughed out loud. They went on to explain that they got together every summer for a few days of fishing, and this year they'd chosen the Big Horn River for the site of their rendezvous. The young men clearly enjoyed their friendship. In fact, Joe couldn't help but think of Donny, and how much he enjoyed Donny's company, when he listened to Mike and Jay joking with each other.

"So is this your first day on the river?" Joe asked.

"Third day. Last day!" Jay replied. "We're going home tomorrow." His expression began to darken as he spoke. "We've only caught one fish in two days. Hell, Mike is still '0 for the Big Horn'—he's still skunked! We were told what a great trout stream this is, but we haven't done shit! That's why we hired you!"

"Really?" Joe asked.

"Really!" Jay replied.

Joe immediately turned the boat toward the riverbank and began to pull on the oars. He dropped the anchor when the bottom of the boat began to scrape the small rocks along shore.

"Two days...and one fish?" Joe asked when the boat was at rest.

"Yep," Jay replied.

The pressure began to settle on Joe like a heavy weight. Now what? These guys had fished this river twice as long as he had and been skunked. And he was their guide? Now they were looking to him to solve their problems and salvage their fishing trip. He knew they looked forward to their time together for almost a year, and the success of their vacation now hung in the balance. If they didn't catch any fish today, their Big Horn vacation would be a memorable bust, and he'd be a failure.

"OK," Joe started slowly, "how were you fishing? What were you doing?" he asked.

"We used dry flies. Neither of us likes to use those damn bobbers!" Mike answered.

"Strike indicators, not bobbers," Joe smiled as he corrected Mike. He knew some fly fishermen preferred to fish only with dry flies, on the surface, and felt disdain for any fish that wouldn't rise to take a dry fly.

"Actually, we don't know what we're doing. We used dry flies because it's easier, and we thought that eventually we'd start catching fish. But it never happened," Jay confessed.

"Well, OK. Let's do this," Joe started. "Mike, you rig up with a strike indicator about six inches from the end of your fly line. Use a nine-foot tapered leader and put two small pieces of lead at the end of the leader. Tie on about three feet of tippet, then tie on a fly that looks like this. No! Use this one. It's called a San Juan Worm. It's supposed to look like an aquatic earthworm. You're just gonna bounce it along the bottom where all the trout are lined up, waiting for lunch to pass by in front of them. Trout think this looks like a pork chop!" Joe said, and he held up the San Juan Worm.

Joe reached over, took the end of Mike's fly line, and began rigging the line for him. When he'd finished, he handed the rod back to Mike and turned to Jay. "All right, Jay, you're gonna rig up the same way as Mike, except you're gonna use a scud, or a freshwater shrimp, instead of a San Juan Worm. This river is filled with freshwater shrimp and other aquatic invertebrates. For now, you guys are just gonna put something in front of the fish on the bottom. Then, later on today when we start to see some mayflies hatching, then we'll fish dry flies. OK?" He nodded at both Jay and Mike, then took the end of Jay's line and prepared it just as he'd described.

When he passed Jay's rod to him, Joe asked if he was ready. Jay nodded and said "yes." But it was clear to Joe that neither of the fishermen in his boat had any confidence in what they were doing.

"OK, Mike. You flip your line out there on the left side, since you're in the front of the boat. Jay, the guy in the back fishes on the other side. That should cut down on tangled lines. You OK with that?" Joe asked as he worked the oars to position the boat properly.

Joe knew that giving simple instructions and speaking with enthusiasm was all he could do. Although it was now clear that he was a far more knowledgeable angler than Jay or Mike, he still wasn't sure if what he'd just done would actually work. After all, he had almost no experience on this river. It did seem to make good sense, though, and it was just what Marsh had done the day before. Still, Joe had never been in this position, and he didn't really know what to expect either.

———————

The boat drifted in silence for a few minutes. A quiet, calm stretch of flat water lay in front of them like a deserted highway. Joe worked the boat oars efficiently, without disturbing the water's surface. He watched the strike indicator on Mike's line while the boat was carried inexorably along by the current.

The reflection of a small, puffy white cloud shimmered and changed shape on the river's mercurial surface. The blue of the sky, the white and silver of the little cloud, and the green of the cottonwoods along the shore all quivered and blended on the river's glassy surface. A dreamy image of woods and water left Joe staring into the river.

"Ooo!" Joe groaned when he noticed Mike's strike indicator twitch and then dart under the surface. "You just missed one, Mike. Anytime you see that strike indicator move, you gotta raise the rod tip and set the hook." Joe's words had the effect of an alarm clock on the two men. Both of them had been lulled into daydreams by the silent river, and they'd become inattentive. They shuffled their feet along the boat's floor and straightened in their seats.

Joe's words were hardly out of his mouth when Mike's strike indicator darted once more. Mike raised his fishing rod into the air, then felt a weight at the other end bend the rod in half. The surprise and excitement that mingled on Mike's face reminded Joe Mix of the look on his own sons' faces not so many years ago when he'd shown them how to fish.

"Nice one!" Joe said with a smile. Mike was clearly surprised at his good fortune, but he was trying desperately to appear calm, as though this was no big deal. Joe understood, however, that the ecstatic smile of an eight-year-old was straining to burst across the face of a grown man.

The battle between Mike and his first Big Horn trout lasted only a minute, and Joe found it hard to look away from Mike's face as the struggle unfolded. The fish made several runs in the current. Then Mike reeled in the slack line when the trout grew tired. Mike never spoke, and his eyes only left the spot where his fly line entered the water once: to be sure his friend Jay, in the back of the boat, was watching him catch a fish.

When Joe finally slid a landing net underneath a thick, brown trout and raised it from the water, he turned a glance toward Mike and watched the joyful smile of a small boy spread across Mike's face. In the instant he saw the joy in Mike's eyes, Joe understood something that clarified much of his own struggle over the past few months—maybe his lifetime struggle: Mike was just a little boy who'd caught a fish, and that was all he wanted to be for now.

Mike was looking at his fish and talking, but he'd reached far into his childhood to recall a memory. "My cousin Geno..." He stopped himself. "Geno and I used to catch trout in a little stream behind my grampa's farm. We dug worms in the garden and put the worms in a can, then sat by a little stream and caught trout." The same smile still covered his face.

"Well, then, hold this big boy up and I'll take a picture for you to send Geno!" Joe said as he handed the fish to Mike and took Mike's camera from the backpack he'd stored under his seat.

"Nice fish. Nice fish!" Jay said when the picture taking was finished and the trout had been released. Jay was happy for his buddy, but he was anxious to return to fishing and see what the river held for him.

The plan, in Joe's mind, had been to pull over at the top of a riffle just ahead, then walk the bank for a while and carefully fish several holes Marsh had shown him the previous day. But in the time he'd been anchored in the current and taking photographs, another boat had passed him and was now sitting where he'd intended to stop.

Joe was disappointed initially that one of the few places he was certain he wanted to fish was taken. As his boat approached the riffle up ahead, Jay caught and released two smaller trout. Then Mike hooked another nice trout while they were drifting through the gurgling water in the middle of the riffle. The Big Horn seemed to hold fish everywhere, so Joe decided to pull over in the slack water at the tail of the riffle and fish from shore for a while. He couldn't remember if Marsh had said to stop here or not, but it looked like a spot that should hold some fish.

All through his life, Joe had learned over and over again to fish the changes—the spots where fast current sped by slow, protected areas, or where the bottom dropped off and shallow water plunged into a deep hole. That was where the fish would stack up and wait for lunch to float by. Trout learned to face upstream and rest behind rocks or stumps or drop offs, then wait for the river to carry things to them so they didn't have to fight the strong current while they waited. They liked to dart into the faster current and gobble whatever came along, then quickly return to calmer waters to wait for another meal.

Joe positioned Mike along the seam where the faster, deeper water in the middle of the riffle moved past the slower, calm water along the riverbank. Mike was standing in about two feet of water, and Joe stood right next to him as he explained that the trick was to flip about thirty feet of fly line, along with the fly, lead weight, and monofilament leader, into the current upstream from him. Then all he had to do was watch for movement in his strike indicator as the current carried everything downstream toward him. If he hadn't caught a fish when the fly line and fly had moved past him and were directly downstream, he simply had to flip the fly line back upstream once again to let it pass by the fish in the riffle again. Joe assured Mike that there were plenty of fish just a few feet from him and told him to keep casting. Then he positioned Jay along the same seam in the current about forty yards downstream and gave him the same instructions.

While Joe was standing next to Jay, Mike caught and landed two more fish. "Maybe I should move up there, closer to Mike," Jay suggested as he flipped his line upstream and stepped one step closer to his friend.

"I'm pretty sure there's fish right..." Before he could finish his sentence, Jay's strike indicator jerked out toward the current, and the second after Jay set the hook, a thick, brown trout erupted from the river only a few feet from them and tried to spit Jay's hook.

The size of the fish surprised Jay at first. He began to fumble with his reel as he attempted to reel it in.

"All right, Jay. That's a nice fish, and I'll bet he's gonna run downstream to use the current against you. Let's just back up toward shore and see if you can lead him out of this heavy current so he can't use the power of the river against you."

Jay and Joe both walked slowly through the shallow water as they eased themselves and the big trout into calmer, slower water. By the time Jay was ready to have Joe net the trout and take a photograph, Mike had joined them.

"Joe? My fish was bigger than Jay's, wasn't it?" Mike asked. Then he nodded in agreement with himself as Jay's trout swam back into the current after he'd released it.

"Oh, shit. That little thing you caught? That was..."

"There's cold beer and a couple sandwiches for you in the boat," Joe interrupted. "Let's have lunch while we discuss it. Then we'll cover some new water."

While they sat in the boat resting on a gravel bar and eating lunch, Joe took several flies from his fly box and attached them to the fleece hat band he'd put on his Stetson. Then he retied all the leaders on Mike's and Jay's lines so that their gear would be in good order for their last afternoon on the river.

During the time they sat there on the gravel bar and talked, several boats drifted past them, and Joe noticed that many of the boats had the logo of "Big Horn Adventures" or one of the other fly shops painted on the bow. As more and more boats from the various fly shops passed, Joe began to notice that most of the guides piloting them were staring at him. Some of the guides waved at him as though he was one of them— perhaps part of a fraternity of river guides. He waved back at them.

Several times he tipped his cowboy hat. Life was funny, he thought. Maybe it's always kind of like Halloween. Here I am, just dressed up like a river guide, and I've fooled my clients and the other guides. Joe smiled as he listened to Mike and Jay discuss their successes on the riffle behind them. Then he turned and waved at another passing boat.

———

"Joe! Hey, Joe! Wait a minute," Marsh called from the doorway of the fly shop as Joe opened the driver's door of his truck.

Joe turned to face Marsh after he'd let Jake jump up onto the truck seat. He stood beside his truck and waited for Marsh to approach him.

"You must have had a pretty good first day! Those two guys just booked four days out here next summer, and they requested you to guide them every day. Must have been a good day, huh?" Marsh repeated.

"Yeah, I thought it was a great day. Those two caught fish all day long, and we had a lot of laughs. Every place you marked on the map held fish, too. You made it pretty easy. I found a few other places too!"

"They said you got 'em onto some dry fly action, too?" Marsh asked.

"Yeah," Joe said as he reached into his pocket to find his truck keys. "Right there along those Russian Olive trees along the bank, by that cow pasture. You pointed to it yesterday. There were a few trout rising when we got there, so we rigged up with a small Baetis pattern and caught a few fish. Nothing of any size, but it's a pretty piece of water. Those guys had fun."

"They sure did," Marsh nodded, then turned to go back inside the shop. "See you tomorrow morning. I have another good day lined up for you. Be here at the usual time," he called over his shoulder.

Joe swung the door to his truck open and then stopped himself. He called out, "Hey, Marsh?" When Marsh turned back to look, Joe walked close to him and said softly, "Hey—Molly seemed angry with me just now when I came to get Jake. She was fine this morning, and then...I don't know. Did I do something I shouldn't have? Was she OK with taking care of Jake today?"

"No." Marsh shook his head and sighed. "That's just Molly. Every now and then her mood turns a little dark. I know her about as well as anyone around here does, and I see her get like that from time to time. Don't worry about it," Marsh shrugged. "Hell, she's a woman! You figure her out. She had fun with Jake. Don't worry about it. See you tomorrow, Joe," Marsh said, and then he was walking back to the shop.

Late-afternoon sunshine poured through the windows on the west side of the trailer and lit the small kitchen/living room with a yellow glow when Joe stepped inside. The place smelled like the open bag of dog food Joe had left on the kitchen table, and Jake nosed around every corner of the room before he started begging for supper. After Joe fed Jake, he sorted through the various canned goods that he'd transferred from his cooler to the cupboard. He opened a can of chili beans and ate a few spoonfuls from the can, then poured some taco sauce into the can and mixed it around before he ate the rest of the beans. When he was finished with the beans, he opened the refrigerator and drank directly from the plastic milk bottle until the milk was gone.

He tossed the milk bottle into the same trash container where he'd thrown the empty can. Then he turned to Jake and said, "I'll do the dishes!" He licked the spoon that he'd used to eat the beans and flipped it onto the kitchen countertop. "OK, that's all done. Let's go outside and make a fire in the backyard, Jake."

The colors of the Montana prairie were softening in the yellow twilight as a little campfire began to dance and crackle inside the circle of stones under the cottonwoods.

Joe settled into the rickety lawn chair. He stirred the fire and poked at it with the weathered handle of the old broom whose business end had been lost long ago.

Joe liked this place. He liked the trailer, the river, his job, even this little fire pit behind his trailer. Tonight this place was just quiet, not so lonely. Little sparks floated up into the cool evening air when he jabbed at the fire, and the cottonwood leaves above him rustled in a gentle breeze. This probably wasn't the place he'd always dreamed of, but it was pretty good. It seemed like it could be his home. The Crossman Ranch had been all right too, but here he had his own place where he could, well, just sit by a fire and scratch his dog. He might be able to be happy here. For the first time in a long time, he wasn't planning to press on— to get to something else. He wasn't counting down the days until he could be finished with the job at hand. He was just happy to sit here and poke at the fire and think about how he was going to enjoy the next day.

Jake wandered over to Joe's chair again and begged for more attention. He nudged Joe's arm and then rested his muzzle on Joe's leg while he begged for his ears to be scratched. "I guess the dentist is dead, huh, Jake?" he sighed. "Now what?"

Joe tossed two more pieces of firewood onto the fire and leaned back in his chair again. He looked into the fire as if there was a message for him somewhere deep in the coals and flickering tongues of flame. Maybe, just maybe, his whole life was an ember about to billow.

———•———

Fishermen, clients from Big Horn Adventures, began to fall into several categories for Joe as the next two weeks rolled by. Most of them were just men who were taking a break from their lives for a few days of fishing with old or new friends. They showed up at Fort Smith with smiles on their faces and some money in their pockets, looking for a good time. Most of them were pretty good fishermen, too. Guiding them was easy, even for an inexperienced guide like Joe. He just helped them with specific tackle requirements and then showed them where the fish were. He tried to stay out of their private conversations, and from time to time his clients would talk to each other as if Joe was either deaf or just not there. Sometimes he was included in the conversation, but he always made a point to ask his clients about themselves and never offer his opinion or talk about his own life. Just as it was back in the dental office, he didn't suppose people were hiring him to talk about himself. He began to develop casual friendships with many of his clients, and he was always surprised when, at the end of a long day, they'd open their wallets and tip him generously, with a smile, for being part of a pleasant experience. That certainly never happened in his old life.

Just when Joe thought he knew what to expect from clients, two unique women walked through the front door of the fly shop. Two Catholic nuns, who'd never been fishing before, drove six hundred miles from their church in Nebraska and hired Joe Mix to take them fly fishing for a day. They'd read about it and they'd seen the movie *A River Runs Through It*, so they'd decided to give it a try. They'd just decided to expand their horizons a little bit and spend a day on a trout stream. Initially, Joe had been overwhelmed by the challenge of finding fish they could catch. But he found out soon enough that novices—people with no bad habits to unlearn—were easy to teach. The two forty-year-old women listened carefully to Joe's five-minute explanation of how the whole process worked, and they both caught fish before their boat had rounded the first bend in the river. In many ways, it was Joe's best day in months. He was able to talk a little religion, some philosophy, and the nuns asked countless questions about the birds, insects, and the river, which Joe was only too happy to talk about. Joe, in turn, asked the women questions about the nature of salvation, the role of women in the church, and the book of Revelation. By the end of the day, all of them wished they had another day to spend together.

When Joe drove up to the front of the fly shop that day, hours after he should have returned, he and the nuns were still talking and laughing. As he unhooked the boat from the hitch on the back of his truck, Joe noticed that the nuns were searching through their wallets, collecting money for his tip.

"Hey, girls," Joe said quietly after he'd pushed the boat back in line with the other Big Horn Adventure boats. "Let's do this a little differently today." With that, he opened his wallet and handed them $200, his tip from the previous day's client. The nuns protested for a moment until Joe interrupted them. "Listen, here's the deal," he said as he pushed the brim of his cowboy hat up with his index finger. "I know this is backwards, but I'd like to thank you two for a great day! When you go home tomorrow, you're gonna need money. But me? I'm a rich man." He looked over his shoulder across Fort Smith Trailer Park. "No, I've got money. What I don't have is friends like you." Both the nuns stared at him, trying to think of something to say. They still looked uncomfortable with this financial arrangement. "It's OK," Joe added. "I'm a rich man! You keep the money." He raised his eyebrows and grinned. "Hell, use it to come back and fish with me next year!" Then he gave them each a hug and got back into his truck. As he drove off, he waved and called out, "Bye, girls! Thanks for a great day!"

Joe continued to enjoy his other clients as the days marched along, and he made more friends, although none were as special as the two nuns. As he became comfortable with his new job, home, and surroundings, he grew confident in his new life. Clients often took Joe's mailing address so they could send photographs and stay in touch with him. Many of them made a point to tell Marsh about the pleasant days Joe had provided for them on the river.

Every day when Joe was finished on the river, he returned his boat to the gravel parking lot in front of the Big Horn Adventures fly shop. He'd chat with his clients for a few minutes, and quite often Marsh would join them for a short visit. Marsh would always make it a point to ask about the fishing and the quality of his client's experience on the river. As Joe got to know Marsh a little better every day, he began to notice something unique about Marsh Clements—something he could never have seen at first.

Marsh took his business very seriously, but he seemed to understand that there was so much of life out there that actually had little to do with his work. All that other stuff in life seemed to rest in balance with Marsh Clements' work, not compete with it. Marsh was content with his job and the place where he'd come to rest—the place where his life would be lived out. Joe hadn't seen that quality in very many men, and he'd certainly never felt it himself. As Joe listened to Marsh and watched him work through each day's challenges, he knew he'd found another man who was searching for whatever meaning there was to be found in life. He also saw that Marsh Clements was a man who was guided by his own set of rules for his life and not the expectations of others.

"Fuckin' rat bastard," Marsh mumbled one morning, then slammed the envelope down on the countertop beside the cash register. Joe's client for the day had failed to show up, so Marsh had put him to work cleaning boats in the parking lot. He looked up from his work when he heard Marsh's rumbling. Molly looked up from her paperwork too. She thought the anger in Marsh's voice was pretty funny, and she was smiling when she turned to look at him.

"What is it, Marsh?" she asked.

Marsh had been opening the day's mail, and he held up an envelope for Molly to see. "Remember that rotten SOB from New York that came out and stayed last month?" he asked Molly.

"Yes."

"Well, the miserable little prick sent me a bad check—for the second time," Marsh said. "He's trying to stiff me for $238!"

Joe wandered in from the parking lot to listen to the discussion. He stood in the doorway and watched Marsh get angrier by the second.

"Forget it, Marsh. Just let it go. It'll cost you more to collect it than it's worth," Molly said.

But while she spoke, Marsh began dialing the phone next to the cash register. He had an entirely different plan. He called the man at his work place and waited politely several times while he was put on hold and his call was transferred around a large office building. "Hello!" Marsh said when the former client answered the telephone. Joe stepped into the fly shop and smiled at Molly, who'd moved closer to the cash register too.

"This is Marsh Clements calling from Big Horn Adventures in Montana. I want you to know that you have four days to make your check good. I mean, I want $238, in cash, by Friday. Saturday will be too late, because I'll be on my way to New York. And when I get there, I'm gonna find you—I don't care how much it costs—and I'm gonna take $238 outta your ass. You understand? Have the cash here by Friday or I'm comin'. I don't care what it costs me once I leave this place, you're gonna pay!"

Molly and Joe exchanged glances for a moment. Then they both looked at Marsh, who was back at work opening mail. "Are you really gonna do it, Marsh, if he doesn't pay?" Molly asked.

"Damn right!" Marsh said without looking up. "That's the only bad check I've ever gotten. I'm not gonna take that shit from some New York asshole!"

The cash arrived in Friday's mail, and Marsh seemed disappointed.

Several days later, Joe saw Marsh do something equally unexpected. The bad-check incident was still very fresh in Joe's mind when he eased his boat and clients up the Big Horn boat access, thirteen miles from the Afterbay, about five o'clock one afternoon. He found Marsh sitting there waiting with his knees tucked under his chin. "You OK, Marsh?" Joe asked while he loaded his boat onto its trailer and prepared to take his clients back to the fly shop.

"Sure," Marsh replied.

"What are you doing?" Joe asked.

"Waiting for some clients," Marsh said.

"Well...why? Why are you just sitting there waiting?"

"They asked if I'd meet 'em here at two o'clock so they could come in a little early."

"They're pretty late," Joe pointed out, although he didn't need to. He expected Marsh to be furious.

"Yeah," Marsh agreed.

"Aren't you getting angry? They've made you wait for three hours...so far," Joe said.

"Nah. They're probably just having a good day—you know, catchin' some fish—and they probably just lost track of time. Hell, they're out here to have a good time. What point would it serve for me to get my undies in a bunch over a little wait?"

"Don't you have other things to do?" Joe asked.

"Yeah, but that stuff will still be there when I get back."

The overdue clients eased up to the landing just as Joe was leaving with his own clients, and Marsh treated them like old friends arriving home from a vacation. Joe had expected him to be furious.

Marsh's response to each of the situations was quite a bit different than Joe's response would have been, but Joe admired Marsh's behavior—both times—and he smiled whenever he thought of either incident.

Marsh Clements wielded an eccentric personality, and he sometimes used his eccentricities to hold others at arm's length. An odd paradox existed in Marsh Clements. Marsh's quick wit and self-deprecating sense of humor drew others to him; everyone seemed to like Marsh. He was always quick with a laugh and a clever comment. But Joe had noticed shortly after he'd arrived that every now and then, Marsh used laughter to punctuate conversations. He let people know in a painless, nonverbal way that some barrier had been reached and they could go no further—the conversation was over. When he wanted to be done talking to someone, he'd simply laugh out loud at something they'd said, then turn quickly and walk away.

Marsh seemed to have a different, closer relationship with several of the locals who were not connected to Big Horn Adventures in any way. He'd seen Marsh standing close to two older women who owned a small restaurant and the tiny woman who worked at the post office, speaking softly to them with no laughter. Marsh valued his friendships with those people who had nothing to do with Big Horn Adventures. Joe had noticed that Marsh's conversations with them never ended in bursts of laughter; only gentle goodbyes. Molly Malone seemed to be one of the few people who had clearance to talk to Marsh in that subdued tone. Joe had seen Marsh and Molly talking several times, their heads nearly touching as they stood by the cash register in the fly shop.

What about Molly? Joe wondered as he got to know her better. She seemed to enjoy spending her days taking care of Jake. Sometimes she was warm and friendly when she spoke to Joe. He liked it when she put her mouth close to his ear and whispered to him in the morning before work. She smelled so good, and she was so pretty. Her auburn hair tickled his cheek when she whispered to him. Even her hands were prettier than other women's, and she fit so nicely into her blue jeans and cotton blouse. But then she could be so distant, almost rude, sometimes when Joe returned to pick up Jake. She never, ever laughed out loud around the shop or when she talked with customers, or anyone else for that matter. Even when she did smile and let those eyes soften a little bit, she retained some distance between herself and whoever she was talking with. Her eyes seemed to invite others closer. But then, if they got too close, her eyes could move people back, too. It made no sense. But there was enough to worry about here besides Molly's moods. He'd just remain cordial, thank her for taking such good care of his puppy, and let Molly be Molly.

chapter thirty-two

It had to happen sooner or later. Joe had seen enough of them around, but he'd just never been assigned to guide two of them. Molly pursed her lips, raised her eyebrows, and smiled an apologetic smile as Joe strode into the fly shop early one morning with Jake trotting along behind.

Joe's face curled into a question, and he walked directly to Molly. When he reached her, he leaned forward and put his face in front of hers, demanding an explanation for the apprehensive look on her face.

"You're gonna have a long day!" she whispered. "Those two guys over there are your clients today." Then she nodded in the direction of the table where Marsh displayed all the trout flies.

Two men, each of them about forty years old, stood beside the table. One of the men was using his index finger to poke through the flies in each of the small boxes on the table, sneering. From time to time, he'd say something about the poor quality of the feathers that had been used to tie the flies, or he'd moan that the color of the fly or the size of the hook was all wrong. His abrasive tone was stabbing through the quiet shop. He was speaking to his partner, but he clearly intended for the other fishermen in the room to notice what he had to say. He was broadcasting his expertise for everyone to hear.

Several other fishermen were milling around the shop, sipping at Styrofoam coffee cups and getting their own gear ready for a day on the river. Joe noticed the other men glance at the blowhard by the fly table, then smile at each other from time to time. They knew they were the target audience for this self-proclaimed expert. Joe noticed one of the other fishermen raise his eyes when the man said something about the poor selection of flies. Then the man looked at Molly, grinned, and shook his head just to let her know that the other fishermen in the room thought the guy was obnoxious too.

"Who are those two guys?" Joe said softly. He enjoyed the act of putting his face so close to Molly's ear that he could feel her hair brushing his lips.

"Just fishermen. From the East somewhere, I think. But they're the kind who know everything, or think they do. Real condescending! They think everyone out here is stupid." She paused, then smiled a wicked smile at Joe. "Marsh hates guys like that! I mean, he really hates 'em! They criticize everything. Marsh says they always travel in pairs. One is the main prick, and he'll always have a lackey boy with him. He'll be a prick too, but his purpose is to be a one-man entourage." Molly shook her head, still smiling. "Those two are a couple dandies. Wait till Marsh meets 'em."

"Marsh hasn't met them yet?" Joe asked.

"No, but we see dozens just like them. These guys just flew in from out east. They spent a few days over in Yellowstone first, then called and arranged to hire a guide just the other day. They've never been here before," Molly replied just as Marsh stepped into the shop.

Marsh was smiling and shuffling, sipping at a coffee cup like everyone else in the shop, when he stepped though the front door. He made eye contact with Molly, and Molly immediately pointed to the two men by the fly table. The look on her face told Marsh everything: those two guys were the new clients, and Marsh could have them.

With an abrupt turn, Marsh veered directly to the table to introduce himself to the men. Marsh continued to smile and nod while the bigger of the two criticized the fly selection. "Pretty sparse selection of midges, and there's too much hackle on those dry flies. Who tied those for you?"

The smaller man never looked up from the table when Marsh introduced himself. He was still sorting through the fly assortment in front of him while his partner continued. "Oh, that's how YOU tie your Caddis flies," the man said with disdain oozing from him. Marsh stood there with his hand extended while the bigger man refused to face him and shake hands for a moment. He seemed to enjoy making Marsh wait to shake his hand. When he finally turned and shook Marsh's hand, he neglected a simple greeting like "good morning" and immediately started to tell Marsh about all the successful fishing they'd had over in Yellowstone Park, and how high their expectations were for today's float down the Big Horn.

Just as Joe expected, when the man paused briefly, Marsh interrupted him with a burst of laughter. While he was still laughing, he added, "Well, you're in luck today! You have the best guide on the river. That's Joe Mix right there. Take 'em fishing, Joe!" With that, Marsh walked quickly from the shop. When he'd turned his back on the men, he looked at Joe, grimaced, and walked out the door.

Molly smiled openly at Marsh's departure. Joe simply introduced himself and led the two fishermen from the East out the door and into his truck. Both Molly and Joe had recognized the contempt in Marsh's actions, and they each thought the whole scene had been predictable. Marsh had actually been rude to the fisherman, but he'd done it in such an artful way that the man clearly thought Marsh found him to be clever and insightful.

"He's kind of an odd guy...your boss," the man said to Joe as they sat shoulder to shoulder in Joe's truck and began the short drive to the boat landing. Then the man smiled for the first time.

"That's a fact," Joe agreed, through a smile that exposed the huge dimple on his right cheek. "So where are you guys from?" Joe asked while they eased the old Ford onto the road.

Marsh re-entered the shop seconds after Joe and his clients had rolled out of the parking lot. He blew on his coffee and watched Joe's truck accelerate toward the boat landing by the Afterbay Dam. Then he leaned toward Molly and said, "Those two steely-eyed gunslingers are gonna eat him up!"

———•———

Molly and Marsh were both standing by the cash register in the shop late in the afternoon when they heard the sound of gravel crunching in the parking lot. They both raised their eyes just in time to see Joe's old Ford roll to a stop in front of the shop. Then they both crept forward with anticipation. They knew Joe would be angry and frustrated after a day on the river with two difficult clients.

Marsh peered out the picture window, staring over the top of his small, bifocal glasses. He watched Joe spring from the truck and unhitch the boat while the two clients gathered their gear after a day on the river. "Steely-eyed gunslingers! I hate those kind of guys!" Marsh mumbled to Molly. "Assholes like that breeze in here like this is some important duel between them and the trout, or between them and other fishermen. I've never understood it. Arrogant pricks!" he groaned.

Molly smiled and turned to look at Marsh. As she did, his face changed completely. The anger and contempt of a moment earlier suddenly morphed into a smile. He'd switched on his happy face. He stepped out from the back of the cash register and got ready to greet his clients at the end of their day. Suddenly, his face was awash with false joy as he prepared to put the proper, happy spin on his clients' day.

Molly had seen this many times before, and Marsh had even spoken about it earlier in the day. Marsh knew that one of his guides was about to come dragging back to the shop after a rough day, and he'd need to smooth things over with either guide or clients or both. "Those two steely-eyed gunslingers are gonna eat him up today!" Marsh had said several times that afternoon while he'd waited for Joe to return.

But the sound of laughter drifted from the parking lot into the shop, and Marsh stopped in his tracks. Molly's eyes moved from Marsh to the scene unfolding in the parking lot. Joe was laughing and shaking hands with the smaller of the men, then the bigger one. Both of the fishermen laughed out loud at something Joe said. Then each of them opened up his wallet and handed Joe a wad of cash. They turned and walked the short distance to their room in the small Big Horn Adventures Motel, which was connected to the fly shop.

Marsh and Molly watched in stunned silence as Joe walked into the shop and whistled for Jake. He looked at them blankly for a moment, and tried to pretend he didn't see the surprise in their eyes, while he stuffed a handful of cash into his wallet..

"What?" he asked finally, demanding that they ask the question he knew was on their minds.

"How did you manage to get along with those two pricks all day?" Marsh blurted.

The dimple in Joe's cheek reappeared in an instant. "I've been kissing asses all day. Hell, my lips are chapped from it!" Joe said gleefully. "The big guy? What an asswipe! He's an ophthalmologist. His favorite subject in the world is himself. He spent the first part of the day explaining what a knowledgeable and skilled fisherman he is. Then, the rest of the day was devoted to explaining how much he knew about everything else. Jeez, it got to be a challenge for me...trying to find something he didn't know all about. Actually, I never did find anything that he wasn't an expert on!" Joe turned his eyes toward Molly and continued. "And the little guy? He was the big guy's junior partner. Whenever the little guy spoke, the big guy's face went blank—you know, like a computer screen when a search engine can't find what it's looking for. Honestly, the big guy seemed to think that the only reason for the little guy to speak was just to give him time to think of some new, profound shit to say. I just kept asking him what he thought or what he knew about all kinds of things. And he kept on telling me!"

"He actually seemed to like you! Steely-eyed gunslingers don't ever like anyone!" Marsh said. He looked bewildered. This time, there was no laughter with Marsh's words. He spoke with admiration. There was awe in his voice, as if Joe had crossed some barrier or accomplished an impossible task, and Marsh hadn't quite been prepared to witness it.

"Well, he should like me. I spent a whole day with my nose up his ass. My only goal for the day was to make him feel good about being here. I learned to do shit like that a long time ago, in my old life. Didn't hurt that he caught a lot of fish either! By the way, he actually is a pretty good fisherman. The little guy is too!" Joe added. Then he turned to leave. "C'mon, Jake, let's go home and eat."

"Wait a minute!" Marsh blurted.

"Yeah?" Joe turned to face him, still smiling.

"You play golf?" Marsh asked, very slowly, and his eyebrows tightened as if he were inspecting Joe for microscopic defects.

"Well, yes," Joe shrugged. "So what?"

"C'mon out for dinner at my place, and we'll play a quick round while you tell me about your day with those assholes," Marsh nodded.

"A round of golf at your place? What are you talking about? You have a putt-putt in your backyard or what?" Joe asked, still very confused.

"Hell, no! We'll be playing..." Marsh started to explain.

"Just go!" Molly interrupted. "He'll make you crazy if he tries to explain. Just go." Now Molly was nodding. "You two might have fun together. Just go."

"OK. Sounds all right." Joe raised his eyebrows and shrugged again. "How about Jake? Can he come too?"

"Sure. I have a great place for him to play. See you in one hour," Marsh said as he turned and walked away. "My driveway is the one with the mailbox that looks like a golf cart!" he called over his shoulder.

"I know!" Joe answered to Marsh's back. He squinted, turned a silly look toward Molly, and added, "My day is getting weird."

"It's gonna get a lot weirder," Molly replied.

———•———

The summer sun was still high in the sky when Joe's truck crept along a narrow road that wound through a large stand of cottonwood trees. The lane from the highway to Marsh's cabin was nearly a half-mile long, and Joe began to wonder if he was lost when the one-lane road suddenly opened into a small clearing next to Marsh's home. The clearing was only about one hundred feet in diameter, but the Big Horn River bordered it on one side, and the open expanse over the channel made the small clearing seem much bigger.

Marsh's cabin was well designed and seemed to be part of the forest, not an addition to it. The siding had been stained a dark brown, and cedar shakes covered the roof. An older Ford tractor with a loading bucket sat off on one side of the clearing, and Marsh's Chevy truck was parked in front of his garage, invisible from the river.

The smell of charcoal briquettes burning in a kettle grill was the first thing Joe noticed when he stepped from his truck. Jake darted around the clearing in search of all the new smells he could find when Joe rounded the side of Marsh's cabin and stepped onto the front yard.

"Hi, Joe," Marsh called, then raised his right hand to wave. "Welcome! You too, Jake." Jake scrambled into the tall grass and brush along the riverbank, already in pursuit of something. "There's a ton of field mice and other critters down here along the river. Jake will have some fun." Marsh was waiting seated on a bench—a common wooden bench like the kind found in any locker room. The bench had been painted bright red, and it sat on the edge of a small patch of unusually lush green grass.

Every other patch of grass in the Big Horn Valley seemed to be burned brown by the summer sun. But this small area in Marsh's front yard was covered in rich, full, green grass. Joe waved back at Marsh, then stood and stared at the green lawn in front of him until he realized just what he was looking at: Marsh had transformed this little area of about twenty feet by thirty feet into a tee box that any golf course in the country would have been proud to claim.

A section of the Russian Olive trees that lined the Big Horn River in front of Marsh's cabin had been removed, revealing the river and a large cow pasture on the opposite bank. The pasture was the one Joe had noticed the first time he'd floated by Marsh's place. Joe assumed that Marsh had hauled in several tons of black dirt to grow the plants he'd chosen to surround the tee box. A purple Clematis clung to a lattice on one side of the tee box. Several rows of flowers grew along the other border. The grass was a sturdy, bent grass that had been cut short.

Then Joe began to notice the signs around the edge of the tee box. A dozen or so handcarved, cedar signs had been mounted around the periphery of the small yard. Each of the signs bore the name of one of the great golf courses in the world: Winged Foot, Turnberry, Spyglass Hill, Baltusrol, St. Andrews, Pebble Beach, Shinnecock Hills.

Marsh Clements was a golf nut, or so it seemed. The place was designed to invoke a sense of tradition—to display a passion for and love of the game. But this tee box just sat there all alone, perched atop a water hazard, and the whole rest of the world was in play just beyond. There was nothing here but one tee box—no fairways, no greens, no sand traps.

"Wow, Marsh. What is this place?" Joe asked with a smile.

"Pretty nice, huh?" Marsh replied. "The clubhouse is right there behind you." He pointed to his cabin. "I built it myself." Then he looked about him. "It's where I play golf. Where would you like it to be?"

"Huh? I don't understand."

"Let me show you how it works here. We'll go up to the clubhouse and eat after the eighteenth hole. I'll just grab a scorecard and we'll get started," Marsh said as he opened the lid on a small cedar box and withdrew a piece of paper that looked like a scorecard. He looked at the paper for a brief second, then smiled. "Good! This is good! We'll play the dream course first." Then he turned quickly and asked Joe, "Did you bring any clubs?"

"No, Marsh. Sorry. I left home in kind of a hurry and I have no..."

"That's fine," Marsh interrupted. "You can use mine."

Marsh stood up, raised his golf bag, and spent a moment searching for the right club. He was wearing blue jeans, a baseball cap, and his moccasin-toed loafers. Joe thought Marsh looked out of place on this immaculate tee box, but that made him feel better about his own inappropriate golf clothing: he was wearing cowboy boots and his Stetson.

Marsh withdrew his driver—a solid black persimmon driver with a Ben Hogan signature on it. He reached into his pocket and produced a white golf tee before he stepped over to a plastic, ten-gallon pail that was filled with about four hundred golf balls. He removed a ball, then stepped to the middle of the tee box and motioned for Joe to have a seat on the red bench. "Quiet in the gallery, please," he said.

"OK, Joe. We're playing the dream course—all the greatest golf holes from all the great golf courses. You're lucky to get to play this course your first time here." Marsh nodded. "Out there…"—Marsh pointed across the Big Horn River—"…out by that big cottonwood in the middle of Mr. Carrigan's pasture? That's the first green at Royal St. George's. It's a 415-yard par-four with no room on the right, so be careful." Marsh bent over, teed up his ball, and then addressed it. He stood over the ball briefly, then withdrew his driver in an unsteady, stiff, hurried backswing that he followed with one of the most unsightly golf swings Joe had ever seen. The ball traveled only about thirty yards before it splashed into the river. "Shit!" Marsh said softly, but with some feeling. "Mulligans on the first hole. I don't care if we're playing St. George's, either!" he added. Then he teed up another and struck it with the same awkward swing. The second ball carried the river, but not by much.

"Helluva shot," Marsh said. "OK, you're up, Joe."

Joe was still confused when Marsh handed him the driver. He found a tee in Marsh's bag and took a ball from the ten-gallon bucket full of balls. Marsh had moved to the red bench and was staring when Joe finally addressed his ball.

"Go ahead," Marsh chided him, and motioned for him to hit the ball.

Joe took a full, easy swing and lofted a high drive to the base of the cottonwood tree far out in the pasture.

"Jesus, what a shot!" Marsh exclaimed. "You've done this before!"

"Some," Joe confessed.

Marsh then stood up and took the driver from Joe's hand. He put the driver back in his bag and produced a four-wood before he took another ball from the large, white bucket and prepared to hit another ball across the river while Joe watched. "OK, we're playin' number two at Medinah: 187-yard par-three, elevated tee, blind approach, water hazard in front, trees and sand all around the green. You'll probably wanna hit a four-iron, I'm guessing."

"Wait a minute!" Joe interrupted. "We didn't finish the last hole."

"Sure we did! You took a double-bogey and I birdied it." Marsh lowered his head and prepared to strike his ball.

"What the fuck are you talking about? You plopped one in the river! Then you barely cleared the damn far side on your mulligan. I knocked mine stiff and rolled it pin high. What the fuck are you talking about?"

"Well, now, just a minute." Marsh put both palms on the top of his four-wood and then leaned toward Joe to emphasize what he was about to say. He spoke calmly, as if he were an elementary school teacher explaining the playground rules on the first day of school. "First of all, a mulligan is a mulligan and it doesn't count. Second, you knocked your drive into the sand trap by the green and took five more to get down: double-bogey." Marsh shrugged and shook his head over Joe's ineptitude. "Third, I made a helluva second shot, then made my putt. Up and down in two: birdie. It's very simple...stupid!" He turned his four-wood around and addressed his ball again.

Joe's eyes began to curl at the corners, and then the dimple began to deepen in the center of his great smile. Now he understood what Molly had been talking about. He began to get a grasp on the game Marsh played—sort of—and he thought maybe he liked it more than the game he'd played with Donny.

Yet again, just before Marsh struck the ball, he stopped himself and leaned on his four-wood. He met Joe's smile with a look of resolve, and he pointed his index finger at Joe. "You see, Joe Mix, you and I have some things in common. We both enjoy the beauty of a difficult thing done well. And you're about to learn something I learned a while back."

"What's that?"

"It don't really mean shit what you do with that first shot," Marsh answered. Then he uncoiled another swing that was so ugly, Joe wondered if Marsh was compensating for some old back injury. His ball skidded down the riverbank and disappeared into the channel. "Shit! Mulligans on the second hole!" Marsh announced as he reached into the white bucket full of balls. Even with his ugly swing, Marsh's second shot sailed gracefully across the river. "Helluva shot. I'm putting for a birdie!" he said as he sat down on the red bench. He sounded so satisfied, Joe thought, as if he were admiring a work of art he'd just created.

"You know, you actually hit the ball pretty well, Joe," Marsh said a short time later. They'd played the third hole at Carnoustie, the fourth at Baltusrol, the fifth at Augusta, the sixth at Melbourne, the seventh at Cajuiles, the eighth at Pine Valley, and the ninth and tenth at Muirfield.

"Compared to you," Joe replied.

"Careful now. Don't rile the guy with the scorecard!" Marsh continued. "We're coming into Amen Corner. You know—the eleventh, twelfth, and thirteenth at Augusta National and…"

"I know, I know…"—Joe joined in the spirit of this round on the dream course—"…where so many players have arrived with a lead and then failed to score well and lost themselves a Green Jacket at the Masters, and all the fame and glory that goes with it," Joe interrupted. The smile he'd been wearing all along as he learned Marsh's game lingered for a moment when he remembered similar chats with Donny.

"So, Marsh, which gives you more pleasure—the thrill of making all these second shots you make, or tallying the low scores?"

Marsh stood up straight and backed away from the ball he'd just teed up. He walked to the edge of the tee box and looked out over the river before he began to speak. "Well, first and foremost, I consider myself a shot maker—a ball striker if you will. I think you can see that." He nodded at Joe but kept a straight face. "Although I do take pride in all the fine scores I make." He nodded again but continued to look out over the river. "In America, we'll always have the people in the media, and the bean counters, the accountants, to tell us who's the most successful— the person who's won the most. But our heroes will always be the ones who may have had flaws, and maybe a little less talent, but they played the game with passion! Like your guy, Natty Bumpo." The humor was gone from his answer, and he let his words carry over the water. "The pleasure? The pleasure comes from swingin' hard and playing out the string. That make any sense to you?"

Joe nodded yes, and Marsh returned to the ball he'd teed up a moment earlier. He stood quietly over the ball for a second, then looked at Joe. "That was pretty good, wasn't it…what I just said?"

Joe nodded yes once again.

"I thought so too," Marsh said as he raised the club into his backswing. He swung through the ball with the same awkward swing as always and knocked it into the river. "Shit!" he groaned. "Mulligans on the eleventh!"

"Good thing you can recover so well here at 'Amen Corner,'" Joe said through a smile when they'd finished the eleventh hole at Augusta.

"Yeah, I guess my short game is pretty good today," Marsh agreed. "I've been recovering quite well once I get off the tee!"

Joe grinned at Marsh's words. He enjoyed Marsh's sense of humor. "So, Marsh, I have to ask you," Joe said. "How do you get your golf balls back? I mean, we're hitting all these balls into your neighbor's pasture."

"See that boat right there?" Marsh pointed to a drift boat on the river bank with several empty ten-gallon buckets in the bow. "I just paddle across to the other side when a couple of these buckets are empty and pick up balls every now and then. I have a couple of those ball retrievers that look like canes, and I walk around for an hour or so until I've picked up everything I can see. Gives me a chance to get the lay of the land and plan my second shots."

Joe stared vacantly across the river when Marsh finished speaking. "Ever been married, Marsh?" He seemed to be lost in his own question.

"Why the hell would you ask me a question like that?" Marsh said, then leaned on his driver while he waited for an answer.

Still staring, Joe answered softly, "Just the thought of having my balls knocked across a river, I guess." Joe turned a wicked smile toward Marsh.

Marsh chuckled softly as he turned and addressed his ball again. He was staring down the shaft of his driver, and he never took his eye off the ball when he spoke. "Get your balls knocked around during a divorce?" he asked. Then he seemed to wait for Joe's response.

"Not so much during the divorce," Joe offered. "But continuously every day for the twenty-five years just prior to it."

Marsh swung the driver and lofted his ball across the river on a high arc that carried it about seventy yards into the short, green grass of his neighbor's cow pasture. "Yeah," Marsh sighed as he picked up his tee and stepped toward the red bench. "That was a helluva shot I just made, by the way." He interrupted himself, then continued in a totally different train of thought. "It's really tough to build a successful relationship—really tough. Here's the driver. Try to avoid the temptation to play this hole on the right of the fairway. Stay left; it'll give you an easier second shot," Marsh added as he handed the driver to a confused-looking Joe Mix. "Yeah, Joe," Marsh continued while Joe pushed his tee into the soft grass and rested his ball on it. "It's hard work building a successful relationship. I know. Hell, I've had hundreds of 'em."

Joe was smiling as he struck his ball across the river. He'd driven the ball high and far in spite of the distraction of Marsh's comment.

"Helluva shot, Joe! That's where Gary Player knocked his drive when he won his first Masters in 1961. That shot will take the water hazard out of play on your second shot," Marsh said as he stood up.

"I'll bet Gary Player worked up quite an appetite that day," Joe said, trying not to hide his sarcasm as he inquired about supper. "I know I sure have."

"Well, you're really gonna be hungry by the time we're done. We're gonna finish with the seventeenth and eighteenth at Baltusrol—two monster par-fives!" Marsh said as he teed up another ball. "But for now, we still have 'Amen Corner' to play. Remember, we're on the tee at the twelfth hole at Augusta, a classic, 155-yard par-three. A classic!" He stood over his ball again and stared down the shaft.

"So what are we having for dinner? Jack Nicklaus's favorite meal—steak and hash browns?" Joe asked sarcastically. Then he watched Marsh use his four-iron to hit his ball into the Russian Olive trees on the opposite bank.

""No," Marsh smiled. "No. That would be prime rib with asparagus and horseradish. That's Jack's favorite meal. But we're having hot dogs. I've already started the grill, up there by the clubhouse. I just hit a fine shot, by the way."

"Hot dogs?" Joe smiled as he took the four-iron from Marsh's hand and prepared for his own tee shot at Augusta National's twelfth hole.

Just as Joe swung the four-iron, Marsh blurted, "Yeah—asparagus makes my urine smell!" Joe nearly collapsed in laughter, and his ball skipped directly into the Big Horn River.

"Gallery interference," Joe laughed as he sat next to Marsh on the red bench.

"Want a mulligan?"

"No, I'm gonna hit a helluva second shot." Joe tapped the four-iron on the ground, just as he had so many times with Donny. "So, Marsh, tell me about your successful relationship with Molly," Joe said.

"Well, Molly is my friend. That's all. To be honest with you, I sort of wondered if I'd have a successful relationship with her when we first met about three years ago. She was managing a fly shop in West Yellowstone when I met her. She was really doing a nice job, but the guy she was working for is really a toad. Anyway, all I could do was stare at her at first. You know, she's so pretty! But then we just became friends. I'm too old for her anyway, and there was never any real attraction there, I guess." Marsh stood up to play the next hole, then added, "Besides that, my father ran a little grocery store for years, and he gave me one piece of advice way back when I was a kid that still rings true for every business." Marsh looked down the length of his driver once more and paused.

"Oh yeah. What was that?" Joe asked.

As he was drawing the club into his backswing, Marsh blurted his answer: "Never keep your meat where you make your bread!"

Joe Mix tried not to give in and smile. He lowered his head and tried to hide the dimple that was beginning to deepen in his right cheek. But the force of Marsh's character was irresistible, and Joe began to laugh out loud.

Marsh took his turn, struck his ball, returned to the little bench, and sat next to Joe, then shook his head. "So tell me about those two gunslingers today. How'd you manage to get along so well?" Marsh finally asked.

"You're not the only person who can sling bullshit. All I had to do was keep telling the big guy how good he was and ask him to tell me the story of his incredibly wonderful life. He ate that shit up with a spoon! You know, I spent twenty-five years trying to convince people what a good thing it was for them when I stuck a needle in their head, drilled on their teeth, and then sent 'em a bill. Takin' somebody fishin'—even an asshole—is pretty easy compared to that."

"You're a dentist?" Marsh asked, as if he'd solved a mystery.

Joe nodded, grinned softly, and confessed, "Used to be."

"Well, I'll be go to hell," Marsh sighed. "You're shittin' me!"

"Fraid not," Joe said.

"You quit that…to do this?" Marsh asked.

Joe nodded. "Well, in a roundabout way I s'pose that's true. If anybody would understand, I guess it would be you."

"So tell me!" Marsh said, and he handed the club to Joe. "Tell me what happened. Jeez, this just keeps getting better and better."

After a bizarre round of golf on the dream course, and after hot dogs with baked beans, they sat on the little red bench, under a nearly full moon, and talked about golf, trout fishing, and successful relationships and their past lives while they watched the river roll by them.

chapter
thirty-three

Through the crystal clear water beneath him, Joe could see the rich green carpet of aquatic grass that grew on the bottom of the river channel. His boat slid along quietly, and he found himself seeking comfort as he watched the river's current sway the lush green grass in a dreamy, undulating dance. Millions, Joe thought—no, billions—of aquatic insects lived in the grass and rocks on the bottom of the Big Horn River, and opportunistic trout lay in wait for them to release their grip on the grass or rocks and try to swim to the surface to continue their life cycle.

Distant thoughts of mayflies, trout, and the current that carried him along had been his escape for most of the day as he sat in the middle seat of his boat and listened to his clients pass their conversation over and around him. A dentist from Des Moines, Iowa, stood in the bow. He fished on the left side of the boat while his roommate from dental school, a dentist from Omaha, Nebraska, sat in a chair at the stern and fished on the right side.

Both men were younger than Joe, and both men were cock sure that their worldviews were completely accurate, and that others could learn quite a bit from them if they'd only listen. The dentist in the bow seemed more concerned with numbers and scorekeeping. He talked incessantly about the dollar amount of his monthly production, his investments, his vacations, and his new home. Joe guessed that the dentist in the stern couldn't quite match his friend's scores regarding money, because he spent much of his time explaining his mastery of clinical dentistry. A stranger would have thought the man in the stern had authored several textbooks on dentistry, but Joe heard plenty of technical errors and inconsistencies all through his client's lecture.

Joe turned away and stared into the water or at the riverbank as often as he could. He hoped he could avoid the conversation around him. It was such a fine day and such a beautiful place...and he had to listen to all this? Why had he spent so much of his life trying to be interested in the things these two men were talking about? Why had he pretended to be like them for so long? He'd never enjoyed the talk of these things. Now, as he thought about it all, he realized he'd never really liked himself very much during all those years he'd tried to be like the two men in the boat with him.

The river continued to offer Joe an escape as the day wound down, and he was happy to take refuge in thoughts of water, trout, and mayflies.

"Hey! Look at that little log cabin!" the dentist in the bow said as the boat eased around a bend in the river and slipped into the middle of the channel in front of Marsh's house. "Do you know who lives there?" he asked Joe.

"No," Joe replied flatly. These two guys didn't deserve to know anything about Marsh Clements, Joe thought. Then he turned toward the pasture on the other side of the river and noticed all the golf balls scattered across the short, green grass. He thought of Marsh's tee box and Marsh's views on keeping score, and he smiled to himself as his clients resumed talking about themselves.

———

"Hi, Jake!" Joe said when he stepped through the door to the fly shop at the end of the day. He was tired, lonely, and depressed after a day with the two dentists. They'd reminded him of just how much he'd hated his old job and his old life. He was glad he'd left it all behind, and he was glad he'd landed here. But damn, he felt lonely tonight.

Jake rushed him, and he bent down to embrace the lanky pup.

"Rough day?" Molly asked. "You look like something's bothering you," she added.

Joe stood up and looked at Molly for a moment. She looked so nice in her blue jeans and knit cotton blouse. Her breasts pushed perfectly at the front of the white blouse, and her auburn hair took on a richer color in the yellow light of an early summer evening.

Molly was folding some papers, and Joe glanced at her long fingers while she worked. He liked the way her skin took on an almost orange-colored tan when she spent time in the sun. He was staring at the soft skin on her face when she looked at him and smiled. He thought of the way Molly made him feel when she leaned close and whispered in his ear in the morning. Just now, after this unhappy day on the river, he wanted to spend some time with her and talk to her, and pick up the conversation right where the morning chats always ended. He missed the sensitivity of a woman's friendship, and he was drawn to Molly. Only a woman could share the company and conversation Joe longed for tonight. Talking with Marsh and playing golf with him were fine. Marsh had become a good friend. But it just wasn't the same as visiting with a woman.

When Molly had discovered Joe staring at her, she'd smiled softly at him. She was still smiling when he asked, "Would you like to come over and sit by a fire and talk tonight?"

"No," Molly said bluntly after a brief silence. The smile drained from her face and she turned away. "No. I don't date guides," she added. Then she turned to walk behind the cash register, and as she did she called over her shoulder. "Your dog was limping all morning, but he's been fine this afternoon. Whatever it was must have healed." Then she was gone. She stepped into the little stockroom behind the cash register and stood there.

Joe was embarrassed, heartsick. He'd only meant to offer his friendship—to visit for a while beside a campfire. But Molly had squashed his feelings. He was stung by the sudden and complete manner in which Molly had dismissed him. She wouldn't even say Jake's name at the end of it all. She'd only referred to him as "your dog," as if she didn't know his name. He stared at the empty doorway into the little stockroom for a moment, then called to Jake.

———

The uneven kitchen floor in Joe's trailer shifted slightly under his weight as he stepped over to the stovetop and poured several scrambled eggs into a cast-iron frying pan.

"Whatya think, Jake?" Joe said to his puppy. "Did I put her on the spot?" He threw a piece of cheese to Jake, who was begging for scraps. "Or is she just a witch, like Jess?" When the eggs were finished, Joe reached into the refrigerator, then poured some salsa over the eggs while they were still in the frying pan. He sat at the table and ate the eggs out of the frying pan while he thought about what had been said between him and Molly.

"Any normal woman would love to come over here and hang out at a place like this, don't you think?" Joe said when he leaned over and held the frying pan on the floor for Jake to finish the eggs. "You're doing the dishes tonight!" he added while Jake licked the pan clean. Then he dropped the frying pan into the sink, walked out to the backyard, and built a fire in the fire pit.

Next morning when Joe returned to the shop, Molly greeted him with a friendly "good morning" as if nothing had been said the night before. But Joe didn't want to pretend that Molly hadn't hurt him. He kept his distance from Molly and sipped at a Styrofoam coffee cup while he talked with Marsh and waited for his clients to arrive.

At day's end, he was cordial with Molly when he had to speak to her, but he couldn't bring himself to make small talk with her. She was kind and businesslike, just as she'd been all along, but Joe no longer felt welcome or comfortable in her company. He kept his distance and spoke to her only when he had to.

Clients came and went over the ensuing days, and Joe grew more and more comfortable with the routine. He played golf several times with Marsh. The strange rules remained the same at Marsh's, but each day they played a new golf course. One day it might be Inverness, the next day Spyglass Hill, the next day Troon. Joe never knew where they'd be playing until he arrived at the first tee, and Marsh kept up a running narration throughout every round.

He never knew what sort of greeting he'd get from Molly either, but he'd lost interest in building a friendship with her now. He kept his distance—maybe in an attempt to punish her and maybe to hide the way she'd hurt his feelings.

chapter thirty-four

"All right, Joe, you know we got our share of celebrities out here," Marsh said, then blew the steam off his coffee. The cool morning air was about to give way to a hot summer day as Joe and Marsh chatted outside the shop and waited for fishermen to start to arrive.

"Yeah," Joe answered while he tightened the tie-down strap that held his drift boat onto his trailer. "So what?"

"Well, today you'll be guiding for Sam Palmer." Marsh stopped himself and waited for Joe's response.

"Really?" Joe said with a smile. "No shit? The movie star? No shit?"

"No shit, Joe. You'll have Mr. Palmer and his agent, or some such person. I don't know just exactly what the other guy does, but he's here with Sam Palmer."

"So how come he's in my boat today? How come he's not with one of the more experienced guides?" Joe asked.

"Your lucky day!" Marsh answered. "Here they are right now. C'mon, I'll introduce you."

Sam Palmer seemed much shorter in real life than he did in the movies. He was actually several inches shorter than Joe. Joe had heard others comment about how it seemed odd when they'd met movie stars and discovered them to be so much shorter in person than they appeared on screen. But Sam Palmer was a handsome man by any standard. He had a rugged, angular face, with short, dark hair that was beginning to gray at the temples. He looked good—no, special, Joe thought. Even dressed in Gore-Tex waders and a work shirt, Joe thought he looked like a movie star.

Sam Palmer had played cowboys and gangsters, and he'd also been a private eye in a successful series of thrillers. It would be great to spend a day on the river with a movie star, Joe thought. But when Sam Palmer shook Joe's hand, he seemed distracted, perhaps even uninterested. He'd known Sam Palmer for only an instant when he began to feel that a day with a movie star might not be so much fun after all.

"I'm Vic Birthler!" the other man said as he thrust his hand toward Joe and smiled. "Looks like a great day for fishing. We should get a nice Baetis hatch this afternoon if we can get a little cloud cover!" Vic Birthler was much younger than Sam Palmer. Joe guessed him to be not much over thirty. His enthusiasm was catching, and he had the look of an outdoorsman. Joe liked him immediately.

"Let's go!" Sam Palmer said while Vic Birthler was still pumping Joe's hand.

"Yeah, you guys get going!" Marsh said. Then he cast a nervous glance at Joe. When Joe made eye contact, Marsh raised his eyebrows and stifled a smile. He let go a peel of laughter to punctuate the end of the morning conversation and turned to walk back into the fly shop. "Have a good one, boys!" he called without looking back at them.

———————

"Do you have any preference, Mr. Palmer? I mean, do you care how I set your rig for fishin'?" Joe asked after he'd slid the boat into the current.

"You're the guide," Palmer replied. His words came along with a tone and a facial expression that Joe could only interpret as indifference. He'd stopped just short of rolling his eyes at Joe.

"I'm gonna start with a San Juan Worm and use a small sow bug as a trailer. Sound OK to you, Joe?" Vic asked as he finished tying his flies onto the tiny tippet and attaching his lead weight a few inches above them.

Joe dismissed Sam Palmer's actions easily—he'd probably just misinterpreted them, he thought. He was surprised that Vic understood the fishing technique so well. It had become popular over the years for Big Horn anglers to attach a second nymph to the first one and fish with two flies at the same time.

"That's what I was gonna recommend, Vic. How did you know?" Joe asked as he rigged Sam Palmer's line in the same way Vic had described.

"I've been here before," Vic replied.

"Are you from Montana?" Joe asked while he looked through a fly box.

"No, California. But I grew up fishing, and I came out here a couple times while I was in college..."

"I'd prefer to use a dry fly," Sam Palmer interrupted, and Joe began to feel an edge to Sam Palmer.

"Well, I suppose you could do that," Joe said apologetically. "But there are no fish rising right now. There are no mayflies hatching now, so all the fish are feeding on the bottom. They're waiting for nymphs and other sorts of trout food to get carried to them by the current. But later today, when the Baetis hatch starts, they'll begin to feed on the surface, and then..."

"I know how it works," Palmer interrupted again. Then he held out his hand for Joe to give him his rod and reel. Joe handed him the rod as Sam stepped into the leg supports in the little pulpit area at the bow and started to pull fly line out of his reel. He must have decided to just go ahead and fish the way I prepared him to, Joe thought.

Sam Palmer stripped a few yards of fly line from his reel and began false casting the line above his head. Joe could see right away that Palmer was a competent fly fisherman but nothing more. When he finished his forward cast and laid the fly line down on the water's surface, his flies, tippet, weight, and strike indicator landed in a pile about twenty feet to the left of the boat.

"Nice cast," Joe said. "That's the perfect place to put it. Just leave it there and I'll get you a good drift," he added.

"Thanks," Palmer said. His cast had been clumsy and his line was probably tangled, but Joe decided not to offer any further instruction. Sam Palmer didn't seem like the kind of man who liked to hear anything but praise.

Joe could feel the boat rocking gently as Vic Birthler false cast his line several times. Joe turned to his right just in time to see Vic lay down a perfect cast with his backhand stroke. The small lead weight and the two flies extended in a straight line toward shore and plopped gently onto the surface. Joe pursed his lips slightly, then winked. He nodded to Vic in a small salute. His cast had been deftly executed and placed in a prime location. Vic grinned and returned the nod.

"So, Vic, what do you do when you're not fishing? What is it that you do for a living?" Joe said as he leaned gently on the oars and turned the boat ever so slightly. "I mean, I know what Mr. Palmer does, but how about you?"

"I'm an editor at Hudson Valley Publishing in New York City," Vic replied. "Mr. Palmer has written a novel, and I've been working with him trying to get the manuscript all finished and ready for publication this winter."

"Wow. A movie star and an author. That's pretty impressive. I didn't know you were so talented, Mr. Palmer," Joe said.

"I've always written," Sam Palmer said flatly.

"Yeah, we published Mr. Palmer's first novel two years ago..." Vic stopped himself and turned quickly in his boat seat as his rod bent with the weight of a fish. "Got a decent fish on here!" he announced when both Sam Palmer and Joe turned to look at him. After a brief struggle, Joe used a hemostat to remove the tiny sow bug from the lip of a seventeen-inch rainbow trout, then slid the fish back into the current.

"Nice one, Vic," Joe offered as he washed his hands in the river. The cool water felt good on his hands. When he leaned back into the boat, he looked up and down the channel in search of a place to pull over and fish from shore for a while. His eyes were still scanning the riverbank when he heard a whistling noise. He flinched just as Sam Palmer's fly line lead weight and flies screamed past his head. He looked up just in time to see Palmer jerk his back cast toward the boat again. In an instant, the lead weight hammered against the side of the boat in a loud cracking noise. The tippet snapped, releasing the lead and the flies to the bottom of the river. Palmer simply handed the rod and reel to Joe for him to re-rig the terminal tackle. The limp fly line dangled in front of Joe, and the wispy remnant of Sam Palmer's leader fluttered in the breeze as Joe took the rod from him.

"If you point the rod..." Joe began in an attempt to help Sam with his casting motion.

"You can't control a fly line in all this wind!" Palmer interrupted to explain.

Palmer's tone stung Joe, as if he was implying that it was Joe's fault the wind was blowing, or for taking him fishing with poor tackle and in such difficult conditions. The truth was that there was only a slight breeze, and Sam Palmer was a weak fly caster. Joe felt himself begin to bristle at Palmer's implication. Other fishermen—lots of other fishermen...two nuns, as a matter of fact—had been able to handle a rod and reel in worse conditions than this. Never once had any clients implied that their own lack of skill had anything to do with Joe.

He decided to try a different tack to win Sam Palmer's friendship. He thought about his next question for a moment while he tied a new leader onto Sam's fly line. He tried to talk to Sam in the same way he'd spoken to the "steely-eyed gunslingers": he'd ask Sam questions about himself. Sam certainly did seem like a man who liked to talk about Sam.

"So, Mr. Palmer," Joe started while he was still working with the monofilament line. "After all the great movies you've made, do you have a favorite?" Joe tugged on the knot he'd just tied and looked at Sam Palmer while he waited for an answer.

Sam Palmer sighed and leaned back in his seat. Much to Joe's surprise, he made a face like Joe had just caused him a great inconvenience. Joe could read it in Sam's expression. Now, he'd have to oblige another fan with stars in his eyes and answer another of the standard movie star questions. Joe couldn't miss the disdain on Sam Palmer's face. He'd only asked a polite question to start a friendly conversation, and Sam Palmer had taken him for a starstruck fan. "Not really," Sam sighed. He'd done everything but roll his eyes at Joe again.

Joe opened a fly box and poked through several rows of flies until he found another San Juan Worm and sow bug. He'd just stop with the questions for a while. He re-rigged Palmer's line and was about to hand it back when Vic caught another fish. When Joe turned to watch Vic reel in his second fish, Sam Palmer leaned over and snatched his rod from Joe's hand, as if Joe had wronged him by looking at Vic instead of returning his rod immediately. Sam's gesture was loaded with nonverbal commentary, and Joe began to feel a deep dislike for the movie star sitting only inches from him.

Joe was able to ignore the urge to confront Sam Palmer only because he was helping Vic land a nice brown trout that measured just a hair under twenty inches. "Nice fish!" Joe exclaimed as he released the trout. Then he turned to Sam Palmer and added, "That was a beauty, huh, Sam?"

Sam Palmer had now lost the respect of a "Mr. Palmer" in Joe's eyes. From now on, he was going to be just Sam—and Joe hoped that irritated Sam Palmer.

"Yeah," Palmer added without looking. Joe turned away in disgust and looked toward Vic, but Vic would not return his glance.

"OK, guys, up here in front of us there's a place the guides call 'The Pig Pen.' It's a nice, shallow run, and it's full of nice fish. We're gonna pull over and fish from the shore for a while. The run is right up here between these two little islands on the left," Joe said as he turned the boat in the current and made for the tip of the smaller island.

Even Sam Palmer, who was turning out to be a self-centered, arrogant man in Joe's opinion, couldn't keep the smile of a child off his face as he started to catch one fish after another at the tail end of the Pig Pen. For a brief moment, when he hooked a big trout that had made a strong run upstream and torn line from his reel as it barreled along the opposite bank, Sam Palmer bore the innocent expression of a boy—just a little boy gone fishin'—and Joe almost liked him. But the fish spit the hook, and in a heartbeat Palmer remembered who he was supposed to be. His countenance turned distant again.

Joe had placed Vic at the head of the Pig Pen and Sam at the tail. He walked back and forth between the two of them for almost ninety minutes while they caught fish in the clear, knee-deep channel between the two small islands. By the time they decided to take a break for lunch, Joe was almost ready to rethink his impression of Sam Palmer. Maybe he wasn't such a bad guy after all. While Sam had been landing fish after fish in the Pig Pen, Joe had actually been able to draw him into some conversation about his younger days and other good times on trout streams. He'd even volunteered some information about a fishing trip to Argentina several years earlier. Maybe they'd be all right if Joe could keep the conversation centered around Sam's skills as a fisherman.

"Would you like a sandwich?" Joe asked when the fishermen returned to the boat for a lunch break.

"Sure," Vic answered as he took a sandwich from the cooler in the boat. Sam said nothing, but he reached into the cooler and withdrew a sandwich also.

"Well, you guys were really puttin' the heat on the fish for the last hour or so!" Joe offered.

"Yeah. I'd like to see the big one that got away," Sam Palmer admitted, almost smiling. Then, in what seemed like an effort to punctuate his sentence, he threw his sandwich back into the cooler with a bite out of it.

"Something wrong with your sandwich?" Joe asked as anger tightened the corners of his eyes.

"Just don't like it," Palmer said while he opened a can of soda.

Joe looked at the broken sandwich laying across the bottom of his cooler. Mustard, salami, and cheese had bounced from the sandwich, and one slice of bread was stuck to the inside wall of the cooler. If Joe had ever done something like that, his father would have been mighty quick with some sort of corporal punishment. The words began to well up in the back of Joe Mix's throat: *"Clean up the goddamn mess you made in my cooler! And be thankful someone was willing to make a sandwich for a worthless prick like you! Who the hell do you think you are?"* But he stifled the urge to blurt it out. Besides, once they were spoken, those words could never be recalled. Sam Palmer was just too important to talk to like that. But he was done trying to befriend Sam Palmer.

As he prepared the cooler and the boat for an afternoon drift, Joe recognized his own feelings of resentment and frustration at not addressing Sam Palmer's bad behavior. He'd felt the same thing toward Jess for years. Now, he was beginning to resent and dislike Sam Palmer on a new and deeper level for making him remember so much hurt and so many injustices from his own past. Hell, Sam Palmer was no different than Jess, he supposed. Sam was just some selfish guy who intended to use Joe for his own needs. If Joe could put him on the fish, that was good…the rest of Joe could be thrown away.

Joe pulled heavily on the oars and moved the boat into the current once again after lunch as both Sam and Vic began false casting their fly lines. He saw Vic's line drop gently onto the water just before he heard a familiar hissing noise and then flinched. This time, the hissing noise was accompanied by a sharp, stinging pain just above his right eye. He heard and felt Sam Palmer's fly line slap at his Stetson and then settle all about his shoulders. He knew right away that the pain by his eye was the result of an impact with the piece of lead shot he'd placed on Sam's line. He reached to his eyebrow to check for bleeding and found nothing but a mouse beginning to raise above his eye.

Joe had kept his eyes closed tightly since the impact with the lead shot and the fly line. He had been, and he still was, concerned about the whereabouts of the two razor-sharp fish hooks that had to be somewhere near his face. When he opened his eyes and peeked out from under the brim of his Stetson, he saw an unrepentant, almost angry Sam Palmer looking back at him. To his shock and dismay, he saw Sam begin to raise his fly rod! He was just about to flick the rod in one violent attempt to free the line from around Joe's head! Joe had only enough time to close his eyes and wait for whatever came next.

Fortunately, he could feel no fish hooks piercing his flesh. But he did feel the orange fly line that had been draped around his head begin to hiss as it slid along his Stetson at a frightening speed. He felt his hat lift off his head briefly, and in the same moment, he heard what he could only assume was a San Juan Worm click as it glanced off something and screamed past his face in a tight orbit around his head, just before it engaged his polarized sunglasses. Then...pfffttt! The forty-dollar sunglasses were gone, splashing into the river about twenty feet from the boat, and his Stetson flipped off his head and landed at his feet.

The thing Sam had done was so inconsiderate and thoughtless that Joe could scarcely believe it. "What the hell was that?" Joe said angrily as he reached for his Stetson.

"Worked out OK," Sam Palmer said over his shoulder.

"Well, I wouldn't say that. My shades are on the bottom now, and the brightest part of the day is yet to come!" Joe said, still struggling to understand what he'd seen and been part of.

Sam Palmer's only response was to shrug his shoulders while his back was turned to Joe and offer, "Sorry."

Joe turned a hateful, questioning glance in Vic's direction but said nothing.

Vic merely shrugged, nodded, and made a face to acknowledge Joe's anger. Vic's eyes revealed that he was basically powerless over Sam Palmer's behavior.

By God, there would be no more stopping to fish any of the good fishing holes Joe had found in the past weeks. That prick in the front of the boat wasn't going to get any more red-carpet treatment. Joe bristled with anger but managed to hide his feelings.

It was still a pretty day with a soft, warm breeze blowing, Joe told himself. He'd find solace in the river, in just being here, as he'd done before with the two dentists he'd disliked. He steered the boat around an island, then another, as his clients fished in silence. Then, unbelievably, Joe heard the familiar hissing sound of a San Juan Worm and a piece of lead shot screaming directly at his head. Sam Palmer was making yet another awkward, dangerous cast. Joe ducked when he first felt the fly line slide along the top of his Stetson, then he flinched when he heard the violent sound of the lead glancing off the gunwale of the boat just to his right. The next thing he felt was a stinging pain in the back of his thigh. When he opened his eyes, he saw the San Juan Worm buried in his leg up to the curve of the hook.

Once again, Sam only stared at Joe. But this time, he seemed willing to wait until Joe had removed the fly from his leg before he began casting. Joe stared back at Sam for a moment, then removed the hemostat from his pocket and gripped the San Juan Worm by the curve, just above its shank. Even though Joe had bent the barb back just in case something like this ever happened, the barb on such a large hook was still big enough that it pulled some muscle and skin and ripped the Gore-Tex waders when it came loose.

Joe was left with a red hole in his waders and a deepening dislike for Sam Palmer as he held the bloody hook in the hemostat and showed it to Palmer.

"Careful, Sam, there are a couple other people in this boat with you!" Then he threw the San Juan Worm at Sam and said, "Let's go fishin'!" as angrily as he dared. He wanted to insult Sam Palmer, to attack him verbally, but he still felt that was somehow impossible and Sam would always be off limits.

Before the boat had drifted another five hundred yards, Sam announced that he had to go to the bathroom. Joe found the statement rather humorous, and he said simply, "Hang your dick over the side and let 'er fly, Sam."

"That won't do," Vic said from the back of the boat. He hadn't spoken for some time, but now he seemed to be truly concerned that Sam might piss over the side of the boat.

"Why not?" Joe asked.

"Sure as hell, some photographer from the *Enquirer* will be hiding in the bushes and get a picture of Sam, and...you know," Vic said.

"OK," Joe replied, "I'll pull over right up here. But I would like to see myself on the cover of the *Enquirer*, even if I was just posing next to Sam's pecker." Joe chuckled at his own words while he leaned on the oars and manned the boat toward shore.

Sam disappeared into a clump of Russian Olive trees as soon as the boat was secure on shore, and when he was out of earshot Joe turned to Vic and said, "You're his handler, aren't you?"

"What do you mean?" Vic replied.

"You know what I mean. You're the monkey wrangler. You're like the guy who makes sure the chimpanzee doesn't shit on the rug or fuck another chimp on TV. You're here to maintain damage control and preen that guy's ego, aren't you?"

Vic lowered his head and admitted, "It's not quite that bad. We are working out the story in his novel. But I wound up here on this working vacation because I had some knowledge of this place and he wanted to come here. My boss thought Sam might be a little easier to work with in a place like this."

"Vic, you're the low man on the totem pole at Hudson Valley Publishing, aren't you? You got sent here because nobody else can stand this prick, right? I'm just guessin', mind you, because I'm the low guy at the fly shop, and I'm pretty sure that's how I got Sam in my boat."

"Yeah," Vic said with his head lowered. "Probably." Joe leaned back in his boat seat, folded his arms across his chest, and stared at Vic Birthler for a moment before he spoke.

"I'm surprised we even pulled over here like this," Joe said.

"Whadya mean, Joe?"

"I'm surprised that prick didn't just order you up to the front of the boat and then piss in your hat, then maybe send you over the side so you could swim to shore and throw the piss up in the woods."

"It's not that bad, Joe," Vic replied, but he shuffled his feet and looked away as he spoke.

"I think it is that bad, Vic."

"Well, there are some things a guy just has to do. My company stands to make a great deal of money on Sam's book." Vic looked around to be sure Sam was still nowhere near the boat, then he leaned forward. "I need to keep this book deal together and bring the manuscript to press. We're gonna sell a lot of books just because Sam Palmer is the author." Vic glanced all around again. "It's not because the book is that good. It isn't any good either, Joe. It sucks, as a matter of fact, but that's not the point." Vic sighed, then smiled a weak smile. "There are just some things you have to do...for the money, I guess."

"Yeah, I suppose so," Joe agreed. He liked Vic Birthler and felt sorry for him, and he knew there was some truth in what he'd said.

Footsteps and some rustling of the brush along shore alerted Vic and Joe that Sam Palmer had finished his business in the woods. When Sam had stepped into the boat and taken his seat, Joe leaned heavily on the oars again and moved the boat into the current once more. "Everything come out OK, Sam?" Joe asked with a chuckle, but Sam didn't answer.

Joe assumed he'd finish the day in an easy drift and make stops only at the popular, well-known fishing holes. He had built a strong dislike for Sam Palmer in just a short time, but the day would be over in a couple hours, he thought. He could finish things with no problem now, and he didn't want to make Vic Birthler's job any more difficult than it already was.

"OK, Vic. Now over here on the right, where you're fishing, there's sort of a little slot right there about ten feet from shore. If you can get your fly..." The now familiar and frightening hiss of fishing tackle screaming through the air at the end of yet another careless cast from Sam Palmer caused Joe to flinch in midsentence. He'd managed to close his eyes just before impact as the piece of lead shot on Sam's line struck him just behind the ear. The collision of lead against his skull made a sharp noise, and his right ear began to ring immediately. In the same instant, he felt a large section of fly line begin to coil and settle around his shoulders. Joe opened one eye just in time to see the last two feet of monofilament fishing line swing around his Stetson and the tiny sow bug at the end of it sail directly toward the middle of his face.

He flinched a second time and felt the tiny fly bounce off his upper lip and into his left nostril. He could feel the tip of the tiny, razor-sharp hook resting against the tender skin on the inside of his nose.

Joe remained frozen for a second, then opened both eyes. Several strands of fly line and monofilament crisscrossed in front of his eyes, but other than that there was no real problem. This was getting old. He was angry at Sam for making yet another careless, inconsiderate attempt to cast his line. Sam clearly didn't care how much he irritated or inconvenienced or injured other people.

But he could let it go, Joe thought. If Vic could make such an effort, then he could too. Joe remained still while he tried to assess the situation. The only thing that really concerned him was the little sow bug nymph in his nose. Well, he wasn't quite sure where the San Juan Worm had come to rest, but he couldn't feel its large, heavy hook imbedded in his flesh anywhere. He'd just slowly uncoil this mess of fly line, tippet material, flies, and lead shot. Then he'd caution Sam to be more careful. He figured he could rub his ear for a minute and it would stop ringing. This day would be over in a couple hours, Joe reasoned. He tried to convince himself that this would be all right.

Joe reached ever so slowly toward the little nymph in his nose. He didn't want to accidentally bump into any fishing line and drive the hook's point into the tender skin on the inside of his nose.

The thumb and index finger on his left hand had just settled over the little nymph, and he was cautiously moving the sharp hook away from his face when his eyes began to focus just beyond the tangle that surrounded his head.

As he groped carefully for the San Juan Worm with his right hand, his eyes found Sam Palmer's eyes staring back at him, and he was shocked at what he read in Palmer's eyes. There was no apology there, no sense of embarrassment, no contrition. There was no anger or even contempt.

In Sam Palmer's eyes, there was a complete disregard for Joe Mix or anyone else. At the very same instant that Joe recognized Sam's lack of concern for anyone else, he saw that Sam was about to act on it. Sam Palmer's right hand was raising slowly. He'd waited long enough for Joe to untangle himself, and he was about to give his fly rod a violent flick in an attempt to cast the tangled line off Joe's head and shoulders and back into the river. The thought that one or the other of the two flies might be driven into Joe's flesh, or into his eyes—which were now unprotected because Sam had lost his sunglasses while doing a similarly thoughtless thing earlier—never occurred to him.

Sam's hand seemed to move backwards in slow motion now. Joe knew he was at risk, and he had to stop Sam Palmer. Suddenly, the same volcanic anger that had erupted when Jess had shown a similar contempt came over him again.

Joe stood quickly and grabbed Sam's right arm, just above his wrist. The sound of his hand grasping Sam's arm made a loud slapping noise. Joe was seething with white-hot anger, and his face was inches from Sam Palmer's, when he spoke.

"Don't move!" Joe growled. He could see in Palmer's eyes that Sam was afraid of him now and that he was hurting Sam. "You give that thing a flick and I'll rip your head off and shit down your neck! You understand me?" he said with a growl that came from deep in his chest.

Joe paused for a moment and stared into Sam Palmer's eyes. He released Sam's arm with a shove, then quickly lifted the tangle of fly line off his head and shoulders.

As he was still throwing fly line to the floor of the boat, Joe hollered, "REEL IN! REEL IN, GODDAMMIT! YOU SONSABITCHES ARE FIRED!"

Joe sat quickly—heavily—into his boat seat and grabbed the boat oars. He pushed the left oar forward and pulled the right oar backward. The boat spun violently in a clockwise motion. When the stern was pointed downsteam, Joe pulled heavily on both oars and the little boat seemed to lift out of the water. With each powerful stroke from Joe's arms, the boat gained speed.

"I'm gonna take you worthless bastards to the boat landing and drop you off. Then I'll send someone to pick your sorry asses up. But not one word from either of you," Joe barked. "I can't believe what a sorry piece of shit you are, Sam! Who the hell do you think you are?"

Sam looked like he was about to speak, but Joe stopped him.

"Not one word! Not one word from you! Or I'll kick your ass 'til your nose bleeds, then throw your ass over the side and you can swim for it. I shit you not, Sam Palmer. I'm the captain of this ship, and I've seen enough of you and people like you. Don't even talk to me."

Joe rowed the boat for forty-five minutes until they reached the boat landing where his truck and boat trailer were waiting. Then he simply raised his boat onto the trailer and drove off, leaving Sam Palmer and Vic Birthler at the river's edge by a small gravel parking lot.

The anger in Joe's heart took nearly an hour longer to subside. He'd called the fly shop and told Marsh what had happened, then driven to a stand of cottonwoods along the river and waited. He flipped small stones into the river and tried to think about what was going to happen next. He'd done the unthinkable: he'd fired clients—important clients— while he was on the river, then abandoned them. Surely he'd be fired. He'd wrecked his friendship with Marsh. Marsh would be pretty angry, with good reason. But, by God, he'd done something that needed to be done. The only thing he could do now was move on once again. But he really didn't want to. He sat by the river and watched the current and tried to think, but there was no solution to this.

———————

Gravel crunched under Joe's wheels when he finally rolled into the parking lot. Through the window in the front of the shop, Joe could see heads turning to look at him when he rolled to a stop. He stepped out of his truck just as Jake ran to greet him. Then he unhitched the boat and rolled it in line with the other boats, as he did at the end of every day.

When he turned to face the fly shop window, Marsh was already walking his way. Sam Palmer had been giving Marsh an earful for over an hour, and now Joe knew he was about to pay for his behavior. Joe hunched his shoulders and grimaced as he braced himself for the punishment he knew he was about to receive. As he watched Marsh walk toward him, he could see Palmer, Molly, and Vic Birthler staring out of the shop window at him.

"Jesus, Joe! Did you actually do it?" Marsh asked as his eyelids tightened.

Joe nodded.

"Did you say all that shit, and threaten to kick his ass and throw him over the side?" Marsh grew more animated as he talked.

Joe nodded once more.

"C'MERE, GODDAMMIT!!" Marsh barked, then gestured violently for Joe to follow him about fifty feet farther out into the gravel parking lot. Joe followed Marsh, and Jake followed Joe.

Marsh kept his back to the fly shop window, and when Joe approached him, he put both hands on his hips and made an angry gesture for Joe to walk around in front of him.

Marsh made sure to stand with his back to the fly shop for a moment and stared at Joe, shaking his head. "You did that shit—really?" he asked again.

Joe nodded once more.

Marsh sighed heavily, then breathed. "Well, nice work! I wish I could have seen it," he added quietly.

"Huh?" Joe said.

"Look over my shoulder, Joe," Marsh commanded. "Are they still looking at us?" Joe looked back at the shop and nodded. "OK, then, just stand there and don't say shit!"

Marsh began to circle slowly to his left, still facing Joe. He raised his hands as if he were totally exasperated, then hollered, "WELL, YOU'RE FIRED, YOU DUMB ASS!! HOW COULD YOU DO THAT?" When he'd made a complete circle and his back was to the window again, Marsh lowered his voice and said, "Not really, Joe. That dickhead is watching, and he thinks I'm reaming you a new asshole. What you did was great! I had a hard time not laughing when he was tattling on you. Is he still watching?"

"Yeah."

"WELL, PACK YOUR SHIT AND GET THE HELL OUT OF HERE! NOW!" Marsh hollered. Then, just under his breath, he added, "OK. Tomorrow after work, we're gonna play the Royal and Ancient golf course at St. Andrews; tee time is 6:30 p.m. The clubhouse chef—that would be me—is preparing a special dinner of hot dogs and beans. I'm gonna want to hear all the details of your day with Sam Palmer."

"No asparagus?" Joe asked with a grin.

"NO, GODDAMMIT! AND WIPE THAT STUPID SMILE OFF YOUR FACE!" Marsh screamed. "Is he still looking?" Jake followed at Marsh's heals as he circled Joe.

"Yeah," Joe replied.

"Take the day off tomorrow. Just lie low for a day. I'll spend this evening smoothing Sam's feathers, and I'll guide for him tomorrow. He's the biggest tipper we've ever had around here you know."

"I didn't know that."

"WELL, HOW WOULD YOU KNOW THAT? YOU'RE A TOTAL DUMBASS!" Marsh hollered and waved his hands. "Is he still looking?" he added under his breath.

"Yeah."

"How am I doing?" Marsh whispered.

"Pretty good," Joe replied. "But you might want to give me a good sendoff."

"Right! Yeah! That's good, Joe," Marsh said as he nodded his head in agreement. "That's a good idea. Here we go."

Marsh spun on his heels and thrust his finger at Joe. "YOU CAN PACK YOUR FUCKIN' BAGS...YOU'LL NEVER WORK IN THIS TOWN AGAIN!" he hollered.

"That was perfect," Joe whispered as he hung his head and turned toward his truck.

"My place, 6:30," Marsh whispered to Joe's back, then hollered, "AND DON'T FORGET IT!"

Joe was fighting back a smile as he and Jake climbed into the truck in front of the fly shop. "'You'll never work in this town again!' That was perfect," he said with a chuckle when the old Ford rolled out of the parking lot. Joe laughed all the way to his trailer. Marsh's reference to the old Hollywood threat about "never working in this town again" had been inspired.

—•—

Afternoon shadows were beginning to darken as another Montana day eased itself over the western horizon. Joe leaned forward and threw several pieces of scrap lumber into the fire pit at his feet, then reached into a little cooler beside his old lawn chair. The wood began to crackle in the fire as Joe withdrew a diet soda from the cooler, straightened his legs, and leaned back in his chair.

"Mr. Mix? Joe?" a timid voice called from behind the corner of Joe's trailer. Joe recognized the voice immediately and turned to see Vic Birthler standing in the shadows, sort of asking permission to come forward. Jake sprinted over to greet Vic. He jumped up with both front paws and licked at Vic's hands.

"Hi, Vic," Joe said with a grin. "C'mon over and sit with me. I won't bite."

"Well, I really can't," Vic said as he inched forward into the growing light of a young campfire. "I don't have time. We're actually working on Sam's book. But I sneaked away for a minute because I wanted to talk to you. That pretty woman from the shop...?"

"Molly. That would be Molly," Joe interrupted.

"Yeah, Molly. She told me where you lived. And I just wanted to come over and say I was sorry."

"Sorry for what? I'm the one who acted badly. I'm sorry, Vic."

"No, no, you were pretty much right, and I'm sorry you lost your job, and..."

"It'll be OK, Vic," Joe smiled.

"Well, I just wanted to tell you I was sorry."

"You know, Vic, I had to bark at both of you," Joe explained. "I know you were doing just fine, but if I'd hollered at just Sam, and not you...well, you'd be in deep shit tonight too. I'd have put you on my side of it all, and Sam could never have tolerated that. You'd have lost your job too. Understand?"

"Sure, but I still feel bad about it all, and what happened to you," Vic added.

"Don't let it bother you, Vic. I'll be OK. Hell, you're the one who has to go back there and work with Sam," Joe said with a sigh.

"Well, I just wanted to tell you I was sorry. I need to get back. Goodbye, Joe," Vic said as he turned to leave.

Joe stood up from his lawn chair. "Come back here," Joe called, then he extended his hand. "Thanks, Vic. Maybe we'll meet again!"

"Yeah," Vic smiled, "that would be good." Then he turned and left the circle of light around the campfire.

It had been an odd day filled with conflict, Joe thought. But then he'd had a lot of odd days since he'd left his old life. The anger he'd felt today when he'd snapped at a movie star, while floating on a trout stream, was exactly the same anger that had finally overflowed and driven him from Jess. That was pretty odd, he thought.

He began to think about Jess as he listened to the fire grow. He didn't miss her. He didn't hate her either, as he'd thought for a while after he'd left her. The only thing he felt toward Jess was apathy. But then how could that be, he thought, because apathy meant nothing, and how could something be nothing? He stared into the fire and smiled about words and the power of words. That thought made him think once again of how he'd felt pain when Jess had said the words "fuck you." But he felt joy and laughter when Donny or Marsh or even the guy at the gas station in Hardin said the very same thing: "fuck you." Yeah, he thought, words were funny; they had power.

And people—what about people? Joe wondered. There in the embers, he began to see the faces of Murdo, Slats Mulligan, Mary Crossman and James Bond, and the Duncan brothers. He saw Tom the horse, too, then the Kadoka Kid. He smiled at the Kadoka Kid, and all the people of his old life began to mingle there in the embers of a little fire with all the people of this new life.

The fire glowed orange and red, and the burning coals crumbled slowly while dreams of his life drifted in front of him, somewhere there in the fire. Joe Mix was lost for a moment, just floating along and recalling the people he'd seen there on the riverbank while his life's current carried him along on this odyssey.

From the darkness behind him, beyond the circle of light from his small fire, Joe heard footsteps approaching again. Jake scrambled to his feet and bounced over to meet whoever was coming to join them. Joe expected Vic Birthler or Marsh, or maybe one of the guides he'd become friends with, to be standing behind him when he turned his head.

"Hi, Joe," Molly Malone said from the shadows.

Joe turned back toward the fire. "Hi, Molly," he answered flatly. He poked a stick into the fire but said nothing more.

Molly found the other lawn chair leaning against Joe's trailer, unfolded it, and sat next to Joe. She stared into the fire for a moment, then said, "I just stopped over to talk a little."

Joe would not look up at her.

"So who are you, Joe? What's your story?"

"You hurt my feelings," Joe said, ignoring the question.

Molly sighed, looked at her feet, and nodded. She knew what she'd done.

"Why do you care who I am?" Joe paused, then he continued. "You hurt my feelings," he added. Then he turned to look at Molly and said cynically, "Thought you didn't hang around with guides."

"I said I didn't date guides," Molly corrected without looking back at him. She scratched Jake's ears while he nuzzled against her leg and begged for affection, oblivious to their conversation.

"I didn't ask you for a date. I asked you to maybe come over here and talk, like this." Joe turned his palms up and looked at the fire, then back at Molly. "Aren't you afraid someone will see you with me? Maybe you'll be shunned by the elite social crowd here at Fort Smith Trailer Park."

"I'm sorry, Joe," Molly said softly. "But you need to understand that all these fishing guides and quite a few of the clients..." She stopped and seemed to be choosing her words carefully. "Well, most of what they say to me is designed only to test the waters—to see if I'm interested in a roll in the hay."

"I asked you to sit by the fire and talk." Joe still stared at the fire. "You didn't have to talk to me like that."

"Well, I came over here to talk tonight. And I am sorry if I hurt your feelings."

"I don't think you're sorry! I think you're a dented can! One minute you're polite and friendly, the next minute you're downright mean-spirited. I think maybe you're just the autistic woman who works at the fly shop. You don't seem to have any feelings. You don't care about me. Hell, you took a little extra effort and wiped your feet on me. I didn't deserve that." He turned away and dismissed her.

Molly covered her mouth with one hand, then stood up and began to walk away. She'd nearly reached the edge of the circle of firelight and disappeared into the dark when Joe stood up and called to her. "Molly, wait!"

Joe hurried over and stood face to face with her in the dim light. "I'm sorry, now. I am. I just wanted a pound of flesh. I wanted to get even. I'm sorry, Molly. Please come back and sit with me for a while. Please?" Joe touched Molly's arm and led her back to her chair by the fire. "Please?"

"OK," Joe said when they were both seated by the fire again. "Can we forget all that stuff and start over?"

"I know how I act sometimes, Joe. But I have reasons. I am sorry. And you're right, you didn't deserve that kind of treatment," Molly said.

"Fair enough. But you were right too," Joe said. "You know, I could have invited one of the other guides over if I needed someone to talk to that night. But I enjoy those little visits you and I share in the morning. And to tell the truth, I wanted to talk to a woman." Joe leaned back in his chair, stretched his legs toward the fire, and looked away from Molly. "Sometimes it's just better to talk to a woman. They see things and say things that a man just doesn't, or can't. There's something soothing in a conversation with a woman." Joe looked over and grinned a sheepish grin. "Besides that, I think you're pretty—really pretty. I just wanted to stand a little closer to that fire, too. Can't blame me for that, can you?"

"See! That's what I mean, Joe. Nobody says things like that!" Molly leaned back in her chair and relaxed. "I wanted to talk to you too, Joe, because of the things you say and do. But I have...well, it's just hard for me to let people get very close. It's...I." She stopped herself. "I am sorry for the way I spoke to you. It's..."

"It's over. Forget it, Molly. I'm sorry too. Now forget it!" Joe said.

"OK. So now tell me who you are?" she said.

"You tell me who you are," Joe shrugged. "I guess I'm about like every guy who rolls in here—just someone looking for a place to rest."

"No. No, that's not true," Molly said slowly and shook her head. "The other men that live here are doing it because they're young and wild and reckless. Living here for a while is just part of that lifestyle. But you...well, I don't think that's you."

"Oh?"

"No. That first afternoon when you pulled up to the shop in your truck with the snowplow? I could see that you were way different."

"How?"

"When I watched you get out of your truck and walk to the shop? I just thought you were a cowboy driving an old truck. But then I watched you walk for a few steps and I knew you weren't a cowboy." She smiled when she stopped talking.

"Oh?"

"Yeah. They're all beat up and hunched over, and they walk like they're dragging something along behind them when they're your age."

Joe thought of Mr. Crossman and Murdo, and he knew instantly what Molly was talking about. "Go on," Joe said when he turned toward Molly. "And just how old do you think I am?"

"Well, not that old! It's just that if you'd been a cowboy your whole life, you wouldn't look as good as you do. Your face would be scarred from fighting and a rough lifestyle, and your hands would be all gnarly and broken. Look at your hands. They look…"—she paused—"…young! You look young. You couldn't have been a cowboy."

Joe accepted her assessment with a nod.

"And the way you asked about a job? You hadn't planned to apply for work. You just did that on a lark. You had no place to go, did you? That was strange. And then, remember, I caught you sleeping in your truck?" Molly kicked at a rock by the fire pit, then continued. "The first thing Marsh said about you…know what that was? He said you were a little odd! Coming from a guy like Marsh Clements—who really knows about odd, in case you hadn't noticed—well, that was interesting. But you never struck me as 'odd.' Lost, maybe, but not odd. You just don't seem to be like the others who find their way here." Molly nodded for a moment as she stared into the fire. Then she bent over and held her face against the soft fur on Jake's neck. She'd interrupted herself to hug the puppy. When she was ready, she sat up and continued reciting her list of reasons why she'd been curious about Joe.

"You got along so well with those 'steely-eyed gunslingers' Marsh hates so much. I saw you give a tip to those two nuns—that actually was a little odd! In fact, they raved about you. All they could talk about was how much fun they'd had talking with you about books and religion and all kinds of philosophical stuff. Marsh has you out to his place and plays his crazy game of golf with you and comes back and tells me over and over again how much he enjoys having you out to his home. As far as I know, I'm the only one who's been there more than once, by the way." Molly stopped to reorganize her thoughts.

"But today, when you fired Sam Palmer? That was it! I just had to come over and talk to you. He's the biggest tipper we've ever had here, and you fired him! You got along so well with the gunslingers, Marsh and I both thought you'd do well with Sam Palmer. What happened?" Molly asked.

"Well," Joe said after he'd thought about it for a moment, "he was rude, and selfish—really selfish—and condescending. He treated me badly, and I got angry. That's about all, I guess. I just didn't want his money bad enough to put up with everything else."

Molly shook her head and asked, "So just who are you, Joe? I heard you tell those nuns you were a rich man. Are you?"

"Hmph," Joe smiled. "I have just what you can see; that's all." He looked around at the trailer and then gestured toward his truck. "But I'm rich, and I didn't know it until I said it to those nuns. I didn't know it till I got here."

"What do you mean?" Molly leaned forward with her question.

"Well," Joe started, "one dark night a while back, I was having a soak in a metal livestock tank with six other naked, drunk cowboys." Joe looked over at Molly and grinned. "Got the picture?"

Molly nodded.

"There was a great philosopher named Preston Murdock sitting next to me, and we were talking about getting rich. Well, Murdo just leaned back and looked into the night sky and said something I can't forget: 'The rich man ain't the one who has the most; he's the one who needs the least!'" Joe raised his eyebrows and grinned at Molly. "I realized I was a rich man shortly after I got here. Found that if I could learn to understand the things I need instead of those things I want, I'd be fine."

"That's why I came over here, Joe. That's why," Molly smiled.

"I'm sorry I was rude, Molly," Joe replied, content to leave the talk of philosophy behind.

"But I still don't know any more about you," Molly said.

"Didn't Marsh tell you?" Joe asked.

"Not a word," Molly replied. She leaned back in her chair, and Jake lay down at her feet.

Joe sighed, then kicked a piece of wood into the fire. "Recently divorced. No job. I used to be a dentist," he confessed. "That's why my hands aren't too beat up."

"Really? That is a little unusual. Not many people would walk away from that." She paused for a second, then continued. "Where's home?"

"Right here, I guess," Joe said flatly as he looked into the fire. "Used to be Minnesota."

"So what happened?" she asked.

"It's a long story," Joe shrugged. "Just wasn't meant to be. I was unhappy, so I left."

Molly waited for a moment, then leaned toward Joe. "Drugs? Alcohol? What happened?" she asked. "There's gotta be something more to it."

"Last time I told this story, I had to make up a lie because nobody could believe the truth." Joe grinned as he remembered the rainy night at Cowboy Camp. "But maybe you'll believe the truth," he said.

"Which is?" Molly asked.

"I was just unhappy and in a bad marriage, like I said. I thought life needed to have some meaning. So I guess I went looking for it," he said.

She leaned over and poked at the coals in the fire with a small stick, then tossed another small piece of wood into the fire. "So did you find any...meaning?"

"Hmph," Joe whispered. "Not yet. Probably never will. Who knows?"

"Wow," she said under her breath, as if she couldn't quite believe his answer. Then she turned to him. "You know, Joe," Molly said, "I have met others who found their way out here and said something similar to what you just said. They just decided to go back home and try harder and do their job better and love their wife more..."

"I went down that road several times. One more time would have killed me—that much I'm pretty sure of." Joe felt himself relaxing as he confessed, or explained, his life story to Molly. "I won't be going back." Joe began to chuckle softly. "You know, Molly, I was in a truck stop in Wyoming, trying to explain all this to my brother, and I wound up using the story of Hernan Cortez. When he reached the New World, he made his men watch while he burned their ships so they'd know that retreat was impossible. They had to go on! I like that story," Joe sighed.

"Why were you explaining it to your brother?" Molly asked.

"He's my best friend. He's my only friend besides Jake," Joe shrugged. "And he's sort of handling the disposal of my old life."

Molly and Joe both stared into the fire for several silent moments, each of them letting the glowing embers and flickering tongues of yellow fire unlock visions of their old lives.

"You know, when I left everything behind, I guess I thought I could just collect up all the good things from my life and take them with me—just leave the old life behind. I thought I'd just surround myself with all the good things I could find and live without all the bad things. But the bad things, the failures, they always sort of find their way back to your life too. I guess a shrink would say I still have a few open wounds, huh?" he said.

"Lotta that around here," Molly said.

"So what's your story?" Joe asked while he poked a stick into the fire.

"Oh, about like yours, I guess," Molly replied. "Divorce, some hard times, then I wound up here." She stared at the fire as though she was lost trying to remember something, and she began to speak while she was looking into the orange coals. "Funny thing...I thought I could gather up all the bad and unhappy and painful things and just live here with them. But sure enough, good things start to..." She stopped herself and looked up, as though she'd just remembered something she wasn't supposed to talk about. "I should be going, Joe," she said as she leaned forward. "It's late."

"I'm off tomorrow!" Joe said. "Stay a while?"

"Would you like to have dinner with me Thursday?" Molly asked. "We can talk more then."

"Sure."

"My place, seven o'clock?" Molly asked.

"Sure," Joe shrugged. "It's not a date, right?" he added.

"Correct," Molly said as she began to back away from the fire. And she smiled the smile Joe liked so much. "But we'll have an elegant dinner by Fort Smith standards."

"You mean like where we look into a fish tank and each pick out the live lobster we want and listen to violin music while we eat?" Joe teased.

Molly pointed at him and nodded. "Exactly! We'll do the Fort Smith equivalent," she said as she backed out of the circle of light from the campfire and stepped into the darkness. "Thursday at seven!" she called when she was out of sight.

"Hey, Molly!" Joe stood up and called into the darkness.

"Yes," she answered from the darkness.

"I'm sorry for what I said—really sorry."

"Me too. See you Thursday, Joe."

chapter
thirty-five

Marsh Clements was sitting on the little red bench on the first tee when Joe and Jake arrived. Joe had spent the entire day in his trailer tying flies and playing with Jake while he waited for his time in exile to end.

"So how was YOUR day on the river with Sam Palmer?" Joe asked as he crossed the little green patch of grass and sat next to Marsh.

"It was all right, I guess. I did most of the damage control last night. Stayed up and drank with Sam and Vic for several hours. That Sam Palmer, he is a piece of work; thinks he's pretty special." Marsh shook his head and scowled slightly. "But he's such a big tipper. He gave me a thousand dollars today! Biggest tipper I ever saw! You just have to be nice to him."

"No, you have to grovel and eat shit," Joe said.

"True enough," Marsh laughed. "He was happy to think that I fired you and that you might die in the gutter." Marsh chuckled for a moment, then asked Joe, "So what happened yesterday on the river? I don't get it. You got along with the two gunslingers but not Sam Palmer. What happened?" Marsh asked with a shrug of his shoulders.

Joe reached into Marsh's golf bag, moved the clubs around for a moment, then withdrew the driver. "Where we playin' today?" he said as he took several practice swings and ignored Marsh's question for a moment.

"St. Andrews. The first hole has the widest fairway in golf—actually, a shared fairway with the eighteenth, you know—so you can let the big dog eat. But you'll have to carry the Swilcan Burn with your second shot." Marsh paused, then added, "So what happened with Palmer?"

"Well, I just found him insufferable," Joe said while he swung the driver in long, slow swings to stretch the muscles in his shoulders. "It's not so hard to understand, Marsh. I spent most of my life doing things I really didn't like and didn't want to do. But the moment I decided I'd had enough and I left my old life behind...well, since that moment, something changed. I find myself saying and doing things I could never have done before. I really like the guy who's living in my skin. For most of my life, I would have just sat there and let Sam Palmer stick fish hooks in me and pretend I didn't mind. I just can't do that anymore." Joe shook his head and looked across the Big Horn River. "I just can't do that anymore. I don't care how much it costs me." He stared at the cow pasture on the other bank for a moment, then reached into one of the plastic buckets containing golf balls. "We ready to tee off, Marsh?" Joe asked as he pushed his tee into the ground.

"Yeah, let's play, Joe. But wait just a minute. There's a boat with a couple fishermen in it coming this way." Marsh pointed upstream. "It's considered bad form, a breach of etiquette, both at St. Andrews and the Big Horn, to hit into another group. We'll just wait a minute and let them play through."

Marsh was sitting on the red bench, and Joe was standing by his ball, leaning on his driver, when the fishermen passed in front of them. The two fishermen wore puzzled looks when their boat drifted by the tee box and Marsh and Joe waved at them. One of the fishermen looked across at the other side of the river, then said something inaudible when the boat had drifted past them.

"OK, you're up, Joe," Marsh said. "Don't push it too far to the right, and when you get to the second hole you'll want to put that driver in the bag. It'll only get you in trouble on this course. The second is a tight fairway that demands accuracy. It's also one of those huge double greens: the people playin' number sixteen will be putting on the same green as us."

Joe hit a powerful, soaring drive that carried far out into Mr. Carrigan's cow pasture and landed at the base of the biggest cottonwood tree.

"Nice one!" Marsh said.

"How do you know all this stuff about all these golf courses?" Joe asked. "Have you played all of them?"

"No. Hell no! Just the finest courses in eastern Montana! But I read a lot," Marsh smiled. "And I have come to enjoy the striking of golf balls. I do appreciate the beauty of doing a difficult thing well, even if I can't actually do it myself." He walked to the middle of the tee box, teed his ball up, and struck a shot that skipped twice along the surface of the Big Horn before it disappeared in the current.

"Helluva shot!" Joe muttered and shook his head. "Helluva shot! You'll carry the Swilcan Burn with your second shot, and then you only need to go up and down in two for a par! Helluva shot!" Joe said while a huge smile pushed his dimple deeply into his cheek.

"Thank you for noticing! And welcome to my world," Marsh said when he returned to the red bench and pulled a scorecard for the Royal and Ancient course at St. Andrews from the wooden box at the edge of the tee box. Marsh folded the card and wrote his score for the first hole. Then he turned to Joe and announced, "You took a bogey there, Joe. Piss-poor second shot. What a shame. Knocked it into a sand trap and took two strokes to get out! Sorry."

"Well, horseshit!" Joe sighed.

Marsh and Joe spent more time talking than golfing for the next two hours. They moved very slowly around the links at St. Andrews, and they had plenty of time to discuss the current condition of the fishing and the mayfly hatches on the Big Horn, along with the subtleties of each hole on the Old Course.

"You hungry?" Marsh asked without looking up as he totaled their scores.

"I could eat the ass out of a dead skunk," Joe replied. Then he stood and waited for Marsh to finish adding.

"We're not having that tonight," Marsh said while he added.

"Well, you never know what's in those wieners," Joe said while Marsh ignored him.

"You shot four over par—lots of missed opportunities out there today, Joe! I was three under—played great!" Marsh simply ignored Joe's comment about the wieners, folded the scorecard, and put it in his pocket. "Let's eat outside tonight by the fire."

The sun was well below the horizon, and only the yellow light from a campfire—like the ones Joe sat around in his own backyard—

illuminated Marsh's tee box, just above the Big Horn River, when supper was ready.

"You put out quite a spread, Marsh," Joe said as he placed a wiener onto a hotdog bun and reached for some potato chips. "Sort of like eating at a real nice gas station."

"All the major condiments and representatives from two of the major food groups are present here. And besides that, it's better than chili beans from a can!" Marsh said as he prepared his own hotdog. "Hey, step inside the cabin and grab that other tray with the lemonade, will you?" Marsh asked.

"What's that thing sitting by the door?" Joe asked when he returned from the cabin with a tray of lemonade and some condiments. "It looks like a long, black tube with a mouthpiece, like the one I had on my trombone in junior high band."

"It's a blowgun," Marsh replied as he squeezed mustard onto his hotdog.

"No. Really?" Joe persisted.

"It's a blowgun!" Marsh nodded, and he continued with his hotdog.

"Bullshit! I don't believe that one," Joe announced with a chuckle.

"Well, go get it, then!" Marsh said from his wooden chair by the fire pit while he took a bite of his hotdog. "Damn fine meal!" he said with a mouthful. "The sauerkraut really tops it off, don't you think? Go get the blow gun, Joe. Bring it over here. There's a few darts right there by the back door—that's where I keep 'em. I'll show you!"

Joe set his plate down and walked back to the cabin. When he returned, he handed the long, black tube and several darts to Marsh. "I gotta see this," he said as he sat in the chair next to Marsh.

"What would you like me to shoot?" Marsh said as he chewed a second bite from his hotdog.

"That sign: the one that says 'Winged Foot,' over there," Joe replied.

Marsh continued to chew his hotdog for a moment, then swallowed deliberately. He raised a glass of lemonade to his mouth and took two swallows in an obvious effort to clear the food from his mouth. "Not good if I blow a wiener down this thing," he said as he pushed a small dart with a feathered end into the blowgun. "OK, Joe. I'm gonna put this in the center of the second 'o' of 'Winged Foot.'" Then he drew a breath, brought the tube to his mouth, and suddenly the sign made a popping noise: the small dart was stuck solidly in the center of the second 'o.'"

Joe Mix smiled a crooked smile, began to stare in astonishment, and then covered his mouth with his left hand and looked over at Marsh.

"Put some more sauerkraut on there, will ya, Joe?" Marsh said as he extended his plate toward Joe.

"So where did you...get that? Where did you learn to do that?" Joe said as he piled sauerkraut on Marsh's hotdog. "What the hell did I just see?" Joe chuckled.

"Well, I spend a lot of time right here. And as you could tell from watching Jake while we were playing golf, there's plenty of mice out here, and mice are expendable. So I salvaged the mouthpiece from MY trombone and found this pipe and these darts at a hobby and craft shop in Billings. I sit right out here and execute mice several nights a week. I'm damn good. A few more potato chips, if you please." Marsh reached his plate toward Joe once more.

"You mean, you sit by this fire and blow darts at mice?" Joe asked.

"Sure. I'll show you! Go get that section of cardboard just inside the cabin door, would you?" Marsh leaned back in his chair and pointed to the cabin.

Joe got up and walked back to the cabin. Then he returned with a section of cardboard about six feet long and one foot tall.

"Unbelievable!" Joe mumbled as he unfolded the cardboard. "Unbelievable!"

"Just put it on the other side of the fire, Joe. Yeah...right over there where the grass is worn away...right there on the dirt, about four feet from the fire pit. That cardboard reflects the firelight just right and lights up Main Street. Now drop some crumbs from your plate in front of it if you would," Marsh requested.

"Unbelievable," Joe said when he sat in his chair next to Marsh and put his dinner plate back in his lap. "Unbelievable!"

Resting on the dirt several feet from the fire, close to the field of tall grass that bordered Marsh's cabin, was the piece of cardboard Joe had carried over. It had been painstakingly fashioned to look like a series of tiny storefronts from an old western town. One storefront read "Marsh's Saloon." Another read "Marsh's General Store." Yet another read "Marsh's Bank." Windows and doors had been cut into every storefront, and the lettering above each store had the authentic look of western print.

"You made that, didn't you?" Joe asked.

"Damn straight, partner! And before you can say 'steely-eyed gun-slinger,' there's gonna be mice a-showin' up in my town. They'll be lookin' for a fight, I reckon. And I aim to show 'em that this town ain't big enough for the both of us." Marsh sat down on the ground by the fire, directly across from Marshville. He raised the blowgun into the air and winked at Joe.

"You see, stranger, this ain't all I blow," he said while he held up the blow gun. "I'm havin' a hankerin' for a shot of reefer, and if'n you'll just pass me that other plastic bag there, by the lemonade, I'll show you how this all works." Marsh nodded and winked at Joe again, clearly enjoying himself.

Joe hadn't noticed before, but there on the tray, next to the mustard, sauerkraut, and lemonade, was a plastic bag full of marijuana, papers, and matches.

"You mean you sit here in the light of a campfire, smoke pot, and shoot mice that wander into Marshville...with a blowgun?"

"Well, not every night. Sometimes I just goof off!" Marsh smiled a wicked smile. "Now, pass me that bag, would you?"

Marsh took the bag from Joe and rolled a fat joint while Joe watched. He lit the joint and inhaled deeply. Then, while he held his breath, he extended his hand toward Joe, offering him the joint.

Joe shook his head no.

"How come?" Marsh coughed, and smoke billowed from him.

"Just never tried it before," Joe admitted with a smile.

"Well, hell, I guess that explains quite a bit. No wonder you had your undies in a bunch for so long." Marsh held the joint out toward Joe once again. Joe stared for a second, then surprised himself: he put his thumb and forefinger together and took it from Marsh. He knew he was just sitting by a campfire, about to smoke some pot. There were probably high school and college kids all over the country doing the same thing. But he couldn't sidestep the feeling that he was about to do the wildest thing he'd ever done.

"Now what?" Joe asked with a smirk.

"Ever smoke a cigarette?" Marsh asked.

"Huh uh," Joe replied.

Marsh closed his eyes and shook his head in disgust, then looked back at Joe. "OK, put that thing up to your lips and take a drag. Breathe in, you know? Pull it right into your lungs and hold it there. It's gonna tickle on the way in, but don't cough. Just hold your breath. Here, give it back to me. I'll demonstrate."

The end of the joint burned hot and glowed as Marsh drew on it. He held his breath and offered the joint to Joe again. When Joe had the joint in his hand, he passed a silent question to Marsh with his eyes. Marsh simply answered by motioning for Joe to "go ahead" with a wave of the back of his hand.

Another new—and not so unfriendly—current began to pull at Joe as he raised the joint to his lips. The smoke and heat burned his throat as he drew it into his lungs. After he'd held his breath for twenty seconds, he offered the joint to Marsh. But Marsh repeated the "go ahead" gesture, so Joe exhaled and took another drag on the joint.

"So what am I supposed to feel?" Joe asked when he'd passed the joint back to Marsh.

"Jesus, a misspent youth doing math problems and shit like that, huh?" Marsh asked.

"Pretty much," Joe confessed.

"Didn't get out and do much bird doggin' either, did ya?"

"No."

"Well, here's to a good second shot!" Marsh said as he took another drag on the joint.

"So what am I supposed to feel?" Joe asked again.

"I believe that someone of your background would refer to it as a mild euphoria," Marsh smiled. "You'll know when it hits. I remember once..." Marsh stopped in midsentence and hunched his shoulders. "Don't move, pardner! There's a stranger in town!" he added softly. He reached for the blowgun with one hand and pointed toward Marshville with the other.

There, in front of Marsh's Saloon on the other side of the campfire, stood a nervous-looking, gray field mouse. The mouse must have entered town through the swinging doors of Marsh's Saloon, Joe thought. As Joe watched Marsh Clements push a dart into the blowgun, then start to aim the gun, everything began to move in slow motion. The thought of a mouse ridin' into Marshville, lookin' for a fight, seemed pretty funny all of a sudden.

Joe watched with an open mouth while Marsh readied his weapon. Marsh's chest expanded ever so slightly, then a small cloud of dust exploded over there on Marshville's Main Street. When Joe turned his head, the mouse lay dead, impaled by Marsh's dart, and both men erupted in laughter as though they'd just heard the funniest joke of their lives. While he was still laughing, Marsh walked around the campfire and into Marshville. He picked up the dart by the feathered end and flicked the dead mouse over the tee box and into the Big Horn River.

"Helluva shot! Helluva shot," Joe laughed.

"I guess I'm a gunslinger too," Marsh laughed. "And I don't miss those little sonsabitches either! Mouse nests in my tractor and car, not to mention the cabin! I don't mind killin' mice. You wanna take a shot, Joe?"

"Maybe another time. I think I've reached a state of mild euphoria. I think I'll just sit here."

"Yeah, I guess that's the way to enjoy your mild euphoria. Everything sounds funnier and feels better—goes great with sex," Marsh said.

"Really?" Joe asked. Then he added, "You're the oldest pot smoker I know! Just seems a little strange to hear you talkin' about pot and sex."

"I like women too! Just like the next man. Even if I am a little older," Marsh said when he leaned back and took another hit. "I got a buddy up in Billings who's a pharmacist. He's a burned-out old flower child just like me. Comes down here fishin' every now and then. Anyway, I've been tryin' to explain to him that he'd have a runaway hit if he could just come up with a drug like...well, let's call it Viagrajuana: you smoke it and you get high, and a boner! Now, there's a winner, huh?" Marsh held the roach between his thumb and forefinger and pointed it at Joe when he spoke.

Marsh's comment struck Joe as the funniest thing he'd ever heard. He sat around Marsh's campfire and laughed until his sides ached.

chapter
thirty-six

The cool river water brought a soothing, icy relief when Joe splashed it on his face. He'd been feeling sweat running down his back, and his head was uncomfortably warm under the Stetson. He walked a little farther into the stream and let the Big Horn River wrap its cold hands around his legs. Then he took his hat off and splashed some more water on the top of his head before he put his hat back on.

Today was going to be a scorcher. Usually, just being on the river seemed to cool fishermen during the hottest summer days. So much cold water so close at hand just kept the summer heat under control. But today, the Montana sun seemed to bring fire from above and then jump back up off the surface of the Big Horn to attack from below. There was no breeze on the river, and the heat was oppressive even at 10:00 a.m.

Joe looked over at his clients for the day and was thankful. A husband and wife from Michigan, they'd never make it for a full day on the river. Certainly they'd be ready to head in by early afternoon. They were already tired of the heat; they'd asked to pull over on the riverbank and sit in the shade for a few minutes.

The young couple seemed content in their midmorning break. While they relaxed, Joe stepped into the current to cool himself and scan the far bank for rising fish. But the trout, his clients, and even the heat vanished for a moment when he remembered that today was Thursday, and he'd be having dinner with Molly tonight. He felt a little twinge of anticipation in his belly when he thought about tonight, and the only similar sensation he could compare it to was waiting for school to be out so he could hurry home and play ball when he was a kid.

The bizarre golf games at Marsh's tee box and the long talks about life that went with them were always fun. Marsh was becoming a close friend. Joe smiled and shook his head when he thought about smoking pot and shooting mice with a blowgun. It had been so odd, Joe thought, such a stretch from his old life. He'd sat beside a campfire holding a joint—the first joint he'd ever touched—in one hand and a four-foot-long blow gun with a trombone mouthpiece in his other hand, while he'd watched his new friend dispose of a dead mouse that he'd killed in an imaginary duel in front of a cardboard cutout of a western town.

What would Donny say? Joe wondered. But he knew he couldn't tell Donny about those things over the phone. It was just out there beyond the scope of experience that could be explained properly to Donny during a phone conversation. Yeah, Joe thought, his growing friendship with Marsh was beginning to reveal some important link between them, but he'd have to keep it to himself for now. Donny just wouldn't understand Marsh and this place quite yet.

All the laughs and long conversations with Marsh were fine, but tonight would be different. Tonight he'd be with a woman, and that was just different than talking with another man. Molly would listen to him differently than a man would, and she'd say things that a man couldn't or wouldn't say. Perhaps, on some level, when a man talked privately with a woman, there was always a hint of sex. Maybe just that remotest of remote possibilities was what made talking to a woman special? No, Joe thought, there was just something deeper—more compassionate— about the way women spoke when they befriended men, and he guessed that most men sensed it too. He'd certainly noticed the phenomenon at the office back in his old life. Women patients listened better, asked better questions, took better care of themselves, and for the most part they'd even tried to make Joe's job easier. Women were just better people than men most of the time.

Joe wondered just what the inside of Molly's trailer looked like and what she might wear tonight. He could see her auburn hair and her smooth skin, and he could smell her perfume...

"OK, Joe, let's go fishing!" called a male voice from the riverbank beside the boat. His clients had returned from their break under some shady cottonwood trees, and they were ready to move along downstream. Joe had been so lost in his own thoughts that he hadn't heard them return.

"All right, climb in and we'll move downstream a ways. I know a nice riffle up ahead," Joe said. Once his clients were seated, he leaned on the oars and moved the boat back into the current. In only a moment, his shoulders were hot once again, uncomfortable under the blazing sun. Then he felt the weight of his hat, and he decided to take the heavy Stetson off for a few minutes. Besides…he'd noticed recently that when he looked in the mirror, the top of his face seemed very white and the bottom half of his face was tanned and dark. Maybe if he could catch a little sun on the top of his head, Molly wouldn't notice such an extreme "farmer tan" on his head tonight.

Several pods of rising trout greeted Joe's boat as it slid around a bend in the river, and Joe silently moved his clients into position along a quiet stretch of current just downstream from the fish. He stepped out of the boat into several feet of water, and the river cooled him immediately. The water's surface along the bank where they'd stopped was smooth; the current was slow and weak right here. The bright sun was glaring into Joe's eyes as he carefully moved his clients within casting distance of the fish. The cold water felt so good as it pressed around him that he waded into even deeper water in search of more relief from the heat.

As far as Joe could see, there were no really large fish rising to the surface to feed. The Baetis hatch was coming off in good numbers— thousands of little blue-winged mayflies were being carried along on the current—but the big fish just didn't seem to be feeding yet.

He separated the husband and wife after he'd moved the husband close to a busy pod of rising trout. The husband was a competent fisherman, and he seemed anxious to fish this pretty little stretch of water beside the riverbank.

The wife, however, was a complete novice and had no chance of catching a fish without the direct supervision of her guide. So Joe moved her to another stretch of flat water and stayed with her. He'd been down this road a few other times with clients, and he knew just what to do. Joe had been hired by a married couple, but he knew that when they found themselves on a productive stretch of water, it was just understood that the husband wanted to be left alone to fish. Then Joe was supposed to take the wife somewhere nearby—out of the way, actually—and devote his time to showing the woman how to maybe catch a few fish. At the very least, he was expected to stay out of the husband's way for a while. It was the best of both worlds, and it worked quite well. The husband got a chance to fish as he wanted to while someone babysat his wife. Maybe she'd learn to catch a fish and come to appreciate this whole thing, and maybe not. Either way, it was fine for the husband. While he'd been doing this for the past few weeks, Joe had noticed a strange dynamic at work. Women would listen to the things he told them about fly casting and fishing and would do the things he said to do, and they'd have success. But if their husbands gave the same instructions Joe gave them, women would fail to listen or in some way resist learning. Perhaps it was that men spoke to their wives differently—more impatiently. Who knew the reason, but it just didn't work for men to teach their wives to fly fish. It was much the same for golf or any number of things. He remembered it from his own marriage too.

From the beginning, Joe had found that he could teach women to catch fish if he could work with them one on one, out of earshot from their husbands. Today was no different: the woman learned to cast a fly line in only minutes and began to catch fish immediately. Joe stood at her side and helped with her hands and arms and her casting stroke for nearly ninety minutes while she caught fish after fish. Every teaching point that was followed by success resulted in more enthusiasm. An hour and a half passed while Joe fished with the woman. She was asking him a pretty insightful question about how he could tell when trout were feeding on emergers when she stopped herself in midsentence. "Wow, Joe! The top of your head is glowing! I think you've sunburned your head!"

The instant she spoke the words, Joe felt the burn she was talking about and realized he'd left his hat off way too long.

"I'll be right back," Joe said as he attempted to smile. He splashed some water on his head and quickly made his way to the boat where his Stetson was waiting on the seat. "Shit," he said under his breath. He knew he'd burned his head badly. The cold river water stung his pink scalp and forehead. He imagined water boiling off his head much like water droplets splashing into a red-hot frying pan. He winced when he pushed his Stetson onto his head. The hat was hurting him, but he couldn't take it off until he got out of the sun. "Shit!" he grumbled as he made his way back to his client's side.

It wouldn't be so bad if he'd burned his nose and ears and maybe his forehead; he'd done that before. But he'd been keeping his fine blonde hair cut very short, and today it had offered no protection against the fierce summer sun. The tender skin on top of his head was throbbing, and he imagined his client had noticed a red glare burning just beneath the short-cropped haircut.

"You OK, Joe?" she asked when Joe returned to the young woman's side.

"Sure. I'm fine," he lied. The hat did shield his now ultra-sensitive head from the searing rays of the sun. But it was no use: even the warm summer breeze began to burn his ears, nose, and forehead. The scalp under his hat felt like it was sizzling.

Mercifully, the young couple decided they'd had enough shortly after lunch. They asked Joe to take them in before they overheated, and Joe was only too happy to comply. He sensed that if he stayed in the sun any longer, he was about to get nauseous himself.

When he stopped at the fly shop to pick up Jake, he made a point to be quick about it and not let Molly see the sunburn on his face and head.

"See you tonight," Molly said softly as Joe walked past her at the counter in the fly shop.

It was all Joe could do to muster a smile and reply. "Looking forward to it, Molly. See you in a couple hours." His head was throbbing.

Molly touched his arm when he passed by her on his way out the door, as if she was trying to keep something a secret from anyone near-by, and she said, "Don't spoil your appetite." She punctuated her sentence with the luscious smile that drew Joe to her. Then, as an afterthought, she called out, "Oh, by the way. Jake should be tired out. He went to a birthday party this afternoon. One of the kids in the trailer next to mine turned six today, and Jake spent part of the day playing with the kids at the party. He ate cake with the kids too!"

"Yeah, that's great," Joe said, trying not to sound too impatient to get home. "See you at seven, Molly," he said as he walked out the front door of the fly shop.

Joe's trailer was hot—uncomfortably hot—and as he opened the windows a little wider, he knew he couldn't cool the little trailer adequately. But at least he was out of the sun, and that felt good. After a cold shower, he plopped onto the little couch in his kitchen/living room wearing only his boxer shorts and aimed a small electric fan at himself.

The top of his head still felt like it was on fire, so he washed four aspirin down with a glass of icewater and sprinkled the last few drops of cold water onto his head.

The sound of Jake chewing on something was the only thing Joe was aware of for the next two hours while he lay in front of the little fan and pretended to sleep. He tried to go to sleep and dream about having a nice evening at Molly's, but for most of the time he lay awake and thought about his head while he listened to Jake playing with something over by the table. He waited for the breeze from the fan to cool him down, but relief never came.

Joe eventually awoke—or maybe just decided to get up. He sat on the couch for a moment with his feet on the floor and his elbows resting on his knees while he let the fan blow directly at his head. When he raised his eyebrows, it felt as if the skin on top of his head might split open and then start on fire. "Mmmm," he groaned. "Shit, that hurts."

He decided to take another cold shower and have a few more aspirin before he walked over to Molly's trailer. Standing in the little bathroom looking at himself in the mirror, he couldn't help but feel good about the way the summer's hard work had restored his flat stomach and his shoulders and arms. But his head...his head looked like a lobster. It hurt him just to look at it. He was half dressed when he walked to the front door and found Jake still chewing on something.

"Aw, shit, Jake! Why did you do that?" Joe said.

At the mention of his name, Jake raised his head and passed a pathetically innocent look to Joe. "What?" he seemed to be asking. But just in front of him lay what was left of Joe's tennis shoes. Actually, Jake had only destroyed the right shoe. He'd chewed the toe and the heel from one half of Joe's only pair of decent shoes.

"Shit, Jake. I was gonna wear those tonight. Shit!"

Joe dressed in shorts, a cotton golf shirt, and one and a half shoes after yet another cold shower. He took a newspaper in one hand to shade himself from the day's final torturous, red-hot rays of the sun, then stepped out of his trailer.

"Lookin' good, huh, Jake?" he said to his dog as he looked at his own feet. He shook his head in disbelief at his sorry condition and grimaced as he held a week-old newspaper up to shade his head. "OK, Jake, let's go. Let's go have an elegant dinner. Thanks for the nice work on my shoes," he added.

The walk over to Molly's took only about three minutes, but Joe held the newspaper between the sun and his scorching head every step of the way. There was no sign of life in Fort Smith other than a couple guides talking in front of one of the fly shops, and no one recognized Joe.

Molly was smiling when she swung her door open, but when she saw Joe standing on her doorstep holding a newspaper up to shade his flaming red face and head, she stepped back and stared for a second.

"Oooo, Joe! Are you all right?" Molly asked. She stared as if Joe were a little boy who had just been beaten by bullies.

Joe stood on her doorstep, still holding the newspaper to shade his head, after she'd opened the door to her trailer, and cold air rushed out to greet him. "You have air conditioning! Oh, Jesus, that feels good!" was all he could say as he stepped into her home.

"What happened?" Molly said as she closed the door behind Joe and Jake. She was still unable to hide the surprise and concern in her voice. Jake was panting from the heat when he followed Joe through the door. Molly bent over, scratched his ears to say hello, and repeated, "What happened?"

"Left my hat off for a while today; just forgot about it for a while," Joe said when he lowered the newspaper.

"Oooo, that looks like it hurts," Molly said while she inspected Joe's sunburn. She put her right hand on the back of Joe's neck and pulled his head forward so she could get a better look.

"You got that right," Joe sighed. He wanted to tell her how soothing it felt just to have those beautiful hands touching him, even if it was only so she could check out his sunburn. While his head was tilting toward the floor, he noticed the white cotton sock poking out the front of his mangled shoe. "Jake ate my shoe too," he added.

"Well, sit down, Joe. Is there anything I can get you?" Molly said while she led him to a small couch and sat down beside him.

"No. I'm OK. But the air conditioning in here is wonderful!" Joe closed his eyes and leaned back on the couch.

"Would you like a drink?" Molly asked.

"No, thanks. I'm not much of a drinkin' man. But you go ahead," he replied with a polite smile.

"Well, I don't mind if I do!" Molly said as she stood up and walked over to her small kitchen. When she turned her back, Joe's eyes moved up and down along her figure. She was wearing shorts, and Joe had never seen her wearing shorts at work. Her legs were lean, and the muscles in her calves tightened with each step. Joe couldn't help but notice the color of her skin. Like most redheads, she had a creamy, soft color. But when she tanned, her skin seemed to take on an orange cast. It looked to Joe that she'd chosen her leather sandals because they matched the color of her tan so well.

Her hair—the beautiful, rich auburn hair—always caused him to stare at her. That hair seemed to cascade down onto her shoulders. Just below the hair, her breasts were straining gently against her cotton blouse. When she raised herself onto her toes and reached up to take a bottle from the top of the cupboard, Joe couldn't look away from her.

When she brought the bottle back to the countertop, she turned her soft brown eyes to Joe and caught him staring. Joe didn't care; his head hurt and he'd had a hard day. He smiled back at Molly and actually enjoyed letting her know that he'd been staring. When he noticed she was holding a bottle of Cutty Sark Scotch Whisky in one hand, he let go of another old inhibition and blurted, "Hey, I changed my mind. If you're gonna have some of that, I will too." He was looking at the green bottle with the yellow label and the picture of the sailing ship on it, and he remembered his last night at Cowboy Camp.

"Good. I hate to drink alone," Molly said. As she made their drinks, Joe looked about Molly's trailer home. It was a cheap, older-model mobile home, and Joe was pretty sure she was renting it for almost nothing. But it was infinitely nicer than his. The walls were white, and the windows had delicate curtains. The kitchen was neat and clean, and the carpet in the small living room looked almost new. Molly's furniture was comfortable. She'd arranged things so that even this little trailer seemed roomy. She had a small stereo and TV sitting on a shelf made of bricks and boards, like every college kid has in their first apartment. A lava lamp and several candles sat on the top shelf next to her TV. Joe thought the place had a look and feel that only a woman could give it. Molly didn't have much money, but she'd sure made this little trailer seem like home. He remembered the open bag of dog food that he kept on his kitchen table, the waders that always hung from a hook next to his chair, and the sand that seemed to be ground into the cheap red carpet in his living room. He'd have to straighten things up a little if he ever had Molly over for dinner, he thought.

The sound of ice cubes bouncing around inside a cocktail glass had a friendly, happy sort of ring to it for Joe. When Molly brought his scotch and water, she sat next to him on the couch and touched her glass against his. "Here's to air conditioning!" she said.

"I'll drink to that!" Joe said. But when he looked at Molly and smiled, he winced.

"What's the matter, Joe?" Molly asked.

"My head," Joe confessed. "Did you hear it? Sounded like somebody crinkling newspaper into a ball, didn't it? Feels like fire. Just a simple smile makes the skin on top feel like parchment—like it's gonna split open if I smile any bigger." He stopped and tried to stifle an embarrassed smile as he looked at her. "I'll be fine."

"I know something that will work," Molly said.

"I'll be fine," Joe said. "Really."

"No. I know what we're going to do," Molly said. She stood quickly and lifted a pink umbrella from a nook by the door. Then she extended her hand to Joe.

"Where are we going?" Joe asked.

"Well, I had planned that we'd walk over to Yellowtail Grocery and pick out our lobster or some such thing," she said with a huge smile. "And now we have something else to pick up too." She motioned to Joe to come along.

"What's the umbrella for?" Joe asked as he stood up.

"To protect your head from the last and hottest sun of the day. Let's go!"

Molly held the umbrella in her left hand and protected Joe's head from the setting sun as they walked together along the gravel road toward Yellowtail Grocery, Fort Smith's only retail outlet that wasn't a fly shop. Molly's trailer was only about two blocks from Yellowtail Grocery—but then everything in Fort Smith was only about two blocks from Yellowtail Grocery. They left Jake behind, lying on the cool floor by the door.

"They don't have lobster in there," Joe said. It was more a question than a statement of fact.

"I know," Molly replied. "They don't really have much of anything. But I said we'd have an elegant dinner by Fort Smith standards, and we will!"

When Molly and Joe stepped into the store, they were the only customers. A teenage girl who clearly wanted to be somewhere else stood behind the cash register reading a *National Enquirer* magazine, and she refused to greet them. Four plywood shelves that had been painted with a pale aqua color displayed a very limited variety of groceries, and there was plenty of empty shelf space surrounding the products that could be found.

"OK. This is the meat section. C'mere and take your pick," Molly called out to Joe after she'd wandered around the store for a moment.

Joe found his way to her side and stared briefly at the display Molly had found.

"Spam?" Joe said.

Molly raised her eyebrows and nodded. "Spam! They have three cans to choose from. Which one do you like best?"

"Oh, this one for sure!" Joe said. He picked up the can in the middle. "Just look. It's got...well, anyone can see it's the best one." He puffed his cheek out and blew a small cloud of dust off the can, then nodded to her.

Molly took the can from his hand and walked directly to the small shelf with personal hygiene products. She selected a tube of Preparation H, then turned to Joe. "Let's go make an elegant dinner."

"Preparation H?" Joe asked when they stepped outside the door. "Is that for you or the Spam?" Joe asked.

"It's for you!" Molly replied with a smile.

"Huh?"

"About two years ago, some other guy sunburned his head out here. He was a huge, fat old retired doctor from Iowa. Anyway, he was almost sick his head hurt so bad. He had me go get some of this for him. Said it felt great! Took the pain away and let him enjoy his last day of fishing before he went home."

"You mean he put that hemorrhoid medicine on his ass and his head felt better?"

"I'll forget you said that," Molly smiled. "You know it has an anesthetic that would make sunburn feel better."

"Yeah," Joe smiled, then winced as the smile pulled at his sunburn. "I suppose I can give it a try. Do I rub the Spam on my head too?"

"No. That would be our elegant dinner. We're gonna barbecue some Spam! Like I said, by Fort Smith standards, this is elegant."

When they returned to her trailer, Molly led Joe directly to her kitchen and sat him down at one of the kitchen chairs. She stood in front of Joe and removed the cap from the tube of Preparation H. When she stepped toward him, he sat straight in the chair. Her breasts were inches from his face when she started using her index finger, ever so gently, to rub the cool gel around the top of Joe's head and down onto his forehead.

"Feels cool," Joe admitted.

"Looks nice, too!" Molly said, then began to chuckle. It was the first time he'd ever heard Molly laugh, and it was such a pleasant sound that he lifted his eyes up to look at her for a second.

Joe could feel his short, fine hair begin to swirl and stay plastered down with the greasy medication, but it felt so good he didn't care. Maybe it was the anesthetic beginning to work, or maybe it was Molly's index finger softly touching his head and face. What did it matter? It was worth a sunburn if he could have her touch him like this.

"Hey, Molly?"

"Yeah?"

"If I told you I thought it was erotic the way you're applying hemorrhoid medication, what would you say?" Joe asked.

"I'd say that was a wonderful compliment, and the strangest thing anyone ever said to me." Molly laughed again, and the sound of it was as soothing as her touch.

As Molly finished with Joe, she put the top back on the tube and handed Joe his scotch. "So tell me, Joe Mix, how did you wind up here in Fort Smith?" Molly moved to the couch and waited for Joe to join her.

"Hmph. I don't really know how I wound up here," Joe said as he stood up and followed her. He sipped at his scotch and bent over to look at himself in a little mirror on the wall beside the door. Then he closed his eyes and groaned, "I really know what the ladies like." He pointed at his own hair and made a face. His short hair was plastered to his head with a shiny layer of grease, and he knew he looked ridiculous. He sipped at his scotch once more and sat on the couch.

"Tell me, Joe. Tell me," she said.

"Well, it's like I said the other night. I guess I just chose the wrong profession. Lots of people do it," Joe shrugged. "Happens all the time."

"Yeah, I told you I see a lot of men out here talking on and on about how much they hate their job or career, then they just go home and get back to work. As if coming out here for a vacation just sort of recharged their batteries, and they let off a little steam in the process. Maybe all you ever needed was some time off?"

"No. That kind of attitude was killing me, that much I know for sure. I tried that—you know, going back after some time off—and every time I went back, I hated my job a little more. You asked me all this the other night by the fire. I already told you."

"But how could you just leave all that? How could you?" Molly asked.

Joe sighed heavily, then took another sip of his scotch. "Mark Twain said, 'The man who does not read good books has no advantage over the man who cannot read them.' Think about that for a minute." The ice cubes in his glass clinked against each other when he paused to sip at his scotch. "What good would it do me to know that my life was a mess if I lacked the courage to do anything about it? At that point, I'd be better off if I was just a happy idiot. Right? I told you, I NEVER liked dentistry. I made a bad choice when I decided to do it, and I knew right away I'd done wrong. But I was making some money, and other people kept telling me how happy I should be. I just kept on telling myself I must be happy because everyone said I was." Joe stopped himself. He held his glass up to his lips but took it away before he started speaking again. "Changing careers? Changing lives so late?" He sighed heavily again. "Yeah, I can't help but regret that I spent so much time on and went so far down the wrong road. I feel bad. I feel ashamed that I didn't have the good judgment to choose the right road or the courage to turn around sooner." He sipped at his scotch and then shook his head. "But I didn't." Joe shook the ice cubes in his glass and listened to them clink on the side of it. Then he stared at them for a moment. "You know what else really bothers me? That I managed to keep happiness at arm's length for most of my life. I just kept thinking that I'll get happy tomorrow or next week, but I had to get some obstacle behind me before I could get happy." He sighed softly and clinked his ice cubes again. "Then I just kept finding new obstacles to keep happiness away. Maybe I wasn't sure if I'd like being happy. That make any sense to you, Molly?"

"Yes," Molly said.

"I ran down a thousand miles of highway, trying to get away from me, I suppose. But everyplace I went, there I was. Before I stumbled into this place, I worked on a ranch for a while. I lived with some cowboys—even tried to be one. If it hadn't been for the horses and the cattle and all that work, I'd have made it too!" Joe laughed as he recalled his time on the Crossman Ranch. "But you know, living there with those cowboys, I guess I found a part of me I liked. I started to get up every day and like my life. Wish I'd have done that a little sooner. But then, maybe it was all meant to be this way."

Joe stood and walked to the kitchen countertop where the bottle of Cutty Sark rested. While he stared at the label on the Cutty Sark bottle, he said quietly, as if he were talking to himself, "My dad used to call me the Kadoka Kid." He turned the label a little bit and tipped his head. "I found the Kadoka Kid again when I was out there with those guys. How 'bout that?"

He dropped two more ice cubes into his glass, along with some tap water and some scotch, then turned back to Molly. "I guess all of our lives are filled with regrets, aren't they? I had to leave my old life, Molly. I had to know if my life was justified. I had to look for some meaning to it all." Joe stopped and looked around himself. "And I do think I've pretty well got it together now. Just look at me. My head's covered in butt medicine, my dog ate my shoe, and I'm living in a trailer court at the end of the road. I'd say I've pretty well tied up all the loose ends in my life. But that's enough about me. How'd you wind up out here, Molly Malone?"

Molly laughed softly at Joe's summary of his life, then considered her own words carefully for a moment. "Well, after my divorce, I left Denver. I sort of drifted around for a few years. I wound up in West Yellowstone, working at a fly shop. One day, Marsh came into the store and we struck up a conversation. He said he had a shop out here and asked if I'd like to come and work. I guess I was looking for a place—a change of scenery, maybe—somewhere a little more remote than West Yellowstone, so here I am."

"Any kids?" Joe asked.

"No."

"How long have you been here?"

"Three years."

"You and Marsh?" Joe asked.

"Hmph," Molly laughed. "No. Never."

"Don't you ever get lonely?" Joe asked.

"No." Molly looked like she was about to say something, then interrupted herself. "Never." She stared at the floor for a second, then added, "Let's eat!"

After a Spamburger and a bowl of pistachio ice cream, Joe leaned back in his chair and exclaimed, "Boy, I don't know who puts out a better spread, you or Marsh."

"You had hotdogs and beans at Marsh's, I'll bet?"

"Several times."

"Well, then this SHOULD actually seem elegant," Molly grinned.

"Well, actually, I think everyone does like Spam. They just won't admit it," Joe smiled.

"It's that way with a lot of things," Molly said.

"And I never had the opportunity to walk into a grocery store and select my own can of Spam before," Joe added.

Molly smiled and was about to say something more when she pointed at Jake. "I think Jake needs to go out. He ate a lot of candy and who knows what else at that birthday party today. He's acting kind of funny."

Joe stood up and opened the door, and Jake shot past him. "Could be my shoe that upset his stomach," Joe said.

When Joe and Molly had cleared the table and done the dishes, they both went to the door and peered outside at the same time.

"Oh oh," Molly moaned slowly, and then looked at Joe. Jake was hunched over, trying to do his business in the vacant lot next to Molly's trailer, but things didn't seem to be going well for him. He'd hunch up and push for a minute, then try to bite at something near his rear end, then take several clumsy steps, hunch up, and push again. The process repeated itself for several minutes while Joe and Molly watched from the front door. Finally, Jake turned his body just right, and in the fading twilight both Molly and Joe could see the problem. Molly covered her mouth, then laughed out loud and looked at Joe. Joe could only shake his head in disgust and then turn away.

As Jake moved and pushed, even in the dim light Molly and Joe could see a blue birthday balloon—or, rather, about four inches' worth of blue birthday balloon—hanging from Jake's rear end.

"Now what?" Molly laughed. "The birthday feast from earlier today must have worked its way..."

"I think you know what's next," Joe said as he lowered his eyes and shook his head. Joe walked out of the trailer, stepped onto the small vacant lot, and walked directly toward Jake. He simply walked up to Jake and put his legs on either side of the puppy's head while Jake was facing him, so that Jake's head was locked between his legs. Jake could not move forward or backward, run away, or struggle in any way. Then Joe bent over and grabbed Jake's tail in his left hand. He lifted Jake's tail up until he could clearly see the segment of blue balloon flopping around while Jake tried to struggle. When Joe turned his head to look at Molly, he wore a look of disgust and revulsion. Molly returned Joe's glance with a howl of laughter from deep in her chest. Joe only shook his head, grimaced, and returned to the job in front of him.

He began to pull on the balloon, and as he did, Jake responded to what must have been a fairly unpleasant sensation by struggling even more vehemently. Joe was aware of peals of laughter coming from Molly, but he couldn't look at her. He pulled more and the balloon began to stretch. Then it began to move slowly out of Jake's behind. The balloon grew longer and the suspense more palpable. Other things began to appear alongside the balloon. Both Joe and Molly knew that at some point, the balloon was going to snap out of Jake's ass. But neither of them knew just when that might happen or just what might accompany the balloon. Molly was sitting on the top step of her doorsteps convulsing with laughter, while Joe was squinting and preparing to flinch. The balloon finally burst free with a loud snap, and Joe flinched a fraction of a second too late.

"Oh, Jesus, a shit storm!" Joe mumbled to himself as Molly covered her face and squealed. Joe was standing with his hands at his sides, and a ten-inch-long blue balloon between the fingers of his right hand, when Molly wiped the tears from her eyes and called to him.

"Oh, Joe," Molly laughed. "C'mon inside and we'll clean you up."

Joe threw the balloon over his shoulder and stepped toward Molly wearing a look of disbelief. Several dozen small flecks of dog shit dotted Joe's right hand and forearm and his face.

Still laughing uncontrollably and stumbling with her own laughter, Molly led Joe into the tiny bathroom in her trailer. She sat Joe on the toilet, took a washcloth from the small closet, and began to clean the shit from Joe's arm and face. She laughed continuously as she washed out the washcloth, put more soap on, and wiped another speck of shit from Joe. "I've never seen anything quite like that before," she said over and over. She washed, blotted, and laughed out loud, then repeated the cycle several times while Joe sat silently on the toilet. As she finished the cleanup, Joe finally offered, "I bet Jake is wondering just what that was all about too." And Molly started laughing all over again.

"Would you like another drink, Joe?" Molly asked when the cleanup chores were done.

"No, thanks," Joe said slowly. "I think that's the way this day should end: sunburn on my head, covered with greasy-ass medicine, one mangled shoe, and dog shit on my face."

"I got the dog shit off you," Molly corrected.

"There's a sentence I bet you didn't plan on saying tonight," Joe said, and Molly started laughing again.

"I'll just go home now," Joe said, but he stopped by the front door when Molly touched his arm.

"Wait," Molly said.

"Huh?"

"I had a nice time, Joe. I haven't had a talk like this, with anyone, for such a long time. And I laughed! I can't remember the last time I laughed like this."

"My pleasure." Joe pursed his lips and nodded, then let his face curl into a smile. "I had a nice time too, Molly. I never thought it would feel so good to have someone rub hemorrhoid medicine on my head. There's a sentence I didn't think I'd be saying tonight," he shrugged.

"So what will you do on your day off tomorrow, Joe?"

"Well..."—Joe stood in the doorway and paused—"...don't laugh, Molly. But I bought a box of books just after I started on this odyssey, and I've been working my way through the books all along. I've sort of rediscovered the power of words, and I think I'd like to write something of my own."

"Why would I laugh at that?"

"Just seems odd to hear myself say something like that, I guess. My brother actually embarrassed me when he told me I thought like an artist."

"I think he was right," Molly said. She looked at Joe as if she'd never seen him before and repeated, "I think he was right."

Joe stared at Molly's soft, brown eyes for a tiny moment, wondering if he should kiss her goodnight. The moment came and went like a flicker of faroff lightning, and Joe decided that if he had to think about such a thing, then he probably shouldn't do it. Besides: she probably wouldn't want to kiss a man who only recently had been covered with dog shit. "Probably see you tomorrow," Joe said as he turned and walked down the wooden steps outside her door. "Thanks for dinner, Molly."

"Joe?" Molly called down to him.

"Yeah?" he said when he turned around.

"Let's do this again," she said.

"All this? Spam? Dog shit?" He pointed to the grease in his hair. "Fort Smith is a wild town! I don't think I can keep up this pace."

"No, not everything, I guess." She smiled as if she were apologizing for the evening. "But I enjoyed talking to you. Let's do this again."

"Sure thing, Molly. I had a nice time too. Well, sort of." And Joe walked off into the darkness, with Jake prancing along at his heels.

"Nice one, Jake," Joe said when they were out of earshot from Molly's trailer and covered by darkness. "I mean, the shoe thing and the balloon thing. Nice work!" Joe finally chuckled at the thought of what he'd just done.

When he reached his trailer, Joe swung the door open and turned to Jake one more time. "Did you hear her laugh, Jake?"

chapter thirty-seven

The world on the other side of Joe's eyelids throbbed with light, and he was awakened by the sound of the cheap aluminum door to his trailer swinging open. Someone had stepped into his trailer, but he couldn't say who it was. He was awake, but not really, as the morning light from outside his trailer splashed all around inside it. The thing that really seemed to draw him from the dark world of his sleep was the sound of Jake's tail thumping against the leg of the kitchen table. Even while he was still emerging from the stupor of a deep sleep, he recognized the sound of a happy dog welcoming a visitor.

"Oh, did I wake you up?" Molly asked when she sat on one of the kitchen chairs. "Hi, Jake," she continued as she scratched Jake's ears.

Joe squinted when he let the first of the morning light into his eyes. His head hurt, probably from that last scotch, he thought. He'd only made it as far as the loveseat in his living room when he'd come home last night. He'd kicked off his shoes, turned on the little fan, and crumpled onto the well-used loveseat, and that's where he'd stayed for the night. Now, he forced himself into a sitting position while Molly took a seat nearby on one of the aluminum kitchen chairs.

His head hurt more when he was rightside up, but nowhere near the way it had after his first drunk at Cowboy Camp, and he was aware that something nearby his head just wasn't right.

"Nice," Molly said. She seemed to be nodding and smiling as the fog cleared in Joe's head.

"Huh?" Joe asked.

"Nice. Looks nice!" Molly pointed at something near Joe's head.

When Joe reached up, he found that one of the little pillows from the loveseat was still stuck to the greasy medication in his hair. Joe simply pulled the pillow from his hair and returned a blank stare at Molly.

"I brought you something," she smiled. Then she reached inside a brown paper grocery bag and produced a laptop computer. She held it up, then put it on the kitchen table and opened it. "It's for you! Marsh bought it for himself about two years ago, but he never uses it." She smiled and nodded. "Thought you might be able to use it when you start writing your story. It has a word processor, but that's the only software. I have to go back to work." She paused and grinned a silly grin. "Marsh wants to know if you're up for a round of golf tonight," she said as she stood up. Then she bent over and put her hands on her knees. Her face was close to his as she looked at him for a second, then kissed him softly on the lips. "I wanted you to kiss me last night," she added. Then she stepped out the door and closed it behind her.

Joe drew in a deep breath, then let it out all at once. Molly was gone, and the trailer was quiet again except for the sound of Jake's breathing. Joe simply tipped back over sideways onto the couch and waited for a better reason to get up. As the little wakeup call played itself over and over again in Joe's mind, the dimple in his cheek appeared in the middle of a tiny grin.

"So, Marsh, what do you think it means when Jake limps like that? You think there's something wrong?" Joe asked.

"No, he's a pup. Just growing pains," Marsh replied while Jake chased around in the tall grass between the tee box and the huge stand of cottonwoods surrounding Marsh's cabin. "Look at him! Looks OK to me," Marsh added when Jake pounced on a mouse.

"Yeah, maybe so. But he limps really bad sometimes for a day or so at a time, and then he's fine. He got kicked by a horse a few weeks ago. S'pose that could still be bothering him? Makes no sense. He gets these little bumps around his neck and chest for a few days every so often too."

"Just growing pains and bug bites, bumps and bruises...could be the horse kick...who knows? Let's tee off," Marsh said as he reached into the cedar box and withdrew a scorecard. "Looks like we're playing Shinnecock Hills. This is one course that will give a guy like you some advantage over me—if you can hit your driver straight and far, that's a big help here," Marsh added.

"Good. I feel strong today!" Joe replied.

"How's the sunburn?" Marsh asked while he stood over his ball and prepared to hit.

"Much better today. But if it weren't for the cloud cover, I couldn't be out now. Direct sunlight, even the stuff at the end of the day, feels like someone's pouring fire on my head still," Joe said. "It's a good thing we got some clouds."

Marsh struck his ball just as a rumble of distant thunder rolled over them from across the river. The ball sailed high and faded off to the left as it crossed the water. "Shit. There's heavy rough on the left side of number one here at Shinnecock, but I think I can come out in good shape," Marsh said.

"No doubt," Joe grinned as he teed his ball up and stood over it. He looked across the Big Horn, then straight up into the sky. "Geez, Marsh, it's really getting dark fast. I think it's gonna storm." Thunder boomed again, this time much closer and louder, just after Joe struck his ball and returned to the little red bench.

"Nice one," Marsh said as he stood up. "Oh oh. I just felt a raindrop." He looked up to the sky and grimaced. "It's gonna storm, Joe." Even as he spoke, the rain began to increase and large, heavy raindrops started to pelt the leaves on the nearby trees. "Let's go on inside. Screw the golf for today!" Marsh added while he scrambled to grab his golf clubs and then ran for the shelter of the cabin.

Large raindrops were splashing against the roof of the cabin by the time Marsh, Joe, and Jake let the screen door on the porch slam behind them.

"Whew, that one blew up in a hurry!" Marsh said. He shook the water off his hat, then opened the screen door that led from the porch into the kitchen, and Joe followed.

Marsh's kitchen was neat and clean, and the countertops were immaculate. But the kitchen table, which sat in a little bay window and looked out at the tee box, was mounded high with colored chicken feathers, colored pieces of deer hide, fish hooks, and hundreds of various fly-tying materials. Several large stacks of golf magazines rested on the floor next to the couch, and books about golf lay strewn across a coffee table also. One large book featured color drawings of famous golf courses and challenging holes. Magazines with color photographs of golfers wearing the loud, almost comical pants, sweaters, and hats of the 1970s and '80s lay open on the kitchen table. Several black-and-white photos of golfers sporting knickers and tweed jackets from the 1800s had been pinned to a bulletin board in the kitchen. Marsh sat on one of the oak chairs and motioned for Joe to do the same. "Someday, I'd like to get myself some golf clothes like that!" Marsh said when he noticed Joe staring at a photo of a golfer from the 1970s wearing plaid pants and a knit shirt with a large collar.

"Yeah, that's pretty snappy all right," Joe offered sarcastically.

"How 'bout this?" Marsh said, and he pointed at one of the black-and-white photos. "Can you imagine how good I'd look playing the Old Course at St. Andrews wearing knickers and a tweed jacket? Handsomer than shit! That's what I think." He nodded in agreement with himself, then asked, "Want something to drink?"

"Yeah, I'd have a diet soda," Joe answered.

"They're in the fridge. Grab one for me, too, will ya?" Marsh said.

When Joe returned to the table, he handed the can of soda to Marsh and asked, "How long have you lived here, Marsh?"

"Fort Smith?"

"Yeah."

"Twenty-some years—closer to thirty now that I think of it." Marsh moved some of the feathers on the table in front of him, then attached a fly-tying vice to the table. "I think I'll tie a few flies while it rains. Feels nice now that it's cooled off, doesn't it? Gimme that package of dubbing there, will you? The olive-colored stuff."

Joe tossed a small plastic envelope filled with finely cut beaver hair that had been dyed olive. "Twenty, thirty years—that's a long time," Joe said.

"It's gone pretty fast, actually. It was the twenty years before that that were a drag!" Marsh placed a tiny hook, no bigger than a question mark on a printed page, into the vise and began wrapping fine black cotton thread around it. "Gonna tie up a few Baetis."

"Any regrets about coming here?"

"Whadya mean?" Marsh said without looking up from the tiny fly he was creating.

"You know—ever feel like you did the wrong thing? I remember you telling me how you stood there outside the grocery store and called

478

from that pay phone to quit your job." Joe smiled at Marsh and leaned forward. "How did that make you feel—to make that call? Was there any sense of triumph in the making of that call?"

"Oh, yeah. Briefly," Marsh replied as he reached for a hackle pliers, a tiny, spring-loaded tweezer designed to handle the tiniest of feathers. He twisted a nearly invisible blue/gray feather around the little hook before he continued his answer. "But I left some things behind. I paid a price."

"Yeah?"

"Yeah. The woman I was living with, she was nice. We might have made it together. But she wanted no part of this place or this life. She had visions of a little house with shutters and a picket fence, stuff like that. I nearly broke her heart."

"Whatever happened to her?"

"She told me she just couldn't come with me on this one. Said she'd be there if I ever came back."

"Still see her?"

"She married somebody else about two years after I left."

"Sorry, Marsh," Joe offered.

"It's OK, Joe. That's life," Marsh shrugged, then finished the tiny fly. "Hey, toss me that gray-colored dubbing, will you? I'm gonna try one of those emergers you like to use. You know, Joe, the sad part is that her life didn't turn out so well. The guy she married was bad news, and the marriage didn't work. She wound up moving to Florida. Never got that house and picket fence."

"Do you still think about her—you know...in that way...like when you were together?" Joe asked.

"No." Marsh looked up from the fly-tying vice and feathers. "No, that's all past me now. Well, that's not exactly true. I think about her sometimes. Everyone thinks about their old lovers now and then. Sometimes I feel bad, I guess. I wonder if I just feel bad about getting old, though." He shrugged. "I don't know. But I don't pine for her and wish it was all different, if that's what you mean. Sometimes I wonder what else I could have done with my life if I'd chosen not to do this."

"How about when you started your business? Ever have any second thoughts? Ever wonder if you were doing the right thing?"

"Shit," Marsh groaned. "Second thoughts?" He finished the Baetis emerger and leaned back in his chair. "That's a nice little emerger pattern. Glad you showed me! Now, throw me that other plastic bag there, will you?"

"Thanks," Marsh said when he opened the bag. He drew out some cigarette paper and rolled a joint with the pot that was in the bag Joe had just passed. Then he took the tiny hackle pliers and clipped it to the joint after he'd taken a long hit. "Want a toke?" he wheezed as he drew in a cloud of cannabis smoke. He offered the joint to Joe and held his breath.

"No, thanks," Joe smiled.

"Suit yourself," Marsh coughed. "But this shit really slows me down. I'm gonna hafta switch to some bigger flies now. These tiny little flies require too much concentration and coordination. I'm gonna switch to streamers." He took a second hit from the joint. "Thisstuffmakesmestupidand-Idon'twanttoomuchtothinkaboutrightnow," he wheezed while he held the smoke in his lungs. He let the smoke out in one large cloud, then began to reorganize the feathers in front of him on the kitchen table. "Second thoughts?" He nodded while he looked down at the table. "You wanna know about second thoughts? Well, how's this?" Marsh looked up and pointed the joint at Joe. "The first winter I was here was a pretty cold one. I was painting the inside of the fly shop, doing all the remodeling myself, trying to get ready to open this place in the spring." He paused for emphasis. "Now, remember, I was all alone. I'd quit my job, said goodbye to a fine woman, and put all my money into building a fly shop on an Indian reservation so I could cater to a bunch of fishermen that I THOUGHT might be coming. The only other business in this little fart of a town was the Yellowtail Grocery Store." Marsh paused and nodded at Joe to emphasize what he was about to say. "So I'm painting, and it's cold in there—because, after all, it was just a shitty old garage I was remodeling. Anyway, I'm painting and I've got a cassette tape playing and it's a Willie Nelson tape, and Willie's singin' 'Blue Eyes Cryin' in the Rain.' With me, Joe?"

Joe nodded.

"So Willie is singin' and I'm paintin', and it's pretty cold. And all of a sudden, Willie just stopped singin'. The tape deck just froze solid. Really caught me by surprise! It was plugged in over by the door. I stopped paintin' and walked over to check it out, and when I saw that the tape deck was froze solid, I looked up the road one way as far as I could see. I had a paint brush in my hand, and I just stood there. Then I turned and looked up the road the other way as far as I could see. And

I didn't see one damn car go by for about an hour! I stood there for a while and thought about what I'd done. I began to think I'd made a huge mistake, and I started to cry. And that's no shit, Joe. I stood in that doorway and cried." Marsh nodded at Joe again. "Second thoughts? Bet your ass!" He looked away and asked, "You having second thoughts about what you did?"

Joe thought for a moment, then said, "No, not anymore. Not really. I wouldn't want my old life back. I'm OK with what I did. I couldn't tell you why, but I am. You know, Marsh, I gave up a lot too. I came to almost hate my wife, and I gave her everything—the house, the cars, our savings, everything—and I left a profitable business because I hated that, too. I just wanted to be rid of it all."

"You gave her everything?" Marsh said.

"Yup! All I got was my truck and my fishin' gear and some cash."

"Well, then, you definitely don't want to smoke any more of this!" Marsh said, holding up the roach for Joe to see.

"Why?"

"You're already a colossal fuckup! You can't afford to get any stupider."

Joe smiled a weak smile. "It was what had to be done. And I'm tired of regretting the things I did. Mostly, I suppose I regret the things I DIDN'T do."

Joe looked at Marsh for a second, then blinked. He reached for the telephone on Marsh's kitchen countertop and dialed a number as he looked at Marsh and waited for the phone to ring. After several rings, Marsh offered the joint again. Joe shook his head while the phone rang.

"Molly?" he said when she answered the phone.

"Yes."

"This is Joe."

"I know."

"When is your next day off?"

"Why do you want to know?"

"'Cause I'd like to spend a day with you. Not a date. Just a day to talk, like the other night."

"It can be a date."

Her words brought a grin to his lips. "OK," he nodded.

"Next Tuesday," Molly said.

"Huh?"

"Next Tuesday. I'm off next Tuesday, and so are you. I'm looking at the schedule right now."

"OK, it's a date, then."

"What are we going to do?" she asked.

"Well, we live so close to this fine river. Let's pack a lunch—no Spam—and spend a day on the Big Horn."

Molly made no reply for a moment, and Joe worried that he'd set his sights a little low and insulted her by proposing a day in her own backyard, so to speak. "Still there, Molly? We can do something else."

"I'm smiling. I've never been on the river."

"Really?" Joe looked bewildered. "Never?"

"Nobody ever asked me," Molly said.

"OK, then, it's a date?" Joe asked.

"Sure!" Molly replied.

When Joe hung up the phone, he turned and looked at Marsh for a moment. Marsh stared back at him for a while before he spoke. "Good call," Marsh said.

"Thanks," Joe replied.

"Molly told me about your adventure with Preparation H and Jake's balloon," Marsh said as he stared at Joe.

"Yeah?" Joe asked

"Definitely don't smoke any more of this shit!"

chapter thirty-eight

"So this is your first time on the river? Really?" Joe asked
Molly as he pushed the boat off the boat trailer and into the Big Horn.
Jake ran out into the river up to his shoulders, took a drink, then ran
back to Molly's side and shook the water off his coat.

Molly nodded and held onto the bow line as the drift boat rocked
gently in several inches of water next to the boat landing. While Molly
stood on shore and held the boat still, Joe lifted a cooler from the back
of his truck, then placed it in the boat. "I just can't believe that! You
seem so knowledgeable when you talk to fishermen back at the shop."
Joe stood with his hands on his hips and questioned her.

"I am knowledgeable! I just don't have experience. I just listen to what
the guides and the fishermen all say, then repeat it," Molly shrugged.
"You believed me when I talked about what flies to use and how to fish
each hole, didn't you? And what I said worked, too, didn't it?"

Joe smiled but didn't reply. He stepped into the truck, moved it away
from the boat ramp, and walked back to where Molly was standing.
"Jump in—the boat, I mean—and we'll go." He was still smiling from
before. "Let's go. You too, Jake."

"Where's your fishing gear?" Molly asked when she sat in the bow
seat and faced Joe.

"I'm not fishin' today. I'm on a date," Joe grinned. He pushed the boat
out into the current and threw his leg over the gunwale, then found the
middle seat. After three sturdy strokes with the oars, the boat was glid-

ing across the surface of the river, and Joe lifted the oars to let the boat slide freely along in the current.

"You could have brought your fishing gear," Molly said.

"Why would I do that? I'm on a date with the prettiest girl in Montana."

"I thought men like you wanted to fish every time they had a chance."

"Men like me? What does that mean?" Joe asked while he pulled on the oars.

"Well, fishermen—all fishermen, you know?"

"I think fishermen are all different—too different to lump us all together. But I think we do have a life cycle, just like mayflies," Joe said.

"Oh?"

"Sure. You've seen it before. The men that come into the shop...they'll all be at one of five different stages in the life cycle of a fisherman." Joe worked the oars gently to keep the boat pointing downstream and waited for her to ask about the life cycle of a fisherman.

Just as a breeze picked up and threatened to toss it off her head and into the river, Molly reached for the baseball cap she was wearing and adjusted it. When she'd pulled the cap a little farther down over her brow, she leaned back in her chair, folded her arms, and raised her eyebrows with a question. "Life cycle?"

"Yeah. The first stage is the novice, where everything is new and the fisherman just wants to catch a fish—any fish. He just needs to prove he can do it. Sometimes, he may stay in this stage for a while because he has to prove it to himself a few times. That was a fun time in my life. I still remember the first trout I caught on a fly rod. It seemed like I'd cracked some sort of cosmic riddle and endless possibilities were suddenly available." Joe smiled a satisfied smile and raised his eyebrows.

"Then comes the stage where he wants to catch a lot of fish. Then the stage where he's after big fish. It takes years to properly work your way through these two stages, but along the way, a fly fisherman begins to discover the legend and lore of all this. He also pushes his marriage to its limits and finds it would have been cheaper and easier to just start a heroin habit than take up fly fishing. He'll have a closet with about forty thousand dollars' worth of rods, reels, and trendy doodads. Over in the corner of his office, he'll have a fly-tying bench stocked with thousands of dollars' worth of rare chicken feathers, polar bear hair, and laser-sharpened hooks." Joe eased the boat past two other fishermen and waved at them. When he'd passed by them he continued. "I knew one guy who was looking for some urine-stained hair from the peri-anal area of a mountain goat! You have to ask yourself just how much hair a goat has on his nuts."

"And how you're gonna get it," Molly said seriously.

"Exactly," Joe nodded and pointed at her.

"So did your friend find his hair?"

"No. But he's one of those guys who's stuck in stage three and will never move on."

"What's stage four?" Molly asked.

"Well, at some point, after a fisherman begins to sense that he can catch fish just about anywhere, he begins to feel a need to stalk the difficult fish. Usually these fish are big. Sometimes they're just average-size, but they're the ones that require insight and skill. They're the bruisers that hide behind that rock just out there beyond the normal guy's casting range, or the spooky fish that's sipping tiny dry flies along a cut bank with tree boughs hanging over—the one that requires a perfect cast on the first try. The fisherman at this stage is closing in on Nirvana."

"Oh?"

"Yeah. He's beginning to truly understand that the joy of it all, the real joy, comes from doing a difficult thing and doing it with some skill and class."

"OK, Joe, then what's a stage-five?"

"That's the guy who's lost interest in the gear he's using. I mean, it's all the same to him if he's fishing his old two-dollar Herters reel and a cheap rod, and he'll probably have a few patches on his waders. He's a 'master.' He's sort of risen above the fray and doesn't feel any urgent need to catch fish. He'll walk along a river until he finds a nice stretch of water, and he'll sit on the bank and watch it all happen. He might not even go fishing. He'll smoke his pipe and study the current for a while until he knows where the fish are lying. Then he'll watch as a mayfly hatch begins. He'll notice the trout start to feed on the emergers, then the dry flies, and he'll feel a sense of satisfaction that he's spent so much time learning to appreciate such a great thing."

"Is he the one who shows up driving a shitty pickup?" Molly asked.

Joe had been looking downstream over Molly's shoulder, but when she said those words, he knew she'd paid him a heartfelt compliment. His eyes quickly found hers, and he caught the full measure of the most beautiful smile he'd had smiled at him in…ever, he thought. "That's a nice thought," Joe replied.

Just beyond Molly—just beyond those rich, brown eyes and the auburn hair—it seemed that every bit of Montana's big sky was being reflected from the blue surface of the Big Horn. The steady breeze broke the blue water into a billion shimmering diamonds. The tall cottonwoods and the Russian Olive trees and all the underbrush along the shore swayed in the wind, and all Joe could do for a moment was stare at Molly. She looked as if she'd planned to reveal herself to him like this—smiling, carefree, and framed by the Big Horn River.

"I know you, Molly Malone. I know you. But why is that? We've never met."

"Maybe we should know each other, Joe. Maybe we're opposite sides of the same coin," Molly said, and her smile faded slightly.

"Huh? Why would you say that?"

"Pull over up here, would you, Joe?" Molly asked.

Small rocks and gravel scraped against the bottom as Joe slid the boat ashore at the head of a long riffle. Jake jumped over the side and began to sprint up and down the riverbank in search of something, anything, to play with. It seemed to both Molly and Joe that the joy of splashing water was enough to keep Jake busy for quite some time. "I hope he doesn't find any skunks to play with," Joe said.

"Or balloons," Molly laughed, and she turned to look at Joe.

"Yeah, the other night while I was brushing my teeth, he yakked up a blackbird. It looked like something from a Steven King novel. Makes you wonder just what he might be thinking that would make him eat a balloon or a bird," Joe chuckled. He watched Molly's smile fade again as Jake scampered off in pursuit of a butterfly.

"What's the matter, Molly? You seem like you can't decide if you're happy or sad. C'mon, let's have a nice time. I just want you to like me."

"It's too late, Joe. I already like you." Molly smiled softly.

"So what's the problem?"

"How did you wind up here?" Molly sighed. "What brought you here?"

"Wanderlust…good Karma?" Joe grimaced. "What do you mean?" he asked with a shrug.

"Look! You left your home and your life because you're one of those men who needed answers, needed meaning, needed to know that your life was justified. As you said the other night, you were willing to pay the price for it. You know, just a moment ago you talked about a guy you know who was stuck at stage three." Molly stopped.

"Yeah?"

"Well, I see that all the time here. Men come out here hinting that they're looking for some deeper understanding or illumination. They get a little drunk sometimes and imply that they've found it too. But down deep, they're terrified to really go search for answers because it might cause them to let go of something comfortable. So they go home and put their brains back in neutral and cling to the safety of their familiar old lives. They claim to be recharged. But the truth is that they stood on the edge for a moment, but didn't have the courage to step off. But you did! Why?"

"I'd like to tell you that I knew it was time to just do the right thing, but the truth is that I was probably pushed into it by the people and circumstances of my old life. I'm not even sure that what I did was such a good thing. I..."

"That's not true," she interrupted. "It might have been true once, for a short time, but you know what you did was powerful, and you're proud of it. You're just afraid of how you're gonna come out of it. And that's to be expected—that you'd be concerned about what's next." Molly waited a moment, then said, "You're proud of what you did. I'm right, aren't I?"

"Yeah," Joe admitted. Then he smiled as though she'd caught him in a fib. "You're pretty good, Molly," Joe nodded. "Yeah, I'm proud of what I did, and I like the man I found along the way, and I'm a little afraid," he said, then stared across the river for a minute.

"OK," Joe started again. "Now you tell me something. You said a while ago that we were opposite sides of the same coin. How do you figure that?"

"Well, I ran away from my life too, and I'm afraid. I've been afraid for several years that I may never get back on my feet. That puts us on the same coin." She paused to collect her thoughts. "Remember that night," Molly continued, "when you said you gathered up all the good things in your life and ran away, and you hoped to live out your life surrounded by only the good things but the bad things kept finding you?"

"Yeah, and I remember what you said..." Joe answered.

"And I said I'd come here hoping to surround myself with the bad things but that the good things kept finding me," Molly interrupted.

Then she stopped again. "Opposite sides—can't you see it? I thought a man like you would like that analogy."

"I guess so," Joe nodded. "So tell me about the life YOU left behind," Joe said.

During the short time they'd been sitting beside the riffle and talking, large, billowy white clouds with gray bottoms had drifted over them and sealed away the sun.

"Looks like it might rain," Molly said. She turned her back to Joe and walked along the riverbank for a ways until she came to a stretch of gravel and sand with a long run of Russian Olive trees hanging over it. She stopped, filled her lungs, and said, "Mmmm. Can you smell that, Joe? Can you smell the Russian Olive trees? There's nothing like that. They smell sweet, don't they?"

"Sure," Joe said. He knew she was stalling for a moment to arrange her thoughts.

Molly sat down on the riverbank, about ten feet from the water and ten feet from the overhanging Russian Olive trees behind her. She raised her bare knees up under her chin and stared into the river when Joe sat next to her. She stared at something far beneath the surface, far away from the peaceful river, and Joe left her alone in her silence for a moment while she considered whatever it was she was about to share with him.

"I grew up in Denver," Molly started. She still seemed to be staring at some faroff place. "I sat right next to the most handsome boy in school, Mike McCarthy." Molly stopped, then smiled a faint smile. "Hmph," she laughed, but she never looked over at Joe. "It was a Catholic school, and we always had to sit in alphabetical order. Malone, McCarthy...lots of Irish kids, you know?"

"Anyway," she continued, "we always just belonged to each other, and everyone knew it. Everyone knew we'd get married when we got older. You must have had kids like that in your high school?" she asked, but she still stared ahead.

"Yeah," Joe answered with a whisper.

Molly drew in another deep breath. "I got pregnant when we were seniors. We got married, like everyone always said we would, and Ryan, our son, was born around Christmas the year after we graduated. Then Sean was born about a year and a half later." Molly paused for a long moment and breathed heavily twice. "We were happy, I guess. We had a little house in a nice neighborhood, and Mike had a good job."

"One winter day when the boys were about eight and six, we got a heavy snow," Molly continued with no emotion in her voice. "The boys wanted to go out and play in the snow for a few minutes before supper. Their dad wasn't home yet, so I said OK, but they had to come right in for supper when their dad got home. I was just finishing supper when Mike pulled into the driveway." Molly stopped as if something was standing in her way. She swallowed once, then went on. "When I went to call the boys, that's when I saw the flashing lights down the street—police cars, an ambulance. That's when I knew...I just knew." Molly wore the look of a soldier who'd seen too much combat—the one-thousand-yard stare. "I ran out to the street, but I knew...I just knew. The boys had slid down a large hill on their sled. But they couldn't stop when they came to the street."

When Molly paused, Joe wished she would simply quit talking altogether. He knew what was coming, and Molly's telling of the story was as relentless and destructive as the story itself.

"They slid right into the path of a delivery truck. They were still in the street when I got there. I saw everything." Molly was numb when she finally turned to Joe. "Wanna guess what I see every time I shut my eyes?"

Joe looked away and didn't answer her. He'd seen a nightmare on her face.

They sat together silently for nearly fifteen minutes, each of them lost in their own thoughts. In every other similar situation that Joe could remember, he had always been able to find words and continue the conversation when a friend had told a tragic story. A small expression of sympathy and maybe a few words of support...there was always a way to help assuage the grief. But this...this was unbearable to listen to. He couldn't imagine what pain Molly was dealing with.

A raindrop thumped against Joe's Stetson, then another, then another. The pace of the rain began to quicken, and Joe and Molly stood up. As Molly began to walk toward the boat, Joe grabbed her arm. "Wait" was all he said. He pulled a large, flimsy, cheap yellow plastic rain poncho from his pocket, covered both of them with it, and fashioned it as if it were a shelter for them to stand under. He put his arms around Molly and pulled her into his chest. As he did, he kissed the auburn hair on the side of her head and held her close. The side of his face rested against her hair. He kissed her hair and softly rubbed his hands over her back, and in that moment he felt something in her relax. She turned her cheek and rested it against his chest before she sighed and wrapped her arms around his waist.

The cheap rain poncho kept the rest of the world away from them as they stood together on the bank of the Big Horn River. They'd crossed a boundary together, and now they stood together, hidden from the outside world, huddled closely under the poncho and holding each other. Joe closed his eyes and smelled her shampoo. He kissed her hair every now and then. And in spite of the awful story she'd just told him, he was content to be here, just standing here with her in the rain. She'd let him share something important—maybe the pivotal moment in her life—and he was happy she'd been willing to open herself up like that. He guessed that she didn't do it very often.

The rain grew into a downpour for a short time, then eased back to a steady shower. Joe lifted up the poncho and peeked at the western sky after a few minutes. "There's blue sky in the west. This shower is gonna pass over us pretty soon. Let's just wait it out under these Russian Olives, OK?" Joe asked.

A sweet aroma from the small, overhanging trees surrounded them when they'd fashioned the flimsy poncho into a rain tarp and slid themselves under the branches along the riverbank. Jake joined them after a moment and played at their feet while they watched the river slide by.

"Thanks," Molly said after a while.

"For what?" Joe replied.

"For not trying to say something to comfort me."

"Sometimes words have no power. What could anyone say?" Joe shrugged.

The weight of Molly's grief and terror began to lift. She picked up a small stone and rubbed it with both hands for a moment.

"You'd be surprised," Molly said. "Several people told me at the time that I was young and I'd be able to have more children—like that made everything all right."

"They meant well," Joe said. "People usually do."

"Yeah, I suppose. But I got so that I didn't want to talk to anyone," Molly said.

"So what happened to your husband?" Joe asked.

"He blamed me for everything, and I suppose he was right..."

Joe interrupted, and he raised an index finger to make his point. "That's a lot of baggage to carry, Molly. You know that isn't right."

"Yes, I know that now. But nonetheless, he blamed me and made no secret of it. Our marriage couldn't survive that. I heard once that the death of a child is a common cause for divorce." She shook her head and shrugged. "We divorced about a year later. I sort of lost myself about that time—rediscovered drugs and alcohol. Mike and I had been heavy users when we were in school. I took a series of nothing jobs, lived with a couple different men, wound up in West Yellowstone living with a guide. That's when I met Marsh. Back then, I would have moved in with Marsh too—anything to get me away from what I'd been doing for about seven years. But Marsh was never really interested in me in that way. I think he saw me as sort of a stray puppy that needed a home. I was already managing a fly shop, and he needed help here. Marsh made me an offer and I took it. Like I said, I knew I had to get away from the way I'd been living, and down deep I guess I thought I could come here and live with all my regrets and pain like I deserved. Does that make any sense to you?"

"Sort of," Joe answered. "But what about your family, your parents?"

"My parents?" Molly scoffed. "My mother married my dad just to get out of a bad home. Her life wasn't very easy. She always seemed overwhelmed by her husband, her family, the life she found herself in. She had no idea what to say to me when all this happened. And my dad? I was just another mouth to feed. He had no expectations for me."

When Molly said the word "expectations," Joe couldn't help but think of his own father, and he wondered whether it was better for a parent to expect great things or nothing from his children. His brow tightened and he shook his head slightly.

"What?" Molly said. "What is it?"

"Nothing, really, I guess. Well, I was just thinking. My father had all those great expectations for me, and I spent my whole life trying to fulfill them, and it didn't work out. And your father expected nothing of you, and now here we are, in the same boat—so to speak," Joe smiled. "Maybe it doesn't matter what we expect; we just get what comes our way. What do you think about that?

"That's too much to think about," Molly said. "Looks like it's stopped raining. Should we go?"

Gravel scraped at the bottom of the boat when Joe pushed it out away from shore and into the current. He stepped over the gunwale and settled into the middle seat as the current began to swing the little boat around and pull it downstream. As he worked the oars and straightened the boat, he looked up into the front seat and found that Molly was staring at him.

"What?" he smiled.

"Tell me about your wife."

"What would you like to know?"

"What does she look like?"

"Pretty. Very pretty. And I think she's my ex-wife by now, but I'm not sure."

"What happened between you?"

"Hard to explain," Joe sighed, and he turned the boat slightly. "I think she married me because she was counting on me to give her a better life than what she came from. I don't know if she ever loved me." Joe looked at Molly and shrugged. "Probably happens all the time. You know: a young woman marries some guy in the hopes that he'll rescue her from her parents' home. Maybe your mother did the same thing, huh?" Joe turned the boat and peered downstream, then turned it back so it was straight in the current. "Anyway, she used her feminine ways to turn my head." Joe smiled and his dimple flashed. "She gave me sex in order to get security." Then he paused again. "I just wanted the sex. Hell, I didn't care what I had to give up to get it. Took me years—years—before I realized there was something really missing in the equation."

"What was missing?"

"Love! Passion! Friendship! Joy! All that good stuff that's supposed to come along before the sex," Joe shrugged. "I was stupid. Well, I wasn't thinking. Maybe I was distracted." He smiled sheepishly and Molly smiled back at him.

"So what about your job?" she said. "Do you not have any second thoughts, really?"

"No. Not really. It's hard to explain. Marsh and I talked about that the other day." He leaned back in his seat and pulled both oars out of the water. The boat began to swing gently in the current, out of control. "I tried to like it; I truly did. But I just grew weary of people begging me to be less."

Molly stared, then shook her head to show him she didn't understand.

492

"OK, let me try that again. Think about it this way." Joe smiled and tried to start over. "You get up every day and go sit in a tiny little room and drill tiny little holes in tiny little teeth, and pretty soon you start thinking tiny little thoughts!"

Molly crossed her arms over her chest, furrowed her brow, and stared at Joe.

Joe raised an index finger into the air for emphasis. "Life, all of life, needs to have some passion and joy. Dentistry is a great profession for geeks and for those who don't care to do much independent thinking." Joe paused. "Oh, there are people who do become masters at dentistry, that's for sure—but very few of them! I knew I was never going to be one of them. I had no passion for it. Dentistry was making me stupider!"

Then he put the oars back in the water and turned the boat so it was straight in the current once again.

"Being a cowboy and a fishing guide...that's making you smarter?" Molly smiled.

"I never said that," he grinned. "But I'm happy, I guess. I'm starting to see life as a little sweeter and more precious than I did before. I actually went from one part of my life to the next waiting and hoping, for years, that this part would get over soon so I could get on to the next one. I started grousing about why life had to be so long. Now, I'm not in a hurry for it to be over."

"You felt that way too?" Molly blurted. She was surprised at her own words. Joe had given a voice to the dark feelings that had followed her for years, and the words leaped from her.

"Sure. I felt really bad about thinking that, too. There's a whopper of a contradiction in those feelings. I thought I was the only one who felt like that. Nobody is supposed to think that life is too long."

"I know exactly what you mean," Molly said flatly.

Carried by the current and the wind, the little boat drifted and swung in the grip of the Big Horn River for several hours while Joe and Molly talked of their families, jobs, world events, politics, religion, and life cycles. They talked of everything except their futures. The past and the present, even for Joe Mix and Molly Malone, seemed more safe than the future.

———

"OK, what kind of pizza do you like?" Molly asked when they reached the boat landing and Joe winched the boat up onto the trailer.

"Dinner—you and me?" Joe asked.

"Yeah. Let's have another try at it. But nothing quite so elegant tonight. Pizza OK with you?

"Aren't you tired of me yet?" Joe asked while he straightened the boat on the trailer.

"Nah, we still have a lot to talk about," Molly said as she stepped into Joe's truck and slammed the door.

Jake leaped onto the truck seat and Joe followed him. "Well, that's good, Molly." Joe reached over and took her hand in his and slammed the door shut behind him. "'Cause I was just gonna ask you if you'd have dinner with me. But I was afraid to ask."

"Aren't you tired of me?" Molly asked.

Joe only shook his head no and grinned. He reached across the truck seat and took one of Molly's beautiful hands in his. He gently stroked the back of her hand with his thumb and whispered, "I'm havin' a good day."

"So what kind of pizza, Joe?" she asked.

"You decide. Check that—hold the Spam," Joe added.

———•———

A warm, late-summer rain was falling, and the raindrops tapped steadily at the aluminum roof of Molly's trailer. Gray clouds had covered the river several times during the day and brought showers. Then the clouds had cleared and revealed a brilliant blue sky, only to return with more rain after a while. They'd landed the boat under a slate sky while thunder rumbled toward them from the west. Now, they were relieved to be indoors as the heavier rains began to fall.

"You should have brought Jake over for dinner," Molly said while she opened a cupboard door and looked for a cookie sheet.

"No. He had a big day on the river. He was tired and limping badly. He got kicked by a horse back when I was trying to be a cowboy, and it still seems to bother him. Besides that, he sort of stole the show last time, and I'm just not up for that again," Joe said as he leaned against the small kitchen countertop. "He's fine. He was happy to lay down in his own bed over at my place."

Molly continued to open cupboard doors and remove pots and pans. She stopped in front of Joe and opened the refrigerator door, then stepped in front of him again with pepperoni and cheese under one arm as she placed the ingredients for pizza on the countertop.

The trailer was a little crowded with just two people in the kitchen, and Joe thought of the tiny bathroom in his trailer where he'd just showered a few minutes earlier. It sure wasn't anything like his bathroom in his former life, with the tile floor and the elevated bathtub overlooking the wooded backyard. But it was clean, and he was happier here than he'd ever been in that big house. Even the tiny kitchen in Molly's trailer was nice. It was cozy.

"Can I help you with anything?" Joe asked after he'd nearly collided with her twice. He was standing behind Molly and trying to stay out of her way. But he wanted to be in her way too. Maybe she'd touch him when she walked by. She was barefoot and dressed in very well-worn blue jeans. They were almost threadbare in several places. Everyone has a pair of old blue jeans like that, Joe thought, but not everyone looks that good in them. Molly also wore a loose-fitting, linen blouse with red roses embroidered on the front and back. Joe was certain she wasn't wearing a bra, and a little twitch of sexual tension stirred in his belly.

Molly's back was toward Joe and she was fumbling with a jar of flour when she answered, "No, I'm OK. I'm gonna make this pizza from scratch. I'm pretty good at this too. You're gonna like it," she said enthusiastically. She was only inches from him when she turned on her heels to face him, as if she had something more to say. She made eye contact with him briefly. She was so close to him she could smell his aftershave, and she froze for an instant.

Then it happened. It was powerful, unstoppable, and she had no control over it. A clear strand of drool rolled over her lower lip, hung there for a second, then dropped all the way to the floor.

Her eyes were still locked with Joe's as a stunned look of embarrassment flashed across her face. She stared at him for a second, not quite sure what to do. In the next instant, she collapsed like a rag doll onto her own kitchen floor and began to laugh uncontrollably.

Joe struggled for a brief moment to stifle his own laughter but found that to be impossible. A deep, loud roar of laughter rolled up from his belly, and then another, and then another. Tears began to well up in his eyes, and he wiped them away several times as he laughed. Molly was coiled into the fetal position on the kitchen floor. Her hands covered her face, and she shook with laughter. He reached down and grabbed

Molly under her armpits and lifted her to her feet, but she refused to stand up. She just hid her face in Joe's chest and let herself remain limp, as if her central nervous system had short-circuited from embarrassment, and he struggled with her slumped body.

"Nice," Joe said as they both continued to laugh. "That was nice," he said again. In a moment, Molly stood under her own power but kept her face buried in Joe's chest to hide her embarrassment. He continued to laugh, but as he did, he began to stroke her hair with his right hand. Then he began to kiss her hair again, as he'd done on the river. She reached her right hand up to her face and wiped away her tears of laughter, then locked her hands around his waist.

"OK," she said after a moment. "I'll clean up the drool. You can go sit over there while I make the pizza." She pointed to the couch, then stepped away from Joe and began to chuckle softly when she resumed her chores with the pizza.

Draped over the couch and the loveseat in Molly's living room were paisley slip covers. Her television rested on the bookshelf made of bricks and boards. The lava lamp and several candles sat next to the TV. This place had the little touches that only a woman could bring. The white curtains and the little knick-knacks were charming. But there was something else here, Joe thought: it was the essence of the 1960s counterculture. "So, Molly?" he said after he'd looked about for a moment.

"Yeah?" she answered.

"If you had been around at the time—the sixties—you'd have been a hippie, wouldn't you? You were a bit of a wild one, weren't you?"

"Yeah. Probably," she smiled. "Not you, huh?"

"No. I was the kid who missed parties in high school and college so I'd be sure to finish the classroom projects I was doing for extra credit in chemistry and physics."

Over the noise of her kitchen chores, Molly said, "The parties weren't all that great."

"Neither was the chemistry and physics," Joe mumbled. He doubted whether Molly heard his reply. Then he watched while she dropped several ice cubes into two glasses, added some Cutty Sark from the green bottle, turned down the lights, and walked over to him.

Molly handed one of the glasses to Joe, then sat next to him—so close that she was touching him and he had to put his arm around her.

She raised her glass to his and clinked them together. "Pizza will be ready in twenty minutes," she said. "It's my own special recipe."

She took a drink of her scotch at the same time Joe sipped at his drink. Then, when Joe lowered his glass, she brought her mouth to his. Her lips were so soft, Joe thought. Then her lips opened and she slid her tongue into his mouth. She was delicious. He could taste the scotch, and he could taste Molly. Her tongue was cold from her drink, and he loved the way it felt when she moved it around inside his mouth.

"Mmmm," Joe sighed as Molly kissed him. Then she moved her lips away from his and curled up at his side. They both leaned back into the couch, propped their feet onto the coffee table in front of them, and stared at the blank TV.

"You know how you like to talk about the life cycles of mayflies and fishermen and everything?" Molly said softly.

"Yeah?"

"You're an emerger," Molly said, then sipped at her scotch. "You're just about to arrive at the surface, dry your wings, and fly away," she said wistfully.

"I'd like to think that's true in some way," Joe said. "What about you?"

"I think I am too. You know how you talked about time being like a circle or a straight line? That's nice; it's good! I think it's a circle too. But I have to tell you that when you have something really awful happen—when every part of your life that will come after you is cut off—then you begin to feel as though you exist outside of time and the rest of the world."

"Yeah, I think I can understand that. Is that the way you've felt for these past few years?" he asked.

"Yes," Molly said before she sipped at her scotch.

"Anything changing?" he asked.

Molly shrugged, then thought for a moment. "I haven't laughed this much, like I laughed the other night when you were here or like just now, when I almost drooled." She looked at him and grinned. "Since I don't know when—and I like it."

"Well, you know..." Joe nodded. "Studies have shown that the thing that turns women on the most—the thing they find most attractive in a man—is his sense of humor." Joe nodded again.

"Really?" Molly said. She shifted her weight and moved her face closer to his. "You know the sexiest thing about you?" she said as she moved her hand along his thigh.

497

"What?" he swallowed.

"Your bachelor pad and your wheels!" she said. She raised her eyebrows, then kissed him softly on the lips.

"Well, I do pride myself on my appearance, too. I thought you were going to mention my grooming aids—Preparation H and dog crap!"

While she was still smiling and looking into his eyes, Molly brought her mouth to his again and lifted her arm around his shoulder. Her sweet, familiar taste and the odd sensation of her cold, wet lips and cold tongue in his mouth were wonderful. He moved his hand under her linen blouse and raised it slowly, over the exquisitely soft skin of her stomach, until her round, full breast filled his hand.

The oven timer began to blare and startled both of them. "Saved by the bell," Joe whispered.

"That's only round one," she said when she stood up to take the pizza from the oven. A steady rainfall continued to tap at the windows and the metal roof of the trailer as Molly placed the pizza on the coffee table in front of the couch.

"What are you thinking about, Joe?" Molly said when she lifted a slice of pizza off the pan.

"I think you know," he smiled.

"So tell me about your first time," Molly said.

"I don't kiss and tell," Joe grinned.

"All men do. Tell me!"

"You go first," Joe replied.

"It was in a sleeping bag..." Molly started.

"It was Mike, right?" Joe interrupted.

Molly shook her head sideways and grinned.

"You're a nasty one," Joe laughed.

"He was one of my brother's friends. He was older, and he knew what to do—exactly what to do," she said with a wicked grin.

"So it was pretty good?" Joe asked.

Molly only nodded and smiled.

"I'm gonna blow up here, Molly. I can't take any more of this," Joe laughed and dropped his pizza onto the coffee table.

"Now you tell me," she said.

"Party at my friend's house; somebody's friend from Chicago was visiting. We had the whole place to ourselves, all alone with no chance for anyone to bother us..."

"Like tonight?" Molly asked.

Joe reached for his scotch and swallowed, but his throat was still dry. "Yeah," he croaked.

———•———

Joe walked quietly to the living room and sat on the couch again. Rain still tapped on the roof, and thunder rolled off in the distance. The room was illuminated only by the lava lamp, and Joe stared at the red clump of lava that rose and fell, changed shapes, and cast its odd shadows across the little room. He was naked now, and he covered himself with a pillow from the couch while he watched the lava shift, rise, and fall.

The sex had been spectacular, unbelievably erotic. He'd risen from Molly's bed and walked out to the living room to think about things while Molly lay sleeping. They'd talked softly, touched each other, and kissed gently for a while after dinner. Then Molly had begun to undress him, and one thing had led to the next. He'd wanted to push things along and take the first steps, but he'd felt, for some reason, that that should be left to Molly. Rain steadily brushed the windows as Joe stared at the lava lamp. The only thought that came to him was how isolated and secure he felt. He was alone in the middle of nowhere, on a dark and rainy night, with a beautiful woman, and no one could possibly bother him. He thought of her round, smooth breasts and the round curves of her behind and how she'd felt in his hands.

Molly had accepted him tonight. She'd granted him a closeness, a tenderness that he'd never known with Jess. Maybe that was just the nature of sex—that a woman would accept a man. But Molly had taken him in on several different levels tonight. Her touch had seemed to coax him, to urge him to another place, then beg him to linger for a while before she led him even closer.

"You OK, Joe?" Molly interrupted the silence. She was tying a terrycloth robe around her waist as she walked toward him.

"Yeah. Fine," Joe smiled. "This is so nice, to be here like this."

Molly laid down with her bare leg across Joe's lap and her head at the far end of the couch.

"What are you thinking about?" she asked.

Joe moved his right hand slowly up and down her legs but said nothing at first. He just touched her legs ever so softly and stared at the lamp.

"Do you think that was wrong what we just did?" Joe asked. "I mean, I don't even know if I'm divorced yet."

"Aw, Joe," Molly said. "Do you need some lawyer to tell you when you're divorced?"

"I guess not."

"Joe, we're just two lonely people who've found something pretty good in each other's arms—and I don't mean just the sex."

"I know, Molly," Joe said as he continued to stroke her leg. "I know." He slid his hand up her leg, over her bare stomach, then back down her other leg, and she shivered at his touch.

"Wrong?" Molly sighed. "Did you say 'wrong'?" As if she couldn't believe he could say something so stupid. "Wrong?" Joe could tell she was smiling by the way she said the word "wrong?" Molly raised her foot and used her toes to turn Joe's head away from the lava lamp and toward her. "In case you didn't notice, it was absolutely right for me—about six times there, right at the end. That thing you did? Right at the end there? Both times? That was amazing!"

"Oh, that," Joe smiled, and he thought of Murdo and the Velvet Half-Nelson. "I used a screwdriver to twist a tooth out for a drunk cowboy one night, and he was so grateful that he showed..."

"Whoa there, cowboy! That's about all I need to know!" Molly laughed.

Joe smiled and continued to move his hand along Molly's leg and onto her stomach.

"You make me laugh, Joe Mix. I like that," Molly said softly.

"Me too. I love it when you laugh," Joe said. "But I have to ask you something, Molly."

"What's that?"

"You know when you nearly drooled there before supper?"

"Yes." She was straining not to smile.

"Was that about me or the pizza?" Joe asked.

"The pizza was a little salty," she said slowly. "But you tasted just right."

Joe covered his face with his hand and said, "You're a nasty one, Molly."

"Well, I have one question for YOU," Molly said, then paused and waited for Joe to respond.

"Yeah?"

"That thing you did there at the end?" Molly's robe fell open as Joe stroked her leg, revealing the tan lines her clothing had left behind. The white outline around her breasts and hips was faint in the shifting light, but the sight of it stirred him once again.

"Yeah?" Joe said, then cautiously gulped back a rush of excitement.

"Think you can do that again?"

"Uh huh," Joe slowly said. "But we don't have enough room right here. We'll have to..."

Molly stood up and took Joe's hand. She kissed him and led him back to her room.

chapter
thirty-nine

Marsh pulled heavily on the boat oars, sending the drift boat away from the cow pasture and back across the Big Horn toward his cabin. Six large, plastic buckets were filled with golf balls and spread all around the boat, while Joe and Jake sat in the rear seat of the boat and watched.

"Ever think about just hitting the balls back across the river?" Joe asked. "You wouldn't have to pick up so many balls."

"Tried that." Marsh leaned on the oars. "Bad idea." He leaned again. "Put one IN my kitchen. Broke the shit out of the big window. Bad idea." Marsh pulled on the oars once more, then spoke again. "'Sides that, it's way easier to pick 'em up over there in the short grass than in this tall grass and brush and forest over here on my side." He made one more long, heavy stroke with the oars, and the boat ground onto the gravel of the riverbank in front of his house. "OK. Let's carry 'em up to the tee box and tee off."

"Where are we playin' today, Marsh?" Joe asked as he trudged up the small incline of the riverbank with a bucket of balls in each hand. Jake ran ahead and started chasing mice in the tall grass.

"Pebble Beach," Marsh answered quickly. "Days are getting shorter here, and winter isn't too far away. Pebble Beach always makes me think of nice weather."

The afternoons had remained warm—sometimes very warm—as they do in the autumn in southeastern Montana. But the days were growing shorter, and the evenings were much cooler.

"So when does the pace slow down here, Marsh? When do the fishermen give it a rest?" Joe asked as he walked.

"Well, this is a tailwater fishery, as you know, and the water temperature in the channel remains about the same all year as it gets released from the reservoir up above." Marsh put his two buckets of golf balls down at the back of the tee box, then continued. "The fishin' is fine year round, but the shitty weather in December, January, and February pretty much thins out the crowd. Don't worry, though, you'll have clients to guide all winter."

"Wasn't worried," Joe said. "I'm plenty busy."

Marsh drew a driver from the bag of golf clubs and leaned on it with both of his hands covering the end before he spoke. "Yes, you have been busy. Molly has too, for about a month, ever since you burned your head." Marsh stared at Joe and waited for him to reply.

It had become an endless summer for Joe. Here at the Big Horn, he'd found a quiet place where he could live cheaply thanks to Marsh's generosity. Marsh had never charged him anything for rent on the old trailer with the pitched roof and shingles. He told Joe it would be like charging a bum to sleep under a bridge.

Joe had found a job that suited him too. At least the job gave him time to think about his future. More than anything, the job as a guide on the great trout river had provided an opportunity—the first opportunity he could remember to get comfortable with the man he was, the man he'd always wanted to be. He didn't come home from work angry and frustrated anymore, except for the one day with Sam Palmer. And he had a chance nearly every day to talk with someone new about life, death, business, religion, philosophy, or whatever. He could see the world around him, all the life and the life cycles. He could engage someone new in lengthy conversations almost every day, without having to run from one tiny room to the next and listen while people begged him, ordered him, not to do good work—just to do something less, to be something less.

He'd been reading more than ever. And he'd begun to write, using the laptop word processor Molly had given him. He'd realized soon enough when he'd started to write that he had nothing profound to say. He had, however, come to enjoy the use of words to tell a story—just the written word, with no help from his voice or hands. He was still discovering the power of words.

He'd grown close to Molly also—close in a way he'd never thought possible. Their evenings together were usually quiet. They read, they talked, they held hands and walked. They sat together on the couch with the paisley slipcover in Molly's trailer, Joe holding Molly close while they talked and laughed. And that time with Molly, Joe knew, was what Marsh was asking about.

"Marsh..." Joe smiled up at Marsh from the red bench on the tee box. "Molly is special. She's smart, and she's great to talk with. She says things I wish I would have said, about life and people. And there's a tenderness there that I just can't turn away from. She's as fine a friend as I've ever known. So yeah, I guess we've been busy. But it's OK."

Still leaning on his driver, Marsh started cautiously. "I know, Joe, but I just don't want Molly to wind up with a broken heart, and maybe leave here and return to something like what she had in West Yellowstone. Do you know what I'm saying?"

"Yeah, I do," Joe admitted. "I've thought about that too."

Marsh waited for a moment, then began to address the ball for his drive on the first hole at Pebble Beach. Just as he was about to raise the club into his backswing, he heard Joe's voice from the little red bench.

"I love her," Joe had said. When Marsh looked over at him, Joe was staring at the ground in front of him. He seemed oblivious to Marsh and the fact that Marsh was about to start play. Joe never looked up at Marsh. He kept his head down, staring at something just in front of him, and spoke again. "We all get a broken heart sometime, don't we?"

Marsh and Joe had played eighteen holes at Pebble Beach and wound up having a few laughs. But today, golf had seemed to be just a distraction for Joe. When the golf was finished, he begged off on another meal of hotdogs and baked beans. He drove back to his misshapen trailer home and tried to call Molly. When she didn't answer, he assumed she was out walking or in the shower, and he decided to just try again later.

The darkness in his backyard was nearly total as a cool evening had settled over the Big Horn Valley. Joe started a fire inside the circle of stones in his yard, and yellow sparks popped into the air when the fire crackled. He stood beside the fire for a moment and raked the coals into an even bed, then went into the trailer.

Molly was waiting just outside the door of his trailer when he swung the door open with his foot and carried the awkward thing out.

"Hi!" Molly smiled.

"Hi!" Joe answered. He bent over and kissed her, with the clumsy thing that looked like an end table in his arms. Then he turned toward the backyard, and Molly followed. When he reached the fire pit, he gently lowered the thing into the fire.

"That's your dad's trout," Molly said. "Why are you burning it?" She took his hand in hers and waited for an answer.

"It's not mine," Joe shrugged. "It was another man's trophy. Maybe it meant something special to him. But he's dead. He's gone—has been for a long time. I brought it halfway across the country. I kept that thing around all these years because I thought it has some special message for my life." He turned and looked at her. "Well, it doesn't. It just represents another man's dreams, and it dawned on me over the summer that I can let go of other men's dreams."

"It was your dad's, don't you want to keep it?" Molly said as she stroked his hand with her thumb.

"No. I'm not throwing my dad away. Just the ratty old fish. It was time. A man shouldn't spend his life looking after another man's dreams and prizes. It's not right. It's good to let it go." The fire grew around the plank and the stuffed fish that was connected to it. Joe added some more wood to the fire as he and Molly watched the fish disappear.

"You're burning more than a stuffed fish here—more than another man's dreams, Joe. You're doing more than letting go of your dad."

"Oh?"

"You're burning one last ship, like Cortez on the shore of the New World," Molly said.

Joe raised her hand, still locked with his, up to his mouth and kissed it. "You're the only person I know who would say something like that, Molly." He kissed her hand again, then stood and stared into the fire for a while.

"Opposite sides of the same coin...you and me," Molly sighed.

"So, Molly...do you have ships to burn too?" he asked.

"I never thought about it until I met you," she replied.

"The story you told me? About your boys? That was the most painful thing I ever listened to. It hurt me just to hear you say the words."

"I could tell." She leaned her head on his shoulder.

"So how do you do it? How do you go on every day?"

"I struggled for a long time; just about didn't make it. It got a lot easier when Marsh came along, though, because I knew he needed me." She looked into the fire. "He needed me to run the shop and tend to the details around here. He needed me to be at my best—better than I ever was in West Yellowstone." She reached her hand over and touched her palm on Joe's chest. "You need me too!"

Joe nodded his agreement.

The stuffed trout was gone. There would be no returning to Kadoka to rewrite the story of Ray Mix. Ray Mix could just be Joe's dad now, a good man who did the best he could. And Joe Mix could get on with his own life, too. Joe and Molly stood in the flickering light and watched the coals shift at the bottom of the fire pit for several minutes.

"Hey, look what I found in one of the drawers in the trailer," Joe said. He reached into his pocket and produced a small transistor radio that appeared to be about 1960s vintage. He clicked the radio and used his thumb to turn the dial while he searched for a station with a strong enough signal to reach Fort Smith.

"You're not gonna have much luck, Joe. We're a long way from the nearest radio tower," Molly said. But as soon as the words left her mouth, a babbling whir of static and partly audible music and voices cleared in an instant, and the refrain from "Never My Love" sounded.

Joe raised his eyebrows and smiled. "You were saying?" he said sarcastically as he rested the tiny radio on the ground next to the fire. He laughed when he found that the reception disappeared if he turned the radio ninety degrees. He carefully moved the radio to just the right position for maximum reception, then stood up and put his arms around Molly. "Remember that?" he said softly "Remember when you had to turn the radio just right or you couldn't hear anything?"

"That was before my time," Molly laughed.

"Right," Joe sighed. He put his lips by her ear and began to sway ever so slowly, as if they were standing in a crowd at a high school dance. "I love this song," he whispered.

"Me too," Molly said softly, and followed his slow movement.

Joe wanted to say the words. He wanted to say, "I love you, Molly." But he couldn't do it. He was afraid. He wondered what she was thinking. He wondered if she wanted to hear the words or wanted to say them. Here he was, standing by a little fire next to a run-down trailer house on an Indian reservation, dancing to music from a crackly, cheap old radio. After all he'd seen and done, he was in love. He wanted to say it, but he couldn't.

"Never My Love" ended after the haunting organ refrain, and Joe kissed Molly's ear. The spell was broken in an instant as Sammy Davis Jr. began to sing "Candy Man." Joe spun in one quick move and kicked the little radio over. "I hate that damn song!" he said.

Molly laughed briefly, then held Joe closer and pushed her face into his chest. After a while, she raised her lips to his and kissed him firmly. Her lips and tongue tasted wonderful, Joe thought.

"Life is strange—really strange—isn't it?" Molly said after a while.

"Yeah. What do you mean?" Joe said.

"After all the things that have happened to the two of us, over all the years, here we are tonight like this." She paused for a moment. "I needed you to come along, Joe. The Kadoka Kid," she whispered.

"I needed you, too." He closed his eyes and sighed.

"You wanna go inside, Joe, and...make some noise?" Molly asked, then raised her eyebrows and smiled a wicked smile.

"Let's go," he answered.

———•———

Cool night air eased its way into Joe's bedroom through a tiny opening in the window. Molly lay next to him, sleeping. But Joe still felt flushed and sweaty; the cool air felt good. He looked at Molly's naked body and tried to make sense of it all. She was good to him. She was smart. When she was with him, he liked himself better. She was lit only by the moonlight that came through the small window with the late-summer breeze. He reached his hand to her back and moved it slowly down her soft skin until he found the perfectly round shape of her behind, which fit so wonderfully in his hand. Then he moved his leg in between hers and pulled her toward him. If he fell asleep like this with their legs entwined and his arms around her, well, that was fine. If Molly woke up and wanted something, well, that was fine too. Holding a woman like this was something new for Joe. Jess had never liked it, and he'd begun sleeping in his den or a recliner or the guest room several years before he'd left her, just to give her some space. Now, he looked forward to those quiet nights with Molly just after sex or just before he rolled out of bed in the morning. He liked to lay with his arms around

Molly and feel her soft skin touching his. Sometimes, he just lay there with her and wondered if she was awake. Holding Molly like this in the half-light of a darkened bedroom was a fantasy that came to him countless times during his work day.

For now—for this quiet moment with a sweet, cool breeze lifting the small curtain away from the bedroom window and drifting over them—he intended to hold on to Molly. He wanted to hear her say the words. "I need you" was nice—it was where love started, Joe supposed—but it wasn't the same as "I love you."

chapter
forty

Molly rose early the next morning, showered, and went to work. When Joe awoke thirty minutes later, he shuffled into the kitchen, fed Jake, and made himself some breakfast. Sunlight was peeking into the trailer. Joe could smell Molly's shampoo and the perfume she'd put on before work. The smell of his coffee mingled with the scent of Molly, and he thought of the way she'd looked last night in the dim light of his tiny bedroom. This was turning out to be a fine summer—a long summer. The days were still pretty warm. He liked this place; he was happy. Marsh had become a good friend, and Molly filled him with a passion he'd never known. He liked going to work in the morning, and he liked knowing that Molly would be waiting to talk and laugh and hold him when he stepped out of the river at day's end.

Jake pranced into the fly shop looking for someone to play with, and Joe followed close behind. Earlier in the summer, Jake had sprinted from Joe's truck into the shop and made so much noise it sounded like there were several dogs bursting through the door. But now, over the past couple weeks, Jake seemed to be losing some of that wild enthusiasm that very young dogs always display when they greet people. He wagged his tail and trotted slowly across the showroom to the counter where Molly stood talking to a fisherman.

Joe held a cup of coffee in one hand and followed Jake over the threshold of the door. He knew he had only one client for the day, but he didn't know who the person was or where he was from. Joe scanned the fly shop for a moment looking for Marsh. Must be in the back room,

Joe thought. Then he caught Molly's eye, and she smiled openly and waved. He waved back, but he thought something looked funny in Molly's smile. He turned back toward Molly, and when he did he got the surprise of the summer. The fisherman Molly was talking with turned and faced Joe.

It was Donny.

Joe stared for a second, then started to smile. Then his face began to bend and his eyes filled with tears and his lower lip began to tremble. Without a word of greeting, he stepped into Donny's waiting arms and began to sniffle. Neither brother spoke. They held each other in a bear hug for nearly a minute, each of them sniffling and patting the other on the back. Then Joe took a deep breath and kissed Donny on the cheek.

"No tongues!" Donny said, and Molly laughed out loud.

When they separated, Molly handed each of them a Kleenex, then wiped her own eyes dry and looked back and forth between the brothers.

"What are you doing here?" Joe asked.

"Fishing," Donny shrugged. He was dressed in Gore-Tex waders, a fishing vest, and a wool baseball cap that said "Big Horn Adventures" on the front. "I have to come way out here just to go fishing with my brother, you know?"

"You knew about this, didn't you?" Joe said to Molly.

"Yeah. Donny asked Marsh and I to keep it a surprise, but it was so hard not to tell you!" Molly confessed, then changed the subject. "Your little brother was just telling me all about you."

"It was all good, right?" Joe asked.

"Thought maybe you'd like a chance to pay for the withholding of certain other information, though," Donny interjected with a grin.

When the surprise of finding Donny in the fly shop began to pass, Joe understood that Donny had made a pilgrimage to visit him. This visit was perhaps in some small way about fishing. But it was more about Donny wanting to assess the current state of Joe's existence, and his own need to reaffirm their love and friendship.

"No, but you're gonna have to pay to go fishing with me. How 'bout that? Course, I should have been charging you all along for all the secrets I told you about fishing!" Joe reached over and put his arm around Donny's shoulder again. "God, it's good to see you, Donny."

Donny nodded, and Jake limped over and put both front paws on Donny's thighs, begging for some affection. "This is the dog you picked up along the way?" he asked while he scratched Jake's ears.

"Yeah." Joe stood and gloated for a moment, as though Jake had just done a trick.

"What ever made you want to have a puppy at that point? You know—your frame of mind had to be a little shaky. Then to be taking off on a roadtrip of such uncertainty, in that shitty old truck," Donny said, still holding Jake.

"Well, I needed him. Just seemed like the thing to do. Maybe I needed to replace your presence in my life. Jake's a better listener, and he doesn't talk back."

Donny looked at Molly and grimaced, then turned to Joe. "I think I've rented you for the day, so why don't you pick up my stuff and take me fishin'. We have a lot of catching up to do."

"See you later," Joe said to Molly as they turned to leave.

Molly watched and listened as Joe and Donny walked to Joe's truck. Joe still kept his arm around Donny's shoulder. "God sakes!" Donny said when they were outside the shop. "I just spent about six hundred dollars, and you could put all the shit I bought in a coffee cup!"

"Quit your bitching. I'm gonna take you out for the best day of fishing you ever had."

"Hey, you two! Dinner at Marsh's tonight," Molly called from the doorway.

"Will it be elegant?" Joe called back. Molly nodded and waved goodbye.

Both truck doors slammed in a moment, and a thin cloud of dust swirled across the parking lot in their wake as they made the short drive to the boat landing at the Afterbay.

"You actually create the illusion of competence quite well," Donny said after Joe had moved the boat into the Big Horn's current.

"Just wait," Joe smiled. Then he rigged Donny's fly line with a strike indicator, some weight, and a tiny pheasant tail nymph. He handed the fly rod back to his brother with a satisfied look and added, "You're fishing now, Donny. Toss that over the side. We're on top of fish right now."

Donny looked at Joe's hands, the way they gripped the boat oars. He looked at Joe's posture and the way his shoulders had grown while his belly had disappeared. And he caught the light in Joe's eyes as he worked the boat in the current. He hesitated when Joe leaned toward him, then made a strange face and leaned back away from Joe. "This is Joe Mix I'm talking to, isn't it?" Donny said. He tilted his head as if he were studying a painting in a museum. "You're different, Joe. You ARE different now; you've changed." Donny looked at Joe as if he were seeing him for the first time.

"Of course I've changed," Joe started softly, slowly, while he worked the boat oars. "That's why all this stuff had to happen: so I could be different than the man I was trying to be all those years. But I think I'm still the same, too. Does that make any sense?"

"So, Joe. What if I had a toothache right now?" Donny asked, as if he wasn't quite satisfied with Joe's answer or wanted more affirmation.

"Well..." Joe leaned on the oars and straightened the boat. "I guess you'd be fucked, wouldn't you?" Joe chuckled. "Why don't you start fishing? This is a good run through this next riffle."

Donny grinned at Joe's reply, then added, "You look good. You've lost some weight. Looks like you've been working out." Donny lofted several false casts above the boat, then laid his line down on the river's surface.

"Just working, not working out," Joe corrected. "But thanks for noticing."

The boat bounced along over the choppy surface of the little riffle, and Joe worked to get a good float for Donny. When they reached the calm water at the tail end of the riffle, Joe mumbled, "Everybody catches fish in that riffle. Everybody. You still suck at this!" Then, when the river seemed to be totally quiet, Joe asked, "How are the boys?"

"They're fine, Joe. I had dinner with them the other night. They're both doing fine—girlfriends, school, plans for life after college, all that stuff."

"I talk to them pretty often," Joe said. "But it's not the same...not the same as being there." Joe seemed suddenly melancholy.

"Well, both your boys are at that age when they really don't have a lot of need for parental supervision, if you know what I mean. They're just discovering their own lives. But something else is going on there inside those heads. I see it every time I talk to them." Donny shuffled his feet and glanced at Joe before he looked back at his strike indicator.

"Remember when you were that age and you did something stupid, and then you thought to yourself, 'Oh, yeah, that's what Dad was talking about—that's why he told me not to do that'? Well, that's where they are now. They verbalize stuff like that all the time, you know? They'll tell me about some lesson they just learned the hard way, in spite of what their dad had warned them to do or not do." Donny shrugged, "Hell, we all did stuff like that. And then, when it was over, we could hear our father's voice telling us how to get around whatever problem we'd just created for ourselves. Your boys were joking about it just the other night. Chris even mentioned Mark Twain's line: 'When I was fourteen, I thought my father was the dumbest man alive; when I was twenty-one, I was amazed at how much he'd learned in seven years.'" Donny smiled. "Your boys are OK!"

Joe smiled as if he'd just been told he'd won the lottery. "So they were listening all along, and I didn't ruin their lives when I left?" he asked. "No need to hurry them off to see a shrink?"

"Not hardly. Oh, they miss you, and they're looking forward to Christmas when they plan to see you. But they're OK. We talk about things."

"Thanks, Donny."

"It's OK. I love your boys too. But I do have some news about your ex-wife that I wanted to give you face to face."

Joe stopped working the oars and looked at Donny.

"She's getting married," Donny said, then waited for Joe's response.

"Oh?" Joe said. "Who's the lucky guy?"

"Omar Hagen," Donny said flatly.

Joe blinked, then tilted his head. "Really?"

"Really! The instant he heard Jess might be available, he dropped his wife like a bad habit and made a move to upgrade. It's really pathetic, Joe." Donny reeled in, folded his arms, and leaned back in his seat. "She sold him a dental practice he can't handle, for way more money than it was worth. Then she made him sign a prenuptial agreement that virtually...well, suffice it to say he's been making some poor decisions."

A devious smirk settled onto Joe's face. "You know who's been making his decisions for him?" Joe's tone was evil. He turned his head and hunched his shoulders. He looked both ways, as if he had a secret to share and didn't want anyone to hear it.

Donny returned a knowing smile. "A little short guy? Wears a Nazi helmet? Lives down there?" And he pointed at his crotch.

"That's the guy!" Joe blurted, and they both burst into laughter. While Donny was still chuckling, Joe pulled heavily on one oar and turned the boat sideways in the current. Then he muscled the boat across the river toward a small island.

"Let's stop and fish this little run over here. It always holds some nice fish," Joe groaned as he worked the oars.

Donny watched his brother move the boat easily across the current. He watched the way Joe moved and studied the clarity in his eyes as he worked the oars. He noticed strength in Joe's hands, a power he'd never seen before. "Any regrets, Joe?" Donny finally asked in a subdued tone.

Joe turned his eyes to Donny and furrowed his brow, considering his answer. "Seems like I've been talking about regrets for too long." He paused. "No. None."

"You know...Jess...the practice...anything?" Donny added.

Joe stopped rowing for just one stroke and looked at Donny. He paused for another second, then pursed his lips and shook his head, as if that question didn't need more of an answer. A shake of the head was enough; the answer was "no," and that was that.

"How you gonna live, Joe?" Donny asked seriously.

"Live? I never lived better than I have this summer." Joe hesitated. "I've had to cut back a little on my spending, but I'm doing all right. Hell, I'm a rich man!"

The boat ground itself onto a ledge of gravel, and Joe dropped the little anchor off the stern to hold the boat in place. He waited for a moment before he spoke again, to emphasize what he was about to say. "The trip out here was hard, Donny. Damn hard. Hardest thing I ever did. But I'm OK. I'm done with my guilt over failing at dentistry and marriage and everything else I was worried about. I'm done with it. You can worry about it if you want, but don't talk to me about it anymore. It doesn't interest me. Regrets? I'm sick of the talk. I have no regrets anymore." Joe folded his arms across his chest and continued. "Donny, I'm fifty years old, and I don't know what I want to be when I grow up."

"Does that bother you?" Donny asked.

"Hell no! I think that's sort of cool! The only thing that bothers me is that you keep asking me shit like that. Let's go fishing!"

"This is amazing, Joe!" Donny exclaimed. He reached his hand under the belly of a thick, sixteen-inch rainbow and then used a hemostat to remove the tiny nymph from its mouth. "I'll bet I've caught ten fish in this little run, and all of them have been nice—sixteen to twenty inches!" he said as he released the trout back into the slow current at his knees and turned to face Joe.

Like Donny, Joe was standing knee deep in the Big Horn, about forty feet downstream from his brother. Both of them were poised at a seam that separated fast water from slow, at the tail end of a small island.

"Yeah, this is a good run through here," Joe agreed. "But there's a lot of nice runs on this river—a lot of them. This is just a typical day here." Then, as an afterthought, he added, "Things are really gonna pick up this afternoon. There'll be a Caddis hatch this afternoon that you won't believe. The big trout start pacing about midafternoon, waiting for supper." Joe smiled and shook his head. "You just won't believe the action." Donny nodded and began to cast his line upstream once again. His orange strike indicator bobbed along gently as it passed by him several times. Each time it started to swing in the current downstream from him at the end of its drift, he lifted the tip of his fly rod and flipped his line upstream for another cast.

"Hey, Joe?" Donny called without looking.

"Yeah?" Joe answered.

"Remember those little black-and-white mayflies we used to see in the Root River? Little tiny things. Remember those?"

"Tricos. They're called Tricos. Tricorythodes something or other. Yeah, I remember."

"Anything like that here?"

"Apparently there used to be," Joe started. "Used to be clouds of 'em. Used to be one of the special hatches out here. Billions and billions. Actually like clouds, so they say," Joe said. "But they seem to be gone or almost gone."

"What happened?" Donny asked.

"Well, there has been serious low water for a while here, and if the river channel isn't full, the water temperature just never rises very much. The Tricos need a water temp of sixty to sixty-five degrees to hatch in big numbers, and it just hasn't happened for a few years." Joe shrugged. "It's a cyclic thing, I suppose. The Tricos will come back when the river is ready. Even a river seems to have a life cycle, huh?" Joe said. But when he looked up from his own strike indicator, he saw Donny had hooked another trout and probably hadn't heard much of his response about mayflies and rivers. He reeled in his own line and then walked slowly to the riverbank.

The air was warming nicely, and the gentle morning held the promise of a clear autumn afternoon. Donny appeared content there in his own world, Joe thought. He was catching trout at a rate he'd never experienced before. From his place on the river's edge, Joe thought Donny looked like a small boy, totally engrossed in the little patch of river current in front of him, working feverishly to harvest all the thrills and secrets the river would offer up. Donny was still stuck in the second phase of a fly fisherman's life cycle: he was after as many fish as he could catch. The river gurgled softly and glistened in the morning light as Donny cast his line. He was surrounded by the blues, greens, and yellows of the beautiful river, and he was working to lift something from the moment.

Joe turned away and left Donny alone with the riffle. He put his fly rod into the boat, withdrew a bottle of water, and drank heavily. When he screwed the cap back on the top, he filled his lungs and tried to draw in the smell of nearby Russian Olive trees. They seemed to be losing much of their sweetness as autumn wore on, but it would be back again when they bloomed in the spring. This was a good day, Joe thought. When he looked up on the riverbank, he saw that some small, yellow wildflowers still grew there in the underbrush, and he decided to climb the bank and pick some for Molly.

Everyone had always said that wildflowers smelled better than domestic, garden flowers. But Joe couldn't tell the difference. He picked a handful of flowers with long sturdy stems and arranged them in his right fist. He sniffed at the flowers and began to think about Molly. He saw her brown eyes, her long, pretty fingers, and he began to feel her hair brushing at his face. He felt the softness of her lips just barely touching his in that way she always held herself close to him at first. He loved the way she passed her tender, baby-soft lips over his for a few seconds when he greeted her now. She hardly touched her face to his at first. She just moved her lips over his ever so softly before she opened her mouth...

"Hey, what are you doing?" Donny's voice stole the moment from Joe. "Let's move on. I bet I caught twenty fish in that little run. Let's try some new water." He was standing by the boat and calling up the bank to Joe.

Joe nodded his agreement and began to walk down a narrow cow path that led to the river. He'd walked about fifty feet back toward Donny when he saw it. He stopped in his tracks and turned immediately toward Donny. Luckily, Donny was looking at him. Joe signaled urgently for Donny to come to him, then put his index finger over his lips to demand silence.

Donny approached slowly, as Joe had directed him. When he stood at his brother's side, Joe used the flowers in his right hand to point at the trail in front of them, but he chose not to speak.

"What?" Donny whispered.

"Look!" Joe urged softly.

"What?" Donny craned his neck and bent over.

"Right there on the cow path...THAT'S a rattlesnake!" Joe said loudly, and the dimple on his cheek hosted an enormous smile. He stomped his foot and startled a large rattlesnake that had been sunning itself on the cow path. The snake slithered off into the brush beside them in an instant, and Donny bolted for the river.

"Goddammit, Joe! Why do you do shit like that?" Donny hollered as he ran back to the boat.

Joe pointed the flowers at Donny as he walked toward the boat, where Donny was now seated and waiting for Joe. "Just trying to help you learn about all the flora and fauna of this beautiful river," Joe smiled. Then he stepped over the gunwale and into the boat with his brother. "Just trying to widen our horizons."

Donny leaned forward, opened the cooler, and drew out a can of Coke. He drank most of the Coke in several long swigs, then sat straight in his boat seat. He looked into Joe's eyes and said, "That's why no one likes you"—then belched a loud, wet belch with his mouth open.

Joe laughed out loud as he pulled back on the boat oars until the Big Horn's current took control and the boat began to move with it. He laughed with every stroke for nearly a minute. Donny drank the rest of the Coke, belched once more, and concluded with "asshole!" as the boat slid around a bend in the river.

—·—

By midafternoon, Joe and Donny had fished most of the water that Joe wanted to show his brother. Joe was trying to situate Donny and himself on a good spot for the evening Caddis hatch, which Joe guessed would be spectacular.

"Let's just rest for a few minutes, right here on this little bar," Joe said. "When the Caddis start coming off in about an hour, this is gonna be a prime spot to fish." Joe nodded in agreement with himself.

"So what do the Caddis flies look like?" Donny asked.

"Like little black moths. Their wings lay down over their backs, not like mayflies whose wings sweep up. They're just another aquatic insect that God created solely as trout food. There'll be millions of 'em in the air soon," Joe said.

"Joe," Donny said as he started down a totally different road. "I have to tell you...I had something happen during your divorce proceedings that I've never seen."

"Oh?"

"Yeah. You know...I made it clear to the judge that your wishes were to give everything to Jess, right?" Donny said.

"Uh huh," Joe agreed.

"Well, when it came down to it—to the final dividing of things—the judge started giving you money. Not a lot, mind you, but nonetheless he'd turn to me and say something like, 'Mr. Mix will take this because it's due him.' I couldn't believe how odd that felt. You know, all those years of fighting for money and property, thinking your client is really entitled to something, then having the judge decide otherwise. This time, I just rolled over and he started giving it back! I played golf with him after it was all done, and he said how odd it seemed too." Donny shook his head, then added, "Anyway, I have about $80,000 in an account for you back in Rochester."

Joe remained quiet for a moment. Then, while he was staring at his boots, he tipped his head to an angle and asked, "When you were playing golf, did you see Slats Murphy?" Donny's story about the divorce and the money had apparently gone unnoticed.

"Well, yes—yes, I did. I see him quite often," Donny stammered. "And he says to say hello, too. He also said he'd received a nice note from Win Westby, and that Win was still in Georgia and doing well."

"Win Westby," Joe uttered in a wistful voice, still staring at his boots. "Now, there's a gentleman, Donny. A real thinking man, too. An artist!"

Joe smiled at his boots and thought of Win Westby. "If a man ever needed a hero..."

"Never met him," Donny said. "But I hear the old-timers talk about him still. Is he anything like the Old Cowboy...like Dad?"

Joe thought about Ray Mix, the Old Cowboy, for a moment. He wondered if he should tell Donny the things he'd learned from Ralph Webster on his way west or if he should just let Donny find those things out as he had. Maybe Donny would never discover them. "How much do you know about Dad?" Joe asked.

Donny waited so long to answer that Joe wondered if he'd heard the question. "Are you asking me if I know about Rose, or are you asking if I know that his business practices were a little shaky?"

"You knew?" Joe sat up straight in the boat.

"I was there, Joe, for some of it. I was still a kid, but I suspected everything. I guess on some level, I was aware of all that, as kids can be sometimes. Kadoka is a small town, and Dad had become the center of some colorful rumors. Whatever I didn't know for sure, my classmates filled in for me."

"Why didn't you tell me?"

"I don't know. I guess you seemed happy with your understanding of everything, so I left you to it." Donny shrugged his shoulders. "I don't know. Maybe I should have told you. Ralph Webster let you in on that stuff?"

"Yeah," Joe answered.

"Figured he might," Donny sighed. "He's the guy you needed to hear it from anyway."

"Yeah, I guess that's true," Joe agreed.

Joe stepped out of the boat and into the knee-deep water. He tipped his Stetson back and splashed some water on his face. Then he used his thumb to blow his nose. After he'd dried his face on his sleeve and put his Stetson back on his head, he leaned against the boat for a moment.

"I was angry at the Old Cowboy, Donny—angry that he'd let me down. I guess I needed a hero," Joe said.

"He's still a hero."

"I know, Donny. But it took me a while to understand. I had to forgive him for not being John Wayne—for being an average man. Once I let go of all those childish expectations, I was able to see his life, and mine, in a different light. I guess it's all right to be...just a man, huh?" Joe said.

"Yeah. I guess you do the best you can and love your friends and family just as they are," Donny said.

Joe reached for his fly rod and began to clip and retie some knots. He removed the orange strike indicator. "You know, Donny, through it all, the one thing that bothers me, the one thing I can't get around…know what that is?"

"What?"

Joe still fumbled with the rod, but he paused for a moment and looked at Donny. "I just don't know how he could love two women. I don't understand."

"Happens all the time, Joe. But sooner or later it all comes apart. Somebody has to choose, or somebody finds out something they weren't supposed to. Cheating? That's one thing, and I guess that's probably easier to get over. But for the person you love to be in love with someone else at the same time…that would hurt. That's when hearts start getting broken. In Dad's case, people just started to die."

"That's too much to think about. I'm going fishing," Joe said. Then he grimaced, turned, and trudged into the current. "I'll never understand."

———•———

"You should have seen it, Marsh!" Joe exclaimed. "I'll bet Donny caught another twenty fish during the Caddis hatch."

"Just another day on the Big Horn," Marsh shrugged.

Donny, Joe, and Marsh stood on the tee box in Marsh's front yard and prepared to play a round of golf in the fading light. Marsh drew a driver out of the golf bag and started to take some practice swings, while Joe and Donny took a seat on the little red bench.

"Best day of fishin' I ever had, Marsh, 'cept I had to listen to my brother yammering away all day," Donny exclaimed. Then he looked around a little, trying to figure out just where Marsh planned to hit the ball he'd teed up on the tee box.

"It was pretty good, Marsh, even by Big Horn standards. I put Donny on the tail end of that little bunch of islands, just down from Marsh's Run. The air was just filled with Black Caddis when the hatch was at its peak. I'll bet there were a thousand rise forms every minute, all within casting distance of Donny. Even Donny was looking like a star for a while there. There he was, silhouetted against the yellow hills in the late-afternoon sunlight. That's how I'll remember this day," Joe said.

"Catch any big ones?" Marsh said as he raised his club into a back-swing. Then, immediately after the whack he made when he struck the ball, he mumbled, "Fuck! Mulligans on the first hole" almost before his ball started its descent to the bottom of the river.

"No. No big ones," Joe said. "Where we playin' tonight?"

"Baltusrol," Marsh replied, then struck his mulligan across the river. "Helluva shot," he said as he picked up his tee.

Marsh handed the driver to Joe after he'd hit the mulligan and said, "First hole is a long, straight par-four. Don't go right or left off the tee."

Donny was growing confused. Marsh's ball had barely cleared the far bank and seemed to have rolled to a stop in the cow pasture across the river, and the conversation about the fishing had ended so abruptly.

Joe took the driver from Marsh and teed his ball nice and high like he always did. When he struck the ball, it sailed high and far, then struck a tall cottonwood tree in the middle of the pasture.

"Nice one," Marsh said. "You should be able to reach the green in two."

Joe stepped toward the red bench where Marsh and Donny were seated and extended the driver toward Donny. "You're up!"

Donny took the club and stood up. When Joe sat on the bench, Donny shook his head and admitted he didn't know what to do.

"We're playing Baltusrol. The first hole is a 469-yard par-four, pretty straight. The green is over there." Joe pointed to the far side of the river and motioned for Donny to hit. Donny shrugged his shoulders and reached into one of the buckets for a golf ball.

Donny teed the ball up and struck it far past Joe's ball. Then he walked back to the bench and gave the club to Marsh just as Marsh was writing on a scorecard.

"Nice drive, but you hit it way to the right! What the hell were you aiming at? Short game let you down; you took a bogey," Marsh said.

"How'd I do?" Joe asked.

"Par," Marsh answered.

"And you?" Joe asked.

"Birdie. Went up and down in two. Made a helluva long putt!" Marsh replied. Then he reached into a half-full ten-gallon bucket and withdrew another golf ball. When he'd teed the ball up and addressed it, he said, "Number two is a tricky little par-four with a lot of sand—big bunker on the right about three hundred yards out."

As he sat next to Joe on the little bench, Donny began to look all around himself.

"What are you looking for?" Joe asked.

"Rod Serling! Jesus, Joe, we are IN The Twilight Zone!" Donny whispered. "I can just hear him: 'An unsuspecting man is thrust into a bizarre threesome and has just struck his golf ball into...The Twilight Zone.'" He enunciated each word carefully.

"Just play along," Joe said.

A car door slammed, and several seconds later Jake scampered around the corner of Marsh's cabin, onto the tee box. He greeted each golfer with a sniff, then disappeared into the tall grass in search of mice.

"Supper's here!" Molly called as she rounded the corner of the cabin with a brown paper grocery bag under one arm. She'd come from work, with groceries and Jake.

Joe stood instantly and picked up a small vase filled with the bouquet of wildflowers he'd picked for Molly. She took the flowers without a word, then dropped the grocery bag on the ground and put her arms around Joe's waist. They stood face to face for a moment and didn't seem to care that the others were watching. Molly closed her eyes and brought her lips to Joe's for a moment, but never seemed to kiss him. "Mmm," she moaned for a moment before she opened her mouth and pulled Joe to her. She moved her hips slowly for a second, then separated her hands and squeezed Joe's rear end with her empty hand.

When she stepped back from Joe, she looked at the flowers again and said, "Thank you." Then she turned to the others and said, "We'll eat in about half an hour. You guys finish your golf. I'll get it ready."

"Hotdogs on the grill?" Marsh asked. "And beans?"

"What else?" Molly answered as she started to fumble with a bag of charcoal briquettes on the porch.

Donny looked at Joe, then raised his eyebrows with the obvious question.

"She's my...girlfriend," Joe said with a smirk.

"Really? I wouldn't have guessed it. Looked like somebody from work just dropping by. That's how all the women at the office greet me."

"I'll tell you all about it later," Joe smiled.

"Cat's out of the bag, Joey. Not much more to tell." Donny tried to stare seriously into Joe's eyes. "Were you ever going to tell me, or just let me watch her molest you again? Jeez, Joe, in Denmark I'd have to pay to see stuff like that."

"I love her, Donny. I was gonna tell you about her tonight."

The strength in Joe's words caused Donny to stop and look directly into his brother's eyes. He could see Joe was serious, and he could see a twinkle there that he'd never seen before.

The moment was soon lost when Marsh called out, "Shit! I'll take a Mulligan! I need some new clubs."

When they'd finished the seventeenth and eighteenth at Baltusrol, the two monster par-fives that Marsh had included on his dream course, Marsh sat for a minute and tallied their scores. "Even par for me. Joe, you didn't play well; you finished ten over. Donny, you struggled there at the turn, but you finished strong; six over. OK, let's build a campfire and set up Marshville. We can eat on the porch. Then, after dinner, we'll get the blow gun, sit by the fire, and drill some mice."

"Now there's a sentence you don't hear back at the office very often!" Donny said to Joe. He turned a suspicious eye to Joe, then deliberately let Joe watch him turn his head from side to side, obviously looking for Rod Serling again. "'The hotdogs were ready...in The Twilight Zone,'" Donny mumbled.

———

A fire crackled in the fire pit, and the sap from some cedar boughs snapped and tossed sparks into the dark of a night sky. Molly, Joe, Donny, and Marsh all sat on blankets beside the dancing flames and leaned back against stacks of firewood after dinner.

"You know, Marsh, I thought maybe the cheese had slipped off your cracker when I first got here tonight," Donny said. Then the joint turned red as he drew in a lungful of smoke. He passed the hemostat that he and Marsh were using as a roach clip back to Marsh.

"Yeah, and I thought maybe you were some uptight bean counter, out here to rain on Joe's parade," Marsh replied.

"No..."—Donny breathed out a cloud of cannabis smoke—"...I'm a helluva guy! But I still think I might have been right about you." Donny and Marsh both laughed out loud.

Joe and Molly sat on the ground holding hands, staring into the fire pit while they leaned back on small stacks of extra firewood. Donny and Marsh sat next to each other, also propped up against extra firewood, and shared a joint. The four of them had finished supper and then adjourned to the after-dinner ambiance of a fire. Now, the yellow light flickered and jumped across the cardboard facade of Marshville's Main Street as the four of them waited on the other side of Marshville for a mouse to arrive.

"I can't believe you got Joey to have a taste of the devil weed," Donny laughed. "What a quantum leap! Hell, I couldn't even buy him a beer."

"I've just been searching for my boundaries, as they say," said Joe, pretending to be serious. "I've found that I can have one scotch, maybe two, before I reach a state of 'mild euphoria.'" Then he added, "One new vice at a time."

"Maybe a couple new vices," Molly said with a smile, then kissed Joe and ran her hand along his thigh.

Donny held his left hand up as if it were a blinder, suggesting to Molly and Joe that he didn't want to see them fondling each other. He was clearly stoned, and he was having fun.

"Hey," Donny said, "I'm gonna throw some more cedar on the fire. I love the way that stuff crackles and pops in a fire. Lemme just reach over and..."

"Don't move!" Marsh whispered hoarsely. "There's an hombre a-headin' into Marshville." Then he slowly reached for the blow gun and placed a dart in the tube.

"Well, pardner?" Donny said quietly when he saw the mouse. "Do you think he's a-hankerin' to have his way with the new school marm? Or will he mosey on down to the saloon and wash down the trail dust with a shot of red eye?" Donny took a long, deep hit from the joint, then watched along with the others while the mouse inched toward a pile of crumbs over on Main Street. Donny breathed out a cloud of smoke when the mouse began to nibble on the scraps.

Joe covered his own mouth to keep from laughing out loud. He could hear Marsh chuckling, and Molly's shoulders moved while she struggled not to laugh out loud.

Marsh raised the blow gun to his mouth as the little gray mouse inched along toward the end of Main Street.

"He's come a-gunnin' for you, Marsh, since you're the law in this town and you're the one who kilt his brother." Donny was narrating as the duel in Marshville began to unfold, and the others were all trying not to laugh out loud and scare the mouse away.

"I hear you're fast—fast with a gun," Donny said, unable to hide his own laughter. Molly laughed louder and the mouse froze for a moment, then stepped closer.

"My friend, here—the shitty golfer—he says you're a low-down sidewinder, and he aims to kill the shit outta you." Donny paused. "Slap leather!"

That was it for Molly; she sat up with a peel of laughter.

Marsh puffed once, and the lethal dart drove the mouse through the swinging doors of Marsh's Saloon with a whiff of dust.

"Whoa!" Donny hollered. "Nice shootin.'"

Marsh got up, flipped the dead mouse into the river, and sat down next to Donny again. He reached into his pocket and started rolling another joint, grinning the whole time.

Donny put his hands behind his head and said, "And to think that only a couple hours ago, I worried that maybe you guys were a little off center."

"Quite a day, yesterday," Donny said before he blew the steam off his coffee. He rested both elbows on the small kitchen table in Joe's ramshackle trailer and sipped tentatively from a white coffee mug.

"Yeah." Joe's face spread into a satisfied smile. "It was a good day."

The rich smell of coffee filled Joe's trailer as early-morning sunshine tossed a yellow glow around the kitchen and living room, which were actually the same room. The place had acquired a significant sense of clutter since Joe had moved in. The laptop computer and a bag of dog food rested on the kitchen table, along with Joe's and Donny's coffee mugs. Several fly rods were stacked in a small corner along the kitchen countertop, behind an overstuffed chair. Several pairs of shoes, one of them Molly's, lay scattered across the floor in front of the sway-backed couch that stretched from the east to the west side of the trailer, and three rain jackets hung from different nails on the wall by the door.

"Remember that last time on the Root, Joe? When we talked about what it would be like to get paid to play golf or go fishing? Remember?" Donny asked.

"Sure."

"So what's it like?" Donny asked.

"It's OK. I like it," Joe shrugged. "It's actually hard work. But I like the people for the most part. They're here to have fun, and it's my job to help. Not quite the same as dentistry." He smiled. "I sure don't drive around before work trying to think of reasons not to go to the office. I guess it won't be my life's work, but I like it," Joe said.

"So what do you want, Joe? Where are you headed from here?" Donny asked.

"Right here is good for now," Joe said.

"You gonna just stay here in this palace, fish, and smoke pot with your buddies for the rest of your life?" Donny grimaced.

"You looked like you were doing all right last night with my friends. It all seemed to suit you last night," Joe said.

"Jesus, Joe, last night was a chance for me to kick back with my brother, like we always did when we went fishing. But today I'm going home, back to my job. The real world! Remember, I'm the one who just put an end to your life back home! You have nowhere to go now. Nowhere! You have a tiny nest egg and a piece-of-shit truck. And you live...well, you live here." Donny leaned back in his chair and looked around, mocking the trailer.

"Did I ask you to come here and straighten things out for me, Donny?"

"No. You asked me to help you, though, and to support you. All I'm trying to do is get a sense of what's going on in your head. I love you, Joe, and I'm afraid you might be in a nasty downward spiral. Do you have any idea what you want to DO?"

"No, not yet. But I plan to enjoy this short time in my life. I plan to thrive. I like this little stop I've made. I spent my whole other life in a hurry to get things over with so I could get on to other things. Each phase, each step, each THING wasn't there to be enjoyed. It was just a barrier, or a hurdle, before the next thing. I like this place, and I'm happy here."

"I'll have to admit, Joe, you do seem all right—better than I expected to find you. But this place? What can you do here?"

"I doubt if you'd understand the changes in my heart—the changes in the way I see things. You know, all those years I spent sitting in a little room, just connecting the dots...that was killing something in me." Joe paused, then pointed at the computer. "I've even been writing some things. I sort of rediscovered the written word."

"Jesus, whatya gonna do? Write a book?" Donny blurted. His tone was heavy with contempt.

The words stung Joe for a second. But before he could respond, Jake wandered over and put a paw on his thigh. Joe turned to him and pulled the gangly young dog onto his lap, pushing his coffee cup across the table and splashing coffee over the rim. He put his arms around Jake's chest and buried his face in the fur of Jake's neck. He breathed in deeply. "Smell that?" Joe asked when he raised his head from Jake's neck. "That's my dog!" He pushed his face back into Jake's fur and inhaled again, then looked up at Donny.

Donny stared blankly.

"We're really not any closer together on all this than we were the day I left, are we?" Joe asked.

"I don't think so." Donny shook his head.

"Is that OK, Donny? Can you still love me, even though I've failed to live up to your expectations too? Like you said, we need to love our friends just where they are. Can you do that?"

"It's not like that..." Donny said. His grin had vanished quickly.

"Sure it is," Joe interrupted, "and it's OK, too! I'm just not gonna worry about that stuff anymore. You deal with it. I'm trying to find my own expectations for myself. Then I'll know what to do." Joe shrugged and sniffed at Jake again.

"It's not like that..." Donny started.

"Sure it is, Donny. How could it NOT be like that? I guess there'd have to be something wrong with you if it weren't like that. You probably should still be worried about me. But I'm OK." Joe nodded. "You'll see," he said softly.

"Don't get married, Joe. Don't make that mistake," Donny said. Then he started to backpedal immediately. "I mean, Molly is nice, and you seem to have something good between you. But these things like this that start up so fast, so soon after a divorce...they just don't work very often," he said as if he were trying to explain a riddle—something Joe couldn't possibly know about—and ask for forgiveness at the same time.

"Donny," Joe smiled, "how old do you think I'll have to be before I figure this stuff out for myself? I'll be OK." He nodded to reassure Donny. "I'll be OK."

"You're right, Joe." Donny sipped at his coffee again and let go of the subject of Joe's future. "I'll be leaving for the airport in about an hour. What are you gonna do for the rest of the day?" Donny asked.

"Since I have the day off," Joe answered, "I'm gonna go fishing. I hardly ever get to spend a day just fishin."

———◆———

Joe struggled against a steady wind that blew up the river channel and wrestled with the boat whenever he let up the pressure on the oars. He planned to float to a little side channel about a mile downstream, where a high bank and a thick stand of cottonwoods would shelter him from the wind. It was a nice little riffle. It always held large fish, and not many of the guides liked to stop there. Maybe there would even be some dry-fly action if the wind would just die down a little.

The feel of the wind blowing through his shirt while he gripped the boat oars and rode the steady pull of the river was wonderful. Every day now when he swung his feet over the side of his bed in the morning, he began to long for those things he could only feel on the river.

As the boat slid along in the current, Joe turned his head from side to side, searching for pods of rising trout in the shallows next to the riverbank.

It had been great to see Donny and talk to him. But just as he'd told Joe that he could see changes in him, Joe saw that Donny had remained the same. The visit with Donny gave Joe a clear look at what he'd left behind. Donny still saw the world in terms of winning and losing. Joe turned to Jake and said, "But he's still my little brother, and I'm gonna love him just where he's at."

Faint little squeaks, hundreds of them, caught Joe's attention, and then the squeaks quickly grew louder and closer. He looked up just in time to see a large group of ducks, goldeneyes, buffleheads, and other divers riding the wind, barreling upstream to the Yellowtail reservoir. He always liked the squeaky noise the ducks' wings made when they flew up and down the channel. Jake bent his head back to watch the ducks pass by too.

"This long summer's about over, Jake. Divers are here already," Joe said as he straightened the boat into the wind once again. "Cold weather usually follows the divers."

The little finger of water wandered away from the main channel as if it were sneaking away with a secret, Joe thought. It created an island about a half-mile long as it wandered away through another cow pasture, then rejoined the main channel of the river. Joe tied the boat to a tree somewhere near the middle of the long, narrow island and stepped out of the boat. He reached for his fly rod, climbed the short, grassy riverbank, and whistled for Jake to follow. He'd walk a couple hundred feet across the wooded island to a secluded pool on the far side where he knew some nice trout were waiting.

"Whatya gonna do? Write a book?" Donny had said, and the scorn in Donny's voice stung Joe again. Jake walked slowly along in front of him, investigating every new scent he found along the way. Twice he stopped to watch flocks of ducks pass by, then looked weary and uninterested after they'd passed.

"Whatya gonna do? Write a book?" Donny's words came back to him. It was all right that Donny was concerned about him. But those words and the way he'd spoken them kept coming back to Joe now as he walked across the island with Jake.

A hen pheasant exploded from a thicket just ahead of Jake, and the gangly pup flinched once before dropping his tail and scampering back toward Joe. "You're a born hunter," Joe said with a smile when Jake retreated to his heels and followed him for a while, afraid of just what else might jump from the tall grass.

Joe began to walk slowly and look for the opening in the trees where he always stepped down into the placid little back channel of the river. He bent over to hide his profile from any wary fish when he came to the opening in the trees, just below a quiet pool. As he stepped close enough to see the surface of the water, his face bent into a smile. "Holy smokes, Jake! We've got fish workin' here," he said.

The pool and the stretch of river channel in the immediate area were protected by a high bluff and the old cottonwood trees on the island. The only disturbance on the water's surface came from the fish moving just underneath it.

Joe rested his fly rod against a tree and sat quietly on the edge of the riverbank about six feet above the water. His movements were deliberate and steady so as not to show himself to the fish.

Jake ran to Joe and planted his wet nose against Joe's face, then immediately dropped onto his back so Joe could scratch his belly. "Look

529

at that," Joe whispered as he gently scratched at the baby-soft skin on Jake's belly. "Those are dorsal fins. Those fish are taking emergers—must be a midge hatch starting soon," he said.

"Whatya gonna do? Write a book?" Joe heard from time to time as he watched the fins break the surface from below and leave gentle rings to grow, then fade as they spread across the calm water. Maybe he could write a book. Wouldn't it be a challenge to compose a long, involved story and tell it with only the written word—no help from his hands or voice or eyebrows? A man would really have to love words to tell a story that way, Joe thought. The circular rise rings continued to appear, then spread, then disappear as the current carried them away. Yeah, maybe he could tell a story that way.

Jake alternately slept and then nudged Joe to plead for some more scratching while they sat beside the pool and watched the trout feed for the next hour. Lips, instead of dorsal fins, began to break the surface of the water and pluck the tiny black midges. Still Joe sat with his feet crossed, caressed his puppy, and considered the challenge of writing a book.

The rise forms were clearly made by snouts, and the rise forms covered most of the pool. The hatch was on. Jake rolled over and scrambled to his feet when a pair of Mallards circled by only a few feet above them, then fluttered out of the sky and dropped onto the pool. The hen quacked loudly several times, and Jake flinched as though he thought he should do something. When Joe waved his Stetson and showed himself to the ducks, they jumped straight up from the water as if they'd been pulled away on strings. "That'll spook the fish some, Jake," Joe said as he sniffed the fur on the tip of Jake's head. "It'll take about five minutes for 'em to start rising again."

Twenty minutes later, Joe groaned as he stood up and reached for his fly rod. "We'll come back and catch those fish some other time, Jake," Joe said. He'd sat for ninety minutes watching trout work a hatch of midges, tiny black insects, and never cast his line once or even stepped into the water. He'd watched the water and dreamed of words. "Let's go," he said to Jake.

The wind seemed to be letting up as the afternoon wore on. Joe quietly wound his way past other boats and waved at the guides. He pulled over several times to let Jake run along the shore and swim, and he heard Donny's words over and over again: "Whatya gonna do? Write a book?"

Russian Olive trees hung over the riverbank, and a large gravel bar extended about fifty yards out from shore, just below a high bluff, as the boat came around a bend in the river. Joe had seen trout working, rising to feed on dry flies, many times just under the overhanging Russian Olive, but he'd never fished the spot before. The little run required some difficult wading to get into position to cast. Then, only an expert fly caster could put a fly over the trout's feeding lanes. The "steely-eyed gunslingers" were the only clients he'd taken into the spot all summer, and they'd been unable to land a fish there.

As if to tempt Joe, or dare him, a trout rose inches from the bank under the Russian Olives. It was a showy rise to a dry fly, and water splashed into the air. Joe watched for a moment as another trout did the same thing. He answered the challenge in a heartbeat. He leaned heavily on the oars and urged the boat into the placid water just downstream from the Russian Olives.

The water's surface was now littered with Baetis, or Blue-Winged Olive adult mayflies. Joe looked into the water by the boat and watched them stream past him. "OK, Jake, looks like those bruisers up there are hittin' on Baetis," he said as he rigged his fly rod accordingly. When he'd finished preparing his rod, he looked out over the river in front of him and swallowed hard. He'd have to wade through some deep, slow-moving current, then some shallow-but-fast current. The approach would be very difficult, and his cast would have to be long and low.

Jake sat in the boat and watched when Joe set out. The wading was easier than he'd expected. But when he reached the place he'd planned to cast from, he knew he couldn't reach the fish. He looked about for a moment, then bent over and crept a few steps toward the fish. Then he dropped to one knee and inched along the river bottom on one foot and one knee. When he finally reached a place where he knew he had to stop, he looked around again. He was kneeling in about eighteen inches of water, and the river around him was smooth as glass. He knew he could move no farther without spooking the fish, but he still wasn't sure if he could cast far enough to reach them. He looked over along the far bank once more. As he did, three fish made splashy rises, one right after the other, right along the river's edge. Each one threw a spray of water into the afternoon sun, as if to challenge him again.

He kept the tip of his rod as low as he could while he fed line into his false casts. The loops above his head were still tight and low when he reached the point where he could control no more fly line. He pointed the top of the rod about four feet upstream from the place where the first of the fish had risen, then lowered the rod. This was it. He might only get one cast before he spooked the fish.

The fly lit in just about the right spot, and the Big Horn began to carry it toward the fish immediately. It passed over the first, then the second, then the third fish. Nothing. "Shit!" Joe hissed as he let the line and the fly swing in the current. "I spooked 'em. Shit!"

Just then, the first fish made another splashy rise, as if to tease him again. He hadn't spooked them; at least one of the fish still didn't know he was here. He knew he was using the right fly. Maybe he hadn't placed it directly over the fishes' feeding lanes. All he could do was feed a little bit more line into the cast and hope to slip it in there, just beneath the Russian Olives. These fish would test the limits of his skill. He feared that just as he was about to make the perfect cast, he'd flip the fly into the tree above the fish, or catch a tree behind him with his back cast, or do something else clumsy, and then spook the fish. He'd left dry flies hanging in trees all over North America, and he knew that if he wasn't at his best, he'd do it again now.

He lowered the rod tip to something like a sidearm cast to keep everything low and away from the trees. Each false cast required just a bit more snap as he prepared to let fly.

When the moment came, he lowered the rod tip and let the last bit of fly line shoot through his left hand. He knew he'd made a fine cast. His line uncoiled, and the tiny Baetis fluttered to the surface even closer to the shore than they did the first time. He watched, ready to strike, as the fly went sliding along the feeding line under the branches. It passed the first fish. Nothing. The second fish. Nothing.

Then a snout appeared, as if it planned to steal something. It sucked the little fly off the surface and was gone in less than a second, leaving only a rise ring on the water's surface.

Joe lifted the rod tip firmly with his right hand and felt the fish turn. The line in his left hand tightened when the trout made its first run upstream. He fed line to the agitated fish until he could play it from the reel. He could see the fish racing around in the shallow water in front of him, trying to decide just where to run.

"That's a nice fish!" Joe said to himself. He followed the trout upstream and landed it after several long runs. It was a thick, nineteen-inch brown trout. Before he released it, he turned it one way then the other and tried to drink in all the color and beauty of a trout that was about to take on its spawning colors. The red, gold, and white along the yellow sides of the trout were spectacular. Joe knew he could never find the words to describe that beauty to his brother. But he'd try to savor it in his own mind. "Take a good look," he said to the trout. "And when you get back over there under that limb, you remember it was the Kadoka Kid who you met today." Then he released it. He could feel its power as it left his grasp and slipped back into the current. The lovely trout still looked mysterious and wild as it swam away into the current and disappeared.

When he stepped over the gunwale, he dropped heavily into his seat and reached for Jake. He rubbed the back of Jake's neck and scratched his ears for a moment. Then he bent down, put his forehead against Jake's, and said, "What are you gonna do, write a book?"

chapter forty-one

The tips of Molly's long fingers were soft—exquisitely soft—as she passed them over Joe's eyelids, forehead, ears, and chest as though they were feathers. "Mmm," Joe moaned as she touched the top of his head and then ran her fingertips over his face and onto his neck.

"Your brother is worried about you," Molly said. "Actually, I think he's worried about me." She lay next to him covered only by a fleece blanket, her head resting on the pillow next to his.

"He loves me," Joe replied. "He's only worried that I'll do something...something..."

"Something that involves me," Molly said, finishing Joe's sentence.

"Yeah, probably," Joe conceded. "I put him through a lot in the past few months. I guess it's all right that he's concerned." Joe's arm lay underneath Molly's naked torso, and he pulled her close. "I don't want to talk about my brother," he said, his lips nearly touching hers. Her bed bounced gently as he shifted his weight to move his leg in between hers. Her smooth legs aroused him and he moaned softly again. He moved his hand onto the roundness of her behind and pulled her closer again.

"The weather's changing," she said. "It's getting cooler at night." Then she reached for the fleece blanket and tried to cover herself.

"I don't want to talk about the weather," Joe whispered.

"Well, you know what they say?" Molly left the question out there for Joe.

"I don't want to talk about the cold weather," Joe whispered again.

"Yes, you do." She paused, but the tone of her voice let the moment rest on the peak of anticipation. Joe felt himself preparing for the laugh that was coming. "When the frost is on the punkin…" Molly started, then stopped.

Joe smiled but did not reply.

"It's time for dickie dunkin!" Molly laughed. She swung her leg over Joe and straddled him, then held perfectly still for a moment. She brought her lips to his and touched them with a feather touch, as she'd done with her fingers a moment before. Joe moved his hands gently along her bare back and waited for her to initiate the lovemaking.

———•———

Molly exhaled heavily and rolled onto her side when Joe released her. She was exhausted and covered with sweat, just as Joe was. The sex had become so urgent that they'd knocked the lamp and several books off the night stand beside Molly's bed. Joe had been concerned that Molly's neighbors might hear her cries as she responded to the Velvet Half-Nelson. Now, the only sound he could hear was his own heart beating as he lay beside her.

He closed his eyes and saw Molly's face, smiling at his jokes. He saw the way she laughed at the silly things Jake did. He saw the intelligence, the insight when she opened up and talked with him about her life. He saw the way her eyes urged him on, and he saw the same face twisted with ecstasy, whispering to him. Still flushed from sex, spent and ready for sleep, Joe lay beside Molly while she drifted off. She'd changed so much in just the few weeks since they'd become intimate. When he first saw her standing there in the fly shop on the day he'd arrived in Fort Smith, she'd hardly spoken to him. She'd begun to offer her friendship in bits and pieces over the next few weeks, but as soon as he reached for it she'd pull it back. It had all happened so fast, so easily, once she'd let her guard down for a moment and taken the time to know him.

Joe rolled onto his side and held Molly's back against his stomach. The auburn hair brushed against his lips when he pulled himself close to her. He reached his arm around her so he could hold her breast while he waited for sleep to come. "When the frost is on the punkin, it's time for dickie dunkin!" she'd said, and then she'd laughed that laugh that came from way down inside her. He nearly laughed out loud at the memory of it all. He knew she'd never have been able to joke and to say something like that before all this had begun. She'd been unable to laugh—to really laugh—for years. She'd changed because of the good things she'd found in him, and he liked that thought. He closed his eyes and kissed her hair once more. In that last moment of the day, before everything faded to darkness, Joe saw the Kadoka Kid tip his hat as he rode past on the red rocking horse. "I love you," he whispered to her, then waited and hoped to hear her say it back to him. But she was asleep.

———•——

Several fishermen milled around the fly shop early on a dark and rainy autumn morning when Joe and Jake entered. Joe was wearing his waders and looking to pick up his clients for the day. Jake followed along at his heels, then greeted every fisherman in the shop.

Molly raised her hand in a silent hello as Joe nodded to her. When he reached the cash register, Molly leaned toward him and said softly, "You've been spending a lot of time at the computer lately. You hardly spoke to me last night. What have you been doing? You were sitting there at the computer when I went to bed, and you were sitting there when I got up. What's that all about?"

Words wouldn't come right away, and Joe could only stare as if he had an embarrassing confession to make. He wore a silly smile when he stepped even closer to her and whispered, "I started writing a story just after Donny left." He stepped back and shrugged when Molly looked at him.

"Really?" Molly said. "I don't know anyone who ever wrote a story." She looked at him now as if she'd never seen him before. "Why?"

"Don't know," Joe shrugged again. "Maybe it's because I've been thinking about the power of words so much over the past year. Then, when Donny was here and I watched him sit around the fire and tell stories that night...he's good!" Joe smiled. "But I started to wonder just how hard it would be to tell the same stories with just the written word—no voice fluctuations, no hand movements, no eyebrows, you know?"

Molly stared for a moment as if she couldn't quite focus on Joe's face. "So were you the smartest boy in your class?" she asked.

"No," Joe shook his head. "I was the smartest boy in my school." Then he smiled, his dimple expanding as the smile crept over his face.

"When do I get to read it?"

"It's nothing, really."

"So I can't read it?"

"Wait till it's done. I'm afraid you'll laugh. Maybe it's no good."

"I doubt that," she replied.

"So where are my clients?" Joe changed the subject.

"Right over there." She pointed toward two gray-haired, well-dressed sportsmen who looked to be about sixty-five, standing by the fly table. Molly watched when Joe walked over to introduce himself.

"Mr. Wells?" Joe asked one of the men.

The man turned and looked at Joe, then stuck out his hand. "Budji...Budji Wells!" he said while he shook Joe's hand. "And this is Fizz..Fizz Mariner."

Molly watched while a smile spread across Joe's face. She could see the good humor in his eyes when he spoke again, and she knew the two fishermen could too. "Well, today is a first for me: the first time I ever went fishin' with a 'Budji' and a 'Fizz.'"

As he started to explain the nicknames, the first man raised the index finger on his right hand, then put his finger on his own chest and looked over his bifocals at Joe. "Carlton," he said solemnly as he pointed to himself. Then, still looking over his bifocals at Joe, he slowly placed his index finger on the other fisherman's chest. "Forest!" he said as he raised his eyebrows.

"OK, then, we'll stick with Budji and Fizz!" Joe blurted, and all three men began to laugh. Molly had never seen a man make friends as easily as Joe Mix did. She'd asked him about it once, and she didn't think she'd ever forget his reply: "I spent twenty-five years sticking needles into people's heads and drilling holes in their teeth, then asking them for money. So many of those people never got to know me, or came to simply dislike me because of what I was. For the time I have left on this earth, I'd like to see just what it is that makes us who we are."

She felt an unexpected wave of melancholy roll over her as she watched Joe escort his clients out the door. So much of his life had existed so far from hers—maybe too far, she thought.

Who is this guy? Molly wondered when she watched him laugh with the new clients. He put others at ease so quickly, and he laughed with strangers as if they were old friends. Making friends seemed to be getting easier for Joe as the summer came to an end, too. Who is this guy? He reads books and talks about the meaning of life. He'd left a big home to live in a crummy little trailer on an Indian reservation. His ex-wife was beautiful, and he'd left her because…Molly had never really understood that either. Now he was writing a book; that was odd. And just a moment ago, she'd known he was absolutely correct when he'd joked that he was the smartest boy in his school. He'd made friends with the nuns and fired a movie star.

Molly felt a powerful attraction to Joe on many levels. He was good to her, and he cared about her feelings. He made her laugh—oh, how he made her laugh—and he was a tender lover. But she often wondered just how well she really knew him and how well she could ever know him and just what it was that held their lives together.

Just as Joe was about to open the door of his truck and drive his clients to the boat landing, he turned back and looked at Molly. He walked back toward her, and when he was in front of the cash register, he leaned over and took her hand in his. He kissed the back of her hand softly and whispered, "I love you, Molly."

"Yeah, me too," she said with a startled look on her face. Joe hadn't waited for a response. He'd just kissed her hand as if the little gesture was merely unfinished business, then walked back toward the truck.

Joe stopped in the doorway and waved to her, and she waved back. Then she remembered something and called to him. "Hey, Joe? Do you think Jake has been acting OK recently? He seems tired all the time."

"He's still a pup. He should be tired all the time. All he does is run around and chase things," Joe said over his shoulder. "See you later, Molly."

He smiled like a little boy going out to play, then turned and walked away.

———•———

"Hey, Marsh, where's Molly?" Joe asked when he returned from his day on the river.

"Bad deal," Marsh said. He was standing by the cash register looking through some papers. He looked up over his bifocals and added, "Her ex-mother-in-law died this morning. Funeral's in a couple days. Apparently she was close to the woman. She felt she had to get going right away when the call came. Said she'll be back in a few days."

"Sorry to hear that," Joe said. He knelt beside Jake and stroked him several times before he put his face in Jake's fur and breathed in deeply. "Did she take the news pretty hard?" Joe asked. "Was she all right?"

"She cried a little. Then she said she needed to go. She looked OK," Marsh said without looking up from the papers.

"I wish I could have said goodbye," Joe replied.

Initially, it wasn't so bad not having Molly around. Joe spent the first day on the river with new clients. The day passed pleasantly. But when he came off the river that night and found himself all alone with no one to talk to but Jake, he thought his little trailer was eerily quiet. He ate supper with Marsh the next two nights, but when he returned to his trailer after supper, he was greeted by silence that reminded him of his nights camping on the roadside back when this journey began.

He missed Molly more than he thought he would. There was no one to talk to over meals and at bedtime. He missed listening to the laugh she'd rediscovered. He missed the comfort of their small conversations, and he missed her touch. It just wasn't right for her not to be there when the alarm went off. He liked it when they lingered in each other's arms for a few minutes before they got out of bed and started the day. Joe needed her, and he knew it now.

Molly called on the fourth day and said she'd be staying a while longer. She'd been in the middle of a large crowd and only had a few minutes to speak to Joe. She said there were a lot of family issues to deal with. She hadn't seemed very willing to talk, and Joe supposed she had quite a few friends and family around that she needed to spend time with. When he said goodbye, he simply asked her to call when she could; he'd be waiting for her.

The story, or the book, or whatever it was, began to tug at his thoughts while he was on the river with clients. When he returned to the quiet trailer after work or after dinner with Marsh, he was usually looking forward to settling into his chair at the kitchen table and losing himself in the written word.

He pulled an all-nighter once, like he'd done in college while studying for final exams, then spent a miserable day on the river dealing with his sleep deficit. The next night, he crashed into bed early, then followed up with another all-nighter. After the third cycle of all-night marathons at his kitchen table, he made a decision to set his alarm clock for 2:00 a.m., then quit for the night no matter how much he wanted to continue. Recovering from the all-nighters was proving to be far more difficult now than when he'd done it in college.

The sixth day came and went with no word from Molly, and Joe began to sense that something was wrong. He called her cell phone that night but could only leave a message on her voice mail. She should have called more than once; there had to be something wrong. But then, who knew? There had been a death in the family, a family with a fair amount of baggage. She was probably just dealing with some long-term family issues that finally needed to be dealt with.

Eight days passed with no further word from Molly except the one phone call. Joe knew something was wrong. Was it Molly's mother, or father? Was she dealing with the death of her sons in the way that combat veterans struggle when they revisit a battlefield years after the terrible event? Joe had no idea what was happening. He could lose himself in his book for a while at night, and he could keep his mind somewhat busy when he was with clients during the day. But he knew something was wrong with Molly—really wrong.

Molly would certainly be home today when he returned his clients to the fly shop after a day on the river, Joe thought. It had been ten days. She'd have a lot to tell him when she finally returned. He'd still had just the one phone call, and now even Marsh was beginning to act a little strange whenever Joe mentioned her.

He dropped his clients in front of the shop and had a short chat about their day on the river before he uncoupled his boat and drove out of the parking lot. Daylight was beginning to slip away a little earlier every day now. He was anxious to see Molly, and he decided to drive by her trailer just in case she'd returned.

The autumn sun had nearly slipped over the horizon when Joe turned down the short street where Molly's trailer sat. He stared for a second, trying to comprehend what he saw on the front of her home. A large utility van with the words "McCarthy Plumbing and Heating" was backed up onto her small front yard. The back door of the truck was open, but Molly's Subaru was nowhere in sight.

Did she buy some new appliances? Joe wondered. This whole thing was beginning to bother Joe. Molly had no need for new appliances. She probably couldn't afford them, and she didn't even own the trailer. He circled the block, then drove back toward his own trailer, and all the pieces of the puzzle fell into place before he'd turned off the ignition switch of the old Ford.

Molly's car was parked by his trailer. She was standing next to it, waiting for him. Joe sat in the driver's seat and stared at Molly before he opened the door. Her eyes were red and swollen, and her face was wracked with anguish.

McCarthy Plumbing and Heating? That was Molly's ex-husband. He was here, and they were loading her things into his truck. She was leaving—she was going back to her husband.

Joe felt a terrible certainty begin to tighten inside him. He read the truth in Molly's eyes, and he raised his left hand to cover his mouth. He'd wanted to burst out of the truck and greet her with a kiss, but now all he could do was stare at her. Everything he'd had with Molly was gone. She'd known for days, and this was how she'd decided to tell him. All he could do was hold his hand over his mouth and feel his throat tighten.

Molly saw that Joe understood what was happening. She held her arms across her chest and began to sob.

When Joe opened the door of his truck and slowly stepped out, he felt the tightness begin to pull at the back of his throat. His legs felt weak and heavy. He walked over to Molly and put his arms around her. When he held her, she wept heavily and pressed her face into his chest. Finally, she uncrossed her arms and wrapped them around Joe's waist and squeezed as hard as she could.

"Why?" Joe asked quietly.

His question caused Molly's chest to heave, and she began to cry with ugly, heaving sobs from somewhere deep inside herself. She tried to step away from him and speak twice, but her face was covered with tears and snot, and she only began to weep again.

She eventually began to speak while her face was still pressed against his chest. "I saw Mike at the wake the night before the funeral. I knew I'd see him, but I thought it would just be like before. He hated me for years after the accident. He wouldn't even talk to me." Molly wiped her eyes and nose with a handkerchief, then stepped away from Joe. "But we had a nice chat. Then, after the funeral, we talked some more. Then...then..." She started to cry, but not with so much pain this time. She drew in a deep breath after a moment and continued. "He was my husband, the father of our children. He was my first love. I still love him," she said softly. Then she looked into Joe's eyes.

"What about me?" Joe asked.

"It's too hard, Joe," she said coldly.

The words crushed him. "It's too hard"? She was going to destroy his love and then explain it with "it's too hard"? This couldn't be happening. The last time he'd held her, he'd been totally secure. Now this. "I don't understand," he said.

"It's too hard and it hurts too much. I have to go," she said, as if she was trying to dismiss him like a difficult assignment. She tried to step back from Joe, but he pulled her close and held her and kissed her hair.

"Say the words, Molly," he whispered. "Just once."

"Let me go." She closed her eyes when she spoke, and Joe let his arms fall from her. Molly walked to her car and was about to get in when Joe raised his voice to her.

"Molly!" Joe called. "You're giving up? Because it's hard? Take a chance, Molly. Risk it all! I lived out my whole life...I made this crazy odyssey and landed here. It took fifty years to fall in love! I love you! Jesus, say the words before you go. Just once," Joe pleaded.

Molly lowered her eyes, stepped into the car, and drove away.

Joe lowered his eyes also; he couldn't stand to watch her drive off. The world was suddenly colder and grayer. It was over. Just like that. It couldn't be, but it was. He'd been betrayed, forsaken. While he'd been pining for her, she'd been falling in love with someone else, and she'd been...he couldn't think about what she'd been doing. How could it all be over that fast? Would this numbness inside him ever go away? There was a pain inside him, deep inside, that was surrounded by a huge, heavy emptiness. So this was a broken heart. He stumbled into his trailer and dropped into a kitchen chair. All there was to do was stare at the little kitchen table. The trailer seemed more empty than he could ever remember. It was more empty now than it was the first day he moved in. No place had ever been as empty as this place was now—not the road that led here, not Kadoka, not Rochester—and the silence made it worse. Now what? There was nothing left.

Jake stood by his side for a moment, then began to beg for supper. Joe poured some dog food into Jake's dish and then stared at the table some more. He didn't know how long he'd been sitting there—maybe a couple hours. It was dark when he stood up and walked outside into the cool evening to take Jake out.

Lights were on at the fly shop and Marsh's truck was still parked in front, so Joe decided to walk over and see if Marsh wanted to talk. He needed to talk to somebody, anybody.

"You knew she was leaving, didn't you?" Joe said when he reached the open doorway. Marsh was still standing by the cash register, still going through a stack of papers. When he heard Joe's voice, he pushed the papers away and looked up at Joe.

"She called me three days ago," Marsh said flatly. "Told me she was going back to her ex-husband and asked what she should do about you. She was a mess."

"Why? What happened? How can this be happening?" Joe asked

"I don't know, Joe. I guess she still loved her husband." Marsh shrugged and shook his head. "I don't know."

"I never knew what it felt like until now. I broke someone's heart once, I think. I saw it from a distance before, but I had no idea," Joe said. He'd lost the need to talk, and he backed out of the doorway. "See you tomorrow, Marsh."

"Joe," Marsh said. "I'm sorry. She was my friend too, as fine a friend as I've known. I was afraid something like this might happen."

"Yeah," Joe nodded. "I'll see you tomorrow," he said as he turned again. But he didn't want to go back to his trailer. This night would be darker than all others. There was no moon, and a bank of clouds obscured even the stars. A handful of weak streetlights and the lights from inside a few trailers were all that lit the tiny village now. No one was out on the street.

Joe's feet turned in the opposite direction of his trailer and began to carry him toward Molly's trailer. He knew she'd be gone by now, but he was drawn to her. He had to go and look at her place. The trailer was dark. Both the Subaru and the McCarthy truck were long gone. His hands in his pockets, Joe stood in the street outside Molly's home and stared at it for a moment. This just wasn't right. The whole place seemed like a ghost town now. Molly's home was dark, forever, and the whole world was empty. Fort Smith had felt like a bustling little town filled with promise only a few hours earlier. Now, he felt completely alone here.

He walked over to the wooden steps in front of her door and climbed them, with Jake at his heels. He tried the door, and to his surprise it swung open. When he flicked on the lights, the world got a little emptier yet. The lava lamp, the TV, the boards and bricks, and all Molly's possessions were gone. Only the couch remained, where they'd sat and read, laughed and talked—where he'd softly stroked her legs by the tumbling light of the lava lamp.

Only one thing remained in the kitchen: a bottle of Cutty Sark with a note taped to it. The countertops were all bare, and it made Joe feel painfully alone just to be there in the empty trailer. He glanced at the floor where Molly had collapsed after she'd drooled. Even that memory hurt now.

The note on the bottle was addressed, simply, "Joe." She'd rejected him, abandoned him. She'd opened a wound he didn't think could heal. He thought about just leaving the bottle and the note, but he couldn't do that. The note was begging him to pick it up. He opened the envelope and found the words:

> *Joe,*
>
> *This is so difficult. I never saw any of this coming. But this is my second chance and I have to take it.*
>
> *Our time was meant to be short and then never again. You spoke once about Cortez burning his ships so there could be no retreat. And I watched you burn your ships. Now, I must burn mine. I never want to see you again. It can be no other way if I'm to be happy in my life as it is now. No retreat!*
>
> *I will always regret that I couldn't say the words. I'm so sorry for all that could never be.*
>
> *You will emerge from all this and do great things. I've known that all along. And I know I wasn't meant to be there with you. Opposite sides of the same coin...remember?*
>
> *Goodbye,*
>
> *Molly*

She still couldn't say the words. All those times when they'd held each other and laughed and shared the things lovers share...and she'd never loved him?

The dark of night, the quiet streets, and the hurt inside him made the short walk home seem like twenty miles.

He held Molly's note in one hand and the bottle of Cutty in the other. How could she never have loved him? How could that be? How could she just leave him like this?

The large cottonwood leaves that tapped against each other on summer nights were long gone. Tonight, the winter wind brought no subtle rustling in the trees; it only stabbed icy fingers under his collar. Only a short time ago, life had seemed so full of promise. Now what?

Joe lay on his back with both hands behind his head for a moment after he switched off the small light beside his bed. Then he called for Jake to join him. When he felt Jake settle next to him, he knew that in spite of the whole long journey and all the changes in his life, he was still just a lonesome boy holding his puppy—and maybe that was all he'd ever be.

chapter
forty-two

Lights were already on inside the shop at Big Horn Adventures when Joe and Jake rolled into the parking lot at 6:00 a.m. The morning chill raced under Joe's collar when he stepped from the Ford. But it felt good, Joe thought. He raised his chin to let the brisk autumn morning wrap itself around him for a moment.

The cowbell above the door clanged when Joe and Jake stepped inside the fly shop. Marsh was standing behind the display counter next to the cash register pouring coffee into two cups when Joe closed the door behind him. "Thought you'd be in a little early this morning," Marsh said. "Get any sleep?"

"Some," Joe shrugged, then lifted one of the coffee cups off the counter, blew the steam off, and smelled the rich aroma for a moment before he sipped at it. "I thought about getting drunk, but that never seems to solve much."

"We talked for about an hour before you got off the river yesterday," Marsh said as he sat on the tall stool behind the counter and held his coffee cup in both hands. "She didn't even look like herself, she was so wracked with anxiety over telling you."

"Well, she kept it pretty short," Joe said.

"She had to, Joe."

Joe only nodded, then sipped at his coffee again.

"She was a mess. She talked for a while about her life before her boys died. She talked about how she'd married her childhood sweetheart, and all the 'history' she had with him. I met him too, by the way. Seemed like a nice guy," Marsh offered.

Joe shrugged and shook his head as if he didn't quite know what to do with that information. "I hope so," Joe offered.

"She had a life with him, Joe. That has weight. Then, when his mother died...well, apparently his mother had been close with Molly, and she'd been trying to get the guy to forgive Molly all these years. Anyway, the funeral, the passing of time...something seemed to have turned for him, and he came and talked to Molly for the first time in years. I guess it's good in a way. It has to be, Joe," Marsh said. "I saw all this comin', Joe. I knew something like this was gonna happen. Nothing could have prevented it either. It's just life."

"Marsh," Joe started without looking up, "I had more laughter, more romance, more sweet, soft moments with Molly during the past couple months than I had with my ex-wife in twenty-five years." Joe stopped. "I'm not going anywhere with all that, I guess. I just had to say it. I was in love for the first time," Joe sighed.

"We talked about that, too," Marsh said. "She knew that."

"So what do you think, Marsh? For the rest of her life, when she's with her husband, will she think of me?" Joe asked. "Or can she just forget me—blank all that out?"

"Don't know, Joe. Nobody knows," Marsh said. "I don't know if it makes a man feel good or bad to think about stuff like that either."

"Wanna know the hardest part, Marsh? The thing that makes the whole world into a big, empty room and makes your feet heavy, and puts a lump in the back of your throat like you're about to cry but you can't because you just can't feel anything?"

"What's that?" Marsh said.

"You know that whole thing with a love triangle, and how writers and philosophers have been posing the question for years about just how one person can be in love with two?"

"Yeah," Marsh replied.

"Well, that's a fine topic for books and movies and chats around a campfire. And there's plenty to think about for everyone involved." Joe stopped and looked into Marsh's eyes. "But I'm the one who didn't get chosen; I got left behind. You just can't know how this feels. She didn't love me enough to take a chance. She didn't love me at all. She chose someone else. I took a chance and failed. What do I do now?"

Joe stood for a moment longer, then took his coffee and stepped out the door onto the covered wooden boardwalk outside the fly shop. He sat on a wooden bench much like the one on Marsh's tee box and sipped at his coffee.

The door to the fly shop opened, and the cow bell clanged again when Marsh followed Joe onto the boardwalk. He walked around the little bench and sat next to Joe. Then, with one gesture, he spoke more eloquently than if he'd used a million words: he put an arm around Joe's shoulders and squeezed him. They looked like little boys sitting on a roadside curb, waiting for something to pass in front of them. Marsh left his arm around Joe, sipped at his coffee again, and leaned back against the front wall of the fly shop.

"Life's funny, huh?" Joe said, and his face softened a little.

Marsh crossed his legs, kept his arm securely around Joe's shoulders, and stared at the bulging orange glow along the eastern horizon. "No shit."

An hour later, Joe Mix eased his life back onto the tracks. Fishermen began to wander into the fly shop about 8:00 a.m. in groups of two or three, talking of the day that was about to be. Most of them knew nothing about Molly; they had no idea she'd ever existed. There was laughter and small talk, boasting about the previous day, and predictions about the day to come. Several times Joe turned toward the cash register, reflexively looking for Molly to answer some question or maybe just to steal a glance at her as he'd often done. Each time he turned to where she was supposed to be and then saw that she was gone, a deep feeling of loneliness squeezed at his chest. This would be a hard day, Joe thought as he prepared to take his clients fishing. He scratched Jake's ears and said goodbye for the day while Jake sprawled out on his rug by the cash register.

"Just a minute, Joe," Marsh called as Joe was moving toward the door with his clients. "I want you to take tomorrow off," Marsh said when he was alone with Joe. "Just get out of here for a day. In fact, I'd like you to pick up some things for me in Billings. All right?"

"I guess so," Joe nodded.

"And while you're there, take Jake in to see a vet. He doesn't look right. Haven't you noticed that he lies around an awful lot?"

"Yeah, I have. And he's got a couple lumps around his neck, too. I wonder if something bit him. I really wasn't worried until about the last week or so. I just thought he'd get better," Joe shrugged.

"I know a vet up there. I'll call him and make an appointment for you. He's probably got some sort of intestinal bug from all the horse turds and mice that he chews on," Marsh chuckled. "Probably a bug bite or something."

———•———

All these people in Billings and no one knows me. I don't mean a thing to anyone, Joe thought while he sat in the small and smelly waiting room at the pet hospital, flipping through magazines. He'd lived in Montana long enough that he'd come to think of Billings as a big town. He smiled at that thought, but he was comfortable with it. He was glad he lived in Fort Smith. It was a tiny place, a village so small it almost didn't qualify as a village. But Joe was happy there; the pace was incredibly slow, but he met new people from all over the country every day. He was exposed to people from totally different backgrounds than his, and he listened to storied of other people's lives all day. It was the best of all possible worlds for Joe—a tiny, simple place with few distractions but filled with interesting people who just traded places in his boat. Each day, someone new drifted with him, then gave up the seat in his boat for someone else the next day so he could make a new friend.

He'd spent the entire day running errands in Billings after he'd dropped Jake off here first thing in the morning. Now, he'd just pick up Jake and some medicine and try to get on with things. Tomorrow he'd try to...

"Would you like to come back to my office, Mr. Mix?" the veterinarian asked politely. Dr. Stanley Gordon was a nice man, Joe thought. He'd been very polite at their first meeting. He'd worn a big smile when he'd asked about Marsh, then asked Joe to greet him. He'd taken Jake into the office right away, and now he stood with a friendly smile as he extended his hand.

Joe was trying not to pass judgment on the doctor based on his appearance, but he couldn't help it. Dr. Gordon was about sixty. His thinning gray hair looked like he'd combed it in a hurry. Strands of hair stuck out in several directions. Dr. Gordon wore a plaid shirt that was pulled tightly around a soft belly, and his glasses kept slipping down his nose.

Odd, heavy smells filled the reception area of the pet hospital. Joe could smell dog food and a medicinal smell and maybe some sort of disinfectant. Above all else, he could smell dog: dog piss, dog shit, a heavy dog odor from the kennel at the back of the office. At least no one had ever shit in his waiting room back in his dental practice. Well, the Loomis kid had puked out there once. Joe made himself stop thinking about that. He'd be back on the river tomorrow, and that would be good.

Joe stepped between two anxious-looking golden retrievers as he crossed the waiting room and shook hands with the veterinarian, then followed him back to a small office behind the reception area.

Dr. Gordon sat quickly at a desk that was covered with books, papers, and plastic models of dogs' hip joints, dogs' jaws, and dogs' internal organs. He pushed all that debris aside and turned toward Joe.

"You have a very sick dog, Mr. Mix," Dr. Gordon said as Joe sat in the chair next to his desk.

"Oh?" Joe tilted his head with the question.

"Jake has an aggressive form of cancer," the doctor said bluntly.

"Jake?" Joe said with surprise. "Little yellow lab? About eight months old? My Jake?" Joe could scarcely believe what Dr. Gordon had said. He'd been expecting to hear about an intestinal ailment or an insect bite.

Dr. Gordon nodded. "Those lumps about Jake's neck? Those are enlarged lymph nodes. He's been very lethargic lately also, hasn't he?"

"Yes," Joe said. "But I thought he was just a puppy and he should sleep a lot because he was growing." Joe felt a need to explain why he hadn't brought Jake in sooner.

"There was nothing you could have done, Mr. Mix. Nothing at all," Dr. Gordon said bluntly.

"Are you sure about this?" Joe asked.

"Absolutely. The blood work and radiographs all confirm the diagnosis. It's called Canine Malignant Lymphoma, or Lymphosarcoma."

"What's the treatment?" Joe asked.

Dr. Gordon leaned back in his chair and tossed his glasses onto his desk. "Canine Malignant Lymphoma is always fatal. I'm sorry."

"So that's it? We do nothing?" Joe could feel a familiar tightness in the back of his own throat. The world was conspiring against him again.

"Not necessarily," Dr. Gordon said. "There are various courses of treatment, and some of the treatments may add some time to your dog's life. But between you and me, oftentimes I wonder if I'm doing the right thing by pursuing an aggressive treatment. Many times I think it only adds several months of miserable time to the dog's life and causes him to suffer even more. I do understand when a person wants to do whatever they can for their pet. But in this case, I certainly wouldn't recommend chemotherapy."

"Where is Jake?" Joe asked.

Dr. Gordon leaned forward and pushed a button on his phone. "Mary Ann, would you bring Jake Mix in here?"

In just a moment, a tiny high school girl stepped into Dr. Gordon's office with Jake on the end of a leash. Jake's tail began to wag the rest of him, he was so excited to see Joe. He ran to Joe and put his front paws on Joe's lap. The young girl removed the leash and left the room while Jake shook with excitement and licked at Joe's hands.

The words Joe wanted to say next stuck in his throat. He felt himself losing control, and he began to weep while he scratched Jake's ears, and his sorrow became a flood he couldn't hold back. He wept openly for several minutes while Jake played with his hands and tried to crawl into his lap.

"Oh, fuck! I don't want to hear this," Joe said angrily. Dr. Gordon handed him a tissue, and he wiped away his tears and blew his nose. "He looks so good right now." Joe seemed to be pleading for Dr. Gordon to offer some hope.

"He's happy to see you," Dr. Gordon said. "And he'll still have some good days."

"So how will all this play out, doctor? What's gonna happen next?" Joe asked, returning to the reality at hand.

"Most untreated dogs die within one or two months," Dr. Gordon offered.

"Fuck, I don't wanna hear this," Joe sighed.

Joe looked down at the cheerful puppy in his lap and closed his eyes. "How will the end come?" he asked finally. The words tried to stick in his throat. He stroked Jake's fur and struggled to hold back any more tears.

"He'll get very lethargic, he'll be suffering, he won't eat...you'll know." Dr. Gordon paused. "Bring him in and I'll put him down for you."

The words hammered at Joe. They seemed so harsh, so final. Joe covered his eyes with one hand for a moment as if he could hide from it all. He breathed in deeply and shook his head. "No. It's not gonna happen that way—not for my friend. I'll do it."

"What do you mean?"

"I mean, you're gonna sell me the things I need to put my dog down, and I'm gonna do it myself. We're gonna go to a nice place I know. I'll do it. There's no need to bring him here—to scare him and have this place be the last thing he sees on this side of the grave."

"I can't sell you those things. It's a state law..."

"I don't give a shit about the state law, doctor." Joe wiped away his tears and continued to sniffle. "This puppy here has been my friend through some hard times—my only friend. I owe him a better ending."

"But..."

"Listen," Joe interrupted. "I did dentistry for twenty-five years. I know how this works. Jake is gonna get a lethal dose of some anesthetic that will just stop his heart." Joe had to stop and cover his eyes again. He removed his hand and continued after he'd choked back the lump in his throat. "I'm not some nut case in here looking for drugs. All you need to do is show me how to find a dog's vein with an IV needle. I can do the rest."

"But..."

"I'm begging." Joe covered his mouth with the back of his hand and blinked away more tears. "I'm begging. I'm begging you to let just one thing in this world be right. Let me do the right thing for my friend. Please?"

Dr. Gordon stared for a moment, then acquiesced. "OK, Joe, this is how you find the vein," he said as he leaned forward and took Jake's front leg in his hands. When he was finished with the demonstration, he stood up and said, "One more thing, Joe. I usually see people about three weeks after I should: they just wait too long and let the poor dog suffer. You'll know when the time is right. If you change your mind, just call me. OK?"

Joe nodded. "Thank you."

Dr. Gordon dismissed himself from the office for a moment, then reappeared with a paper bag containing a small brown bottle, an IV needle, a small tube, and a syringe. He stepped toward Joe, put his arms around him, and patted him on the back. "Good luck, Joe," he said as Joe left his office.

"Hey. Thank you, doctor. Thank you for...this," Joe said, and held up the bag.

"I've been where you are, Joe. Just don't tell anyone I sold you those things."

Joe had walked into the pet hospital expecting to pick up a healthy puppy and some pills. But now the world had turned in such a short time—again. He'd be without Jake soon. Nothing…nothing was fair.

———•———

"All right, Joe, I'm up first," Marsh said as he pulled a driver from his golf bag. A gray sky covered the Big Horn Valley and threatened to spit snow at the golfers on Marsh's tee box. "All this shitty weather makes me think of the British Open. I think we'll play the Royal and Ancient club at St. Andrews. Founded in 1754, the Old Course is considered the home of golf. On the first hole…"

"I know: the second shot has to carry the Swilcan Burn. I played this hole with you before," Joe said.

"How did you score on it?" Marsh asked while he steadied his ball on a wooden tee.

"Not well. I hit a nice drive but followed with a poor second shot," Joe said as he rummaged through the other clubs in Marsh's golf bag.

"I remember now. Your game has improved all summer, though. Try to play it the way I do." Marsh raised his club in an awkward backswing, then struck the earth about six inches behind his ball at the end of a vicious swing. His drive barely made it to the river. "Fuck! Mulligans on the first hole!" Marsh said angrily and reached for a new ball. As he was addressing the ball preparing to strike another drive, he said to Joe, "How's Jake?" He swung easier the second time, and the ball cleared the river easily.

"Lookin' pretty rough," Joe said while he drew a three-wood from the golf bag. "I have to help him in and out of the truck every now and then, and he's got a lot of those lumps on him now." Joe took a practice swing. "He had an accident in the trailer the other night. That was a first." Joe pointed to the clubhouse where Jake lay sprawled out on a large pillow. "He sleeps a lot." He struck his ball high and far across the river, then returned to the bench.

"Perfect shot!" Marsh said. "You put yourself in great position to par the first hole, and you did," he mumbled while he wrote their scores on the scorecard.

"What'd you get?" Joe asked.

"Birdie," Marsh replied matter of factly. Then he added, "Your brother's a lot better golfer than you" while he walked over to tee up another ball.

"Might even be better than you," Joe said just before Marsh started into his backswing.

"No way," Marsh replied while he was in his backswing. "Shit! Mulligans on the second hole!" he grumbled after his drive sliced far out to the right and plunked into the river. "So whatya been doing with all your free time? You've been holed up in that luxurious home of yours quite a bit lately," he said after he'd hit his second ball across the river.

"Well, don't laugh, but I've been writing something. Just sitting at the computer and writing. Gives me plenty of time to be with Jake, too," Joe replied. He was still sitting on the bench when Marsh returned and sat beside him.

"Writin' a book?" Marsh crinkled his face with the question.

"Hell, I don't know. I just started writin' a story, and I'm having some fun with it," Joe said. "The whole thing has kind of taken on a life of its own."

"Can I read it?" Marsh asked.

"No. Too many big words in it for you," Joe replied. "No pictures, either."

"You mean big words like 'triple bogey'?" Marsh said while he wrote in the scorecard again, then put the little card back in his hip pocket. "Hey!" Marsh continued, "speaking of books, did you ever finish that big 'ol box of books you were keeping by the couch at your place?"

"Yeah. Quite a while ago. That's one nice thing about being broke and not having any friends: you have a lot of time to read. Actually, I've found that I really like words. I've been driving up to garage sales in Billings from time to time, looking for more books."

"So you're writing a book—really?" Marsh seemed intrigued by the possibility.

"Told you, I don't know. For now, I'm just telling a story," Joe said with a shrug. "I would like to get some new books, though." Then he stood up to take his turn at the tee box. "You know, I bought all those books for five dollars," he said just before he drove his ball across the river. "At a garage sale."

"Got a good deal there," Marsh said while Joe was walking back to the bench. "Out here in Montana, good literature'll cost forty to fifty cents a pound!"

chapter forty-three

A shower of yellow light flowed from the desk lamp on Joe's kitchen table, surrounding Joe and the laptop in a soft, amber glow. Joe could feel a gust of December's first real cold snap shake the trailer every now and then. He shivered from a cold draft sneaking through the cheap windows. He hunched over in front of the small computer, tapping words into the keyboard and then staring at the words on the screen for a while before he tapped again.

Jake lay on the couch sprawled out like a king, oblivious to Joe's typing or the chill wind swirling outside in the thick darkness of early evening.

Joe typed for a moment, read what he'd typed, deleted it, typed something else, and then smiled when he read it. "There, that's pretty good," he said to Jake when he stood up. It was all Jake could do to open his eyes. He couldn't muster the strength to raise his head off the couch. Joe walked slowly to the couch and stood over his friend for a moment.

Joe sighed heavily and knelt beside the couch. He put his face on the fur around Jake's neck and stroked the dog with a soft touch. He feared Jake just might crumble under a heavier hand. Then he stood up and walked into the kitchen.

He held the bottle of Cutty Sark by the neck and used the bottom of the bottle to push the remnants of two chicken potpies and a can of sliced peaches across the counter and out of his way. The ice cubes bounced around inside a tall, plastic cup and nearly filled it as Joe poured it half full of scotch, then topped it off with water.

When he settled back into the chair, he took a sip of the scotch and began to stare at the computer screen again.

He should have seen it coming, but he didn't. He should have known that life just wouldn't be that easy, that simple. But why did Jake have to get sick so soon after Molly had left? Bad things did come to find him here. Maybe good things had come to find Molly, too, just as she'd said. He'd been working at the computer more than ever since Molly had been gone. It kept him from thinking about her all the time. He stared at the computer screen and waited for words to come.

The thump on the door next to the kitchen table scared him, and he flinched when he looked over at the door. He assumed it was Marsh, stopping by for a drink after he'd finished his day's work at the shop. "C'mon in!" Joe said, smiling at the way he'd jumped.

A burst of cold air blew papers off Joe's desk when the door swung open, and Vic Birthler stepped into the trailer. "Hello, Mr. Mix," Birthler said as he extended his hand. "Marsh said to just come over and say hello. I was going to call you. He said to just come over," Vic shrugged. "Hope that's OK."

"Sure, Vic. Come in!" Joe said as he shook the young man's hand and then bent over to pick up the papers that had blown off his table.

"Actually, I stopped by the fly shop to see Marsh and ask him whatever happened to you after you got fired last summer," Vic said while he took off his coat. "Imagine my surprise when he said you were still living here and still working at Big Horn Adventures." His face opened into a smile. "That routine in front of the shop that afternoon was all for Sam's benefit, huh?"

Joe returned a smile, then chuckled, but said nothing.

"And here I thought you were all washed up in this town!" Birthler said in reference to Marsh's tirade the day he'd pretended to fire Joe. His smile told Joe that he understood exactly what had been done that afternoon in July.

"Would you like a drink, Vic?" Joe asked.

"Sure would! Whatever you're having!" Vic replied.

"Well, have a seat and I'll get you something." Joe walked into the kitchen and felt the warped, uneven floor of the trailer shift under his weight. The mostly-eaten potpies and the empty can of peaches still littered the countertop. Joe tried to clean up a little without being noticed. He saw that Vic was watching him bus the garbage over to the open wastebasket beside the refrigerator, and he said, "Fort Smith Gourmet Club met here tonight—too bad you missed it" as he dropped the mess into the basket.

"So what are you doing here?" Joe asked as he handed the scotch to Vic, then sat down next to Jake on the couch.

"Took my vacation in early winter so I could come back for some streamer fishing," Vic said, then raised his glass in salute before he took the first sip. "Just didn't think I'd see you again," he added. "I'm really sorry for that day."

"It's OK," Joe said. "I was wrong to wipe my feet on you, too. Sam was the problem. Whatever happened to him, by the way?"

"He's still an asshole. A rich and powerful asshole. Some things never change." Vic looked at Joe and shook his head. Then he changed the subject. "How's the fishing been?"

"You're just in time. The fish are just turning on to streamers. You're gonna have some good fishing. The lower stretch, after Big Horn Landing..."

Joe was interrupted by the ringing of his phone. When he saw that it was Donny calling, he motioned to Vic that he was going to answer it and talk to Donny from his bedroom. "Make yourself at home. I won't be long," Joe said, just before he picked up the phone and turned down the narrow hallway that led to his bedroom.

From behind the flimsy bedroom door, Vic could hear Joe speaking in a subdued tone, and he heard laughter occasionally. He looked at Jake sleeping soundly over on the couch, then looked at the laptop on the kitchen table. He craned his neck as far as he could to read the words. The lines appeared to be double-spaced, like a manuscript, which piqued his interest. So Vic decided to set himself down at the kitchen table to have a closer look while Joe was talking on the phone.

"Yeah, I'll be home for Christmas," Joe said as his bedroom door finally swung open after a five-minute conversation.

Vic stood up from the kitchen table quickly and moved back to the saggy, overstuffed chair he'd been sitting in before

"Huh? Oh, the fishing has been good, Donny. The trout are starting to hit streamers pretty good." Joe listened for a moment. "Streamers! You know...big, fluffy, flashy-looking flies that slip through the water like injured minnows, I suppose, and trigger the trout to make aggressive strikes. It's pretty easy. Even you could do it." Joe listened again. "You too!" he said finally, then hung up his phone. He sat in the kitchen chair in front of the computer and took a sip from his scotch. "Sorry. Where were we?"

"What did you do before this?" Vic asked with a furrowed brow. He leaned back and questioned Joe with his eyes as if he'd already caught him in a lie. "Before you were a guide?"

"Did some ranch work," Joe replied.

"Try again," Vic shook his head and frowned. "No ranch hand wrote that." He pointed to the computer screen.

Joe tried to think of what to say.

"That's your story, isn't it? That's you?" Vic pointed at the computer with his drink.

Joe made no answer, and Vic began to recite from the first page of the story.

"'He didn't want to go to work today or any other damn day, ever. He hated his job, and he was ashamed because the expectations of others would not allow it.' That's good, and you're the dentist, aren't you?" Vic asked.

"No. Not anymore," Joe grinned. He was no longer reticent to share his past with others. In fact, he seemed proud to have left it all behind.

"That's you there in that story, isn't it?" Vic said as if he were cross-examining a witness in a courtroom.

Joe nodded. "Yeah, pretty much," he said, then smiled. He was pleased that Vic had figured it out, and he sensed Vic liked it.

"It's good, Joe. Really good!"

"It's doodling! I started playing with a story, and it's just taken on a life of its own. Now, the characters do what they want, not what I try to make them do. It's been fun, but..."

"No. It's good. It has passion, and you make good sentences. I read hundreds of manuscripts every year. This is pretty good."

"It's just my story of the past few months, with a liberal amount of bullshit thrown in!" Joe said.

"Well, I liked it. S'pose I could show it to my boss at Hudson Valley?"

"No. Well, maybe. You mean you'd publish it?" Joe cocked his head at an angle.

"Maybe. I'd like to read the whole thing."

"It's not done yet," Joe said.

"Can I see what you've done so far?" Vic asked.

"I guess so," Joe shrugged. "Sure."

"Great. Now tell me about the fishing," Vic said.

"That's easy: brown-and-yellow streamers—put 'em as close to the bank as you can, and fish the entire top thirteen miles. Every inch is fishin' good," Joe grinned. "There's bigger fish in the next few miles, but fewer of them."

The talk of big fish taken recently and which streamers to use and what stretches of river to fish lasted until Vic tipped his scotch up and felt the ice cubes slide down the glass into his lips.

"Would you like a refill?" Joe asked.

"Sweet talker," Vic said with a grin, and handed the glass back to Joe. Then, while Joe added more ice to both of their glasses, Vic leaned back in his chair. "I'm serious about your book, there, Joe! It's good! It's a uniquely American story."

"Jeez, don't get too literary on me now, Vic. It's just a story," Joe said when he returned a full glass to Vic.

"Ever heard of Zane Grey?" Vic asked.

"Sure! He wrote *Riders of the Purple Sage*, one of my favorites," Joe answered.

"Did you know he was a dentist?" Vic asked, then raised his eyebrows and sipped at the scotch.

"No shit?"

"No shit," Vic nodded. "Turns out his father pushed him into a career in dentistry, but he always wanted to be a writer. He took a trip out west and then wrote a story about the places he'd been. Created a great hero and threw in some fine bullshit. Then he got rich and famous writing books. Spent all his time fishin'!" Vic raised the scotch in salute. "You think about that!"

Vic stopped and reached into his pocket when his cell phone began to ring. "Now I've got a call," he said while he fumbled with his phone. "Looks like it's my buddies back over at the hotel. I'd better get back over there, Joe." He put the phone back in his pocket without answering, then stood up. "Will you be our guide tomorrow?"

"No," Joe said, then he looked at Jake. "My friend over here is sort of in hospice care, and I won't be leaving his side for a few...until...you know," Joe stammered.

"Yeah, Marsh said the pup was sick. I'm sorry, Joe. I'm sorry you won't be guiding us, too. But I'll stop over before I leave. Thanks for the drink, and I'm glad you're not finished in this town." Vic smiled, shook hands, and stepped out into the cold evening. "Remember, I'll stop over and pick up that manuscript before I leave!" he said just as he was about to close the door.

"Remember to pound the riverbank with your streamers! Keep 'em close to shore, as close as you can get 'em!" Joe called before he shut the door.

Joe walked over to the couch and sat down next to Jake. He put his feet up on the scuffed coffee table and began to pet the yellow dog. "How 'bout that, Jake?" He stroked the fur on Jake's side. "Zane Grey! Now, there's a hero!"

chapter
forty-four

Marsh watched through the front window of the shop when Joe's truck rolled to a stop. He could see Joe's breath curl into puffs of steam when he stepped out of the Ford and walked across the parking lot toward the fly shop. He turned around to pour some coffee for Joe so that his back was still turned when the cowbell clanged and Joe entered. He started talking before Joe was through the door. "It's gonna be a nice day when the sun gets a little higher in the sky. Definitely a chill in the air this morning, but the sun is gonna warm things up. It's supposed to rain tomorrow..."

"Today's the day," Joe interrupted as Marsh turned around. Joe stood at the counter, expressionless.

"Jake?" Marsh said.

Joe nodded. His Stetson was pulled low, just above his eyes, and when he looked at the floor Marsh couldn't see his face. "He hasn't kept anything down for two days, and he's really moving slow when he moves at all. It has to be today." When Joe raised his eyes and looked at Marsh, he couldn't hide the despair in his heart.

"Anything I can do?" Marsh asked.

Joe shook his head. "No, I'm OK. I'm gonna take him to a quiet spot on one of the islands and..." His lip began to quiver, and he turned for the door.

Through the front window, Marsh watched Joe wipe his eyes with the back of his hand as the truck inched out of the parking lot. Jake sat on the seat next to Joe looking out the window, and the handle of a shovel extended over the tailgate.

The shallow water at the boat landing splashed gently against the boat while Joe reached over the side and placed a cooler on the floor. Then he lifted the shovel into the boat and turned to look at Jake. He was preparing to lift Jake over the gunwale and place him on the boat seat. "OK, Jake, lets…" And with that, Jake leaped over the gunwale and climbed onto the seat next to Joe's, where he always sat.

Joe closed his eyes and wondered if he was doing the right thing. Maybe Jake wasn't ready yet, he thought. No, he was at the end, Joe knew. He hadn't eaten in two days. This had to be some burst of enthusiasm triggered by the boat and the river. Nonetheless he sat, ready for a day on the river, just like all the other times with Joe. Why did this have to be so hard? Joe thought.

He sat down and put his arm around Jake. "You're not making this very easy, Jake," Joe sighed when he finally pushed the boat out into the current. Jake sat there as he had so many times before and looked across the water's surface while Joe allowed the Big Horn River to move the boat along in silence.

The mouth of the small back channel where the two of them had watched trout rising to feed on tiny mayflies slid past them quietly, and Joe began to maneuver the boat close to the island where he usually beached it when he came to this place.

Jake waited until Joe stood in the water beside the boat, carrying both the cooler and the shovel. But when Joe turned and began to climb the several steps to the top of the bank, Jake leaped over the gunwale again. He splashed through the ankle-deep water and climbed the riverbank at Joe's heels.

It was impossible for Joe not to question all this once again. Was he really doing the right thing? When he saw Jake scramble up the little hill as he'd always done, he looked just fine! But before he could even give his feelings a voice, he saw Jake's tail fall between his legs, and his head became too heavy to hold high. The small burst of energy was Jake's last. He walked slowly to Joe's side, then trudged along when Joe began to make his way to the small pool on the other side of the island. It would be their last walk together.

One fish rose as if to greet them when Joe and Jake reached the pool and looked down from the bank. This just isn't right, Joe thought when he glanced at the weary dog. "I can't be doing this," he said to himself. He stood on the riverbank, overlooking the pool and holding a shovel and a cooler, and tried to make sense of what he was doing.

He had to continue with it, he knew, and he looked around for a place to start digging. A clear, level spot between two large cottonwood trees caught his eye, and when he walked over to the clearing, he knew it was the right place.

He set the cooler on the ground and leaned on the handle of the shovel in the same way Marsh leaned on his driver. He had to start digging, but the absurdity of the whole thing was overwhelming. Jake, his best friend, was going to be there watching while Joe dug his grave.

The reality of what he was about to do settled over him like a storm cloud that would never move away, and he felt a lump begin to grow in the back of his throat again. When he stepped on the shovel and pushed it into the earth at his feet, Jake walked over to inspect the dirt Joe threw on the ground. There was still enough puppy in Jake that he was drawn to play in fresh dirt, and today would be his last day. Why did this life have to be so hard? Joe thought. He turned over several more shovels full of dirt, and Jake lay down next to the expanding pile of earth.

Every time Joe glanced at the lethargic dog stretched out by the hole growing next to him, his face tightened and he averted his eyes to the shovel at his feet. With each plunge of the shovel, Joe knew he was drawing inexorably closer to the terrible thing he had to do.

The hole was nearly four feet deep when Joe decided it was deep enough. He dropped the shovel on the ground, stood with his hands on his hips, and waited to catch his breath. Marsh had been right, he thought: it had turned into a warm December day. While he was looking over the little pool in front of him, the wingbeats of a large flock of ducks racing up the river channel caught his attention, and he looked up to see them pass by.

Jake hadn't noticed the ducks. His eyes were open—maybe he'd seen them, or heard them—but he didn't have the strength to raise his head anymore. What did it matter now, anyway? It was time.

Joe opened the cooler and found a plastic cup. He took the cup down to the small pool just below the grave he'd just dug and scooped up some river water, then returned to the cooler and dropped a handful of ice cubes into the glass too.

Joe reached into the cooler one more time and found the bottle of Cutty Sark.

He sat down on the ground and Jake did what he always did when Joe sat on the ground: he walked over and sat next to Joe. Then he lowered himself to the ground and rested his head on Joe's thigh.

"We're gonna have a moment for ourselves now," Joe said as he twisted the top off the bottle of scotch and poured a tall shot into the plastic cup. "Here's to you and me, Jake. We made it! Yeah, I don't know where we made it to either, but here we are, so I guess we made it." Joe took a sip from the cup and ran his other hand up and down Jake's side. The lumps were everywhere now, just under the skin, and the biggest lumps were around his neck and behind his shoulders. Joe held the cup for Jake to sniff, and Jake licked from it briefly.

"And here's to you, Jake." Joe raised the cup. "Here's to all the things you did that made me smile. That balloon trick—that was my favorite!" Joe managed a faint smile before he took another drink.

He raised the cup again. "Here's to all the things we never got around to." He rubbed Jake's belly for a moment, listening to Jake's labored breathing and trying to summon the courage to do what he had to do next. His own breaths were turning into long sighs.

Joe reached into the cooler and withdrew the paper bag that held a brown bottle, an IV needle and tubing, and a syringe. Before he opened the bag, he climbed onto his knees and leaned over Jake so he could hold the puppy one more time. The heaving in his own chest started when his face touched the fur on Jake's neck. In a short time, his eyes were clouded with tears and it was impossible to swallow. "It'll be all right, Jake. Pretty soon this suffering will be over," he whispered.

With his knees resting on the ground beside Jake, he began to search for a vein on Jake's left front leg. He was beginning to question whether he had the resolve to do this, and he forced himself to carry on. When he felt he was ready, he introduced the needle as gently as he could. But Jake yipped in pain and flinched his leg away from Joe. "Oh, Jesus. I'm sorry, Jake," Joe sobbed. "I'm sorry, I'm sorry." He reached for Jake's leg and rubbed it softly for a moment. He sighed heavily, twice, and decided to try again. When he introduced the needle a second time, Jake never moved. "That's a good boy," Joe said as he stroked Jake again. He sat down beside Jake one final time and held him for a moment. Then he connected the syringe to the IV needle and tube as he looked at his puppy's face once more. It was time.

"You had a good life, Jake. My friend." He knew he could wait no longer; it was time. Then he pushed the plunger down into the syringe.

Jake's eyes drifted shut in a moment. Then he grew limp and lost control of his bladder. "Oh, Jake! Oh, Jake! Oh, Jake!" Joe sobbed as if he could call him back. He squeezed his puppy and cried while Jake slipped away.

Joe carefully lowered Jake's body into the ground and stood up. He wiped his eyes and looked about for a moment, then sighed heavily and continued with what he had to do. He looked at the things laying around him, and life seemed so complicated. Now, he was all alone too.

One last extraordinarily painful chore was waiting for Joe: he had to bury Jake. When he tried to lift Jake's body and place it into the grave, he was surprised at how difficult it was to handle a limp, lifeless body. Just as he was about to lower Jake into the bottom of his grave, Joe lost control of the body and it dropped heavily for the last foot or so. Jake's jaws slapped together loudly, and he lay in a hideous, twisted posture for a moment. The fall and the impact were shocking, and Jake's contorted position was unbearable for Joe to look at. Joe felt as though he'd failed his friend and dishonored him in his last moments by dropping him. The sound of Jake's jaws slapping together when he'd landed in his grave made Joe feel sick. "Oh, Jake. I'm sorry," Joe whispered as he reached into the grave and positioned Jake on his side as if he were sleeping by a fire. "I'm so sorry, Jake. I'm so sorry," Joe kept repeating as he lay beside the grave. He reached his arm to the bottom of the grave and stroked Jake's lifeless form. How could he possibly say goodbye forever and do what he had to do next?

Finally, he stood up, took the shovel in his hands, and lifted some dirt. Before he began to spread the earth over his friend, he took one last look at Jake. Jake's motionless body now rested in a hole, as it would forever. Joe stepped back to look one more time at the hideous sight. He wanted Jake to look peaceful, but he didn't: he looked dead. Joe leaned back and looked away before he lifted the shovel. When he spread the first shovel full of dirt over Jake's body, an awful gasp escaped from Joe's throat. He couldn't stifle the gasp. It was just a tiny cry, but he couldn't help it. This was the hardest thing he'd ever done. And with each succeeding shovel full of dirt, another small cry rose from his chest. He shoveled slowly and gently so that the dirt wouldn't hurt Jake when he covered him. "Uh," he whimpered with each shovel of dirt as he watched his puppy disappear in his grave one shovel full of dirt at a time. When the last bit of yellow fur was hidden beneath the dirt, Joe sped up the shoveling and finished as quickly as possible.

The shovel in one hand and the plastic cup in the other, Joe looked at the fresh grave beside the little pool. He drank what was left in the cup and tossed it in the cooler.

"Goodbye, Jake. I'm gonna leave you now," Joe said. He tipped his hat, picked up the cooler, and wept every step of the way back to his boat.

When Joe's boat rounded the bend in the river just upstream from Marsh's cabin, Marsh stood on his tee box, leaning on his driver. Joe had both hands on the oars as he steered the boat down the middle of the channel and passed by Marsh. The sight of Joe alone in that boat, with a shovel leaning against the gunwale, told Marsh all he needed to know. He raised his hand to Joe, and Joe raised a hand in return, then drifted on by.

chapter forty-five

Joe's hands and the tip of his nose were cold, and he blew into his cupped hands to try to warm himself. He reached over to the thermostat on the wall, and when he turned the dial up, he heard the propane valve open and felt the small furnace begin to hiss.

It was cold in his trailer, but it never took more than a few minutes to warm the place up. He blew into his hands once more, then opened one of the small cupboard doors to look and see what he might prepare for supper.

He'd worked all day, a long day on the river with two good fishermen. He enjoyed the clients who had just enough skill so they didn't need a lot of handholding and instruction. Today's clients had been two chiropractors from Michigan. Both of them had many years of experience fly casting. The day had actually been fun, and he'd been able to put Jake and Molly out of his mind from time to time. But it had been a long day, and now he was cold and hungry and he couldn't find anything but macaroni and cheese or Ramen noodles to prepare.

A fist pounded twice against the door, and the door swung open with a blast of cold air that blew all the feathers off Joe's fly-tying bench along the wall opposite the door.

"D'ja eat yet?" Marsh said from just outside the door jamb.

"Shut the door!" Joe barked as he motioned Marsh into the trailer. "It's cold out there!"

Marsh stepped up from the ground outside the trailer, then slammed the door behind him when he entered. "Colder'n shit. We got a little front comin' through." Marsh set a paper bag on the kitchen table and took off his coat. "Love what you've done with the place!" he said with a smile as he looked about the trailer.

Two pairs of neoprene waders hung from the wall beside the kitchen door, and half a dozen fly rods, along with a shotgun, stood in one corner of the living room. A small desk with a fly-tying vise, covered with feathers, fur, hooks, and small spools of thread, sat between the couch and a well-used, overstuffed chair. Jake's unfinished bag of dog food rested on the kitchen table next to the laptop computer.

"So, did you eat yet?" Marsh asked again.

"No," Joe replied.

"Got any butter?" Marsh asked.

"Yeah."

"Ketchup?" Marsh continued.

"Yeah."

"Cutty?" Marsh asked as he reached into the paper bag.

"Yeah."

"Good! Then we're in business. Make me a Cutty and water, then sit down. I'll make dinner," Marsh said. "An old buddy just dropped off some elk meat," he added as he reached into one of the cabinets and found a cast-iron frying pan. "We're having elk tips and tater tots. The ketchup is for the tater tots. Anybody who'd put ketchup on elk needs a kick in the nuts. Zat scotch ready yet?"

Joe handed Marsh a glass filled with Cutty and ice and grinned when he remembered the girl his father had tormented over the same ketchup issue many years before.

"Thanks," Marsh said. "Now, go sit down. You're in my way."

The bundle of elk meat was wrapped in freezer paper. It thumped onto the kitchen table when Marsh put it down. He produced a bagful of frozen tater tots from his coat pocket and began searching for something. "Got a cookie sheet?" he asked as he crouched on one knee and looked in the cabinet next to the oven.

"I don't make cookies very often," Joe replied, then sipped from his own glass of scotch.

"I used to keep one...there it is!" Marsh said. He grabbed the cookie sheet and scattered the tater tots onto it. He turned on the oven, dropped a large spoonful of butter into the frying pan, and opened the package of elk meat. "Elk tips, fried in butter! Damn good eats. You don't wanna overcook elk..." He stopped in midsentence and looked around. "Where's my scotch?"

"On the table," Joe answered, then pointed.

"Oh yeah," Marsh sighed. He dumped the entire two-pound package of elk tips into the frying pan, stirred them around with a fork briefly, then turned back to Joe. "So! Good day on the river?" he asked.

"Yeah, it was a good day," Joe answered.

"I thought about you all day," Marsh said, then turned to put the tater tots in the oven and stir the elk pieces in the frying pan again.

"Oh?"

"Yeah, the office was pretty busy. Next summer is already pretty booked up for you," Marsh said.

"Good. That's good," Joe nodded.

"You OK, Joe? I mean, are you all right? You've had a lot to think about in the past couple weeks. I just thought you might wanna talk," Marsh said.

"Yeah, I'm glad you came over," Joe smiled. "I guess I'm OK. But I get lonely."

"Me too," Marsh said over the sound of frying elk tips. "I never used to get lonely, but with Molly gone and you leaving for home in a couple days...well, like I said, I thought about you all day."

"I am home, Marsh. I'm just going to see my boys for Christmas. I'll be back in a couple weeks. This is my home now."

Marsh turned one of the aluminum kitchen chairs toward Joe and sat heavily on it. "That's what I was waiting to hear you say. I sure hope that's true, Joe. I haven't made a lot of close ties, you know. Living out here and doing this doesn't really lead to a lot of deep friendships. I'd have to say Molly was as good a friend as I've known. But you are too, Joe. I need you."

Joe's face slowly curled into a smile, and the dimple began to dent his cheek.

"I don't want a date or anything," Marsh shot back. "But I sure have had some fun this summer! Clients like you too. But more than that, I don't want to lose another friend."

"Well, I need you, too, Marsh. And I don't want a date either." Joe raised his glass in salute to Marsh, then took a drink.

Marsh stood up and began to stir the sizzling elk tips. "Get two forks and some ketchup," he called to Joe. In a moment, he reached into the oven and withdrew the tater tots. He dumped them directly into the frying pan with the elk tips and carried the frying pan to the kitchen table. Then he set the cast-iron frying pan with the elk tips and tater tots directly onto the old kitchen table and pulled up a chair. Each man had only a fork, and they both ate from the frying pan.

"Mmmm," Joe said when he put the first bite of elk in his mouth. Then he squeezed some ketchup into a corner of the frying pan and dipped a tater tot. "You're a good cook, Marsh," he said as he leaned over and stuck his fork into another elk tip.

"Pretty hard to fuck up elk," Marsh said as he surveyed the frying pan and searched for another piece of elk for himself.

Neither man spoke for a moment. Each of them rested an elbow on the kitchen table and leaned over the frying pan. They each held a fork in one hand and used it to pick up a bite of elk meat, then a tater tot or two.

"Really, Joe—how are you doing with the whole Molly thing? Are you all right?"

While he was chewing a bit of elk, Joe began to nod slowly. "Yeah, I'm OK." He shrugged his shoulders. "I have to be, don't I? But you were right. Molly was right. Donny was right too. It all just burned too hot; it couldn't last. Probably one of those things that just wasn't supposed to be, I guess. But I loved her, Marsh. It was worth the pain. I'd do it all again."

"You know..." Marsh said when he finished eating. He dropped his fork into the frying pan, then leaned back in the kitchen chair and lifted his scotch from the table. "Molly said something about you that I just can't get out of my mind."

"Oh?" Joe asked without looking up. He searched among the remaining elk tips for another morsel.

"She told me what you said about the life cycle of a fisherman. I like that, by the way. Then she said you were a 'master.' You know, like the fisherman who's reached stage five? I think so too," Marsh said.

"Oh?" Joe asked again, chewing on a bite of elk and still not willing to look up.

"Yeah, you are pretty good out there." Marsh pointed in the general direction of the river. "But all this isn't about fishin'. It's way more than that for you, isn't it? You need this place in order to find what you're REALLY after." He said the words with a finality that caused Joe to look at him, and he paused for a moment.

"We all need to draw strength from something. Well, maybe 'strength' isn't the word. 'Insight', maybe, or perhaps 'vision.' Anyway, I know this place, this life, the river—it all holds something special for you. But it isn't really this..." Marsh gestured at the fly rods and fly-tying materials. "This is all just a window that lets you see into a place that only you can see, and THAT'S where you draw your strength from." Marsh nodded and raised his glass.

"That's pretty good, Marsh," Joe smiled.

"Yes...yes it was," Marsh agreed. "I'm sixty-six years old, and I've seen a lot of men come and go out here. You're among the more interesting. You'd have been a success at just about anything you tried because that's the kind of man you are. But a master? A master river guide or fisherman? So what? That's just fishin'! I know you're after something more." Marsh paused and shook his head. "And I know now why you could never be a master in dentistry! I know why that didn't work for you."

"Why?" Joe asked. "Why do you say that?"

"Well, it's like I just said: we all need to draw strength from something. Maybe it's from God or some internal source or nature," Marsh shrugged.

"Yeah."

"Well, some people don't have that ability to tap into God or their own inner strength...call it what you will. They just seem to walk around with a vacuum hose and hook it up to all those people around them—anyone who'll let them hook up, anyway. They just suck the life out of that person and move on to the next. They continue to hook up and suck the life out of anyone who'll let them."

Joe looked at Marsh with a furrowed brow and considered his words for a moment.

"You never could truly be a master in your old life because you let everyone who came along hook up to you and suck the life out of you. You just let 'em. You couldn't shut it off, could you?" Marsh raised his eyebrows with the question. "That's what was holding you back."

Joe looked away and thought about how the petty arguments between the women on his staff used to leave him feeling exhausted. He thought of all the stress that had been piled on him by unscrupulous insurance companies and worthless government bureaucracies. He remembered all the times he'd come away from patients nearly trembling with anger or frustration because he was expected to care more about them than they cared about themselves. "Yeah, that may be true,"

Joe agreed. "That's good, Marsh!" Joe nodded. "That's good. I take back some of that terrible shit I said about you. That was good."

"Sure it's true!" Marsh smiled. "And when you got here, for some reason you were able to take the next step—continue on your life cycle. You learned to stop letting people and circumstances suck the marrow out of your life. I think Sam Palmer would agree with me on that."

"OK," Joe said. "Now what do I do? I like where I'm at now. I don't want to move on again."

"That's exactly what I'm sayin'," Marsh said. "I'm saying this place, this life, may not be the answer for you, but it's the window that will allow you to see yourself. You need to stay here. Don't move on because of Molly and Jake! We all have people that come into our lives and only stay for a short time. Then some people stay in our lives forever. One person might show up and have a huge impact on our life in just a short time, while others sort of glance off our lives and maybe redirect our journey. People come and go from our lives! That's OK. It is what it is."

"That's a lot to think about, Marsh," Joe sighed.

"I know! I do say a lot of insightful shit, don't I? Now, don't get a headache thinking about it all," Marsh said softly. Then he stood and raised his voice. "Let's play one more round of golf before you leave for the holidays! My place. Tomorrow morning!" he said as he touched Joe's shoulder and walked to the door.

"See you tomorrow," Joe said when Marsh opened the door and let in a mighty blast of cold air.

chapter forty-six

The steady, cold wind had died away before midnight, and now all Joe could hear was the gentle ticking of a small clock on the kitchen countertop. A calm, dark night lay quietly outside his trailer while Joe sipped at his coffee and stared at the small computer screen on his kitchen table.

The transition to a life without Molly and Jake had been quick—too quick. Life had taken another turn he just hadn't seen coming. It had been almost as sudden as his decision to leave his other life behind. But at least he'd had some say in that matter. Molly's leaving and Jake's death had come at him like sucker punches. He'd been foolish enough to assume that there was some sort of unspoken assurance they'd just be there indefinitely. He'd felt that by enduring the pain and sacrifice in this whole odyssey, he'd paid a price and purchased a happier start in life, which he was entitled to. That certainly hadn't proven to be true. Joe leaned back in his chair and rubbed his face. "Not fair," he sighed. "Not fair."

He'd risen early—actually it was the middle of the night—to work on his story, or book, or whatever it was. He was compelled to fix the sentences, to find the right words, and he was having a cathartic experience each time he sat down at the little kitchen table in the trailer and typed something new into the laptop. He'd found that from time to time, when one of the characters in his story said something to another character, it was actually something Joe needed for someone to say to him. In the telling of his story, Joe seemed to be explaining something to himself, too.

The sun was still well below the horizon when Joe slid his chair away from the small table and walked across the tiny kitchen to pour himself another cup of coffee. The bag of dog food still sat on the table next to the computer, and two empty bottles of Cutty Sark, along with a full one, rested on the small kitchen countertop. A very still December morning was about to dawn as Joe looked around the little trailer searching. His eyes brightened and he reached for his wallet. He began to fumble through the small stubs of paper next to the cash until he found a crumpled napkin with a phone number on it.

"Hello?" answered a voice on the other end of the line.

"Murdo?" Joe asked.

"Who's this?" the voice replied.

"It's Joe...Joe Mix!"

"Well, how 'bout that! Goddammer, Joe, it's good to hear your voice. Where did that old piece-a'-shit truck of yours finally stop rollin'? Where you at?"

"Not too far from you, actually. Still in Montana." Joe paused for a moment. "So where are you, Murdo? The number I called isn't your place, is it? I thought I called the number that rings in the barn, the kitchen, and Robert and Mary's house."

"You did. We had alotta dern changes here since you left. Lotsa changes!"

"Like what?" Joe asked.

"Well, for starters, I'm living in the ranch house now. Just after you left, Robert decided to run off with some gal from Denver. He don't want any more to do with the ranch business. He took a job in Denver," Murdo said.

"How's Mary?" Joe asked. He closed his eyes and remembered the anguish on her face when he'd said goodbye.

"Well, she left soon after. Took up with a man who teaches college up in Missoula. I guess they knew each other when they was younger. How's that for a shocker?"

"That's too bad. How's Mr. Crossman taking it?" Joe replied. He'd seen it all coming and he suspected Murdo had too, but he said nothing about that.

"Purdy good, actually. I think he always knew this wasn't the place for Robert, and he's all right with that part of it. But he sure took it hard when Mary and Robert split. He really loves Mary."

"Yeah, that's a bad deal," Joe sighed.

"But we worked out a way for me to buy the ranch—or part of it, anyways. Sort of a long-term agreement between Mr. Crossman and Cletto and me. That's why I'm living here now."

"Well, I'm happy for you, Murdo. I hope it all works out for you. You'll do well. Maybe you'll find a nice girl and settle down," Joe said.

"I ain't looking for nice girls," Murdo replied.

"That's OK too, I guess," Joe laughed. "And how's Cletto?"

"Fine, he's fine," Murdo answered.

"And Norm and Junior?"

"Fine. Long as I keep breaking shit so they got things to fix."

"And James? How's James?" Joe asked.

"James only works here part time now, for the next year or two," Murdo said. "Strangest thing, Joe. He met a gal and went back to school."

"Really?" Joe smiled.

"No shit. He took up with some gal—met her at the library! She's a librarian! Ain't that something? Goddammer, I laughed when he told me that! But she's a nice gal, an' 'nen James decided to enroll at the vocational school up there in Billings and get some formal education about livestock breeding and ranch management. When he finishes school, he plans to come back here and take my old job. How 'bout that?"

"Great. That's just great, isn't it?" Joe replied.

"Sure is!" Murdo paused, then asked, "So whatever has happened to you, Joe?"

"Well, I had a good summer after I left the ranch. Wound up working at a fly shop, guiding fishermen. I like it." Joe didn't think Murdo wanted to hear much more than that.

"And Jake?"

"Jake didn't make it. He died a while back."

"Oh. I'm sorry to hear that, Joe. He was a handsome pup. He was...shit, I gotta go! Cletto just pulled in here driving an eighteen-wheeler. We're gonna move some livestock today. I gotta go, Joe!"

"Hey, before you go...did you ever get your teeth fixed?" Joe asked.

"They don't hurt," Murdo said.

"Murdo, you..." Joe stammered.

"Don't get yer shit hot, Joe. I already heard that lecture. I just wanna wait till something hurts real bad like that other one did. 'Nen I'll call you and you can stick a screwdriver in my dern head and tell some more dirty stories," Murdo said.

"Love to help you when the time comes," Joe sighed. "I'll stop and see you sometime."

"You do that, Joe. We'll have some fun, goddammer!" Murdo said.

"Bye, Murdo."

"Bye, Joe," Murdo said.

The gray sky brightened only enough to announce that another dark winter day had dawned, and three hours passed easily after Joe hung up the phone and returned to the laptop and the story he was telling. Many of the characters in the story had become composites of people he'd known in real life. Others were people he'd heard friends talk about, and still others he'd simply created because he liked them. The story was basically his, but he suspected that millions of others could see themselves in it. He drank coffee, typed, smiled at times, and stared blankly at others while he searched for the words to tell the story.

His coffee was gone when he looked at his watch and pushed himself away from the little table once again. He shut the computer off, lifted a large bagful of colorful packages from the loveseat in his trailer, and carried it to his truck.

——·——

The woman behind the counter at the Fort Smith post office was so short that all Joe could see of her above the scuffed and worn wooden surface on the counter was her head and shoulders. "Here you are, Joe," she said as she reached up and slid the letter to him. "Where you headed?" she asked.

Mabel Whiteman was a full-blood Crow Indian who'd lived her whole long life within thirty miles of Fort Smith. It had taken all summer for Joe to draw her into a relationship that would allow for such excessive conversation, and Joe was proud that he'd won some measure of friendship. One of her front teeth had been lost years ago, and when she smiled, its vacant space sat in the middle of an adorable smile. She looked like a small, innocent child when she curved her shoulders over in a shy posture and sighed. It made no sense, Joe thought, but this shattered smile was charming.

"Thanks, Mabel. I'm headin' over to Marsh's for some smart talk," Joe said as he took the letter from her. The letter had drawn his interest away from Marsh Clements just now. He didn't get much mail anymore, and he was anxious to see who had written. "Vic Birthler, Hudson Valley Publishing" the envelope read when Joe turned it over.

"You're smiling, Joe," Mabel said in her tiny voice. "You always tell me you don't have any friends, but it looks like you do!" she added as she hunched over and began to grin at him.

"Maybe," Joe nodded and returned a little grin. "Thanks, Mabel," he said again as he turned to the door.

"Wait a minute, Joe, I almost forgot! Looks like you have two friends!" Mabel said. Then she reached under the counter and lifted a large, flat, rectangular box about five feet long, and pushed it across the counter top. "Santa Claus send you that?" she asked, grinning even wider now.

The box was light—only a couple pounds. It was long and flat, and Joe had no idea what to expect. He flipped the box over to check the return address and the dimple jumped into his smile. "Win Westby, Augusta, Georgia," he whispered to himself. A package from Win Westby after so many years!

"I know you got some friends now!" Mabel said. "I can see that dimple." She pointed a crooked finger at him.

"Thanks again, Mabel," Joe said as he turned for the door. "Maybe you're right."

"Hey, you wanna take Marsh's mail, too?" she asked. She was already pushing a bundle of mail across the counter. Joe assumed that either Mabel or he was breaking some postal laws, but that sort of thing was OK here. Mabel knew everyone in Fort Smith and where they lived.

"Sure," Joe nodded as he reached across the counter for the third time. Then he asked, "Is that everything?"

Mabel stepped back from the counter and looked first to the right, then to the left, then under the counter, and finally behind her. She shrugged, turned up her palms, grinned her toothless grin, and said, "That's all."

The Big Horn Valley was cloaked in an eerie quiet now that the first winter squall had passed. An inch of new snow covered the ground, and all of the cottonwoods and Russian Olive trees along the riverbank were coated with white. A low, gray sky hovered over the silent valley and hinted that more snow could come at any time. Nothing moved in the woods, and no sound carried up or down the channel. The new-fallen snow deadened all sound as Joe walked around the corner of Marsh's cabin. He couldn't hear even his own footsteps.

He opened the door and found Marsh sitting at his kitchen table tying flies and drinking coffee. A handful of golf magazines lay spread out underneath a layer of feathers, thread, and fur.

Joe simply placed Marsh's mail on the table in front of Marsh, then poured some coffee for himself without any type of greeting. He placed the flat box and his letter from Vic Birthler on the table, then sat down across from Marsh.

"Thanks," Marsh said. Then he reached for his mail and started thumbing through it while Joe opened his letter and began to read it in silence. There had been no real plan for the day. Marsh and Joe had only decided to have coffee, maybe breakfast, and maybe a round of golf if the weather held before Joe left to spend the holidays with Donny and the boys.

The snow had put an end to their thoughts of golf, and now they each read their mail and waited for the other to say something about breakfast.

After several minutes, Joe began to clear his throat a little bit louder every few seconds. When Marsh finally looked up from his own mail, Joe tossed the letter from Vic Birthler in front of him. "Read it," Joe said.

Marsh adjusted his bifocals and reached for the letter. He sipped at his coffee and read it to himself while Joe watched. When he was finished, he tossed the letter back to Joe and took off his bifocals. "Wow," he said. "They want to publish your book?"

"How 'bout that." Joe made no effort to hide the surprise and satisfaction; he smiled openly. "Who would have guessed?"

"Says they want to see the ending? You're not finished yet?" Marsh asked.

"Just finished it," Joe said.

"They're talking about a pile of money there," Marsh added.

"They're also talking about a large advance on another book," Joe said, shaking his head.

"What are you gonna do?" Marsh asked.

"What do you mean?" Joe replied.

"Did you give 'em a happy ending or a sad one?"

"A happy one...hmph," Joe sighed. "This whole book is a happy end-ing to another story. That's pretty much how life goes, huh? Just one story after another. But yeah, it's a happy ending." Joe took the letter from Marsh's hand, then stared at it again. "Do you know what this means, really?"

"What?" Marsh asked.

"It means I made something out of nothing. I created something, and now somebody wants to pay me for it! Maybe I did something good. How 'bout that?" Joe continued to smile as if he couldn't believe it him-self. The talk of money just flew right under Joe Mix's radar. The joy was in the telling of the story and someone enjoying it.

Joe held the letter for Marsh to look at. "You were right, Marsh! This is it. This is what I've been searching for when I've looked through that window you talked about last night."

"Well, here's to you, Joe," Marsh said as he raised his coffee cup in salute. "You're a writer! What's in the box behind you? Did the people at Hudson Valley Publishing send you flowers, too?" Marsh smiled.

Joe reached across the table and began to tear at the tape on the box from Win Westby. "I almost forgot," Joe said. "Remember I told you about the guy who made my bamboo fly rod all those years ago? Well, this is from him. I'm sure he got my address from somebody back in Minnesota. Donny must have told someone about his visit out here, and the word got to him. Wonderful guy...an artist, a master! Maybe you can meet him someday. I'll bet he made me another fly rod," Joe said as he opened the box.

When Joe lifted open the top of the cardboard box, the spectacle of what lay inside drew them both forward for a closer look. The grain of the wood and the beauty of the leather were rich, the color warm and deep. A hickory-shafted golf club—a driver—with a grip of soft, brown leather rested before them like a museum piece. The head of the awe-some golf club was made of persimmon wood and had been stained a reddish brown to bring out the rich grain. The head was secured onto the shaft with a tight winding of black wool yarn, which had been bound into place with several layers of varnish. The handmade driver had been crafted by Win Westby to duplicate the look of the classic golf clubs from the nineteenth century.

"Jesus, Joe. This guy IS an artist," Marsh said as he reached a tenta-tive hand toward the club. He leaned forward cautiously, as though he might need to get permission from someone before he could handle such a work of art, while Joe found an envelope and read the enclosed note from Win Westby.

> *Joe,*
>
> *I hope this finds you in good health. Slats Murphy told me all about your leaving Rochester and gave me your current address. He said your brother told him that you'd found your golf game, at long last. From what I could understand, it sounds like a fine game for you.*
>
> *You will no doubt be searching for something more than golf or fishing. I was when I left Minnesota all those years ago, and I could see the same struggle inside you even then. I have no insights for you, but I wish you good luck. I know you always appreciated the beauty of a difficult thing done well. Please enjoy this driver. I made it for you, my favorite golf partner. Perhaps we'll play again one day?*
>
> *Hit 'em straight!*
>
> *Win Westby*
>
> *Win Westby*
> *Westby Gallery, Fine Furniture, Fly Rods,*
> *and Wooden Golf Clubs*

Joe dropped the letter onto the table and lifted the club from the box. It was a little heavier than any modern golf clubs he'd handled, but the balance of it was perfect. He stood still, addressing an imaginary ball, then turned his head very slowly to look out the window.

"It needs to be done!" Marsh said after he'd read Joe's mind. He raised his eyebrows and looked over the top of his bifocals. "We need to do it!"

"Yeah," Joe nodded. "We need to play," he said. Then he handed the club to Marsh. "I'll be right back. This reminds me—I forgot something in the truck. This is perfect. It's like a message from God," Joe added.

"What's in the truck?"

"Your Christmas present," Joe called over his shoulder.

"Now I'm embarrassed. I didn't get you anything," Marsh said.

"It's OK. When I got yours, I liked it so much I went out and found something for me, too," Joe said.

"You bought your own Christmas present?"

"Yeah, I knew just what I wanted. I'll be right back."

When Joe reappeared from his dash to the truck, he was carrying the large bag of packages. He sat down at the table once again and began to fumble through the packages. "Don't get nervous, Marsh. It isn't much." Then he handed a colorfully wrapped box to Marsh. "Merry Christmas," he said.

"Thanks, Joe," Marsh said as he opened the package. Then he turned a questioning glance to Joe.

"It's a tweed golf jacket!" Joe shrugged. "Just like the ones in those old photos in your magazines and books! Remember when you said some-day you wanted to dress like they did in Scotland, at the Royal and Ancient Club? Today's the day! Now open this one." Joe tossed Marsh another package.

Marsh held the package for a moment, then opened it. "Knickers?" he smiled.

"No shit! Now this one," Joe laughed.

"Argyle knee socks and one of those Scottish stocking caps with a big floppy tassel on top!" When Marsh had the box open, he held the con-tents out and examined them for a moment. "This is great! Where'd you get this stuff?" Marsh chuckled.

"Garage sale in Billings. Thought of you right away when I saw it," Joe said.

"So what'd you get for yourself?"

"Well, since I'm a little younger than you, I thought I'd outfit myself from a more recent era. Actually, I was at another garage sale in Billings, just after I bought your stuff, and I found this. I was looking for books again, but when I saw this I just couldn't pass it up." Joe opened one of the packages and produced a pair of bright pink, double-knit pants.

Marsh covered his eyes as if to protect them and stepped back.

"Circa 1972, I'm guessing," Joe said. "Wait till you see this." Then he opened the last package and removed a bright yellow-and-aqua sweater and a pink ball cap that matched the pants. "Ugliest shit I've ever seen! I'll either look like a golfer from the seventies or a pimp! And it was all my size. We're teeing off in ten minutes, so get dressed," Joe said.

———·———

"You look quite dashing, Marsh," Joe said. Marsh had found a white shirt and a necktie with a trout on it to wear with his olive green tweed jacket and knickers. His cap was tipped at a jaunty angle, and he crossed his legs to show off the argyle knee socks. "The only weak link in your ensemble is the cowboy boots," Joe grimaced. "They just don't work with the knickers."

"I might say the same for you," Marsh replied. He guessed that Joe's outfit, especially on a soft, gray day like today with a blanket of new snow, would be visible from anywhere in the Big Horn Valley. "I'm getting nauseous just looking at you. Even when you stand still it looks like you're vibrating."

"Too much coffee, that's all," Joe smiled.

"OK. Today let's play the course at…" Marsh said.

"Today I get to choose! I'll be giving you the scores today, too," Joe interrupted. "We're playing The Oaks in Rochester, Minnesota. A delightful course of medium length with plenty of trees and trout streams running through it. I think you'll find it challenging. The pin placement can be difficult, and with today's snowfall I don't think you'll get much of a roll, so keep your ball up." Joe grinned. "And I'm up first!"

Joe carried the broom from Marsh's porch out to the tee box and swept the snow away until he'd exposed a small green area.

More fluffy snowflakes had begun to drift silently onto the tee box, the river, and Mr. Carrigan's pasture as Joe took some practice swings with the new hickory-shafted driver in an effort to loosen his shoulder muscles and back. "Feels nice," he said to Marsh. "Totally different than the newer clubs. You'll want to slow your swing down." He held the club close to his face and looked at it one more time. "OK, first hole is a long par-four with water on the left and a little dogleg to the left. Everything is gonna roll to the right. Just try to stay in the middle." He was still talking as he lifted the club back slowly. The persimmon head of the driver struck the ball perfectly and made a noise like a wooden bat striking a baseball. "Mmmm," Joe said. "That felt good." The ball sailed across the river and disappeared in a puff when it hit the new snow in the cow pasture.

"Nice one," Marsh said as Joe handed him the driver.

"Yes it was," Joe replied.

Marsh took his turn and addressed the ball as he usually did, then started his herky-jerky backswing and promptly knocked the ball into the middle of the Big Horn. "Fuck. Mulligans on…"

"Jeez, you take a lot of mulligans," Joe blurted.

"Why would I NOT take a mulligan every now and then?" Marsh replied. "It's not like the scorekeeper's gonna mind," he added while he held the scorecard up for Joe to see, then slid it back into his own pocket. "And after all, I'm just trying to get it over to the other side."

"Then hit it right the first time," Joe shot back.

"If I could do that, I wouldn't need to take so many mulligans. I'm trying here, Joe. I just can't do it. Besides, life isn't like that. We just don't hit that first one straight every time." Marsh stopped, then his face tightened when he added, "And look who's talking! Your whole life is a mulligan! Nowadays, every morning when you roll out of bed and start your day, you're playin' that mulligan. You're not keepin' score, either. You're tryin' to strike the ball artfully, that's all." Marsh paused and nodded. "I know you, Joe Mix. You're just the same as me."

Joe looked at his feet for a moment, then his face began to brighten and a large smile tugged at the corners of his mouth. He stared at Marsh but said nothing. He just smiled openly. "You do say a lot of insightful shit!" he said finally. "So hit your mulligan and we'll keep playing."

Joe led Marsh on a tour of The Oaks as they played their bizarre fantasy round of golf. Joe gave his scores to Marsh for a change, and as the round evolved he found himself duplicating the round Win Westby had played on the day he'd set the course record. Joe went to great lengths to describe every hole, every shot of that round to Marsh. He relished his own description of chipping in by banking the ball off a tree, and of striking the ball through a cluster of trees as he went for the course record. Somewhere during the round, he became uncertain: was he describing his own game or Win Westby's? He felt good inside when he understood that it might just be the same.

A silent snow fluttered down ever so gently on the odd-looking pair while they played The Oaks together. They laughed quietly and spoke only of the golf as ball after ball disappeared into the snowflakes, the gray fog just beyond it, or the white cow pasture waiting beyond the fog.

"You look fine—handsomer than shit, actually—in your golf attire," Joe said as they made the turn and prepared to play the back nine. "But those cowboy boots really don't work with argyle socks and knickers. We'll really have to switch to golf shoes in the spring."

"Well, pink double-knits don't really work tucked into your boots either," Marsh replied. "But other than that, you've captured the essence of your era."

Large snowflakes drifted slowly onto them as they finished the back nine, and when Joe finally sat next to Marsh, each of them had a dusting of snow resting on their hats. "Helluva day!" Joe said as he sat down and tallied his score. "Up and down in two from the rough on the eighteenth! Course record—a fifty-nine! I knocked that fucker stiff. Nobody thought I could do it. Through the trees from two hundred fifty yards—I did it, didn't I? I risked it all and I won."

Marsh tilted his head and stole a sideways glance at Joe. "Ever heard of Ed Furgol?" Marsh asked with a strange look on his face.

"Huh?" Joe's face crinkled with his question.

"Ed Furgol was leading the 1954 U.S. Open by one stroke when he teed his ball up to play the eighteenth. They played at Baltusrol that year—you remember those two monster par-fives, the seventeenth and eighteenth?" Marsh asked. "We've played 'em a few times this summer."

"OK," Joe said, still confused. "I remember."

"You remind me of Ed Furgol. He knocked his drive into some deep shit on the left of the fairway; no shot at the green. He was screwed; no chance to salvage his round. Found himself in the same boat you were in back there in Minnesota. The people he was playin' with just wouldn't tolerate a mulligan, so he did something else: he remembered that just up the hill from him was the upper course at Baltusrol. They have two complete courses—the upper and the lower, you know. Turns out nobody had ever decided that the upper course should be out of bounds! So Furgol asked for a ruling from one of the judges. When they told him that the upper course actually wasn't out of bounds, Furgol turned around and knocked his ball completely off the lower course to get a better look at the eighteenth hole. Hit the next shot back onto the right course, pin high, sank the putt, and won the Open—by knocking his second shot completely off the course! That's what you've done." Marsh sighed and waited for Joe to reply. But when Joe held his silence and stared into the snowflakes above the river channel, Marsh said, "You knocked your second shot right off the golf course and onto another, separate golf course...then you came back to win!" Marsh shrugged, "Ed Furgol! With me?"

"Yeah," Joe nodded.

"So now that you've righted yourself and maybe even won something, are you sure you'll be coming back?"

Joe tapped the hickory-shafted persimmon driver with the burgundy, calf leather grip on the ground several times, then stood up without a word. He took a ball from the plastic bucket full of balls and prepared to strike it. "Ed Furgol, huh?" he said with a soft smile. Then he swung an easy, full swing and stroked the ball into the sea of white, out over the river. "Yeah! I'm coming back."

He dropped another ball onto the tee and hit it. "Of course I'm coming back. This is where I want to be." He walked to the bucket and withdrew several balls, then stood over one for a moment before he added, "You were right. When I'm standing right here, I can see what I want to be." Then he struck another ball through the white veil over the river.

"So have you found it?" Marsh asked. "After all this, have you found it?"

"Huh? Found what?"

"What you were looking for—the meaning of life," Marsh said.

"The meaning of life?" Joe looked at the ground in front of him and smiled as he repeated Marsh's question. "No," he said after a pause. He teed up another ball and addressed it. As he stood over the ball waiting to strike it, he continued. "But I know I'll never waste another day—you know, sit around and wish today would be over so I can get on to something else." Joe shrugged. "I'll never count down the days of my life again. I was letting too much get away from me." He struck the ball into the snow flurries and teed up another.

"Hmph," Joe chuckled as he remembered the question. "The meaning of life? No. I'm still looking for that. But I think I know where it all starts. I think I know where meaning begins."

"Where's that?" Marsh asked.

"Well, the times when my life has been the richest have been when I needed someone—my sons, those cowboys, my brother, my parents, Molly, Jake...even you." Joe smiled at the way he'd included Marsh after Jake. "We were better, life was better, when we needed each other—and we knew it. I think that's where the meaning in our lives begins. You have to need someone, and you have to know it." Joe swung easily and stroked another ball into the snow. "I'll get back to you when I have the rest of the meaning-of-life thing figured out."

"You say a lot of insightful shit too, Joe," Marsh said.

Joe grinned for a moment, then dropped another ball onto the tee box and prepared to strike it. "Look at us," Joe chuckled, then struck another ball. "Couple 'a shot makers, aren't we?"

"Yeah," Joe continued, "I'm gonna come back here and forgive myself for just being an ordinary man. I'm gonna play golf with you and Ed Furgol, and I'm gonna catch a few fish. I'm gonna take a mulligan every so often, and I'm gonna write another book..." He struck his ball and watched it until it disappeared into the white snowflakes. Joe stared into the snowy sky for a moment, then glanced downstream.

He dropped another ball onto the thin layer of snow that was beginning to cover the area he'd swept. He stood over the ball for a second and said, "Yeah, of course I'll be back. I'm gonna stay here by this mighty river and keep on lookin' for my life."

Joe swung the driver and watched the ball sail into the white snowflakes. "I might just make a stop on the way back here, though. Maybe I'll see just how long I can ride a nasty-tempered old blue roan named Billy, and I think I'll stop and have a word with a red-headed cowgirl over by Ennis."

Joe dropped another ball onto the tee box, then addressed the ball for a moment. As he swung the club through the ball, he lifted his eyes to watch the ball rocket away into the snowflakes and then be lost in the distance. Instead, he shanked the ball and sent it skipping into the river. He reached into his pocket and grinned when he tossed another ball down. "Mulligan," he whispered.

Joe Mix leaned on the driver and watched for a moment as silent snowflakes drifted from a white sky and then disappeared into the relentless current of the Big Horn River. He wondered just where the current would take him next.